THE SAXON SHORE TRILOGY
THE COMPLETE SERIES

JOHN BROUGHTON

Copyright © 2024 John Broughton

Layout design and Copyright © 2024 by Next Chapter

Published 2024 by Next Chapter

This book is a work of fiction. Names, characters, places, and incidents are the product of the author's imagination or are used fictitiously. Any resemblance to actual events, locales, or persons, living or dead, is purely coincidental.

All rights reserved. No part of this book may be reproduced or transmitted in any form or by any means, electronic or mechanical, including photocopying, recording, or by any information storage and retrieval system, without the author's permission.

THE SAXON SHORE

THE SAXON SHORE TRILOGY
BOOK 1

CHAPTER-BY-CHAPTER GLOSSARY

CHAPTER ONE

Batavians = Germanic people on a large island between rivers in the Rhine-Meuse delta.

CHAPTER TWO

Trireme = a war galley with 3 banks of oars, each oar manned by one man.
Corvus = a boarding ramp taking its name from corvus – the raven, owing to its spike like a beak.

Menapian = a member of the Belgic Menapii tribe dwelling near the North Sea in the Roman period.
Classis Britannia = provincial naval fleet of the Ancient Roman navy, its purpose to control the English Channel and the coastal waters of Britannia.
Bagaudae = groups of peasant insurgents in the later Roman empire who arose during the 3rd Century.
Cornu = Roman horn.

CHAPTER THREE

Capsarii = Roman doctors taking name from doctoral bag – capsae.
Corbilo = important trading port of the Veneti on the Loire about 2 leagues below Nantes.

CHAPTER FOUR

Branodunum Fort = ancient Roman fort to the east of modern Brancaster in Norfolk.

CHAPTER FIVE

Solidus = highly pure gold coin issued in the late Roman and Byzantine Empires.
Denarius = 4.5 g silver coin – 1/72 of a Roman pound weight.

CHAPTER SIX

Antonine Itinerary = a register of the stations and distances along Roman roads compiled for Emperor Antoninus (86-161 AD).
Camulodunum = modern Colchester.
Venta Icenorum = modern Caistor-St-Edmund, Norfolk.
Sitomagus = a town 30m south of Venta Icenorum on the road to Londinium.
Combretovium = present-day Coddenham in Suffolk.

CHAPTER SEVEN

Glevum = present-day Gloucester.
Dalmatia = a region of modern Croatia.
Mauretania = a region embracing more than modern Morocco.

CHAPTER EIGHT

Deva = modern Chester.

CHAPTER NINE

Gesoriacum = modern Boulogne in France.
Ulpia Noviomagus Batavorum = modern Nijmegen in the Netherlands.

CHAPTER TEN

Regulbium = Roman fort near modern Reculver in Kent.
Canti tribe = Britons in Kent.
Portus Lemanis = Roman fort at modern Lympne in Kent.
Vectis = the Isle of Wight.
Metatores = a Roman civil engineer.
Gromatici = Roman surveyors.

CHAPTER ELEVEN

Tamesis = River Thames.
Durovernum = modern Canterbury.

CHAPTER TWELVE

Civitas = citizen community.
Praetorium = high army officer's headquarters.

CHAPTER THIRTEEN

Vindelis = modern Portland Island, famous for Portland stone.
Anderitum = modern west end of Pevensey in Sussex.
Ander Forest = the Weald.

CHAPTER FOURTEEN

Porta decumana = Decuman gate opposite the praetorium, generally the rear gate.
Portus Adurni = fort situated at the north end of Portsmouth harbour.
Ballista ball = ballista, an ancient missile thrower which launched great balls of stone a considerable distance for use against fortifications in a siege.
Clausentum = a small town in the Roman province of Britannia. The site is believed to be located in Bitterne Manor, which is now a suburb of Southampton.

CHAPTER FIFTEEN

Verulamium = modern St Albans in Hertfordshire.
Cornicen = a junior officer in the Roman army, whose job was to signal salutes to officers and sound orders to the legions.

dextrarum iunctio = the joining of right hands in wedlock.

CHAPTER SIXTEEN

Dubris = modern Dover.
Liburnia = a type of small galley used for raiding and patrols. It was originally used by the Liburnians, a pirate tribe from Dalmatia.
Othona = Roman fort near modern Bradwell-on-Sea in Essex.

CHAPTER SEVENTEEN

Chauci = an ancient Germanic tribe living in the low-lying region between the Rivers Ems and Elbe, on both sides of the Weser.

CHAPTER EIGHTEEN

Teutoburg Forest = is commonly seen as one of the most important defeats in Roman history, bringing the triumphant period of expansion under Augustus to an abrupt end.

CHAPTER NINETEEN

Rutupiae = modern Richborough Castle near Sandwich in Kent.

CHAPTER TWENTY

Constantius = Flavius Valerius Constantius "Chlorus" (ca. 250 – 25 July 306), also called Constantius I, was Roman emperor from 305 to 306.

CHAPTER TWENTY-ONE

Liburnae = used as cargo ships in the later Roman empire.

CHAPTER TWENTY-TWO

Principia = headquarters building. This building was in the very centre of the fort. It was where the commanding officer would issue orders to the soldiers, and the clerks would have offices. Also, there was the strong room where the pay was kept.

CHAPTER TWENTY-THREE

Ballista = Roman catapult for hurling massive stones.
Illyria = north-western part of the Balkan Peninsula.
Infera Insula = the legendary once fertile low-lying island of Lomea – the modern Goodwin Sands.
Testudo = a packed formation covered with shields on the front and top.

Gariannonum = Roman shore fort probably at modern Caistor-on-Sea, Norfolk, guarding the Yare estuary.
Rutupine shore = Roman name for the coast around modern Sandwich, famous for its oysters.

CHAPTER TWENTY-FOUR

Noviomagus Reginorum = modern Chichester, West Sussex.

Calleva Atrebatum = modern Silchester, 5 miles north of Basingstoke, Hampshire. Well-preserved Roman walls and amphitheatre.

CHAPTER TWENTY-FIVE

Isca Dumnoniorum = modern Exeter, Devon.

Eboracum = modern York, Yorkshire.

Dumnonia = the Latinised name for a Brythonic kingdom covering modern Devon and Cornwall that existed in Sub-Roman Britain.

Drepana = Helenopolis, a Byzantine town in Bithynia, Asia Minor, on the southern side of the Gulf of Astacus (present-day Turkey).

Samhain = pagan festival, marking the Celtic New Year, the end of summer, and the end of the harvest season.

Mediolanum = present-day Milan in Lombardy.

I

A SMALL UNNAMED VILLAGE ON THE SOUTH BANK OF THE RIVER WAAL, BATAVIA AD 286

VALDOR BENT TO HAUL HIS EEL TRAP ONTO THE RIVER BANK when a hand clamped over his mouth and a familiar voice hissed, "The Romans are hunting for Faldrek; you've got to help us find him. He's only killed a centurion, and the whole legion is hunting for him. Look over there! They've even got dogs to help sniff him out!" The rough hand of the smith's apprentice released its grip. "You're his best friend; you'll know where he'd run to."

Several ideas tumbled through Valdor's mind, but there clearly wasn't time to evaluate which was best.

"I know what I'd do in his place, Heidar," he told the apprentice. "Are you three willing to come with me? We'll take my uncle's boat, find Faldrek, and sail it out of the estuary into the open sea."

"My father's boat? The North Sea?" Johar gasped. "Then what?"

"Then we take our chance and see where the gods, time, and tide lead us."

"Are you mad?" Johar, the youngest of the four by one winter, protested. He was comfortable with the older youths because he could run and throw as well as them, and his muscles were just as well developed from hauling wet, laden nets of fish onto his father's boat.

"I'll come with you, Valdor. There's nothing for us in the village now the Romans have seized our tribe's treasure, and they've forced my master, Thragnor, to work the forge for them. I'll not stay to be a

Roman slave! Besides, Faldrek is my friend, too. If the Romans seize him, they'll torture him and maim him for killing a centurion."

"Are you coming with us, Johar?" Valdor shook his cousin's arm urgently. "Look, some of them are splitting from the main force and coming this way."

"Since it's my father's boat you're planning to steal, I'll come so that it isn't seen as theft. Let's go!"

Hidden by the steep river bank from the approaching Romans, the three youths dived into the river and struck out for the islet opposite. Batavian boys all learned to swim like otters in their infancy, and the men were renowned for their incredible ability to swim even in armour, thus taking an enemy by surprise. So, it was not a hard task to arrive at the far bank, scramble up, cross the islet to reach Johar's father's boat, moored in its usual place, and decide there what to do next. The distant yapping of hounds made them hasten their deliberations.

"You two get in," Johar said. "I'll push her off the mud, and you can haul me aboard. We'll row to where we're going for now. We can't risk hoisting the sail; it's white, and the Romans will see it and be after us in a trice."

He gave the boat a mighty shove, but it failed to budge, so he tried again while Valdor used an oar to push into the silt. Johar had to dive into the river again and strike out after the boat that was already being swept along by the current. Strong arms reached for him, and soon he was hauled into the belly of the boat. Valdor had already taken charge of the oars and was pulling strongly with the current, parallel to the bank but in the direction of the village and hence towards the Roman soldiers.

"What do you think you're doing, Valdor?" Heidar grumbled. "You'll have us all taken prisoner."

"Nay, Heidar, you take the tiller and head us out into midstream while I do the hard work."

"Give me an oar; I'll help you," Johar said fiercely. With the two youths hauling on an oar each, the boat shot forward swiftly.

"Now where?" the tillerman asked.

"Torik Isle, over yonder," Valdor pointed. "That's where we'll find Faldrek."

"Never! He'd never have swum that far," Johar argued.

"Listen, Faldrek is a stronger swimmer than any of us, and he was desperate. Besides, I know a place where he would hide."

Gradually, they approached the low-lying holm, a refuge for every conceivable type of seabird, but uninhabited by the Batavians as it was so prone to flooding.

"There's nowhere for him on Torik," said Johar querulously. He was a little jealous of his elder cousin, who had now assumed command in what by right was his boat.

"You'll soon see; I'm not given to flights of fancy, cousin."

The low line of the coast, which was the bank of the Waal, could be seen from Torik, but the movement of anyone ashore was invisible at this distance. Conversely, this was a guarantee that the three of them and their boat could not be seen by the Romans. The value of Johar's advice not to hoist sail was evident now. They ran the boat into a small inlet, where there was slightly firmer ground in the shallows made up of shingle. The boat scrunched into it, and they leapt out to drag it higher, making it impossible for the vessel to be lifted away by the tide.

The turf was springy but not marshy in these summer months, so they set off confidently towards the middle of the islet. The forces of nature had created a hollow at the centre, and as they approached, they saw a thin wisp of grey smoke curling into the air to be instantly dispersed by the sea breeze.

"I told you!" Valdor said triumphantly. "It must be Faldrek!"

The three youths appeared over the brow of the hollow, where their friend leapt to his feet, brandishing a gladius—a short Roman sword. "Hey!" he cried. "What are you doing here? Don't you know, I'm an outlaw?"

"Whose law?" Valdor said truculently, smiling grimly. "We've come to share your fate."

"You can share my dinner, too!" He pointed to a rudimentary turnspit where two seabirds were skewered and dripping fat, hissing in the flames of a small fire made from salvaged driftwood. "Puffins. I caught four. I still have to prepare the other two."

In their village, puffins were regarded as a delicacy, so Valdor's stomach was already rumbling.

"What happened exactly," he enquired of his friend.

"I was grooming our horse when that swine of a centurion crept up behind me. The first thing I felt was a hand on my buttocks, and then he spun me around and started kissing me on my mouth. Yuk!" He dragged me into our house and pushed me onto the bed. Luckily, mother was out; she'd gone to Aunt Ysilis' to help make bread and prepare some crabs. Then he started to strip off his armour until he was naked." Faldrek's voice broke, and his lip trembled. "It was clear he wanted to rape me. In fact, he said that if I was a good lover, he would see that I was well-treated in the legion. They plan to round up all our people aged over sixteen winters because, he said, we make the best warriors in the Empire—"

"So, that means us as well," Valdor looked meaningfully around his companions' serious faces.

"Ay, anyway, that was when I surprised him by leaping up to grab this," he brandished the gladius, "and plunged it into his heart."

"Good riddance," said the apprentice smith, "I'd have done the same!"

"Hang on," Johar looked astounded, "Are you saying that you swam all this way carrying the sword?"

"Ay, what's the problem?" Faldrek replied proudly. "You just have to keep a tight grip on it."

He used the murder weapon to slice the puffins, but it made no impression on the hungry youths, who devoured the fowl with relish as their host prepared the other two birds. Soon the fat was spitting in the fire again as Heidar, expert with flames, added just the right amount of wood for good roasting without burning the flesh.

Chewing on his meat, Faldrek swallowed and asked, "I suppose the Romans are hunting for me?"

"Ay, they are, but I reckon they won't think of scouring the various isles and islets because they won't think anyone could swim this far. I think they'll search the nearby villages and while they're at it, they'll round up lads of our age and older as auxiliaries in their army.

"So, what are we going to do? We can't stay here too long."

"We have our boat," Johar said proudly, and Valdor's plan is to sail out of the estuary into the North Sea."

"Aye? But what then?"

"We'll leave it to the gods to decide our fate, my friend."

After much discussion, they decided to spend the night on the holm, also because not even the Romans would attach importance to a white sail in the early morning, which would be seen as a fisherman sailing out to cast his nets. The mild season permitted them to sleep under the stars, and the hollow hid the glow of the fire from the mainland so that they could sleep around its warmth. Heidar organised the collection of driftwood and maintained that he needed little sleep, so he would keep the fire burning through the night. The other three were weary from their efforts and soon fell into a deep sleep.

The following morning, Valdor gathered his friends together to make a solemn oath. His grey-blue eyes, typical of his tribe, stared intensely into others of the same hue, except Heidar's, which were an unusual deep blue.

"We must swear before the gods that whatever we have to face, we'll endure it together, united: each individual should act for the benefit of the group, and the group should act for the benefit of each individual."

Four arms stretched out in unison and hands clasped over the other, "I swear!" they chorused and grinned into each other's faces: each face that of a young man who had grown through infancy and childhood together. Trust for each of them was of supreme importance and in the comforting glow of comradeship, at least momentarily, they were able to dismiss the frightening thought of what a future far from the reassurance of their village, family, and the routine of their chosen trade might bring. A moment's thought told them that was no longer any reassurance. For Faldrek, a return certainly meant a cruel death and for the others, a harsh life in the Roman legion under Emperor Maximian.

Valdor, who had tacitly assumed command of the little group, said, "Come on, men, the sun is lighting up the river, it's time to row out into midstream and raise sail. We'll be out in the North Sea by noon. Look, there's an ebb tide to help us and the current is in our favour!" He hadn't mentioned the breeze, but when they hauled in the oars and, as before, Heidar took the tiller, when Johar ran up the sail, it flapped and filled with the wind. Since the breeze was contrary, coming from the North Sea, Johar called to his tillerman, "We'll need to tack downstream. Keep the bows in that direction for the moment. I'll tell you when to turn."

Nobody questioned his decision because among them, he had the most experience of sailing. If they were to survive this voyage, they would have to heed his advice. The fisherman's son settled down in the bows to keep an eye on the direction and perhaps any debris that might damage the small vessel.

By midday, they had reached the choppy water at the mouth of the estuary, sliced through it and into the calm water in the lee of the islands positioned like sentinels guarding the entrance to the great river complex. From the bows, Johar pointed excitedly, calling to Heidar to change course. They headed towards an area where the sky was full of mewing gulls and diving gannets. The diving birds were plunging into an area of water that seemed to be bubbling and boiling. "Mackerel!" Johar shouted and pointed excitedly as the boat ploughed into the area, the fisherman's son twirled a net over his head and cast it among the easily netted fish.

Moments later, he had hauled the bulging net aboard, tipping the teeming fish into a writhing, glittering heap on deck. His exultation was brief, as a large gull swooped down and snatched one in its bill, soaring away with its prize. Soon, all four youths were using oars as weapons to fight off the famished persistent predators. Johar was the first to use his wits instead of his muscles, grasping a mackerel and flinging it into the sea, diverting at least a dozen of the gulls to swoop and compete for the prey. His friends joined him, throwing squirming mackerel into the sea. The breeze came to their aid, driving them towards the shore of an island. Johar seized the respite to cover the fish with old cloths so that the gulls, unable to see fish, mewed and sped off in search of prey elsewhere.

Valdor took charge now, "Heidar, take us into that inlet, we have more fresh fish than we can eat for lunch."

Johar had a gutting knife on board, so he prepared selected fish whilst Heidar took charge of lighting a fire on the sandy beach. Never had they eaten so much fish in one meal, and they had plenty to store in a barrel of salt that Johar's father kept on the boat for occasions when he had fish that advanced beyond the requirements of the village. "In this way, we'll have rations for when we can't catch fresh food," Johar explained.

"Let's sail over to the outermost island," Valdor said, "we can spend the night there and above all, we can find a freshwater spring or we'll die of thirst. Have you got an empty barrel on board for water?"

The following morning, they found a spring oozing from a cleft in the rock and slowly filled a medium-sized cask with fresh water, blessing

Johar's father for the useful equipment found on board the vessel. They carried the cask aboard and then shoved off into the relatively placid waters of the bay. Strong strokes on the oars took them around the northern tip of the island and into the face of a strong south-westerly wind. The sail filled with a snap and the boat shot forward.

Johar approached Valdor, grasping his arm, to turn him so that he faced back towards the land they had left.

"Now what? Cousin? It's all very well leaving our fate to the gods, but should we not have a *plan*."

"I was thinking that we should cross the North Sea and try our luck in Britannia. They say the people there are similar to our tribes."

"But Britannia is under Roman ru—"

Valdor followed his cousin's gaze and understood why he had broken off mid-sentence and was standing, mouth open, peering into the distance. A rectangular sail clearly stood out against the horizon and it belonged to a much bigger ship than theirs.

2

THE NORTH SEA, AD 286

As soon as the large vessel came into sight, the four companions realised to their dismay that it was a Roman war galley. That observation was not exact because the galley was a Carthaginian trireme captured in battle during the Carthaginian war, little more than a score of years before. Still, it contained a complement of 190 men and was a formidable fighting vessel armed with a ram, catapult, fire pots, and archers. It possessed a tower from which to direct attacks and reinforced wooden sides. An innovation was the *corvus*, a thirty-foot-long boarding plank, four feet wide with a spike at one end. As the trireme neared the fishing boat, the corvus came crashing down to impale the wooden deck, just missing Johar standing in the bows. Roman legionaries swarmed down the boarding plank, at least a dozen of them, wielding swords and wearing armour. The four youths had one sword between them. Resistance was out of the question and, laughing, the legionaries herded them up the ramp into the galley. The remaining warriors searched the vessel, but the only thing they removed was the barrel of salted mackerel, which they carried up the steep ramp, taking it aboard the trireme.

Valdor gazed with amazement at the ranks of seated rowers and the drummer in the stern, there to beat time for the coordination of the many oars. He imagined that the galley could fly through the water without the aid of the large rectangular sail that now flapped uselessly in the breeze because the crew had slackened the stays for the boarding. The crew were now busily engaged in recouping the *corvus*—no easy task because the spike had embedded deeply into the wooden deck of the fishing boat. It required a team of twenty men to release it by hauling on ropes. With a squeal of steel on wood, the spike came free and, at last, the fishing vessel, of no interest to the Roman commander, was allowed to drift free. The fate of Johar's father's boat was in the lap of the gods, whereas the fate of his son and companions was firmly in the hands of the galley commander.

Forceful hands pushed them towards the tower in the stern and half-shoved, half-hauled them up the ladder. The legionaries thrust them before the commander of the galley. Here was their next surprise because the curly-haired and curly-bearded stocky man in full Roman regalia was not a Roman, neither was he a patrician. His coarse-featured visage spoke of humble origins and his accent was known to the youths. Before them stood a Menapian, a member of a tribe the Batavians figuratively 'rubbed shoulders' with in Belgic Gaul.

The rough-mannered commander grinned, "Well, well, what a prize! Who would have thought it? We close in on a fishing boat; nothing more than a tub containing a few salted mackerel and find a real treasure —four Batavian warriors!"

Faldrek was about to protest that they weren't warriors when Valdor nudged him in the ribs, and he swallowed his objection.

The commander, who had noticed the gesture, fixed his eyes on Valdor and astonished him by addressing him in his own language. "You have something to hide from me, young man, but Marcus Aurelius Mausaeus Carausius has a way of finding out everything. Do not dispel my goodwill. Tell me what you are doing so far from home?"

"Commander Carausius, sir," Valdor gained confidence because he could use his own language freely, "we are fugitives from the Romans, who seized our village, but one of my dear friends here slew a centurion who tried to rape him."

To his surprise, Carausius laughed heartily, "Ay, some Romans, especially those of noble families, have this peculiar vice." He slapped his thigh as if sharing a joke, "I prefer women to satisfy my carnal needs as I expect you four healthy Batavi do, as well. Am I right?"

"Ay, sir, you are. Will you not punish us for the death of a centurion?" Valdor asked meekly.

"Listen, young man, it would be a waste! I know the worth of Batavians in battle. I venture you are all horsemen who can swim, too?"

"Indeed, we grew up with those skills, lord."

"I knew it! I will give orders for you to be equipped, and you will form part of my bodyguard. That is a special privilege. As for the centurion, I am not interested; the swine had it coming to him!" Carausius spun to face Faldrek. "It was you who slew the Roman, was it not?"

"H-how did you know?" Faldrek stuttered.

The commander guffawed. "Easy, you are the pretty boy of the four! If you like, I can scar your face to spoil your looks, you just have to ask," he roared with laughter again. "I'm only joking, don't worry!"

"Thank you, lord," Faldrek found the wits to add. "We'll serve you faithfully."

The commander shouted orders in what they recognised as the Latin tongue, and the galley stopped wallowing in the waves to shoot forward under the power of 120 oars, to the pounding rhythm of the insistent drum. More orders and the crew stretched the rectangular sail by hauling and fastening the stays.

Suddenly, the commander looked at the four companions and switched to their language again. "You rascals took me out of my way, but I believe you were worth it!" He addressed Johar. "That boat was yours, was it not?" Johar's jaw dropped in amazement. "Ay, sir, but how could you know that?"

Carausius bellowed with laughter again, a trait they would come to know and appreciate. "Easy, one should always pay attention, especially in the presence of strangers. I saw how your eyes followed the tub as we set her adrift."

"It was my father's livelihood, lord, but I expect he will not need it now that the Romans have seized our people."

"Think no more of them," Carausius said, casting a weather eye to the south-west. "A new and better life awaits you. Your father will find his place in the legion if he is anything like his son. You four and I will become friends." He shouted orders in Latin again. They did not understand, and the sharp-witted commander recognised this. "I have ordered them to kit you out with armour and weapons. As of now, you are part of my bodyguard. Soon, I will summon your superior officer. He is a good man but does not suffer fools gladly. You'll find him brusque but fair."

"Suits me!" Valdor murmured, not intending Carausius to hear, but the officer's hearing was as sharp as his wits.

"I'm glad we deviated to pick you up," he said. "I'm more at ease with my own kind. We are on our way to meet the *Classis Britannica*. I am to command that fleet in the English Channel to eliminate the Frankish and Saxon pirates who have been raiding the coasts of Armorica and Belgica." He stared hard at Valdor, meeting his puzzled eyes. "Why me in command? You might well ask, young fellow. I'll tell you. We Menapians are fierce fighters like you Batavians, and although I have no great fondness for the Romans, I distinguished myself," he beat his chest proudly, "during Maximian's campaign against the Bagaudae rebels in Northern Gaul, earlier this year." He smiled grimly. "Add to that my previous career as a pilot in these waters, and you see, there's nobody better to command the fleet."

Modesty might not have been his strong suit, but the commander had impressed the four youths, each of whom was eager to seize the opportunity Fate offered him. To strengthen this feeling, four legionaries deposited arms and armour at their feet. These same soldiers helped the lads strip out of their dirty clothes and pull a deep crimson *tunica* over their heads, next they strapped a *balteus*, a kind of apron belt, around their waists, from which dangled the *baltea*, studded leather straps. "These are the insignia of my bodyguard," Carausius said. "The mere sight of them should instil terror in the foe," he grinned wolfishly. Expert hands positioned a leather cuirass over their torsos so that, with the steel *lorica segmentata*, all four took on the appearance of fully fledged Roman soldiers. Two details were missing: the *caligae*, the army sandals, and the *galea*, the helmet. The eight men on the tower had a good laugh because the *caligae* fitted them perfectly, except for Heidar, whose feet were too big; not only that, the *galea* was too small for his head. The legionary hurried away to fetch replacements as Carausius guffawed. "Friend, what is your name?"

"Heidar, lord."

"Well, Heidar, you are a big lad for your age; it must be hauling all those nets that have built you up."

"Pardon, commander, but I am no fisherman, but a smith by trade."

"A smith! By all the gods! Today is my lucky day! I know we will give you many opportunities to practise your trade in the months to come. Ha! Here are your sandals and protection for your head."

As soon as Heidar was fully kitted, Carausius spoke again. "As part of my bodyguard, you are exempt from pulling on the oars. If you hear two blasts of the *cornu*, you drop everything and rush up onto this tower, swords drawn. You'll notice that for the moment you have no *scutum*, no *gladius*, and no *pilum*." He saw the confusion on their faces. "You'll soon learn the terms for your equipment. In our tongue, I refer to shield, short sword, and javelin in that order. When you meet your centurion, Galenus Cato, after his sleep," he smirked, "he will issue you with arms and no doubt, sleeping quarters since he's an expert on the subject." The smirk reappeared. "Meanwhile, off you go down on deck and familiarise yourself with the ship. If you see a soldier with the same *baltea*, make his acquaintance at once, for he will be your comrade at arms. Besides, you might need to find your way back with all speed."

The four companions gingerly, but noisily, stepped down the ladder to the deck, getting used to the clattering hobnails under the soles of the *caligae*, which made it easy to slip on wooden surfaces.

Once on deck, Valdor held up his arms, looked down his body ostentatiously, and then peered at his friends. "Will you look at us! Proper Roman soldiers, who'd have thought it this morning when we were filling our water cask?"

"Who indeed?" Faldrek said. "It looks like my career of killing centurions has come to a sudden end."

"Hush! Only our commander must know about that," Johar said anxiously.

"My cousin is right, the least said about that, the better."

"Isn't that the coast of Britannia?" Heidar asked.

Valdor resisted the temptation to gaze at what might otherwise have been their destination and said, "The commander seems a fine fellow."

"Aye, we're lucky. He's a Menapian—almost one of us," Johar said.

"Take nothing for granted," Valdor cautioned. "We'll have to show our worth. He's as likely to send us to our deaths as protect us. He's a quick-witted type, that's for sure. He notices the slightest detail, so let's strive to show him our true worth."

They wandered right to the bows, where a sentinel stared at them. "Here, aren't you those fishermen we rounded up earlier?"

Valdor wasn't going to let the opportunity pass. "Fishermen, nay, we are part of the commander's bodyguard, so show some respect or my comrade will throw you overboard."

"The commander might not take too kindly to losing the sharpest eyes on the ship," came the sour retort.

"Sharpest eyes?" Valdor tormented him. "Then, why haven't you spotted those sails in the distance?"

The man spun around, a look of anguish on his face, his hands reached for a *cornu* dangling from a leather cord, which he unhooked and blew two shrill blasts. "Thank you," he smiled at Valdor, who in turn, spun around and startled his comrades by setting off at a dash, jumping over anything in his path. His companions, suddenly realising their duty, chased after him to reach the tower in the stern. Valdor took the ladder two rungs at a time and almost stumbled at the commander's feet, but the willing hands of other bodyguards hauled him to his feet.

"What the devil? Why has the lookout sounded the alarm?" Carausius snarled.

"Because I spotted sails in the distance, over yonder, Lord. Aye, see over there beyond yon headland!"

Carausius's eyes narrowed as he peered. After a moment's concentration, he said, "By the gods, lad, you have sharp eyes. And you say that *you* spotted them, not my lookout?"

"To be fair, Commander, we distracted him with our presence in the bows. If not, I'm sure he would have seen them first."

"What's your name, lad? I like your honesty."

"Valdor, Lord."

"Valdor, eh? Men, this is Valdor and he is Heidar, a smith. They, with their friends, are your new comrades."

Valdor stepped in quickly, pointing, "Johar and Faldrek. We are Batavians," he said proudly.

"Ay, and Batavians are not to be messed with," the commander said sternly. "You will treat them as brothers."

The red-plumed helm of a centurion appeared up the ladder.

"Ah, Centurion Galenus Cato," the commander said. "We have four new recruits, Batavi, worth their weight in gold in battle. This one, Valdor, out-spied my lookout, hence the warning."

"We'll see their battle worthiness if those are enemy ships," the centurion said grumpily, his sleep disturbed, glaring at Valdor, who met his gaze without flinching.

3

OFF THE COAST OF EAST ANGLIA, AD 286

THE TRIREME DREW CLOSER TO THE FLOTILLA OF SHIPS waiting a mile off the coast of East Anglia. Valdor counted nine vessels, all war galleys. His commander ordered a small boat to be lowered to carry a messenger, instructed to summon the nine captains and their escorts aboard the Carthaginian flagship. Soon, several small boats arrowed towards them.

In moments, a swarthy Roman officer stood before Carausius, and next to him a crimson-plumed centurion. The captain's lip curled, and in a sardonic voice, he said, "What's this? Are we to take orders from a barbarian thug?"

No sooner had the words left his mouth than Valdor's sword was in his hand. The centurion reacted just as quickly, drawing his gladius. "How dare you draw your sword at a Roman officer, barbarian?" He leapt forward, delivering a scything blow, which but for Valdor's agility would have been fatal. As it was, it left a gash in his leather cuirass without penetrating his flesh. Valdor's same nimbleness allowed him to jump, twisting off the deck and deliver a downward chop by surprise, which severed a tendon in the centurion's wrist, causing him to scream and drop his gladius with a clatter on the wooden boards. In a flash, as the centurion held his useless, bleeding arm to his chest, Valdor's sword was at his throat. The Batavian glanced at his commander, who reacted quickly, "Spare him! That kind of wound is two a sestertius in the army, and we have the *capsarii* to stitch him up and have him fit for combat in no time. It would be a shame to lose a centurion on my first day in charge, Valdor."

Valdor glared at the centurion, removed the blade, and bowed to his commander.

By now, other captains had reached the command tower, and word had rapidly spread about what had happened. The swarthy captain now changed his tone, "Commander, I believe you were about to give us instructions; pray continue."

Carausius also glared at the offending captain, but in a loud clear voice declared, "Caesar Maximian has named me commander of the *Classis Britannica*, tasked with cleansing the channel of Frankish and Saxon pirates. So, we'll sail in search of them off the coast of Armorica. My ship will lead the flotilla, and I expect you to remain within hailing distance of each other. When we sight the enemy, I will issue further orders. We sail upon three blasts of the *cornu*."

There was nothing to question, so the captains, murmuring sullenly among themselves, beat an orderly retreat to their small boats, which were hoisted aboard the galleys. As soon as the last of them was on board, Carausius raised three fingers to signal to the lookout to give three blasts of his horn. That done, he shouted crisp orders to get the galley underway, leading the small fleet south-eastward towards Armorica.

On the voyage, the commander took Valdor aside and confided, "I will not forget your action, my lad; it made an immediate difference to my acceptance as commander. Those captains realise that if a commander inspires such loyalty in his men, he is to be reckoned with. You have a great future ahead; you have my word."

"Thank you, Lord. May I seek out my friends?"

"Ay, but remember, two blasts of the horn and you are to be back beside me on the instant."

"So be it!" Valdor bowed and descended the ladder, turning over Carausius' words in his head with mounting excitement. A matter of days ago, he was a nobody even in his own village; now, it seemed, he was a favourite of a high-ranking Roman officer.

In the open sea, they passed the occasional Roman trading vessel, but there was no sign of pirates. They scoured the north-western coast of Armorica, paying particular attention to the great estuaries.

Valdor spotted a comrade with the insignia of the bodyguard and strolled over to speak with him. He was in luck because many of the crew could not speak his language, but this man, a seasoned mariner, had picked up enough over the years to hold a rudimentary conversation. After rounding a large headland and changing course, the older man said to him, "We're heading to a great river we call the Liger that the locals call the Loire. There are several ports at the mouth, but the most important is Corbilo, the busy trading station of the Veneti tribe. I say, is it true that you chopped the hand off a centurion?"

"People exaggerate," Valdor said. "I had to disarm him, so I cut into his wrist, but the last I saw, he still had his hand. He attacked me first."

"I heard you defended the honour of our commander. That will stand you in good stead with all your comrades. So, it's true that the Batavi are great warriors."

"Well, we need to be put to the test in battle for you to decide that," Valdor said modestly. "But you remind me, I must seek out my friends."

"The other Batavi? I saw them playing dice at the front of the ship not long ago. Stay strong, my friend."

"You, too."

Valdor gazed at the bustling port of Corbilo, which held his attention for a while. Lumpers carried crates of fish from boats up steep steps to the quay, while others rolled barrels into warehouses. He had never seen such a busy place and on so large a scale. He thanked the gods that his life had changed so dramatically. His reverie came to an abrupt halt at the twin blast of the horn, so he skipped over coiled ropes and hastened to the ladder. Again, he was the first of his original companions to mount the ladder, but once on the tower deck, he was met by the broad grin of his new friend who, in a lowered voice, said, "Look over there, the other side of the estuary!" He pointed to a fleet of ships tied together. "Those are Frankish vessels or I know nowt about ships! If I'm right, they'll be raiding in Namnetes territory. That's a valley area full of rich country houses. But let's hear what the commander has to say. The other captains should be here for orders, soon."

His words proved correct, but Carausius' orders did not please them.

"Hark! We'll not chase inland after the pirates. We'll let them plunder and bring back their spoils, which we'll relieve them of in a trice. We'll slay them in battle hereabouts. Meanwhile, we'll sail across the estuary to cut loose their ships, which will be lightly guarded and we'll use our rams to sink the lot of them. Any questions?"

One bold white-haired captain stepped forward to express the perplexity doing the rounds among his colleagues. He stared down his aquiline nose, saying, "Commander, I fear the emperor's wrath when he learns that you did nothing to protect the Namnetes' villas."

"Captain, do not dare question my orders. *I* am the voice of the emperor here and as such, I tell you that when he learns we have destroyed a whole Frankish fleet and its crews, he will be more than satisfied."

Muttering among the captains caused Carausius to lose patience. He bellowed, "Return to your ships and carry out my orders! Within the hour, I do not want to see a single Frankish ship still afloat."

Valdor marvelled that his commander did not take part in the operation but contented himself with a watching brief. Ramming was not so straightforward as he had imagined. Each galley was equipped at the bows, below the waterline, with a long spike, essentially a sharpened tree trunk. But to use it effectively, the attacking vessel needed considerable speed, generated with the sole intention of caving in the side of an enemy ship so that the seawater flooded in and sank her. The first ship had the easiest task because she targeted the outermost of the moored vessels and, sail filled by the strong breeze, drove into the smaller craft with a mighty crashing of rending timber. Valdor listened to the orders being called and watched as scores of oars backed the galley away from its victim. Panicked shouts came from other Frankish ships, whose skeleton crews attempted to cut their boat free. The first to drift out into the estuary was immediately rammed by an incoming galley surging forward at high speed.

The smaller, lighter and therefore, more manoeuvrable Frankish vessels were able to avoid ramming, but not the grappling irons that flew towards them. Roman soldiers poured aboard and overwhelmed the undermanned vessels. Working at great pace, the boarders soon scuppered the ships by springing the planks below the waterline. In these operations two or three Romans drowned because they were unable to flee the onrushing waters in time and went down with the ship, but the number was negligible compared to the Frankish losses. Soon, not a single Frankish craft of the twenty-two moored vessels remained afloat. Even the irascible Carausius expressed his satisfaction and hailed the nearest captain, telling him to moor where the Franks had tied up previously. Shortly, all ten galleys were moored alongside each other so that it was easy to step from one craft to the next, which Carausius did to congratulate his captains in turn. To each, he ordered a scout sent inland to look out for the returning pirates and with instructions to report back without being seen as soon as they spied the foe.

Carausius sent out Johar with another of the older bodyguards. When they returned together, all smiles, the older man reported to the commander. "Before sunset lord, look the sun is low, by the time it touches the sea, they will be here. I estimate that there were eight hundred of them and they were carrying a large box on two poles."

"Ha, the booty!" The commander turned to Johar, "do you agree that the enemy has eight hundred men?"

"Aye, I'd say that's about right, lord."

"Then, we outnumber them for sure," he smiled grimly.

The accounts of the other scouts tallied, so Carausius ordered three blasts of the *cornu* and led his crew onto the shore. He employed the tactical system based on small and supple infantry units called maniples. Each maniple numbered 120 men in 12 files and 10 ranks. The maniples drew up for battle in three lines, each line made up of 10 maniples and the whole arranged in a chequerboard pattern. Nobody organised this better than Carausius, hence his burgeoning reputation as a military strategist.

The Franks possessed high-quality weapons, especially their long swords, but unlike the Frankish professional soldiers, did not wear chain mail. This was an advantage for the Romans along with their superior numbers. Had their commander brought horses, he would have used the cavalry to protect his flanks. Instead, he urged his captains to position their hardiest men on the right flank and took his bodyguard to hold the left.

Johar whispered to his cousin, "I'm scared, is there anything I should know?"

"Aye, that we are stronger than they, and will win the day. Keep your shield high and meet force with force. Remember, I'm next to you and will guard your flank. Look, Heidar is on your other side. You no longer need to be scared."

The Franks came at a rush, hurling insults, oval, colourfully-painted shields raised. Their first mistake was to hurl throwing spears and axes at the solid wall of Roman *scuta*. These formidable curved shields proved impenetrable, causing the weapons to fall harmlessly to the ground. The Romans did not waste their spears, preferring to use the *hastae* to stab the onrushing enemy between shields. So, the Franks crashed onto a wall of spikes. The survivors were forced backwards by the *scuta* and the *gladii*, the famous short swords used so effectively in close engagements.

The chequerboard line-up of the Roman formation proved devastating as the Frankish pirates had never encountered anything similar. They were already outnumbered and, adding disorientation to this, the battle was soon swinging towards a Roman victory. To combat the Roman formation, the Franks split their force to attack the flanks. It was the worst thing they could have done as the central maniples swung out behind them to drive them from behind onto the well-formed flanks. The four Batavian companions acquitted themselves bravely, a fact noted by their equally ferocious commander. Three of them killed for the first time, the strong Heidar, several times.

At last, an eerie silence, broken only by the shrieks of scavenging birds, fell over the battlefield as the twilight brought by the setting sun enveloped the survivors, casting long phantom-like shadows before them.

"Quickly, you four," Carausius indicated the Batavians, "come with me." He set off through the bodies at a run until there remained no more corpses. The comrades had no idea what he was about until in the distance, about four hundred yards ahead, they spied four Franks each holding up a pole, transporting a large chest.

Carausius pointed, "Their spoils, ours now!" They redoubled their pace and within shouting distance, the commander warned them fluently in their own language, "Set down that chest if you want to live and disappear from my sight. We'll slaughter you like swine if you make a fight of it."

Evidently, the Franks' greed outweighed their wisdom, for they drew their swords and stood shoulder to shoulder. The sight of their gore-spattered adversaries should have terrorised them, but they were determined to keep their ill-gotten gains.

The sheer ferocity of Carausius and Heidar was probably enough for victory without the support of Valdor, Johar, and Faldrek, but it was the latter who first struck down and killed a foe. The engagement was short and sharp and the outcome inevitable. With all four Franks dead on the ground, Carausius ordered the Batavians to hoist up the poles and carry the chest to his ship. They laid their *scuta* neatly on top of the chest and weary, fit to drop, plodded back to the battlefield, where many Romans were picking weapons, especially the prized swords, and items from the corpses of fallen Franks. To the relief of the four companions, their commander called four of his bodyguards who took over carrying duties. Even so, they had to help them load the chest onto the galley as it needed lifting high to clear the gunwales. That accomplished, they were entitled to rations of wine and bread.

But Valdor could not enjoy his refreshment in peace since he spotted the captain of the neighbouring ship storming aboard, his expression wrathful. Sensing trouble, Valdor set down his beaker and tossed his remaining crust overboard for a swooping gull to devour before hurrying to the tower ladder.

He was in time to catch the same puce-faced, patrician captain shouting at Carausius, "First, you let the pirates rampage at will through the province, then, not satisfied, you seize their bounty and bring it aboard *your* ship. We *all* fought in the battle." He thrust his contorted face into the commander's so that their noses were almost touching as he shouted, "Do you think we'll passively accept this? Well, you're mistaken!"

The commander stepped back and wiped his spittle-flecked face, leering at his enraged subaltern, and said, "What are you going to do about it?"

"The emperor will hear about this!" He raised a huge fist and took a step forward to deliver the blow, but Valdor's hand clamped around his wrist and hauled him, off-balance away from Carausius. Valdor meant to take advantage of the man's loss of equilibrium to toss him to the deck but, as misfortune would have it, the captain's sandal caught in a small gap between planks and he staggered at the moment Valdor heaved. The result was disastrous because the captain precipitated down the ladder, striking his head on the way to lie still at the foot of the steps, his head at an unnatural angle. Valdor shot down and placed two fingers on the officer's neck searching in vain for a pulse.

Carausius joined him and the Batavian shook his head, "I-it was an accident, I didn't mean to slay him."

The commander placed a fatherly hand on his shoulder, "I saw that it was an accident! But where were the rest of my bodyguard? Only you,

Valdor came to ensure my safety and I shall not forget that. Now, I'm twice in your debt. Hurry, find and fetch four of your comrades with a blanket. They'll carry the body back to his ship. I'll accompany him to appoint a new captain and explain how this one lost his temper and stormed away in a blind rage, losing his balance and falling down the ladder in a terrible accident that was his own fault."

"Thank you, lord."

"Nay, thank *you*, my brother!"

4

BRANODUNUM FORT, NORFOLK, 296 AD

Luckily, Carausius could not hear the murmurs of discontent on the other vessels of his flotilla. His own crew thought the world of him because they admired his strategic military superiority compared to previous generals.

As they approached the coast of East Anglia, the commander summoned Valdor to the tower. They were alone up there, and Carausius spoke with confidentiality to The Batavian.

"Valdor, I can only imagine the grumbling on the other ships. You see, I made my name as a land-based soldier and led my men to victory against the Bagaudae rebels, using the same tactics as against the Franks at Corbilo. These naval types have never taken me to heart, and they resent me holding the Frankish spoils." He placed a hand on Valdor's arm and stared into the earnest grey-blue eyes. "Why am I telling you this? For two reasons: to urge you to watchfulness because those sailors would as soon slit my throat as shake my hand; secondly, because I don't want you to judge me ill. I do not lust for treasure any more than the next man; indeed, I intend to share the Frankish loot with my crew and with—oh, never mind, you'll find out soon enough."

"Lord, I promise to be watchful and will also speak about the need for alertness to my three friends."

"Look, yonder is the fort of Branodunum; can you see its walls? Severus Alexander built it and two others along the coast some three-score years ago to help protect traders from pirates. At the moment, the garrison is made up of *Equites Dalmatae*, Dalmatian cavalry. I remember you saying that you and your friends grew up riding horses."

"Ay, lord, it's true, although—"

"Tell me."

Valdor hesitated as if reluctant to criticise anyone. "My cousin Johar is not as proficient as we others because he had to spend much time at sea with his father."

"I'll bear that in mind. I have a surprise for you and Heidar once we set foot in that fort. See, to the west and north of it is the *vicus* where the civilians live and work outside its walls. The inhabitants belong to the Iceni tribe. I have a lot of time for them; they are fierce warriors if you get on the wrong side of them, as their queen, Boudicca, proved by defeating a Roman legion and burning Londinium to the ground, but that was in a past century. The southern wall, facing the sea, is on the shoreline and it serves as a harbour. I have brought the fleet here as I will not tolerate mutiny in the ranks, and I have a special fondness for cavalry."

I wonder why he is telling me all this?

Once moored at the harbour, Carausius issued orders that only his crew should disembark, while the others were to remain aboard their respective ships. The commander inspected the loot obtained from the Franks and called several of his officers to whom he handed coins and gems to distribute among the crew. Valdor and Heidar each received a large Byzantine gold solidus, whereas Johar and Faldrek were happy with a smaller Roman gold *solidus* bearing the portrait of Augustus Diocletian.

At a certain point, the commander closed the trunk and ordered it to be carried ashore. The lookout, on his command, strode with his horn to the southern gate and blew a peremptory blast, at which the doors swung back and Carausius marched his men, carrying the remainder of the spoils into the rectangular fortress. At the eastern end, there was commotion with many men cheering and laughing.

A couple of officers strode to greet Carausius. Judging by their elaborate crimson plumes, they were of high rank, Valdor thought. His conjecture proved correct when they introduced themselves respectively as the camp prefect and a tribune. To them, Carausius delivered the spoils to be shared among the cavalrymen.

"What's going on over there?" The commander pointed to the raucously cheering assembly.

"Ah, yesterday we received a new consignment of horses," said the tribune, "and among them is a spirited black stallion. Nobody has managed to break him in yet. Assuming anyone succeeds in mounting him, the beast bucks so hard that it is impossible to stay on its back. Remember, I have some of the finest horsemen in the Empire and yet..."

Without asking permission, Valdor strode over to the compound, leaving Carausius to deal with the camp officials. He pushed his way through the crowd to the front, just in time to see an unfortunate cavalryman thrown backwards off a stomping black stallion, its muzzle flecked with white foam. Valdor climbed into the compound over a three-barred fence without consulting anyone. Meanwhile, a soldier had snared the stallion with a lasso, so Valdor walked up to him and took the free end of the rope. "I'll ride him," he said confidently. The soldier, like the rest, had never seen this cocky fellow before, so, not knowing him, tamely handed over the rope.

Valdor strolled carefully over to the stallion, making sure to keep well within the horse's sight. The stallion was stamping and snorting angrily, but Valdor's first action was to remove the noose from over its head and then, he gently caressed the restless animal's muzzle. He put his head close to the horse and, smiling, looked him straight in the eye before slowly, slowly, moving to whisper in its ear. The onlooking crowd had become rapt in silence, which helped him soothe the beast. He continued to pacify the horse with gentle words before again, slowly, slowly, moving to stand, arms outspread in front of him, gently clicking his tongue. An awed murmur came from the gathering when the stallion steadily stepped towards the stranger and nuzzled his chest. Again, Valdor whispered in the horse's ear and suddenly, sprang onto its back, threading his fingers into its mane, leaning forward and whispering his magic words into its ear. With a proud neigh, the stallion responded to the gentle heel kicking of its rider and to the astonishment of the assembly, set off around the compound at a trot. Valdor sat upright and, holding tightly with his knees, waved to the crowd, which raised a cheer. Valdor's delicate pat on its head kept the stallion calm, and he let it trot where it wanted as there was no bit nor reins to guide it. Soon, the splendid mount stopped of its own accord, and Valdor leapt down to caress the sleek coat and speak more calming words. Another nuzzle and their friendship was sealed. "Thank you, my friend; I shall call you Sparax," he said to the stallion, earning himself another whinny and a happy toss of the head.

Ignoring the pressing questions in a language he could not understand, Valdor broke free and came face-to-face with the broadly-grinning Carausius.

"Well done, Centurion," the commander said.

"Lord, I don't understand."

"Centurion Valdor, you have been promoted, and the tribune has gifted you yon stallion since only you, it seems, can domesticate it."

Valdor, for once, was speechless. "W-what?"

The tribune, an officer of considerable learning, came to his rescue. "Come, Centurion, I will accompany you to withdraw your new equipment," he placed a playful finger in the slash in Valdor's cuirass and tugged. "By all accounts, you owe the legion a new centurion! The camp prefect is designating the seventy-nine men under your command. You know that a century is made up of eighty men; well, your Decurion is also withdrawing his uniform, there, with him, that makes eighty."

"Heidar, my decurion?" Valdor had regained his tongue.

"Aye, but expect him to be excused service whenever the prefect requires him to man the forge. I believe there's some call for an able smith."

"Oh, Heidar is able, alright, for he learnt from Thragnor, the best smith in Batavia."

"You Batavians are full of surprises, but take my advice, young man. Your feat with the stallion has earned you much goodwill, but don't underestimate the Dalmatians; they too are a fierce race of combatants. They will expect you to be better than them in courage and compassion, not merely in horse-riding. You are evidently young and will be viewed with diffidence."

"Rightly so, I have never commanded men."

"*Hard, but fair; kind but hard.* Make that your motto, and I'll have to look over my shoulder lest you rise further!"

Valdor laughed, but his head was spinning, yet, he sagely managed. "Lord, you need never fear for my loyalty."

"So, I gather from your commander. I do not suffer fools and would not have consented to your early promotion if I did not agree with Carausius. He is a fine general. I'm sorry that he might leave us so soon."

"I know nothing of that, lord."

"I know, but here we are. Greet your decurion, and I'll requisition the armour with a centurion's insignia."

The tribune marched into the building Heidar had just vacated.

The former smith greeted him. "Valdor, you'll never guess!"

"I will. You're a decurion, and you can't believe your luck!"

"H-how did you know?"

"I know because I am your centurion. From now on, you obey my orders, Decurion!"

Heidar mock-scowled. "Nothing new, then! Oh, by the way, the prefect is giving me a horse!"

"I like your feathers, very impressive!" He pointed to his friend's plumed helmet, tucked under his arm.

"Ay, but I can't wear it yet; apparently, it's not the done thing in the camp when we're off duty."

"I must go; the tribune's calling me!" He dream-walked into the building and, several minutes later, emerged with a *galea*, distinctive with its traverse crimson crest, and carrying a vitis, the vine-stock that a Roman legionary centurion wielded as a cane with which to punish his soldiers. *Hard, but fair; kind but hard,* he told himself, *I'll probably never use this on my men, except on Heidar!* But that was a private joke because a centurion would never, surely, punish a decurion with a whip!

The two friends strolled aimlessly around the fort, taking in details like the rounded corners with internal turrets backed by earthen ramparts that strengthened the walls, not less than four feet in thickness, built of stone, brick, and tiles used together.

The troops were housed in timber-built huts. The quarters of the tribune and the camp prefect were spacious buildings of brick, and although the friends had not yet seen inside, the latter might almost have been a mansion in Rome itself thanks to its handsome chambers with tessellated floors, its baths, and underfloor heating.

There was a central street, in which provisions, clothing, and trinkets could be bought. The Romans did not permit the dealers to remain within the fort after sunset, but the shops were tenanted by day and did well for business, not only with the soldiers but also with the neighbouring Britons. Many of the women in the soldiers' huts were Britons. "I'll bet their children will be soldiers, too, when they grow up," Heidar said.

From the nearest corner turret, Carausius emerged.

"Centurion, Decurion!" he bellowed at them, "Over here, smartish!"

Taking time only to exchange glances, the friends ran at once to their commander.

"Quickly, up the tower! I want you to see something."

Together with Carausius, they gazed down at the harbour. "What do you see?"

"Our ships, lord," Heidar said.

"Ay, but what don't you see?"

Heidar frowned, looked puzzled, and glanced at Valdor, who said, "Eight-*nine*! One is missing!"

"Exactly! What does that mean?"

"One of the captains has disobeyed orders and sailed—"

"Correct, Centurion, and I know why."

"You do?"

"Ay, we must prepare for war. He'll have sailed off to meet Emperor Maximian's forces in Gaul to denounce me for not protecting the Namnetes from the pirates and for keeping the spoils to myself." He bellowed a laugh. "He would be angrier if he knew I had given the bounty to the Dalmatians. But I need the loyalty of these cavalrymen."

"Those other four ships did not come with us," Valdor pointed at four identical two-masted vessels, smaller than the galleys but with deep rounded hulls.

"They will join our fleet because they are specially built to transport horses. In our next battle, Centurion Valdor, you will command a cavalry unit. Those ships have stalls below deck along the whole length of the boat, and above deck, there are slings designed to restrain a nervous horse even in the heaviest seas."

"I think Sparax will be better off above deck in the open air."

"Sparax?"

"Ay, my stallion. I would like to travel with him at sea to keep him calm."

"Nay, you travel with me to keep me calm! Or do you have a short memory, Centurion?"

"You are right, lord, my primary task is to guard your safety."

"Those ships look smaller and slower, but in reality, they have two triangular sails that drive them forward at a faster rate than our galleys.

Having cavalry available in battle will make my strategy so much easier. Do you remember how our best soldiers covered the flanks? Well, that task will go to the Dalmatian cavalry."

"Do you truly think that Emperor Maximian will declare war on you?"

"I can't be sure, but the captain who has fled is the highest-ranking in the *Classis Britannica*, apart from myself, that is. He's resentful of me and renowned for his political manoeuvring, so I expect he will persuade the emperor that I am a traitor."

"But that's ridiculous!"

"Ay, Valdor, we know that, but my friend, the corridors of power in Rome are awash with the blood of innocent men.

5

BRANODUNUM FORT, NORFOLK, 296 AD

Several weeks passed in which Valdor and Heidar refined their respective roles with helpful advice from fellow officers. Valdor took delight in training his cavalrymen to form up as required by Carausius. He found ways of putting the formation to the test by mock battles and stressed the importance of keeping a tight formation. A revolutionary aspect was his insistence on occasionally training without horses. Other cavalrymen might have resented this, but Valdor had a way of gaining support through his personality. *Hard, but fair; kind but hard*. The Dalmatian horsemen fulfilled his demands, and he was convinced that he had an elite group ready to face the most testing circumstances in battle.

Relaxed, he conceded himself more free time, so that one bright morning, he decided to survey the view from the top of the south-western tower. He saw a sail and watched a galley anchor close to the South Foreland point. He recognised the vessel as the *Leopard*, the galley that had fled the harbour months ago. His eyes narrowed as a small boat with a single occupant and two oarsmen started to row towards the approaches of the harbour.

He hurried to find Carausius, who took the news badly. "We must intercept that boat before its captain can turn the fleet against me. He must be confident of Maximian's support to sail boldly back here.

Centurion, I have noticed you training your Dalmatians to fight without horses, bring them aboard my galley. We'll seize his messenger and then face Captain Leander Russus before he can overturn me."

The oarsmen carrying the messenger did not know that they were in a race against time, an advantage that Carausius possessed. Swiftly, Valdor urged his Dalmatians aboard, their morale high at the thought of impending action even without horses. Carausius soon had the full complement of oarsmen in position and the galley cast off, shooting out of the harbour. Valdor stood in the bows with a coiled rope in hand. In a deep voice that belied his stature, he called down to the rowing boat, "Here's a rope, climb aboard at once, or we will ram you and send you to the bottom to feed the crabs!" He was close enough to see the expressions of fear and horror on the three faces. Moments later, one of the oarsmen grabbed the rope and jumped into the sea. Three strong Dalmatian cavalrymen hauled him to the galley and up its side until he jumped onto the deck. Valdor coiled the rope again, and although he misjudged his cast this time, it fell close enough to the boat for the second oarsman to dive into the sea and grasp it. Valdor's third throw was perfect as the rope landed on the boat. The messenger was soon hauled onto the galley and confronted by Carausius.

"You will tell me what message you bring and for whom it is intended."

The messenger's face was a picture of misery. "Lord, my message was not intended for you, but for Captain Cyrillus Drusus."

"As I feared. But you can confirm that the vessel you sailed on and now standing offshore is the *Leopard*, commanded by Captain Leander Russus?"

The messenger did not meet Carausius' eyes but lowered his head and muttered, "Ay, I can vouch for that."

"I command the *Classis Britannica*, so any message for Cyrillus Drusus is also of concern to me. So, you will tell me your message at once."

"Nay, lord, I cannot. My captain said it was for Drusus' ears only. I dare not disobey orders."

Carausius glared and snarled, "If you care for the lives of your companions and your own, you will give me that accursed message." He signalled to the two Dalmatians who each had an oarsman by an arm. They dragged the unfortunate fellow to stand trembling before the enraged commander, who drew his gladius and pressed its blade to his throat.

"Wait!" The messenger cried desperately. "I'll give you the message, lord, but I beg you to recognise, I am but the bearer of tidings."

Carausius withdrew the blade from the oarsman's throat, and he, who had steeled himself for a mortal blow, visibly sagged with relief, held up by the two cavalrymen.

"Out with it, then!" the commander roared.

The messenger wiped his brow with a shaking hand. "Caesar Maximian declares that Marcus Aurelius Mausaeus Carausius is..." his voice caught, and he paled... "a traitor to the Empire and decrees," as if to shed a great burden, the messenger shrieked, "his immediate execution!"

"This means war!" Carausius bellowed, and raised his voice to a roar everyone on board was meant to hear, "I, Marcus Aurelius Mausaeus Carausius, declare myself Emperor in Britain and Northern Gaul, which area will be known as the *Imperium Britannicum*. There are now three Augusti: salute Imperator Caesar Marcus Aurelius!"

The Dalmatians drew their swords and raised them above their heads. "Hail Caesar!"

The oarsmen on each deck beat their fists on their benches and repeated the cry over and over.

"We have our Emperor of the North," Valdor said to Heidar. "And now, it's off to war."

The new emperor heard him and grinned. "Too true, my friend, and with stalwarts like you, I shall prevail." He turned to the Dalmatians. "Put these three in irons, for the moment, they know too much! Prepare for battle, Centurion, we'll attack Russus' galley."

Valdor ensured there were four javelins for each of his Dalmatians and inspected them as they lined up behind their shields.

"Shall we prepare the catapult and pitch, Lord?" Heidar asked.

"We shall not, Decurion. I do not wish to destroy or sink the galley. It will be useful in the forthcoming war. Neither do I wish to annihilate the crew. Those who can be spared in victory will follow me! I want Leander Russus' head. A *solidus* goes to he who severs it from his body." Only the men close to Heidar heard this, but the words engendered a great ferment among them. A gold solidus was the equivalent of six months' pay for a legionary, few of whom had even touched such a coin, as their pay came in silver denarii.

Normally, a war galley approaching an anchored vessel would steer amidships to ram the stationary ship, but their new emperor had been explicit; he wanted to preserve the *Leopard* at all costs.

Instead, they came swiftly alongside, observing the pandemonium aboard the enemy vessel, whose rowers rushed to gather arms. Carausius ordered the *corvus* to be dropped. The long spike knifed into the deck, and the emperor watched as the first across was the man with the transverse plume: Valdor. He was closely followed by the decurions. He smiled grimly; the role of a centurion in the Roman army was not all prestige. On the whole, they were short-lived for this very reason; they put duty and glory before personal safety.

Valdor, and the rest of the vanguard knew they would find Leander Russus on the tower at the stern, overlooking events to send tactical orders to the men on deck. Having disposed of the first onrushing defenders, Valdor pushed Heidar forward, took several steps backwards, and issued orders. The response to his command was a hail of javelins falling into the oncoming defenders followed by his Dalmatians forming into a wedge as practised on the training ground. He placed himself at the head of the wedge and set the pace with a slow forward march.

The sight of the relentless and deliberate oncoming wedge formation unmanned the relatively inexperienced crew, who responded by dropping their weapons and squatting on the deck, despite the hysterical shouting from the tower and the flailing vine whips of the centurions, determined to make a noble fight of it. Valdor chose the nearest centurion, still busily flogging a recalcitrant man, and slew him, distracted with his arm raised. Heidar led the wedge around the squatting and, in some cases, bleeding men. "Go to the bows!" he shouted. "You will be spared."

The demoralised crewmen needed no further encouragement but fled from the vine whips past the grinning foe to stand huddled in the front of the ship. A Dalmatian decurion broke formation, first to slay a resisting enemy centurion, then to bound up the steps where several bodyguards defended their captain. Fortunately for the decurion, inspired by lust for a solidus, several other decurions followed his example to make an even fight of it. Valdor hastened to join them, but with the difference that he bellowed, "Halt, lower your weapons, the

Emperor Marcus Aurelius has decreed that those among you who wish to join his legion will be spared today. Look below on deck, there is no further resistance. The day is lost, and the emperor's victory is secure. Join your brothers and fight for the glorious Emperor of the North!"

He read uncertainty on the faces of the bodyguard surrounding their captain, so added, "I, too, was a captain's bodyguard, a nobody, but raised to centurion by my generous emperor. So, I know how hard it is for you to abandon Leander Russus, but remember, the traitor was he, not our new emperor. He deserted the fleet to run off with falsities to Maximian. The bounty we won was shared among the men."

"Pay no heed to this liar!" Russus shrieked. "Fight like men!"

"The cause is lost, lord," one of the guards said to the corpse of Drusus, who had fallen to the blade of a Dalmatian decurion while everyone was distracted by the debate. The same decurion was now busy hacking the head from the body. Valdor took charge *Hard, but fair; kind but hard*, "Come, my comrades, we must return to port." He led the way down the ladder and addressed the cowering crew, "The battle is over, you now serve the Emperor of the North, Caesar Marcus Aurelius," he had a moment of inspiration, "who promises you a donative within the space of a month."

These words were greeted by raucous cheering, handshaking among themselves, and wide grins.

"But now," bellowed Valdor, pointing to the victorious galley, "Greet your Caesar and then back to stations. We will raise the *corvus*."

As the 'Hail Caesar' rang out, to be met with the recognition of a hand wave from the swarthy, stocky, curly-haired and curly-bearded figure on the stern tower, Valdor took Heidar aside. "I'll leave you with your thirty men to guard this ship, although I don't expect trouble. Have them sail to the harbour and then row to their berth." He turned to others of his men. "Prepare ropes around the *corvus*. We'll cross it, back to our ship and free it to stand upright."

The struggle to free the *corvus* was as difficult as expected, but after adding extra muscle, they succeeded.

Valdor hurried to his emperor, "Caesar, it is clear we won the day, but at a cost."

"What? I saw none of our men fall."

"Thank the gods, that is true, but I promised the crew a donative within the space of a month, to obtain their loyalty."

Carausius slapped him on the back and grinned. "My friend, you are a diplomat and should wear the imperial purple, but don't let my words go to your head! What you promised to these rebels, I'll extend to the other crews immediately. Oh, what's this?"

"The head of yon galley's captain, Caesar," said the decurion, "I slew him myself and removed the head."

"I shall keep my promise, Decurion, but I will need you to bring your grisly trophy to a captains' meeting that I will call in port."

"So be it, Sire," the decurion bowed and moved away to show the head to the few curious Dalmatians.

The two galleys arrived together in the harbour, gliding perfectly into position. Carausius spoke quietly to Valdor, issuing commands for their arrival on the quay.

The first of these was to convene the captains on the quay. The second was to intimidate them by encircling them with Dalmatian troops, and this was followed by the decurion, bearing the deceased captain's head by the hair, breaking through the ring of steel, accompanied by Valdor. The centurion raised his voice, "In the name of your emperor, Caesar Marcus Aurelius, I inform you that any of you who do not swear allegiance to him will meet the same fate as the traitor Leander Russus." On cue, the decurion raised the head of the rebel captain and showed it at close quarters to the aghast assembly.

"But," continued Valdor, "those of you swearing allegiance will receive, along with all your crew, a donative within the space of a month." He watched as the captains put their heads together, and before a conspiracy could brew, he added, "the same news has been delivered to your ships."

As Providence would have it, at that very moment the raised voices of eight galleys chorused repeatedly, "Hail Caesar Marcus Aurelius!" The crews' loyalty had been obtained by blatantly appealing to their desire for silver. One of the captains stepped forward and in a loud voice called out the same refrain. He was soon followed by the others, except one, a white-haired fellow with a swarthy complexion, Cyrillus Drusus, who drew very close to Valdor and thrust out his chin, "I'll not follow a barbarian with the features of an ape." No sooner had the words left his mouth than Valdor's blade had pierced his heart. Although he had slain him, Valdor could only admire the man's courage and loyalty, if not his folly. He wiped the bloody blade on the captain's cloak, then sheathed his sword and, with a nod, dismissed his men, remaining alone with the captains. "I need not remind you that today you have sworn loyalty to the glorious Emperor of the North. I will make it my personal mission to destroy any of you who reneges on their word. I swear this by all the gods!" *Hard, but fair; kind but hard.* He drew his gladius and kissed the blade to solemnise the oath.

6

BRANODUNUM FORT, NORFOLK, 296 AD

THE FOLLOWING MORNING, THE GARRISON AWOKE TO THE sound of hammering. Shaking off his sleepiness, Valdor peered out of his window to see the carpenters erecting a dais in the courtyard. He correctly imagined that the emperor meant to address his men. So, it came as no surprise when the southern gate opened to admit an orderly procession of sailors from all the galleys. Soon, they were joined by the soldiers of the garrison, including the Dalmatian cavalrymen.

Everyone waited in anticipation for the new emperor to make his appearance, and he came, with the cloak of imperial purple thrown over his shoulders and with a peaked diadem of office upon his head. Suddenly, the throng of soldiers and mariners fell silent as the emperor raised a hand.

"Comrades, I renew my pledge of a donative within a month. But let us not be deluded; we know that there are now three emperors: myself, Maximian, and Diocletian. I can count on the goodwill of Diocletian because last year, here, in Britannia, I won a famous battle after he assumed the title of *Britannicus Maximus*, and he is grateful and respects me. But, influenced by lies, Caesar Maximian has decreed my execution, which means he is preparing for war. Well, let him know that I can count on three legions here in Britannia, all of which are superior in discipline and strength to anything he can muster. Comrades, we shall prevail. But first, before we move, I shall honour my pledge. I ask only that you bear with me for a few weeks because, as you know, it takes time to gather a decent amount of silver. It is my priority!"

These words were greeted by a thunderous roar of approval, which stopped as if by enchantment when the emperor raised a finger and thumb above his head, holding a gold solidus that caught the sunlight and flashed brilliantly.

"Comrades, see how Caesar Marcus Aurelius honours his word. Step forward, Decurion!" bellowed Carausius, turning to grasp the arm of the Dalmatian decurion. "This man slew my enemy, the treacherous Captain Leander Russus, who spread poisonous lies against my person and turned Maximian against me. I pledged a solidus to the man who brought me his head. Here is the coin, Comrade, take it with your emperor's gratitude." He embraced the embarrassed soldier to deafening cheers. Carausius enjoyed and milked the moment, waving to the approving throng. Suddenly, he raised a hand and silence fell again. "I seek an artist, one capable of capturing my portrait. It is an opportunity for one of you to gain some coins. If there is a competent artist among you, step forward!"

Three men stepped out of the crowd and approached the dais, stopping to bow before their emperor.

Valdor felt sympathy for the three men. He considered Carausius his friend, but by no stretch of the imagination did he have godlike features; rather, his were coarse and pug-like. It was difficult to gaze upon Carausius and not consider him a barbarian thug, as expressed by the late, unlamented Captain Drusus, of Roman patrician birth.

Rather they than me! But why does he want a portrait, now?

He was soon to find out. An hour after the parade ground dismissal, Carausius summoned him to his chamber. He found the three artists there, charcoal in hand and portraits ready for exhibition.

"Ah, Centurion! Come in, I require your opinion. Which of these three portraits, place them on the table, Comrades, do you prefer?"

Valdor looked at the honest renditions with some trepidation but, after a brief hesitation, pointed to the one on the left. "I find this one captures you well, Sire."

"Ah, then we are in agreement, good Valdor," Carausius said, to his relief, a sentiment he kept closely hidden. "Even so, I am grateful to you other two. Here is a smaller recompense for your efforts, which anyway, will grace my wall." He handed them each two denarii. "As for you," he said to the chosen artist, "I require your further services. Take another vellum and draw a large circle. Imagine it to be the reverse of a coin but it must show three profiles: mine," he laid two silver denarii on the table and tapped each with his forefinger, "those of Maximian and Diocletian — a new version of a Triumvirate and underneath, the legend CARAVSIVS ET FRATRES SVI— Carausius and his brothers."

When the artist had finished, the emperor said, "Now, back to my portrait, write the legend PAX AVGGG, the peace of *three* Augusti."

Mmm, cunning devil! That implies that he is recognised by the other two current Augusti, thought Valdor, *smart move!*

He didn't have time for further reflections because the newly self-appointed emperor turned to him, "As you see, Centurion, I will have my own coinage, and it is your duty to take all of your cavalrymen to the mints in Londinium and Colonia Claudia Victricensis, and I want none of their excuses. If need be, slaughter the lot of them, but come away with all of their reserves of silver and gold transformed into my coinage. Your Dalmatians will ensure safe transport back to Branodunum. Do not fail me, Centurion Valdor. You are becoming my right hand!"

"I am humbled, Caesar, and your wish is my command."

The artist rolled up the two sheets of vellum and bound them together with a red ribbon before scooping up the six denarii given to him by his generous emperor. Valdor felt the gold solidus in his pocket and decided to visit the stalls in the camp to change the coin into more practical silver denarii before departing the fort. He bowed out of his emperor's presence, bearing the precious sketches. At a stall, he bought an expensive whetstone, costly because it had two degrees of roughness so that sharpening a blade could be done more precisely. This enabled him to change his coin easily. At another stall, for just one denarius, he bought a pendant image of Epona, the sole Celtic divinity worshipped in Rome itself as the patroness of cavalry. He took off his helm, bowed his head, and allowed the British woman stallkeeper the satisfaction of looping the leather thong over his head. *Epona, may you protect me in battle!*

Next, he summoned Heidar. "Assemble the century. All my men are to ride to Colonia Claudia Victricensis on an important mission. Encourage them by telling them we are going to collect the emperor's donative. Soon, they will receive it, but only if we return with it safe and sound."

He wandered over to the stables, realising that he hadn't seen Sparax for several days, a rarity because he loved his stallion as he might a brother if only he had one. There was a married sister back in Batavia. He wondered if he would ever see Alodia again. Would he have nephews or nieces that he would never see? His destiny was now in the hands of a terrestrial god, namely, Caesar Marcus Aurelius, or as he knew him first, Carausius. His emperor pressed a map into his hands.

"Use this, it is a copy of Iter IX of the Antonine Itinerary and the only reliable guide to our roads in Britannia. If you ride south to *Venta Icenorum*, you will have the precise route to *Camulodunum*, the site of the first mint and thence to *Londinium*, where the second mint is located."

Valdor took the map gratefully and saluted his emperor with a clenched fist to his chest.

At the stables, he caressed Sparax's sleek coat and pressed a silver coin into the young Briton's hand, the one which groomed his stallion so assiduously that the horse's forelock felt like silk thread. He whispered to the stallion, whose gentle whinnies showed him how much his horse had missed him. "We're going a long way, my beauty, but fear not, I'll look after you."

His century set off out of the southern gate and took up a gravel-surface road some fifteen yards wide with a ditch either side and headed southwards to *Venta Icenorum*, the trading capital of the Iceni tribe. Their early morning departure meant that they arrived in sight of the flint defensive walls by mid-afternoon, by which time, every one of them and his steed was weary from the ride. The town, with its forum, two impressive temples, and baths was a thriving combination of Romano-British activities. Rather than thinking of relaxing in the baths, Valdor thought of the well-being of Sparax and the other horses, so it was a relief to find a welcome in the Roman fort, where willing servants rubbed down, fed, and gave drink to the animals. The camp prefect told Valdor that the walls had just been completed in response to constant Saxon raids. Valdor reassured him that the *Classis Britannica* was on hand to deal with the pirates and that his mission was to fetch the pay for the fleet.

Having seen to the well-being of their horses, Valdor and his decurions and some of the legionaries availed themselves of the hot and cold baths to reinvigorate their aching bones. Afterwards, Valdor and Heidar joined with Johar and Faldrek to find a tavern with acceptable red wine. Their first attempt had them spitting vinegar in disgust and threatening the innkeeper, who blamed the Saxon pirates for the depredation of his best wine. However unwillingly, he told them where to find a tavern that had enjoyed better fortune than his. The streets took them past a temple with massive stone pillars. Valdor wanted to look inside, but his companions were not enamoured of the idea, so he gave Heidar three denarii and told him to start without him. He secretly hoped to find a shrine to Epona, but wasn't to know that her altar was in the town's other temple, so he contented himself by making his devotions to the helmeted statue of Minerva, the Roman goddess of war and wisdom. He prayed to her to watch over him and his close friends in battle and to give him the wisdom to fulfil his centurion duties with sagacity.

The latter part of his prayers took an immediate blow as he allowed himself to drink more of the excellent red wine than could be legitimately described as wise. As an incentive for their continued consumption, the innkeeper provided them with salted meat, cheese, and bread.

The next morning, Valdor ensured that his dearest friends rode close to him because apart from the previous evening, he and Heidar had rather lost touch with the other two. Their long-standing friendship meant that there was no envy or resentment about the promotions the other two had enjoyed. Before them, but on good roads, stretched a ride of 54 Roman miles to reach *Camulodunum*. After 30 miles, they came to *Sitomagus*, an important market town as the name *long market* suggested, the stalls stretched along the road for almost two miles, in which Valdor allowed those of his men who wished to peruse and purchase to do so without reprimand. They could always gallop to catch up with their comrades.

Apart from this brief diversion, the journey proved to be uneventful. Fortune favoured them at *Combretovium*, a Roman fort, which was garrisoned only by cavalry. This fort was at the crossing of the River Gipping and, as the camp prefect lamented, it was undermanned also because nothing ever happened since the Britons in the area were pacific and largely civilised. The official was happy to accommodate his visitors for the night and allow his grooms to pamper the steeds.

Over another excellent wine imported from Ostia, and fortified by fermented British elderberries, the prefect and Valdor hatched a plan. On their return from Londinium, whenever that might be, the entire garrison would forsake *Combretovium*, unite with Valdor, and ride to swear allegiance to the Emperor of the North. Their conversation was not as private as Valdor imagined because as he was retiring to his quarters in a rectangular timber building, he encountered three centurions who eagerly pressed him: "Is it true that we'll transfer from this godforsaken place to Branodunum? And will there truly be the prospect of an engagement? We're fed up with rotting in this place, Centurion."

"Valdor is the name, I'm Batavian by birth. But goodness, how quickly news travels in *Combretovium*!"

"So, it *is* true!" said another eagerly. "When do we leave?"

"Within the month when I stop here on our return."

"I'll bet our good prefect did not tell you the whole truth, Centurion."

"Hush!" said another, arousing Valdor's curiosity.

"Hold your tongue, Marcellus!" said the other, making it imperative for Valdor to discover what was afoot.

The one called Marcellus stuck out his chin defiantly, "We have nothing to be ashamed of, Centurion Valdor, but it's like this: the men here are a part of the disgraced 3rd legion, punished by being disbanded in 238 and sent to useless places like this because of its role in putting down an African-based revolt against Emperor Maximinus Thrax in favour of the provincial governor Gordianus. Capelianus was a legate in the legion and the officer who was falsely accused of misusing his legion to attack Gordian. It was a necessary action and I blame Maximinus for the current crisis in the Empire. He was the first emperor who hailed neither from the senatorial nor from the equestrian class. Now we have your Carausius..." Valdor's hand strayed to the hilt of his gladius, a reflex noticed by the others. Marcellus added quickly, "...of whom I have heard only good things.

"Centuriones, our emperor will be delighted to welcome you into our ranks and I, who have fought under him, can assure you that he is a great general. I, too, will welcome you as comrades." He extended a hand and had his wrist clasped three times in time-honoured fashion.

"It is time I retired because we have an early morning start, so I'll bid you goodnight." He set off for his quarters but soon heard a footfall behind him, so he spun around just in time to see the flash of a blade and throw himself to the ground. Rolling over before springing to his feet, gladius in hand, he crossed swords with a helmeted figure—the single plume indicated a decurion. The idle life at Combretovium could not match the disciplined training at Branodunum, so Valdor rapidly gained the upper hand and sent his opponent's gladius clinking on the paving stone. Pressing his blade to the decurion's throat, he uttered one word, "Why?"

"Because you wish to dishonour the 3rd legion, by inducing us to desert our duty."

"Truly, the 3rd is dishonoured already, festering here, doing nothing. My intention is to restore honour to your legion by placing you in the forefront of battle. But you'll need training to be ready, judging by what I've just seen. Since we are in the throes of a misunderstanding, Decurion, I am prepared to accept an apology and let the matter drop." Valdor slowly lowered the blade but kept a tight grip on the weapon.

"Forgive me friend, I misjudged your intentions. The 3rd legion has a glorious reputation and my only desire is to uphold it."

Valdor sheathed his gladius and smiled, offered his hand and they clasped wrists. "We need more honourable men because war is in the offing with Maximian, not to mention the Saxon and Frankish pirates that infest the Channel." He slapped the decurion's upper arm before bidding him goodnight, said, "Reassure others who might share your earlier doubts that they are uniting with a formidable fighting force. Good night, Decurion."

Pleased with the outcome of his visit to Combretovium, and departing on refreshed horses, the journey was easy on a gravel road whose ditches were 60 feet apart. Before noon, they arrived at the river Colne, where five temples graced the crossing point. Delighted by how things were faring for him and his men, Valdor was convinced that he had been guided by Minerva to the agreement at Combretovium and was determined to visit her shrine to give thanks in prayer. Rightly, he chose the largest temple and immediately found himself face-to-face with the larger-than-life statue of the helmed goddess. "O Minerva, I beg you to continue to guide your humble servant so that he accomplishes his mission to the glory of Rome," he whispered.

"Lead us to glory in battle and preserve us," came a deep voice behind him, and Valdor turned in time to see Heidar's bowed head.

"Come, let's cross the river and find what is in store in Camulodunum."

His fearless stallion waded across the ford confidently, setting the tone for the other horses so that, soon, they were before the north gate of the stone-walled town. Valdor called his *cornicen*, the horn blower, who produced a prolonged, deep vibrating sound from his curved horn. It proved immediately effective as the gates swung back and the cavalry rode into town. Valdor, who had not imagined such a bustling city existed in Britannia, led his cavalry along the *Cardo Maximus*, the well-paved main north-south street with drainage channels and fronted by houses and shops. It included footways, and the rest of the Colonia was gridded into about forty blocks known as *insula*, all with paved streets and colonnaded paths between. Valdor was impressed while at the same time concentrating on his stallion's hoofs skidding on the paving stones. They certainly slowed his progress as he did not want any of the horses to slip and become lame.

The vast, busy population reminded him that this city enjoyed the status of *Colonia* rather than *Municipia*, meaning that legally, it was an extension of Rome and its inhabitants were Roman citizens. Many of them were, in reality, retired legionaries. Next to one of these greybeards, Valdor halted his horse and called down, "Good fellow, where is the building where coins are made?"

The man saluted the centurion and replied, "Continue to the main crossing of the *Decumanus Maximus*, the main east-west street, turn right, and it is the second building on your left."

This information proved correct, meaning Valdor and Heidar entered the main portal, leaving his cavalry at ease but on call in the street. Clasping his rolled vellum, Valdor mounted the stairs to the first floor, where he found an official. He handed over the drawings and gave instructions.

The man looked uncertain and even rebellious, "But you don't have written authorisation, and we cannot utilise all of our reserves to produce what you want."

"What need is there for written authorisation when our emperor's profile speaks for itself? Dare you disobey him?" Unsheathing his sword, he said, "Decurion, go back downstairs and bring the whole century up here to persuade this disobedient servant of the empire that we mean what we say!"

"Centurion, that will not be necessary," blurted the official, "I'll set the die cutters to work at once and fire up the forge."

"That's better! And make sure that each denarius weighs precisely four and a half grams. I shall check carefully. When will the coins be ready?"

"The die will be prepared directly on the anvil, and the forge will rapidly melt the silver. Hark, Centurion, if you want a vast quantity of coins, we'll have to debase the silver somewhat with copper. It's normal practice. We can treat the coins with acid to bring the shiny silver to the surface; even an expert will not know the difference. The die cutter can hammer the mould, producing one hundred coins an hour."

"I want at least 40,000 denarii, so decide how many die cutters to use. The emperor requires me to go to Londinium to have more coins minted. I shall return in six days and expect to find that many coins, so calculate well; otherwise, it will go badly for you, as our emperor has authorised me to slaughter anyone who does not cooperate in this important matter. Let me remind you that I have a century of bloodthirsty Dalmatian cavalry outside just waiting for an excuse to use their weapons."

"Go to Londinium in peace, Centurion. Upon your return, your coins will be bagged up and waiting for you."

"They had better be!" Valdor snarled and marched out of the room.

7

CAMULODUNUM TO LONDINIUM AND BACK TO BRANODUNUM FORT, AD 286

VALDOR LED HIS CAVALRY THROUGH THE MONUMENTAL archway of the west gate and remembered the camp prefect's words. This was the *Porta Clausa*, built to commemorate the crushing victory of Emperor Claudius in 61 AD when he terrorised the local tribesmen by using war elephants. The name of the city in Latin was *Colonia Claudia Victricensis*, so named after Claudius' victory, whereas Camulodunum was a Romanised version of the Brythonic name, just as the *Balkerne Gate* was the Porta Clausa to the locals. The past glory of the Empire in Britannia could still be read in such Camulodunum structures as its vast circus, but Valdor had plans of his own to re-establish Roman supremacy in Britannia under Carausius. If that meant riding to *Londinium*, which by all accounts was as large and important as Camulodunum, so be it!

The Antonine Itinerary indicated a road running westwards called Stane Street, which led to a three-way interchange, one of which led directly to Londinium and was known as the Great Road. An engraved milestone indicated 70 Roman miles—70,000 paces of a Roman soldier. He sighed at the thought of the 139-mile return journey awaiting them, stretching back from Londinium to Branodunum Fort. But that was in the future, for his mission was less than half completed at this stage. But would he achieve success in time for his emperor?

The journey was swift and uneventful, owing to the remarkable work of the Roman engineers who had made a road surface ideal for rapid military transfers. The journey remained uneventful until the Great Road brought them to the Thames crossing, where an entire Roman cohort emerged onto the north bank. Valdor blinked; there was something different about this force. In an instant, he understood—the skin colours! These legionaries were, for the most part, black, others brown. The centurion who rode towards him and hailed him was not black but distinctly swarthy.

"Hail friend, we are the *Auxilia Palatina,* fresh from victory on the Danube. I am Centurion Ibrahim Ibn Attab—that's my true name in my own language. Emperor Diocletian, in his infinite wisdom, has rewarded us by sending us without pay to the confines of Britannia." His voice dripped with sarcasm, and his dark eyes were hard. "This valiant cohort is to garrison the Aballava Fort at the western end of the wall, built when Emperor Hadrian reigned." His sincere disapproval became obvious when he said bitterly, "What sense is there in all this? It's freezing cold here, so why send men from Mauretania to the frozen north of this accursed land to act as *limitanei*? But enough of my moaning. What of you?"

"I am Centurion Valdor, a Batavian, but my men are the *Equites Dalmatae*, Dalmatian cavalry. We are on an important mission for Imperator Caesar Marcus Aurelius, Emperor of Britannia and Northern Gaul."

"Hold!" the Mauritanian interrupted, his expression revealing his perplexity but also hope, "Are you saying there is a new emperor? Where is he based, in Londinium?"

"Nay, we are with the *Classis Britannia,* the fleet based on the coast 140 miles hence."

The Moor's eyes glinted with slyness. Half-turning in his saddle, ensuring that his men had joined him, he said, "Well, this changes everything. But tell me, maybe our new emperor will spare my men from chill exposure in the northern fastnesses. Why are you heading for Londinium?"

Valdor looked at the centurion from head to toe. *I cannot trust him. I will not tell him!*

"Centurion Ibrahim," Valdor smiled, "as I said, we are on an important mission for our emperor that will detain us several days in the city."

"It must be *important* to send so many men to accomplish it. What is the nature of your assignment?"

I'm damned if I'll tell you.

"I am not at liberty to reveal it."

The unmistakable irritation was plain in the swarthy countenance. Although his eyes did not, Ibn Attab's mouth smiled, "I'll tell you what we will do. We shall make an encampment hereabouts and await your return after these *several days,* then, we'll accompany you north to the emperor, for I wish for an audience with him."

Valdor hid his feelings and gave the Moor a friendly smile, all the while eyeing the newcomer's cavalry and massed infantry. "Very well, Centurion, I cannot be certain how many days it will take, but we'll meet here when my mission is fulfilled," he lied.

I must devise a plan. I cannot risk the coins with a whole cohort of Africans in the offing.

The officers clasped wrists, and Valdor then led his cavalry to the great river Thames, across it and south to the Aldgate, one of seven gates in the Roman-built walls girdling the city.

His encounter in the mint was even more hostile than that received in Camulodunum. This time there was bloodshed, not only inside the building but outside, too, the Dalmatians had to fend off a part of the garrison summoned urgently by the mint officials. Their resistance disappeared like slush in the rain when Valdor, without hesitation, struck down the obstructing prefect in charge of the mint. Suddenly the obstruction ran away like melting snow and changed with the sun into cooperation. Valdor displayed the sketches of the emperor's profile and demanded haughtily of an official, "How soon before you provide me with the 40,000 denarii?"

"If we work also at night with all our available men, I can have them done within forty-eight hours, Centurion."

"Mmm. See that you do; otherwise..." he jerked a thumb at the blood-soaked corpse and left the rest unspoken.

"Have no doubts, Centurion. I'll oversee the production myself."

"Good man! Two days is enough for us to obtain a solid cart and two strong carthorses. Hark, I need to know, apart from the Great Road, is there another that leads to Camulodunum?"

"Ay, there is. You can take the Ermine Street, which leaves through the Bishop's Gate."

"Perfect!"

Centurion Ibrahim Ibn Attab, you'll not get your thieving hands on our silver coin!

Two days later, Valdor selected thirty Dalmatians, took them to a tavern, and bought them each a couple of beakers of the best red wine to ensure their goodwill, returned to the mint, and oversaw them load the new cart with bulging bags of silver coins. Prior to the loading, he had them accompany him upstairs to the production centre, where he ordered the weighing of a randomly chosen denarius. It was exactly 4.5 grams, which satisfied him. The brutish features of Carausius on the coin seemed to smile up at him in approval.

Unfortunately, on exiting the main door, Valdor and his decurions did not spot the black-faced figure lurking in a shady portal of a nearby building, so they set off for Bishopsgate without undue preoccupation. The Ermine Street crossed the river just below Cricklade and would have taken them to Glevum, but they found the intersection with its milestone indicating Colonia Claudia Vitricensis.

They had been on this road at the steady pace dictated by the sturdy carthorses for a while when in the distance, the drumming of galloping horses assailed their ears, and, swivelling in his saddle, Valdor saw a cloud of dust raised by the selfsame hoofs. He rapidly issued orders: "Halt! Defensive formation around the cart, weapons drawn!"

Centurion Ibn Attab's eyes were anything but friendly, "Centurion Valdor, you broke our agreement! Did you think you could elude my spies? I now know your mission was to obtain coinage for our emperor. But hark, instruct your men to sheath their weapons because we come in peace and wish to *buy* from you and not steal your coins. We wish to buy the emperor's goodwill by pacifically accompanying you to your base wherever that is."

Can I trust this man?

"Where are your infantry, Centurion Ibn Attab?" Valdor asked, scanning the road behind him.

The Moor laughed, "They are fast, but cannot keep pace with my cavalry. I will leave a horseman to order them to march to... where, Centurion?"

"To Camulodunum, but beware, Ibn Attab, do not incur the wrath of Caesar Marcus Aurelius. His coins must arrive undiminished at our base."

I'll not inform you where that is until I'm good and ready!

"And so, it shall be! I do not blame you for your mistrust, brother. I would have done the same." The deep brown eyes were sincere and met Valdor's grey-blue eyes without faltering.

As one, the Dalmatians sheathed their swords at Valdor's gesture—in itself, an impressive display of leadership—and the Moors, obeying Valdor's command, delivered in Latin, much to his satisfaction, formed up behind his Dalmatians, and the steady advance continued. For a while, he chatted with the Mauritanian centurion, without revealing their ultimate destination because he had a plan that depended upon his calculations: *Ibn Attab commands these eighty cavalrymen, but he has a cohort, so there will be 400 infantrymen. They must not know that our destination is Branodunum until I gather reinforcements at Combretovium.*

First, however, they had to add to their load by calling at Camulodunum. A surprise awaited them there. The western gate, the one with the monumental archway, by which they had left the town and now approached, had been bricked up during their week's absence. Valdor could see no structural purpose in this as the monumental archway revealed no lesions or other reasons. Since the walls contained three other gates, Valdor led his men around them as far as the southern entrance. He halted them there, distant from the mint, and took his most loyal Dalmatians, the ones from the tavern, with him in case of trouble, and the carthorses and cart. The bricking of the archway, he discovered, was simply a precaution to strengthen the walls, for it was regarded as a weak point. After checking and withdrawing the coins, he had them loaded with those from Londinium and returned to the bulk of his force, where a shock awaited him.

He had left just over a hundred men but now found five hundred! The Mauritanian infantry had arrived, and he was in time to hear Centurion Ibn Attab address them in Arabic—loyally, although he could not know it—: "Men, we are no longer going to Hadrian's Wall…" he had to raise a hand for silence such was the positive murmuring caused by his words. "…and we are no longer serving Emperor Diocletian, but the new Emperor Marcus Aurelius, who will recompense you for your toils." This remark was greeted by unrestrained cheering until Ibn Attab raised his hand again, now, for the benefit of Valdor, he spoke in Latin, "as from this moment, you will obey the orders of Centurion

Valdor, your new commander." He pointed him out, lest anyone was in doubt. Again, these words were greeted by murmurs, this time a neutral sound. "I have promised them a reward from the Emperor of the North," Ibn Attab explained to the new commander.

"I shall see that they will have it if they obey me," Valdor replied.

It was just after noon, so Valdor went to the camp prefect and asked about the possibility of spontaneously feeding nearly 600 men. He expected a rebuff but was surprised to receive a positive reply and, to ensure the Moors' loyalty, Valdor was able to accommodate them in the refectory in turns of 50 men. Fresh bread and seasoned cheese accompanied by red wine was simple fare, but manna to the famished infantrymen. They gobbled the food, so the turnaround was fast. Within an hour, Valdor was ready to lead the 25-mile march to Combretovium. The infantrymen could march at almost three miles an hour; the well-disciplined *Auxilia Palatina* neither flagged nor complained, so thankful for the long hours of daylight, Valdor brought his men across the river Gipping and across the triple ditches of the Roman fort of Combretovium as twilight cloaked the land.

When the approaching force sounded a triple blast of the *cornum*, the gates swung open and the camp prefect rode out on a fine white charger.

"I am pleased you honoured our agreement, Centurion Valdor, although I expected no less from you. But I see you are now leading African legionaries."

The interrogative tone of this statement made Valdor answer in Latin for the benefit of the Moors within earshot, "Aye, we met at the Thames, where Centurion Ibn Attab and his valiant men decided to follow your example by swearing allegiance to the Emperor of the North. But, heed me, Prefect, the men are weary after tramping this morning from Londinium."

"By the gods! That's some feat! They can sleep in the fort as we have many unoccupied beds in the barracks. Pray give orders," he wheeled his horse, waved a signal to the gatekeeper, and the second door swung back.

To obtain the loyalty of men, sometimes it is more important to be lucky rather than a capable commander. Valdor was endowed with both virtues. His arrival with extra men coincided with the Roman desertion of Combretovium, so there was no problem about eating and drinking what provisions remained, for the Provisioner was not concerned about the morrow. After the previous lean days of near-famine, the Mauritanians felt that the gods had supplied them with the best officer in the world. Even if Valdor could not speak their language, the flashing white teeth of ready smiles soon convinced him of his popularity among his new troops.

The following day, at the halt station of Venta Icenorum, he endeared himself further. In possession of 80,000 denarii, he felt it incumbent upon himself to issue one silver piece to all of his new additions, which cost him less than 1,000 denarii. He allowed his troops an hour's break to do as they wished with their pay. Most drank it away, others paid for sex, but he saw some at market stalls purchasing trinkets. Wherever he went, he was greeted with joyous smiles and friendly nods.

They arrived at Branodunum Fort in ordered ranks, the cavalry flanking the infantry at both sides. Never had Valdor dreamt that he would lead men and never had a sound rung so sweetly in his ears as the triple blast of the *cornum* outside the northern gate. Proudly he led his troops into the fortress to be greeted by his beaming emperor, who asked: "What do you do on a mission, Centurion, breed soldiers?"

"They need pay, Sire."

"We all do, Centurion, and so it shall be!"

Valdor was glad to be home but he was not alone as Sparax whinnied a happy neigh as the three Batavians hurried to embrace their returning friend. They managed this without taking their eyes off the bulging money bags. In this, they were not alone, as soldiers and sailors alike waited for the emperor to fulfil his promise.

8

BRANODUNUM FORT, NORFOLK, AD 296

THE EMPEROR ORDERED A ROOM TO BE EQUIPPED WITH shelves, groaning under the weight of bags of silver coins, with a desk where an official doled out denarii after entering the recipient's name in a ledger. Upon receiving his shiny coins, each man signed his name or placed his mark against the sum. It was a long process, for all the legionaries, whether established or newcomers, were in line to receive their pay together with the sailors. The centurions collected first, followed by the decurions before the lower ranks entered. As one of the first to get his pay, Valdor decided to pass the time by climbing the south-eastern lookout tower to breathe in the sea breeze, and from where he could survey the harbour and its approaches.

He was surprised to see the increase in moored vessels since his absence. Undoubtedly the fleet had swollen due to the capture of pirate ships. He recognised the shallow-draughted Saxon vessels and the shape of the Frankish two-masted river craft, which somehow the marauders managed to keep afloat in the rougher North Sea. To add to this mixed score of shipping were Roman trading vessels. Had they been captured or levied by the emperor? He didn't know for sure.

His surprise increased when his eyes shifted to a shipyard. Faintly, he could hear hammering. One galley was near completion and four others under construction, one of them little more than a keel. *The emperor must be concerned about Maximian's threat. I need an excuse to speak with him, especially now that he has given me command of both the Dalmatian and Mauritanian cavalry. I'd like to know how close we are to war.*

His excuse came in the most unexpected form. As his eyes turned inland, he saw a legion marching on Branodunum. A well-disciplined march it was, too. He could see the SPQR eagle standard from his tower and, unless he was mistaken, another with II proudly displayed. So, this was the legion II Augusta, stationed in *Glevum*, the Cambrian frontier town the Britons called *Caerloyw*. The question was, did they come as enemies, loyal to Maximian, or as deserters prepared to throw in their lot with the new emperor, Carausius?

Valdor dashed down the winding stairs and to the emperor's quarters, which was no more than a spartan chamber equipped with a bed in one corner and a desk under a window. A fire burnt in the centre of the room, for the sea air had freshened now that summer had given way to autumn. It was difficult to imagine what luxurious quarters Emperor Diocletian must enjoy when he gazed at this rudimentary room, little better than the legionary's barracks.

"What is it, Valdor? Have you not been paid your fair share?"

"As to that, lord, I am more than happy. Nay, I come to warn you of the arrival of an entire Roman legion. I believe it to be II Augusta but cannot be sure until it is right under our walls."

"How come it is always you who informs me, Valdor? Are you the only one awake in this fortress! How long before they reach us?"

"I'd hazard a quarter of an hour."

"So soon? We'd better prepare the men."

"They won't like that! They are being paid."

Carausius roared with laughter. "That's true, so we'll bar the gates and anyone, like you, who has received his pay will take his arms and draw up behind the gate."

Valdor decided that now was the time to raise his query.

"Caesar, I also saw that you are building new galleys and have added to the fleet. Are we about to sail to face Maximian?"

Again, came the bellow of a laugh.

"How can Maximian assemble a fleet? He gave me his! Nay, *we* do not sail, *you* sail with your cavalry, Valdor."

The conversation terminated abruptly as three sharp blasts of a *cornum* rang out from outside the gates.

"More of that later, Centurion. Quickly, I must wear the purple! We'll mount the gate tower and see with what we have to contend." He snatched up the imperial diadem and rammed it on his head. It lent the coarse features an undoubted dignity and authority. Valdor ran to keep up with the emperor's stride. Stocky, he might be, but he could move rapidly, as under the toga were thighs of iron.

Standing at the battlements before Valdor arrived breathless, Carausius said, "Look at the emblems, every shield bears the Capricornus and the other emblems are Pegasus and Mars. You were right, this is *Legio II Augusta*."

"I like the horned goat on the shield," Valdor said irrelevantly, "I must acquire one."

"When we've defeated them, my friend."

But there was no need. A hand pointed up to the battlements and a strong voice cried, "Hail Caesar, Imperator Marcus Aurelius: Legio II Augusta at your service!"

"Valdor, put on your helmet, go out the gate, and see if we can trust them enough to welcome them into our ranks."

"I'm on my way, Caesar." Valdor beat his chest with his fist in the standard salute and hurried down to get his plumed helmet. Confidence increased by wearing the insignia of his rank, he ordered the gates to be opened and rode out on Sparax to meet the commander, who introduced himself as Legate Vitulasius.

"You have a fine steed, Centurion, my congratulations. I thought I saw our emperor over the gateway?"

"Indeed, lord, he came to see whether II Augusta had come in peace and friendship."

The legate smiled, "Your emperor will be pleasantly surprised because, to my knowledge, XX Valeria Victrix, based in Deva and, therefore, not far from the territory of the Silures, whence we came, will follow our example and swear allegiance to the Emperor of the North."

"You know that it may mean war with Emperor Maximian, Legate, are you prepared for that eventuality?"

"I have spoken with my counterpart in Deva, and he fully understands the implications of our decision."

"You are most welcome in the *Fortress of the Crows*, as many call Branodunum. I shall not presume to command your horn blower, but the gates must be opened to your legion."

The legate bowed in acknowledgement of the courtesy and cried, "Three blasts, *Cornicen*!"

Even as the third resonant note faded, the great gates swung back.

"Your men will be weary, I'll see to refreshment for them, but first, I must accompany you to the emperor, ride with me."

Once they arrived inside the compound, stable boys met them and led the beasts away while Valdor took Legate Vitulasius to Carausius' quarters.

The newcomer knelt before his new emperor and, having formally given his name and rank, said, "I have come to deliver the Legio II Augusta to you, Caesar. As their commander, I swear allegiance."

"Let it be known, Legate, that any disloyalty in the ranks will be punished by death," Carausius said bluntly.

The high-ranking officer looked around the spartan quarters and said approvingly, "Reports do not lie, you are a true soldier—hard but fair."

I have heard that before, thought Valdor and smiled.

"You are most welcome to Branodunum, Legate. I have only one other condition to stipulate. My centurion here desires a *scutum* of the II Augusta. He has a liking for goats!"

The famous bellowed laugh surprised the legate, but soon he would grow accustomed to it; meanwhile, he assented immediately, "I shall find you a *shield* without battle scars, Centurion."

Valdor felt that circumstances were favouring his emperor day after day, and with his good fortune, his own went apace. Now was not the time to ask what the emperor had meant earlier by *you sail with your cavalry.* That could wait until the morrow. Now he had to see to the welfare of the II Augusta. No one knew better than he what toll a cross-country march took.

Once he had dealt with that, he was free again.

Although the three friends from his village were still dear to him, it was inevitable that he had become closer to Heidar, his trusted decurion. There had to be a certain detachment from Faldrek and Johar to avoid rancour among the other legionaries. Valdor was well aware that he should display no favouritism, but an opportunity arose to draw nearer to them when Carausius summoned him the following day.

"Have the II Augusta been adequately accommodated, Centurion?"

"Ay, they have, Caesar. It's just that—"

"What?"

"It's not in my place, but since Legate Vitulasius informed me of the likelihood of *Legio XX Valeria Victrix* coming to swear allegiance—"

"He did not tell me this!"

"Forgive me, Sire, he must have believed I had referred the matter…"

Carausius smiled, "Well, it *is* good news."

"Ay, lord, except—"

"Except?"

Valdor was hesitant as he didn't wish to risk the wrath of his fiery emperor. He did not want to overstep the mark. But he knew that keeping Caesar waiting for his reply was a sure way to arouse his temper, so he blurted, "We are overcrowded in Branodunum as it is, Sire. With XX Valeria Victrix, we'll need to construct new barracks."

The roar of laughter, always a possible reaction from Carausius, surprised Valdor.

"When you said it was not in your place, you seemed as timid as a serving wench, Centurion. I do not doubt your courage or spirit, so I take it that your emperor intimidates you," he smiled smugly.

"Nay, Sire, not *intimidate*, it's a question of respect."

"Well, let me tell you something, young man, your emperor respects your views, so be bold and air them whenever you see fit. As proof, now I shall order work to begin on constructing ten *contubernia* with larger officers' quarters attached." Again, came the formidable roar of laughter, followed by, "Also, *you* and your cavalry will ease the problem."

"Sire?"

"Think about who you wish to take to *Gallia*. Precisely to *Gesoriacum*—the place your people and mine call Boulogne—my spies tell me that Maximian is building war galleys there in preparation for an invasion of Britannia. Your task, Centurion, is to reduce the new vessels to ashes. Once you have done that, my orders are to proceed to your old village and to destroy any of Maximian's Romans in the area. I will not have an enemy on my doorstep. As yet, I have not worked out the details of my invasion of Gaul. I've decided to wait for news that the enemy ships are burnt. Then, likely I'll join you in Gallia with all the men at my disposal. Let's hope the news about XX Victrix is correct! I also have Frankish allies I can call upon."

He has truly taken me into his confidence.

As if he had noticed Valdor's concentration stray, Carausius said, "I want you to take all four horse transports because it'll be strictly a cavalry campaign until further orders, but you may also take two galleys both for defence and attack," he said enigmatically. "Why don't you take the Moorish infantry, they covered themselves in glory on the Danube. I've discussed that campaign with their commander, Centurion Ibrahim Ibn Attab. He has the makings of a fine general; Diocletian did me a favour sending him to Britannia. Oh, and take your Batavian friends with you. They know the area between the Rhine and the Waal; they could prove useful to you in capturing the area. Go and make preparations, you sail at dawn tomorrow. Judging by the red sky, it'll be a fine day tomorrow. Fare thee well, my friend, and," his pugnacious face thrust into Valdor's, "do not fail me and keep me informed."

"Your will is mine, Sire."

Valdor took his leave, bowing out of his emperor's presence, smiling wryly at the bustling courtyard where only the Mauritanians were undergoing drill. *They'll be glad to get some action.* With this thought, he hastened to find Heidar. After discovering that he had finished in the forge for the day, he reflected and had a good idea where he would find him. His intuition proved correct but with a bonus. His friend was, like himself, as a child brought up by the sea. Military discipline meant that he could not leave the fortress to wander along the shore at will, so the next best thing was to watch the sea from a tower. He found him on the south-eastern turret, beloved of Valdor, in the company of Faldrek and Johar. All three were staring out to sea when Valdor made them jump by saying, *"Ave Socii,"* translating, "Hail comrades," for the benefit of Faldrek, who had difficulty grasping the Latin tongue.

"Valdor!" they exclaimed in unison.

"Will the sea be calm tomorrow, cousin?"

Johar smiled happily. He had overcome his initial jealousy at Valdor's rapid promotion and now felt that his cousin bowed to his superior knowledge on matters regarding the sea.

The former fisherman looked at the sky, sniffed the air, and said, "I'd stake my life on it!"

"Good, because I bring orders from the emperor. Tomorrow, we sail at dawn and that's not all, the latter part of our mission will take us to our village."

"I doubt we'll be welcomed with open arms," Faldrek said grumpily.

"The gods only know where the menfolk are, but I'd love to see my mother and my aunt,"

Johar looked pointedly at his centurion cousin.

"We'll be on a mission, and while we mustn't be under any illusion about the womenfolk's well-being, we'll make time to find out. That's a promise, Johar. Now, orders! Heidar, have the Dalmatians accommodate their horses in the transport ships. Johar, Faldrek, take your horses on the ship and decide whether to place them above or below deck. Sparax will travel above, I've decided, especially because the weather will be fair. I must away to organise the Mauritanians, Centurion Ibn Attab will add his cavalry to ours."

"The Moors have fine steeds and know how to handle them," Heidar said.

Johar's eyes were still fixed on the sea, but he said, "I wonder if they are used to sailing, though."

He needn't have worried because Ibn Attab was quick to point out that Mauritania boasted two seas: the Mediterranean and the Atlantic. "We also have desert and mountains," he said wistfully. "But shall we see action, Centurion?" He asked this with the same yearning in his voice.

"We're not going to so much trouble not to wield our arms, my friend."

"My men will be overjoyed."

Valdor gave instructions for the cavalry and explained, "I will command the cavalry, but the emperor has chosen you to command the infantry. It seems you won his admiration when you told him about the Danube campaign."

"And he mine because his questions were astute, which only a competent general would have asked."

"Excellent, we sail at dawn, Centurion. Please explain the arrangements to your cavalrymen. Then, it's each to his respective tasks."

Among Valdor's first tasks, to the perplexity of his men, was the sequestration of every small rowing boat they could lay hands on. These were carried aboard each ship along with many bales of straw, covered with oiled cloths to prevent them from becoming damp.

The following morning, with dawn's orange-streaked sky and millpond sea, encouraged not only the mixed crews and horses to settle but also the purple-clad figure standing on the battlements, watching his ships leave the Fortress of the Crows. Of all these souls, perhaps he was the only one who wished that he was aboard one of the ships. However, wisely, he didn't embark because he wanted to assure the allegiance of XX Victoria Victrix, which, according to his scouts, was only an hour's march away. The imperial diadem sparkled orange in the low sunlight, and Valdor, on the stern tower, pointed it out to his bodyguard, Faldrek. The centurion waved and, although uncertain, thought that Carausius returned the salute.

9

GESORIACUM AND ULPIA NOVIOMAGUS BATAVORUM, GALLIA, AUTUMN, 286 AD

ON A HIGH CLIFF NEAR THE BEACH STOOD A TWO-CENTURIES-old lighthouse, built on two storeys in the reign of Emperor Caligula. Once spotted from the sea, Valdor had confirmation that they had reached their destination, but Carausius' words came to mind, "My scouts tell me that the new ships are being built on a beach of white sand, some twelve miles north of the port." To find the beach, Valdor veered his flotilla of six vessels northwards and scanned the coast for the tell-tale white sand.

The improvised shipyard was easy to find, and while his keen eyes sought signs of defence, his lookouts confirmed what he had seen for himself: there were no or few defenders. Carpenters went about their business, hammering nails and carrying a shaped wooden bulkhead to construct the hull of a galley. Others were adding what appeared to be the finishing touches to four complete war galleys, as yet without masts. Valdor calculated that the position of the low sun suggested there was an hour of daylight available before it set. It made little difference to him whether he destroyed the galleys before or after sunset, given the poor state of defence.

Logically, if he attacked immediately, he could make use of the port of Gesoriacum on the Liane estuary overnight. It would be more comfortable moored in the placid harbour than riding at anchor offshore, and the harbour was, after all, the official base of the *Classis Britannica* and, therefore, theirs, not Maximian's, by rights.

Decision taken, Valdor ordered pitch to be melted and poured over the straw filling the rowing boats, thus arousing the crews' curiosity. As soon as his men completed these preparations, the six ships towed two rowing boats each close to the completed galleys, half in the sea and half-stranded on the beach. Within twenty yards of the prey, confusion reigned in the shipyard as carpenters abandoned their tools and ran for the safety of the shore, screaming warnings. Valdor's archers picked off most of them while he ordered the straw to be lit. Black smoke puthered into the air, to be swept away instantly by the sea breeze, but before long, the fire caught, and the legionaries propelled the fire-boats among the war galleys. The effect was devastating: twelve blazing rowing boats crashed into the new hulls so that the raw wood caught instantly.

Carausius wanted the galleys reduced to ashes, and that was what he would obtain, judging by the leaping flames, snapping and crackling along the hulls. Valdor regretted that he had not reserved a fire-boat for the last of the galleys—the one the majority of carpenters had fled, so he improvised, sending a standard rowing boat with six men and three fire tubs filled with molten pitch. He watched as his men carried the tubs onto the beach and smeared the structure of the emergent galley with pitch before setting it alight. The late daylight turned artificially to night by the black smoke shrouding the beach, but the flames from the completed hulls provided a flickering red light for the coughing legionaries to carry out their task. Valdor's scrupulousness was repaid as the pitch caught and the last of the galleys became the pyre to Maximian's carpenters' efforts. The task completed, Valdor had only to wait to survey the extent of the damage.

To do this, he ordered the ships to stand off—blessedly far enough from the choking smoke to the relief of his crews and the few restive horses on deck. The last of the flames coincided with the sunset. The hulls remained little more than useless charred and smouldering skeletons, quite beyond salvage, so Valdor ordered his oarsmen to veer the ships to head for the estuary while keeping a wary eye on the headland, now illuminated by the lighthouse.

Arriving safely in port, the six vessels tied up together at the wooden quay. A surprise awaited them there, as an arrow thrummed into the tower deck at Valdor's feet. "Scuti!" he cried as one nearby crewman fell dying, clutching an arrow embedded in his chest before everyone sheltered behind raised shields. Valdor rapidly ordered his men onto the quay in serried formation to seek and exterminate the archers. He went to Sparax and led him onto the wooden jetty, mounting the stallion and taking command of his Dalmatian cavalry, who were quick to join him. Their mobility allowed him to find the fleeing enemy rapidly, who consisted of less than a score of Roman archers. The horsemen quickly surrounded them; the archers wisely did not attempt to shoot their arrows at such a superior force. The odds were overwhelmingly in Valdor's favour, so he ordered the enemy to lay down their bows. A decurion disobeyed and raised his weapon, determined to kill this arrogant centurion who had destroyed the new fleet. Before he could shoot the arrow, Johar's javelin had pierced his chest, and he fell to the ground.

Thank you, cousin!

"Hark! In the name of Emperor Marcus Aurelius, *Restitutor Britanniae*, unite with us and be saved, or fall on your swords!" Valdor bellowed and thought, *A score of archers will be useful.* But this wishful thought was not to be because three archers had the nerve to kill themselves by holding a gladius to their chests and falling upon the blade. He ordered the remaining comrades to fling the corpses into the harbour and regretfully watched the three bodies splash into the depths—food for crustaceans.

Suddenly, a Dalmatian scout galloped up, swivelled in his saddle, and pointed back over his shoulder, "Centurion, an entire legion is marching this way from the garrison!"

Valdor quickly ordered Ibn Attab to form his infantrymen into ranks and flanked them with his cavalry. He was ready to confront the enemy legion.

Soon, hundreds of flickering torches held aloft, made of reed fasces dipped in sulphur and lime, appeared over the dunes. The fiery light reflected off the shiny steel armour, but what intrigued Valdor was the absence of spears or drawn swords. His men had spears and swords at the ready behind their shields.

A tribune rode forward alone, hand raised in a gesture of parley. He selected Ibn Attab as the centurion to speak with, but the Moor gestured towards Valdor, who urged his stallion across.

"Centurion," said the tribune, "We are *Legio III Gallica* and come in peace. We know you are sworn to the Britannic emperor and that you burnt the new ships constructed for Emperor Maximian. In theory, we are sworn to serve him, but we are without pay, except for debased, worthless bronze coins with a silver wash. The men are restless and have no stomach for a fight with their brothers. Yet, I cannot surrender Gesoriacum to you as you probably wish. Is there no manner of avoiding bloodshed?"

Valdor smiled grimly, his thoughts racing: with the burning, he had accomplished the first part of his mission. This legion outnumbered him, so avoiding a fight appealed. He replied, "Tribune, as you say, neither do we wish to fight our brothers. If you agree, we shall stay in the harbour overnight and sail away to northern Gallia at dawn. Does that suit you?"

"We can always claim that we never saw who burnt the new ships and leave it at that. But hark, if you wish your men to be more comfortable for the night, we have entire *contubernia* vacant, as the old fortress was razed and a new one built in 274. Since then, we have never been at full capacity."

"It's a kind offer, Tribune, but for an early departure, it's better my men are onboard rather than in your barracks." *Besides, I don't trust you!* The two men clasped wrists in a sign of agreement, and the naval garrison of Gesoriacum wheeled and tramped back to their fortress.

At dawn, Valdor led his flotilla northwards, and his thin smile greeted the sight of the blackened remains, stark against the white sand. His heart sang, not only because they'd accomplished their mission so thoroughly, but also because they were now directed to his home village on the Waal. Hopefully, he would see familiar faces, but he was prepared for the worse.

By early afternoon, driven by a favourable south-westerly breeze, bearing an irritating drizzle, his ships turned into the Rhine estuary and then, into the Waal, its confluence also at the mouth of the Rhine. Valdor explained to his excited Batavian comrades that his idea was to moor near their village and swim the horses ashore. Each would then ride to his own house, with hope in his heart.

Johar expressed what they all felt, "Likely, there'll be nobody to welcome us, we must be prepared for disappointment."

The ships moored, and Valdor urged a reluctant and restive Sparax into the water. The stallion's huge lungs kept him afloat, and instinct had his legs trotting underwater so that soon, the relieved animal was climbing the low bank of the Waal. Familiar terrain and sights moved Valdor almost to tears. Although not even a full year had passed, much had happened since they fled to Torik Isle. His stallion thundered into the village's only street, and at the sight of a Roman centurion, young children bravely stood their ground and stared while the few womenfolk screamed and fled indoors. Relieved to see life in his village, Valdor rode directly to his parents' home. The door was firmly closed, so he tied his reins to a fence and knocked.

His mother, arms white with flour up beyond her elbows, squealed in fear at the sight of a centurion, but suddenly, her jaw dropped, and she cried, "Valdor, my son!" He gently backed her into the house and closed the door behind him with his free hand. His nostrils breathed in the mouth-watering aroma of baking bread.

"Why are you dressed like that? Did you slay a Roman centurion and take his uniform? The gods forbid!"

"I have done that, too, mother, but I wear this uniform as of rights. I left you as a simple country lad, now, I return as an important Roman officer: I'm the emperor's favourite," he said proudly. "It's a long story, but in the name of Jupiter, what are all these sacks, and what are you doing?"

"Every day, the Romans bring sacks of flour from the fortress, and I bake bread for the legion based there. They give me a pittance for my trouble, but I do it for your father and the men of the village, who form part of the garrison. My bread is appreciated, and, in this way, I'm allowed to enter the fort once a month to see your father."

"So, he is alive and well! The gods be praised!"

"Ay, and most of the others, too. He tells me that he has a hard life, always drilling and occasionally marching to fight insurgent tribes inland. Do you remember the smith, Thragnor?"

"Ay, of course."

"Oy! Now look, this bread needs to come out of the oven, or it'll be ruined," she took a long-handled wooden peel and saved the well-baked loaves, sliding them onto a table containing at least another dozen. "... anyway, as I was saying, sadly, Thragnor died from a spear thrust between his ribs when they fought a Germanic tribe last month. Our men—if we can call a Roman legion such—won a crushing victory but lost the poor smith—is Heidar...?"

"Ay, he is well. What of his family?"

"His mother and younger brother still live down the street," she jerked her thumb before sliding the peel under a raw loaf and transferring it into the oven. At the same moment, Johar walked into the house, his expression glum.

"Greetings, Aunt Namuta! My heart sings to see you well. But my house stands empty, Valdor."

"Your mother died of the ague last spring, Johar, I'm sorry. It was just after you boys left. The Romans had captured our shaman, so there was nobody to cure her. But your father is well. I saw him a few days ago."

"Well? Where is he?"

"In the fortress of Noviomagus, a league or so up the river. He's a legionary, like my Caurus."

"Are they well?"

"Ay, until they fall in battle."

"Mother bakes bread for the legion, Johar," Valdor waved a hand at the mountain of loaves, "but hark, I have a plan. I'll tell you when Heidar and Faldrek get here." He turned to his mother, "Ma, do you know which legion is stationed at Noviomagus?"

"I seem to remember *Legio XXII*... something or other."

"Thank the gods! *Legio XXII Primigenia*—"

She turned, her brow glistening with sweat as she removed the loaf from the searing oven and added the bread to the pile. She turned to gather two short logs and placed them on the fire under the stone hotplate, speaking as she did so, "Ay, that's them...XXII Primigenia."

"When do the Romans come to collect the bread?"

"Any time, soon. They exchange the bread with fresh sacks of flour."

"Well, today is your last consignment," he said enigmatically.

A knock at the door ended the conversation. "That'll be the carter to take the bread." But she was wrong, as in walked Heidar, followed by Faldrek. "A sight for sore eyes!" she cried as Heidar embraced her.

"What are you doing? There's enough bread here to feed a legion!"

"Exactly!" she chuckled, and Valdor explained. When he had finished, he put an arm around Heidar's shoulder, "Good and bad news, my friend, Thragnor died in battle, but our fathers are safe in the garrison at Noviomagus, a league hence. You will see them soon." He explained his plan.

"Do you think it will work?" Johar asked anxiously as he watched the tears of joy roll down his aunt's cheeks.

"Legio XXII Primigenia is an old-established legion with a proud story, and that alone gives me hope. Ma, when your carter arrives, carry on as normal and say nothing about our visit. You three, outside with me! We'll ride down the road towards the fortress to greet the carter."

"What about our mothers?" Faldrek asked hopefully.

"Later, once we've completed our mission in Noviomagus. Ha, look! Unless I'm mistaken, here comes the carter."

A chestnut draught horse clopped towards them, hauling a cart laden with sacks. "Whoa!" cried the carter, bringing his horse and vehicle to a halt.

"Hail, carter!" Valdor greeted him, "we'll give you a hand to unload at Namuta's house."

"How do you know—"

Valdor laughed, "It's a long story, but come, we'll ride beside you and you can answer my questions as we go."

In this way, Valdor discovered that the commander of Legio XXII Primigenia was a prefect named Gnaeus Cordius Nolus, and Valdor was delighted to hear that he was a veteran of the Danube campaign. Also, the legion was not at full strength, boasting six, instead of ten cohorts, so slightly fewer than 3,000 men. This information suited Valdor's plan perfectly.

At his mother's house, the four soldiers each shouldered a sack of flour and delivered it into the delicious aroma-filled kitchen. The carter went outdoors, only to return with empty sacks, which he began to fill with fresh bread. When his sacks were full, Valdor hugged his mother and whispered instructions, "We'll be back tomorrow morning, early. Have them here and ready," he ended.

Outside the house, he said to the carter, "We'll accompany you to Noviomagus, friend. Decurion, ride to the ships and tell Centurion Attab to join us." Heidar thumped his chest and rode off to fetch the Mauritanian.

When he drew near the ships, he saw that the men had created an encampment by the river. He made his way to the centurion's tent and passed on his instructions. The Moorish officer called for his charger and leapt on its back. Together they galloped after the bread transport. Fine as Heidar's steed was, it had a struggle to keep apace of the sleek Arab mare. Head-to-head, they came within sight of their comrades and the cart. Ibn Attab slowed to a gentle trot to Heidar's relief since he did not want to injure his stallion or himself.

Valdor turned to wave over the centurion, noting, not for the first time, the pleasant but stark contrast between the Mauritanian's swarthy skin and the fine white transverse plume of his helmet. The white was the insignia of officers of the *Auxilia Palatina* and made a welcome change from the standard crimson that Valdor and Heidar and the officers of most other legions vaunted.

"Centurion, we are making for the fortress of Noviomagus, the stronghold currently held by the Legio XXII Primigenia and commanded by an old acquaintance of yours, unless I err."

The Moor looked perplexed, "As far as I know, I have no friends in the XXII Primigenia."

Valdor laughed, "Be that as it may, but when we arrive and you greet the prefect, you might have a surprise! I hope that I am correct, however, because our task is to persuade Legio XXII Primigenia to accompany us to Britannia."

"Excuse me, Centurion Valdor, but do we have sufficient berths for an entire legion?"

"Doubtful, but they have six cohorts. It will be a squeeze, but the crossing is short to Branodunum. We'll manage, somehow." But both centurions calculated without being in possession of all the information they needed.

Apart from lying close to the border with Germanic tribes, the fortress of Noviomagus had a splendid strategic position on high ground, surrounded by other hills; it commanded views over the river Waal and Rhine valley.

As a daily habit, the carter trundled straight to the main gate, and the small unit of legionaries rode beside him. The carter was worried that he might be reprimanded for bringing strangers into the fortress, but the camp prefect's curiosity was aroused by the white plume and dark skin of Ibn Attab. When he strode up to the Arab steed, he gazed at the newcomer and cried, "So it is you, Centurion Ibn Attab! Do you not recognise an old comrade from those glorious days on the Danube?"

The Moor's flashing white teeth answered before he spoke, "Centurion Gnaeus Cordius Nolus! But I see they have elevated you to a prefect—congratulations!"

"There is little to congratulate, old friend. I am here in command of a mixed bag of Italians and auxiliaries. We have at least two cohorts of barbarians! And don't get me started on the weather," he cast a baleful eye at the dark rain clouds that merely threatened a downpour but instead offered a dispiriting damp mist-like drizzle.

"You will be grateful then, Prefect," Valdor seized his opportunity, "to obey Caesar Marcus Aurelius' order to bring your men to Britannia with my small fleet." He held his breath, but when the reply came, it was unexpected.

"Welcome to Noviomagus, Centurion. From your accent, I hear that you are Batavian, so I should welcome you more correctly to Ulpia Noviomagus Batavorum: the name given this fortress by the great emperor Trajan some two hundred winters past. The Batavi make fine soldiers and have all my respect," he smiled ingratiatingly at Valdor.

"Indeed, your legion contains my father, uncle, and friends, Prefect. I am anxious to reacquaint with them when our business is done."

"Do you have written orders for the transfer, Centurion?"

"I do not. Take my word as your guarantee. I can also warrant for better weather in Branodunum." He looked at Heidar for confirmation, but the decurion looked uneasy and, keeping his head down, muttered, "Not much better!" At which, the prefect guffawed, "Any improvement will be welcome."

"I doubt you will have time to enjoy the British sunshine, Prefect, for Carausius—er, I mean, Emperor Caesar Marcus Aurelius—is on the verge of war with Maximian."

"Splendid! At last, real warfare! We're tired of walking into cowardly traps and ambushes in the German marshes and forests. I hear Carausius is a remarkable general."

"You have heard correctly, Prefect."

"He has the good sense to appoint Batavian officers, so it is settled!"

"It is. We shall accompany you to Britannia. I fear it will not be a comfortable crossing for your men as we have but two galleys and four horse transports."

"You say that because you have not strolled around the harbour. We have two triremes in the port."

The look of sheer relief on Valdor's face made the prefect guffaw again.

He's sure to get on well with Carausius! Our poor ears!

"Heidar, ride back to the ships. They are to be ready to sail an hour after dawn."

"Nay," the prefect caught Heidar's arm. "There is time before nightfall for you to reunite with your father and to eat with my officers. We have the delicious fresh bread you brought from your village and good red wine from Italy."

Only Ibn Attab did not have relatives in the legion, but he spent a pleasant couple of hours with Gnaeus Cordius Nolus reminiscing about the Danube campaign.

The others did not have to seek out their relatives, who had sidled up to the small party and lurked a discreet distance away from them until the prefect dismissed them.

"Valdor!" his father cried and almost tripped in his haste to embrace his son. There were tears in the older man's eyes, "Your mother and I were unsure we'd ever see you again. Yet, here you are—and a centurion, too! I hope you treat your men better than some of these!"

"Hard, but fair, father, kind but hard. But we have a lot to catch up on. I have spoken to mother today, so I know most of your news. You will hear mine. But the best is that I am taking you to Britannia with mother and will find you employment far from the battlefield."

The next two hours passed in an instant, it seemed. The same was true for Valdor's three friends until they were all called to the refectory for simple but wholesome fare and the welcome red wine. Prefect Cordius Nolus joined Valdor, his expression anxious.

"I understand the emperor's need for my men, but surely, it is not his intention to leave Noviomagus ungarrisoned?"

Valdor thought quickly. He had pondered the problem on the way from the village, but his local knowledge was too limited to be precise. He said, "I believe we have Frankish allies who wouldn't hesitate to take command of this fortress, although I confess, I don't know how to approach them."

"Your emperor is wise. It is a splendid idea. I will send an emissary at once to the Franks' chieftain. Tomorrow, he will find the gates open. I'll give orders to embark at dawn."

"I have only one request, Prefect, and it is in your power to grant it if you are so minded."

Prefect Cordius Nolus looked askance at Valdor, for he was not used to granting favours, but pulled an earlobe and looked down his nose, "Ask, then."

"Prefect, will you grant the transfer of our relatives to my legion? It is a question of but ten men or thereabouts."

"Is that all you ask, Centurion? You have my immediate assent!"

"Thank you. I hope we shall become friends as well as comrades. I'll gather the men concerned and ride back to our ships. Will your ships join us soon after dawn?"

"They will. Take the bread cart to transport your relatives; our cavalry has no spare horses."

The two men clasped wrists, and as he organised the men into the cart to transfer to the ships, Valdor thought, *Things are falling nicely into place for we four simple Batavian country lads!*

10

BRANODUNUM FORT, NORFOLK, AD 286-287

Valdor expected to be charged with another mission when he returned to Branodunum, but the emperor embraced him warmly for what he had achieved and quipped that on every mission, his centurion returned with more men to strengthen his position in Britannia. He did not, however, keep the XXII Primigenia Legion and their two war galleys but sent them to the south to strengthen the garrison of a shore fort called *Regulbium* in the area of the Canti tribe, known as Kent. This, he explained to Valdor, was for practical purposes because Branodunum was now overcrowded and Regulbium understaffed as a garrison.

Now that the autumn had advanced, there was little danger of pirate incursions, Carausius explained, citing an old rhyme passed down from seafarer to son:

> *"Never let your keel be wet*
> *When the Pleiades have set;*
> *Never let your keel be dry*
> *When the Crown is in the sky."*

Certainly, most maritime traffic ceased by the end of October, for the North Sea could change rapidly into a raging beast as sudden gales whipped its surface into huge waves capable of capsizing even the most stable round-bellied trading vessel.

"When the spring comes, Valdor, I mean to sweep the Channel free of Saxons and Franks."

"I'll enjoy that, Sire."

"*You?* You will do no such thing! I have another task for you, but I shall not inform you until I make my announcement at the end of Yuletide."

Valdor knew better than to object because it was unwise to stir up Carausius's wrath. Yet, he yearned to tell the Emperor of the North that he had acquired sea legs and a certain prowess as commander of a war galley; still, wisely, he held his tongue.

Carausius lit the Christmas brand—or Yule Log—on Christmas Eve to mark the end of the 40-day Advent fast and the start of the midwinter feast. The log burnt for the next 12 days, which were a holiday for everyone—bar slaves and bonded labourers.

The fire in the hearth crackled as a living symbol of the household's prosperity, and a special midwinter fire was a tradition also on the Continent, including pagan areas. When it was over, the emperor ordered the ashes to be scattered outside the walls of the fortress as protection against storms and weather damage, as he looked to prolong the magic of the midwinter fire.

This ceremony enacted, to Valdor's surprise, the emperor summoned Caurus and took him aside, far from intrusive ears. Valdor watched, peered across the hall, as the Emperor of the North embraced his father, clasped his wrist, and handed him a bulging bag of coins. The centurion waited until the emperor dismissed his father before hurrying after him to the small house he had managed to have allocated to his parents in the *vicus* outside the walls.

He watched his father slip into the building and hesitated outside the door, listening to his mother's delighted squeal, and his bafflement increased. He knocked and walked in without waiting to receive permission to enter. His mother's triumphant expression on seeing him startled him somewhat. "Father, what's going on? I saw the emperor embrace you and hand you a bag of coins."

Caurus first looked uncomfortable, then ran his fingers across an eyebrow, bowing his head in thought, but Namuta spoke eagerly, "Your father is in difficulty because the emperor has ordered him not to speak about what he has decided. You will have to hear it directly from his mouth, my son. Oh, I'm so proud of you! Be patient and all will become clear."

"But, mother, all that money?" Valdor pointed to the bulging linen sack with drawstrings his father had set down on the table. "What is the meaning of this?"

"My dear son, it is a fee the emperor has paid me to honour a long-standing Roman tradition. He needed to compensate me in return for my agreement. I'm sorry I am not at liberty to explain. As your mother said, be patient and have faith, for it is a marvellous thing! Emperor Marcus Aurelius is truly a great man!"

"Ha!" Valdor was extremely irritated—*after all I've done for them, they shun me and will not share a secret!*—he glared, turned on his heel, and strode out the door, slamming it behind him.

The centurion brooded all afternoon and asked himself a hundred questions. What would his father do with the money? Why was his mother proud of him? What did Carausius have in mind? Given his parents' reaction to the emperor's scheme—which he could only describe as ecstatic—it had to be something extremely positive involving him. Yet, the emperor himself had excluded his participation in the forthcoming Spring campaign. He would not gladly accept the role of camp prefect here at Branodunum. What use was a promotion if it meant a static life organising the daily routine of a shore fortress?

Suddenly, a thought struck him; tonight, the emperor had organised a feast to mark the end of the advent fast. At last! After forty days without a glass of red wine, he could indulge, but it was not the thought of wining and dining that gripped his imagination, but the memory of Carausius's words. He would make an announcement concerning his future in the Spring. He need only be patient for an hour or two.

It was less than an hour before he learnt something directly from the emperor. The Emperor of the North repeated an earlier gesture by taking Valdor aside as he had done Caurus before him. Instead of the usual booming voice, Carausius pushed forward his somewhat brutish face close to Valdor's and spoke low: "Centurion, from the day I met you, you have been loyal and true. You have shown concern for my well-being and, not only that, you regularly demonstrate how much you care that my reign is a success, by reinforcing my position at every opportunity." He paused, and his eyes pierced Valdor's, who muttered, "I only do my duty, Caesar."

At last, the bellow of laughter had everyone in the hall turning to stare, so the emperor gently pushed Valdor out of the glow of the torch in its sconce on the wall and into the shade, where he lowered his voice so much Valdor strained to hear him.

"Hark! Everyone does his duty, even I do! But it's *how* one goes about it that counts. You have been exceptional, Valdor, my boy! So, I have decided to adopt you as my son. I have paid your father as *pater familias* the requisite compensation according to Roman law. All that remains is for you to agree and for us to sign and seal a document with the lawyers. What do you say?"

"Caesar, I am lost for words! It is an honour for me to be your heir. I am shocked."

"Do not be! Did not the great Emperor Hadrian adopt not one, but two sons, at different times? But heed me well, your new position will bring enemies that you do not yet have. Do not speak of this to anyone until my announcement during the feast."

"But—"

"Enough! Come, take your seat at my right hand. The camp prefect can sit to my left!"

The meal passed in a blur for Valdor as his stomach readjusted to the ample rich food and strong drink. The emperor had ordered a priest to recount the Nativity, which further aroused Valdor's perplexity. He had not been baptised, although the idea had crossed his mind on occasion; like his father, he was still a pagan, and his bafflement came from the concept of a god that allowed his son to incarnate only to die cruelly— Valdor had seen the victims of crucifixion first-hand—and all this, without seeking vengeance on his oppressors. Thor would have smitten them with his hammer, sending lightning to burn his tormentors on the spot like a smith's steel sends sparks flying. Valdor had seen mighty oaks split and charred by lightning. Many in the hall were Christians and, overawed by the tale of angels, a comet, and shepherds, crossed themselves in awe. The priest ended the tale for the ages and sat beaming around the crowded gathering as, with one hand, Carausius called attention to himself by banging his wooden beaker hard on the table several times, and with the other, hauled Valdor to his feet.

"Friends," he boomed, "today is one of the happiest of my life for I have decided to adopt Centurion Valdor as my son and legitimate heir. Behold Caesar Valdor Aurelius!" This announcement was met at first by a stunned silence, which Valdor took to mean envy and hatred. His emperor's words still rang in his ears. *Your new position will bring enemies that you do not yet have.* But he need not have worried: not yet, at least, for suddenly people rose to their feet and bellowed "Hail Caesar! Hail Caesar Valdor Aurelius!" applause thundered around the hall. Men copied the emperor and banged beakers on tables until the noise was deafening and only stopped when the emperor raised his hand.

Valdor looked around the high table and only grins met his gaze. He was a popular centurion, but it pleased him most that there was no sign of envy on his close friends' faces, just simple happiness for his lot.

The emperor cried, "Friends, I have not yet finished with my announcements. There is more! As you know, our coasts are infested by pirates from Saxony and Francia. It is my task to liberate Britannia from these marauders and to facilitate this task, I have constructed more war galleys and thanks to my son, we have more legions to man them and sweep the brigands from the seas. Besides, I now announce the new office of my son. I appoint him Count of the Saxon Shore—*Comes littoris Saxonici per Britanniam*," he announced solemnly in Latin so that everyone would understand.

Valdor's jaw dropped, but quickly he controlled his gaping. After all, such an expression was unworthy, but the position was dignified of the next Caesar. But what did it entail exactly?

That was what the emperor explained as they finished the roast swan and conversations became private again.

"I almost envy you, my son; my campaign cannot begin until the North Sea calms in the spring. You can begin work as soon as you wish, tomorrow if you want! I'll prepare a document stating your role explicitly with my seal attached, so that you meet no internal obstacles."

"But father, what exactly does my role entail?"

"It's complex; we have three shore forts: here, at Regulbium and at Portus Lemanis in the land of the Canti. These fortresses all guard estuaries against Saxon incursions, but I need them also to protect us against an attempt at the reconquest of Britannia by the Empire. I task you to study these three forts and to build at least another six at strategic estuaries as far as the Insula Vecta or *Vectis*—the large island on the Solent. Then, we'll need signal stations with roads to them and strategically placed depots. You will be entitled to withdraw and use the necessary funds, my son."

"As always, I shall carry out the task to the best of my ability, father, and hope that I'll see some action as a result."

"Always the man of action, like myself! I feel sure you will be called upon to fight Maximian unless I can first deal with him. There's news of him gathering troops in *Gallia*. I'm convinced that his first move will be to retake your old homeland, Valdor. In that way, he'll be a constant threat to Britannia, not to mention the other side of the coin, he'll want to defend the Rhine and Waal estuaries from a possible invasion on my part. I have to decide whether to surprise him by moving first. It's painful to me to have to wait for the fair-weather season."

"On the other hand, there's no sense in losing men to a watery grave. Anyway, father, I think I'll walk around this fortress to understand its construction, seen through different eyes. Tomorrow, I'll take Sparax down to Regulbium. I'm told that it is exactly a day's ride from here. I can renew some old acquaintances and confront the layout there with this fortress."

"Nay, stay a few more days so that we can get to know each other better."

"Thank you for everything you've done for a poor country lad."

"The merit is all your own, Count Valdor. In any case, you have to wait for documents to be drawn up—not least, the one that will enable you to withdraw the huge sums needed for building. They'll also prepare another one, entitling you to levy taxes in my name. Only to be used in absolute necessity, mind. It's easy to lose popularity when money raising enters the equation." The famous roar of laughter echoed rather hollow with concern.

Valdor decided to pace out the length and breadth of the fortress and concluded that the walls enclosed an area of roughly two and a half hectares. He had already considered the height and strengthening of the walls but noted that each side of the rectangle was interrupted by a gate, each flanked by two towers. The necessary buildings and the road layout next concerned him. The main road was paved and ran from north to south; at its centre was the *praetorium*, the headquarters building because it housed the *praetor* or base commander and his staff. Just strolling around the camp, Valdor realised the scale of the task he was about to undertake and at once realised he could not do it on his own.

He had to create, not one, but at least, six fortresses like this—so, he would need to call on experts. Upon enquiring for an engineer, a soldier led him to a grey-haired man, who had laid out this very stronghold some score years before. He was one of the experienced officers called *metatores,* who explained to him that a camp could have one of two basic shapes: a square, or a rectangle like this one. The rectangular layouts were larger and designed to contain two legions, not one, each legion being placed back-to-back with headquarters next to each other. Laying it out was a geometric exercise conducted by the metatores, who used graduated measuring rods called *decempedae*—10-footers— and *gromatici* who used a *groma,* a sighting device consisting of a vertical staff with horizontal cross pieces and vertical plumb lines. The lined face grew even more wrinkled as Valdor explained the need to construct several camps. He said, "Count," surprising Valdor by using his new title, "you will need to gather a group of expert engineers and begin ideally in the centre of the planned camp at the site of the headquarters tent or building known as the *principia*. Streets and other features are marked with coloured pennants or rods. We can oversee the work done by legionaries drafted for the manual labour," he smiled, confident in his ability to undertake this phase of camp construction.

"You will ride with me tomorrow, my friend. I'll place you in charge of creating my first *castrum*. The prune-like, wrinkled countenance activated smile lines around the eyes and mouth. "Lord, you do me a great honour, for it has been too long since my services have been required."

Valdor had made a mental note of the layout of Branodunum Fort, the roads, buildings: the tribunal for courts martial and arbitration, the guardhouse, the storehouses for grain (*horrea*), for meat (*carnarea*), the barracks, stables, workshops, and the *questorium* for the safekeeping of plunder and cells for captives or hostages. A sudden thought struck him, and he turned to his companion, "Won't we first have to find running water, maybe a stream to divert for the latrines?"

The visage again cracked into a smile, "Ah, I see you are of a practical bent, Count. Fear not, one thing about Britannia we cannot deny is that this soaked country of rheum and agues does not lack water! Another of the first things to be done will be to dig a well for drinking water—again, not an arduous task."

"I take it you can ride, Engineer?"

"Ay, Sire,"

"Then, meet me at the stables at dawn. We'll take an escort of a dozen men to Regulbium. *I'll take all my friends.* When we arrive there, we'll confront the two fortresses and together decide whether there are improvements we can make on our first fortress. I'm sure you'll find gromatici and metatores among the men there, and I'll make it clear to them that they'll work under you. We'll discuss your pay and rank once we start work on the first project." *I make it sound easy, but first I'll have to identify the site.*

Before anything else, he went to find his Batavian comrades to tell them to prepare to leave at dawn. He worried about the reception his new status would reserve for him, but he need not have. His cousin was the first to remind him, "Remember the oath we took on Torik Isle: *whatever we have to face, we'll endure it together, united: each individual should act for the benefit of the group, and the group should act for the benefit of each individual.*"

"I have not forgotten, Johar, and now that I am a Count, I have the position to raise you all in rank. Each of you will be a centurion. I will accompany you to withdraw your uniforms, new galea, and the necessary *vitis*, but friends, make my motto yours, I implore you: *Hard, but fair; kind but hard.* Remember this, and you will be successful officers like me. Now, decide for yourselves, each of you will choose three trusted comrades to ride with us at dawn to Regulbium. Once there, you'll each take command of a century."

"Am I dreaming all this, cousin?"

"Nay, Johar, ask former decurion Heidar whether this is a dream. Together, we'll do great things. As the new Count, I know that I can rely on tried and tested comrades, or better, on old friends."

The four repeated the gesture of long ago on Torik and placed hands one on the other and grinned as of yore.

II

REGULBIUM FORTRESS. KENT AD 287

THE WINTER MADE THE BRITONS' TRACKWAYS IMPASSABLE quagmires, but the Roman engineers, the best in the world, had created arteries that had a metalled curved surface off which the rain ran into lateral ditches. The band of legionaries already knew the route to Camolodunum from Valdor's previous journey. Nevertheless, the long ride south was dismal in the incessant downpour. It dampened enthusiasm for conversation, enabling the cloaked Valdor, under his hood, to reflect on his life.

He dwelt on his new responsibility and, above all, on his youth. He had been catapulted to prominence thanks to the affinity he had evoked in the emperor. That, too, was curious because Carausius would not have become emperor had he not rebelled against Maximian. How strange was Fate! Now, he was effectively the second highest-ranking person in Britannia and was still only on the threshold of his twentieth winter. Therefore, it was reasonable for him to harbour doubts about his capabilities. He would have liked to take the route south along the coast to consider which estuaries might need a new fortress, but the bad weather had botched that idea. This setback did not help his self-confidence. He needed the gods to send him something to ignite the flame of self-assurance.

Whether it was the work of the gods or of Fate (were they one and the same thing?) the event came in the most unexpected way. They had travelled the old British track, the splendid Watling Street, made wide and practicable by the Roman engineers—the rain had eased off for some time—and they were drawing close to Regulbium when smoke darkened the already dull sky: a village was in flames! This could only mean one thing in these troubled times—a pirate incursion! Valdor led the gallop, intent on fighting the raiders, but when they came to a rise overlooking the great river *Tamesis,* Valdor saw that the Legio II Augusta, his old comrades from the garrison of Regulbium, had the situation in hand.

He stared in disbelief, the barbarians were surrounded and fighting desperately for their lives, but among them, surely there was a woman! A female warrior! Was that possible? He galloped over to the fray and in ringing tones ordered the centurion to halt the combat. The tigerish woman had affected him so deeply that he could not understand his own actions.

"If they lay down their arms, take them as slaves, Centurion. Whoever they are… I want that woman."

Valdor's imperial purple confirmed the rumour that had reached the centurion's ears. Here in person was the emperor's adopted son. There could be no gainsaying *him*.

"They are Jutes, lord, barbarians who use women in battle—whoever heard of such a thing?"

The surviving Jutes, standing among their fallen comrades, realised that they had to choose between feasting at Odin's table or remaining alive, laid down their arms. "Bind the woman! I want her for my slave," Valdor ordered. He grasped the trailing rope from her bound wrists to force her to walk beside Sparax or be dragged along the ground. She walked. He could not see the hatred in her eyes because she had smeared a pigment from ear to ear that created a black band across and around them.

The centurion rode beside Valdor to offer gratuitous advice. "Do not underestimate the ferocity of the woman, Sire. The Jutes call such demons *skjaldmaer*, or as we would say, *shield maidens*. She will attempt to strike you with any blade that comes within her reach. Taming her will be harder than trying to skin a wildcat alive!"

I shall tame her if it's the last thing I do! His next words did not reflect this thought: "I'll bear your words in mind, Centurion. Thank you for obeying my orders in the heat of battle. I'll not forget it; indeed, I'll have Legate Vitulasius promote you."

"It was my duty to obey, lord. The legate will appreciate some hardy slaves, in any case. There's maintenance work to be done in the fortress and it will fall to them as soon as the weather permits. The gods only know what folly drove them to risk drowning by crossing the North Sea in this intemperate season."

Valdor completely forgot about his mission to study and compare the layout of the Regulbium fortress. He was too obsessed with his female prisoner. After greeting Legate Vitulasius and explaining his mission, he ordered four female slaves to bathe the captive and dress her in clean clothes.

When they brought her back to him, he was struck by her beauty without the black mask and her proud bearing. Neither did it escape him that the biggest of the slave women now had a red gouge running down one cheek. He would certainly beware his untamed tigress' claws.

The fact that he was Batavian helped him, for she was impressed that so youthful a barbarian warrior had risen to power; also, she found him most attractive. He had little difficulty understanding her Jutish tongue although a few words escaped him. As he admired her long barley-coloured hair flowing in waves over her shoulders and cornflower blue eyes, he realised that this was the first woman he had ever been attracted to. He discovered that her name was Svafa, the daughter of a jarl. Her slim, but muscular arm shot out and, grasping him behind his neck, hauled him towards her. Before he could react, her tongue was inside his mouth. He had no experience of kissing a woman and this lascivious action rocked him to the core, but he loved it! Without realising it, he was responding with his tongue, engaging in a loving battle. At that moment, although he knew it not, Valdor had found the love of his life.

Despite the soft breasts pressing against his chest, he broke free. He needed to find out more about this siren from the north before surrendering to her undoubted charms. He led her to his chamber and was impressed by her strength when he resisted her attempt to push him onto the bed. Her eyes burnt with resentment and anger, but he soothed her, "Svafa, if you are to be my woman, I need to know more about you, and you about me."

"What do you need to know, Valdor? I am a woman and you are a man! I am Jarl Hibald's daughter and will not give myself to just anyone."

"I am the second most important man in Britannia. I command everyone except my emperor, Caesar Marcus Aurelius. Will you concede yourself to a future emperor?"

"You are younger than I. How old *are* you, emperor's son?"

Strangely ashamed of his youthfulness, he conceded defensively, "Almost twenty winters, and you?"

"I'll wager you have never been with a woman! Are you afraid of women, Valdor? I'm five and twenty."

"Nay, I'm afraid of no one. But if a woman were to frighten me in battle, it might be you! I saw you fighting near the village your people raided and was impressed and..." he said slowly, "...attracted, I suppose."

"Batavians are fierce warriors. I dare say you are a mighty one. Why don't we wrestle?"

He laughed, "We'll do that when I'm ready. First, I want to know why you left your homeland."

Her lip curled, "*Me?* Because my father ordered me. He is in Valhalla now, thanks to your Roman friends. But he sailed to escape the doom of our village. The sea has engulfed it and there is no tillable land to support our folks. That is why we sailed over the raging sea. I grew up with tales of how fertile this Britons' land is and how we would one day take it for ourselves. The dream didn't quite match the reality, did it, Valdor?"

"Let's wrestle!" He kicked her leg from under her and threw her off-balance onto the bed before diving upon her. She snarled and wrapped arms and legs around him, writhing so forcefully that she overturned him and pinned him down. They struggled, trading move and counter-move. Valdor could not believe the strength and vigour of this apparently slight jarl's daughter. At last, exhausted, they lay still, and she paid him a compliment, "Only my brother could beat me in a wrestling match in our village. You have not beaten me, but I could not overcome you, either."

"How come you, a woman, are so strong?"

"Training. As a girl, I lifted rocks, increasing their weight with every passing year, and wrestling the youths and even the men. Do not underestimate me, Valdor," she echoed the centurion's warning, "I have killed men in battle, at least two today! Have you fought in battle?"

"Ay, and killed my share of foes."

"I knew it, emperor's son. Come, love me!"

Again, her tongue sought his, and her thighs locked around him. What did he know? He was still a virgin but would never admit it. Nature took its course. With this wildcat, how was he to know that lovemaking could be gentle and slow? Svafa was uninhibited, passionate, and demanding, but Valdor adored what her body was doing to his. If he thought maybe he loved her, now he was completely in her thrall. The gods had answered his prayer for self-assurance. He had it now when the Jutish goddess whispered in his ear, "You are my first lover and I could not wish for better."

"I could have said the same words," he confessed, sending her into a renewed frenzy of lovemaking.

Two days passed sweetly before Valdor returned to his senses and remembered the task assigned to him. When he told her that he had to begin work, she said, "I will not be an ornament or a wallflower when you enter battle. I wish to fight alongside my man."

He gazed at her earnest expression and said slowly, "The Count of the Saxon Shore should be different from other men. He should have his own *skjaldmær*," he pronounced the word awkwardly, "I'll have you fitted with a legionary's armour and find you a decent horse. You can ride, can you not?"

"Can a jarl's daughter ride? What do you think?"

He would not tell her his true thoughts at that moment, which were that he had been forced to tame the two creatures he loved most in this world, Sparax and Svafa, where others had failed! He was not sure she would appreciate him comparing her with a stallion, however wild. He imagined how she would look in a legionary's uniform and liked the thought, so he took her to the armoury and had her fitted. First, he had to warn the armourer, "Do not say what you are thinking, soldier. This is my bodyguard and she can kill with her bare hands, so obey my orders in silence." *What a shame to hide such a splendid body beneath a cuirass* was his principal thought.

After which, his attention was immediately given to how best to compare this fortress to the one he had left in the north. He called over a legionary, one of his Branodunum party, and told him to find the *metator* who accompanied them.

Some minutes later, the wrinkled countenance was beaming at him before disappearing in a deep bow. "Show me around this fortress, my friend, I have been—*ahem*—somewhat busy and have had no time to explore. Perhaps you can point out the salient features of this fortress and we'll see how it differs from Branodunum.

"First, its history, Sire, this was a small fort built directly after the invasion of Britannia in the reign of Claudius, protected by earthworks. It was connected to *Durovernum*, the capital of the Cantiaci, by a road. It was strategically located at the mainland side of the entrance to the mile-wide Wantsum Channel, which separates the Isle of Thanet from the mainland. We'll see from the ramparts, and in yonder corner, once stood a lighthouse. Later garrisons did away with that because it was of more use to Rome's enemies." His dismissive laugh seemed to speak of earlier follies, but then he added, "Some four score years ago the decision was taken to build this stone fortress on the ancient Claudian site, so in some way acknowledging the sage choice of our forefathers."

"The first difference I noticed, Master Metator, is that this fortress is square-shaped, unlike Branodunum."

"You are right, lord, and this depends upon a choice you must make regarding the accommodation of a single legion, as here, or two legions as at Branodunum. Yesterday, I paced out the size of the fort. By my calculations, it covers an area of just over three hectares. I also measured the walls: the single rampart is ten feet thick at the base, tapering to eight feet at the top, with a height of twenty feet. It is a solid construction, which we should imitate, lord, following this example by the additional strengthening by an interior earthen rampart. The entire wall is surrounded by two external ditches, which I think you'll agree is an arrangement difficult for a foe to penetrate."

"Excellent, let's walk around the interior and you can indicate anything you believe worthy of consideration."

The two men took the buildings for granted, so the only feature the engineer wished to point out was the aqueduct.

"This runs inland to a freshwater spring, Sire. I believe the laborious choice was dictated by the marshy nature of this terrain, which might have dissuaded the choice of not digging a well, owing to the insanitary nature of the groundwater."

"I see. This kind of observation makes me realise that choosing a site for a fortress is not quite so simple a matter as I'd thought."

"Fear not, Count, I have found two qualified engineers in this fortress and we shall unite our expertise to your choice."

"Before choosing another site, we'll make a further comparison by riding to another nearby stronghold at *Portus Lemanis*, which I believe is but some 40 miles to the south from here and guards a large bay on the Channel coast. By drawing on the best features of all three, we should be ready to construct some new forts. I think we'll start here in the south, towards the west, before considering the east coast." He paused and smiled at Svafa, who had struggled to understand the long conversation. Next to her stood the legionary who had brought the metator. Valdor addressed him, "Legionary, find all the members of the group who came here and tell them to be ready to leave at dawn. Engineer, you tell your two colleagues the same message. Svafa, you and I will find some food and drink. We'll need an early night if we are to leave at dawn." He said this with a degree of innuendo that was not lost on her, and she leered at him.

12

PORTUS LEMANIS, KENT, AD 287

Valdor's Antonine Itinerary took them through *Durovernum Cantiacorum*, the capital of the Cantiaci tribe. The *Duro* in its name spoke of a stronghold, and as they approached, they could see why. The strong stone walls with the interspersed towers were enough to dissuade any random band of roving pirates, although an organised army might be a different proposition. The thriving and bustling town contained a mixture of timber and stone buildings, but its role as a Romano-British *civitas* was clearly defined by the forum and basilica at the centre, the temple enclosure, and theatre. Sparax's shod hoofs clattered along the main road through the town while Valdor gazed anxiously at Svafa, but she seemed in complete control of her chestnut mare, despite the tendency to slide on the paving stones.

Although neither of them referred to this difficulty, they were glad to exit through the southern gate and take the crushed gravel road to Portus Lemanis, according to the Itinerary, some 16,000 legionaries' paces to the south, which was, therefore, sixteen miles away and could be easily reached before darkness cloaked the land.

Valdor realised he was nearing their destination when the invigorating salty sea air filled his lungs. He wondered whether Carausius, given the clement late-winter weather, was preparing to sail southwards. It occurred to him that if he did, he would be able to see the *Classis Britannica* sail along the Channel. He would much prefer to be commanding a war galley than organising the construction of a chain of forts.

The difference between Portus Lemanis and the previous two forts was immediately evident to him as Valdor approached the gate. He had been informed that the fort had been rebuilt as recently as twenty years ago, and the novelties introduced included the projecting towers. He could count ten of them from his vantage point beside the road, although later, he was able to ascertain fourteen. Another curiosity struck him when he entered the fortress—the shape—whereas the other two had been regular, either square or rectangular, this fort had the unusual form of an irregular pentagon. Also, there was only one gate to enter the stronghold, but he noticed several posterns.

One attractive feature was the presence of a heated bath, where men and women mingled in unconcerned nakedness, luxuriating in the steamy water. Not for the first time, Valdor admired the ingenuity of the Romans and the civilising effect they'd had on the world. Certainly, the aches caused by the hours in the saddle eased in a delightful torpor. This lethargy was interrupted unexpectedly when an underwater invader grasped his genitals. Valdor removed the hand and, taking the wrist roughly and irritably, hauled the offender to the surface, only to stare into the beaming face of his woman. "Svafa! You're lucky I didn't break your arm!" She looked different with her bountiful locks transformed into lank dripping rat-tails, but she was still beautiful to his eyes.

"We've been in this water long enough. Come, we must dry ourselves and dress, for it is time to meet the fortress officials."

They walked naked, arm in arm, over a mosaic floor, depicting the god Neptune, back to the *laconicum*, a dry hot room, where towels and their clothes hung from pegs.

"I'll rub you down," she offered.

"I'm not a horse!" he objected, but allowed her to dry his back and to sprinkle a scented liquid over him. Feeling clean and invigorated, he went to retrieve his imperial purple cloak and diadem from his travelling chest. There were two sides to this decision: first, he had not worn them on the journey to avoid arousing unwanted attention; second, he now wished for the authority they would bestow in the presence of the unknown fortress commanders. So, dressed as the emperor's son, he headed across the compound, receiving closed-fist salutes from the soldiers. A carved stone near the wall caught his eye.

Valdor stood in contemplation in front of the altar stone dedicated to the god Neptune. Of course, he knew all the Roman gods and the tales surrounding them. The long-haired, long-bearded god holding his trident was the god of the ocean, and everyone knew about his violent temperament and lustful urges. Ocean storms and earthquakes were due to Neptune's bad temper, which was why the Roman naval legion, based here, sought to propitiate him at every appropriate opportunity.

As he stared at the carved dolphin and the sea horses surrounding the god, Valdor recalled his turbulent love story with the water nymph, Amphitrite, whom he had spied dancing on the island of Naxos. Upon seeing her, Neptune fell madly in love with her and had to take her for his own. Valdor had a similar tale to tell, but Svafa wasn't dancing; she was engaged in deadly fighting; still, like Neptune, he had lost his heart and had to possess the ferocious Jutish beauty.

Apart from dolphins and other oceanic creatures, Neptune was associated with horses and bulls. Valdor decided that he would ride Sparax up to this altar stone before departing this fortress to ask for the god's protection. He could not be too careful since he had to worry about Svafa's safety in these dangerous times as well as his own. His hand sought hers and gave it a squeeze, before he offered his arm and they walked together to the *praetorium* and, despite his high rank, Valdor felt nervous. Perhaps he was conscious not only of his youth but also of his barbarian origins so evident in the Jute on his arm. He knew that barbarians had risen to become generals in the Roman army, some had become senators and some, like Carausius, even emperors.

Much depended on the origins of the officials because there was still a minority of patricians who felt the purity of their Roman blood entitled them to feel superior. Luckily, the fort was garrisoned by troops raised in Tournai, the three hundred men based there known as *numerus Turnacensium*, with their officers of the same origin. The base commander, the *praetor*, was a consul, who, as Valdor had planned by his appearance, was honoured to welcome them and, as soon as pleasantries were exchanged, issued orders for a sumptuous meal to be prepared.

Valdor explained that his commission as Count entailed the building of further forts and, warming to this argument, Consul Titus Attius Marsus, was forthcoming.

"I have been in command here for four years, in which we have been subjected to pirate raids. When the barbarians decide to sail into our harbour, it is an easy matter to vanquish them. However, when they land in a bay farther west of here, it is a difficult task to move my men quickly enough to protect the settlements. I am sad to say that many peaceful farmers lost their livestock and property to these raids, not to mention the cost in lives in desperate attempts to repel them. The construction of more fortresses to the west, if located well, with perhaps a signal tower between us, would enable us to catch raiders in a pincer."

Aware of the precious nature of this testimony, Valdor listened carefully before adding, "I'm sure this can be done as a priority, Consul, but I must ask, do you have metatores in your ranks?"

"I'll call for him, at once. Perhaps you did not know, Count, that rebuilding began here in 270 and was only finalised some ten summers ago, before my arrival. The old fort was demolished and the stone reutilised in the new walls."

They continued conversing, especially about the Count's adoptive father because the consul knew very little about the new emperor. A man entered bowing to interrupt the dialogue, his neatly-trimmed grey hair, short and brushed forward to his brow, and his deeply lined face made Valdor smile. *Perhaps all engineers look alike!* he thought. As they spoke, Svafa lifted a domesticated weasel onto her knee and stroked its brown fur. Valdor wasn't sure whether he would have risked exposing his hands to those razor-sharp teeth, but the consul smiled and said, "This little fellow keeps us free of pests; he deserves petting." The Count smiled and said, "Honestly, I prefer cats, although I imagine the weasel is faster and fiercer."

"Ay, and can squeeze through narrow openings more easily. But let's return to more serious matters; Master Metator, the Count wishes to question you about the building of our fort."

"Sire, the fort was rebuilt on the site of a smaller and weaker one. As you will appreciate, the location is ideal as we stand on a hill overlooking the sea, so that we have excellent visibility over the Channel. You will have passed through the *vicus* that bestrides the road to Durovernum. The people can flee within these walls at the first sight of danger. The walls are twenty-six feet high and the ramparts almost thirteen feet wide." Valdor caught the pride in his voice. "We used recycled stone bonded with brick and some roof tiles to enclose 3.4 hectares."

"It's an impressive construction, Metator, but tell me, what would you improve if you had to start afresh?"

The engineer looked uncomfortable, "I'm somewhat a traditionalist, so I'd prefer a more regular shape, and although, fortunately, we have not been tested by a superior force, I can't help but think that against such a foe, we would need another larger exit than the several small posterns provide. I feel sure that our layout is limiting for a strategic response, but, Sire, we were conditioned by the terrain, hence the irregular shape."

"I see, but did you not gain by the location on top of the hill?"

"Precisely, Lord. Also, at the time of building, there was considerable danger in the offing, and by remaining on the same site, our defensive capabilities were not compromised."

"Consul, are you prepared to let your metator lend his expertise by coming along with my party to choose a site to the west?"

"How could I refuse such a worthy request?"

Before Valdor could continue the conversation, the weasel leapt off Sfava's lap and sped across the hall in a brown blur. The animal must have sensed the presence of a small rodent. The consul laughed, "Just doing his duty, as we all do, Sire."

"Even on weasels was a great Empire built," Valdor laughed. "We shall leave at dawn, but tell me, how far away is the bay you believe needs safeguarding?"

"To the west, 44,000 paces, lies a bay with a long sandy beach, which makes it easy for pirates to run their shallow vessels ashore. To make matters worse, it is at the confluence of three rivers, one of which is navigable, allowing inland penetration," said the consul.

"It's true, Sire, I know the bay," added the metator, "there is a peninsula projecting into a tidal lagoon and marshes. A small river runs along the north side of the peninsula." He smiled smugly, "You could say that the place is as ideal for a fortress as it is for an enemy incursion."

"We'll leave as the cock crows on the morrow to make a definitive decision. With a little luck, in the form of the gods sending us kind weather, we can begin levelling the terrain and digging the ditches. Consul, I'll need a large part of your men to work as labourers. Should raiding vessels approach your harbour, your men will be only a day's march away."

"The pirates will not know that we have reduced the garrison and will not dare attack the fort. I can spare two hundred and eighty men, for a score of men on the ramparts will be sufficient to give the impression of a full complement."

"Then, it is agreed. Master Metator, you will lead us to this bay. What is the state of the roads?"

"There is a ridgeway that will take us almost to our destination, while the last stretch onto the peninsula is sound. We have to avoid the surrounding marshland to the east, which will make an extra defensive feature. If we leave at first light, we can be there well before nightfall."

13

THE NEW CONSTRUCTION AT ANDERITUM, AD 287

WHILE VALDOR BUSIED HIMSELF BARKING ORDERS AT HIS hard-working men, he endeared himself further by grasping a shovel and setting an example—an emperor's son who cared little that his feet were covered in the mud at the base of the fifteen-foot-deep trench he was helping to dig. The men might not have been so happy had they shared in the conversation between Valdor and the metator: "By my estimation," said the engineer, "it will take 160,000 man-days to build the fort, which is another way of saying that it will take our 285 men two years to complete it."

"Then, I'll waste no more time in conversation," the commander said, grasping the shovel and leaping with a squelch into the trench. True, his manual contribution was useful, but the building work required all his organisational skills. He arranged for carts and oxen to be available to teams of woodcutters in the woodlands to the north of the peninsula. They loaded felled oaks for transport to the trenches, where these great trunks were driven as piles into the soft earth, destined to support the weight of the stone walls. Rubble and timber were thrown between them to aid in solidifying the foundations. Several weeks passed before the metator expressed himself satisfied with the preparations and declared the trenches ready to receive the stone needed for the walls.

"Regarding the stone, Sire, I calculate that we'll need eighteen vessels for a continuous supply over a working season of 280 days."

"Where will we get the ships, and what about the stone?"

"It's a question of 600 boatloads of stone, which I dread to think about how many wagon-loads that equates to: I'd hazard 49,000! So, we'll need oxen to haul them, too. All this must be done without delay, for every day is valuable."

"Ay, but where will we quarry the stone?"

"There is an isle that lies to the west, which provided the stone for Regulbium. It is the finest quality material, and the isle is known as Vindelis, which lies just over 100 sea miles from here. I have taken the liberty of sending a message for transport boats from Regulbium. Instead, Sire, you have the authority to requisition oxen and wagons from the surrounding area."

"I shall set groups of men to this task; it will come as a pleasant change from toiling in the trench."

After several days, the lowing of the oxen became a common sound, but the voracious cropping of the grass within the interior of the trench created another problem—that of obtaining sufficient fodder. At the last count, they now had 1,500 oxen and 250 wagons.

They were still waiting for the transport boats to arrive when a cry from a lookout warned Valdor that ships were in the offing. It did not require his sharp eyes to determine soon that these were not transport barges but war galleys. Approaching the harbour under full sail was the Classis Britannica. *Does Carausius think it necessary to inspect my work?* The thought made him angry, but he could not greet his adoptive father with a sour face. Before the emperor could disembark, he had time to wash and change into his imperial *sagum*. Besides, the heavy purple cloak would warm him, even if he had become used to the fresh wind off the sea. Sfava insisted that he wear the diadem, too. She seemed more excited than he to see the emperor.

"Father! How wonderful to see you, but what brings you here?"

Carausius bellowed one of his famous laughs and thumped Valdor playfully on his shoulder, "To see you, of course, my son!" The two men embraced.

"Not to check on my progress?"

Again, the trumpeting laugh, "Not at all! I know that you will deliver; indeed, at a first glance, I see you have made great progress, and the Spring is not yet here. Nay, I sailed into Regulbium to fill our casks with fresh water and found the place nigh on deserted. They told me that you were here with your wife. Now, I did not know that you were wed and so, I decided to come and see the spouse for myself."

"Father, I am not wed, but I have a woman. Sfava! Where are you? Come here!"

"Ah! A fine barbarian beauty! Just like you, Valdor! That makes sense, but why are you not wedded? You are a Jute, are you not, my dear?" Carausius' pug-like face came close to her, and he inspected her as a plebeian farmer might inspect a mule.

"Sfava is the daughter of a jarl, father, and she is a shield-maiden."

Carausius roared his laugh, drew his gladius, and lunged at the woman. Adroitly, she skipped aside and snatched Valdor's gladius from his belt in one motion. In a moment, feet apart and shoulders forward, she was ready to fight.

"Hold!" ordered Valdor, "You cannot fight your emperor!"

All work in the camp had ceased as the men gathered around to see their emperor, and now with these events, the atmosphere was heavy and tense. Carausius' bodyguard had drawn their swords and placed themselves between their ruler and the impertinent barbarian.

Once more came the guffaw, and the emperor ordered, "Put away your weapons, I like the girl's spirit! Valdor, she will give you a formidable heir! You must wed her at once before I sail away. Did you know that Maximian is preparing for an invasion of Britannia?"

"You will vanquish him, father. But about this wedding…"

"You're right. Things should not be done in haste. Besides, it takes time for a priest to convert pagans."

"By the gods! Father, do you expect me to become a Christian? Why?"

"Because one day, you'll rule the Britons. Diocletian is persecuting Christians, covering them in oil and using them as torches to illuminate the streets of Rome. The Britons rightly will not tolerate such inhumanity. I am popular because I am the restorer of the true spirit of Rome, Valdor. When I have defeated Maximian, you will wed your Jutish wildcat with a Christian rite."

His arm around Sfava's shoulder, they watched the Classis Britannica sail away to war in Gallia.

"I like your father; he is one of us," Sfava confided, "but I'll not abandon my gods for him."

"We don't know if and when he will return," Valdor said. He had foreseen her objections but said in a low voice, "I will wed you by handclasping when the walls are completed, and we'll have a great feast. Let's leave this Christian business to blow away in the wind."

Two days after the fleet's departure, the lookout called to Valdor—"The barges, Sire!"

Urging oxen onto barges is no simple feat, but all eighteen barges sailed for Vindelis with three oxen and the same number of wagons to each vessel. The beasts would be needed to transport stone from the quarry back to the barges. They would remain on the isle until 600 boatloads of stone had arrived at the peninsula. The name of the completed fort would be *Anderitum*, named after the great Ander Forest to the north that stretched across most of the south of Britannia.

Three days passed before the lookout repeated the same cry. Valdor broke off sparring with Sfava with practice swords. She hurried over to him to inspect his right forearm, where she had delivered a hefty thwack.

"It's nothing!" he insisted, eyes watering and jaw clenched, but when she touched it gently, he pulled his arm away, "Ouch!"

"You'll have a nasty bruise tomorrow. I'll go to collect the arnica plant in the woodland. I saw a cold well-drained place where it grows. I can make an ointment. You're lucky we weren't fighting with steel blades."

"Do not think you'd have got near me with a real sword, woman!"

She could see that his pride was hurt, but she would earn his respect on the battlefield when they fought side by side. She hoped that day would come soon. There was little work the men in the fortress would allow her to do; at least, searching for the herb would be more interesting.

On her way back to the woods, she noticed again that the fortress occupied all of the peninsula so that there was no room for a *vicus*, meaning that if Britons decided to live near the stronghold, they would have to build their settlement in the woods.

She left behind hectic activity as men toiled to unload blocks of stone from the barges in the harbour onto the wagons on the foreshore. This operation was made wearisome by the soft ground, which meant putting shoulders to the carts until they reached the harder ground of the winding track up to the heights of the peninsula. The quarrymen had faced the stone blocks and also provided sacks of broken tiles and bricks to be mixed with cement for the binding courses.

As soon as the first barge was empty, it sailed away again as if the respective captains were in a prestigious race. Inside the perimeter of the trench, the metator spoke with Count Valdor, "Sire, I think it would be best if we pace out four lengths of wall and mark them with pegs. Each length will be apportioned to a gang of labourers and be twenty-six paces long. What do you think?"

"You are the expert, Metator. Will the wall be the same height as at Regulbium?"

"This site is more easily defended, but it would be wise to keep the height."

The months went by and the three adjacent lengths were completed, with three more lengths started when a small boat carrying a messenger arrived with the news that Carausius had won a victory in Gallia, retaking possession of Gesoriacum, meaning that he had complete control of the Channel. Maximian did not have the ships necessary to challenge him at sea. Given the Emperor of the North's military skills on land, the Western Emperor was forced to sue for peace.

Valdor celebrated this news by giving his men two days off work and declaring a celebratory feast. Work resumed three days later when an unexpected visitor arrived. The well-dressed individual rode a fine grey stallion. He declared in a ringing voice: "I have come to seek Caesar Valdor Aurelius!"

"I am he!" Valdor strode towards the bearded individual, who dismounted and bowed. On closer inspection, the newcomer had grown a full beard to hide to some extent a severe wound that ran diagonally from under the left cheekbone across the mouth. A blade had slashed both lips, leaving the man with a permanent disfigurement that appeared to be a constant sneer.

"I am Allectus, Sire, treasurer to Caesar Marcus Aurelius."

I suppose you've come to see why I am spending so much money. Valdor thought, but said, "You are welcome to Anderitum, Allectus, although, as you can see, it is little more than a building site at the moment. Still, you may come to my tent and share a bottle of red wine and some bread with me."

"I thank you, Sire. I can see why you have been drawing considerable sums from the treasury. May I compliment you on your choice of location for what is going to be a fine fortress?"

So, I was right about your visit. He said tightly, "It is commendable that a finance minister has come to ascertain that the imperial coffers are not being wastefully drained."

"It is my duty, Count, as the emperor spoke of a series of similar strongholds along the coast. Judging by the state of progress of this fort, I can suppose it will be finished next year?"

"Our aim is to finish Anderitum by the autumn of 289."

Valdor found that he could not help but look at the scarred lips, which created the unsettling sneer, but now, the smirk increased as Allectus smiled, revealing the damage to his teeth caused by the enemy blade.

"In that case, there will be some respite for our treasury this coming winter before you start again, Count."

"Unfortunately, Jutish and Saxon pirates are directly responsible for draining our coffers. Defence comes at a cost, Minister."

"As we are well aware, Sire. I can see that you and your men are doing a magnificent job. This will be an impregnable fortress against the raiders and, undoubtedly, will stand the test of time." He raised his beaker of wine, "Here's to confounding the raiders and the future of Anderitum!"

"The future of Anderitum!" Valdor echoed. "I don't wish to be indelicate, Minister, but where did you receive your wound?"

"Fighting with Carausius, my general, in Maximian's campaign against the Bagaudae rebels. Those peasants were better armed than we imagined and although I slew my enemy, he wielded a fine Frankish sword to some effect," he pointed ruefully at his mouth. "I expect he'd taken it from a nobleman's corpse. I know, I took it from his, and sold it for a tidy sum." His laugh was harsh and bitter. "We won a crushing victory, you know. Isn't it absurd that Maximian, the ungrateful dog, has turned on his greatest general?"

"The latest news is that my father has defeated him and that he sued for peace, which was granted. My father now holds Gesoriacum."

"Mars be praised! Holding that port means that Britannia cannot be invaded."

Why the strange expression, then, Allectus? I'm not sure that I entirely trust you! Still, father clearly does.

Smiling in a friendly manner, Valdor offered his visitor another beaker of wine and the talk moved on to future foreseen expenses, which at this point, were little more than legionaries and quarrymen's wages.

The discussion did not prove to be problematic and the Count and the Minister parted on amicable terms. Deep down, Valdor was pleased to see him go, although he could not explain his antipathy. After all, the unsightly wound had been gained honourably, fighting for the Empire.

He was pouring his third beaker of wine when the tent flap opened and Sfava came in, carrying a bunch of yellow-petalled flowers and a linen cloth containing animal fat. She spread her treasures on the floor and sat, her legs curled behind her, as she shredded the petals into the fat and mixed them with the point of her knife. Valdor poured her some wine; she took the beaker in her left hand and drained it in one draught like a true warrior. He grinned, but she grabbed his arm, making him grimace.

"Sorry," she lied with a fierce grin, gently pulling the offended arm towards her. She smeared her blade in the greasy ointment and spread it along the outside of his forearm. Then, with a circular motion, rubbed it into his skin.

"There, you'll feel better tomorrow. Soon we'll be able to practise swordsmanship again and I'll do the other arm!"

"Unless I swipe you so hard across your arse that you won't be able to sit down for a week, balm or no balm," he growled, glaring at his shieldmaiden. But she laughed and, by surprise, kissed him ferociously.

Her wild, untamed nature had captured his heart. *See, she loves me or else she wouldn't have made the arnica ointment — the little vixen!*

14

ANDERITUM FORT, SEPTEMBER AD 289

THE COUNT OF THE SAXON SHORE SURVEYED HIS MEN'S achievement. The Anderitum fortress was now completed except for minor details. Some men were tamping gravel to make the walkway around the parapets sound underfoot. The walkways ran for each of the fifty yards between turret and tower. The towers were 28 feet tall and so that the users could move around undisturbed while carrying long weapons, the height between floors was 9 feet. Having only one floor over the 9-foot-high wall, the second floor of the towers was at a height of 20 feet. The killing range of a javelin hurled from one of these turrets was reckoned at 35 feet, so the area from the walls to the first of two ditches in front of the fortress was kept entirely clear. Some men were putting the finishing touches to the two ditches, the inner one was a *fossa fastigata* 20 feet wide and 6 feet deep and contained a drainage ditch or ankle breaker, 1 foot by 1 foot, to facilitate maintenance. The outer ditch was a *fossa punica*, 20 feet wide and 5 feet deep. Its outer slope made an angle of 30 degrees with the vertical and the inner one, 19 degrees with the horizontal. Woe betide any foe advancing on the stronghold out of the woods. He closed his eyes and imagined the excitement of defending the fortress against an advancing enemy. He realised that it was more likely that the garrison would leave the fortress through the 20-foot-wide gate of the *porta praetoria* to catch the raiders in a pincer trap. *Ay, all told, we've done an excellent job. It'll seem like child's play now to construct a signal tower between here and Regulbium. Then, I'll choose another site and begin all over again, farther down the coast.*

After the walls were completed, the legionaries had rapidly constructed timber buildings, which he now surveyed with pride: beside the road running through the *porta praetoria* were two important buildings—on the right a hospital and on the left the latrines. Between those and the stables in the corner was a stockyard. Across the road and beside the hospital were the baths next to a storehouse in the corner of the fort. All of these buildings were separated by the via principalis—which joined the two gates, the left and the right— from the headquarters that contained his room and those of the high-ranking officers. This building was flanked on either side by the barracks. Two more buildings behind the headquarters and between it and the last of the gates, the *porta decumana*, contained a granary and a workshop. Valdor fully intended to build another six of these forts copying this exact layout in the years to come.

(PORT OF GESORIACUM, SEPTEMBER AD 289)

Carausius stood abaft his flagship on the tower with Centurion Heidar beside him. The Emperor of the North had been so successful as a general also because he listened to his trusted men and sought advice. "The question, Centurion, is should I accept Maximian's offer of peace or press on to destroy him?"

"Sire, better the enemy you know. The Western Emperor is in disarray, and having defeated him so emphatically once, you can do it again. The Romans produce great generals all the time," he said prophetically, "one can never be sure from where or when the next one might emerge and prevail."

"Sound advice, Heidar. I shall accept Maximian's plea."

"Also, because, my Emperor, whilst you hold this port as tonight, there is no question of Maximian invading Britannia."

Carausius guffawed and slapped his thigh, "That's true enough, but we cannot stay here indefinitely, the men will get restless, not least me! I need to see my son wedded and wish to admire the fortress he has built."

For his part, Maximian realised that he could not defeat Carausius in Gaul and that he would have to indefinitely shelve his invasion plans, but he had no intention of losing the last battlefront—that of the ancient Roman art of intrigue—even as Carausius and Heidar discussed whether to accept his offer of peace, one of Maximian's envoys discussed treason with a bearded man of the disfigured mouth.

In the next four years, much would happen under Carausius' rule. Elsewhere, Diocletian continued to persecute Christians and, at his insistence, Maximian applied his co-emperor's first edict in his part of the Empire, which ordered the burning of the Scriptures and the closing of churches. The Western Emperor was reluctant to engage in the horrific excesses of Diocletian against the person of the Christians in his territory.

(PORTUS ADURNI, AUTUMN AD 289)

In Britannia, informed of the persecutions, Carausius engaged in encouraging the Church to convert pagans. For this reason, he visited his son, now engaged in building a square fort at Portus Adurni on a commanding position at the head of a large, safe harbour opposite the large isle known as Vectis. The emperor followed his adopted son into the praetorium, a timber construction made comfortable for Valdor as the walls, built of coursed flint bonded with limestone slabs, rose around them at a faster pace than had been possible at Anderitum.

"It is the beginning of October, son, I have no complaints whatsoever about the progress you are making with the forts—"

Valdor interrupted his emperor to describe eagerly his plans for further forts and their possible locations. Carausius listened indulgently and offered a few shrewd comments about locations and watchtowers, but Valdor could see that something was on his father's mind and that he refrained from broaching it while the Count so keenly outlined his future plans.

"Father, I can see that something is troubling you, will you not share your thoughts with me?"

"Ay, that is why I have travelled thus far, Valdor."

"What is it, then?"

"Are you informed about events in the wider Empire?"

Valdor shook his head, "Occasionally, something seeps through. I know, for instance, that you brilliantly defeated Maximian in Gaul. How I wish I had been there to play my part."

Carausius, typically, roared with laughter and thumped Valdor's shoulder, "There was no need for your strength, my boy. Your fortress at Anderitum is a much greater contribution; by the way, I've issued orders for it to be garrisoned by the *numerus Turnacensium* from Portus Lemanis, whereas that stronghold will receive surplus troops from overcrowded barracks elsewhere."

"Splendid! But that is not what is weighing on your mind."

"Nay, I confess that my heart is heavy for the sins of my co-Augustus."

"Maximian?"

"He is but a puppet manipulated by the demon, Diocletian. That is something I refuse to become! Do you have any idea of what he is about? I do not doubt that he is an able general; indeed, he was proclaimed emperor by his troops. Just this year, he defeated the Alamanii and usurpers in Egypt. But it is his persecution of Christians that concerns me. He claims to do the gods' will on Earth and calls himself *Jovius*. He organises games and feeds Christians—men, women and children— to wild beasts in the arenas. He crucifies many and, I hear, crosses line the main roads into Rome. Others are burnt alive to light the streets of Rome. I will have none of this in Britannia. We should never lose sight of what happened years ago when the Britons, led by the Iceni, defeated Rome under Queen Boudicca. Many Britons, my people, have adopted Christianity through baptism and I wish them to practise their religion freely in my empire." He paused and asked for wine, draining his beaker in one gulp. Valdor scrutinised him, convinced that he had not yet heard what he had come to say. In this, he was correct, for Carausius went on to say as if he had not paused: "Which is why I have been baptised and pray for Diocletian to mend his ways—"

"What! You are a Christian, father?

Another bellow of laughter rent the air, "Exactly! You should see your face!"

Valdor placed a hand upon the table for support as his head began to spin. He could not easily absorb what he had heard. "But what about the old gods? Have you renounced them? Do you not fear their wrath?"

A long discussion followed in which Carausius echoed the words of the priest who had converted him. He was persuasive, but Valdor thought about his birth parents and their forefathers' beliefs. He satisfied himself that his adoptive father had no intention of persecuting pagans and was ready to let the matter drop when Carausius delivered a blow worthy of a *ballista* ball. "I want you and your woman to convert and be wedded in the Church by Christmas. Nay, I'll hear no objections! Either you do this, Valdor, or I will disinherit you and strip you of your rank and titles." Sfava, who had followed the debate with interest, buried her head in her hands but remained silent.

"I need to speak alone with Sfava, father."

"By all means, but I want an answer before long. I'll await it in my cabin aboard ship." He glared from one to the other and neither doubted that he would fulfil his threat.

When he had marched out, Sfava grabbed his empty beaker and hurled it at Valdor's head. He just managed to dodge out of the way. "I'll not abandon my gods," she screamed and rushed out of the praetorium and through the fort to the main gate, where she slipped out and ran towards the woods.

Valdor realised that it was pointless chasing after her, but he felt a hollow sickness in his stomach and his heart was beating too fast. He had experienced a similar feeling before his first battle. He wondered about whether he would ever see her again, for the one thing he knew about her was that she was as fierce in her beliefs as in her behaviour. Would she abandon Freya for the love of him? He doubted it, and his uncertainty increased as the day gave way to night. She was still somewhere out there in the forest, wild beasts and all. Maybe he would mourn over her mangled corpse sometime soon.

His immediate choice was whether to sit in self-pity or to get drunk, so he opted for the latter. The strong red wine, reinforced by fermented elderberry, which grew locally and saved the imported wine from Ostia from becoming little more than weak vinegar, miraculously did not cloud his powers of reflection. His sense of loss for Sfava gave way to rage at her selfishness—did his position as the emperor's son mean nothing to her? Well, he thought, *I can convert to Christianity to please father and find a pretty woman to wed.* Even as he thought this, he knew that no other woman could ever replace Sfava in his heart. He roared and hurled his empty beaker at the wall. Should he go in search of her? But it was dark and moonless that night and the forest was endless. She could be anywhere, assuming she managed to avoid the beasts. He thought of the irony: Diocletian threw Christians to wild animals and Carausius had driven a pagan to their fangs and claws. He shuddered as a wolf's howl rent the night air.

Slowly, he stood and bent to retrieve his beaker, hiccupped, and poured another measure of red wine and watched the bubbles winking at the brim before draining it in one gulp as he had watched his father do. After several more beakers treated similarly, he slumped across the table, his head resting in the crook of his elbow and he snored, oblivious to the world and his woes.

Dawn came and went and still he slept until a hand shook him roughly out of his comatose state. Slowly, he sat up, bleary-eyed and with a painful cramp in his right arm. He shook it to restore the circulation the pressure of his head had impeded. The brusque movement made him groan, fighting back the urge to vomit. But who had awakened him? He turned to gaze into the grinning face of his woman. "Sfava!" His tongue felt furry and twice its normal size and the word came out thickly but his heart leapt. She had come back to him! In her left hand, held by the ears was a dead hare—thank the gods, the only victim of last night had been her prey, not the other way around. But what would she say to him?

"Valdor, I cannot live without you. The night brought me counsel. I will do anything to stay by your side."

He rose unsteadily and accepted another beaker of red wine. "It is the best cure," she said as he looked doubtfully at the red liquid that had made him feel so bad, but he downed it and immediately felt better. As usual, she was right. "Wash and clean your teeth," she said. He obeyed and the cold water invigorated him and the sage-leaf paste made his mouth sweeter.

When he came back to her, he said, "We must go down to father's flagship and break our news. He loves hare, Sfava, make him a gift of it before we give him our consent."

"I can always trap another one," she said blithely.

"Weren't you afraid of the wolves, Sfava?"

"Ha, I can climb trees, wolves cannot!"

His laugh might have competed with Carausius' bellows, for he was truly relieved and happy; as was Carausius when he learnt of their decision. He accepted the hare with almost as much enthusiasm, summoning a cook at once. The next person to respond to his summons was a priest. "This is Father Wymond, he will instruct you in our faith. Centurion!" he bellowed and Heidar hastened into the cramped quarters.

"Centurion, tell the Count," Carausius grinned.

Heidar frowned in concentration and then, hesitantly in Latin, orated:

> *Credo in Deum Patrem omnipotentem,*
> *Creatorem caeli et terrae.*
> *Et in Iesum Christum,*
> *Filium eius unicum, Dominum nostrum,*
> *qui conceptus est de Spiritu Sancto,*
> *natus ex Maria Virgine..."*

He paused as if struggling to remember when Father Wymond came to his rescue, finishing the Apostles' Creed: *"passus sub Pontio Pilato,"* the priest droned on uninterrupted until the final *"Amen!"* Thus, giving Valdor time to think and ask: "Have you, too, then, Heidar, forsaken the old gods?"

The centurion removed his helmet and beamed happily at his old friend, "Ay, brother, and I hope you will join us. Father Wymond baptised me together with your father, our emperor. Eternal Life awaits those who believe in Christ."

Valdor turned to the priest, "How long will it take to prepare us for baptism, Father? We wish to wed in the faith," he put an arm around Sfava's shoulder. Before the priest could reply, Carausius intervened, "This is what we will do: Valdor, you take Father Wymond to your headquarters and he will prepare you every day until he considers you ready. When he does, he will baptise you in the creek that runs into the sea, yonder," he pointed vaguely at the cabin wall. Then, we shall prepare a great feast at Yuletide to be eaten after your wedding, which will be celebrated in the small Church of St Mary in *Clausentum*," again he jerked a vague thumb at the wall, "just up the river is the settlement. You are popular there, Count Valdor, because Saxon pirates sacked the place twice in the past and the inhabitants can see that your fortress will protect them henceforth."

15

PORTUS ADURNI, OCTOBER-DECEMBER, AD 289

LEFT TO HIS OWN DEVICES, VALDOR MIGHT HAVE EMBRACED the cult of Mithras like many of his men. But he owed all his privileges to his adoptive father, not a man he would cross lightly. So, he followed Father Wymond's tutoring with great attention and ardour, paying special attention to the Annunciation and the Virgin Birth.

Yet, Valdor was endowed with curiosity and could not accept the priest's certainties when he retained the smallest doubt.

"Father, if the Archangel Gabriel was sent to Mary by God and she, a virgin, conceived Jesus, we must assume He was a divinity on Earth from His birth. Why, then, was it necessary for Him to be baptised in the Jordan River?"

The priest was a simple man and ill-prepared for such theological complexities, so he begged the Count for time. He hurried to search for the proselytiser who had baptised him. If anyone could explain these intricacies to the sceptical Count, it was Amphibalus. Father Wymond found the priest in Verulamium talking with a young follower called Alban. Amphibalus, a Roman Christian, had fled Diocletian's persecutions and recently baptised the ardent Alban. He recognised his convert, Father Wymond, and was intrigued to hear about Count Valdor. Here was a golden opportunity, he believed, to settle the mind of the emperor's son and complete poor Wymond's mission.

Several days later, the priests arrived and Valdor repeated his perplexity to the theologian. Amphibalus was perhaps the only person in Britannia capable of providing an answer. He listened carefully to Valdor's argument and complimented him on the intelligence of the question.

"Count, some of the leading minds in the Christian community over the last century have debated this very point, *in primis*, Irenaeus of Lyons and Justin the Martyr, who explained the events at the Jordan as necessary only for the sake of humanity; Jesus was not personally in need of the descent of the Spirit. For Justin, the Gospel narratives show evidence of the fruits of the Spirit in Christ, gifts that were later passed on to humanity in virtue of the baptism of Christ. Likewise, the baptism in the Jordan was and is a manifestation for the Christian community of the graces of the Spirit that are bestowed on Christians through immersion."

Valdor pursed his lips and frowned, gnawed at his thumbnail for a moment, then his expression cleared into an engaging smile. "Well, that makes sense, and I presume, priest, that if I submit to lustration in the freezing waters of the Itchen, I will receive the grace of the Holy Spirit, too?"

Now it was Amphibalus' turn to frown, and he said cautiously, "It behoves me to preach that the only begotten Son of God comes here, in order that whoever believes in Him should be saved, and whoever does not believe in Him should be condemned." He stared hard at Valdor, making sure that he had understood, but to be quite certain, added, "What I am saying is, ay, the Holy Spirit will come to you, Count, but any relapse into pagan practices or failure to renounce Satan's wiles, and the vessel of your body will be deemed unworthy to house it—"

Valdor cut the monologue short, "Your faith is demanding, priest, and I am but a poor, ignorant man. I wonder whether—"

Amphibalus took Valdor's hand and stared into his grey-blue eyes, "Nay, Count, for one thing you *are not* is ignorant, maybe you are insecure. Remember from Father Wymond's teachings that God the Father spoke thus: 'This is my beloved Son, in whom I am well pleased,' as if to reassure His Son. If our Lord needed reassurance, wouldn't you know *you'd* need it?"

Valdor laughed, "Priest, it takes more courage to enter your religion than to go into battle!"

Amphibalus squeezed the hand and, finally, let it go, "You *are* going into battle, but against the invisible Forces of Darkness. Faith and prayer will sustain you, and you will not lose the war."

Valdor had much to reflect upon and, that night, for the first time in his life, prayed to the Christian God. It troubled him that he might not be ready to embrace this religion, but he woke in the morning with the conviction that he and Sfava should literally take the plunge into the gelid waters of the nearby River Itchen. Sfava's decisive nature and lesser propensity for intellectual struggle meant she had waited patiently for Valdor to decide for them both.

The Count accepted Father Wymond's plea to allow Amphibalus to conduct the ceremony, although he, too, would be in attendance to watch proceedings. The exiled priest surprised everyone by not leading them to the river, but to a small church between the fort and the stream. He explained that before baptism, the catechumen should renounce Satan and receive a first anointing with the oil of exorcism.

"Is that because you believe us to be possessed by evil, priest?" the quick-witted Count snarled.

"I wish you to do great deeds, son," Amphibalus reassured him, adding "and your jarl's daughter is by nature ferocious," he murmured this so low that not even Wymond standing beside him understood. He raised his voice, "Now it's down to the water for a triple immersion and the confession of faith."

Valdor and Sfava stripped naked on the banks of the Itchen and while he entered the freezing stream little-by-little, she flung herself with a great splash into the icy river, causing him to wince as the spray struck him. He managed not to curse, recalling that this was a spiritual moment. Amphibalus waded in and cupping his hands poured the water over the waist-deep Valdor's head while uttering prayers. He repeated the action twice more, then gave his attention to Sfava. When the Roman priest had finished, the goose-pimpled newly baptised, shivering and teeth chattering, grabbed the cloths offered by Wymond and rubbed themselves dry vigorously. They dressed hastily and Valdor turned to Amphibalus and glared. "Apart from cold, I feel no different, priest!"

"Nor should you, my son, the test will come and you will *know*. Now, let us go back to the church."

Inside the dimly-lit, simple wooden building, Valdor's eyes adjusted and he stared at the altar with its simple wooden cross. Amphibalus made his two converts kneel before it and, uttering a prayer, smeared them with the oil of thanksgiving, saying, "I anoint you with sacred oil in the name of Jesus Christ." He then laid his hands on their heads in turn and, again, applying oil, said, "I anoint you with holy oil in the Almighty Father, in Christ Jesus, and in the Holy Spirit."

It was at that precise moment that Valdor *knew* something had changed within him. Later, Sfava put it into words, "I felt a golden glow pass from the top of my head through my body to my toes. At last, I felt in touch with the divine."

"Ay, with the Godhead," said Amphibalus triumphantly and explained to her, "Daughter, you felt the Holy Spirit entering your corporeal body. Pray that He will remain forever within you. Do good deeds and love your man and your neighbours."

She began by acting as a nurse to injured labourers, bandaging blisters and making tinctures for sprained ankles. Valdor, instead, eased the pressure on the masters, whose exhortations had produced astonishing progress. On the sabbath, without explanation, he gave everyone a day's rest, which the men appreciated and redoubled their efforts the following day. In this way, the fort neared completion as advent approached. Only Valdor and Sfava knew what this meant, but they were surprised when, as the last gateway tower neared completion, a horn sounded to announce the approach of a ship. Valdor bounded up the twin tower at the other side of the east gate and peered seawards. Indeed, there was a ship, he smiled, recognising the vessel as his father's flagship. Disembarked, Carausius led a small party up to the east gate, where three blasts of a horn opened the great oak doors to admit the emperor and his contingent into the square, 9-acre enclosure.

As he embraced his father, Valdor peered over his shoulder to espy with pleasure the features of the priest, Amphibalus, whom he had not seen for months following the baptism.

"My dear son," Carausius began, "I am well pleased. This fortress is almost completed and, although you have not yet been called upon to fight, we have destroyed countless pirate vessels in the east coast estuaries. Don't worry, I predict that you'll be honing your blades in the spring to repel the marauders, who are coming in waves." The emperor turned and gestured to Amphibalus, who hurried to stand next to him. He addressed Valdor with "Greetings in the name of Christ our Saviour,

Count. I hope you have said your prayers and read the Bible that I left you."

"I have, and expect some lively discussion with you, priest. But all in good time. Come, you must be weary, let's enter the praetorium, where you shall have warmth, food and drink."

Gathered around the hearth, supping Valdor's fine red wine, served by Sfava, the conversation soon turned to their conversion.

"Amphibalus survived my co-emperor's persecution of Christians in Rome. Some friends hid him and smuggled him aboard a trading vessel directed to Britannia. He tells me that you have a fine mind and posed him some acute questions before he baptised you."

"I'm thankful that it was he who performed the rite, father, because I know it was efficacious."

"Good, you may ask why I brought Amphibalus with me."

"Why, father?"

Carausius roared his typical laugh, "To add to your sacraments, of course."

Valdor looked puzzled, "I don't understand."

Again, the bull-like bellow of laughter, "Holy matrimony! There's no reason that you and Sfava should not marry in the Church. Yuletide is in the offing and Christmas is a good time for your nuptials. Who better than Amphibalus to conduct the service?"

"There is no church in the fort," Valdor said gloomily.

"Nay, but he tells me there is one down by the river. It's enough that it's consecrated. Afterwards, we'll have a great feast. I've brought a host of cooks with me. We should go a-hunting in the forest together tomorrow. I have a fancy for venison," another roar of laughter made Valdor smile. "It's a splendid idea, father. They say that bear steak is exquisite, but I've never tasted it. Sfava found a bear den while collecting herbs to treat men's aches and pains. She can lead us to it." He turned to his woman, "Can you find it again, do you think?"

Her quizzical expression made his smile widen, for he knew she was challenging him. "I reckon that means ay, you can!"

"If you're after bear, we'll need spears, not just bows and arrows," the emperor mused. As if remembering something important, he turned to his cornicen, "Outside by the gate," he jerked a thumb, "three blasts if you please!"

The soldier picked up his horn, draped it around a shoulder and hurried out.

Three resonant blasts followed, and Valdor wondered what their purpose could be.

Soon enough, the cornicen returned, leading a small group into the building. To his immense pleasure, Valdor recognised his Batavian friends: Faldrek, Heidar, and his cousin, Johar, accompanied by Father Wymond.

Carausius howled another of his laughs, "You should see your face! Close that mouth and welcome your brothers in Christ!"

"What! My friends have become Christians?"

"Ay, fully-fledged, thanks to Father Wymond. I thought it best that my most trusted bodyguard shared my faith. When they heard that you had converted, they decided to do the same."

Valdor leapt to his feet and embraced them each in turn. He called Sfava. "This is my woman, Johar, it's time you found one like her," he paused and considered, "well, perhaps a little less savage!" Sfava backhanded a slap, but Valdor was ready and caught her wrist, "See what I mean!" and Carausius bellowed again.

Amid the hilarity, Faldrek looked serious and said, "When we came through the gate, I couldn't help but notice—it's ingenious."

"What?" asked Johar, "I didn't notice anything."

"You have a good eye, my friend," Valdor smiled at Faldrek, "but I take no credit. It was my metator."

"What are you talking about," Johar asked grumpily.

The emperor, too, looked intrigued and stared at Valdor expectantly.

Valdor smiled and said, "Faldrek's right, the gates of Portus Adurni are of particular interest: they are indented inwards, so as to trap the enemy in an area exposed to walls on three sides. That is, if we ever get the chance to fight the pirates," he added gloomily.

"Cheer up, my boy, I'm sure you will, for these Germanic tribes are coming in increasing numbers to these shores. Thank the Lord they cannot venture forth in these winter months, so we can enjoy our firesides," he stretched out his hands over the hearth.

Christ's Mass approached and Carausius busied himself with organising the ceremony unbeknown to Valdor. The first he knew of any such arrangements was on the day itself, the eve of the celebrations for the birth of Christ. Carausius ordered them to march down to the small church by the Itchen. Valdor gazed with curiosity at a plump matron dressed in white and at his bride, who wore a veil over her face. He wondered at these oddities. The Romans were as reluctant to surrender their gods as the pagans were, so in these early days of Christianity, Carausius made sure to appease the old divinities at his son's nuptials. The ceremony was simple and conducted by Father Wymond. However, the matron chosen by the emperor took Valdor's right hand and placed it in Svafa's, the *dextrarum iunctio*. The matron was the personification of Juno or of Concordia. She only backed away when the priest wrapped his stole around the joined hands and declared the couple man and wife. Then he addressed God in prayer, citing Tobias, "You made Adam, and for him you made his wife Eve a helper and support. From these two the human race has sprung. You said, 'It is not good that the man should be alone; let us make a helper for him like himself.'" Then, the priest blessed the couple and they exchanged the gold rings Carausius had provided. It was that simple and, amid the well-wishers, Valdor and Svafa returned to the fortress. There, they found more surprises.

The emperor had been busy with craftsmen for some time. He presented the couple with a large gold glass medallion. Their likenesses were beaten into the gold foil before it was encased in green glass, the couple stood, half-turned with right hands joined and between their heads was the *chi-rho* symbol. The magnificent piece was intended for display on a high table and it certainly caught the light and affirmed the Christian marital status of the spouses.

The surprises did not end there because the emperor presented Svafa with an exquisite silver cosmetics case, its lid inscribed with the slogan *Dulcis Anima Vivas*—Sweet Soul May You Live! —a nod to the concept of Eternal Life.

Carausius brought to an end the wedding occasion by announcing that they should be in the forest before noon to hunt for the bear or a deer. The Batavian centurions, Valdor and two of his preferred officers each withdrew a heavy spear from the storeroom as did the emperor.

The ever-practical Johar also coiled a rope around his shoulder and down to his hip. Svafa, instead, not wishing to carry a heavy pole, withdrew three javelins. Some of them also carried a bow and wore a quiver of arrows. These were more suitable for deer hunting should the bear not be found. Svafa led the way into the forest and pointed out various herbs to her husband, explaining their doctoral use until she came to a clearing, where a track led away through dense undergrowth. It was narrow, so they were forced to move in single file behind her. After following this trail for several minutes, she stopped and spoke to Valdor behind her. "This fork to the left leads to a small clearing where there is an outcrop of rock. There are signs that a bear has dug a den under the overhanging rock. We should move swiftly and silently if we want to slay the bear." Valdor passed the instructions back and Svafa took the fork, halting when she reached the glade. "It might be a little early for hibernation," Valdor said doubtfully. "But if we wake the beast, it will be enraged. I see the opening under the rock." He pointed out the crevice to Heidar. "I'll go and poke my spear into its den," said the centurion. "Usually they are not very deep, just big enough for the creature to turn around on its litter of leaves."

"Be careful, Heidar, we'll have our spears ready in case the animal attacks."

They moved forward silently, Svafa hanging back slightly as the men approached the den.

Heidar lowered his spear, holding it parallel to the ground, his left hand grasping the pole ahead of his right. He assumed a half-walking, half-squatting position and drew near the entrance. Only a foot away from the hole, he thrust his spear forward. The other men formed an arc behind him, their spears all pointing at the den.

A squeal followed by a growl came from the den and suddenly, Heidar fell backwards as the spear was knocked sideways out of his hand. Before anyone could react, the brown bear emerged, preparing to pounce on the supine figure of Heidar. Even as the moaning bear sprang, a javelin thudded into its chest, rapidly followed by another. This second strike was enough to send the creature toppling backwards, which was when Carausius lunged forward and buried his spear deep into the beast's chest. To make quite sure, Valdor plunged his spear into the bear's throat and there could be no doubt that it now lay dead.

Johar dropped his spear, leapt forward and bound the bear's front paws together. He hacked through the rope and proceeded to bind the hind paws. That done, Valdor inserted his spear so that two men at each end could raise the prey onto their shoulders to transport it back to the fortress, where it would be skinned and butchered.

Heidar, somewhat pale, got to his feet, his first thought being to thank Svafa for her prompt reaction that had likely saved his life. But the emperor reached her first to congratulate her on the accuracy and power of her throwing. "After all, I see that my son's claims were not exaggerated. You are truly a shield maiden and I thank you for saving my centurion."

The fierce light in her eyes thrilled him and he knew why Valdor had chosen her to be his woman. But her words pleased him even more. "Lord, I wish only to fight beside my husband in your cause."

"You are as impatient as he is, but trust me, the pirates will come in the spring and worse for them if you are to greet them, my daughter!" he guffawed.

They trudged back to the fortress eagerly anticipating the two evenings of feasting that awaited them. Tonight, they would sample bear steak for the nuptial feast and on the morrow, roast geese for the Lord's birthday.

16

DUBRIS, KENT AND THE SOLENT, AD 289-90

CARAUSIUS, A MENAPIAN COMING FROM THE LOWER RHINE, was a seasoned sailor and already knew the ways of Frankish raiders. He enjoyed his peaceful Christmas and shared his fireside reflections with his son.

"I have experienced considerable success against the pirates, Valdor, but it cannot last unless I change things."

"You'll have to explain, father, I've been fully occupied with fort building and know little about your maritime adventures."

"It's a question of ships, my boy. The Frankish vessels have much in common with the 'Celtic' shipbuilding methods of my area of the Rhine. I have captured several and studied them. They have a strong keel and are carvel-built. The Romans use the immensely strong but time-consuming Mediterranean method of shell building," he explained the two techniques to the ill-informed Valdor. "So, you see, if we adopt the Rhine building technique, we can produce more craft quickly to match the increase in pirate numbers that I expect."

"But doesn't that building method mean that the ships are less watertight?"

Carausius roared with laughter, "The priest is right! You ask astute questions, my boy! It does! That's the importance of caulking. We'll stuff the joints with fibres and smear tar over them. That solves the problem. There are other gains, too. Let me explain. The mast step takes the form of a heavy transverse frame with a notch to hold the mast. The mast can take a light, lateen sail and there are twenty-six oars and a steersman. The vessels I captured are sleek with a shallow draught, drawing only about eighteen inches of water. They are about sixty feet long by ten feet broad: fast and manoeuvrable."

"Certainly, more so than our lumbering war galleys," Valdor mused.

"Exactly! But if we match them, we can intercept and defeat them. At present, they can easily escape us even by rowing up shallow rivers. I have ordered the building of scores of a ship type called a *scafa exploratoria*—a fast, 20-oared, camouflaged warship to be used for scouting and interception. I'm afraid that the triremes and Liburnians are no longer of much use to us. We must and will adapt! Since I became emperor, the land has prospered, to become largely free of piracy."

"I can see the benefits of the new ships," Valdor scratched the back of his head, "they will be cheaper and easier to build with a good performance—"

"Ay, and they'll require only a third of the crew of a Liburnian, meaning I can deploy my manpower more efficiently."

"Is the rumour true? Has Maximian taken Gesoriacum?"

"True, but much worse, he has defeated our Frankish allies to gain control of navigation on the Rhine. My scouts tell me that he exploited the tribal rivalries and is forming a fleet up at Trier. When spring comes, he'll proceed to the mouth of the Rhine and launch an invasion of Britannia." Carausius smirked, "But we'll be ready for him, son. During the next few weeks, I'll rearrange my legions, they will man your shore forts. You will be ready to counter any attack that sets foot on our shores. I will have every available vessel gather in the east coast estuaries but will send you a patrol for the Solent Channel. Together we'll defeat Maximian and confound his intention to re-take Britannia." The emperor of the North did not bellow his famous laugh, but frowned and stated prophetically: "Sooner or later, the Western Empire will find itself a better general than Maximian. My boy, do you know how many emperors have been murdered due to their lack of success? Failure in battle means loss of confidence and shortage of pay. My men have a lack of neither. Learn from me how to cultivate popularity." Now he trumpeted his famous laugh.

"How many?"

Carausius looked puzzled, "How many, what?"

"How many emperors have been murdered?"

"I don't know the exact number, but it goes as I said: defeat, lack of pay, debasement of the coinage to find the silver with a consequent inflation in prices, then revolt. Look, as recently as Gallienus, about the time you were born, he alone had to suppress 18 usurpers in his nine-year reign, only at the end to be murdered by his own officers. The empire was on the brink of collapse, then along came Diocletian and his reforms, of which I am proud to have played my part." He peered at Valdor and placed a hand on his arm, looked apologetic, and said, "This is your heritage, my son. Only success is acceptable."

"Then, it is success we'll achieve, father."

The emperor kissed his son's hand and agreed, "We'll have success!"

Winter gave way to spring and Valdor finished the work on Portus Adurni. He was considering what to do next when the warning blast of a horn sent him scurrying to an observation post. His heart thudding in his chest, he peered out to sea, relaxing at the sight of two familiar triremes leading half a dozen lighter ships into his harbour. His father had kept his word about reinforcements. He remained patiently at his vantage point and watched the pleasant sight of an entire legion disembarking from the two triremes. He identified the Capricorn shields of II Augusta and the figure of Legate Vitulasius leading his men to the trail up to the fortress. Valdor hurried down to wrap his imperial purple cloak around him and place the diadem over his fair locks.

To the usual three blasts, the great gate swung open and Valdor hurried to greet his welcome visitor. "Legate, you are just the person I would have wanted to take command of this fort. I'll soon leave you in charge." He explained the novelty of the defensive gates and how best to lure the enemy to destruction then, went on to negotiate for the ships. "I suggest that my cousin, Centurion Johar takes command of the triremes and patrolling the Solent. I will command the six smaller vessels and take them to the site of my next fortress."

After much reflection, he had decided on a strategic location facing Gallia—at a place named Dubris—the site of the estuary of the Dour. The planned fortress would, therefore, be in close contact with Portus Lemanis to the south and Regulbium to the north.

He was delighted when the shallow draught of his flotilla allowed him to moor in the River Dour. At this site, two lighthouses called the Pharos stood on the eastern and western heights. They were constructed soon after the Roman conquest of Britannia. Valdor chose the western heights for his fortification and climbed up to inspect the 80-foot-high lighthouse to see whether it could be incorporated into the planned defensive walls. His metator urged him, instead, to consider constructing, as the earlier Classis Britannia fort, below the western heights on the west bank of the Dour, but building anew, ignoring the old fortress. When the metator marked out the line of the foundations, the corners of the two forts did overlap. The older fortress would be a profitable source of stone for the new one. The new fort enclosed a number of civilian buildings to the north of the earlier fort and the west wall went straight through the west end of a Painted House. Valdor also inspected this *mansio*, which the metator considered in an ideal position for his fortress. The army came first, so he would sequester the building, demolish it, and incorporate its foundations into those of the 10 feet thick walls. The foots of the *mansio* walls could be embodied into the ramparts. He inspected the many multi-coloured panels framed by fluted columns, each with a motif dedicated to Bacchus, the Roman god of wine. As a Christian who appreciated wine, Valdor was saddened to tell the owner of the *mansio* of his decision.

"Friend, it is better to lose your home to the Roman army, than to lose it to Frankish raiders along with your life. Defence of the Channel is paramount. I will see you are compensated."

Demolition and the beginnings of the foundations began the next day. The surplus stone from the *mansio* was immediately built into the wall foundations. Valdor was pleasantly surprised to find baths quite close to the *mansio* and made good use of them, soaking himself while his metator took control of the layout of the fortress. The worthy engineer decided to reinforce the walls at intervals along its length with great stone bastions and ditch nearly 40 feet wide and 10 feet deep. Within the walls, he planned a dozen timber-built structures, metalled roads, and a postern gate with a footbridge. The ancient military bath house would be reused within the walls, which would delight his commander, the Count.

(THE SOLENT, AD 290)

Initially, Johar was irritated at being fobbed off with the two lumbering triremes while his cousin and commander took a sleek *scafa exploratoria* and the other five to Dubris. He sent the other trireme to the eastern approach of the channel and stationed his own at the western entrance. He understood that the two vessels guaranteed safety to a long stretch of the south coast and this made him feel better about his appointed task. During the first six weeks of patrolling, he was first startled by the strong and variable currents, which he studied intensely until he knew them intimately. At this point, he began to hatch a plan to defeat the pirates. He was certain that when they approached from the east, they would see his sister ship and deviate course to pass the northern coast of Vectis to then veer into the western entrance.

His scheme involved subterfuge. He would let the raiders believe that he was frightened of them and make as if to flee.

Everything went to plan when a dozen lateen-rigged Frankish ships appeared and Johar apparently fled. But he led them in hot pursuit into the treacherous currents where his three banks of oarsmen were able to pull out of danger. Alas for the raiders, each with only a third of Johar's available rowers, they were unable to save themselves from being dashed and wrecked on the rocky shore. The Franks who survived the devastation to reach the land were slaughtered by the II Augusta legionaries, who had been warned by their watchtower of an imminent incursion.

A more successful patrolling of the Solent was unimaginable, and Johar rejoiced in his feat, giving his crews three days' respite in the harbour.

(DUBRIS, KENT AD 290)

The fortress was half built when Valdor received news of a likely raid on his stretch of coast. It was extremely difficult to foresee where the pirates would choose to penetrate the land. However, he took his six ships deeper into the Dour estuary where a reed bed grew and backed his camouflaged ships among the tall canes. From the water, they were practically invisible. He had left instructions with a horn blower placed on the seventh floor of the western lighthouse to alert him with three blasts if he spotted pirates entering the Dour estuary.

The wait was long and boring, hardly relieved by the teeming fowl that occupied the reed bed. The men were becoming restless, the tedium made worse by Valdor's strict orders not to speak. He did not want voices alerting the enemy. At last, three horn blasts came from the

Pharos, but Valdor held up a warning hand, ordering his crews to wait. He wanted to see the foe for himself to evaluate the odds.

He saw eight vessels rowing towards them, which made the stakes about even. He had the advantage of surprise, so he dropped his arm, and simultaneously his six vessels shot forward abeam of the foe. His archers in the prow had easy pickings, decimating the enemy crews before they realised they were under attack. The current swung Valdor's ships parallel to the Saxons so that his oarsmen hauled in their oars and became javelin throwers. These wreaked more havoc than the archers. Valdor's was the first boat to grapple an enemy and heave it to his hull. The commander himself, closely followed by Sfava, jumped aboard the enemy craft, swords drawn and shields raised. There was no need for shouted orders. His men knew their roles, and they followed their two leaders to overcome the marauders. The beauty of his success, repeated along the river by the others, was that not only did they slaughter the enemy, but they also seized the Saxon ships undamaged, thus more than doubling the size of their flotilla.

Valdor ordered a celebratory feast for all his men, including those in the garrison who had not been involved in the triumph. Sfava boasted that she had slain one more Saxon than Valdor's three, and he knew this to be true, although, as he pointed out to her, she had run a risk with the fourth that he would not have taken. She laughed; "I only did it because I'm more agile than you, and the swine was about to strike you from behind with his axe. I saved you, my darling commander." He knew that this was true, too, and was grateful and indebted to her, but knew that she had exposed herself to the very peril he had faced. She was indeed more agile, but on a blood-smeared deck, footholds were uncertain. He would have to think long and hard about taking his shield maiden into another battle.

(BLACKWATER ESTUARY, ESSEX, AD 290)

Built shortly before Carausius came to power, the fortress of *Othona* at the edge of the Dengie Peninsula was ideal for control of the estuaries of the rivers Blackwater and Colne, the latter leading to the important city of Camulodunum. It was here that Carausius had taken his newly-built fleet of fast interceptors and here that he added to his crews, reinforcing them with the *numerus fortensium* of the garrison. Before leaving Branodunum Fort, he had made arrangements to reinforce all the east coast garrisons because his scouts were certain of Maximian's invasion. The scouting patrol ship he had sent out sailed at great speed into the Blackwater Estuary and rowed over to the flagship. "Sire, the invasion fleet is on its way. I believe it is heading for the Yare Estuary. If we move quickly, we can trap them there."

"Excellent!" Carausius grinned. "I have added to the garrison at *Gariannum*, so we are well prepared. We sail at once!"

Whether Maximian expected to be opposed by cumbersome triremes or was ignorant of Carausius' new fleet, he was caught cold by the manoeuvrable interceptors and, much as had happened almost contemporaneously in the Dour Estuary, his fleet was overwhelmed by the disciplined troops who grappled and triumphed over Maximian's vessels. The engagement was short and bloody and ended with Carausius deliberately allowing his co-emperor to escape with six other vessels.

"Why, Sire, did you let your sworn enemy escape?" asked Centurion Heidar, who shared the emperor's confidences.

Carausius bellowed his famous laugh, "Because, my friend," he said triumphantly, "he will never again dare to launch a seaborne invasion after today's debacle." In this, Carausius was correct and far-seeing. For the moment, at least, Britannia was firmly in his grasp.

17

NORTHERN GAUL, AD 290

Carausius slapped Heidar on the back. "You're going home, Centurion!"

The former smith's apprentice stared at his emperor slack-jawed. What had he done wrong to deserve exile? He had thought that his commander was in an excellent mood after his crushing defeat of Maximian. Strangely, the deafening laugh seemed to confirm as much.

"You should see your face, my boy! Anyone would think that you don't want to return home. We're all going, you know."

Heidar's mouth shut with relief. "To Batavia, Sire?"

Another slap on the back. "That's where you are from, isn't it?"

"Ay, but—"

"*But* Batavia is in Maximian's hands, you were about to say. And that's the point. He was able to invade Britannia because he could sail unimpeded out of the mouth of the Rhine. We have to put a stop to that. We don't want him making a habit of it!" He bellowed another laugh at his joke. "The sea conditions are fair. Gather your men and bring them on board my flagship. I want you by my side, Centurion."

As predicted, the crossing was calm for the season, and Heidar, standing in the stern with his emperor, enjoyed the breeze ruffling his hair and breathing in the salty tang, and, to crown his enjoyment, he was going home. But that, in itself, promised to be problematic. He turned to the stocky, curly-haired figure beside him and shared his doubts.

"Sire, I have spoken to some recent recruits from Batavia, and they tell me that the sea level has risen and that the land has subsided. Together it means a higher water level of twelve feet. Good farming land has been flooded. A decurion told me that agriculture has been ruined by inundation together with a lack of manpower. People are leaving to seek a better life elsewhere. He said that the area between the Scheldt and the Rhine is so wet and swampy that it cannot truthfully be described as 'land' anymore. I dread to think what has become of my village, Sire."

The emperor frowned and ran a hand over his curly blond beard. "Heidar, you have provided me with one of the reasons for all this piracy. These fellows want plunder right enough, but I'll wager that given half the chance, they'll seize good farm land in Britannia without thinking twice."

Heidar nodded thoughtfully. "You can't really blame them, can you, lord?"

"Our duty is to protect our people. If the new settlers clear woodland and pay their taxes, while living peacefully beside our people, I can see no harm in their permanence. You know I've been recruiting men from your area. They prefer to fight for me than to struggle to make a living. After all, I guarantee them pay and food!" The sea breeze carried away his guffaw.

On entering the Rhine, Heidar gazed with trepidation at the flooded fields. Where crops once grew, waders splashed in search of worms or small fry. Carausius' new vessels handled beautifully in the river, so steering into the turbulent confluence of the Waal was no problem. Heidar looked longingly ashore as they rowed past the small group of houses that once comprised his village. What he saw was desolation. Not one emitted smoke, but that was hardly surprising as they had moved their families to Britannia and to a better life. Water, at least a foot deep, lapped against doors and walls.

"Look, sire, that building yonder, it was once the smithy where I toiled, but now the roof has caved in!"

"Times change, Centurion! Surely, you have no regrets?"

"None, Sire. But life plays certain tricks. If Faldrek had not fled from his Roman pursuers, who knows? I might still be beating red-hot iron bars in that hovel, or sweeping out muddy water. Soon, I'll use these arms to beat your enemies, God willing."

"Ay, my friend, it's not far now to Noviomagus Batavorum if my memory serves me well. We'll enter the harbour and then besiege the fortress, for it controls the whole reach of the Waal and Rhine lands."

Heidar blew out his cheeks and released his breath slowly.

"What?" said the emperor. "Do you think it an impossible task?"

"Well, Sire, we have brought no siege engines."

Carausius' lips curled. "Then we shall pray for ingenuity. Look! Up there is the fortress!"

The dominating site of the citadel did nothing to ease Heidar's fears. This wasn't the homecoming he'd anticipated when they set sail from Othona.

On arrival in the port, they found three of Maximian's warships. Onboard, the scuttling around suggested anxiety at seeing such a large naval force entering the harbour.

"These are three of the vessels that we allowed to leave with Maximian. So, news has arrived of his defeat," Carausius nudged Heidar. "Centurion, go to the ships and find out whether they wish to join our fleet or die a noble death. Put it to them in those terms."

"Ay, Sire, we'll see how faithful they are to their emperor."

As a Batavian warrior, Heidar considered loyalty a prime and immutable quality, so he prepared himself to receive insults and, as a neo-Christian, was prepared to turn the other cheek with dignity. At his approach, he was surprised, therefore, when a decurion scrambled up the ladder to the quay to meet him. Heidar delivered his message, and the decurion laughed bitterly. "Centurion, you should know that my crew are on the verge of mutiny; they have received no pay from the emperor even after they traversed the North Sea twice at his command. The other two ships will tell you the same tale. Indeed, they detached from Maximian to berth here as we did. I believe that the other three ships have rowed upstream to Trier."

"Are you saying, Decurion, that you accept to join on the Emperor of the North's terms?"

"I presume from his reputation that Caesar Marcus Aurelius Mausaeus Carausius will pay my men for their service?"

Heidar smiled: "Nobody among us ever speaks against our emperor because he pays in good coin punctually. Rest assured; I shall intervene personally on behalf of the three crews."

The two officers clasped wrists and grinned at each other. Heidar could not blame his erstwhile enemies for not following a leader who exploited their loyalty without reward.

"One last thing, Decurion, has news of Maximian's defeat reached the garrison?"

"Ay, it has, and it must be said that the commander and his men are largely auxiliaries raised by the same emperor and transported here from Dacia. I think you'll find no love among them for Maximian."

Heidar hurried back to his emperor to assure him that the three ships would unite with his fleet. He explained the price for their loyalty. Carausius roared mirthfully, "The world is made up of men who want the same thing—money to buy strong drink and women!" He ended his homespun philosophy with a guffaw. "Centurion, fetch your comrade Faldrek to me. He can help carry the bags of silver to the ships. You have given my word, and it will not be broken: a promise is a debt, my friend."

Soon, Heidar withdrew three bags of silver coins and took them with Faldrek to the moored vessels, where cheers from the crew greeted them along with cries of 'Hail Emperor of the North!'

Carausius listened to this with pleasure, even if his smile was cynical. These were not the first, nor would they be the last men he had brought into his ranks with undebased silver coins bearing his portrait.

When the two centurions clambered aboard, he called them over.

"Hark, my most trusted and able Batavians, I have another task for you. Go up to the fortress and deliver this message. 'The Emperor of the North has no quarrel with them, but if they do not surrender the fortress, no ships will be allowed to unload wheat. They will be permitted only barley for their bread.'"

Bread was made from barley, but in Italy, almost all bread was made from wheat, and barley was usually reserved for animals. Forcing men to eat barley—the lesser grain, the grain of beasts—was nothing more and nothing less than a way of underlining a unit's shame and exclusion from the rest of the army.

The two centurions exchanged a grim smile, bowed, and set off up the winding track. The message was insulting, and Heidar worried about their reception. Had not the decurion stated that these men were mainly Dacian auxiliaries? Dacians were renowned for their fierce pride. He discussed this with Faldrek as they approached the gate.

"Let's hold back on the barley and use it *in extremis*."

"Very wise," his comrade agreed.

The fortress commander, a Dacian consul, received them amicably, with a jocular smile, "So, the conquering heroes have arrived!"

"We bear a message from our emperor, Caesar Marcus Aurelius Mausaeus Carausius, Consul. He wishes to make it clear that he has no quarrel with the garrison here, but, as you are aware, needs control of this stronghold to avoid further attempts at invading Britannia."

"Until now, this fortress has been under the sovereignty of Emperor Maximian, Centurion. Yet, we have been ineffective because the emperor had no interest in preventing pirates from leaving for Britannia. Indeed, I'd say he positively encouraged certain Germanic tribes to depart for your shores; hence his stubborn refusal to equip us with interceptor craft. However, his defeat to your illustrious emperor—a great general, by the way—changes everything. Most of my men are Daci and feel no particular loyalty to the Western Emperor. Of course, the same could be said for the Emperor of the North. The difference is that your Caesar pays his men, whereas Maximian provides coinage the traders snub. It is practically worthless. I have a message for Carausius," the centurions noted that he pronounced the name with due respect. "Tell him that Noviomagus Batavorum is his, on one condition, which is that my men receive a fair indemnity for the surrender of a fortress that they have loyally garrisoned for his foe."

"We shall bring you his answer within the hour, Consul."

Carausius agreed to these terms but with a condition of his own. The Dacians would be replaced by a cohort of Batavians led by Centurion Faldrek. The Dacians would receive their pay but would serve in Britannia after swearing loyalty to the Emperor of the North. The Dacian troops greeted the announcement of these conditions with a raucous cheer and the chanting of the emperor's name. Heidar surveyed the strong walls and thanked the Lord that taking Noviomagus had not come to a battle. He blessed his intuition not to insult the Dacians by comparing them to animals.

The consul made his way to the flagship and spent a considerable time speaking with his new emperor. Heidar was not privy to their conversation but noted Carausius' keen interest in the other's words. It would not be long before Heidar knew more than he would have liked about the consul's discourse. The emperor called him over to explain.

"The consul is going to fetch his men, who will return to Othona with me. Your cohort of Batavians will remain here under your command, Heidar, but such a fortress cannot be governed by a centurion. I am raising you to the rank of consul."

Heidar knew he was too young for this rank, but if that was his emperor's wish, who was he to argue? Also, he was confident of his relationship as centurion with his men. They would give him unswerving loyalty. His musings were interrupted by the emperor's next words: "I'm leaving you half of the ships, Consul, for it is time to go on the attack. I learnt from the garrison commander that the largest number of pirate ships leaving the Rhine are from one tribe in particular—the Chauci. I want you to row upstream, raid inland and slaughter the lot of them, seizing every available seaworthy vessel. Once that is done, you will regularly patrol the estuary, making sure that no bands of pirates sail for Britannia. Any questions?"

"None, Sire. My men will not disappoint you."

"I am sure of it, Consul Heidar. Now, gather your troops and lead them up to the fortress."

Heidar's 480 men filed past the descending garrison, making the new consul realise how seriously understaffed his garrison would be. He knew that some Roman consuls commanded an army of 20,000 men, but at a quick assessment, he could see that the Noviomagus garrison was no greater than 800. A rapid exchange of information with the retiring commander proved informative. Heidar particularly appreciated the suggestion of enrolling auxiliaries from the Chauci, once he had defeated their chieftains. One important fact also emerged: it appeared to the Dacian consul that the Chauci had been largely absorbed into a Saxon confederacy, so Heidar might have to press as far inland as the upper Weser. The friendly officer summoned four men from his ranks. "These men are expert scouts and know the Germanic territory well. They will be of no use to me in Britannia, so consider them my parting gift to you."

No sooner had Heidar established himself in the luxurious praetorium and ensured that the emperor's bags of silver were locked into a steel-banded chest with no less than four locks—the departing consul had consigned him a key ring and a cynical witticism about poor-quality coinage—than he summoned the four scouts and seated them at a large table. Across this, he spread a map of the river systems in the area. The men seemed perplexed.

"What is your worry, good fellow? Share it with me."

"Consul, we'll need to reach here," his finger jabbed the chart midway down the upper Weser. "Marching there would be folly, as the land is dense with impenetrable woodland and the tribes are expert at ambushing enemy incursions. We need river craft, but—"

"You were going to say *but* we have no ships. That's where you are wrong! The emperor is leaving half his fleet in the harbour for our use."

The relief on the scouts' faces was palpable. One was already tracing a route with a finger along the river Elbe.

At dawn, Heidar stood on the ramparts and watched the fleet sail out of the harbour. As he stared, he felt a pang, realising that the departing Carausius was more than his emperor, for he had become his friend. He and Valdor, and his other two close friends, owed everything to this remarkable man: their rank, place in the world, wealth, and safety of their families. He would serve his emperor-friend to the best of his abilities. As the departing fleet became dots in the distance, his eyes moved to the vessels Carausius had left him. He counted them and considered that, again, the emperor had shown his military acumen. He knew how many men Heidar had at his command and had calculated the necessary number of ships. Tomorrow he would lead the expedition to re-establish his lord's military presence in Northern Gaul. His only regret was that Valdor and Johar were not here to share in the glory, but he did have Centurion Faldrek. He collected the invaluable chart of Germania and summoned him to his room, where he outlined his plan to take the Saxon chieftains by surprise.

18

LOWER SAXONY, AD290

HISTORY HAS A WAY OF REPEATING ITSELF, WHICH IS WHY A good general should be a student of its military aspect. Heidar was not a scholar, but history also allows for the idiosyncrasy of individuals to emerge. The Batavian was inexperienced but had the instincts and intuition of a great general. Knowledge of what had happened in the Teutoburg Forest in the autumn of 9 AD might have made him even more cautious when he disembarked on the Elbe and pressed into the forests of Lower Saxony. It may have been that Publius Quinctilius Varus had been inept or unlucky, but the Germanic leader Arminius had ambushed and slaughtered three Roman legions in the woods. Heidar, aware of his inexperience, arranged his men so that battle formation could be achieved in moments while still making progress along the trail. He sent scouts, now forging ahead, who explained that they had found the heartland of the Saxon confederation between the Elbe and the Weser.

Heidar was correct in thinking that a surprise attack could not be launched from the water. The forest cloaked their approach and kept them safe in an overnight encampment. The new day brought them to a large settlement made of primitive turf houses dug into the earth, their roofs only a few feet above the ground. At a quick glance, Heidar estimated 200 houses. In the centre of the community stood a larger wooden building that must have been a hall, perhaps, hoped Heidar, the chieftain's residence. He decided to attack that building, giving instructions to slay anyone who resisted.

The Saxon warriors who emerged from their bunker-like homes were tall, strong blond or red-haired men. They wielded axes or long swords, but charging Heidar's steadily advancing defensive formation, they were no match for the disciplined Batavian regiment whose swift gladius stabs took a deadly toll from behind their curved shields as the Saxons raised their weapons to strike.

The cries and screams had alerted the occupants of the hall, who barred the stout oak door. Since access without a battering ram was impossible, Heidar ordered straw and wood to be piled against the walls and fires lit. But before striking the tinder, the men used their blades to hack away the dried clay daubed between the wooden uprights so that they could smoke out the occupants, or they could alternatively choose to choke to death.

Meanwhile, he was content to allow men to run away into the forest. His vague plan was to take an important hostage and, in any case, to provoke other tribes into emerging to seek vengeance. It was easier to provoke the enemy into coming to him than to find their lairs in these dense forest lands.

The dry wood caught and crackled, and soon Heidar's men were backing away from the flames and smoke. After a while, the sound of an iron bar hitting the floor rang out, and the doors swung back. The gigantic form of a blond warrior emerged, trying not to cough, but snarling as he crouched over a battle-axe held at the ready in both hands.

"I want him alive!" Heidar shouted, which made his men's task much harder. Their discipline and training paid off as half a dozen curved shields cramped his swinging room and pushed him back against the wall. Persistent short stabs to his bare, muscular arm made him drop the axe, and the sag of his shoulders meant the encounter was over. Heidar ordered him to be bound, ignoring the stream of oaths in an unknown tongue. Five other men staggered out of the building, coughing and spluttering, careful to lay their weapons at their feet. They had emerged in time because the roof had caught fire, and the whole structure was now in flames. Again, Heidar shouted orders to secure the captives and gave further instructions to ignore the women and children peering fearfully from their tiny doorways. He had achieved what he wanted and, as a Christian, was not prepared to slaughter the innocent.

He led his men back into the forest, sending out scouts as a precaution and ringing a clearing with guards. His next move involved interrogating the prisoners. He tried speaking to them in his native tongue and noticed that there was comprehension in the eyes of the captive, but he obtained no cooperation. He wanted to know where the enemy kept their ships and where they were based. His questions met with a stony silence and even a spit, which stirred him into slapping the offender across the mouth with the back of his hand.

Not achieving anything, he ordered a small fire built near the prisoners. As the branches caught and created glowing embers, he seized the bound spitter by the hair and dragged him towards the flames. Holding the man's face for a mere second over the heat, he said, "You will tell me what I need to know; otherwise, I'll hold your face in the flames." He was prepared to do this, but fear loosened the fellow's tongue. The language was not so different from Heidar's own, close enough to understand. The captive revealed that there was a river basin some miles to the west, where the Saxons kept their vessels moored. He added death threats, revealing that the tribes had united their forces in the area and their numbers were far greater than Heidar's puny force.

Restraining a desire to cut the man's tongue in retaliation, instead, he asked who the giant prisoner was. "That is Arnulf, son of Fulbert, the chieftain of our tribe and one who will make Rome pay for what it has done today."

"Always assuming that Arnulf, son of Fulbert, survives this day," Heidar said sourly—Batavians showed no fear to their enemies. He called over the only scout remaining in the camp and referred to the news of the river pool to the west. "I want you to find it and return to me with its precise location and distance from here." The scout departed, well aware of the danger of his mission without the consul's dire warnings.

The danger of lingering in the forest became clear towards the end of the day when a score of Saxons intent on rescuing their leader were surprised in their furtive approach by the Roman watchmen. A skirmish ensued, which showed how closely matched, in terms of valour, were the tribesmen and Heidar's force, which sustained its first casualties. Only when alerted to combat and the disproportionate numbers overwhelmed the would-be rescuers did the fighting end in the slaughter of the Saxons. Heidar ruefully ordered the burial of his six dead comrades and the burning of the Saxon corpses.

If he had not learned about the Saxon vessels, he would have beaten a hasty retreat from the perilous area he had penetrated. It was now crystal clear why Maximian and others before him had established a line of fortresses along the Rhine-Danube axis and rarely ventured beyond it into the densely forested area. As he lay on his heavy woollen sagum, trying to snatch some sleep, he pulled the cloak closely around his shivering body; his restless thoughts also kept him sleepless. It would be futile to retreat without completing his mission, which was now so near and yet so perilous.

Towards morning, when he at last had sunk into sleep, a gentle hand shook his shoulder.

"Sorry to wake you, old friend, but first light is nigh, and our scout has returned with news." Heidar shook his head to chase away the sleep and peered blearily into Faldrek's concerned visage.

"Fetch him to me, Centurion, I need to splash some cold water on my face to clear my thoughts." In truth, he wanted to pray for guidance. He had seen what the Saxons were capable of and did not want to blunder into danger.

His scout was reassuring, up to a point. "Lord, the Saxons have placed a guard upon their ships, but I counted only a dozen. There are sure to be more. If we move early, we can reach them by noon."

"Good work, my friend, you will lead us, but a small advance party will accompany you to look out for danger in all directions."

"Ay, that would be as well, lord." The scout approved of the commander's wise precautions.

As the sun rose to almost overhead, with Heidar wondering how much farther to the river, a runner from the advance party bent double in front of him to catch his breath. When he straightened up, he pointed in the direction from which he had come, gasping, "A trap, Consul, but we can circumvent it. There's a track off to the left, which will take us to the enemy's rear. There are at least a hundred Saxon warriors waiting for our arrival, but I killed their scout myself." Heidar stared at the bloodspattered forearm of his scout and congratulated him, "Well done, friend, you've earned extra pay. Now, lead us to the fork in the track and we'll attack from the rear with javelins."

The Saxons were hiding in a hollow not far from the main track, which made the javelin throwers' task easier. At the silent lowering of Heidar's arm, more than 400 javelins hailed down on the unsuspecting backs of the lurking force. The survivors turned and ran, shouting up the slope to be met with the second wave of javelins. Many were parried this time, but some achieved their purpose. Heidar wasted no time in forming his troops into seven eight-square phalanxes.

Even with matching numbers, the Saxons would have struggled against this defensive formation, but with Heidar's skilful manoeuvring, their task became impossible. His Batavians surrounded and annihilated the enemy force in less than half an hour. Heidar's scouts assured him that the way to the river was now clear.

A small fleet of some thirty vessels lay moored in the calm water of an ox-bow lagoon formed by the meandering river. The consul's cohort raised their shields and lined up along the bank. They were met by desultory and ineffectual archery. Heidar had Arnulf pushed forward in front of the shields and called out, "Surrender your ships or we'll cut his throat here and now!"

The stunned silence that followed made the consul fear that his threat would be ignored until a voice shouted, "We'll exchange the ships for your captives."

"We agree to this proposal!"

One by one, the boats rowed to the bank and were occupied by legionaries. When the last one was taken, Heidar and his bodyguards handed the captives to a tall, red-haired Saxon with a livid scar down his right cheek.

"Tell your fellow chieftains to stay away from the North Sea, for we shall destroy any vessel intent on leaving the Rhine Estuary for Britannia. We'll be ready and waiting in strength." Heidar said, thrusting his face into Arnulf's before bounding aboard one of the boats.

One of his four Dacian scouts explained to Heidar how they had to follow a long detour, taking a circuitous route necessary because the Wadden Sea, with its shoals in the area between the Weser and Elbe estuaries, was unnavigable. They rowed well into the evening until the dim light made navigation impossible. A temporary camp was established and, aware of the danger of a night-time attack, Heidar tripled his guards and arranged for regular rotation.

Apart from distant wolves' howls, the night passed peacefully. An early morning start brought them to the turbid waters of the Weser estuary, where they raised sail and travelled westwards into the mouth of the Elbe. They rowed for hours upstream until they came to the place where they had left their ships days before. Heidar was relieved to find his small crews untroubled and the ships unharmed. The guards reported having seen only three men the day before. From their sooty aspect, they believed them to be charcoal burners, out collecting wood with a small handcart. Anyway, the entire fleet was now ready to make the return journey to the river Waal.

The consul was confident that his force could handle any adversary except a united tribal army, but he expected to arrive at Noviomagus unscathed with a fleet sufficient to patrol and dominate the estuaries on the North Sea, exactly as Carausius wanted. In addition, the Saxon fleet had been depleted and the enemy would have to rebuild its naval strength. Heidar smiled wryly at the thought that the Saxons might now gather together and launch a revenge attack upon Maximian's border fortresses to the south. He doubted they were bright enough to understand that Noviomagus should be their objective.

19

BRITANNIA, AD 291-293

THE COUNT OF THE SAXON SHORE WENT ABOUT HIS DUTIES largely untroubled for a long period in which raids had become infrequent. He toured the fortifications, old and new, adding reinforcements of men to garrisons where necessary. Among his other activities was the construction of intermediate watchtowers, either in stone or timber depending on the availability of material. On three occasions, his enforced absence from combat persuaded him to join in the pursuit of sporadic pirate incursions. Twice, he led by example and wetted his sword, but on the other occasion when the Saxons veered and headed back towards the Continent, he called off the pursuit, considering it wiser to remain in British coastal waters.

In April 292, Sfava bore him a son—*his little warrior*, the proud father called him—and his world offered him everything he had ever wanted: a beautiful family, power, status, and wealth, friends, and respect. This blissful state of affairs could not last, he told himself many times, for he lived in a harsh world liable to sudden shifts and dangers.

The first erosion of his solid foundations of happiness arrived when the news that his cousin Johar had been smitten by a Saxon axe while intercepting a raid. The message came to him while on a visit to Rutupiae, where he had gone ostensibly to supervise the last of the work completing the new fort. His real reason was to sample the famous oysters—renowned as the best in Britannia—and to attend a gladiatorial contest in the amphitheatre with its capacity of 5,000 spectators.

Rutupiae, with Dubris close by, made a perfect supply station for the whole south-eastern area and the twin presence of the fortresses ensured prosperity to the Canti, now free of marauders.

As is often the case, the more carefree and entertained an individual becomes, the more Life seems challenged to swipe an unexpected low blow. A messenger rode into the fortress, sought out Valdor, and informed him, "Sire, your cousin is grievously wounded and struggling between life and death; he is asking for you."

"What happened? Where is he?"

"At the new fort at Portus Adurni. A Saxon axe laid him low and now, the doctors are fighting to save his arm if not his life."

Valdor took three ships and sailed to the harbour, making sure his crew comprised two capsarii.

Entering the sick room, Valdor gazed at the fevered brow of his cousin and at the pallor of his cheeks. His two capsarii were already in conversation with the doctors of the base. After what seemed an eternity, one of them came over to Valdor and spoke gravely. "Lord, I wish you to give me one last chance to preserve the arm. The doctors here have given up on saving it and decided on amputation. They fear the onset of gangrene, but my examination reveals that there is still time to intervene. In our capsae, we have the necessary potions. If I can sedate the patient, staunch the bleeding more effectively, and remove some rotten flesh, who knows, the gods may smile upon us."

"Let it be so!" Valdor waved everyone out of the room except his two capsarii. He sat on the edge of the bed and took his cousin's hand, feeling its unnatural coldness. He closed his eyes and preferred to pray to his Christian God that the two doctors might succeed. The one he had spoken to explained as he mixed scopolamine with red wine before operating, that the plant extract caused drowsiness and amnesia. Leaving nothing to chance, given the gravity of the patient's condition, he took out a phial of clear liquid and carried it to the patient's lips, pouring a few drops into his mouth. Valdor watched his cousin swallow while the doctor explained, "It is an extract of the seed of the poppy. Under its sedating influence, he will feel nothing. Now we must operate on the arm, Sire, will you see that we have a brazier and a searing iron as well as boiled water? It will be of greater use than holding the centurion's hand, for see, he is quite insensate now." Valdor sprang up and hurried to organise the necessities.

On his return, he watched as the doctor took a scalpel and began to remove dead flesh around the gash. Next, he soaked a cloth in vinegar and applied it to the wound to disinfect it and prevent infection. He called out, "Honey, wine, and olive oil!" A legionary brought them on a tray and, as the doctor mixed them, he explained, "This will stop inflammation and prevent the wound from going bad." After applying this mixture, he cauterised the slash, then took a curved needle and fine catgut and stitched up the wound. "He'll be lucky to boast about this scar to his sons!" the doctor grinned. "Sire, we have done all that is possible; the rest is in the lap of the gods. Do you want us to organise a sacrificial rite?"

Valdor gazed severely at the doctor. "Nay, you have done what you can. I shall say my own prayers as I vigil over my cousin. Go! I'll send for you if his situation changes."

The doctors bowed out of the room and murmured, unheard by Valdor, that the Count had abandoned the gods of Rome. Would he be punished with his cousin's death for this? For his own part, Valdor took his hand again and peered at the sutured arm. Undoubtedly, his capsarii had done a precise job on it. *If only we had come sooner!*

Valdor reflected on the importance of having specialist doctors in every fortress. The local doctors had done their best but faced with a severe wound had blundered around. His capsarii, instead, had operated swiftly, *but is it enough?* He looked lovingly and doubtfully at the young fisherman's son with whom he had shared his childhood. The Count sat for hours in this attitude, but his restless mind was working on establishing a school for capsarii. His project was to have a competent surgeon in each Saxon Shore fortress. Lost in these thoughts, he suddenly realised that Johar had been unnaturally still for too long. He placed a finger under his nose, hoping to feel breath upon it. Nothing! Having no doctoral knowledge to speak of, he leapt up and called for his doctors, who came running.

He pointed at the supine figure, "I fear he is dead!"

A doctor sat on the bed, still indented from where Valdor had been moments before. Gently, he did what the Count had failed to think of doing. He pressed two fingers to the patient's wrist and felt a weak but steady pulse.

"Sire, he is alive! The unnatural stillness is due to the opiate. It will help with the recovery. Your centurion is strong, but even he will require time for healing and convalescence."

"The Lord be praised, he lives! Thank you, thank you!"

The hours passed until Johar groaned and his eyelids opened. He tried to speak but only made a croaking noise, yet he managed to squeeze Valdor's hand. The Count called for the doctors, who had expected some sign of revival and were ready with a beaker of mead. Gently, one placed it to Johar's lips, easing him more upright with an arm behind his shoulders. Valdor stared on in approval and wondered if he imagined the slow return of colour to the cheeks.

"Let him sleep, lord, you can talk tomorrow."

"Ay," Valdor acquiesced, thinking that maybe his cousin had overcome the worst.

Once out of the room, a doctor halted him. "When he is back on his feet, he'll need to rest that arm for some time. It will be a slow healing process."

"I understand. Hark, doctor, what do you think about teaching your profession to eager young men? We can begin here in this fort if you consent. I want rigorous standards, mind you. You must work only with those who show promise."

"I consent, lord. It is a splendid idea."

"I fear that I will bring you more patients for them to practise on, since my aim is to clear these waters of raiders."

For the rest of the sailing season, Valdor assumed command of naval operations around Vectis. He was driven by the twin desire to rid those waters of the pirates and to avenge his cousin who was convalescing and recovering well. The Frankish pirates, in particular, proved able seamen and difficult to capture. However, in the first month of his command, he overcame two pirate vessels and, although he would have been happy to enrol the crews or enslave them, he was compelled by their ferocity to slaughter them.

The first boat they encountered in the next month brought Valdor a memorable unpleasant incident. Warriors do not wish to be reminded of their mortality, but that is what happened. Upon grappling and boarding the Saxon vessel, Valdor came face-to-face with a gigantic chieftain. He wielded an axe and, despite himself, Valdor thought about Johar's wound and took an involuntary step backwards. This was the first time he ever hesitated in battle. Hesitation is usually fatal and would have been on this occasion, except for the quick wits of Valdor's centurion, who hurled a javelin with all his might that impaled the Saxon under the raised arm about to deliver the fatal blow. The great Saxon toppled and fell to the deck, and such was his strength that he tried to pull the dart from his body. In a mist of rage, no doubt associated with his cousin's injury, Valdor leapt on the Saxon and finished him with his short sword, effectively breaking the Saxon resistance.

Four of this crew agreed to enrol in the Roman army as auxiliaries, two flung themselves into the sea and drowned. The others surrendered and awaited their fate; Valdor set them labouring tasks, such as building a defensive wall around the high-status villas on the nearby Isle of Vectis at a place called Brerdynge by the locals, or working on raising the height of the old lighthouse on the prominent headland.

Vectis had no towns, but was a fertile isle with a mixture of wealthy farmers and a smattering of poorer peasants who worked the less productive land. The new slaves eyed the recent construction of an aisled farmhouse with a mixture of wonder and envy. In their wildest dreams, they could not compare this stone-built marvel with their wattle and daub homes in Saxony. They were not allowed inside, or their eyes would have boggled at the mosaic floors with their images of dolphins and sea nymphs. What they saw was enforced because they had to work the furnace used to parch the crops of Celtic beans that they had previously harvested and carried back.

Valdor's brush with death did not dishearten him, but he had to find time to inspect the new lighthouse and purchase some red wine directly from the press because the islanders took advantage of the south-facing aspect and light, chalky soil to dedicate themselves to viticulture and bottling and storage of wine. Argue as he might, Valdor did not pay for the several flagons he had chosen because the farmer was so honoured to provide for the emperor's son that he insisted on making a gift of the wine and pressed on him a variety of fresh produce, which had to be carried to his ship. This perishable cargo gave the Count a good reason to return to nearby Portus Adurni to check on his cousin's progress, where his wife and son provided companionship to Johar as he convalesced.

As he strode through the gates of the fortress, he found Johar fighting a legionary, both using practice swords.

"Johar! Are you crazy? It's too soon for this!"

"I'm going easy on him, Sire," grinned the legionary.

"Oh, aye?" snarled Johar and redoubled his efforts. In moments, the legionary's wooden sword sailed through the air, and the blunt tip of Johar's pressed against his adversary's throat.

Valdor clapped, "Very impressive, cousin, but aren't you liable to spring your stitches with all this vim and vigour?"

"You've lost track of time, cousin. How long have you been at sea? The doctors removed my stitches weeks ago, and I began by lifting weights. I wanted to see if I could fight again, but this apology for a warrior has scarcely made me break a sweat. What I need is a tall Saxon chieftain!"

The Count shuddered, "That's exactly what neither of us needs! Come indoors, and I'll tell you about my meeting with one such over a beaker of Vectis wine."

Little Caurus, named after his grandfather, flung himself into his father's arms.

"I swear you have grown since I sailed out a few months ago. Where's your mother?"

The tiny finger pointed towards the kitchen. *Of course, she's sorting the vegetables.*

Slowly savouring the wine, Valdor stared hard at his cousin, "Are you completely healed with no pain?"

"It's as good as new!" Johar flexed his arm and waved it around extravagantly.

"Just as well I didn't arrive a day later, cousin, those butchers had decided to amputate. That's why I set up the doctoral school."

Johar's mouth dropped open. "Really? They were going to amputate?"

"Ay, in their ignorance, they wished to prevent gangrene. But if it makes you feel better," he gazed around to make sure Sfava wasn't in the offing, "I found myself in the exact same situation as you—facing a giant Saxon chieftain. If it hadn't been for my centurion's quick reactions, I wouldn't be here now. I hesitated, something I never do, and he would have finished me but for Livius' javelin."

"It seems we were both fortunate."

"Ay, but good fortune cannot last forever," Valdor said ominously through clenched teeth, but as it would turn out, with prescience.

20

PORTUS ADURNI AND BRANODUNUM FORT, AD 293

For a number of years, Carausius had maintained that sooner or later a competent general would emerge to sustain the western Empire. Following Maximian's failure to invade in 289, an uneasy truce with Carausius began. Valdor wondered whether when that day came, it would be with or without the presence of Emperor Maximian? Maximian tolerated Carausius' rule in Britain and on the continent but refused to grant the secessionist state formal legitimacy. Neither Carausius nor Valdor understood that Maximian was not the main threat to their newly established equilibrium, but Emperor Diocletian. For his part, Carausius was content with his territories beyond the Continental coast of Gaul. However, Diocletian would not tolerate this affront to his rule.

Valdor had established hearth and home in the fortress of Portus Adurni, where the milder climate and bracing sea breezes, with the strategic outlet into the Solent, granted him the possibility of controlling the south coast of Britannia and the approaches to the Channel.

He watched his son grow sturdy and headstrong—a miniature Valdor but with Sfava's fierceness—would he ever get to know his father's homeland? On occasions, Valdor would sit and reflect on his early life in Batavia. In truth, he had left his village when he was no more than a boy. The world he had grown into was dominated by Rome. And

Rome, in the shape of Carausius, had evaluated him, seen his worth, and promoted him to wealth and rank beyond his imaginings.

To maintain his position and enjoy it in peace with Sfava, Caurus, and the newcomer, the bouncing Lavinia, was his heart's desire. He had his cousin based here, although Johar spent much time at sea, patrolling the coasts of Vectis—too much, because he hadn't found time to choose a wife. As his commander, Valdor felt responsible, for it was he who sent Johar forth to sweep the sea clear of pirates. Often, he would join the fleet, leaving the command to his relative. He had seen him frolic with a slave girl on his last sojourn in port. Yet, as a centurion and commander of the fleet, Johar had the wealth and stability to set up home with the daughter of some high-ranking citizen. The problem was that Johar used Valdor, or rather, Sfava as his model, and where did one find such a spirited goddess? Valdor made a silent promise to search for a bride for his cousin.

He also missed Heidar but was happy for his best friend, who had become his adoptive father's closest counsellor. Carausius had decided that given Valdor's preference for the south coast, he would establish himself at Branodunum Fort on the east. He recalled Heidar from Noviomagus, replaced him with Faldrek, whom he also raised to the rank of consul. The distance to Branodunum meant that visits were increasingly rare and, indeed, Carausius had not yet seen his new granddaughter.

As for Faldrek, he was clearly doing his job, which could be seen from the reduced number of Frisian, Frankish, and Germanic raiders leaving the Rhine estuary. Valdor missed his old friend and wondered when they would meet again. Did Faldrek enjoy breathing the air of home? One thing was sure, their homeland was not what it had been in their youth. There was little or no possibility of recreating the fertile fields of yore. Where crops had once grown was now marshland or worse. Building a villa on Vectis and farming there in their old age was more appealing. But would events allow such a peaceful outcome? A man could dream, but Valdor had seen and done enough to differentiate between fantasy and reality.

The most unlikely component of a reunion was Faldrek; ironically, he was the nearest to their origins, but the farthest from his friends. Rome, in the shape of Diocletian, remained vigilant and, faced with Carausius' secession and further challenges on the Egyptian, Syrian, and

Danubian borders, he realised that two emperors were insufficient to manage the Empire. Carausius' prediction that a new formidable general would emerge came to fulfilment.

On 1 March 293, at Milan, Maximian appointed Constantius to the office of Caesar. On the same day, Diocletian did the same for Galerius, thus establishing the *Tetrarchy*, or 'rule of four'. The reforming emperor made Constantius understand that he must succeed where Maximian had failed and defeat Carausius.

As a general, Constantius was everything that Maximian was not, and he met expectations quickly and efficiently, and by the summer of 293 had expelled Carausian forces from northern Gaul.

Constantius stood under the gateway to Noviomagus and spoke directly to the commander, Faldrek, inviting him to open the gates, "Consul, as Emperor, I wish to laud you for the commendable work you have done in clearing the Rhine delta of pirates. This has not gone unnoticed in Rome. However, you will realise that you cannot continue in the service of the usurper, Carausius. I order you, in the name of the Empire, to open the gates."

Faldrek looked with concern at the four legions disembarked on Batavian soil and considered his position. He owed everything to Carausius. It would be the meanest betrayal to surrender the fortress to his rival. He wondered whether he could negotiate passage to Britannia for himself and his most trusted men? This thought prompted his reply: "Caesar, I require a few minutes to parley with my senior officers. My reply will soon be forthcoming." He turned away from the rampart to do so and had no time to defend himself as three Dalmatian officers drove their swords into his chest and stomach.

Together, they hoisted his body to the rampart of the gate tower and flung it down under the hoofs of Constantius' rearing horse by way of reply. The Batavians, faithful to their consul, could do nothing except watch as the great gates swung slowly open and Constantius rode triumphantly into the fortress followed by the eagle standard bearers. Rome had retaken possession of Noviomagus Batavorum at the expense of one of Batavia's most eminent sons.

Meanwhile, not only was Constantius preparing to overthrow Carausius, but Maximian also plotted to do the same. As autumn headed into winter, Heidar and Valdor separately learnt of their friend's demise and the fall of Noviomagus.

Carausius cursed and warned Heidar, "We have to reckon with a *real* general." He wrongly added, "We have nothing to fear from Maximian, but we must ensure that all our shore fortresses are completely garrisoned and ready to resist this so-called Constantius I. We'll see who is the more capable general—he or I. I want you to travel swiftly to Count Valdor and explain my requirements." Neither man would realise what a portentous decision this would prove to be and how mistaken Carausius was, for once, in his assessment of the political situation.

Heidar decided that sailing down the coast and rounding Kent was a better solution than riding across country. Although autumn had shaken the leaves off the trees, the sea was grey but relatively calm. His voyage was undisturbed by raiding vessels, his only sightings being Roman trading vessels legitimately plying their trade.

When, at last, he reached Portus Adurni, after the usual pleasantries, he exchanged versions of Faldrek's demise. The two accounts differed: Valdor had the correct version, but Haidar insisted that their friend had led his forces out to engage Constantius and had died gloriously in battle.

"Who told you this?"

"A Batavian trader."

"Well, there you are, then. One of our own, wishing to glorify Batavian prowess. Look, knowing Faldrek, if he'd had any chance of making a stand or escaping, he would have taken it. Nay, he was disloyally betrayed, as I learnt—it's the only explanation."

"Ay, you're right. First there were four. Now we are three! Where's Johar?"

"My cousin is patrolling the Solent. I dare say he knows of your arrival and will join us when he can. But come, see my treasures." He led Heidar to his private chamber where Sfava was playing with the children. She leapt up and embraced Heidar before lifting Lavinia and handing her to the warrior to hold.

"Heidar, you are another, like Johar, who needs to find a good woman to give you children as Sfava has to me."

Heidar ran his fingers through the silken blonde hair and let the little fingers twine around his large forefinger. "I have thought about it; indeed, your father is insistent, but Valdor, how can I make such a move when our emperor is under threat? First, we must secure Britannia for him, then I'll set about hunting for a wife. I have a fancy for a red-haired Briton!"

Sfava laughed, "I'll say one thing for you Batavians, you do not care for an easy life. If Valdor thinks he's tamed his wildcat, just because I've borne two children, he's got another think coming! Graahr!" She bared her teeth and made a feline scratching gesture with her hands.

The following day, to Heidar's delight, Johar's fleet docked in the harbour below. The commander brought a surprise with him. It was not unusual for the Classis Britannia to capture prisoners and enrol them as auxiliaries. Most of these men were either Saxons or Franks, but on this occasion, Johar brought Jutes and handed them over to a centurion to be whipped into shape. He brought his real surprise with a rope tethered around the neck like a mule: another captive shield maiden. His first thought was to make a present of her to Sfava, who would be sure to welcome a compatriot, and one as fierce as herself. Things did not quite work out as planned because he was not expecting the presence of Heidar.

While the old friends embraced, Sfava directed her attention to the crouching creature staring with malevolent grey eyes, who now addressed her, "What are you doing here with the enemy, Sfava Hibaldsdottir?"

"You know me!" Sfava cried incredulously.

"Your father and mine fought often enough over land, back home. Ha! Now they are both dead and we are here."

"You are Jarl Egred's daughter, but which one? Estrith or Inga?"

"Inga, but what is it to you, who cohabit with the foe?"

"These men are Batavians, Inga. So, not so different from us. They have served Rome to make Britannia safe and risen as reward for their valour. My husband is the emperor's adopted son."

Inga spat on the floor. "Give me a sword and I'll kill him!"

"The only sword I'll give you is one between your ribs!" Sfava leapt forward and drew Johar's blade before he could move. Now she held everyone's attention as she circled the red-golden-haired woman like a prowling cat ready to pounce. But Johar jerked the rope attached to Inga's neck fiercely, pulling her off-balance and causing her to stagger straight into Heidar's welcoming muscular arms. He pinned her to his broad chest and refused to release the writhing, spitting Jute.

Valdor drew his gladius and placed himself between his wife and the newcomer.

"Hand me that blade, Sfava, it's an order!"

A stream of oaths greeted his words, but she could hardly fight the father of her children, whom she dearly loved. "Punish her then," she sulked, handing the gladius back to Johar.

A momentary silence fell over the hall, although Inga tried stamping on Heidar's foot. This only made him squeeze her tighter and, breath forced out of her lungs, she ceased her writhing to sag forward in his arms. It was he who spoke, "Sfava, Johar gifted her to you. Let me buy her—this is the red-haired woman for me!"

Sfava snorted, "Buy her? Nay, I'll *give* her to you. I don't want her!"

Heidar unclasped his arms and gently eased the chafing rope from the captive's neck. No sooner had he raised the noose above her head than Inga dodged sideways and flung herself on Sfava, bringing her crashing to the floor. Her fist raised to smash into Sfava's face, when a giant hand clasped her wrist. The former smith, always strong to those who knew him as a youth, had become an athletic and mighty warrior. Now, he picked up Inga and raised her in the air above his head, oblivious to her venomous kicks that had no effect on his cuirass.

He looked her in the face and said, "Isn't it enough for you, foolish woman, that a consul wishes to take you for his wife?"

"Wife?" the Jute echoed, all the fight going out of her body as he lowered her and bent his face to hers. He half-expected her to spit in his eye, but instead, her lips sought his and she kissed him passionately as Sfava called for ale. The first beaker she offered was to a beaming Inga, who quaffed it in one wild gulp, her eyes sparkling.

"We shall be friends, Inga; you have chosen the best man in the fortress, bar one," she said hurriedly, glancing at Valdor, who smiled. Soon, influenced by drink, they danced and caroused until Valdor brought an end to proceedings.

"Heidar, Johar, I need to speak with you about serious matters," he panted happily, "we can leave Sfava and Inga to catch up on their various news, always hoping they don't harm each other," he added, warily eyeing the two wildcats. Sfava was more interested in showing off her children, so he need not have worried, since Inga had helped her mother raise Estrith and Hild, her younger sisters. Capable of slaying a warrior in battle, Inga was gentle and playful with children.

Valdor made sure to take a flagon of Vectis wine to a table and, seated around it with his lifelong friends, poured three beakers full to the brim. He raised a beaker in a toast before his thirsty friends could move, "To Faldrek!" he said simply.

They echoed the toast, and Heidar said gloomily, "If Carausius hadn't recalled me to Britannia, it could have been me in his place."

"We'll talk about Faldrek in the days to come, first we have our duty to consider," said the Count. "It's clear that now Constantius will not halt at Batavia. From there, he'll strike at Britannia." In this, he was incorrect, for something more terrible would happen first.

Unable to see into the future, Valdor divided the shore fortresses into three groups, keeping those nearer home to himself and sending Heidar to those more north-easterly, culminating in Branodunum Fort. Johar, principally, would deal with the Kentish strongholds. "We must each ensure that every fortress is well-armed and its garrison up to strength ready for when the invasion comes. Be prepared to move men quickly from inland stations to reinforce the coastal contingents. Also, ensure that watchtowers are properly manned and supplied with coal to act as visible beacons. That's it for now. When you have finished, report back to me."

"Not to the emperor, Valdor?" Heidar asked.

"Nay, to me. I might have to organise a land army in conjunction with sea manoeuvres. I need you both here."

"Very well. I'll tell Inga I'll wed her," his voice slowed and he sounded doubtful, "...when I return. But that's a problem, isn't it?"

"Nay, Heidar. You'll wed her with her customs. Later, calmly, you can persuade her to convert to Christianity, just as Sfava did."

"Do you think she'll consent?"

"I don't know, but you'll be wed anyway!"

"Now, let's set about what we must do so that we are ready for any eventuality." They would have been, except for the unexpected upsetting Valdor's plans.

Fortunately for the timing of subsequent events, Heidar decided to start at Branodunum and work his way down the coast, not on the contrary. His motivation was to reunite with Carausius to describe his new granddaughter and to share his news about Inga. He considered the emperor as close a friend as Valdor and could not wait to share a glass of wine and these confidences.

While Heidar sailed north, Carausius and his treasurer, Allectus, were discussing the apportioning of pay to various garrisons. The treasurer's disfigured smile unsettled most who encountered it, but Carausius paid it no attention, considering it a badge of honour. Unfortunately, there was nothing honourable about Allectus' intentions. He had been in constant contact with Emperor Maximian and had his head turned by false promises. Allectus, as his scarring testified, was a valiant warrior proven in combat, but he was also a coward. He knew that he could not overcome Carausius in a fair fight, which was why, with insinuated doubts, he led his emperor to the steel-banded coffer containing the imperial treasure. The locking system required four separate keys and the final one held by Carausius himself. After the treasurer had opened the four-lock sequence, the emperor bent to insert his key in the central lock. Swift as a striking serpent, Allectus plunged his sword with all his might into his emperor's back, hissing, "Die, usurper!"

He now had to enact the next part of his plan. Over the past few weeks, Allectus had gathered a group of Frankish mercenaries, sufficient to seize the fortress. The coffer was open and he could pay his accomplices, so the leaders came in, as arranged, and, leaning over the body of Carausius, he grasped three bags of silver and handed them to the Franks. He cleaned his bloody blade on a drape and said, "We need to find a scapegoat for the assassination."

The Frankish chieftain hurried out of the room and returned moments later hauling a pale-faced slave, a callow, gangly youth, who had never shaved. He flung the poor creature over the body of the emperor, pushing him into the blood pooling around the body, and grinned at Allectus and nodded. The treasurer did not hesitate but plunged his sword into the slave's defenceless body three times. The Frank took his own sword, dabbed the blade in the blood, and forced the slave's fingers around the hilt.

"I'll swear the slave stole my sword while tidying my room. You will say that you caught him in the act of murdering the emperor and dealt with him on the spot. Now let us go to conserve these bags of silver. Give us some time before calling for help."

The Franks left the strongroom and Allectus smiled grimly. He helped himself to the emperor's key and closed and locked the treasure chest with all five.

His wild cries for help brought guards running; as speechlessly, Allectus pointed at the bodies. When a centurion arrived, Allectus grasped his arm. "When I came into the room, I found this wretch—what is he? A Briton? If only I had come a few moments sooner, I could have saved our beloved emperor. Where did he obtain that sword? What now, Centurion? We must appoint a new emperor."

"Caesar Marcus Aurelius was a fine general. We need someone as worthy as he," the centurion said thoughtfully, keeping his counsel for the moment. "We should deliberate carefully, but let's fling this wretch to the crows and wash and prepare the emperor for entombment."

From the doorway came a loud cry, "Long live Emperor Allectus!" It was the leader of the Frankish mercenaries. Figures half-shrouded in the gloom of the corridor behind him took up the cry, and they, too, had a Frankish accent. The Centurion wisely continued to keep his thoughts to himself, for he favoured the emperor's son, Caesar Valdor Aurelius, but he sensed that nominating him would lead to his demise and bloodshed within the fortress. There had been too many Frankish auxiliaries taken on lately for his liking.

At the first opportunity, the centurion sidled out of the room and went to seek several trusted officers to share the news of the murder. They took a fortuitous decision by slipping down to the harbour with other trusted men. It was a lucky move because as they prepared to sail southwards to find Valdor and proclaim him emperor, Heidar's ship nosed into the harbour. The centurion recognised him and waved him over.

"Caesar Marcus Aurelius is dead—murdered—they are blaming a British slave, a mere youth, but I say it was the treasurer, Allectus! They are declaring him Emperor. Beware, friend, the fortress is in the hands of Frankish mercenaries."

Heidar stood in stunned silence for a moment. It was hard to take in that he had lost a dear friend as well as his emperor.

"Never! This cannot be!" Heidar cried. "Quick, we must return south and install Count Valdor as Caesar. It is his right: Carausius declared him Caesar Valdor Aurelius." The two ships sailed away, their occupants unaware of the coup taking place in Branodunum where the Franks, rewarded with bags of silver, ensured that Allectus was pronounced Emperor of the North. The few foolhardy dissenters were immediately slaughtered.

21

PORTUS ADURNI, AD 293

Valdor stared white-faced, his hands balled into fists as Heidar explained the events in Branodunum. He passed through such a range of emotions in mere moments that he determined to avoid making an impulsive decision. For the moment, he would push vengeance to the back of his mind. With Carausius dead, his position most definitely had changed, but he needed to think calmly about his next move.

"Heidar, my old friend, ahead of us stretches a road with at least three forks: the question is which route to take? Remember our oath back on Torik Isle? Each of us would always support the others until death intervened. Faldrek is dead, so whatever we decide, we'll commit to as a threesome."

"Where's Johar?"

"Back out patrolling the Solent."

"When he returns, we'll sit down and consider the different options together."

"Ay, I'm in no state to choose right now. I just want to slay my father's murderer. Oh, the irony! A usurper accusing Carausius of usurpation."

"The only urgent decision I wish to take," Heidar said, "is to wed Inga as soon as possible."

"Not today, my friend. In the midst of tragedy, we'll have a celebratory feast for your wedding. Hold off a couple of days so that I can make arrangements."

As if a dark thundercloud had rolled away and the sun blazed forth, Heidar's countenance cleared, sporting a broad grin. "I'll go and tell Inga the news!"

Valdor sent a ship to bring Johar back to the harbour, little realising that the few days' grace he had insisted on would prove so momentous. Rapidly apprised of events in Branodunum, Johar spat, "We should march north at once, gather legions, and destroy the murderer."

Valdor put an arm around his cousin's shoulder and said calmly, "Ay, that's one option, but remember the oath we took on Torik. Whatever we do will be the result of a joint decision and, you wouldn't want to miss Heidar's wedding, would you?"

Two days passed, in which Valdor and Sfava made arrangements for the great feast. On the eve of the wedding, the praetorium fell silent relatively early as everyone took to their beds. Valdor was in a dark mood owing to the emperor's murder and, a rarity this, repulsed Sfava's amorous advances. She, instead, lay drifting in and out of sleep, which was fortunate because she perceived movement in the bed-chamber. She always kept her sword on the floor next to the bed and, although she was uncertain about whether she heard breathing, her hand grasped the hilt and she threw back the covers, swinging out her legs and standing upright. This movement provoked an onslaught by the intruder, and the dim light cast by the moon piercing the small window high in the wall saved her, for she was able to parry the thrust of a gladius. The clash of steel and her scream to Valdor for help roused him from his slumber.

Without a moment to spare, he was on his feet, drawing his gladius from its sheath and springing at the second interloper. Valdor was at a disadvantage because he was barely awake and naked down to the waist; the price he paid was a slash across his upper arm, luckily not his weapon arm, but a shock that enraged him, waking him completely. Even so, he was pressed backwards by his armoured assailant and would likely have been killed had not Sfava smitten her opponent's throat, sending him crashing lifeless to the floor. She immediately saw Valdor's predicament and leapt onto the bed, bringing her Frankish sword down with all her might onto the nape of the infiltrator's neck.

"I am cut!" Valdor spat. "Father was right, by adopting me, he placed me in danger."

"I'll light a taper, we need to—oh, God! The children!" Sfava dashed out of the room to the children's chamber. She almost tripped over a dead body, and her heart seemed to leap into her mouth. She burst into the room, sword raised, and discerned a figure. Gently stroking Caurus' head with one hand and sword in the other, stood Inga, her white shift spattered with blood.

"Inga! What? —"

A throaty laugh preceded the Jute's words, but it held a bitter tone. "I heard the clash of steel and your cry. My first thought was for the babes. She pointed at the corpse, "He had come to slay little Caurus, but it is *he* slain!" Valdor arrived with a blazing torch to light the scene. "The children?" he could barely utter the words for anxiety.

"Safe, thanks to Inga! She's no longer my friend, but my sister! She saved our son."

Valdor laughed, "More than a sister, just look at you two! Twins more like!" He had a point; there they stood, in matching white blood-spattered shifts, swords in hand and hair tousled. Sfava's concern had shifted, "The children are asleep, come on, let's move the body! Oh, let me see that wound! Straight to the hospital with you! You were so insistent on opening an infirmary, but pull a cloak around you!"

Sfava and Inga, smiling at each other like true sisters, dragged the bodies of the legionaries out of the praetorium to find the guard on the door slumped with his throat cut, which explained much.

The following morning, that of Heidar and Inga's wedding day, the time had come to take a decision. The three Batavians sat together and considered the events of the previous evening. "It's Allectus' handiwork," Valdor said, "without a shadow of doubt. He knows that if I make the slightest move, I'll have the legions in Britannia behind me, whereas he can only count on his Frankish allies. He sent men to kill me and my son because, as the legitimate heirs to Carausius, who was so popular with the legions while alive, we'd be a constant threat to his position."

"Well, it's clear then," Heidar said, "we should move north and gather men like a rolling snowball gains in size until we have an irresistible force. Then we can oust the usurper."

"Then what?" Valdor replied, "You seem to forget some important facts, my friend. Diocletian was unwilling to tolerate Carausius, and now he has a competent general, raised to Caesar, readying an invasion of Britannia: I refer to Constantius. It will be his task to overthrow Allectus."

"So, do we wait, defend ourselves, and then defeat this Constantius?" Johar, who was the slowest of the three, asked.

"Nay, cousin. We cannot hope to combat the Empire. Besides, I have no wish to become emperor. I have already risen beyond my wildest dreams."

"Speak plainly, Valdor, what is it you intend to do?"

Valdor pursed his lips, "It is easier for me to state what I *don't* mean to do. I will not remain in Britannia while Allectus is in power. That can only lead to our murders—where he has failed once, he will try again, or as an alternative, I'll be forced into a civil war to take his place and, as I said, I don't want that."

"So, where will you go, cousin?"

"Don't lose patience, Johar. Have we not seen how leaders will gladly accept reinforcements? I propose to take a legion and sufficient ships to Gesoriacum and offer my sword to Constantius. My long-term aim is to return in some role to Britannia. Are you both with me, or do you have alternative suggestions?

His friends sat in silence until Heidar grudgingly said, "If Constantius respects our ranks, joining him will gain us all revenge on the traitor Allectus. That sits well with me."

"Me, too!" Johar said quickly, who found agreeing far easier than ruminating.

In the afternoon, the hand-clasping ceremony, held in the courtyard in front of the ranked legionaries, by its very nature was a rapid affair, culminated in the throaty cheers of the rank and file. The heartiness of the roar, sufficient to drown the ubiquitous mewling of the ever-present swooping gulls, reflected the popularity among the men of the newly-wed centurion. There was scarcely a man present who would not willingly have changed places with Heidar as it was universally acknowledged that Inga was a Nordic beauty. Word had not yet circulated about the death of the emperor, so the prospect of a celebratory feast and indulgence in wine on such a splendid day, clear enough to see Vectis Isle from the fort, created a joyous atmosphere.

Valdor doubled the watch for the celebratory feast much to the disgruntlement of those chosen, but he did not want Allectus sailing into the harbour with an army and attacking during the revelling. He ensured they received food but did not allow them wine until the end of the watch that coincided with the onset of night. It was a long night. Valdor deliberately allowed the stock of wine to be entirely depleted, for he did not intend for anyone to remain in the fortress in two days.

As the Count of the Saxon Shore, he had every right to send to other fortresses, requisitioning ships. He would need a numerous fleet to transport the entire garrison to Gesoriacum.

The day after the feast, not only Heidar was the worse for wear but also most of the garrison. Valdor had expected this and contented himself watching the harbour fill with the *scafae* that was the basic warship of the Classis Britannica. The fleet was completed by several horse transport vessels and the *liburnae* to transport food and drink for the legion.

By the afternoon, the hangovers were cleared by the fresh sea air so that the ships could be loaded and Valdor chose a suitable moment to address the men, assembled in front of the praetorium. He chose to speak from Sparax's back, which enabled the men to see and hear him better. He began thus: "Soldiers of Rome, it is my solemn duty to inform you of an act of treason. On the eve of our recent nuptial celebrations, an attempt was made to murder me and my family in our beds." The reaction, although not deafening, was loud, for it is a notable noise when thousands murmur chorally. Valdor allowed this to sink in before raising his bandaged arm for silence. He indicated the binding, "I was lucky enough to receive only a scratch, but you will wish to know who was the principal behind the attempt. Let me inform you..." he paused and called for water, his throat refreshed, he shouted again, "...it was none other than my father's murderer—ay, Imperator Caesar Marcus Aurelius is most foully slain—his treasurer, the traitor Allectus. This coward has declared himself the Emperor of the North. Be it known, that I, your legitimate commander have, like you, sworn loyalty to Rome, not to a usurper. I have brought ships to sail to the headquarters of the Western Emperor Constantius I with the aim of uniting my forces to his to reconquer Britannia. You must choose, brothers, whether to remain in this fortress or to sail at dawn with me."

Now the incomprehensible shouting was deafening, and it took Valdor much effort and coaxing to control Sparax. Valdor lifted his wounded arm again and winced. He cried: "Fellow soldiers, you will each go to your centurion and communicate whether you will stay or will sail with me." He touched his chest with his right hand and then his forehead in a sign of respect. By jumping from Sparax, he made it clear that his speech was concluded.

Valdor was much loved and respected by men he had commanded, even those in other garrisons, so it was no surprise when a series of centurions entered the praetorium, hobnails ringing on the paving stones. Their message was always the same—the men were faithful to him and to Rome; they would sail at dawn. The Count was gratified, knowing that the backing of an entire legion made his bargaining position incontestable, not to mention the fleet of *scafae exploratoriae* and sundry quinquiremes he had available.

The sea was rougher than of late, but Valdor did not want to delay departure. Many men suffered sea sickness, but generally, the mood was good with much speculation about Emperor Constantius. The discipline of Valdor's sailors meant that despite the heavy sea, the fleet was not dispersed. By mid-afternoon, the water had become less choppy until by evening and their arrival in the estuary, the harbour water was calm. Valdor retrieved Sparax, mounted him, and disembarked, prepared to open a new chapter in his life.

22

GESORIACUM, AD 293-294

THE UNANNOUNCED ARRIVAL OF A FLEET AND AN ENTIRE legion caused alarm in Gesoriacum. Valdor rode with a small group of officers, including his trusted friends. The approach of a dozen horsemen made the serried ranks in front of the shore fortress appear absurd. Valdor had chosen not to dress in his imperial purple cloak and diadem but wore the crimson cloak and helm of a centurion.

At the sight of what was clearly a peaceful encounter, Constantius urged his horse forward to meet the newcomers. Valdor halted his a few paces ahead of the emperor and sprang to the ground, holding Sparax's reins. Reciprocally, Constantius dismounted, which gave Valdor the opportunity to kneel before him.

"Hail Caesar, we come from Britannia, and I, Valdor, *Comes littoris Saxonici per Britanniam*, bring you an entire legion and fleet in the service of Rome. I also bring news. My father, the Emperor of the North, was treacherously murdered by his treasurer—"

"I am informed, Count, and I gladly accept your men and ships, but cannot say whether I accept *you* until you have answered some questions."

"Sire?"

"Your father fought against his emperor, Maximian, and defeated him. Did you take up arms with him against the legitimate ruler?"

"Impossible, Caesar, for I was charged with constructing defensive fortresses, and that is what occupied me during the battle."

"Can you honestly say that you have not fought against the imperial army?"

"I can. Although I fought on occasion with Carausius, it was always against Rome's enemies, including pirates, with some success."

"Finally, Count Valdor, if I accept your sword, what are your expectations?"

"Sire, I renounce any claims to my adoptive father's inheritance but would appreciate my officers and myself maintaining our ranks."

"I see you wear the helm of a centurion. I confirm your ranks. If you conduct yourself well, Centurion, I may well confirm you as Count when we re-conquer Britannia."

"Thank you, Sire, I would ask for no more."

"Bring your men into the fortress. We shall talk further in the Principia when they are settled in."

Valdor looked around him, whatever doubts he had about the fortress accommodating his Legio XX vanished. To his expert eye, Gesoriacum was about twelve times bigger than Dubris. The two men walked side by side into the Principia.

Soon seated facing each other across a table, the emperor and Valdor talked about the political situation.

"You have Batavian origins, is that not so?"

"It is true, Caesar."

The emperor smiled, "That could be useful since my first task is to reclaim Batavia from the Franks."

Valdor frowned, *Surely you took Noviomagus when Faldrek died.*

As if he could read his thoughts, or alerted by his perplexed expression, Constantius said, "It is true that I took Noviomagus, but since then, I have been diverted from the task of retaking the rest of the country. Maximian's most urgent priority was for me to recapture Gesoriacum, which I did. There remains unfinished business beside the Rhine. Have you not heard that the Franks have retaken Noviomagus?"

"Nay, that's news to me."

"We shall have to march north to re-conquer Batavia. That will be your first campaign with me. Only once the Rhine delta is in our hands can we contemplate an invasion of Britannia."

"But surely, Caesar, if you hold Gesoriacum—"

"Are you not aware that the usurper, Allectus, has made an alliance with the Franks? He's an astute devil, not to be underestimated. Nay, we have to march on Batavia first to nullify the Frankish threat to our rear."

"The year is drawing to a close, and the weather certainly not improving, Sire. At this time of year, we can expect heavy rain and when I was last in my homeland, not so long ago, I was appalled at the flooding, mostly due to a rise in sea level. Rain will make matters worse. I suggest postponing the campaign until spring."

Constantius snapped, as if resenting the advice he had sought, "I had already decided that we'd await spring. How I detest sitting hand in hand!"

The rest of the year passed uneventfully, although Constantius began to appreciate Valdor's intelligence and became more confidential in his conversation. Early in the New Year, Valdor was wandering around the port with Sfava and Heidar's wife, Inga. The women were interested in buying cloth for dressmaking. Allectus had spies in Gesoriacum, who had received instructions to eliminate Valdor when a suitable occasion arose. It was difficult, if not impossible, to act while the centurion was safely within the Roman fortress. Wandering the chaotic streets of the port among traders' stalls was another matter, especially since he was accompanied by two women. The three spies considered it an easy task to dispense with the women and then slaughter the centurion. To make sure, they enrolled a couple of Frankish mercenaries. Five men against a man and two women seemed to promise only one outcome.

Sfava studied a sample of silk imported from Asia and, despite her apparent distraction, out of the corner of her eye, noticed suspicious characters approaching Inga from behind. She had no time to draw her weapon, but swung the bale of silk forcefully into the midriff of the nearest assassin. It was enough to save Inga and alert her companions, whose swords flashed forth in seconds. The would-be killers were unaware of the prowess of Jutish shield maidens—to their cost. So, surprised, one Frank and a Roman spy fell dying to the ground. Now, evenly matched, Valdor overcame another of Allectus' spies, and most likely the two women would have prevailed, except that a patrol from the fortress came running to restore order and, recognising the centurion, captured the assailants and marched them back at spear point to the stronghold. Warily, Sfava continued her scrutiny of the gaudy silks.

Having purchased material to her liking, the trio returned to the fortress, where Valdor was immediately summoned to the emperor, who said, "This is Allectus' handiwork. But well done, Centurion, you slew three of the assailants and protected your womenfolk as a true Roman officer should."

Those two don't need my protection!

Constantius stared hard at Valdor as if assessing his value. Measuring his words, he said, "The question now is, what to do with the two prisoners. I could have them crucified outside the gates, but I have an idea. Little escapes my notice: it is clear that the men of your legion hold you in great esteem, but you have to win the respect of the other legions here. This is my proposal; nay, my command. Centurion, you will fight both adversaries in the arena outside the port at dawn tomorrow. In that way, the men will see what a valorous centurion they have and will be willing to follow you in battle when need occurs. Besides, it will alleviate their boredom. To incentivize your opponents, I will promise them their freedom if they overcome you, which they will not!"

"They tried to murder my woman, Caesar, I need no other motivation to slay them." Valdor bowed and hurried away to hone his *gladius* and break the news to Heidar.

"But that's unfair, two against one," his friend objected. "I'll plead with Caesar to let me fight by your side."

"If you value our friendship, you'll do no such thing. I ask only that you look after my family if I fail." Valdor explained why the emperor wanted him to fight superior odds.

"It makes sense only if you have to lead a ragbag legion of auxiliaries, Valdor. Our men would follow you into the jaws of Hell."

"Ay, the emperor knows that."

Heidar frowned and said, "The Frank had a long sword when he was captured. If they give it back to him, you'll need a good shield."

"I've already thought about that; I have my Capricornus shield gifted to me by Legate Vitulasius of the Legio II Augusta. As yet, I have never used it in battle. It's sure to bring me luck and, at least with the Roman, intimidate him, for the fame of *that* legion precedes it."

"Good, and whatever you do, seize the initiative, Valdor. Do not hesitate!"

"You mean well, old friend, but you begin to annoy me! I am away, I must make sure the tip of my *gladius* is well honed."

Invigorated by the sea air and watching the sky from behind a barred gate on a fair, somewhat variable day, with clouds scudding across the sky, sending sudden beams of light through the breaks in the murky grey patches, Valdor waited patiently as the stadium filled with rowdy legionaries. There was excitement in the air as men took or placed wagers. Staring out across the arena's ground of beaten sand, Valdor saw his opponents stride from another gate into the centre of the circus. The Frank was a head taller than the Roman, and both were fully armoured and wearing helms. Valdor's body was well armoured, too, and he smiled grimly as he adjusted the cheek-guards of his *galea*. The thought of his transverse centurion plume heartened him because he knew that his aspect would be fearsome for his adversaries. Suddenly, a cranking sound and the squealing of hinges accompanied the slow opening of the barred gate. He did not rush out but allowed the tension to build as a sector of the crowd—his men—began to intone his name.

That enthusiastic noise was nothing compared to the great roar that coincided with his emergence into the arena. It was clear that the spectators wanted him to win. The odds seemed stacked against him, so a good price was quoted for his victory, which, in turn, meant greater vocal encouragement.

He did not need Heidar's advice, for he had already decided not to hesitate. He thanked the Lord that his left arm, supporting his shield, had fully recovered from the first assassination attempt. Merely thinking about the cowardly assault on his family and, now, the repetition the day before, sent adrenaline surging through his veins. His adversaries clearly had a plan because they stood back-to-back, motionless. This allowed Valdor time to devise a countermeasure; suddenly, he ran in a circle past the Roman, ignoring him, turned, lowering his shield to a collective gasp from the crowd, who sat forward as the Frank raised his long sword. Without breaking stride, Valdor swung the shield upwards fast, using the metal-rimmed edge to strike his opponent violently under the point of his chin. He continued running, ignoring the deafening cheers, to stop several yards farther on, sending sandy dust flying from under his caligae. He turned with a raised shield and surveyed the scene. The Roman was vigorously shaking the prone figure of the unconscious Frank. He obviously had no stomach for a fair fight. Valdor realised that it was to his advantage that the Frank remained senseless, so he broke into a run directly towards the legionary, who leapt desperately to his feet, raising his shield.

At the sight of the Batavian centurion charging him, his nerve broke, for he was not a veteran soldier, but a spy hired to enact a cowardly murder. The craven-hearted assassin turned and ran towards the edge of the circus. Valdor, instead, reached the Frank who was stirring. The tall, bearded warrior struggled to stand, but Valdor was too quick for him, kicking his chin and dropping him back to the ground amid shouts and chants of 'kill, kill, kill!'

His opponent was helpless, but so had been little Caurus in Britannia, prey to assassins; thanks to Inga, his son was alive. This thought was enough to make Valdor strike the Frank's throat with the sharp point of his gladius. He sprang to his feet and raised his bloodied blade to the heavens as the sated crowd shouted his name, not just his own men, but the whole stadium rocked to the repetition of *Valdor! Valdor!*

He took a deep breath, knowing that the contest was not over and not yet won. It would be folly to believe it so because the other had run to cower against the perimeter wall. Valdor admitted that it was not a bad ploy because the wretch's back was covered. But he might turn it to his advantage. He would play on the villain's mind. Slowly, shield raised full on, displaying the Capricornus; slowly, swinging his gladius in a nonchalant circular motion, he advanced with slow determination, playing on the legionary's nerves. With every step forward, the crowd chanted his name louder, in time with his step. The slow advance ceased at ten paces from the cowering figure, who nevertheless held his gladius at the ready, only to be replaced by a sudden surprise dash. Valdor sprinted at his opponent, arriving shield-to-shield with a mighty clash and pinning the man's shield with all his might against him, trapping him helpless between the oncoming shield and the wall. His situation impeded him from wielding his gladius so that the centurion, with no such problem, was able to pick off the other's sword arm with a series of short, sharp thrusts that shredded the legionary's forearm, causing him to drop his weapon to the delight of the crowd, which took up again the familiar chant 'kill, kill, kill!'

The beaten man dropped to his knees, letting his shield fall to the ground. He stretched out his arms, one bloodied, in supplication as the disgusted soldiers encircling them bayed for his death. Valdor dropped his shield to free his hand to grab the man by the hair and pull him painfully into the centre of the arena. His eyes sought the emperor and for the first time, he realised that Heidar, Inga, and Sfava were privileged to be seated in his box.

Marching the man to the area in front of the box, Valdor gazed at Emperor Constantius and their eyes met. Almost imperceptibly, the emperor's head nodded, so Valdor tugged at the hair, pulling his head back and swiftly used his razor-sharp gladius to slash the man's throat. A rousing cheer greeted this bloody act and men demanded their winnings. In an act of disdain, Valdor placed a boot on the dead man's chest. He raised his sword, first to Caesar, then to the four quarters of the arena. In an afterthought, he ran to retrieve his shield, which he was certain had played a psychological part in his victory.

He was sure that he would carry it to further triumphs in Batavia in the months ahead.

23

GESORIACUM AND BATAVIA AD 294

THE HARBOUR AT GESORIACUM WAS LOCATED IN THE 'Anse de Brequerecque', a small bay off the Liane estuary located below the fortifications. On the waterfront, Valdor watched a wooden crane swing a large, sturdy net laden with perfectly round stone missiles over the hold of a cargo ship, and a legionary wound a handle and lowered them down. This was the third such netful since he had been in attendance. He strolled over to the labourer to ensure that *ballistae* had been previously deposited in another cargo vessel. He also discovered that they had loaded a battering ram, so, satisfied, he strolled back to the fortress. A sharp cry to the gatekeepers, and the heavy wooden door swung back to admit him.

An acute observer, Constantius could not resist a smug smile as he glanced at Valdor making his way across the courtyard. The idea of a gladiatorial contest had proved compelling. Whoever the centurion passed smiled at him and fisted his chest in respect, and Valdor's proud bearing indicated his appreciation. There and then, the emperor decided to entrust an army to the Batavian's leadership.

In his right hand, he held a suitable provocation to spur Valdor on to greater determination—if he should need it—which he doubted. Nonetheless, he called the centurion over to him and opened his hand, saying, "Centurion Valdor, you might find this interesting." He handed a coin showing the bearded and cuirassed profile of Allectus with the legend

IMP. ALLECTUS around the edge. His expression grim, eyes blazing, Valdor turned the coin and saw a galley under a set of compasses on the reverse. His hand clenched over the coin until his knuckles became white, and he only slowly handed the offensive piece back to his emperor, who said, "This was given in change today at the fish market to one of my cooks. He wanted to know if it was legal tender. I exchanged it for a coin bearing my portrait, Centurion. Keep the coin. It will remind you, if needed, who your enemy is."

"I swear to God that I'll slay him, given half a chance!"

"Tomorrow, you will lead an army to Batavia. Take Noviomagus and drive the Franks out of your homeland. That done, leave a strong garrison and ships in the harbour, then sail back here and we'll invade Britannia. I have the utmost faith in you, Centurion Valdor. There's no need for me to raise your rank, for you are a Count. I'll announce as much to the army."

"Thank you, Caesar, I'll not fail you." *So, he's going to keep me as Count of the Saxon Shore! Thank the stars!*

The following morning, the emperor convened Valdor's *Legio XX* Valeria Victrix and another legion, the glorious *Legio VI Gallicana*, largely made up of Illyrians from the Balkans. These were renowned fighters but they also had a reputation for intolerance towards inefficient officers. Murders had been known. This made the emperor's speech all the more important.

"Legionaries, you sail within the hour for Batavia, where you will retake the region for Rome under the command of my friend and general, *Comes Saxoniae Litoris*, Valdor. Once you have achieved this objective, some of you will return and together, we shall invade Britannia. Comrades, onwards for the glory of Rome!"

Ha! He kept his word and used my highest title.

This short speech was met with thunderous cheers and all eyes turned to Valdor when he drew and raised his gladius, "*Ave Caesar*, Hail Caesar! For the glory of Rome and Emperor Constantius I!"

Ten thousand voices took up the cry and the emperor beamed with satisfaction at his chosen commander, who went to the stables for Sparax and proudly led two legions on the short march or, in 600 cases, short ride, to the harbour.

All aboard, they sailed with a seasonable following wind past the Grey Cape into the Strait of Dubris. To the east, the coast of Gaul, with its cliffs and sandy beaches, flashed in a blur while to the west, the white cliffs made his hand clench over Allectus' coin. The invasion of Britannia and his revenge could not come soon enough. At this fair rate of knots, they cleaved into the North Sea, never losing sight of the eastern coast, thus avoiding the dangerous, well-known sandbank of the *Infera Insula*. Legend had it that this sandbank was once a fertile isle.

Bearing north-easterly, they came to the sodden mouth of the Rhine and sailed into the estuary. Orders were shouted on each ship, sails furled and oars deployed as they rowed into the confluence of the Waal. Fifty-two nautical miles of fatigue to the beat of drums resounded over the water from one ship to another, drowning the cries of waterfowl in the reed beds, stretched before them along the Waal as far as the harbour at Noviomagus, which was their destination.

Arrived at the quay, his men requisitioned oxen and carts before taking command of the loading bays and unloading the weapons and missiles from the cargo ships. His officers had readied the men on dry land so that the two legions were ready to march up the trail to reach the levelled ground under the fortress walls. The eight double-yoked ox carts lumbered uphill after them. At the head of the army, Valdor halted Sparax and ordered the cornicen to blow three blasts of his horn. The gates remained stubbornly shut, but a Frankish officer appeared on the gate tower and refused to admit the Roman army.

"Your decision is the worse for you; this means war!" Valdor cried.

He withdrew his men out of range of archers and javelin throwers, then waited for the ox carts to creak their way to him. Meanwhile, he organised a *testudo* formation around the unloaded battering ram—an oak trunk with a steel sculpted ram's head at its extremity—swinging on leather bindings in its wheeled cradle. The ram thundered against the stout, barred oak doors to no avail as missiles and boiling oil, launched from the ramparts, had no effect on the Roman shields held overhead, effectively creating a protective roof.

Exasperated, Valdor withdrew the testudo and organised the ballistae so that all three were aiming at the same spot on the oak doors, where he believed, from memory, the bar was placed. This took some time, but the veterans were not restless. They knew that alternatives to storming through the gates would be costly in the number of lives lost. Instead, the Frankish onlookers from the ramparts prayed that the barred doors resisted the bombardment. The ballistae were wound to maximum tension and the engineers alerted their commander to their readiness.

He raised and dropped his hand, so, with amazing accuracy, three massive stone balls almost contemporaneously smashed into the oak doors. The noise was reverberant and the only astonishing thing was that the doors were still intact. "Three more!" yelled Valdor. He had a good supply of missiles and was prepared to use them all, but he wanted to concentrate his fire on the same spot. It proved to be a wise decision as the second volley, while failing to demolish the doors, had weakened the steel brackets holding the bar in place and created a small visible gap between the doors, forcing one back slightly.

Encouraged, the Count ordered another volley, whose thunderous impact was matched by the hoarse roar of thousands of legionaries as the doors caved in under the enormous impact. Valdor ordered his cavalry forward at a gallop and the heavy infantry centurions urged their men to run forward, shields raised against missiles from above. But the resistance was weak, both in number and in morale, since the garrison was so obviously outnumbered. More Franks surrendered than fought. The gallant fighters met a bloody end, so their courage and opposition were futile. Soon, the fortress belonged to Valdor. His only task now remained to send scouts along the river in both directions to ensure there were no other Frankish enclaves.

The scouts returned the following day, assuring him their reports were negative. This was mostly due to the sodden terrain and the desertion of farmsteads.

Considering his mission accomplished, Valdor convened the Illyrian commander and explained that he intended to leave the *Legio VI Gallicana* as the garrison with a commensurate number of ships, should they be needed for embarkation. To his relief, the centurion accepted the orders without a qualm, grateful to Valdor for the sound strategy used to capture the fortress-citadel that had left him with minimal casualties.

All aboard the vessels, Valdor's fleet rowed with the Waal's favourable current very swiftly as far as the mouth of the Rhine. There, the choppier water of the river mingled with the tide of the North Sea and an idea came to Valdor.

He could transform the return voyage into a reconnaissance. His knowledge of the Britannia shore forts was second to none, and he might well contribute to his commander's thinking. Thus, he sailed straight across the sea to near the British coast where he surveyed the two forts, which were considered as one site, guarding the entire Yare estuary. Without entering the estuary, which was not his intention that day, he made out the form of Gariannonum Fort, its curious name derived from the Celtic language, meaning 'babbling river.' He remembered that this fortress was commanded by a cavalry garrison, the Equites Stablesiani.

Valdor cursed himself for the thoroughness that had characterised his construction work. The other fort, surrounded by imposing walls, was also protected by treacherous marshland, although on the far side from his viewpoint, there was an extensive civilian vicus. It was one thing to construct a fortress with defence uppermost in mind, another to plan an assault, altogether a more difficult prospect. Perhaps the other fortress, built before he took over responsibility for the Saxon shore, the one guarding the river Waverley confluence with the Yare, might be more vulnerable. He would report this to Constantius. Satisfied with his inspection, Valdor's ship led the fleet down the east coast, where he reached the territory of the Cantiaci. He knew all about these forts, their strong and weak points, and began to abandon his earlier idea of Gariannonum. At the end of the day, much would also depend on the mustering of Allectus' army. Still, any information he could give to Constantius would be useful, especially if the usurper barricaded himself in one of these fortresses. After his experience at Noviomagus, nothing seemed too formidable to overcome with the right approach.

The Count studied the Rutupine shore, whose oysters were considered on a par with those from the Italian Lucrine Lake, or so he had heard fellow officers declare. What he remembered most fondly of Rutupiae was the major quadrifons triumphal arch, one of the biggest in the Roman Empire, which was erected around AD 85 to straddle Watling Street, the main road from the fort to Londinium. He sighed at the memory and the significance of the monument and felt a surge of pride at his role as the Count of the Saxon Shore. He considered himself, justly, a part of the history of Britannia. He closed his eyes and remembered the arch as if seeing an image of it in front of him. Its position and size were due to its being built to celebrate the final conquest of Britain after Agricola's victory at the Battle of Mons Graupius.

He prayed to the Lord that he, too, would win a battle against Allectus, although he doubted that even if it should come about, it would not merit an arch almost 82 feet high with a façade of high-quality Italian granite, adorned with sculptures and inscriptions like that of General Agricola. That arch, which he saw so clearly in his mind's eye, standing as it did between the port and the province, signified formal entry into Britannia. What could he hope to achieve of greater importance? Nothing. He could only hope for victory and vengeance for the murder of his adoptive father.

As the white cliffs of Dubris slipped past, barely registering on his distracted mind, he knew that the time had come to return without further delay to Gesoriacum. He would arrive in triumph with the emperor's promise that on achieving his mission, they would set about the invasion of Britannia. Momentarily, he thought about his birth father, Caurus, and with a pang realised that Namuta had never seen his namesake, her tiny grandson. When he re-conquered Britannia, he would remedy that situation.

24

GESORIACUM, PORTUS ADURNI AND LONDINIUM, SEPTEMBER, AD 296

NATURE CONTRIVED TO DISPLAY EVERY SHADE OF GREY, IN the sea, in the sky, and even in the drawn faces of the garrison. A few adventurous gulls, driven from precarious nests in desperation to seek food, were snatched mid-air by gale-force wind and flung, ruffled-feathered, in a different direction. The winter of 295-296 was the most severe in living memory.

If Valdor had not abandoned the pagan gods for Christianity, he would have thought they were conspiring to prevent the invasion of Britannia. How could it be right that a murderous usurper thrived while his justiciar waited impatiently on the other shore of the raging sea?

If only Constantius had kept his word more than a year ago and allowed Valdor's fleet to sail for Britannia! The irony was that the emperor's scouts had reported on the strength of the shore forts—those he had created. The decision to delay departure apparently provoked Neptune's wrath. The North Sea became unnavigable for Valdor's ships and had remained that way until the summer of 296. Even so, preparations were slow, and only by the end of August, were his daily prayers answered. Constantius' fleet sailed in several divisions, one under Valdor's command, another under the praetorian prefect, Asclepiodotus. The emperor's dithering meant that his division was the last to leave Gaul.

As if to taunt him, Nature decided on one last flourish. She wreathed the approach to Vectis in thick fog. Allectus' fleet was concentrated there, and Asclepiodotus used the conditions as an excuse to sail well wide of the isle to avoid the enemy. Instead, Valdor, knowing the Solent well, sailed recklessly at considerable speed too close to the island. His years of patrolling saved him, as despite the veil of grey, he discerned a dangerous headland. His alertness served a dual purpose: first, it gave him his position, and second, it saved his fleet from certain shipwreck. He changed course, and, sure of himself, directed his ships into the estuary under the fort of Portus Adurni, which he had built.

Since he had conveyed the entire garrison to Gesoriacum, the fortress was weakly defended, commanded by a centurion who had remained at the time on his sick-bed with the ague. Now fully recovered, he had worked miracles to transform an ill-disciplined collection of scoundrels into a respectable unit to hold the fortress. His joy on seeing Valdor was immense, and the gates were flung open to receive the new garrison.

The following morning broke with welcome limpidity. Valdor watched a fishing boat sail out of the estuary into the calm Solent, little suspecting that the wretch had other than fishing on his mind. He wanted to gain good coins for reporting what he had seen to Allectus on Vectis. His mission became more urgent when halfway across the strait, he saw Asclepiodotus' division sail into the natural harbour of *Noviomagus Reginorum*. This fleet almost came to grief, its crews unaware of the shallow spit that presented a navigation hazard at all states of the tide. Fortunately, only one ship foundered there. The others dealt with the fast tidal stream at the entrance to the harbour with considerable expertise. Nonetheless, once his men had disembarked, Asclepiodotus decided to burn the ships. He did not want them falling into the hands of his enemy, and, besides, he was an able general on land and did not care for the restrictions of naval warfare.

From his vantage point on a turret of the fortress, Valdor saw the smoke of the conflagration. He could not imagine that Asclepiodotus had burnt his vessels, but having seen his division enter the north side of the Solent, recognized that the fire appertained in some way to the praetorian prefect.

Meanwhile, on Vectis, the fisherman told Allectus everything he had seen and for his troubles received three silver coins. The usurper, devious and cowardly, stripped himself of outward signs of command, posing as an ordinary legionary, in case the forthcoming battle went against him. Even if he died, he did not want the enemy desecrating his body.

He directed his fleet towards the smoke and, disembarking his force, immediately realised his tactical inferiority to Asclepiodotus. Wily and craven, he ordered his men to retreat aboard the ships, for he knew that the prefect had burnt his and could not pursue him out of the harbour. Reasoning with his own yardstick, he did not expect the other division to leave the safety of its fortress at Portus Adurni. Therefore, Valdor had the advantage of surprise. Allectus knew that he had to remove Constantius' force from its stronghold if he wished to retain his position of emperor of the North, so he disembarked in the harbour under the fortress. Concentrating their gaze inland, his lookouts were slow to spot the oncoming naval division, which had turned about from the high water of the Solent, heading for Noviomagus Reginorum, and veered instead back into the same estuary of Portus Adurni. By the time Allectus' force was aware of the disembarkation of the enemy, its commander, concerned at being trapped between the fortress and the newly arrived force, formed his army into a defensive formation.

Consumed by hatred for his father's murderer, Valdor had only attack on his mind, which, anyway, was his preferred battle tactic. He arranged his veterans of the XX Legion into a wedge formation, placing himself at the front tip of the triangle, leading by example, closely followed by his Batavian officers and then the veterans, attacking the enemy centre. No army in the world could have withstood these able soldiers, and, with the tactic repeated in two other wedges along the enemy front, the three wedges thrust well into the foe. When these formations expanded, the enemy troops were pushed into restricted positions, making hand-to-hand fighting difficult for the less experienced legion of Allectus, largely composed of Frankish mercenaries. This was where the short legionary gladius was useful, held low, and used as a thrusting weapon, while the longer Frankish swords became impossible to wield.

It soon became clear to Valdor that victory would be his, especially because Heidar had wrested the eagle standard from the foe, a sure sign of imminent success. Indeed, the adversary received orders to retreat and, gathering together, headed northwards along a Roman road towards *Calleva Atrebatum*, where undoubtedly, Allectus expected to reinforce his numbers. Valdor was in no hurry to pursue the routed force but sent an envoy to fetch Asclepiodotus' division.

For the moment, the triumph had a bitter taste because there was no sign of Allectus' insignia. Arrogant as ever, and reinforced, Allectus now felt sufficiently superior to Valdor's army to not remain behind the solid walls of Calleva Atrebatum. Instead, he placed his army in the same defensive formation that had cost him dear the previous day. Also, the arrival of the other division took the usurper by surprise.

Valdor spoke rapidly with Asclepiodotus, an experienced general, who nodded wisely in agreement and allowed repetition of the tactics of the previous day. Allectus had fewer Franks in his formation, but the confidence of Valdor's force compensated for the increased presence of Roman legionaries in the enemy ranks. The tide of battle soon swung in favour of Valdor and the praetorian prefect. Even so, there was no sign of his hated foe. The Count wondered whether Allectus was cringing behind the city walls, watching the progress of the engagement, which inexorably swung in favour of his foe—the deceased emperor's adopted son.

The battle still raged and Valdor noticed an enemy enclave seemingly intent on defending someone at its core. He fought his way through and at last found what he sought. Although Allectus wore the armour of a simple legionary, his men were determined to protect him. Had Valdor not had the advantage of having met the usurper, he would not have recognised the disfigured face. There was only one like it, so with a bloodcurdling cry, emanating from suppressed fury at his father's murder, Valdor pressed forward, stabbing and thrusting, closely followed by his most trusted friends and the expert veterans of XX Valeria Victrix.

The coward fought with the desperation of despair as he saw his handpicked bodyguard falling before the fighting valour of his adversary. With horror, he recognised the murdered emperor's son, whose eyes blazed with hatred as he neared him. With his own malevolent yell, Allectus leapt forward to finish the job of slaying father and son. It was his undoing because his foothold betrayed him, slithering on blood, he lost his balance and Valdor, infused with demonic energy, was onto him in a flash. His gladius pierced at least three inches through the leather cuirass, such was the might of the thrust impelled by pent-up rage. The Batavian followed it with a slash to the throat, possibly unnecessary, since the first thrust was mortal, but undoubtedly satisfying as he watched the light of life dull in his victim's eyes. "For Carausius!" Valdor shrieked like a man possessed, and standing astride the corpse, let the fighting proceed around him as he offered a prayer to his deceased adoptive father: *Father, I have avenged you this day. I pray that now your soul may rest in peace at the bosom of Our Lord. Amen.*

Valdor felt a great weight removed from his shoulders and again thrust himself into the fray. Soon, a rout followed towards the town. Heidar lagged behind. He had seen his friend exult over the body of what seemed to be a lowly legionary. He had not seen Allectus; nonetheless, he had heard Valdor describe the disfigured mouth, so he recognised the corpse for whom he was. Unknown to his friend and commander, for love of Valdor, Heidar beheaded the body and carried the head to town. Outside the main gate to the amphitheatre, he sharpened a stake and planted it with Allectus' head impaled on it. "Behold the usurper!" he cried, and numerous legionaries gathered, curious to see.

"Long live Caesar Valdor!" someone called, and the cry was taken up by many voices until Valdor rode up and called for silence.

"Nay," he shouted, "I have sworn fealty to Emperor Constantius. This victory today is in his name. Long live Caesar Constantius I!"

Unknown to Valdor, Constantius' division had been separated by the fog from the others, and he had rowed up the Tamesis, where he saved Londinium from an attack by Frankish mercenaries who were now roaming the province without a paymaster, and massacred them. At the very moment that Valdor declared his loyalty, Constantius was riding into Londinium, where he was hailed by the Britons as a liberator. That very afternoon, he had a die cut for a gold medallion describing himself with the wording: *redditor lucis aeternae*, 'restorer of the eternal light', by which he meant Roman rule.

The triumph was essentially Valdor's and to some extent Asclepiodotus', for Constantius had arrived after the battle. On hearing that the emperor was in Londinium, the two generals marched their men there, where Constantius received them with great honour.

"Centurion Valdor," said the emperor, "I hereby confirm you as Count of the Saxon Shore. You will resume your duties forthwith. It seems I have business in the far north of the land, where trouble is stirring."

"Sire, your wish is my command; forgive me, but my greatest desire is to retire on Vectis with my family. I would like to settle there, build a villa and plant a vineyard to enjoy my old age."

The emperor looked at him benevolently, "I have heard reports of your loyalty, Count. This is what we will do. You will come north to aid me in my conquest of the Picts. That achieved, you will suggest a successor to build more fortresses and fend off the pirates. You will, however, retain the rank of Count for your retirement."

"Thank you, Sire. I could ask for no more. I'll look forward to seeing and pushing beyond Hadrian's Wall. I have never travelled so far north."

"The noble Hadrian found the Picts fearsome warriors. Every time he tried to move into their territory, they successfully drove him back. That was over a hundred years ago. Did you know that they fought completely naked, using only spears? Although, some say they painted their bodies in different colours. Reports have come to me that the Picts are attacking the forts along the Wall."

"We can deal with those savages, Sire. I look forward to it."

25

BRITANNIA, AD 299 - 306

THE EMPEROR EXPLAINED TO VALDOR THAT THE PICTISH crisis had calmed, meaning there was no immediate danger from the north. His scouts were monitoring the situation but as far as Constantius was concerned, he smiled benignly, Valdor could go to Vectis and make a start on his retirement plans.

"Sire, might I suggest Centurion Heidar take over the shore defences? He has worked with me and knows what is entailed. I was going to build a fortress near the mouth of the River Exe to complete the southern line of strongholds and to protect *Isca Dumnoniorum*."

"Then that is what we will do. I'll make him the Count on the understanding that if I should need you—you remain a count—you will come with all haste to *Eboracum*."

"Eboracum, Sire?"

"Ay, I have chosen it for its strategic location, especially with unrest to the north of the Wall."

Valdor had a cart built, making it into a comfortable travelling wagon with a luxurious interior. He requisitioned oxen to haul it and a chestnut mare. With these, he travelled on Sparax to Branodunum, where he arbitrarily removed his parents from their employment, explaining, "Father, I'll need you to take over a vineyard and produce quality wine. Your previous years of farming in Batavia will stand you in good stead. Mother, you will continue to make bread. I'll have an oven constructed according to your requirements. We shall all live together on an island with a milder clime than this east coast, where the wind cuts to the bone: it's no place for the aged."

They travelled south, and Sfava and little Caurus joined Namuta in the wagon, much to his grandmother's delight. The crossing to Vectis was uneventful, except that they were joined by a small craft containing Johar, who had retired from the army. He explained that he wanted to resume work as a fisherman and to live close to his only remaining relatives. In an aside to Valdor, he confided that on Vectis he hoped to find a Briton who pleased him so that he could wed her and start a family. Valdor took everyone to a fertile inland area on a strategically defensible height, known as Robin Hill.

He took his father and Johar aside to describe his vision: "I want to build a bath-house and an aisled building linked by a corridor on this side of a courtyard that will stretch down there to the south. I will have a mosaic floor with a dolphin motif in the bath-house and underfloor hypocaust heating in the main building. Then there will be outhouses, barns..." he paused, "... come over here, father, see how the land rolls away down to the south? Imagine it cleared of trees and planted with rows of vines. I'll bring labourers to start work next week. For a while, we'll have to camp, military style," he chuckled. Johar clapped him on the back, "Who would have thought that you would have become a wealthy landowner in Britannia when we set out to sea with no destination in mind? What folly that was, eh, Valdor!"

"Ay, but we had to save Faldrek. Poor Faldrek! He was unlucky. How he would have loved it here, don't you agree?"

"If only Heidar could join us. I'm going to love it, too, I know. Now I must go to choose a site near the sea for a small house, not a grand villa like yours, Valdor."

"Not too small, Johar. I'll help you with funds, for I have been very fortunate. Besides, I'll regularly send servants down to buy fresh fish from you, so it's in my interests that you establish yourself comfortably."

They laughed, and their enthusiasm for a new lifestyle was evident to anyone, who, like Caurus, could see the joy illuminating his son's face.

The months passed, and the buildings sprang up like mushrooms; inside, however, work was slower because the master craftsmen, the mosaicists, worked with precision and could not be rushed. In the villa, once the hypocaust was installed and the pavement laid, these master craftsmen created a magnificent mosaic of the legendary Medusa, with hissing snakes for hair.

Outdoors, a barn was adapted for a wine press, with large barrels ready for the first grape harvest. Caurus had overseen the planting of twenty-seven rows of 100 vines on a hectare of prepared land. Namuta requested a wood-burning oven, with a granite slab as a baking surface. Valdor organised the transport of the slab from Dumnonia; that done, he oversaw the stacking of wood obtained from the vineyard land clearance.

Johar made his own nets on a frame by the shore. His house, not a villa, but a fine *mansio*, overlooked a bay where he dragged his fishing boat onto a sandy beach when not in use. In that bay, without venturing far, he caught flounder and mullet and school bass, rays, mackerel, and bream in the summer, whereas in late autumn and winter he netted cod without risking turbulent waters.

Inland, Valdor built a small church near his villa and employed a priest from the mainland. Johar's wedding with the Briton, Valda, was the first such ceremony there, followed months later by the baptism of their baby boy, Enyon.

Everything would have been auspicious, had it not been for the news arriving from Rome. Emperor Diocletian had begun persecuting Christians and had issued edicts ordering the destruction of the cult throughout the Empire.

Therefore, when a messenger arrived on Vectis from Constantius, demanding Valdor's presence in Eboracum, he feared the worst. He travelled, determined to fight for his faith, expecting never to return to his family on the isle. He had expressly forbidden Johar from travelling with him, demanding that whatever happened, his cousin should protect his family. His main hope was that the island was too far from the rest of Britannia and his family and small church too insignificant to interest Constantius; yet, he had summoned Valdor to Eboracum.

The emperor's welcome reassured him somewhat and an explanation for his summons was soon forthcoming. The Picts had breached the wall and invaded the north. "You owe me a favour, Valdor. I presume you know about the persecution of Christians according to the imperial edict?"

"I have heard terrible reports from other parts of the Empire, Caesar."

"I have limited myself to demolishing a handful of churches for appearance's sake, but have not harmed a single Christian. My son Constantine and his mother, Helena, are both Christians, which is why I have brought Constantine here. You will meet him soon, for he is marching with us. Helena is hiding, safe in her home city of Drepana in Bithynia."

He assures my loyalty by playing on my Christianity, but he has it anyway.

Constantius studied Valdor's face as if trying to read his mind, but continued, "There are those, notably Galerius, who married Diocletian's daughter, who use my leniency towards the Christians against me with the Emperor, but he will not prevail. I have put plans to work so that when Diocletian and Maximian no longer wear the purple, Constantine will do so."

Now, I understand! He wants me to befriend Constantine and become his trusted general in Britannia.

As if reading his mind, Constantius said, "I am placing you and Constantine each at the head of a legion, and I will command a third. Fetch Constantine!" he bellowed at a servant. "We shall march north at dawn on the morrow; so, we need a strategy to defeat these savages."

Valdor rode Sparax next to Constantine, mounted on an equally fine stallion on the long march north. The Picts retreated ahead of them beyond the Wall, which marvel, Valdor surveyed for the first time, noting how it stretched up hill and down dale for miles.

The Roman forces advanced past the Firth of Forth, razing villages and sending refugees ever deeper into lands where the harvest was already beginning to wane. As the native population became more desperate, the Romans carried out the plan the three generals had devised in Eboracum; namely, they grew better stocked by ransacking the provisions that the fleeing Picts had left behind.

The scheme worked perfectly until one band of Picts decided that the best way to end the Roman advance would be by assassination: this unstoppable army would descend into chaos, they believed, and, leaderless, would hurry to retreat to winter quarters.

The Picts chose to make the attempt during the pagan festival of Samhain. While Roman eyes were dazzled by the bonfires lit to keep wicked spirits at bay, a small group of Pict soldiers adopted the ancient practice of guising: wearing masked costumes to approach a neighbour's house. Under the half-moon, they wandered about, wearing cow heads and hides amid a small herd of stray cattle, which was eagerly snatched up by Roman scouts. By this subterfuge, they entered the Roman camp and evaded the sentries long enough to sneak up to the luxurious tents of the Augustus and his generals. There they shrieked and attacked, slaying everyone they could reach before Valdor and Constantine, fighting shoulder-to-shoulder, cut them down.

The attack did not entirely fail. Among the dead officers was Constantius' son, Constantinus, by his first wife. The emperor, thanks to the harsh clime, had fallen ill, and announced the retreat to Eboracum to mourn. By January, the broken-hearted father also passed away, leaving behind his two younger sons by his second wife, Helena.

Constantius died on 25 July 306, endorsing Constantine as his successor. The legions hailed him as Rome soon broke into civil war.

"I will leave you temporarily in charge of Britannia, Valdor, until I have overthrown my rival Maxentius. I know you dearly wish to return to your isle and you have my benediction to do so as soon as I am undisputed ruler of the Empire."

Valdor arranged to meet Heidar in Eboracum and devised a plan to ensure that Britannia would remain loyal to Constantine. The Picts settled for a period of peace, which made his task that much easier.

"Heidar, I'll make Eboracum my base and strengthen the east coast shore fortresses. You will use Camulodunum as yours, and from there reinforce the southern shore fortresses. We must make certain that Britannia does not fall to other usurpers. Constantine will ensure that our religion is respected throughout the Empire."

A messenger arrived at Eboracum to inform Count Valdor that Constantine had defeated Maxentius at the Battle of Milvian Bridge. The new emperor immediately pushed the Edict of Mediolanum, legalising Christianity. When he heard this, Valdor immediately departed Eboracum for Camulodunum, where he encountered Heidar.

"My dear old friend, I leave Britannia in your hands, for now, unless I have to defend my home and family, my fighting days are over. Since leaving Torik Isle, we have achieved much. Now, the time has come to enjoy my father's first vintage by the fireside with Sfava and my mother, not to mention little Caurus, who will soon be taller than I! Remember our oath on Torik: I expect it still to bind you—when Emperor Constantine allows you to retire, come and join Johar and me on Vectis. Sfava would love to have Inga close by, and we can all live in peace on an isle that does not flood."

THE END

THE GREAT CONSPIRACY

THE SAXON SHORE TRILOGY
BOOK 2

CHAPTER-BY-CHAPTER GLOSSARY

PREFACE

Vectis = Roman name for the Isle of Wight
Portus Adurni = present-day Portchester, Hampshire, 4m north of Portsmouth.

CHAPTER ONE

Cypros = Roman name for Cyprus.
Hibernia = Roman name for Ireland.
Mediobogdum = Roman fortress at Hardknott, Cumbria
Glannoventa = Roman naval base at Ravenglass, Cumbria

CHAPTER TWO

Branodunum = shore fort to the east of modern Brancaster, near King's Lynn, Norfolk.
Laconium = dry, hot room, the Roman equivalent of a sauna.

CHAPTER THREE

Clipeus (pl clipeī) = a light, round cavalry shield
Hasta (pl hastae) = long spear
Lancea = short thrusting spear
Scutum (pl scuta) = large curved Roman shield
Spatha (pl spathae) = long sword, suitable for mounted combat
Exploratorem (pl -es) = Roman mounted advanced scout(s)
Gabrosentum = Roman fort at present-day Moresby, Cumbria
Dalriada = ancient Gaelic kingdom in N. Ireland occupied by the Scoti.

CHAPTER FOUR

Vercovicium = present-day Housesteads Fort, Hadrian's Wall, near Corbridge, Northumberland.
Coriosopitum = Corbridge, Northumberland.
Tungrians = a Belgian tribe.

CHAPTER FIVE

Vallum = an earthen or turf rampart with a wooden palisade on top, with a deep outer ditch.
Classis = Roman fleet.
Comitatenses = the heavy infantry in the late Roman Empire, its legion consisting of 6,000-7,000 men.
Camolodunum = present-day Colchester, Essex.

CHAPTER SIX

Civitas = Latin for citizenship, citizen community, or a free-standing city-state, especially in the imperial period.
Dubris = present-day Dover, Kent.
Domus palatina = early third-century imperial palace in York, probably built for Septimius Severus.
Ostia = the ancient port of Rome, which is now a major archaeological site known as Ostia Antica.
Caledonia = present-day Scotland.
Isurium Brigantum = present-day Aldborough, Yorkshire, capital of the Brigantes tribe.
Cateractonium = present-day Catterick, with Roman fort protecting the crossing of the River Swale.
Concangis = present-day Chester-le-Street, County Durham – a Roman fort on the River Wear.
Aesica Fort = present-day Great Chesters Roman Fort, 6m east of Housesteads.
Brocolitia Fort = Carrawburgh Roman Fort, 5m west of Housesteads.
Magnis Fort = modern Carvoran Fort, Northumberland.
Abus River = ancient Roman name for the Humber River.
Hamian archers = auxiliary archers from Hama in Syria.

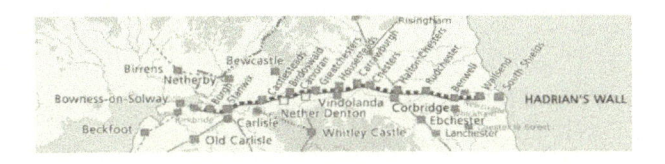

CHAPTER SEVEN

Sagum = warm military cloak.
Alauna Fort = coastal fort just north of modern Maryport, Cumbria.

CHAPTER EIGHT

Bibra = Roman fort on Cumbrian coast near Beckfoot, close to Hadrian's Wall.
Cohors II Pannoniorum = a five-hundred-strong infantry unit from the province of Pannonia, the region of the modern Czech Republic.
Portus Trucculensis = Roman turf and timber fort a few miles to the south of the Wall fort at Bowness on Solway.
Lavatrae = present-day Bowes, Barnard Castle, County Durham.
Vinovia = present-day Binchester, small village in County Durham.
Opus revinctum = interlocking squared stone technique (see below).

Cilurnum = an ancient Roman fort on the Wall at Chesters near the village of Walwick, Northumberland.
Petriana = present-day Carlisle in Cumbria.

CHAPTER NINE

Not applicable.

CHAPTER TEN

Areani = people of the sheepfold, spies north of Hadrian's Wall.
Augustodunum = Autun, a subprefecture of the Saône-et-Loire department in the Bourgogne-Franche-Comté region of central-eastern France.
Hispania = Roman name for Spain.
Helena = Elne, a commune in the Pyrénées-Orientales department in southern France.
Illyricum = present-day Croatia and Slovenia.
Pannonia = modern Osijek in Croatia.
Nauportus = port on the present-day Ljubljanica River, Slovenia.
Cataphract = heavily armoured men and horses, first used in ancient Persia.
Mursa = present-day Osijek in Croatia and site of a great battle in 351.
Oppidum Genua = present-day Genoa in Liguria, northern Italy.
Mons Seleucus = now La Bâti-Montsaléon in Hautes-Alpes, south-eastern France.
Pillars of Hercules = the promontories that flank the entrance to the Strait of Gibraltar. The northern Pillar, Calpe Mons, is the Rock of Gibraltar.
Transitus Maximus = Roman ferry across the Abus estuary.

CHAPTER ELEVEN

Alamanni = a confederation of Germanic tribes on the Upper Rhine River.
Quadi = a Germanic people who lived approximately in the area of modern Moravia.
Sarmatians = a large confederation of ancient Eastern Iranian equestrian nomadic peoples.
Mopsuestia = a city in present-day Adana, southern Turkey.
Banna Fort = present-day Birdoswald Fort on Hadrian's Wall, in Cumbria.
Cambria = Roman name for Wales, from Gaelic Cymru.

CHAPTER TWELVE

Attacotti = Latin name for a people first recorded as raiding Roman Britain between 364 and 368, alongside the Scoti, Picts, and Saxons. Their exact origins and location are unknown.

CHAPTER THIRTEEN

Cursus publicus = the chain of watchtowers and beacons along the coast.

CHAPTER FOURTEEN

Augusta = fourth-century name change from Londinium.
Arbeia = present-day South Shields, the most easterly Roman fort on Hadrian's Wall.
Stanegate = a Roman road running through the natural gap formed by the valleys of the River Tyne in Northumberland and the River Irthing in Cumbria. It predated the Hadrian's Wall frontier by several decades.
Claideamh = early version of the claymore broadsword.
Scian = a long dagger, the forerunner of the dirk.
Caerdydd = Gaelic name for Cardiff.

CHAPTER FIFTEEN

Viroconium = present-day Wroxeter, Shropshire.
Uxacona = present-day Redhill, Shropshire.
Pennocrucium = present-day Water Eaton, Staffordshire.
Letocetum = present-day Wall, Staffordshire at the crossing of Watling Street and Icknield Street.
Manduessedum = present-day Mancetter, Warwickshire.
Venonis = present-day High Cross, Leicestershire, was "the central cross roads" of Anglo-Saxon and Roman Britain and a Romano-British settlement where the Fosse Way and Watling Street intersect.
Maxima Caesariensis = one of the provinces of the Diocese of "the Britains" created during the Diocletian Reforms.

CHAPTER SIXTEEN

Vicarius = deputy to the Comes Britanniarum, responsible for administration.
Votadini = Iron Age Brittonic tribe, occupying the area of south-east Scotland.

Maia = Roman fortress on Hadrian's Wall at modern Bowness-on-Solway, Cumbria.
Habitancum = Antonine Auxiliary Fort at present-day Risingham, Northumberland.

CHAPTER SEVENTEEN

Magnis = present-day Carvoran Roman Fort, Northumberland.
Magister equitum praesentalis = Master of the Cavalry in the Western Empire.

CHAPTER EIGHTEEN

Not applicable.

CHAPTER NINETEEN

Coggabata Fort = present-day Drumburgh fort, built to guard the Solway fords, the Stonewath and the Sandwath.
Wath = ancient British or Scottish name for a ford.

CHAPTER TWENTY

Brigetio = present-day Komárom, in Hungary – a Roman fort on the river Donau.

CHAPTER TWENTY-ONE

Lower Moesia = ancient Roman province situated in the Balkans south of the Danube.
Greuthungi = Goths from the Pontic steppe between the Dnieper and Don in Ukraine.
Thrace = Roman province covering present-day south-eastern Bulgaria, north-eastern Greece, and European Turkey.
Marcianople = capital of Lower Moesia and modern-day Devnya in Bulgaria.
Adrianople = present-day Edirne, a city in Turkey 7 miles from the Greek border.
Dibaltum = located at the mouth of the River Sredetska on the west coast of Lake Mandrensko, near the modern village of Debelt in Bulgaria.
Scutarii = shield-bearing Iberian heavy cavalry.
Nicopolis = Roman town, present-day village of Nikyup in northern Bulgaria.
Beroe = modern-day Stara Zagora at the centre of fertile Upper Thracian Plain in northern Bulgaria.
Imperial scholae = imperial bodyguard.
Foederati = tribes that were bound by a treaty (foedus) to come to the defence of Rome but were neither Roman colonies nor beneficiaries of Roman citizenship.

CHAPTER TWENTY-TWO

Not applicable.

CHAPTER TWENTY-THREE

Vinovia = A Roman fort overlooking the River Wear at present-day Binchester, County Durham.

CHAPTER TWENTY-FOUR

Mona = Roman name for present-day Anglesey Isle, keeping the name in the Welsh *Ynys Mon*, (Mona Isle).

Sirmium = city in Pannonia, located on the Sava River, on the site of modern Sremska Mitrovica in the Vojvodina autonomous province of Serbia.

Alani = were an ancient Iranic nomadic pastoral people of the North Caucasus generally regarded as part of the Sarmatians.

magister equitum = Latin for Master of the Horse.

Lugdunum = Roman name for present-day Lyon, France.

Mons Iovis = present-day Isle of Monte Cristo, part of the Tuscan archipelago.

Armorica = present-day Brittany, France.

PREFACE
VECTIS ISLE AND PORTUS ADURNI, BRITANNIA AD 309-312

Sfava decided that at sixteen, Lavinia was old enough to begin her training as a warrior. For that reason, she commissioned a rawhide whip and mercilessly flicked it at her daughter's ankles and bare feet. If she danced out of the way, all well and good; if not, harsh words and a soothing balm were the outcome.

"It's all about agility, child. In battle, you can't afford to be a statue!"

When she wasn't cracking the cruel lash at her daughter's bare skin, Sfava had Lavinia running with heavy stones until she begged to stop. Daily, she increased the stone-carrying sessions, substituting the weight with a heavier one from time to time until she was satisfied that the girl's strength was sufficient. Throwing was the next skill to develop, so she obtained real javelins and had a labourer build a straw man. Sfava's choice of distance had Lavinia sulking, "It's too far, mother, I'll never hit the target from here."

"You'd better if you don't want to go back to lifting rocks again!"

To her surprise, the young woman pierced the straw man on her third attempt. Sfava, who was never mean with praise, exulted and kissed her daughter, which meant a lot to the girl.

"It's now time you learnt to use a sword. I'll have practice swords made and we'll fight tomorrow. I'll teach you all I know. When you're ready, the smith will craft you a real sword; meanwhile, I think a linden shield like the Jutes use will be better than a Roman shield. I find them so unwieldy. Besides, we don't want a gladius like your father uses. I never got on with them. Also, we won't be fighting Romans, Lavinia, nay, it'll be pirates if anyone, or the pagans on this isle. If I make a good shield maiden of you, I promise you this, you'll have the best Frankish sword that money can buy."

A discreet cough interrupted her discourse. Sfava recognised her husband's cough and looked at Count Valdor lovingly. The outdoor life of a farmer suited him, who had been used to the harsh military life, a veteran of many conflicts. It had given his face a becoming tan that enhanced his grey-blue eyes and, although there were the first traces of silver hair threading his blond locks, he remained a handsome, muscular fellow, even more attractive than the young man she had wed back in 289.

"What's that about a Frankish sword?" he asked.

"I was just telling our daughter that if she continues to make such good progress as a shield maiden, I'll gift her the best Frankish sword money can buy."

"Shield maiden! Lavinia is sixteen! We should be looking for a suitable husband for her, so she can bear us grandchildren. It's my only hope..." his voice choked with emotion, "...now that Caurus is dead. You see, wife, our son wanted to fight for Rome at all costs. A centurion's lifespan is generally not long. They are always at the forefront of battle, leading by example, and Caurus knew no fear. He died an honourable death, but he is no more. Do you want the same for our daughter?"

"A shield maiden cannot be a centurion, Valdor! She can help defend our villa against pirates or pagans. Do you suppose that you, Heidar, Inga and I will be enough against a whole pirate crew or a horde of pagans from the other side of the isle?"

"Our pagan neighbours have shown no inclination to disturb us. Why, they even buy my produce."

There was a lull in the discussion and Lavinia stepped across to the villa wall against which a javelin was propped. With a feline swoop and twirl, Lavinia hurled it at the somewhat battered remains of the straw man, to her father's amazement—if not incredulity—piercing its chest.

"Well done, my girl! That's incredible!"

"Nay, father, I can do that from twice the distance and, one of these days, I'll beat you in a sword fight."

"That day will come only when I'm white-haired and decrepit!"

"It will come sooner than you think, especially if you continue talking about wedding me off against my will!"

"My sweetest girl, I would never insist on anything against your will. I'll leave it to Divine Providence! The day the man of your life walks into it, you'll know and won't resist—exactly as happened with your mother and I—isn't it true, Sfava?"

"Ay, sure enough! I still love the old fool, Lavinia. Pay no heed. Your training is coming along better than I had hoped."

"I'll hold you to that promise of a sword, mother. I can't wait to start practising tomorrow."

Sfava was a pitiless taskmistress. She had grown up in a school of hard knocks with her brothers and their friends in Jutland, none of whom was prepared to risk jibes from his companions that he had been beaten by a girl. Yet, it happened on more than one occasion. Each victory was hard-earned and measured in black and blue bruises, cuts and repressed tears. Her pride would not let her cry in front of a swaggering boy. So, Sfava expected no less than full commitment from her daughter. That she obtained it with such results made her chest swell with pride.

Valdor had not overcome his grief for the loss of his firstborn son. To console himself, he travelled to Eboracum, where Caurus had received a Christian burial. His father's dearest wish was to have the coffin exhumed and transported to Vectis where Caurus had grown up and romped happily as a youth. Valdor had plans for an underground family tomb. He wanted a loculus there for himself next to one reserved for Sfava. His grade as a Count, even though he was retired, still carried weight, so he was able to organise the exhumation and obtain a cart and an escort of four men, led by a centurion—an honour befitting his rank.

The journey was long and slow and conducted with sobriety, which scarcely helped to make the time pass quicker. At last, they sailed across the Solent, unaware that hostile eyes were watching.

The sad procession made the last stage of the journey up Robin Hill to the little church, where the priest awaited to conduct the transfer from coffin to sarcophagus. A score of people: family, friends and labourers and the escort attended the solemn service, carried out with full Christian rites. It proceeded with incense, blessings, anointing and prayers in a most comforting fashion, until the door burst open and, accompanied by war cries and oaths, a throwing axe flew across the sacred space and planted itself between a labourer's shoulder blades. The irony being that the worker was a pagan and only at the service to please his master. In truth, he remembered the deceased as a friendly and curious young man before he travelled north to join the army and wished to give him a personal final salute. He could never have imagined how final.

They were under attack from pagan islanders who could no longer tolerate a Christian church on their isle. It was an affront to the gods even if the Roman farmer was a kind and honest man.

The first to react was Lavinia, who sprang over to the fallen labourer and tugged the bloody axe free from his body. The Roman legionaries were armed, as was Valdor, although none had a shield. Still, as trained fighting men, they soon accounted for several of the intruders. Sfava allowed Valdor to kill one before springing over to snatch up his strange long, curved sword, probably from the east and bartered with a foreign trader. She used it to devastating effect and, before long, the pagans were driven outdoors and the church emptied except for the sarcophagus and the despairing priest. Out of the corner of her eye, Sfava saw Lavinia bend to wrest a sword from the grip of a dead pagan. She knew her daughter could handle it very well, but cursed that she had not had the time to teach her everything she knew. Meanwhile, Lavinia flung the throwing axe with deadly effect, planting it from distance into the forehead of an advancing foe. She had slain her first enemy in a single devastating gesture.

The numbers were now about equal, thanks to the skill and determination of the defenders. Even so, the day might have ended in tragedy had it not been for the escort's centurion. One of the pagans rushed at Lavinia with a spear and was about to deliver a mortal thrust when the quick-witted centurion used his gladius as a throwing weapon and hurled it so forcefully and accurately that it buried its blade deep in the islander's chest. Lavinia's eyes met the centurion's dark grey ones fleetingly in a smile of gratitude. He was now unarmed, so she placed herself between him and an onrushing attacker. To the centurion's amazement, the mere slip of a girl agilely sidestepped the thrusting spear and delivered a backhanded upward swipe of her sword to slash the man's throat. She had killed her second enemy and it had been so easy! Blood lust throbbed in her veins and sent her searching for her third victim. She found him, too, hard-pressed by her mother, but a tall, thuggish-looking brute. Lavinia would take no risk that he might prevail and showed no pity by approaching him from behind like a stalking feline, where she drove her blade deep and fatally into his unsuspecting back.

She gained no recognition, at that moment, from Sfava, who was already turning to continue the battle with one of the few remaining foes. Soon, the battle was over and Valdor, who had admired his daughter's exploits, hurried over to her.

"Well done, my little princess!"

She loved it when he called her this; it meant he was proud of her. She was trembling and he put his arm around her.

"It's normal," he said, "you relax after the battle and all that pent-up tension is released. Sometimes, it still affects me." He lied to make her feel better.

"Lord, your daughter is a tigress!" It was the centurion, but she wouldn't thank him in front of her father for saving her. That would have to wait for another moment. Already, Valdor wasn't keen on her being a warrior. If he thought that she had come close to death in the encounter, he would lock her away for her own safety! She gazed into the centurion's smouldering dark eyes and her heart skipped a beat. Instead, she limited her thanks to him for bringing her brother home and helping to save the church. "If we had lost the battle, the pagans would have burnt the church to the ground," she said gloomily. "I can't understand it, they were our customers, father."

"Not anymore," he said gloomily and pointlessly.

"Centurion, what is your name? I'm Lavinia," she gave him a radiant smile.

"Maximus Decimus, at your service," his smile revealed white even teeth and made him look even more handsome.

"Bring your men indoors, Centurion," Valdor said, "You've earned some draughts of my best wine. We produce it here, you know," he waved a vague hand in the direction of the neat vineyard. "We've lived here for three years and never had any trouble," he said reflectively, as if to himself.

The centurion was profuse in his praise for Valdor's wife and daughter's prowess, saying, "Woe betide any other ill-meaning intruders—word will spread far and wide that Count Valdor's family are a force to be reckoned with," he smiled at Lavinia. "Your brother was my friend, you know? That's why I volunteered to accompany him on his last journey. I'm so glad that I did," his smouldering dark grey eyes left her in no doubt what he meant by that and her stomach felt as if a hand was squeezing it.

Her parents went outside, determined to finish the service so rudely interrupted. Valdor was explicit, "Lavinia, you stay here and look after our guests. Maybe they would appreciate something to eat."

As soon as they went out the door, Lavinia turned to the centurion, "Centurion, forgive me, I have not thanked you for saving my life. What a throw that was! I dared not speak in front of my father. He doesn't appreciate me taking after my mother. She was a shield maiden with the Jutes—the daughter of a jarl."

"Mother and daughter are both formidable. I was just lucky. Would you believe it, I've never thrown a gladius. Let's say, it went well for us; equally, it could have been a disaster. I doubt that it will be a technique I'll refine. I couldn't stand by and allow such a beautiful creature to be skewered!"

"Do you truly find me beautiful, Centurion?" She forced the words out and flushed as she checked under lowered eyelashes that his men were not following their conversation.

"Astonishingly!" he said, it was only one word, but laden with promise to her ears.

"Then, you must come and visit us often. Oh, but it's so far from Eboracum!" she wailed.

"But not far from Portus Adurni! As soon as I return to Eboracum, I'll ask for a transfer. Maybe your father could organise it. He's a count, so I'll be careful not to betray the real reason for my request."

"Oh, he won't mind, Centurion. He would rather that I was betrothed than a shield maiden."

"Call me Maximus. That's it then. I'll ask him for your hand!"

"Oh, come into the kitchen, away from your men!"

She kissed him passionately in front of the burning logs and the affair was settled. Three months later they wed in the villa's little church. After a year of wedded bliss, across the water on Portus Adurni, Lavinia bore him a son, Primus, respecting her father's desire to 'Romanise' the family as he had shown in naming her Lavinia, and not Namuta after his mother. Nineteen months later, she bore him a second son, named Leo because she wanted him to be a little lion. As they grew, she swore that she would prepare them to be warriors just as her mother had prepared her.

I

PORTUS ADURNI, AD 328

VALDOR'S INTENTION HAD BEEN FOR HIS FAMILY TO REMAIN united on Vectis, which he considered a healthy place to live. He sorely missed his daughter and her boys, yet they were only across the strait from the isle, a voyage of less than an hour in favourable conditions. He gazed around at the perfectly ordered rows of vines—not a weed in sight—and his smile was self-satisfied. There was always a price to be paid for such commitment and always work to be done on the farm; leaving his livestock and the plants for any long period of time was out of the question, yet he regretted not seeing Primus and Leo and their parents often enough.

The boys had grown into strong youths, and while he had qualms about his daughter becoming a shield maiden, he had no problem with his grandsons going through the same arduous training routine that his wife had imposed on his daughter. Lavinia was just as hard a taskmistress as her mother had been. There was little to choose between the prowess of Primus and Leo. Despite being nineteen months younger than his firstborn, occasionally Leo could prevail in mock combat over his brother. Both were unbeatable by the other youths in the Roman fortress of Portus Adurni. Lavinia had impressed upon them not to let their superiority go to their heads. "Nothing is more precious than comradeship," she stressed. For this reason, the boys were popular with the others and befriended the bravest among them.

Another reason that Valdor was relatively happy about Lavinia and her sons living in Portus Adurni was that he had overseen the construction of the fortress, and while he knew from his own experience that no stronghold was impregnable, it would take a mighty army to overcome those defences. Also, Lavinia's choice of husband could not have been better; Centurion Maximus Decimus reminded the Count of himself as a young officer: hard but fair and respected by his men.

Portus Adurni was literally a backwater in Britannia, and the Empire was so vast. The news that filtered through to the people living in the fortress came principally through chatting with seamen, especially the traders who infrequently arrived.

Tempted down to the harbour by the arrival of a merchant ship, Lavinia invented an excuse to chat with the owner of the vessel. A corpulent man, his belly stretching his yellow tunic to the extent that Lavinia feared the stitches would cede, the trader's face, ruddy under the weathered tan, split into a broad grin. Only in his unsettled dreams in his small cabin did he meet with pretty young women like this one, so he was eager to chat.

"Whence have you sailed, captain?" she asked.

"We have come from the east, from a distant isle named Cypros. We have goods that might interest a fine lady like you: spices, scents and a special drink. It's made from almonds and orange flower water, you'll love it!"

"I'll buy some of your wares, but first, what news do you have? Is Emperor Constantine well?"

"Never better! You will not have heard of the recent great naval battle in the Bosphorus between him and Licinius. It was a great victory for Constantine, who went on to capture Byzantium..." The shrewd piggy eyes of the trader studied her face, "Of course, you have no idea, I'll wager those names mean nothing to you."

"My husband speaks of Byzantium, but the others..." her voice trailed off lamely.

"What it all means, my lady, is that Constantine has united the Eastern Empire with the Western—all under his own person!" He lowered his voice and gazed around, reminding Lavinia of the washerwomen at the river when they embarked on scurrilous gossip. "Are you a Christian, my dear?"

"Indeed, I am."

"Well, so is Constantine, but don't let him fool you!" He lowered his head so that his double chin reminded her of a drawing of a pelican she had seen in a villa fresco. She stifled a laugh and looked serious, raising an eyebrow, which was all the encouragement he needed.

"Some say that our emperor Constantine was originally a devotee of Apollo as Helios or Sol Invictus and suggest he came to associate him with the God of the Christians. They say he believes that Christianity with its single god can provide the basis for a sole cult that unifies the Empire. He regards the Christian god as a war god, who brought him victory over Maxentius and Licinius. I'm not saying that I believe all these voices, but look at this!" He took a coin out of his purse, and although Lavinia reached out to take it, his podgy hand clenched into a fist around the golden piece.

"Oh-ah, forgive me, it's very valuable. No offence, but just look." The sausage fingers unclenched, and Lavinia leant forward to peer at it, "Well, what of it? Isn't that Constantine's profile?" she asked.

"Ay, it is, but here's the point..." Delicate despite their podginess, two fingers turned the coin over. He explained, "See here, the reverse represents the Daphne mythos to indicate the transformation of the old capital, Rome, into the new capital, Constantinople. The deity might be Victoria, not Daphne, who knows? But she is holding a laurel branch, so my guess is that it's Daphne, and a palm branch, do you see?" His head was almost touching Lavinia's, and she could smell a syrupy sweet scent of almonds on his breath. "Why do you think the goddess is turning away from the captive at her feet?" he asked confidentially. "Does the palm branch stand for Christianity? I'm a Christian, too, dear lady."

"I know very little of what goes on in the wide world, but, captain, you hold proof in your hand that cannot be gainsaid."

He gave her an ingratiating smile, somewhat oily. "I would invite you aboard, but it's no place for a lady. Wait here, I have a surprise for you."

He reappeared moments later, carrying a bottle in one hand and a beaker in another. He emanated the smell of almonds as he spoke. "This here, my lady, they call *the drink of happiness!* It is a syrup made of a barley-almond blend. All you need is to add water, and it's ready to drink. The Cypros natives call it Orgeat Syrup. I'm fond of it myself. To be honest, I can't get enough of it. Here, what do you think?" He handed her the beaker, and she sipped tentatively, but soon drained the lot.

"I'm pleasantly surprised," she admitted, smiling. "I must buy some bottles from you, but oh, I came to the harbour without my wicker basket."

"Fear not, my lady, I have baskets enough and will carry your purchases up there, myself. Here, will you have another drop while I tell you more about the emperor?" His voice lowered again as he carefully poured another beaker at her nodded assent. "Did you know that Constantine has erected a statue of his mother Helena at the sanctuary of Apollo at Daphne in Syria Palaestina? They say it was founded by Seleucus I many, many years ago. It's a most important religious site, and it makes me wonder…" his voice became a whisper, and the small eyes shifted around, "whether Constantine is the Christian he pretends to be. I'm of the opinion that he considers himself the new Seleucus or even," he cleared his throat apologetically, "…the new Jesus Christ, but then, what do I know? Now," he said hastily, "apart from the drink of happiness, can I interest you in the scent of sandalwood? It's really special, and the oil comes from India. I was lucky to find it on Cypros. How many bottles of Orgeat Syrup? Six, ten?"

She had never smelt sandalwood but immediately adored the perfume. True to his word, the merchant followed her up the steep trail with a large basket containing ten bottles of the liquor. Soon, he was red-faced and panting heavily. Lavinia told him to sit on a rock, guard the basket, and wait. She'd find one of her sons and send him running to fetch the burden.

As she continued alone, Lavinia reflected on her conversation. It had been refreshing to hear his chatter about distant places, produce, and politics. She hoped that he was wrong about the emperor still clinging to pagan beliefs. It would be a disaster if he suddenly began to persecute Christians as his predecessor had done.

Standing before the gate, trying to catch a gateman's eye, she chided herself for her foolishness. Diocletian had never been baptised, but Constantine had adopted his mother's faith. Surely, there was nothing to fear. Inside the compound, she found Primus practising archery. The four arrows he had fired were neatly grouped in the centre of his target. She felt a surge of love and pride, waited for him to shoot another arrow equally effectively, and only then said,

"Primus, I need your muscles." She explained, and he thrust the bow into her hand before setting off at a run. She decided to retrieve the arrows and went back to his mark, thrusting the darts into the sandy soil at her feet. One by one, she aimed at the target and smiled at her accuracy, which was not inferior to her son's. *My mother taught me well, and I have done the same for my boy. Boy? Nay,* she sighed heavily, *he's a man and soon he'll fly the nest to fight somewhere, and I'll worry about him!*

In a remarkably short time, Primus returned with the basket and laughed, "Yon great bladder of lard could barely stand from his perch on that rock. I had to haul him to his feet. But he's a kindly sort. He told me that the basket is a gift to you and that he could scarce believe that you were old enough to have a son my age."

"It's not every day I receive a compliment, Primus. Perhaps you could practise on me, so that you'll be ready to win the heart of a maid when you find one to your taste."

Primus did not reply; she saw that he was occupied by staring at the target. He had a fine eye for detail and turned to grin at her, "You fired those arrows! I remember how I clustered mine. But you are a fine archer, mother." He paused and reflected, grinned, and said, "There you are, see, I do compliment you, and my words are sincere."

They both laughed, and she took the basket from him, but he gently retrieved it to carry to their quarters. Alone there, his face suddenly became serious. She recognised the expression, and it worried her.

"What is it, Primus?"

"Mother, has father told you why he's giving me riding lessons?"

"I didn't know he was!"

"Ay, and Leo, too. It's because the army will send for me soon. The Scoti are constantly raiding the coast of Cumbria, and the legion is gathering reinforcements. Father says that we'll go together, but not Leo, just me and him. Leo kicked up a fuss, but father is adamant. He says that Leo is to stay here with you for another two years. Do you know, my brother's sulking. We haven't exchanged a word for three days. It's not my fault, is it?"

"I'll talk to him…and to your father, too. He has no right not to inform me about decisions that affect our family. Do you feel ready to fight the Scoti, Primus?"

"While they are raiding into Britannia, I do. I'm not sure I'd feel the same about invading into Hibernia. I don't think it'll come to that, though."

"Wouldn't it be better if you trained here for another year?" she said hopefully.

"Nay, what's to be gained here? Not even the centurions can match me in practice fights, not even father. I'll be ready as soon as I've learnt to wield weapons on horseback better. At the moment, it doesn't come naturally to me. Father says that it's the cavalry that must stem the incursions along the Cumbrian coast."

I'm only thirty-five, and I can ride. Let's see if Maximus can stop me going to Cumbria!

Lavinia could think of nothing else for the rest of the day and went over her tactics several times until she decided that she would employ all her feminine wiles to get her way. Leo need not be a problem. She had an idea for him, too.

She waited until bedtime to launch her attack on Maximus. Since he didn't appear to be in an amorous mood, she waited until his breathing became more regular before snapping, "Didn't you think to tell me?"

That stopped him falling asleep.

"What, my love?"

"That you are going to take Primus to fight the Scoti and leave me and Leo to rot here!" Her tone was very sharp, so he sat up and lit a candle.

"I was going to tell you when Primus becomes a proficient cavalryman."

"Then, we'll all leave for the north together."

"That's out of the question! Leo isn't ready."

"We'll transfer Leo to one of the forts along Hadrian's Wall, where he can finish his training and grow stronger."

"I won't allow you to risk your life against the Scoti, Lavinia."

"Humph!" She turned her back on him and shuffled to the edge of the bed, shrugging off his advances. She had known all along that it would be a slow process to wear him down. But she had done enough for one day; also, she would let the matter be until he made the mistake of trying to make love to her again.

He probably suspected her ploy because he didn't try for three nights until she had the idea of sprinkling her new sandalwood scent on her bare flesh. He couldn't resist that, so she let his kisses become passionate before pushing him away.

"There's a price to pay, Maximus. Right now, I don't love you, and I'm thinking of leaving for Vectis." She was bluffing and held her breath while her words took effect.

"You don't mean that! In any case, what difference will it make if I am in Cumbria? Vectis or Portus Adurni, it's the same thing."

"Nay, you will not throw away the comfort of a loving wife, just to satisfy your male stubbornness."

As if to prove her words were not empty, she surprised him by straddling him and making passionate love. When they lay exhausted and embracing, she stared into his eyes with an inquisitive expression.

"All right, you win!"

She laughed, "There was never any doubt about that!"

"There are two conditions, though."

"What?" She sat up and stared down at his jutting jaw.

"You promise that you'll fight shoulder-to-shoulder with me against the Scoti."

"I promise. Someone has to look after you!"

"Have you forgotten? It was I who saved your life against the pagans?"

"And the other promise?"

"That you'll take me again like that tomorrow. Now I need to sleep."

He didn't wait for a reply as he was already snoring.

The entire family and four horses took a ship with stable bays for Branodunum the following week. From that fortress, the plan was to ride along a Roman road across the moors into Cumbria and the small temporary fortress of Mediobogdum that commanded the Eskdale Valley and the Roman road to Glannoventa naval base.

2

BRANODUNUM AND MEDIOBOGDUM, AD 328

As their ship nosed into the harbour at Branodunum, Lavinia pointed to the fortress, whose nearest walls came almost up to the quay, and said to her sons, "Your grandfather served here, you know. He was a dear friend of the emperor at the time. It was here that he was raised to the rank of a centurion. At the time, he was only two years older than you, Primus."

"We should get the horses," Primus said grumpily. He didn't want to be compared with anyone, least of all his famous grandfather, who had become Count of the Saxon Shore. He often prayed to the Lord that he would have the opportunity to display his worth, but as he looked sidelong up at the gate towers on his way to the stables, he doubted very much that his chance would come here, at Branodunum.

The entrance to the fort was so close that there was no need to mount the horses. The family of four led the beasts by their bridles into the stronghold.

"I need to speak to the commandant," Maximus said. "You three find yourselves something to eat and drink. I'll join you soon." Branodunum was a sufficiently large fortress to accommodate civilian activities, hence the market stalls and the tavern, where they tied their horses to a railing and ordered a meal. Surprisingly, Maximus joined them after only a few minutes.

"The prefect was very helpful," he said, brandishing a scroll. "He had a fellow copy this for me."

"What is it, father?" Leo asked.

"A rough sketch of our route across the moors. To be honest, he wanted to provide me with a scout, but I turned him down. He tried to convince me to take an escort of ten men, but I refused."

"Why?" Lavinia asked. "Surely, he knows the dangers of this area better than you?"

"True, but I felt that an armed party of fourteen would attract more hostile attention than a group of four travellers."

"In any case," Primus blustered, "We four can fight off a band of twenty ruffians."

"I fear it's not brigands we need to look out for; the prefect spoke to me about Scoti. It seems that they have raided to within a score of leagues of this base. Last year, the Dalmatian cavalry based here won a glorious victory over Irish raiders."

"I wish I'd been a part of that glorious victory," Primus said, although his words were muffled by a mouthful of bread and cheese.

Maximus warned him sternly, "Don't be in a rush for glory, my lad, you'll get plenty of opportunities here in the north and warfare isn't a game, you know." He took a swig of red wine and looked appreciatively at his beaker, "Strong stuff!"

"Let me have a look at the sketch, husband." Lavinia studied it thoughtfully. "It's farther than I thought. At least ninety leagues; that'll take us four days from dawn to dusk! Couldn't we have sailed nearer?"

"The voyage around the north of Pictland to the western coast is too hazardous. As was the Irish Sea route. We'll buy a packhorse, some provisions and a couple of tents this afternoon. Tomorrow, we'll leave at dawn. If you can't face the journey, my love, you and Leo can always return to Portus Adurni on the same ship."

She glared at her husband, "You don't think I'd leave you to ride into danger alone? You know you need me as a bodyguard!"

Primus sniggered and received a playful cuff from his father, "You've drunk enough of that red wine, young fellow! Let's go and make our purchases."

The tents would have been a problem, but a stallholder pointed out that a centurion should be able to sign out a couple of tents at the military stores.

"Of course," Maximus muttered, "we're on army business, after all."

The tents were heavy-duty leather shelters.

"These are proof against this vile climate," the storeman said sourly. "They were specially requisitioned for the north of Britannia. How I miss my warm Sicilia! Centurion, take a couple of sheepskin rugs as barriers against the damp earth, too."

Using the same argument that he was on military business, Maximus saved money by requisitioning a packhorse. He arranged to collect it the following morning. Meanwhile, his family wandered around the market stalls, where Primus bought himself a small crucifix on a silver chain. He kissed the effigy of the crucified Lord and hung it around his neck. "It'll protect me in battle," he explained to his mother.

"Nay, my training will protect you in battle. Always remember, concentrate on your enemy's weaknesses and you'll prevail, but Primus, concentration is the key to overcoming an enemy who wants to kill you as much as you want to slay him."

Listening carefully, Leo shuddered and thought, *maybe it's a good thing I'll have another couple of years before I'm called upon to fight.*

They slept in the barracks that night. Lavinia thought that the hard wooden pallet was a far cry from her comfortable bed back in Portus Adurni, but she didn't doubt for a moment that she had made the correct decision to insist on accompanying her husband and sons.

They travelled sixteen leagues inland on the first day, camping near a brook in a shady dell. The tents proved remarkably windproof and they all blessed the warm sheepskin rugs the storeman had persuaded Maximus to take. Encouraged by the choice of overnight stopping place, the next night, Maximus decided on a woodland clearing, again by a babbling stream. However, it wasn't the wisest choice because during the night, wolf howls close to the tents had them reaching for their weapons. Nothing happened, but it took Lavinia some time to relax and fall back to sleep.

This episode served to keep them alert to possible dangers, although Maximus was blasé about the wolves, saying that they rarely attacked humans. Still, by the late afternoon of the fourth day, they had come to within sight of their destination. At that stage, none of them could imagine what a relief it would be. Maximus had heard tell that the fortress, nestling into a precipitous hillside, was originally built in the reign of Emperor Hadrian, but about a hundred years ago it was abandoned, only to be reopened as a temporary base, housing Dalmatian cavalry from Branodunum. Given its history, Maximus did not expect to find such comfortable accommodation.

"You have had an arduous journey," stated the camp commander, surprisingly a legate, not a centurion. "If you go back out of the south gate to the west, where you entered, you'll find a track off the road at about 200 yards. It takes you to a bathhouse. I find there's nothing quite like a relaxing rest in the *laconicum* after a long time in the saddle. I'll have a servant bring clean towels."

Weary and saddle-sore, they walked slowly to the stone bathhouse, made up of four rooms. At the nearest end, a room contained a furnace, the others, a hot, warm, and cold bath. To the left was a circular structure, which the soldiers called 'the sweat room'. This was the laconicum. Lavinia and Maximus made their way straight there, where they stripped off their dusty clothing. Although she would not have been too bothered because it was normal for men and women to share the facility in communal nakedness, Lavinia was pleased to see that there was nobody else in the room, perhaps because of the time of day. Her sons decided to progress through the three pools from hot to cold. In both cases, the aches and pains accumulated by the long ride were eased, and now they were hungry, but comforted by the legate's invitation to a meal in his residence near the headquarters. This was a stone building at the centre of the fort with its own courtyard. Since they had time on their hands before this appointment, Lavinia suggested a visit to the small temple. This columned building contained the garrison's standards and various dedicated altars, mostly to Roman gods, but Primus immediately strode over to a granite altar, where a silver cross shone in the dim evening light. He knelt and bowed his head. Leo, instead, to his father's amusement, knelt before the altar to Mars—the Roman god of war. He wondered what was going through the youngster's head. Whatever it was, he would ensure a proper military education for him within the safety of the stronghold. It was one of the topics he wished to raise with the legate at dinner. Lavinia joined her eldest son at the Christian altar, where she muttered some prayers. At this point, Maximus, whose devotion was a personal mix of Christian and pagan, bowed before the statue of Minerva, where he whispered a prayer, pleading for the wisdom to decide his family's future for the best.

To the left of the headquarters stood the commander's residence, a large house with a courtyard, as befitting his rank. Before entering, they all strode around the stronghold, familiarising themselves with the layout: the granary, elevated on piers for air circulation and vermin control, and its entrances with raised platforms onto which the carts carrying grain were unloaded. Behind the headquarters were leather tents, like their own, to supplement the accommodation offered by the stone and timber barracks at the front of the fort. At each corner rose a watchtower. These were all joined by an earth walkway behind the external stone walls. The early evening sun, low in the sky, suggested why the majority of stallholders was packing their goods for the night.

Maximus did not expect a delicious meal in such spartan surroundings, although it was no great surprise that the meal began with fresh oysters as the road led straight to the coast, less than an hour away. The roast kid with carrots, parsnips, and celery and bread was a delight for their hungry stomachs. A fig and quince paste with anise, fennel seed, cumin, and toasted sesame wrapped in fig leaves made for a delicious dessert. The meal was accompanied by the familiar strong red wine. The Italian wine was fortified by the fermentation of local elderberries.

Over the meal, the legate made it clear that a new centurion was a welcome addition to his force, not to mention the two young men.

"Nay, Legate, although two is the correct number, one is a woman. My younger son will not fight, he is not ready."

"A *woman!*" the legate spluttered. "You are jesting, surely."

"Tomorrow, choose your champion and pitch him against my wife. If you wish to make the clash more interesting, I can accept a wager."

"By the gods! You are not jesting! Well, we'll see what happens in the morning!"

Maximus proposed one gold piece as the bet.

The following morning, in the centre of the parade ground, just over 200 yards to the east of the fortress, Lavinia prowled in a circle around the tall, muscular figure of a legionary. This man stood still, bulging biceps folded across his chest and a supercilious expression on his face, as if the whole exercise was a waste of time. Egged on by the catcalls and jeers of the encircling ring of comrades, still he did not move. She continued her stalking gait, oblivious to the insults directed her way, her concentration unwavering. Her movement was hypnotic and as she passed for the tenth time behind the statuesque warrior, she suddenly darted sideways and delivered a cracking blow with her practice sword to the nape of his neck. A deafening silence fell on the assembled crowd as their hero staggered forward and collapsed face down in the dirt. She was on him in a flash, smashing blows on his unprotected skull.

Maximus rushed forward, grabbed her arm and hauled her, snarling, to her feet.

"Enough, Lavinia! You don't want to slay a helpless man," he stared into her wild, savage eyes and watched as she emerged from her trance-like state of aggression. She stood, head bowed, hardly aware of the thunderous applause and cheers from the legion, which had recovered from the shock of seeing its hero beaten.

The legate came forward to honour his debt by pressing a gold coin into Maximus' hand. The proud husband whispered in her ear, "This coin is yours. I'll give it to you later."

"Your son Leo will finish his training here at Mediobogdum, but your wife will ride with the cavalry at the next Scoti incursion. Centurion, you will command the third cohort; be careful that the men follow you and not your wife!" The legate guffawed, but he was not entirely joking.

3

MEDIOBOGDUM, CUMBRIA AD 328

THE NEW DAY BROKE WITH A HEAVY DEW OUTSIDE THE fortress, whose interior did not contain a blade of grass except for the odd stray weed. It also began with a discussion between Maximus and the legionary responsible for stabling the horses.

The stubborn set of the man's jaw matched that of Maximus.

"I'm sorry, Centurion, but I'm not allowed to give you back your horses. It's regulations, you see. You'll have to have written permission from our commandant. It's quite clear, all horses withdrawn for a campaign must be the same breed: that is, from Lazio, the *Maremanno*. There's a good reason, they've been specially trained for combat and know how to behave. We can't just introduce other breeds into action alongside them, it would unsettle them. I can give you three Maremanni, no problem."

Maximus nodded mutely, recognising that there was no point in arguing. Besides, he quite liked the look of the sturdy breed with its thick mane and tail and, above all, the robust legs. If its temperament matched its build, it would be a fine mount. This regulation had not reached Portus Adurni—it was the first he'd heard of it—but then, in the south there was little call for cavalry as most raiders were repelled by infantry. He thanked the Lord that he'd heard about the cavalry's role in the north of Britannia. Forewarned, he had trained Primus, and himself, for that matter, to shoot and throw from the saddle—no easy feat because the Equites Romani did not use stirrups—but Lavinia had not joined in their session he reflected. *How will she cope in battle? Why did I yield to her insistence to come?*

These questions became more pressing when they went to withdraw their arms and armour. Lavinia's voice rose to a dangerous pitch, "And I'm telling you that I don't want a *hasta*, it's too long and heavy. I'm a skilled archer and I'll be more use with a bow and arrows."

"The fact is, lady, we attack in formation with spears. If you refuse the hasta, you must take a *lancea*; it's shorter and lighter and you can wield it for thrusting."

"Very well," she lowered her voice, "anything for a peaceful life!"

She was happy to take the *clipeus*, a light round shield. She could easily sling it over one shoulder as she rode and, that at least, removed one worry. She had not seen the cavalry in action and had stupidly regarded the large curved infantry *scutum* with horror. Rightly, she could not imagine managing one of those on horseback. She was also relieved to see the issuing of *spathae*, long swords suitable for mounted combat. *What use would a gladius be on horseback?*

Her husband had pulled on his laminated steel cuirass and she thought he looked magnificent, but she objected, "I can't wear *that!*" she was right, they did not have such a cuirass to fit her slender shoulders and accommodate her ample bosom. Under the guise of helpfulness, the storeman eyed her body with lustful eyes; nonetheless, it was he who found a solution.

"Lady, you cannot go into battle without armour. You would become the target of every enemy archer. Now that would be a shame," he eyed her attractive breasts and she glared at him. Unfazed, he said, "I'll tell you what we can do, I'll find the smallest mail shirt we have and see if we can squeeze you in." His eyes never left her breasts and she wanted to flatten his nose with a punch, but military discipline prevailed. Yet, in his own way, he was trying to help. The storeman lifted the heavy mail shirt over her head and onto her shoulders. She sagged slightly, rather taken aback by its weight. Next, he provided her with a helm, and best of all, a full quiver of arrows and a bow. Its draw weight was 80 pounds, unconvinced, he asked her, "Do you think you can cope?" risking her wrath.

"Were you there when I beat your champion?" she hissed dangerously. "Do not underestimate a shield maiden. My mother could have beaten three of those so-called champions at the same time!"

"Ay, I saw you defeat him. I'll tell you what, lady, I'm glad I'm not one of those Scoti raiders! But look here, I have an idea to help you. Bring your horse and we'll fit him with a leather harness that will carry your lancea so that your hands are free to shoot the bow. Of course, if your officer orders a charge, you'll set aside the bow and take up the lancea."

"You are a good man. I must bring you a present. How about the head of a Scoti?" she showed her teeth in more of a snarl than a smile. The storeman took two paces back and paled before hurrying off to search for the lancea support. He buckled the complicated belt around the horse's neck and flank, inserting the weapon in position himself. "There, see, lady, while the men are carrying their heavy hastae, you will have your hands free!" She slung the clipeus over her right shoulder and unashamedly led her horse to a mounting block because with the weight of her armour, she could not spring into the saddle. Once comfortably seated on her horse, Lavinia comforted herself at the sight of several cavalrymen using the same mounting block. She failed to recognise Primus among them, disguised by his cuirass and helm. She urged her horse close to Maximus' steed. The two animals snorted at the same time. *Was it a kind of greeting?* "So, what's the plan?"

"There are three cohorts, ours is number three. We all leave together and head towards the coast, then we'll separate in three different directions. The legate received reports of a Scoti incursion on the coast to the south of Glannoventa. We'll gallop along the road; do you think you can cope?"

"If anyone else asks me that, I swear I'll slay him on the spot!"

She rode on in silence, brooding on her sense of injustice. Nothing happened until she smelt the tang of salt in the air and saw seagulls wheeling in the sky. Then, the three centurions at the head of the cavalry halted the men behind and consulted each other. As the newcomer, Maximus deferred to the senior centurion in charge of Cohort One. "I'll continue on this road until we reach Glannoventa. You take Cohort Two down this trail and sweep the area between the sea and those hills, and you," he said to Maximus, "take Cohort Three as far as Gabrosentum Fort. You will find another cavalry unit there. The Scoti are not invisible: one of our cohorts will find and slay them. Do not allow them to escape out to sea."

Without wasting time, the three cohorts separated and Maximus dwelt on how best to scout the area designated to him. Before he had gone too far, he halted his force. His cohort contained 480 men. He had no idea how many Scoti had landed in Cumbria, but felt that he could cover more ground by dividing his men. He called over a decurion and, to his relief, saw that he was the champion who had confronted his wife. That defeat was not down to lack of valour but to underestimating a female opponent, so he would not judge him for that. "Decurion, divide the men into three groups. You will take charge of one group and lead them to the north east. Be sure to send out *exploratores* ahead of you. If they find the Scoti, immediately send for me."

He turned to Lavinia, "You will take Primus and keep him close to you. You will be in charge of another division. Lead your men direct north. I will take the final group and ride to the fort, which is on the coast. Remember to send *exploratores* ahead of your force, wife. God be with you."

"And with you, husband." Her earlier resentment had passed with this display of trust in her leadership abilities. She did not ask herself why he had insisted on keeping Primus near her. She supposed he was concerned at the youth's safety, not the other way around. The three divisions separated in the indicated directions.

Lavinia soon discovered that apart from settlements associated with the coastal chain of forts, Cumbria consisted of sparsely populated scattered rural settlements. These were situated where good agricultural ground could be found and were mostly family units. The first such land she came across was in the Esk valley. Her *exploratores* had found a ford across the river, which the horses willingly waded. She noticed that ahead, directly north the terrain became mountainous and rocky, probably unfit for farmsteads. Before long, they arrived at a track that led eastwards towards a lake or tarn, according to one of the men, who had patrolled the area from Mediobogdum Fort. He insisted that the lake made a dead end since the land beyond was uncultivated. It was there that she noticed movement that her scouts had missed or had not followed the trail in that direction. Was the light playing a trick on her, or had she noticed a human form dart away to the right?

She had laid her bow along the lancea, so now raised it and, urging her horse into a gallop, matched only by Primus, headed towards the fork in the trail. Sure enough, when speeding into the new trail, she spied a man running, looking over his shoulder occasionally. She took careful aim, not wanting to kill him, but to bring him to a halt. Her precise arrow took the fugitive in the back of his right thigh. Over the beating hoofs, they both heard his scream and saw him fall, clutching his thigh. Soon they were upon him. Lavinia halted her horse a few paces away from the red-haired man with desperate eyes and called to Primus, "make him talk, but do not slay him. I'll fetch the others." She wheeled her horse and galloped away back along the trail. She found them immediately, waiting at the fork in the trails. A sharp command had them all following her back to Primus, who they found kneeling over the fallen raider.

"Well?" Lavinia asked her son.

"He has a lot to say for himself when I play with the arrow in his flesh. It seems that they came over from the Kingdom of Dalriada in two boats. He was sent as a scout to make sure no Roman force came from the fort where father is bound. They have gone down this trail in search of plunder because they found enclosures with crops and others with livestock."

"Two boatloads. I have 160 men, less the *exploratores*, so 150. We can defeat them for sure." Then, she remembered her husband's words *if you find the Scoti, immediately send for me.* She selected a rider, "Find Centurion Maximus and bring him here." She wondered whether to follow the trail to the farmstead or to deploy her men among the trees north of the track in case the raiders returned. She could ambush them in that case. *Besides,* she reasoned, *I have only the word of this captive, under duress, that there were only two boatloads. What if there were more and we ride into a trap?* She ordered her men to spread out into the trees and to keep their horses quiet.

"What about him, mother?" Primus looked up at her.

"Cut his throat." She did not want him screaming a warning if the Scoti returned.

Primus drew a knife from his belt, but hesitated, so Lavinia nocked an arrow and sent it winging to bury into the fellow's throat. A rapid gurgling cough was the last they heard from him. "At least dump the body in the nettles by the side of the road. We don't want any evidence of our presence. Oh, and Primus, sooner or later you'll have to slay a man if you want to follow in the footsteps of your parents and grandparents."

"Sorry, mother, it's just that—"

"Ay?"

"Well, I'd just been talking to him and it seemed more like murder than a killing in a fair fight."

"Get rid of the body and don't forget that you tortured him to get information."

She trotted her horse up to the trees, where, to her pleasant surprise, she found that the division was extremely disciplined and the experienced cavalrymen had soothed the horses into passive silence. It was as if the beasts could commune with each other and their riders.

She gently stroked her horse's jaw and then threaded her fingers into its forelock and massaged it gently. The horse did not whinny, which would have been normal, but maintained the communal silence, broken only by a twig snapping under the hoof of Primus' returning horse. He reined in beside her and whispered, "that's done. Now what?"

"We wait to see who gets here first, the Scoti or your father."

"How far inland do you think this trail leads?" Primus asked.

"Not far, according to one of our scouts who knows the area. It reaches a small lake and that's it," she whispered. "Is that smoke I smell?"

Primus sniffed dramatically, "I believe it is. I'll wager the Scoti have burnt the farmstead."

They did not have long to wait as the Scoti came marching into sight, driving cattle before them. Some of the raiders carried sacks slung over their shoulders and one of them played a strange instrument made of a pig's bladder, emitting a high wailing sound out of an attached pipe. The instrument and the lowing of the cattle allowed Lavinia to issue clear orders.

"Wait until the last man is level with us, then we charge down with *hastae* lowered and finish them from the rear." After this short speech, she freed her lancea and lowered it as an example. She could feel all eyes on her and appreciated the trust she had gained by overcoming their champion.

She was the first to break cover and plunge her spear into the chest of a surprised enemy, who, on hearing hoofs, had spun around to face the onrushing horse. Primus was next and his long spear impaled a screaming

Scot in the back. Soon, the horses were galloping alongside the running enemy, some of whom attempted to escape off the track, but were pursued and cut down by the *spatha*-wielding horsemen. Lavinia flung her lancea at one such fleeing warrior, missing the target by a fraction. So, she spurred her horse forward and used her long sword to finish him. Only then, on wheeling her horse around, did she consider that the original scout that Primus had tortured had spoken the truth. Luckily, there were only two crews of Scoti and her division had accounted for them in less time than it took to eat a meal. What she did not know was that there had been another six ships from Dalriada and that Maximus was fighting a desperate battle with his depleted force even as she considered what to do next.

The decision was taken for her by one of the returning *exploratores*, who informed her of a battle between the garrison of Gabrosentum and Maximus' division. "The Scoti have taken a defensive position on a marshy inlet into the estuary that reduces the advantage of being mounted," the scout explained.

"Lead us there," Lavinia ordered, "we might swing the battle in their favour."

"We'll be forced to fight on foot, once there," the scout advised.

"At a gallop!" she screamed, fearing for her husband.

They came to the Esk Estuary, where various streams joined the river to create a watery landscape. Quite what the Scoti had in mind when they chose this position eluded her. Was it an attempt to lure the garrison to defeat before plundering the land? Well, if that was the case, they would have a surprise, she promised herself. She heard the screams and other sounds of warfare before she saw the battle. The scout pointed and said, "Lady, it would be better to leave the horses here to graze. We can march into the enemy flank if we cross yon stream."

"Ay, I see it! Primus, you and the *exploratores* lead an attack on the flank. I have other plans!" She grasped her bow and dismounted; running in a crouch as fast as her heavy mail would allow, she splashed across a brook and came to a halt a hundred yards from the raging battle. Drawing back her first arrow, she took careful aim and released, watching with satisfaction as a battling Scot fell before the astonished eyes of his Roman opponent. She looked at her full quiver and decided that she must make every arrow count. As far as she knew, she was the only archer on both sides. She could see Primus leading his 150 men in a wedge formation into the flank of the enemy, but there was no time to waste being proud of her son.

She drew back another arrow and chose carefully as she could not afford to waste a single dart. Whoosh! It flew and buried itself in the axe-wielding arm of a foe. Like a springing lynx, his Roman opponent was on him in a flash, taking lethal advantage of Lavinia's aid. Another arrow pierced the neck of an onrushing Scot before he could strike a blow. Alone, Lavinia slew or wounded a score of Scoti. Her contribution did not win the battle on its own, but played an important role in turning the tide of battle, along with the force led by Primus. She had exhausted all her arrows, so threw the bow to the ground, drew her *spatha* and literally waded into the battle.

Whether the snarling, blue-faced Scot who rushed towards her had realised that she was the archer who had killed his comrades or not, she was not impressed by his size and aggression. She could not be her nimble fighting self, wearing heavy armour and moving laboriously on this swampy ground, but unslinging her *clipeus*, she faced him without fear because he, too, was struggling to keep his footing on the slippery mud. Her mail shirt came down to the elbow, so she had the freedom to use the wrist movements her mother had taught her. Her high-pitched scream altered the course of events.

The Scot suddenly realised that he was attacking a woman and, mistakenly encouraged, he rushed forward, oblivious to the fact that there could be no rushing on this treacherous surface. He slipped and fell headfirst in front of Lavinia. She would not repeat his mistake of over-haste, but could not afford to wait, so she tossed her shield to the ground, grasped the sword in both hands and launched herself forward in a dive that drove the blade like a descending spike between her adversary's shoulders, all her weight plus that of her armour was behind the plunging steel. The Scot died instantly.

Lavinia stood unsteadily, looking around to make sure she was not under attack. She placed a foot on the dead body, expecting it to be beyond her strength to remove her blade, but she was wrong, it slid out so easily that she almost fell backwards into the water. A well-placed leg maintained her balance so that at last, she could look around to see the grinning faces of a dozen Roman legionaries, one of whom, thankfully, was her husband. The battle was over. With various degrees of apprehension, they had watched her account for the great brute who had attacked her.

"You have lost none of your ability with a bow, wife!" Maximus splashed slowly towards her as she gathered up her shield. "Nor with a sword, it seems. I would hug you to me, but that mail shirt is somewhat off-putting."

"I can't wait to take it off," she said bitterly, reflecting that no blade had touched the steel rings. However, she could see Roman soldiers among the dead and recognised that she had played a peripheral part in the day's warfare and perhaps been lucky, although she would never admit it openly. Primus joined them, saying "Let's get back to the horses, I could do with a good soak in the bath-house right now."

"Well, that's a weight off my mind. You are safe, Primus."

She jested, but not too much, "now I could do with a weight off *my* shoulders!"

4

VECTIS AND VERCOVICIUM FORT AD 340-343

LEO'S INTENSE COMMITMENT TO ROMAN MILITARY TRAINING at Mediobogdum Fort saw him rise rapidly to the rank of decurion, but it also saw his transformation from handsome youth to irresistible man. At least, this was true for many of the British women from the vicus who made doe eyes at him. He reciprocated their interest by sowing his wild oats so profusely that claims about the paternity of three boys became the local gossip that partially drove him to seek a transfer to Hadrian's Wall. Partly, too, because he missed his family who were stationed in Cumbria at Glannaventa, the fortress guarding the Esk Estuary. There, Primus, less fancy-free than his brother, courted and married the commandant's daughter, of pure Roman lineage, a Mediterranean beauty named Silvia.

Doubtless because of his connections, the legate soon had his daughter's husband raised to the rank of tribune. About the time, in AD 340, when Leo transferred to Vercovicium Fort, at the centre of Hadrian's Wall, Silvia bore Primus a boy. His parents gave him a Roman name: Gaius. Naturally, Maximus and Lavinia were delighted and persuaded the young couple to undertake the voyage with them to Vectis so that they could show the infant to his great-grandparents.

Sfava took the babe in her arms and said, "I never dreamt that I'd live to see the son of my daughter's son! I have snow in my hair from the seventy winters I've survived. What a lovely name, does it not mean *rejoice?* There is much to rejoice about. Just wait, Lavinia, to see your father's face when he gets in from the fields."

Four years older than his wife, Valdor had outlived his dearest friends: Faldrek was the first to pass, murdered in Batavia while on duty; then, he lost his cousin at sea when a sudden autumn storm drove his fishing boat onto a rock. Johar's body was never found. Instead, Heidar had died on this farmstead of an apoplectic seizure, brought on, some said, by his over-indulgence in the red wine produced in Valdor's vineyard. He lay next to his gallant godchild, Centurion Caurus, sadly lost in action at Hadrian's Wall.

Sfava was correct, the elderly, but incredibly fit, Valdor did not know whom to greet first. He was so happy to see Lavinia and Maximus after all these years, but here, too, was his grandson, Primus, who had gone away as a youth, now with a son of his own—his great-grandson. "God has blessed me not only with a long life, but also with a fine lineage! And not only that, but I have the best land to cultivate in the whole of Britannia. This calls for a celebration! Bring my finest wine!" he ordered Heidar's son, his estate manager, a burly fellow in his mid-thirties.

The men shared anecdotes of battles fought, while the women spoke of child-rearing, although Lavinia recounted her exploits against the Scoti to her mother, a former shield maiden. It brought talk around to the missing member of the family, Leo. "The last I heard; my brother, who was a decurion at Mediobogdum, sought a transfer to the Wall. I think he wants to replicate the deeds of his late lamented uncle."

"What would he say if he knew you were a tribune?" Lavinia said proudly.

"Knowing Leo, he will do everything in his power to surpass me and become a legate."

Valdor's brow wrinkled into a frown and the deep lines were white, offset by the weather-tanned skin. "I'd love to embrace Leo before it's too late for one of us."

"Don't worry, grandfather, I'll make it my business to visit him at Vercovicium Fort. I'd love to embrace him myself. It's not all that far from Mediobogdum. I could get there by horse in a day." As he spoke these words, he could not imagine the circumstances that would reunite them.

Meanwhile, at Hadrian's Wall, Leo learnt of the birth of his nephew and his family's departure for Vectis. Mixed emotions passed through his breast because, in truth, he felt somewhat abandoned by his parents. He knew that they had left him at Mediobogdum for his safety and military education—for his own good—but his gratitude mingled with resentment and, the more he thought about his situation, the more he was determined to do something about it.

Always one with an eye for a pretty face, he decided that the time had come to emulate Primus and find himself a beauty to wed. Gossip spread from fort to fort, so he learnt that Primus' wife was a splendid Roman woman. His brother had done well for himself, but Leo would not choose a wife for betterment but for her allure. He found British women, especially the redheads, winsome. Vercovicium stood on the crest of an escarpment with steep drops on two sides. However, to the south and east lay an extensive vicus, a civilian area full of shops and workshops. The thriving community had its share of young Britons and it was there that Leo would cast his hook. Blessed by his extremely good looks, he was confident that he would succeed.

He wandered into the market area of the vicus to the south, his eyes roving, aware of the need to choose well, but also to charm his way to success. His roaming brought him to a stall where a most attractive redhead presided over a display of curvilinear jewellery. He smiled at her and was rewarded by a broad even-toothed grin.

"My dear," he said, "are these earrings silver?"

"Indeed, they are, decurion"—she understood his insignia, which pleased him— "hand-crafted in nearby Coriosopitum by my brother."

"Be an angel and lean over here, I wish to hold one next to your splendid locks, for my mother has similar colouring," he lied.

She obliged, bringing her face close to his. He moved slightly closer and stared into her deep green eyes, which met his blue ones unwaveringly.

"You are more beautiful than your jewels," he sighed, "don't tell me you are betrothed!"

"I am not, although it is no business of yours, Decurion."

"Call me Leo, what is your name?"

"I am Aoife. Well, are you going to buy these for your mother, Leo?"

"Nay, I lied; she's blonde. I just wanted to get closer to you! I'll buy them for *you*, Aoife; with your splendid locks, they become you."

"For me? But you don't know me."

"But I'd like to. How much? And when can we meet?"

She hesitated and frowned, "They are expensive. I can't afford them, myself—six denarii."

"*Six!*" He grinned, "I've fought Irish pirates less rapacious than you! But ay, I'll buy them, I want to see you wearing them offset by your glorious tresses," he shook silver coins from a bag into his hand and passed them to her. As her hand closed over them, his hand closed over hers and lingered there until she blushed. "Wear them for me," he pleaded. She obliged and asked, "Do you know the White Stag tavern? Meet me there this evening after sunset." She tilted her head in both directions, letting him admire the twinkling earrings, catching the afternoon sunlight that also brought the auburn highlights of her hair into play.

"My God! You are lovely, Aoife!"

"Are you betrothed, Decurion?"

"I am not and, as I'm new to Vercovicium, you had better give me directions to the White Stag."

"You can ask your comrades, many of them go there," she teased and gave her attention to a young woman enquiring about a brooch.

He strolled away without saying another word. *Best to let her worry!* Despite his nonchalance, sunset could not come soon enough. He thought about her glorious hair, oval face and small, upturned nose, lightly sprinkled with freckles. She was not tall, like the rest of her Celtic race, but slender and with even teeth highlighting a cheeky grin that had captured his heart, If Aoife would have him, he would wed her. True, he didn't know anything about her, except that she had a craftsman brother. So, his task that evening would be to find out as much as possible. *What does she do with her jewels at night? There's silver among the items, after all.*

At the fortress, he encountered a fellow decurion and said, "I'm new here, but I've got an appointment at the White Stag. Can you tell me how to get there?"

"Well, I suppose I can, but if you buy me an ale there, I'll take you, so you won't get lost."

"It's a deal! Although I prefer red wine."

"Like a good Roman!" he looked puzzled, "But you don't have Italian looks."

"My father's Roman, but I look like my mother, she's half Jutish and half Batavian."

"You're a right mix! But I'd say the ingredients have worked remarkably well! I'm a Tungrian, myself. The whole first Tungrian cohort is here. Come on, I'll introduce you to our centurion, he'll be pleased because, like you, he has a Jutish mother."

A pleasant fellow, the centurion had a Jutish name, Jerrik, and was quick to point out that Leo was a Roman name.

"Ay, my father is Roman. He's a centurion, too, and his name is Maximus. I think my mother didn't care about a name, but I can tell you, she did care about *fighting*. Like her mother, she was, well, is *still* a shield maiden."

"By the Oracle of Apollo! They are a dying breed, especially now that Christianity has a foothold in Jutland."

"Not much of a foothold from what I've heard, Centurion. The Jutes are still devoted to Woden."

"Whereas, you wear a crucifix, I'm happy to see."

"Tell me, are the Britons hereabouts Christians?"

"Many of the Britons in this area still talk proudly of King Lucius the Glorious. He's credited with introducing Christianity into Britain. But I'm not sure if he was real or a myth. They claim he had all of his people convert to worship Christ and I know that there is a Christian church in Coriosopitum."

"I have found myself a pretty Briton and I'm hoping she's a Christian."

"In the name of the Lord! You don't waste time Decurion Leo! How many days have you been here?"

Leo launched into an explanation about his newborn nephew, occasionally casting an anxious eye at the sinking sun. He made his excuses to the Centurion and called to Tungrian decurion friend, "It's time to go!"

On edge because there was no sign of Aoife in the tavern—Leo drank slowly as he did not want to appear tipsy when she arrived. His comrade from the Low Countries had no such qualms and repeatedly filled his beaker.

"So, who are you waiting for," the Tungrian asked.

"A woman I like, so don't take it amiss if I leave you alone when she arrives.

"I won't be alone. I have my little friend here," he patted the earthenware ewer affectionately.

"It's a deceptive wine, stronger than it seems at first. Don't let it fool you. Ah, here she is! I'll leave you for a while."

Her friendly grin immediately reassured Leo, who rose and took her arm, steering her to a corner table some distance from the decurion and slightly away from the eddy of people coming and going.

"Aoife, what would you like to drink? Are you hungry?"

"A beaker of mead would be nice and they make a nice honey cake here."

She smiled fondly at him when the innkeeper's daughter brought a whole honey cake and a jar of mead with two beakers.

"You are generous, Leo. A slice would have been quite sufficient."

"Only the best for you! Besides, you've been on your feet for hours. You must be tired and hungry."

She cut two slices and handed the larger piece to him. She was right, the honey cake was delicious, not too sweet, it melted in his mouth. Her eyes twinkled at his obvious enjoyment. After the red wine, the mead, however, did not suit him but he sipped at it to keep her company.

"Are you a Christian?" He fired the question by surprise.

"I am, along with all of my family. We are lucky, we have a church near our home at Coriosopitum. I was pleased to see that you wear a crucifix, Leo."

"I prayed the Lord that you would come to the tavern this evening... and here you are!"

Her eyes twinkled again. "Did you think I would not come?"

"There was a moment when it crossed my mind. It was a relief to see you enter, for my comrade, yon decurion, seems bent on getting drunk."

"Maybe he has some reason to be unhappy. You should find out, Leo."

"Not this evening. I don't want to waste a precious moment I can spend with you. But tell me; you say you live in Coriosopitum. Surely, you don't travel there every night?"

"Nay, I have quarters not far from the market. It would be dangerous to carry my wares through the streets, some of which are valuable." She touched an earring subconsciously. "I have a strongroom, where they are safe. I go home to my parents now and again and to pay my brother when I pick up some of his latest creations."

"He is very skilful, Aoife. My brother, Primus, wed a year ago. He made a very fortunate choice because his wife is beautiful, but also his commandant's daughter. It's no surprise to me that he has risen to the rank of tribune—"

"While you are a mere decurion!" she teased him, then, her face became serious, "are you jealous of your brother?"

"Nay, I love him. We grew up together..." he went on to describe how they separated against his will. He ended his account with, "...and now he has a boy...my nephew. I haven't seen him yet and don't even know his name," he ended lamely. Then, his face became determined and his chin raised, "I'll not be a decurion for long."

"How do you know that?"

"Because nobody can match me in a fight."

She looked at his muscular arms and her gaze seemed to weigh him up, "I can believe that. But tell me, do you wish to be like your brother?"

He laughed, "I don't know if my commandant has a daughter. In any case, I'm falling in love with a market trader!"

"Do you mean that, Leo? Isn't it too soon to make certain declarations?"

"Maybe, Aoife, but I've never felt so sure of anything in my life. Hark, it's not as if I haven't been with women before. Perhaps there have been too many, but never one like you!"

"I like you, too, Leo—very much, but I won't be rushed into betrothal." She poured herself another drink and as she sipped it, her eyes met his over the rim. The green seemed deeper by candlelight than it had outdoors in the sunlight, but now, maybe due to the low light, they seemed mysterious.

Is she distancing herself from me? I mustn't seem desperate to her or she'll run!

Despite his intentions, his tongue defied his brain, "Aoife, I'd like to meet you regularly."

"I'd like that, too, my decurion."

"Tomorrow, I'll come to the market, but I'm afraid that I won't buy anything."

"You've spent enough, today and I'm very grateful."

"How grateful?" He smiled roguishly and leant his face close to hers.

A moment's hesitation gripped her before she shared her first kiss. It was very chaste, but he was happy to content himself with that for the moment.

He spent the rest of the evening questioning her about her family, likes and dislikes and found that they shared a love of animals and nature. Gradually, a vision of the future with this woman gripped him and his conviction that she was the woman for him grew by the minute.

After meeting every day for two weeks, compatibly with his military duties, came the breakthrough. Aoife announced that she was going to Coriosopitum for a couple of days.

"I'll accompany you, my love. I'd like to meet your family."

"In that case, you must have serious intentions, Leo. My parents have sound values."

"Heed me well. I want you to be my wife. It's true that we have known each other for a short time, but it's enough. It feels so right to be with you...so easy."

He would have continued, but a middle-aged woman, dressed in expensive clothing and accompanied by perhaps her daughter, demanded Aoife's attention. She chose a pendant necklace for the younger woman and Aoife explained that the alternating stones were jade and jet. She outlined their meaning as Leo listened intently: "jade is associated with nobility and wealth, it is considered a protector of generations, whereas jet stands for good fortune and can bring clarity during tribulations. They are all strung on a silver chain."

"I'll take it," the matron said, "how much?"

A few minutes of bargaining followed, but Aoife obtained her asking price by encouraging the young dark-haired woman to clip the necklace around her neck. She held a mirror for her to admire the effect and the sale was made.

There followed a lull in trade and Leo pulled Aoife into his arms, kissing her passionately. It was their first real kiss and left her gasping, chest heaving. She looked him fiercely in the eyes as if challenging him. "That's it, then, we're betrothed. I will wed you, Leo."

Easier than selling jewellery, she clinched the deal with another kiss and agreed for him to travel to Coriosopitum the following day. He was pleased to discover that she could ride and had a pony that she part-owned with two other women. She had already made arrangements to take it for three days.

"Good, then I'll bring Cirratus."

"Who?"

"My horse. I gave him that name because of his curly mane. You'll see."

"Are you in the cavalry, then?"

"Ay, like my father and brother. We'll ride to Coriosopitum together and see whether your family will accept me."

5

HADRIAN'S WALL AND EBORACUM, AD 343

AOIFE'S FATHER, EARNAN, DEALT IN FURS AND TUSKS SHIPPED from Scandinavia. He made a good living from this trade, enough to set up his son, Aodh, with a fully equipped workshop and the materials to exploit his talent as a jewellery designer. The market at Vercovicium offered an outlet for his attractive creations with the additional benefit of providing work for his daughter.

After his wife's premature death, Earnan missed her; she spent more time in Vercovicium than in Coriosopitum. Yet, she seemed happy selling her brother's jewels, so he did nothing to change the arrangement. When she arrived accompanied by a Roman soldier, he struggled to quell his paternal jealousy. The decurion was clearly intelligent and ambitious but he was not a Briton. Earnan set great store by a traditional saying: *get oxen and spouses from your own town*; in that case, you knew what you were getting. This Leo was unknown to him and a newcomer to Vercovicium. There was no doubt that he was besotted with Aoife and his daughter seemed equally smitten. It was hard for the trader to find a valid objection except that Leo was not a Briton. He was relieved that the decurion was a Christian and impressed upon learning that his grandfather was a count.

The young man stressed that he would rise to a higher rank with a disarming confidence. He told Earnan that his brother, two years older than he, was already a tribune. Also, he had no objection to Aoife continuing her work if it was what the family desired. So, convinced by his daughter's obvious happiness, the trader gave his blessing to the betrothal.

The couple planned to be married within a month, but events north of the Wall delayed their espousal. High among the remote mountains and icy lochs, the Picts were fomenting raids that would take them as far as the wealthy city of Eboracum. They decided that the best place for a surprise attack was Vercovicium, whose garrison was largely made up of auxiliary troops, resentful of their frontier posting and disaffected with Rome. The Picts were well-informed, with many Britons preferring their Celtic 'cousins' to the Roman invaders. In the vicus, alcoves and portals made perfect places to huddle and conspire.

Tattooed with tribal symbols, the Picts advanced furtively at night up the escarpment and across the vallum, culminating in a ghostlike entry and passage through the Roman fortress. Aided by bribed disgruntled auxiliaries, who ensured the gates opened wide enough for this progress, facilitated by the sentinels' greedy consumption of strong wine mixed with appropriate herbs, meaning there was no need for their malcontented comrades to slit their throats. Instead, they would wake with a sore head and nauseous stomach.

The first the garrison knew of the Pictish arrival were reports of cattle raiding and plunder in farmsteads south of the Wall. In all haste, the legion was prepared and Leo, as decurion, was placed under the command of Centurion Jerrik. As a cavalry officer, Leo led a band of horsemen; their commander ordered them to scout the terrain and locate the enemy, then, to report for deployment.

Jerrik was brave and, like most centurions, led from the forefront. When Leo's scouts reported on the Picts holding a hilltop position ready for battle, Jerrik ordered Leo to circle with his cavalry to attack from the rear, but only after the infantry had engaged frontally. Obedient to this command, Leo unleashed his cavalry, himself to the fore, launching javelins from the saddle and hacking with spathae, throwing the Pictish formation into disarray. Despite his involvement in the battle, from his raised position on Cirratus' saddle, Leo spotted the eagle standard and saw Jerrik, next to it, fall to a spear thrust. Impulsively, he galloped to the standard, leapt down from his horse, slapping its rump to send it clear of the enemy. On foot, he took command of the infantry, yelling orders and setting an example by slaughtering any enemy brave enough to challenge him. A hard-fought battle ended in victory for the weary Roman garrison as the raiders' bodies littered the hillside, their typical H-shaped bucklers strewn among them.

Leo whistled shrilly and Cirratus, blessedly unharmed, trotted up to him. Proud in victory, from the saddle, Leo ordered the rounding up of the stolen cattle to have them driven to the fortress. The legion was abuzz with talk of Leo's valour and, as soon as he arrived in the fort, he received a summons to the quaestor's headquarters, where he received congratulations and promotion to the rank of Centurion, but that was nothing compared to circumstances lurking in the offing.

Unknown to those occupying the northern outposts, Flavius Julius Constans, unwittingly the last Roman emperor to travel to Britannia, had arrived in Eboracum. The youngest son of Constantine the Great, he had quarrelled over the sharing of power, which led to a civil war with his eldest brother and co-emperor Constantine II, who invaded Italy in 340 and was killed in battle by Constans's forces near Aquileia. Constans moved on to secure Gaul, campaigning against the Franks, and then, on hearing of Pictish and Scoti incursions into Britannia, decided to sail there and reorganise the administration to put an end to the problem.

Well-informed about events in his colony, the emperor learnt about Leo and his brother and gathered further information about them. On hearing that their grandfather was the famous Valdor, once the Count of the Saxon Shore and a close friend of his father, Constantine, Constans summoned the brothers, who had not met in years, to Eboracum. He had plans to restructure Britannia and these siblings were exactly the kind of people he had in mind for the job.

Before presenting himself to Constans, Leo sought out Primus, who also delayed the audience with the same notion to meet his brother. They embraced joyfully with Leo unable to contain his news.

"I know you are married, brother, and that lot will soon befall me. I am betrothed to a marvellous woman named Aoife."

"A Briton?"

"Ay, but a rare beauty!"

"Congratulations, then. When will you wed?"

Leo's lips pursed. "It depends on what the emperor wants of us. Do you have any idea?"

"Nay, I could have asked you the same question."

"Let's hope that whatever Emperor Constans wants will enable us to spend time together. I would like to meet your wife and my nephew."

Primus laughed, "You are right, surely fate can't keep us apart forever. Mother and father are well and our grandfather is remarkable for his age as is Sfava—she's still a lioness!"

"How I miss them all! Let's go together to see the emperor, Primus. I hear tell that he's remarkably young."

"Is that all you've heard? There are scurrilous tales circulating about his sexual proclivities."

"I give no credence to rumours, brother, especially where emperors are concerned. There are so many envious usurpers lurking in the shadows when it comes to the imperial purple."

"My, my, you have become wise beyond your years!"

Leo's sense of injustice reared its ugly head, "You're only two years older than I! It always was a bone of contention between us."

"Nay, that's in the past. Father was only trying to keep you safe, forget it!"

"I know, but I'm able to look after myself now."

"Ay, so I've heard. You're a centurion, too!"

Leo made no mention that Primus held the higher rank of tribune; he wasn't seeking a quarrel. So, they linked arms and walked to the palace, chatting about family and camp life.

The emperor was young, precisely twenty, so a decade younger than the brothers. Clean-shaven, with an oval face, his slightly wavy hair brushed forward in traditional imperial style since the days of the great Julius Caesar. His ready smile put the brothers immediately at their ease. Educated at Constantinople under the tutelage of the poet Aemilios Magnus Arborius, who instructed him in Latin, Constans was witty and erudite. His gentle, dark brown eyes studied the brothers openly.

"I have heard that you two conduct yourselves with courage and determination, as your grandfather did in his day. I know that he was *comes littoris Saxonici per Britanniam*. The role of Count of the Saxon Shore has remained vacant for a number of years, which is strange now that Britannia is subject to raids around its long coastline. This, gentlemen, is the purpose of my visit here. As Emperor of the Western Empire, I intend to ensure that Britannia is safe from barbarian assaults and, therefore, intend to fill the vacant post. You, Primus, are the new Count and I expect you to use all of your energy to ensure that the eastern and southern coasts are impregnable to barbarian raids. I will make the funds available for you to strengthen the classis and the garrisons. I leave it to you to appoint a new *classis praefectus*."

Primus glanced at Leo, causing the emperor to chuckle, "Nay, not your brother, I do not see him as an admiral. I have another role in mind, a new position." He left Leo in suspense as he turned to a clerk, "Fetch Gratianus Funarius!"

The brothers exchanged glances; neither had heard of him. The clerk returned walking alongside a man of unmistakable Illyrian features. The emperor presented him to the brothers: "This is Gratian, his nickname is *Funarius* because he was a rope salesman in his younger days," he teased. "But he has proved his worth to the Empire in the field. So, this is what I propose: in my absence, you will be the three most powerful men in Britannia. Primus, you are the Count of the Saxon Shore, you Gratian will be *Comes Britanniarum*—the Count of the Britains will have command of the mobile army for the whole of Britannia, but not the frontiers; You, Leo, are appointed as *Dux Britanniarum*, responsible for the area along Hadrian's Wall, including the surrounding areas to the Abus estuary and the end of the southern Pennines. Your headquarters will be here in the city of Eboracum. This will create a buffer zone designed to preserve the economically important and prosperous southeast of Britannia from attacks by the Picts and the Scoti." He paused and looked hard at Leo, "You do not seem pleased, Leo."

"Forgive me, Sire, I am grateful and enthusiastic, but I wish to seek your permission for two important matters."

"Name them!"

"I wish to wed my betrothed before undertaking my new role and," he hesitated, "regarding that, many of the garrisons on the Wall need reinforcements; will there be funds available to me as to my brother?"

The emperor chuckled and looked sternly at Gratian. "All three will have suitable sums, but no need to remind our friend the rope seller that he was removed from the African frontier on charges of embezzlement. Nay, I will not spare your feelings, Gratianus Funarius! It goes without saying that I expect total honesty in the use of imperial finances. The three of you will ensure that Britannia prospers. Leo, bring your betrothed and her family to Eboracum, where you will wed in my presence and in the attendance of your peers," he indicated the other two.

"I will bring our parents, my wife and son, Sire," Primus said, "they will be delighted for Leo and to see their beloved emperor. When will the wedding be?"

"As soon as Leo can reach the Wall and return to Eboracum. He has a better road than you, Primus, so you'd better make haste!" Constans chortled. "Gratian, you will remain here and we'll go into more detail about your role with the *comitatenses*." He waited until the other two departed. "I see your role as commanding an *ad hoc* force to deal with particular situations. You have more experience than the other two, so you can assume overall command if such a set of circumstances arises."

Outside the stables, the brothers embraced before retrieving their horses. Leo mounted Cirratus and clasped his brother's wrist. "Who'd have thought it? We're two of the most powerful men in Britannia."

"Ay, but let's hope it's not a poisoned chalice. These are troubled times and I can't say I took to that rope merchant."

"Oh, he'll be all right; it seemed the emperor took some delight in mortifying him, but if he served on the African frontier, his experience will be invaluable. Give my love to our parents, and see you back here in a few days." With that, Leo abruptly kicked his heels and Cirratus leapt forward, leaving Primus coughing at the dust stirred up. He was confident that he would be back before Leo and in time for the wedding, and, like Leo, spent the first part of the journey reflecting on his brother and their strange overlapping destinies. True, their areas of competence were far apart. *I'll probably make my headquarters in Camolodunum, while Leo's will be in the palace at Eboracum—lucky little devil!*

Leo, instead, worried about Aoife. *Will she be prepared to leave the north for Eboracum? And what about her job?*

He was not worried about the wedding going ahead. Her family would be astounded at his news and a wedding in the presence of Emperor Constans. His head was awhirl. He could not decide whether he was more excited about breaking his news to his betrothed or at the prospect of reuniting with his own family. He had not been a centurion for even a week and now he was a dux and, as such, superior to the quaestor who had raised him to centurion. *I have always known that I was destined to great things and that I would catch up with Primus. It looks like that Gratian is superior to us both if it comes to a full-scale war—but will it?*

As a good Christian, he could not consult an oracle, but as he rode, he prayed that he would fulfil his new role worthily. God knew what the future held and, given recent events, he suspected that it would be complicated.

6

EBORACUM, AD 343

THE NETWORK OF ROADS TO AND FROM THE NORTH-EAST, superior to that linking the north-west to Eboracum, ensured that Leo's party arrived half a day before Primus'. To Leo's relief, Aoife and her family were delighted to travel with the prospect of meeting the emperor high among their expectations. Earnan, shrewd trader that he was, saw opportunities everywhere in the thriving city and wandered in the early morning to the riverside wharves, where his business sense led him to question other merchants. He returned to their lodgings, where he found his daughter and her husband-to-be deep in conversation.

The trader was bursting with his news and didn't hold back from interrupting them.

"Aoife, I'm seriously thinking of transferring to Eboracum. It's a thriving well-connected city with the prospect of allowing me to make more money from the sale of my goods. It won't be difficult to set Aodh up with a workshop either, and he'll have far more clients among the *civitas* here than you can provide in Vercovicium. I've made enquiries, and there is a large, bustling market, which will be ideal for your stall."

"Oh, Leo, you know what this means! We'll be together here in Eboracum, and I already like what I've seen of the city!" she exclaimed.

Leo smiled broadly; Earnan's scheme had removed his one major worry. At last, he would have a family united in one place. He expressed his delight and then added, although it was more thinking aloud, "I wonder where my brother will settle his family? At a guess, it'll be somewhere down south." He looked glum, and Aoife took his hand, "I'm sure we can travel to see them from time to time. They should be here soon; I can't wait to meet your parents and your brother."

"And little Gaius and his mother, Silvia. I've never met them." Leo brightened.

They did not have long to wait, as in the early afternoon Primus, expert at investigations, discovered where his brother was staying and rented accommodation nearby for his family. A sharp knock at the door had Leo scurrying to answer, and he found himself staring into his brother's grinning face.

"Bring your family to our lodgings, Leo. It'll be easier for you to come to our place than to move Gaius; we've just settled him down. I've found quarters around the corner," he said in a rather military manner.

"Come in and meet Aoife."

This first introduction over, Primus led the others to his accommodation. The rented villa was worthy of a high Roman dignitary and his family. Amazed at the beauty of the frescoes and mosaics, Aoife thought Primus must have paid a fortune. At the same time, with a thrill, she realised that she, too, would become accustomed to a life of luxury very different from her modest home in Coriosopitum, even if her father had managed to buy one of the better buildings in their hometown.

Her scrutiny of the surroundings left unfinished; she came face-to-face with Silvia. The two women smiled at each other, both thinking that the other was more beautiful than herself. Aoife broke the ice, "Where is Gaius, Silvia? Leo can't wait to see his nephew."

"Thank the Lord, he's sleeping at last, in a cot. I swear that he didn't give me a moment's peace the whole journey."

"How was the road?"

"Bumpy, and our carriage got stuck twice, but we're here, and the villa has a fine bathroom with hot water, so soon I'll make myself more presentable. By the way, I love your dress."

"Do you think it suitable to meet the emperor?" Aoife asked anxiously.

"My dear, it's fine. Anyway, you could wear an old sack and still look beautiful!"

Those words were the start of a lifelong friendship as Silvia steered the Briton towards her in-laws, where she made an equally positive impression. The various reunions continued apace until Leo and Primus stood before their father, whose congratulations were notably rueful.

"To think, my sons are now my superior officers! I am still a centurion, while you, Leo, have overall command of our fortress and my men."

Leo frowned and took Primus aside, "Hark, brother, we have the power now to promote and demote. Did not the emperor leave you with the task of finding a new *classis praefectus*?"

"Brilliant, Leo! Why didn't I think of that? Let's go together to break the news to Maximus—I'll not take all the credit—the idea was yours."

"Father," said Primus, "How are your sea legs? Leo has had a splendid idea: you are to be the new admiral of the Classis Britannica. It will be your job to clear the channel and the North Sea of barbarous pirates. What do you say?"

"Me? Admiral of the navy? Ay. It suits me very well—thank you, my sons. Where is the classis based?"

"I think in Dubris, but you can sail your ships to any of the many harbours, including here in Eboracum," Primus said pointedly.

It was a happy family that congregated to meet the emperor in the imperial palace, but the surprises had not finished. Primus explained to Constans that Centurion Maximus was the ideal appointment to the rank of *classis praefectus*. The emperor smiled and summoned a clerk, "Put it in writing that Centurion Maximus is appointed as admiral of the Classis Britannica and apply my seal to the document."

There followed conversation in which Constans expressed himself satisfied with what he had found in Eboracum. In particular, he approved of the integration of tribal leaders into an elite group of citizens, who exploited the civitas capital to expropriate surplus over the long term. This was exactly the vested interest that Rome required of its provinces. He explained, "The former tribal leaders are now worthy of being Roman citizens and I see here in Eboracum the creation of public buildings, constructed by the intensive application and extensive organisation of labour."

He means slave labour, Leo thought, but kept this notion to himself.

"In this regard," Constans continued, "I have to return to Italy immediately. There are religious problems to deal with, so let's get you wed, Leo. My present to you is the official consignment of this *domus palatina* to the Dux Britanniarum, where you will live with your lovely bride." He smiled, and his youthful face illuminated as he gazed at Aoife.

With the slightest twinge of jealousy, Leo thought, *I knew he wasn't homosexual*. He didn't have much time to think anything else because Aoife clutched his arm and whispered, "I can't believe it! This palace is *ours*, Leo, thank the emperor."

"Sire, your generosity knows no bounds, I thank you with all my heart."

"Your thanks to me will be the quelling of the Picts, Dux Leo."

"It shall be so, Sire," Leo bowed deeply and with genuine gratitude.

"We must go to the other side of the fortress, to the basilica, where the Sixth Legion hailed my father as Emperor years ago," Constans said, "can there be a more fitting place for your wedding? I doubt it."

Constans had organised everything, brilliant administrator that he was: from the priest awaiting them in the basilica to the celebratory meal in their new home afterwards. The emperor partook frugally because, as he explained during the meal, "I have to sail for Ostia and cannot over-indulge my stomach. Your North Sea, Admiral Maximus, can play unpleasant jests on the unwary." Just the same, he managed to raise a beaker of red wine and quaff it before launching into an explanation. "As soon as I arrive in Rome, I intend to make it clear that Judaism is to be tolerated in the Empire. That is true for Britannia, too," he stared hard at the Illyrian, Comes Britanniarum. "And I'll issue an edict banning pagan sacrifices throughout the Empire." This much was clear to the wedding party, but he lost them when he continued, "I'll suppress Donatism in Africa and support Nicene orthodoxy against Arianism, which is championed by my brother Constantius." They did not understand the intricacies of Christian doctrine, but were impressed by the emperor's grasp of it when he explained, as well as his determination and administrative capacity.

They all accompanied him down to the harbour with his escort before his ship, accompanied by several war galleys, rowed into the wide river before setting sail. Maximus turned to Leo, "Rather Constans than me. He's a fine young fellow, but these arguments over religion can be very bitter." Prophetically, he added, "For the sake of our positions, let's hope that the emperor can avoid warfare with Constantius—it's far better to negotiate than fight in these circumstances."

"Ay, let's pray for his safety after all that he has done for us."

"You should return to your new home and devote yourself to your bride, son," Maximus said with a wink and a nudge.

Such was his devotion that the couple did not emerge from the bedchamber until the following morning. Their appearance was in time to say a heartfelt farewell to Primus, Silvia, and the babe, who were headed for Camolodunum.

Gratianus Funarius consulted with Leo and decided to go to Glevum, where he wanted to form a mobile force that could react rapidly. Leo was impressed with Gratian and could see that he was an able soldier. The emperor had mentioned that Gratian's first command had been as a tribune in Constantine's mobile field army. That was before he supervised the African frontier. So, his experience was ideal for a speedy reaction if the Picts or Scoti raided into Britannia. Constans had also added that Gratian was popular among his men when in active service.

While Leo would have liked to remain in Eboracum to enjoy a life of luxury, other pressing matters led him dutifully back north. First, he had to accompany his wife's father and brother with an armed escort to assure their safe arrival in Coriosopitum; secondly, he had to make his authority known along the chain of fortresses that ran from the northeast coast across the frontier with Caledonia and down the west coast of Cumbria. He needed to discover which garrisons needed strengthening and if there was any simmering resentment over pay or conditions.

"Leo, I am going to settle my affairs in Coriosopitum," Earnan said. "Then, Aodh and I will travel back to Eboracum. My son's baggage will contain valuable materials, and I fear for our safety."

"Nay, I'll arrange for an escort to accompany you, and it would be better if Aoife travelled with you, for I have much work to do along the Wall. She can organise the domus as she thinks best when she returns until I am able to come back to the capital."

Before departing Eboracum, Leo issued instructions for the strengthening of the city's walls. If the Picts ever invaded south in great numbers, it was essential, as Constans had pointed out, that they should not go beyond Eboracum.

The last thing he needed to do in the city was to say farewell to his parents. He presumed that his mother would also travel south with his father, and this proved correct. So, they embraced, and Leo took his father's arm to speak in private. "Father, we have been apart for too long.

I know it was my idea to have you appointed as admiral of the fleet, but it needn't mean that you are always at sea on patrol or based permanently in Dubris. Consider the strategic position of Eboracum. The Ouse is wide and navigable all the way to the Abus Estuary, whose brown waters command the North Sea outlet. From there, you can easily intercept pirates from the Low Countries around the Rhine Estuary."

"Leo, I did not know you had such a command of geography."

"Oh, ay, Grandfather Valdor would show Primus and me charts when we were little. He was proud of his Batavian origins. He used to swim in the river Waal as a youth, you know. If God blesses me with children, you will want to see them from time to time, for it is only natural that a grandfather gives his grandchildren the benefit of his experience."

Maximus' reassurances that he would come to Eboracum made parting sweeter, and once Lavinia and Maximus set off for Dubris with a small escort, Leo decided it was time to head in the opposite direction. So, he led his party through the north gate and out of the fortress, noting how it lay between the rivers Ouse and Foss; they passed the cemetery and took the excellent road to the north direct for Isurium Brigantum, the capital of the Romanised Brigantes tribe, the largest such group in Britain. Having embraced Roman culture, these people also accepted the *pax Romana*, meaning that a peaceful passage across their territory was taken for granted. The road continued to Cateractonium, where a fort protected the crossing of the River Swale.

They broke the journey there, stopping for refreshment for themselves and their horses before departing, still on a good road, towards Concangis, another fort guarding the crossing of the River Wear. They stopped there for the night, as twilight discouraged them from pressing on with a seven-hour ride still ahead of them to reach Coriosopitum, their destination.

Leo left his family in that town and ordered the escort to wait there for two days before reaccompanying them south. In charge of the escort was the Tungrian decurion, who had accompanied him to the tavern for his first meeting with Aoife. They had become firm friends, and although he made no mention of it to him, Leo would make it his business to promote him at the first opportunity. It was good to have a close friend and, above all, for the first time in a long while, a family of his own.

The journey over, he rode to his former barracks at Vercovicium on Hadrian's Wall, where he conducted a discreet investigation into how the Picts had been able to pass through the fort so easily. It soon became evident by careful questioning that the garrison was generally tired of manning this remote outpost of the Empire. He discovered that the Tungrians had been on the Wall for six long years. It was too long, making unrest and even treachery inevitable. So, he decided to relieve them, replacing them with a fresh force from Eboracum. With this in mind, he arranged for their departure to be led by his Tungrian friend from Coriosopitum, who would also take Leo's orders to the garrison commander in Eboracum.

Spies in Vercovicium reported the weakening of the garrison to the Picts, who had to decide whether to launch another attack. Leo, who knew that it would be several days before his garrison returned to full strength, sent for half the contingent at Aesica Fort, six miles to the east, and half that of Brocolitia Fort, five miles to the west. He calculated that in the event of an attack at any of the three points, he would be able to move troops quickly from the central base.

Awaiting the arrival of the replacement troops, Leo rode westwards and found that the garrison at Magnis Fort contained five hundred Hamian archers, the *Cohors Prima Hamiorum Sagittaria*. This was useful information, for as far as he knew, they were the only regiment of archers in Britannia. He sent for a cohort of infantrymen—fifty men from ten other garrisons to replace the archers and transferred them to Vercovicium. They were not in the least disgruntled to move because there were better facilities at their new posting, not to mention the attractions of the vicus.

The usual spies reported on the Dux's arrangements and whether or not it was on the basis of this information, the arrival of the Eboracum troops destined to garrison Vercovicium together with the newcomers, the Picts postponed their attack until the winter. They had their reasons for awaiting worse weather.

7

VERCOVICIUM AND EBORACUM, AD 343

Doninas, the Tungrian decurion and Leo's friend, stared open-mouthed at the Dux. "Are you seriously asking me to act the role of a traitor?"

Leo put a hand on the shorter man's shoulder and said, "Think about it. Who is the least treacherous person in this fort? Who else can I rely upon? Look, Doninas, we know that the Picts have contacts both in the fortress and in the *vicus*. It's true that I've renewed the garrison, but we underestimate the cunning of the foe at our peril. If we know for sure what their plans are, we can make arrangements to thwart them. Besides, I have an incentive for you, my friend." He smiled and waited, but not for long.

"An incentive?"

"Ay, complete this mission to my satisfaction and I'll promote you immediately to centurion."

"You will? Oh, well, everything considered, I think I can play that part!"

Leo's hand was still resting on his friend's shoulder and now it gave a gentle squeeze of encouragement. "Go to the White Stag this evening—what's more natural? They know you there. Oh, and Doninas, here's a perk of the job." He handed him a small bag of silver coins. "I don't want you out of pocket, but, hark, don't get drunk. Slur your speech a little, but stay lucid and, whatever happens, be careful. If anyone suspects you are a spy working for me, they'll slit your throat. You might offer a jug of wine to ingratiate yourself, too."

"I can manage, Leo, I've been going to that tavern for years—before you ever did."

Later that evening, steadily working his way down a jug of red wine, Doninas gazed around the tavern. His eyes met those of a tall fellow, a carter with whom he had previously chatted. Quickly, he looked away, poured himself another beaker of wine, then stared back at the fellow, who didn't look away. So, he raised his cup in a salute. The carter replicated the gesture and Doninas waved him over.

Deliberately slurring his speech, he said, "I might need help with this wine; the jug never seems to finish!"

"I don't mind helping you out, Decurion," the Briton stuck out his empty drinking vessel and the Tungrian somewhat shakily filled it. The mocking eyes of the other assured him that his act was working.

"Don't tell me that a veteran soldier can't hold his drink!"

"Well, this *is* my second jug," Doninas protested, lying through his teeth. "*You'd* give yourself to drink if you lived my dog's life," he slurred.

"I thought Roman officers were well-paid," the thin-faced Briton said, gulping down his wine and boldly thrusting out his beaker for a refill.

"As it happens, I've just been paid, about time, too! You haven't seen me in here recently, have you? Why do you suppose that is?"

"I heard the Tungrians had relocated and I supposed you'd gone to Eboracum with them."

"You're remarkably well-informed, Briton."

The carter's eyes became shifty and he murmured something incoherent.

"That's the thing, you see," Doninas poured himself another cup, deliberately spilling wine on the table and cursing, "I've been in this God-forsaken fort for six years. All my comrades have gone and my superiors have kept me here to train the raw newcomers. Useless lot! I pray that the Picts stay at home in their glens because these recruits will be no use in battle. I'd do better training a batch of—*hic*—Vestal Virgins!"

"Six years, eh? That's a long time to be stuck here."

"Ay, and I'm still a decurion, like when I arrived," he said querulously, before gulping down another draught ostentatiously and spinning unsteadily on his chair. He called in an over-loud voice, "Landlord! Another jug of wine for me and my friend!"

"Do you think that's wise?"

"Wise? Nay, of course, it isn't w.i.s.e! I think I'll get drunk tonight, young fellow. What else is there to do in this—*hic*—God-forsaken place? I'll tell you what, if the Picts were to come knocking tomorrow, I'd let them in myself!"

The carter stared hard at him, "You don't mean that! You've just had too much to drink."

Doninas leant forward pugnaciously, and slurring, growled, "Too much? *Too much?* Not enough!" He grabbed the Briton's arm and hauled him across the table, overturning the fortunately almost empty cup. "Be careful what you say, carter, a man might get offended!"

The Briton adjusted his sleeve and poured himself another beaker. "See here, I didn't mean any offence. I can understand you being fed up. I'd be the same. But did you mean what you said?"

The innkeeper brought another jug of wine, so the decurion kept silent.

"Everything all right, here?" the landlord asked, looking anxiously at the soldier.

"Couldn't be better," his words were deliberately hard to understand. The tavern-owner stared at his fellow Briton, who nodded, so he shrugged and went away.

"What were we saying?" Doninas asked.

The carter put a finger under his chin, covered by a slight downy beard, "I asked you whether you meant what you said."

"And what did I—*hic*—say?"

"You said that if the Picts were to come knocking tomorrow, you'd let them in!"

"And so I would! As they say in Rome, *in vino veritas!*"

"You complained about poor pay earlier. Well, I know someone who'd pay you good money to open the gates to the Picts. It's been done before, you know?"

"It'd serve the—*hic*—bastards right if I did!"

The Briton hesitated, he did not want to push too hard, "Look, you think about it and we'll talk tomorrow. Let's just enjoy this wine for now."

Doninas had to be cunning now because he seriously risked getting drunk and he didn't want that, so he began by saying he needed to use the latrines. That enabled him to gain much-needed fresh air and time without consuming wine. When he got back, deliberately walking with the determination of the truly drunk, his first act was to pour each of them another beaker, but he didn't raise his for a while, closing his eyes and pretending to rub a sore forehead.

"Maybe I should get back to barracks and sleep this off," he garbled.

"Ay, maybe you should, but remember our conversation and come back on the morrow. I owe you a jug. I can finish this on my own."

Doninas rose unsteadily, reached for his beaker and swigged the wine in one long draught. His words ran together as he bade his companion goodnight and swayed out of the tavern. With the door closed behind him, he took a deep breath and strode capably to the fortress, where he sought out Leo and reported on his progress.

Back in the White Stag the following evening, Doninas kept a low profile and sat quietly at an unoccupied table. The innkeeper came over with a jug of red wine, "This is already paid by March the carter."

"Be a good fellow and tell him to join me."

Moments later, the carter drew up a chair and sat opposite the decurion. "Have you thought about our conversation of last night?"

"Ay, once my splitting headache wore off!"

"Have you changed your mind?"

"Why would I?" Doninas made his tone bitter.

The carter smiled thinly, "I thought it might have just been the strong drink talking."

The decurion bridled, "Watch your tongue, March, you're talking to a soldier, not a milksop!"

"Don't take offence, friend, I meant none. It's just that this is a delicate matter."

The soldier lowered his voice, "Ay, it is and I have a couple of conditions if we are to proceed."

The carter stood, "A moment, Decurion, I'll fetch someone who can respond to conditions."

"Be discreet!" Doninas hissed, but the tall carter had weaved through the throng standing in the middle of the straw-strewn floor, and not having heard, did not reply. He soon returned with a shorter man, whose head was buried inside a hood. Given the dim light cast by the single candle on his table, the officer could not make out the fellow's features. The hooded man leant forward and, in a very low voice, said, "I hear that you are prepared to help us, but that you have conditions. What are they?"

Doninas took a deliberate draught of wine before replying and when he did, he stared hard at the newcomer, who in response tugged at the edge of his hood, pulling it further over his brow. "I want twenty silver denarii and a commitment that the Picts will not kill any of my comrades, but will pass swiftly and silently—in through the north gate and out by the south. All done in the early hours of the night, when the world is at its darkest. I want five denarii in advance and will collect the rest a few days after the passage through the fort."

"It is a small fortune you ask, Decurion," the stranger said.

"Nay, you ask me to betray my position and risk my life—I'll not do it for a pittance."

"Very well, I accept your conditions. Here are your instructions. Wait for the first foggy night in November, then, at the dead of night, see that the gates are open wide enough for our men to slip through. As soon as they have gone, ensure that both gates are shut so that no alarm is given, clear?"

"Quite clear."

"Good," the unknown man reached into a pocket and took out a small money bag with a drawstring. He opened it and his fingers wriggled inside, bringing out, one at a time, five silver pieces. Looking around to ensure nobody was taking undue interest, he slid the coins across the table, where Doninas swiftly picked them up and slipped them into a pocket, keeping one in his hand to inspect its quality.

Satisfied, he stood, "Right, it's better we split up. You finish the wine. I'm on my way."

The hooded man caught him by the wrist, saying in a low voice, "Remember, the first foggy night in November."

"I'm not a fool," the decurion growled, "we have an agreement."

He hurried back to the fort to refer it to Leo, who was slightly perplexed, "Foggy night? These Picts are cunning. They mean to slip through like wraiths. I must speak with the commander of the Hamian archers."

Swearing the officer to the utmost secrecy, Leo explained his plan but expressed his doubts, "If it's foggy, will your men be able to hit their targets?"

"It's a question of range, Dux. From the ramparts, the fog would have to be so dense that nothing can be seen, but I doubt that it will totally obscure their forms. Besides, my men are experts and eagle-eyed. They train constantly—you can rely on them."

November proved equally reliable. In those parts, the weather was guaranteed to be bad, whether it was rain, mist, fog, sleet or snow, that month failed only to provide sun and warmth. The third day of November started with a grey shroud over the fortress and continued throughout the day to reduce the shapes of people in the *vicus* to ghost-like entities except for their coughs and sneezes. Leo waited until midnight before deploying the Hamian archers on the southern ramparts, ordering them to sit in total silence with their backs against the wooden palisade. "No talking and not so much as a sneeze," he ordered, recalling the sounds from the vicus, "if one comes, stifle it and the same goes for coughs! We need total surprise. When you hear three hoots of an owl," he imitated the call of a screech owl convincingly, "draw back your arrows and slay the foe. I want no survivors."

The well-disciplined Syrians obeyed to the letter and, Doninas, standing over the northern gateway, peered out over the fog-shrouded escarpment. He pulled his *sagum* tighter around his shivering shoulders and waited.

He had suffered the cold for about an hour when he saw a flaming torch move in an arc, back and forth. *At last, a signal! They are here!* He hurried down to open the gate, which he had ordered to be left unbarred. So, it was an easy task to haul it open on its well-greased hinges, creating a gap wide enough for a man to squeeze through. He raised a hand to Dux Leo, hiding behind the corner of the granary and hurried to open the southern gate in the same way. As soon as he had done that, he hastened to hide, too. He needed a clear view of the southern entry to judge the success of the plan or its failure, so he crouched behind the wall of the infirmary, the nearest building to that gate.

Leo watched the first Picts, bare to the waist even in this weather, slip silently into the fortress. He waited a moment only because the enemy moved fast and silently. A call of a screech owl broke the silence; it was convincing because had such a bird been around, it would have protested at the intrusion of the Picts. In response, the Syrians rose quietly as one, chose a target and loosed a rain of arrows on the unsuspecting enemy. Without armour, the Picts were easy pickings and fell like ripe apples from a tree in a gale. They had no time to turn and flee and, in any case, could not be sure where the archers were deployed. The Dux's plan had produced a slaughter of merciless proportions—not one raider survived. The Syrians came down from the rampart and found three or four Picts still alive. Obeying orders, they immediately dispatched them with a slash of their sharp curved knives.

In the cold light of morning, Leo ordered a mass grave dug on level ground outside the fortress. The toll was 120 Picts buried. The *Dux Britanniarum* smiled grimly. The outcome of his trap would send shock waves through the glens. He was sure that the Picts would not contemplate another raid for some time. His task now was to relocate Doninas from Vercovicium, for surely, revenge would be on the minds of the conspirators. No better way to remove him from their vengeance than to have him accompany him to Eboracum, where Aoife awaited her husband and the Tungrians expected the arrival of their decurion, except that he would appear before them as a centurion. Leo smiled; he would break that to Doninas on the journey south.

The new centurion was not the only one to receive good news. A messenger caught up with the small southbound band at Cateractonium.

"Dux, greetings from the *Comes Britanniarum*, who wishes to inform you of a great victory over the Scoti near Alauna Fort."

"Splendid! Return to the Comes and report our crushing victory at Vercovicium over the Picts." He turned to Doninas and confided, "I believe we are in for a period free of incursions. Emperor Constans will be delighted. We need my father, the admiral, to stem the influx of Saxon and Frankish pirates and Britannia will be safe."

The good news did not end there, for when Leo at last embraced Aoife in their palatial residence, he found her positively radiant. Her mood was not due to the luxurious home bestowed by the emperor, but as she explained, "Oh, Leo, I rise each morning and hurry off to be sick. You know what that means, don't you?"

"You eat too many oysters?"

"Nay," she pummelled his chest playfully, "I am expecting our child, foolish man!"

8

EBORACUM TO BIBRA, AD 343-344

LEO WAS CORRECT ABOUT ONE THING: THERE WOULD BE A lull in Pictish incursions after the November massacre, which circumstances, coupled with the deteriorating marine conditions in the Irish Sea due to winter weather, meant that the north would be trouble-free at least until the spring.

Peace provides time for reflection, and Leo had much to consider, especially recurring thoughts about his grandfather, Valdor, whose tales of his youthful rise to glory remained an inspiration. Yet, Leo, who was on an upward trajectory, knew that Valdor might have remained a simple legionary had he not had the fortune of becoming Carausius' favourite. Leo rejected the self-delusion of believing he had arrived at the rank of Dux, and Primus to Comes, on merit. It was clear that their courage and Lavinia's training had played a part, but most notably, Emperor Constans was impressed by their lineage. Valdor had been Constantine's friend and counsellor—and Constantine was Constans' father. Significantly, Valdor's wisdom to refuse the imperial purple eased Constantine's acceptance by the army. Leo doubted that he or Primus would have set aside their ambitions in this way.

After due consideration, he decided that his desire was to reach greater heights than Valdor and Primus, and this latter challenge was all-important to him. The more he thought of Valdor, the more determined he became that he must convince Aoife to name the babe, if a boy, after his great-grandfather, Lavinia, if a girl.

To stoke his aspirations came the news of the retirement of Gratian Funarius, happy to return to his birthplace to enjoy his reputation as a successful general. Until Constans decided to replace him, Leo would have total command in the north, and he was determined to be ready in the spring to take advantage of any external menace. If he could prove himself as able as Gratian, the emperor might be tempted to promote him to Comes, which would take him to the same level as Primus.

The problem for Leo of being in Britannia was that he was out of touch with events overseas. All his calculations depended on the emperor's continued support. How was he to know that in Rome, court officials had begun plotting to overthrow Constans? The emperor was deeply unpopular, and his failings would be the cause of his downfall: he employed corrupt ministers such as the *magister officiorum* Flavius Eugenius, neglecting portions of the Empire, personal greed, and treating his soldiers with contempt. Although his days were numbered, he would continue wearing the purple for a few years yet, thanks to the fear he evoked because of his undoubted bravery on the battlefield.

Leo watched on proudly as Aoife's pregnancy advanced, even delighting her by arranging for a woodcarver to create an intricately wrought cot, which featured curious animal motifs around its inside edges—they should capture the babe's attention! Countless times, Leo told himself that it did not matter whether his child would be a boy or a girl. After all, his mother and hers had both been shield maidens, capable of fighting the best male warriors on equal terms. Despite his logic, he ardently desired a son to be his heir, also because Primus had been blessed by the birth of Gaius. He believed that he truly loved his brother, but could not overcome the smouldering resentment caused by the enforced separation from his parents when they accompanied Primus on his first campaign. His rational mind accepted that Primus held no responsibility for that decision, but he continued after all these years to brood on being the second son and, therefore, the second choice. It was a state of mind that drove him to continually prove himself, with the intention of superseding his brother's achievements.

The Christmas festivities behind them, and winter giving way to spring, brought Aoife closer to the birth. This period of domestic bliss ended with the arrival of a tired and bedraggled messenger. A member of the *Cohors II Pannoniorum*: an infantry cohort, he had ridden for two days from the *Bibra* garrison. The fellow explained that he had been chosen as the messenger because he was one of the few infantrymen capable of riding a horse. Speed was essential because a large force of Scoti had landed in a bay south of the fort of Bibra and had attacked and plundered the *vicus* lying either side of the northern road. The townsfolk had successfully fled to safety within the fortress, but the raiders from Hibernia were cunning and knew that the increased consumption of water and food would sooner or later force the garrison to surrender.

Leo searched his memory of visiting the Western Sea Defences, which were an extension of Hadrian's Wall, and recalled that Bibra was a fort situated between *Portus Trucculensis*, built on the river Wampool beside the natural sheltered harbour offered by the Morecambe mud-flat, and the Alauna Fort. It would therefore be a disaster if this strategic fortress fell into Scoti hands since where these raiders led, others would follow, and the entire north of Britannia would be endangered.

He needed to move quickly since without the orders of the Dux, the other garrisons would not react independently, for fear that uncoordinated action would lead to defeat against the ferocious Scoti, descendants of the Picts.

Leo summoned his friend Doninas and ordered him to find five other Tungrian centurions because he needed a reliable cohort of horsemen to ride to the north-west. Once arrived at *Glannaventa* fort, he planned to add that garrison to their number and proceed up the coast, collecting more men from each of the other four western coast fortresses to the south of Bibra, swelling their number to create a force capable of overcoming the besieging Scoti.

On the journey, Leo subtly changed his plan by sending a small detachment under a centurion to *Vercovicium*. They would order the Hamian archers to ride to Bibra and, thus, catch the Scoti in a pincer from the north-east. At first, he thought of entrusting the task to Doninas, knowing how capable he was, but then remembered that in Vercovicium there were people eager to gain revenge for the Pictish massacre by murdering him.

The detachment separated from the main cohort at the Roman ford across the Tees on the *Lavatrae* to *Vinovia* road. The ford was made of squared masonry blocks held together by the *opus revinctum* technique. Leo encouraged the commander of the detachment to press on northwards to *Cilurnum*, which they would reach before nightfall if they did not spare the horses; on the contrary, he would rest his men and horses at the waypoint of Lavatrae, ideally placed for the westward ride the following day. The name 'Lavatrae' meant summit because the fort, with its timber ramparts, overlooking the river Greta, guarded the eastern entrance to the Stainmore Pass through the Pennines. Even if the Pass took them well north of Glannaventa, it would bring them close to *Alauna* Fort. He would forgo reinforcements from the garrison at Glannaventa in exchange for fresher horsemen to combat the Scoti. Alauna would provide sufficient men, he reckoned, now that he had conceived the idea of the formidable Hamian archers.

Arriving at Alauna the next day around noon, Leo received a welcome, which became warmer when the garrison troops learnt that they would soon participate in active service. Patrolling the bleak northwestern coast, especially in winter, was a thankless task, far better a hard-fought battle against a redoubtable foe.

The Dux Britanniarum marched a cheerful company along the coastal road. The enemy scouts warned their chieftain about the Roman force's arrival so that Leo found them lined up on the far bank of a beck that provided fresh water to the Roman fort of Bibra. Leo weighed up the situation at a glance; he was not prepared to charge that line across the beck, which was what the cunning foe wanted. The risk of the horses slipping and breaking a leg was too great, so the Dux retreated slowly, approaching the fortress gateway and called upon the commander to send forth his infantry armed with javelins. Each man carried his rectangular curved *scutum*, the layered wooden shield, covered in leather with linen glued on the front and painted red to symbolise Mars, the god of war. Around the boss was the legion's symbol of laurel bay leaves, like a crown, painted in yellow to depict power and victory. Leo took command and had them march slowly, scuta interlinked, towards the beck. Even the forbidding Scoti must have trembled at the sight of their resolute advance.

Perhaps Leo was the first to catch a glint of metal to the north and his heart thrilled with joy. The Dux called his *cornicen* and had him blow a long, lowing blast of his horn. In the distance, came the hoped-for reply, so Leo ordered three sharp blasts. The reply was the thunder of hoofs, which made the enemy spin around in horror to see the approach of hundreds of horses. Far worse for the Scoti, trapped in the jaws of a pincer, were the raining javelins Leo ordered, hurled at their exposed backs, descending contemporaneously with the deadly hail of arrows shot by the expert Syrian archers. Slaughter was a foregone conclusion when the infantry waded across the beck and drove in among the Scoti survivors. Only now did Leo jump his horse across the beck, followed by his entire cohort. The spathae, chopping down on the decimated enemy, took a deadly toll. Any Scot attempting to flee towards the nearby coast was scythed down by multiple Hamian arrows. The crushing defeat was bound to reverberate throughout *Hibernia* and Leo hoped, beyond the other boundaries of Britannia, especially, for his purposes, into *Caledonia*.

Basking in his victory, Leo told himself, *While I am Dux Britanniarum, the Picts and the Scoti will make no inroads into Britannia.* His thought was not an idle boast. He had now outwitted both enemies within a calendar year. If precedent was anything to go by, the desperate Celts would resort to assassination attempts, so maybe it was time for him to consider creating a bodyguard. He had already taken the precaution of strengthening the walls of Eboracum and he had overseen the insertion of a levelling layer of red tiles as the walls grew higher. That work was ongoing, but perhaps he need not fear an assault by a Pictish host as much as a cowardly attempt at murder. *Ay, I will create a bodyguard and a plan of how best to use them. I want to watch my son grow with his loving father to guide him to manhood.*

The first stage of this plan came once back in Eboracum, where Leo summoned Centurion Doninas.

"You are my dearest friend outside of my family, Centurion, and I wish to entrust my safety to you." He saw the perplexity in his comrade's face. "Ay, I know that I can look after myself as well as any soldier, but I am not a god, hence I'm mortal, and not proof against Celtic cunning—I fear cowardly and murderous slyness. I want you to put together a bodyguard of the finest ten men you can assemble. Under your command, Tribune—"

"Tribune?"

"Ay, you are promoted, but hark, a tribune does not only command a bodyguard, but also multiple legions. You will do both because I need a reliable second-in-command if ever it comes to open warfare and, also, I want you close to me if it comes to treachery. Clear?"

"It couldn't be clearer, Dux, and I thank you for the trust you have always given me—"

"And which you have always faithfully repaid!"

The friends embraced, and as they did so, Doninas was already mentally selecting reliable men for the role of bodyguard.

The second stage of the plan came wailing for milk and kicking into the world in the shape of a baby boy. Leo had the son he craved, and within days, he was baptised Valdor in the basilica.

To complete the Dux's happiness was the arrival in the Ouse of the classis' flagship. Maximus and Lavinia entered the palace arm in arm, unaware of Valdor's birth.

"Mother, don't tell me you are a sailor now! I expected you to stay in Camulodunum to enjoy your grandson."

"I was tempted, but do you suppose I could leave this wretch to face an enemy without his fiercest bodyguard?"

"As it has worked out," Leo peered at his mother intently, "You can enjoy your grandson here in Eboracum."

"Why? Are Primus and Silvia here with Gaius?" Her face lit up with joy.

Leo stifled a growl, "Nay, mother, but little Valdor awaits you in his cot." Her joy transformed into sheer delight, and she flung herself into Leo's arms, almost knocking him off his feet. "Congratulations, my dearest son!" Maximus' strong arm steered his wife away so that he could embrace Leo, too. "Can an admiral command a Dux on dry land? If so, I order you lead me to my grandson!"

"Without entering into the merits of command, follow me!"

Leo watched on with delight as his parents celebrated the new arrival with cuddles and caresses—he had matched Primus with another achievement, and he might yet supersede him by giving Valdor a brother!

A peaceful month passed, although Maximus was obliged to resume command of the North Sea fleet. At the end of April, a messenger arrived with a sealed document from Rome. The verbal message that accompanied the parchment was one of congratulations from Constans for the victory over the Scoti. With trembling, eager hand, Leo broke the seal and the contents confirmed his appointment as Comes Britanniarum accompanied by the order to find a new Dux. This latter caused Leo considerable anxiety. His instinct was to appoint Doninas, but would he be sending his trusted friend to the butcher's by returning him to Hadrian's Wall? Whatever he decided, he had become Primus' equal as a Comes.

He thought about appointing Maximus and sending Doninas to sea, but remembered that his friend was a poor sailor, so he took another decision.

"You are no longer tribune, but Dux Britanniarum. The bodyguard you assembled for me will be yours now as I am sending you back to the Wall, but not to Vercovicium: to *Petriana*, so that you can command the Wall and the Western Defences from one place. I intend to remain at Eboracum unless I receive a message from you.

9

PETRIANA AND VERCOVICIUM, AD 344-346

Doninas worked from Petriana, the largest of the Wall forts, in conjunction with the western fortresses, to deal with sporadic raids from Hibernia over the next two years. He understood perfectly that he would have moved to Vercovicium as the more central fort along the Wall had it not been for Leo's consideration for his safety. The Dux became fretful as rumours of a new Pictish uprising reached him. So far, he had been obedient to his orders and remained in and around the north-western extremity of Hadrian's Wall.

He was convinced that Leo would not agree to an eastward relocation, so decided to take matters into his own hands. He had a plan to circumvent any act of vengeance for the November massacre of more than two years before.

During his period in Petriana, he had become a close friend of a centurion named Quintus. The pride and dignity of this officer had caught his eye. In truth, the whole garrison of Petriana was renowned for its qualities of courage and discipline. A 1,000-strong cavalry regiment, the *Ala Gallorum Petriana*—a distinguished auxiliary regiment, whose soldiers had been made Roman citizens for valour on the field of battle—gave its name to the fort, previously known as *Uxelodunum*.

Doninas recognised a kindred spirit in Quintus and confided in him.

"This is a relatively settled period along the frontier, so I believe that we can afford to split the regiment and take half the men and horses to

Vercovicium. Rumours from the north suggest that the Picts are restless. We would be better placed to counter any incursions if our base were in the centre of the Wall, don't you agree?"

"Ay, I've often wondered why you chose Uxelodunum." Quintus used the old name of the fort out of inverted pride. He felt that his company had earned its reputation elsewhere and, therefore, the naming of the fortress after them was mistaken. Still, his regiment had been the principal reason that the fort was later considerably expanded to the north and west to accommodate them. In extending north beyond the Wall, as required by a cavalry fort, they pushed it to the edge of the escarpment and also extended it to the south to the limit of the Vallum. "I suppose it's because this fort stands on a natural platform above the river Eden and guards the Eden bridgehead, overseeing the western route to Caledonia."

"I didn't choose it, Comes Leo insisted on sending me here and what you just said must have been a part of his reasoning. But, may I speak frankly?"

Quintus looked surprised and, at the same time, curious. "What is it that troubles you, lord?"

"You will remember our slaughter of the Picts some two years ago?"

"Ay, when you lured them into Vercovicium and cut them down with archers."

Doninas laughed, but not heartily; there was a measure of restraint that the centurion immediately picked up on. "Was there something about that victory that bothers you?"

"Not that bothers me, but it left a situation that troubles the Comes. He believes that if I go back, there will certainly be an attempt on my life."

"An assassination, you say?"

"Ay, but I have a plan, Quintus, and it involves you."

"Tell me, Lord."

"The reason the Picts hate me so much is that I acted as a spy for Leo, who was then Dux. I found one of their sympathisers, a Briton, a fellow named March who works as a carter in the vicus. Through him, I was able to lure the Picts into a death trap at night. My idea is to have you arrest him, bring him into the fortress and threaten him with a cruel death. When he is certain that he will be executed in the morning, I will come along and recognise him as an old friend and spare him. Thus, regaining his friendship, then, I'll tempt him with riches to betray the Picts. He will be my unsuspected spy among them. What do you think?"

Quintus' brow furrowed with concern. "I don't know if you can trust such a man. Isn't he as likely to double-cross you and enable the Picts to lead you into a trap—the perfect revenge?"

"I think it depends on how effectively you manage to terrify him. If he sees Death with a hand on his shoulder, he will think twice about repeating the experience."

Quintus laughed, "You're right, a carter of a defeated people will not have the courage of a Roman soldier. I'll have to think this through carefully. Is this March a Christian?"

"I believe he is."

"There we are then; I know how to terrify him. Leave it with me! Describe this carter to me."

Two days after arriving in Vercovicium, Quintus, in full regalia, led ten legionaries, each with a gladius ostentatiously brandished, into the White Stag tavern. The previous noisy banter descended into a sullen silence.

Quintus looked around and spotted a tall man standing with a beaker of ale in his hand. He strode up to him and held his gladius to his throat. At a silent gesture from their decurion, the legionaries turned, backs to the centurion and his captive, facing the tavern's customers, their intention to quell any attempt at rescue was obvious.

"Are you March the carter?"

"I might be. What's it to you?"

Quintus raised his voice, "March, you are under arrest, in the name of Emperor Constans, for treason. You are accused of collaborating with the enemy Picts. The sentence for treason is death. Take him!" He called to the decurion. Strong hands seized the carter and hustled him out of the tavern to glowering glances and resentful spitting on the rush-strewn floor: the only protest the cowed Britons dared perform.

Quintus ordered his men to take the prisoner beyond the walls to the north of the fortress to a hollow where a deserted Mithraeum lay. This underground place of worship had been abandoned by the soldiers some years before, made redundant by Christianity. The few Mithras devotees who remained still had cult places such as the nearby Brocolitia Fort. Unlike this one, it had better statues and devotional carvings.

Quintus shoved the captive into the dank cavern and said, "I believe you are a Christian, carter. I might reprieve your sentence if you convert to Mithras worship."

"Never!"

"Of course not, Mithras is a soldier's god. He was the Persian god of light and truth, born from a rock on 25 December brandishing a sword in one hand and a torch in the other. You Christians have stolen his birth date! Mithraism is identified with bravery, manliness, and fidelity, all virtues you lack! Since you are such an avowed Christian, we shall honour you with the Christian death you so much admire. Decurion fetch me crucifixion nails to show to this wretch!"

Quintus kept his gladius in full view of the trembling carter. It was difficult to know whether he was trembling from the penetrating damp of the dim interior or sheer terror. When the decurion returned with two wicked-looking, nine-inch sharply-pointed nails, Quintus was certain that his intimidation had succeeded—that was terror in the carter's eyes.

"Look here!" Quintus held a nail under the carter's nose, "This one we'll drive through here," he grabbed the fellow's wrist and jabbed the cruel point into his flesh just below the hand. A trickle of blood matched the trickle of tears running down the anguished face.

"Please, I'm innocent, don't crucify me."

"Don't worry, you'll not have far to walk," Quintus taunted, "we'll erect the cross outside this old temple. So, you can pray to both Christ and Mithras for your soul. We'll nail you on it at dawn. Have a good sleep!"

Quintus' cruel laughter echoed in the tomb-like cave followed by that of the slamming heavy door that had been part of its adaptation into a dungeon.

The following morning began with the hammering of carpenters creating the cross and March the carter began to cry and pray to Jesus to save him. Doninas arrived accompanied by his bodyguard. He turned his back on the Mithraeum and stood apart from the drama that was about to be enacted. For his plan to succeed, he needed the poor carter to suffer the pangs of approaching death.

March had eyes only for the instrument of his torture and death and did not notice the former decurion with whom he had plotted. Rough hands seized the carter and he was pushed, spreadeagled onto the cross. Muscular hands held him firm and a knee on his sternum stopped him writhing. Slowly, a heavy lump hammer rose above March's arm and the point of the nail had bitten into his wrist.

"Halt!" came a ringing command. "Raise that man to his feet and bring him to my quarters."

March could not see his saviour through his tears, only the blurred uniform of a high officer. They pushed him roughly across the sodden soil towards the gate of the fortress.

Inside the *principia*, Doninas held out a cup of red wine, "Here, you need this! Accept it from an old drinking companion!"

"You! But you were a decurion—" he bit his tongue, better not to provoke the man who had stopped that brute from driving a nail through his wrist. He had stared at the heavy lump hammer in horror.

"Ay. I could not let an old friend die a horrible death. As you see, I have the authority to commute your sentence. I owe you that much for the part you played in my rise. But before we enter into details, I want you to eat that bread and cheese. It'll give you strength. Drink up! There's more wine for you, old friend."

March was a broken man, prepared to do anything to save his skin. In his mind, he still had the vivid image of the raised hammer and the cruel nail held against his arm and, ringing in his ears, the word 'halt!' shouted at the last blessed second. All the signs of stress were there as he raised the cup with a trembling hand, sweat, like dew on the grass, sleeked his brow. Doninas observed him impartially and recognised the moment as favourable.

"Naturally, I have the power to send you back to be nailed on that cross, but, old friend, I also have this:" he tossed a bag of coins on the table, which landed with a satisfying clink. "I want you to leave your job as a carter and work for me for high pay. Today is your lucky day, March. Heed me well, I know what you're thinking, but you owe the Picts nothing. They are not your people any more than I am. The difference is that I can give you riches—they cannot. Go ahead, take the bag."

He saw the momentary greed in the eyes as a shaking hand reached out and clasped the coins.

"Good man! This is what you must do... to the north, outside the fortress is wilderness, frequented by sheep, hence there are sheepfolds. You will make them your home and roam from one to another, keeping your eyes and ears open, collecting information for me." He paused and studied his captive's face. "I will need to know who the enemies' allies are, where they are camped, who is in charge, what their plans are, and how many men they have."

"It will be dangerous," March muttered an objection.

"Ay, but safer than being nailed to a tree. Believe me, carter, that will be your fate if you betray me. You saw the nails. We have them aplenty. Besides, you will not be the only one, we have other prisoners and deserters, so we can verify your words by checking with many others. You will occasionally meet one of them. Instead, every time you report back to me with useful information, you will receive a similar bag of coins," he nodded at the hand clutching the bag and gave him a significant look and encouraging smile. "Do we have an agreement, March, old friend?"

"Ay, we do, Decurion."

Doninas' clenched fist hit the table, "Decurion? That was a lifetime ago!" he snarled. "You will address me as *Comes* and ask for me with that title when you return. Now go! Out of my sight! Go to a sheepfold and give thanks to your God that an old friend saved you from the fate He bestowed on his only son."

As he watched him scuttle out of his quarters, Doninas smiled. His plan had worked splendidly, in one fell swoop, he was now safe in Vercovicium; he had sent a message to the Britons that spies would be arrested and disappear; he would have his own unsuspected spy out among the Picts. All in all, a good day's work!

10

EBORACUM AND THE WESTERN EMPIRE, AD 344-353

THE IMMEDIATE CONSEQUENCE OF DONINAS' CREATION OF A network of spies north of Hadrian's Wall, known as the *Areani* or 'people of the sheepfolds', gave a degree of tranquillity to Leo, Comes Britanniarum. In the spring of 344, his second son, named Maximus after his paternal grandfather, was born. Together with good work by the Dux along the Wall and the Western Defences, Leo experienced a period without military action. In ordinary circumstances, this would have driven him to distraction; instead, he enjoyed family life with his beautiful Aoife and little Valdor, whose idea of play was to imitate a soldier. Leo lost count of the number of times he 'died' in battle under the blows of his little boy. To crown his happiness came the birth of and baptism of Maximus.

This domestic bliss would soon end in the most unexpected way. Unexpected, because Britannia was an outpost of a large Empire and uncertain rumours arrived through loose-tongued traders, or, occasionally, by official messenger. Leo and his brother, therefore, had little idea of how unpopular their emperor Constans had become. Unlike his brother and co-ruler Constantius II, Constans was targeted with gossip about his personal life. Suspicions were fuelled by his unduly favouring good-looking members of his barbarian bodyguard and he was accused by some of pederasty with young barbarian hostages. These hostile slights, probably untrue, when added to serious accusations of personal greed, neglecting parts of the Empire and employing corrupt ministers resulted in the inevitable.

Leo first learnt about these events when his father's flagship docked in Eboracum.

"Leo, we have to make a decision, or rather, *you* have to make it, as my mind is made up."

"What's going on, father?"

"Emperor Constans was on a hunting trip when he heard that General Magnentius declared himself emperor at *Augustodunum* with the support of troops on the Rhine frontier. Worse followed, Leo, because he also gained support from the western provinces of the Empire. Our Emperor Constans was forced to flee to save his life."

"Good God! So, what is it you have resolved?"

"Given that, as he tried to reach *Hispania*, supporters of Magnentius cornered him in a fortification in *Helena* in the eastern Pyrenees of south-western Gaul and slew him after he sought sanctuary in a temple."

"The emperor is dead!"

"I'm afraid so, and we have to make a choice, Leo. Either we support a barbarian usurper, Magnus Magnentius, unrelated to the great Constantine, or we sustain Constantius II, his grandson. I am ready to take the fleet in support of Constantius, but I need cavalry and infantry from you and Primus."

"What does Primus say?"

"He doesn't know, yet."

"Well, I've decided. Give me two days to gather my men. Where shall we join your ships?"

"Let's say at Branodunum."

"So be it!"

Despite his enjoyment of family life, Leo had missed the thrill of a military campaign, only occasionally joining in the defeat of Scoti raiders on the west coast. Here was the potential of real warfare—a Roman civil war. So, he left his palatial home with mixed feelings, kissing Aoife and the children, knowing that he might never see them again. Yet, he was convinced that his father was right. What guarantee was there that his family, known supporters of Constans and Constantine the Great before him, would be confirmed in their positions of privilege by the usurper? Therefore, he boarded the flagship at Branodunum with a relatively light heart, knowing that his messenger had ridden to warn

Doninas of his departure and the consequent weakening of forces in the north.

They sailed south to Dubris, where Leo was united with his brother, who had received his father's message. Primus brought with him welcome reinforcements, so it was a significant force that sailed for Italy. Only in Ostia did they discover that Constantius had marched westward to avenge the murder of his brother. Magnentius, meanwhile, decided to invade Illyricum, and initially his army performed very well.

In Ostia, the admiral explained, "We must sail around the south of Italy into the Adriatic Sea to join forces with Constantius in the Province of *Pannonia*." They disembarked at *Nauportus*, where they joined Constantius. The emperor sought out Leo and rode with him to show him the cataphract cavalry. Leo's jaw dropped; he had never seen anything like them. Constantius chuckled, "I see you are surprised Comes!"

"I am, Sire, I have never seen horses covered in steel plates and their riders, too! They must be invincible in battle."

"That is my hope. As you see, they are heavy and that is why I brought you here. You command light cavalry, but will have an important role in the forthcoming battle. Your men will follow the cataphracts and skirmish around the edges, eliminating the enemy scattered and fleeing from these men and, if there is a rout, you will be the pursuers, slaying the escapees."

"So be it, Sire. I will prepare my men for their role."

On 28 September, 351, the two armies—together totalling 95,000 men—clashed at the Battle of Mursa. With 55,000 casualties, it was the bloodiest battle in Roman history. Constantius lost 30,000 men and Magnentius 25,000. The Eastern Emperor, Constantius, wisely declined to fight and only learnt of his hard-won victory afterwards from the bishop of Mursa. Primus, who did fight, led infantry from the front and died a hero's death. Leo, who saw his brother fall, immediately charged his cavalry at the foes responsible and cut them down from horseback.

Despite his severe losses, Constantius won the battle, largely due to his heavy cavalry, but also to the bravery of the Comes Britanniarum and his mobile horsemen. Magnentius fled to *Aquileia* in northern Italy while Constantius consolidated by regaining control of Africa, Spain, and southern Italy, strengthening his army as he progressed. Meanwhile, Magnentius decided to retreat into Gaul.

Constantius spent his time recruiting troops and retaking towns occupied by Magnentius. In the summer of 352, Constantius moved into Italy, only to find that Magnentius had chosen not to defend the peninsula. Leo and his father had sailed from Pannonia to Ostia and were on the verge of returning to Britannia when Constantius summoned them, "I am sorry for your loss, my worthy generals. This time we shall travel to Gaul together, for it is there that the traitor Magnentius has fled. He has assembled troops in a mountainous area in southern Gaul."

Constantius and his troops sailed to *oppidum Genua* in Liguria and from there marched into the Alpine region. The armies met at *Mons Seleucus* in early August, 353 and, this time, Constantius led his men into battle, again adopting the tactic of placing the light behind the heavy cavalry and holding back the infantry until after the charge of the cataphracts. Again, it was a victorious tactic, but with a more decisive outcome and Magnentius escaped, only to commit suicide, a few days later on 10 August. Following his conclusive battle, Constantius wintered his troops at Arles, where among the guests of honour were Maximus and Leo. The latter suffered the absence of his beloved Aoife and the children, so he begged the emperor to be allowed to return to Britannia. Constantius smiled indulgently, "You will stay for three more days, Comes Leo, for I have planned a surprise."

The highest military honour for a Roman general was a triumph, normally enacted in Rome, and reserved for generals who exceptionally had saved their legion in battle. But Constantius, grateful to Leo and Maximus, held a triumph in Arles. In any case, the festivities would be paid for by the Senate in Rome. Before an exultant, cheering populace, Constantius himself placed the coronae of laurel leaves on Maximus and Leo's heads. This was the most prestigious honour, awarded to soldiers for exceptional bravery on the battlefield.

After the evening's celebrations, Constantius took them aside, "You will still be in mourning for your son, Primus, Maximus, and my heart aches for you. But on a practical level, I need to replace my Count of the Saxon Shore, but have nobody in mind. What are your thoughts on the matter?"

"Sire, I think that the Dux Britanniarum, whom I appointed could take up the position. He has never disappointed in each mission I have assigned to him, while he has a noble and trustworthy centurion who could take up his post, well used to the north of Britannia and its challenges. He is a centurion of the glorious Ala Gallorum Petriana, named Quintus."

"My grandfather, a splendid judge of character, trusted yours, Leo, and his judgement has proved indispensable to me. I accept your recommendations and am prepared to have the documents drafted and sealed in my name."

"Thank you, Sire," Maximus echoed Leo's words.

They left at dawn to march over the Alpine pass with their men and return to Maximus' flagship, still berthed at *oppidum Genua*. It took two weeks to arrive at the port and another delay of a few days of bad weather before they could safely sail through the Pillars of Hercules and northwards for Britannia.

Maximus agreed to disembark Leo directly at Eboracum and would sail back down the coast to Dubris, where he would break the bad news and console Primus' grieving widow. As he said to Leo, "I wonder how his mother will take it?"

"Mother was a shield maiden," Leo said proudly, "She would expect nothing less than the courage my brother displayed when he fell. Mursa was a bloody affair, we were lucky to survive it, father."

"We were and I am lucky to have another son, like you."

Those words resounded in Leo's heart as he hurried to Aoife's arms. She sobbed when he broke the news of Primus' death, but Aoife was anything but a shield maiden. Leo was astonished to see how Maximus had grown. Of course, he had been away for three years in his emperor's service and the six-year-old he had left behind had become a sturdy nine.

"Valdor insists on training with him," Aoife explained.

"Ay, where is Valdor?"

"Likely he is down at the river practising his swimming."

"Not alone, I hope!"

"Nay, husband, I insisted on a swimming trainer—a Batavian, whose boast is that he has swum the Ouse from here as far as the ferry at *Transitus Maximus* on the *Abus* and back."

"Do you not wish to swim like Valdor, Maximus?"

"Nay, father, I prefer to learn to fight. A man cannot fight in a river!"

Leo laughed, "I suppose there's time to learn to swim." He stared hard into Maximus' eyes. "Did you know that your great-grandfather,

Valdor, was a hardy swimmer? His friend escaped the Romans in Batavia by swimming farther than his pursuers thought possible. So, the four friends escaped and came to Britannia. You see, one day, you may need to swim before you become a great warrior like your father." He showed his wife and son his laurel crown and explained how it was the greatest honour a Roman soldier could achieve. Little Maximus wanted to wear it but Aoife stood firm. "You will only wear one of these if you earn it in battle for the same bravery your father showed. Be proud of your father and seek to be noble like him." Maximus, who was about to stamp his feet, thought better of it and, instead, made a silent vow.

"My love, be prepared to host two guests and their escort in the next few days. I'm sending for two of my best men in the north. The emperor has promoted them on my recommendation, so it will be a festive occasion."

"I'll warn the cook and the servants. But there's no immediate rush if your messenger has to ride to the Wall. Anyway, look who's here!"

"Oh mother, you spoilt my surprise attack!" cried Valdor, who was sneaking up on his father from behind. That plan abandoned, he flung himself into his father's embrace.

"I swear you have grown a foot taller!" Leo crowed, delighted, also at the hard muscles he could feel under the tunic. "How old are you now?"

"Eleven, father."

"Well, tomorrow, I'll take over your military training and teach you all I know. You'll be ready to fight real foes when you are sixteen and I'll not hold you back as my father did me! I've proved him wrong many times over," he explained his *corona* to the wide-eyed prodigy.

"I'll make you proud of me, father, you'll see, but I don't know if I could ever win my laurels, like you," he ended modestly.

"Oh, I'm sure you will, Valdor with those muscles and that proud name."

"I've got muscles, too, father," Maximus showed a flexed arm to his smiling family, "but, oh, I'm not called Valdor," he ended, dismayed.

"Ah, but you are *Maximus*, like your grandfather, did I not mention that he won a corona, too?"

"There you are, my pet," Aoife said to her favourite son, "you can do it, too!"

It was a very happy family that retired early to bed.

The days slipped by and on the fifth, Doninas and Quintus arrived at the palace on foot from the harbour, for they had wisely taken a ship from the north-east, thus avoiding the long ride to Eboracum.

"It has been too long, old friend," Leo greeted Doninas. "How's life on the Wall?"

"As dull as ever! While you were away enjoying yourself in Italy, we have been fighting the mist and rain. I swear my bones ache the more with every passing year!"

"Then you will be pleased with the news I have for you both from Rome." He handed the men a sealed scroll each. Hastily, they broke the seals and read.

"But what of Primus?" Doninas asked.

"Died at the Battle of Mursa," Leo said flatly.

"Oh, my dear friend, I did not know. Forgive my earlier crass remark."

"It is forgotten. Quintus, you will take over Doninas' role as Dux and keep me well informed about the situation beyond the Wall."

He could not know that his well-meaning promotion of his friends would lead to disaster because, whereas March the carter was reasonably happy to report on the Picts to his former drinking companion, who had saved his life, he was terrified at the prospect of meeting with the very man who had ordered his crucifixion. March disappeared into Pictish territory, ready to join the enemy and to corrupt the other Areani.

II

EBORACUM AND HADRIAN'S WALL, AD 353-361

AFTER A PERIOD OF MOURNING FOR PRIMUS, SILVIA DECIDED that there was no point in remaining in Dubris without family ties. She was certain that it would be better for Gaius to grow up with his cousins, who were only slightly younger. Besides, Leo and Aoife had plenty of room in the *domus palatina* and their quality of life would be better. As for Gaius, he acted indifferently, but he liked his uncle and admired him from a distance after his grandfather's tales; Maximus had told him about his younger son's valour. Secretly, Gaius wished to emulate him by winning a triumph or a corona or both. Therefore, on the day of his arrival in Eboracum he was impressed by Leo teaching his cousin how to fight a left-handed opponent.

When he begged to be included in the next training session, Leo said, "Of course! If you are anything like your father, you'll be a mighty warrior. Valdor, you'll have your mettle tested." Valdor grinned; he was confident of his abilities and was happy to have his cousin to measure himself against. Gaius, at ten, was a year older and a few inches taller, but judging by his leanness, Valdor believed he had more muscle. *I wouldn't be surprised if Maximus runs him close!* To hear Maximus boasting, it was a foregone conclusion, but Valdor smiled, *he's due to be taken down a peg or two!* He would rather Gaius did it because Maximus had the dislikeable trait of running off and whining to his mother. *Well, he's only seven, I suppose.*

The boys' prowess at sword fighting progressed so that when Leo received the unexpected pleasure of a surprise visit from Doninas, he was proud to have him watch a mock combat between the older cousins. Doninas was impressed.

"How old did you say they were?"

"Gaius will be eleven next month and Valdor is a year younger."

"Good Lord! As these two continue to grow, the enemy would be wise to flee overseas!"

They shared a hearty laugh and left the boys to their labours to discuss more serious matters.

"What brings you to Eboracum, apart from visiting an old friend?"

"That was my main purpose, but I also seek out your advice. I am new to the role of Count of the Saxon Shore and, frankly, can see no need for additional forts. My idea is to strengthen those that my predecessors built. I wanted your opinion, that's all."

"Do you have anything in mind?"

"Ay, well, I thought I'd begin with Othona because it protects the estuary of the Colne, which flows through the important town of Camolodunum. I thought that it would be a good idea to strengthen the walls with bastions, but I also wish to seek men to reinforce the garrison."

"Strengthening the walls is a splendid notion, but I'm afraid I can't help you with reinforcements. More or less on a daily basis, I receive such a request from every fort in the north. Strictly in confidence, I can tell you that the emperor is sapping men. Since the civil war against Magnentius and the heavy losses incurred, Constantius is short of men in the frontier areas. Despite this, he is planning a campaign against the Alamanni and word has it that if he defeats them—as I believe he will—that he will campaign across the Danube against the Quadi and Sarmatians. He's right, of course, the Empire is assailed on all of its frontiers, especially now that the barbarians have understood that internal strife has bled our defences white and that's something I must talk to you about, who are more expert than I."

"How do you manage to get better wine than that of Dubris?"

"I think it's a question of having the right contacts. If you like, I'll summon the merchant who supplies us and we'll see if the Italians can stop off at Dubris on their way here. Now, back to business. I've received alarming reports from Vercovicium."

"What's the problem?"

"Your reliable spy, March the carter, has vanished."

"Do you think that the Picts discovered his betrayal and have slain him?"

"It's a possibility, but it doesn't explain why Quintus' chain of Areani has also disappeared."

"The Picts will have silenced them one way or another."

"Ay, it's a problem because we know nothing more of their plans, whether they're plotting to attack again."

"You could send a raiding party into Caledonia, capture a couple of savages and torture the truth out of them."

"You make it sound easy, Doninas, but you know the nature of the terrain north of the Wall. Remember that the Antonine Wall lasted only eight years before the legions were forced to abandon it and withdraw to Hadrian's Wall."

"The Picts are formidable in their own territory; I'll give you that."

"Frankly, the situation worries me and, to strengthen the Wall's contingent, I've had to weaken some inland forts, which is why, old friend, I can't spare you any men for south of Eboracum."

"I understand. I'll press on with building the bastions at Othona, though."

As Leo expected, the following year, after Doninas' visit, Constantius defeated the Alemanni, although it did not stop him from demanding more men from Britannia.

"If things carry on like this," Leo grumbled to Aoife, "the Picts and the Scoti won't hesitate to invade."

"What can you do to prevent this?"

"I am thinking of raiding into Cambria and taking slaves to train as auxiliaries to strengthen the northern frontier. But nay, it's an unsound plan—a folly. The Cambrian frontier is settled and our garrisons at Deva and Glevum have everything under control. How I wish Constantius would leave us be!"

It was a vain wish, for as predicted, the emperor thrust across the Danube in 357 and the war against the Sasanians erupted with renewed intensity in 359, causing Constantius to travel east in 360 to restore stability after the loss of several border fortresses. As Leo explained to his wife and Primus' widow, "The emperor makes more demands for our auxiliaries and who can blame him? What would I do if we were to lose border fortresses? I wish for a change of policy in Rome."

Maybe that wish would be granted because in 360 Julian claimed the rank of *Augustus*, leading to war between the two after Constantius' attempts to persuade Julian to back down failed. Fortunately, no battle was fought as Constantius became ill and died of fever in November of 361 in *Mopsuestia*, naming Julian as his rightful successor.

In the prosperous and peaceful town of Eboracum, meanwhile, by the time of the emperor's death, Gaius, his lean frame now filled out into a robust eighteen-year-old, expert with all types of weapons, in horsemanship and a strong swimmer for his age, was matched only by Valdor. Both youths pressed for active service in Britannia and, although Aoife and Silvia protested, Leo remembered his treatment when Primus was allowed to go and he was not, sent them to join Quintus at Vercovicium. Despite his hot protests, Maximus managed only to extract a promise that he could join them on his seventeenth birthday, still two years away. To some extent, this mollified Aoife, making her loss of Valdor more palatable.

Leo's decision was based on two important facts: firstly, for the last eight years, the Picts and the Scoti had left the frontiers in peace; secondly, the cousins were unrivalled in martial arts, managing to defeat even veterans in mock combats. Neither of them had bested Leo, yet, although he admitted to himself that it was only a matter of time since he was getting no younger.

As for the youths, they soon settled with their comrades in the spartan, wintry conditions on the Wall. One day, while on sentry duty above the north gate, Gaius stared out over the snowy landscape and whispered to his cousin, "Tomorrow, we're off duty. What say you? Shall we venture out and capture ourselves a Pict? My friend Marcus is on gate duty this week, he'll let us out without any fuss."

"We can't just go without our centurion's authorisation."

"Lucius Sextus would never agree and, in any case, he won't miss us as we're off duty. We can always say we were in the White Stag tavern. That'll probably end up being true, anyway!"

The following morning, early, their breath wreathing up in front of them, the cousins slipped out of the fortress and into the deep snow of the wilderness. Even with their protective clothing and footwear, the cold was dangerous and the going difficult. They had been out less than an hour when Valdor whispered, "Look over there, footprints in the snow!"

They hurried over to examine them, determined the direction, westwards, and followed them. Before long, in the distance, they could make out a sheepfold and a thin spiral of smoke.

"There's someone in there," hissed Gaius, "try to be as quiet as a viper sunning itself in the summer."

Valdor smiled; he could do with some summer sunshine. He nodded and pointed to the sheepfold entrance, signalling with a circling finger, to close on the pen from the back. This they did, climbing up the drystone wall and peering into the interior, where several skinny bleating sheep were huddled around a small fire and a man with a woollen cloak was adding crackling twigs to the scant flames.

Valdor waved his hand in a downward motion and he and Gaius dropped down into the snow, bending over to enter the fold through a rickety gate. This could not be done silently, so the man tried to escape by climbing out the back of the pen, but his smooth leather shoes slipped on the stones and he fell backwards to find Valdor's gladius at his throat.

He was an unkempt, starved Briton and no match for either youth, who hauled him to his feet, thus demonstrating the mismatch of muscles to the frightened captive.

"We'll not hurt you if you come along with us peacefully." The Briton nodded his understanding of Valdor's words. "Try to escape and we'll slay you," Gaius added, his voice and intent harsher than his cousin's.

"I'll be happy to go to a warmer place," the Briton said in an accent so strong that they could barely understand him.

"Ay, we'll give you a bowl of hot gruel at the fortress," Valdor grinned.

"Who are you, Briton? One of the Areani?"

"Ay, that I am."

"Why then do you not report to our Dux?"

"Because he wanted to crucify our leader and none of us durst speak with him."

"Well, that's one fear you'll overcome, friend. You can trust me to intervene on your behalf," Valdor reassured him with a gentle squeeze of the almost absent arm muscle.

Inside the fortress, it was easy to obtain three steaming bowls of oat gruel. They slurped the watery porridge greedily, the food restoring warmth to their chilled limbs. In between spoonfuls, Gaius nodded at the captive, "How are we going to explain *him* to our centurion?"

Valdor frowned and said, "I have an idea! We'll tell Lucius that we were on sentinel duty and we spotted him in the distance, so we slipped out to arrest him. Our centurion doesn't keep the duty roster in his head!"

"You're right!"

"Hark, Briton, it's in your interests to tell our centurion the truth. I can only prevent torture if you cooperate. Understood?"

"Ay," the Briton gulped down the last of his gruel and Valdor noted that although his face was sullen, his eyes were not shifty.

They took him to Centurion Lucius Sextus, a veteran of the XX Legion, and gave their version of events. The centurion was so taken by the capture that he did not think about the duty roster. "Well done, lads! You've only been here two minutes and already you've pulled off quite a coup. As a reward, it'll be you to fetch Dux Quintus. He'll be in his quarters in the *principia*."

The Dux listened intently to Valdor's plausible explanation, all the while studying the strong neck, bulging arm muscles and firm jaw of the youthful legionary.

"You are both among our latest auxiliaries, is it not so?"

"Ay, lord."

"What is your name, legionary?"

"Valdor, Dux."

"Valdor? I know that name! Wasn't he the Count of the Saxon Shore?"

"Ay, my great-grandfather, lord. He lives on the Isle of Vectis, but he's an old man now."

"So, your father is the Comes Britanniarum, true?"

"Ay, lord, he is."

"What the devil! Why did he send you here as a simple legionary?"

"I suppose he wanted us to make our own way. This is my cousin, Gaius, son of Primus, who died in battle not long ago."

"Welcome, Gaius. You boys have started well, but can you ride a horse?"

"Ay, and well, lord," Gaius said, receiving a nudge from Valdor for his immodesty, a gesture that did not escape Quintus' eagle eye.

"Good. I shall not have you remain simple infantry legionaries, but transfer you at once to my glorious *Ala Gallorum Petriana* cavalry regiment. You will both be decurions."

The youths' faces lit up, making Quintus certain of the wisdom of his decision.

"Well, I'll send you to choose from the available horses and to withdraw your insignia. Meanwhile, I'll notify your respective centurions before I go to interrogate the captive."

"Lord, I have impressed upon him to tell the truth, so that mercy can be shown to him, whatever his tale," Valdor said.

"I'll bear that in mind, Decurion."

The Dux strode across the courtyard to the centurion's quarters and greeted his subordinate.

"Ave, Lucius, what does this wretch have to say for himself?"

"Nothing, lord. I thought it best to wait for you before questioning him."

"Ah, good, so we can set off on the right foot. Heed me well, Briton, the men who found you are good fellows and have intervened for you. They tell me that you are prepared to tell me everything you know to avoid any—*ahem*—unpleasantness."

"It's true, sire, I'll tell you everything. But where to begin?"

Quintus snorted, "From the beginning, of course!"

"I was starving, see. Scratching out a few carrots and parsnips when a man gave me a silver coin and told me to get a meal at the tavern. I was so grateful—"

"Who was this man?"

"He didn't give me his name, but he was a Briton and tall. They told me he was a carter by trade. Anyhow, he told me I could earn more silver coins if I did as he asked."

"What did he want you to do?"

The Briton looked uneasy and shifty, "It's not so easy to come and go through the forts along the Wall. I feel as if I could be arrested and killed any day. My job is to report on how many soldiers I see and to try and gain recruits in the *vici*, who are tired of struggling to survive. I found out his name!" he added hurriedly.

Quintus grinned wolfishly, "Who, the carter?"

The Briton gulped, "Ay, lord, his name is March."

"We already know that. I almost crucified him."

Sweat glistened on the Briton's brow. "I know! He talks about it often enough to scare us into doing his will."

"Where will you meet him next?"

"We change places every time, but it's always in a sheepfold and there's usually about twenty of us. We have to be careful not to attract the authorities' attention."

"I'd say you do that very well."

"Next time, we have to meet at a pen north of Banna Fort when it is the half-moon."

"So, in approximately five days from now."

"Ay, lord."

Dux Quintus smiled grimly, "This is what we will do. You will be our guest meanwhile. You can eat and drink your fill. In five days, you will make your way to the sheepfold but you'll wear a red Roman cloak so that we can distinguish you and you'll be unharmed. You can tell the others that you stole it from an empty room. We want to take this March alive and I am prepared to spare your comrades if they cooperate like you, Briton." Quintus' brow wrinkled and he expressed his thoughts, "The Banna Fort, that's the *Cohors I Aelia Dacorum*; they're experienced veterans and should do nicely."

12

BANNA FORT AND ENVIRONS, AD 361-362

Dux Quintus took a strong force out of Banna Fort made up of the *Cohors I Aelia Dacorum* and his own cavalry unit, including Gaius and Valdor. The sturdy horses had little difficulty in ploughing through the snow to encircle the sheepfold due north of the fortress. Quintus dismounted and led his horsemen into the pen. They knew it was the right one because in among the huddled bleating sheep was a glimpse of a red cloak. Shooing the animals aside, they saw the grisly sight of the familiar Briton with his throat slashed from side to side. There was not much blood visible because the crimson woollen cloak had soaked it up, but the gaping slash and the bloodless face of the victim spoke clearly of death.

"They somehow discovered that the poor fellow was working for us," Quintus said grimly. "Quick, search the area for footprints. I want to capture March the carter alive." There was little chance of finding disturbances in the snow because it was snowing heavily and even their hoofprints had already vanished.

The Dacian infantry arrived, so Quintus ordered their centurions to search the vicinity of the sheepfold for any trace of the missing Areani. He remounted his patient horse and ordered the cavalry to fan out in all directions and to travel with speed in the hope of coming across the furtive and wily spies. Logically, they could not withstand the cold by remaining exposed to the snowstorm for long, so it was a question of finding a place—one where they could shelter—another sheep pen or a cavern, or so the Dux thought. The Areani had the advantage of knowing the terrain intimately, whereas the Roman force struggled merely to cope with the harsh weather.

Valdor rode beside his centurion, Lucius Sextus, at the head of twenty riders; Gaius was with another centurion off in a different direction. This was the first time since they came to the Wall that the cousins had spent time apart.

Suddenly, peering through the thickening veil of snow, in the distance, Lucius slowed and pointed. Narrowing his eyes and squinting through the flakes, Valdor saw what the centurion had noticed: a dozen or so orangey-red pinpricks of flickering flames—bonfires!

"We have them!" Lucius exulted, but Valdor's heart sank. He was sure it was a trap to lure them towards the flames. But how could he, with his inexperience, argue with a veteran centurion? Lucius ordered a gallop towards the fires, not that galloping was an option. The sturdy beasts responded as best they could on the soft, energy-sapping surface. It was the reduced speed that saved the company of horsemen. Scanning ahead as best he could, Valdor noticed the curved depression in the snow some fifty yards ahead. Usurping the centurion's rank, Valdor raised an arm and bellowed, "Halt!" The cavalry, trained to obey a superior officer, slithered to a halt.

"What the devil! What's the meaning of this, Decurion?"

"Forgive me, Centurion, but look closely, can you not see yon snow-covered hollow? We're riding towards a trap. Why else would the Picts announce their presence with fires? I'll wager there's an abyss where the snow dips."

"You!" the centurion commanded a rider, "Approach yon depression carefully and check to see if it's crossable."

There was no danger of the horseman plunging headlong into a pit because the conditions slowed his horse considerably; not only that, but the beast's instincts made it stop just before the dip in the snow. The rider dismounted, walked over to a rock and, staggering under its weight, with a superhuman effort, swung it backwards and forwards until he hurled it into the hollow. Being so heavy, it fell only a few feet ahead of him, but the effect was spectacular. The rock created a hole in the snow through which the cavalryman was able to glimpse a cruelly sharpened stake, presumably one of many. Had they ridden into the hollow, the result would have been devastating. The soldier returned to his horse, his movement saving him because a black-fletched arrow buried itself into the snow a few paces beyond where he had stood. Swiftly, he jumped on his horse and rode back to his comrades to report, pursued by arrows shot from beyond the fires.

"Centurion, it's a trap; a pit filled with sharpened stakes and they have archers, firing from beyond yon fires."

"Decurion Valdor, well done! Your sixth sense saved us. That trap is not the work of recent hours, but a cleverly prepared scheme that must have taken weeks. We shall return to our base and hope that the others are as lucky."

Lucius Sextus ordered the retreat, heading directly for the fortress. The route took them back to the sheepfold where the corpse of the unfortunate Briton lay. Whereas the centurion and his other comrades rode straight past, Valdor had half a mind to sling the body of the poor spy over his horse to give the man a decent Christian burial. That was how he found another man lurking inside the pen, huddling up to the sheep to keep himself warm and alive. Valdor put two fingers in his mouth and emitted a shrill whistle, alerting not only the man who tried to escape, but also his centurion. In moments, the shelter was surrounded and the man captured. He was one of the Areani, not a Pict, but it meant their foray into the wilderness had not been entirely in vain.

Seemingly more a bundle of rags than a human, the spy was bound with a rope and dragged behind a horse. Mercifully, it was not far to the fortress. Valdor, instead, shuffled backwards on his mount and ordered two cavalrymen to heave the body of the murdered Briton across the horse in front of him. With the extra weight, the sturdy beast plodded slowly back to the fortress. Once there, Valdor allowed the body to slide to earth and had it covered with snow to preserve it until it could be buried in the presence of a priest.

Gradually, the other parties returned, able to report no gains or losses. Valdor was delighted to welcome back his shivering cousin and together they found a space in front of a log fire and gradually restored body heat, helped by the passing around of a leather bottle containing red wine.

Valdor related the tale of the deadly pit, narrowly avoided, resisting the temptation to take any credit, but stressing the cunning of the Picts.

He also told Gaius about the unlucky Briton whose throat had been slit.

"They probably didn't believe his account of how he had come in possession of a soldier's cloak," Gaius said.

"I'll wager they thought it impossible to leave the fort wearing the crimson of a legionary; it's not as if it's unnoticeable. Maybe we shouldn't have given it to him. Likely, it condemned him to death."

"We can't be sure about that, cousin. Set your mind at rest. But by God, it was cold out there! And all for nothing!"

"Not exactly. Our party has brought back one of the Areani."

"Really? Well, let's hope he proves more useful than the other one," Gaius grumbled. "I don't want to go out there again for a while."

Dux Quintus ordered the poor skeletal figure of the Briton—more bones than flesh—stripped to the waist and bound spreadeagled to a wooden frame in a staged attempt to extract the necessary information required. A strapping legionary with a scourge in his hand stood, muscular arms folded across his chest, awaiting orders while Quintus waited for the faked enactment to have its effect on the trembling Briton.

"We may be able to avoid whipping you, Briton, if you cooperate and tell us what we need to know."

"I'll tell you everything, your lordship. I swear, I will."

The pathetic quaking figure poured out some facts that startled the dux. He sent for Decurion Valdor because he considered him the perfect messenger to ride to warn Count Leo in Eboracum. After a few minutes, Valdor appeared and cast a pitying eye over the wretched captive. Quintus caught the look on Valdor's face and ordered the legionary, "Toss that scourge aside and cut down the prisoner; find him a warm cloak and feed him, for he has provided invaluable information.

"Decurion, be seated. Your alertness at the sheepfold has been repaid a thousandfold. Hark, this is the situation: the Areani met with the Pictish leaders who are a chieftain from the north of Caledonia named Elpin and one from the area north of the Clyde named Uist. It seems that the Areani are not only active in the area of the Wall, but also much farther south, even beyond Eboracum." He paused to let his words sink in. "It is a matter of great concern to me that Elpin and Uist have met. They are plotting a conspiracy that goes beyond our shores and may involve Germanic tribes. Now heed me well, the situation is made much worse because the former emperor Constantius sent an administrator to Britannia, a certain Paulus Catena. This came about when the usurper Magnentius tried to seize power. Constantius needed to root out potential sympathisers of Magnentius in Britannia, but the problem is that Paulus Catena is corrupt. He has been trumping up false charges against rich and peaceful Britons, seizing their villas and possessions in a bloody and arbitrary purge. It is important that your father learns of the activities of this unprincipled Paulus, and what better messenger can I send than his son? I am sure he will be as happy to see you as he will be unhappy to hear the news that the Picts and Scoti intend to profit from the resentment that is stirring among the Britons south of the Wall. Many of Paulus' victims are unjustly imprisoned. Count Leo—"

"Has the power and sense of justice to right these wrongs," Valdor interrupted.

"Your father will also be glad to learn of your promotion, Centurion."

"Centurion?"

"Ay, you saved us from the Pictish trap and then followed it up by capturing the Briton who has provided all this invaluable information. You will take an escort of twenty men to Eboracum. I cannot stress enough that it is essential that the Comes learns about the potential danger that Britannia faces."

"May I take Decurion Gaius, my cousin, with me to Eboracum?"

"You may, but do not overly delay your return, as I fear we will soon be called into action."

Uplifted, Valdor led his band of cavalry without incident south to Eboracum, where he was joyfully reunited with his parents and Gaius with his mother. Delighted to see such a rapid promotion, Leo said, "I sent you to the Wall without any recommendation. I see you have both risen in rank immediately, on merit, exactly as I foresaw."

"Unfortunately, father, I'm afraid I am the bearer of unforeseen tidings." The grave expression on his son's face captured Leo's attention. Valdor explained his role in the arrest of the Briton and delivered the unsettling message that had been entrusted to him.

"The sly devil! How come his activities haven't come to my attention? Valdor, I appreciate that you must return with haste to your post, but I order you to remain in Eboracum for two days until I have dealt with this perverse individual. If reports are correct, the new emperor, Julian, will have no truck with certain behaviour."

Count Leo was as good as his word. Although Paulus Catena's trafficking had escaped his vigilance, his subordinates were quick to react and arrest the malefactor. A centurion was tasked with keeping Paulus under restraint on board a ship that would take him to Rome. In a document, Leo drafted Paulus' official exile from Britannia. The Britons unjustly imprisoned with false accusations were immediately released and restored to their positions with compensation. Leo ensured that justice was seen to prevail. He had a letter drafted for the Dux Britanniarum and entrusted it to Valdor. The parting from their families was bittersweet for both Valdor and Gaius. The one who suffered most was young Maximus, but the promise that he could join his brother at the Wall the following spring lightened his mood.

Back at Hadrian's Wall, Valdor gave the dux the letter from his father, who broke the seal with apprehension, but when he read it, his expression changed. "I always knew that Count Leo was a capable soldier and a brilliant administrator. Valdor, I fear that dark times lie ahead."

The anxiety underlying his conjecture would prove to be well-founded.

13

HADRIAN'S WALL, AD 362-368

THE OMINOUS STORM CLOUDS THAT DUX QUINTUS SAW gathering north of the Wall had still not burst. For the first few months after the capture of the Briton, named Lugh, Quintus ensured that the man recovered his strength and that without catching the eye, he was clothed adequately for the harsh clime. As soon as the dux felt that he was ready to venture out, he made a pact that would keep him informed of events north of the Wall and also allow him to send disinformation to the enemy.

Lugh was able to move freely to and from Vercovicium because that was what other Areani and the Picts expected of him. So, the Briton spent his time gathering snippets of information in the vicus and the fort and providing details of Pictish encounters with other hostile tribes. Gradually Quintus pieced together an appalling picture of what was occurring in Britannia. Count Leo in Eboracum proved the exception to what was a corrupt and treasonous administration; native British troops collaborated with the barbarians and, in general, the Roman military that remained after imperial demands depleted their regiments, often deserted and joined in widespread banditry.

Paulus' destabilisation of the Roman administration in Britannia allowed the hostile Picts and the Scoti to invade and pillage Roman settlements. The enemy used cunning to find entry routes less difficult to overcome than the western defensive chain of forts or those of Hadrian's Wall. These marauders formed bands moving from place to place in search of loot. Count Leo fought a pitched battle against one such band in the summer of 363 and won a crushing victory, but it was an isolated success in a situation of general chaos that made him despair. Eboracum was a safe haven for trade and civic stability but once beyond its walls, the picture was very different. The truth was plain to Leo: there was no longer an effective military force in the province and from what he learnt from occasional messages from his old friend Doninas, now Count of the Saxon Shore, his forces were also depleted by imperial demands as the Empire struggled to defend its extensive frontiers against constant barbarian assaults and an inability to staunch the haemorrhage of desertion.

How Leo longed for the good old days when his troops were not made up of native auxiliaries or barbarian troops lured by prospects of steady food and pay, but by professionals from the Italian peninsula or consolidated provinces.

The immediate problem facing Leo came from within the family. He had a promise to keep and had defaulted by a year. Young Maximus would join his brother and cousin on Hadrian's Wall, but Leo considered Eboracum a safer place for his son than the Wall. Pestered by the youth, Leo recognised the same resentment that he had felt when many years ago, his parents had taken Primus to his first stationing in Cumbria and left him behind with a promise of future deployment. At last, in the late summer of 367 the Count gathered a strong escort and led it himself on the northern journey to Hadrian's fortress of Vercovicium.

The Count considered that his escort of fifty cavalrymen could deal with any marauding band they might encounter. Somewhere in a dale between Isurium Brigantum and Cateractonium, near the river Swale, Leo's attention was captured by swirling black smoke, which came from a settlement in the bottom of the valley. They urged their horses forward only to halt suddenly at the sight of a woman clutching a babe to her breast, who dropped sobbing to her knees. Leo was the first to dismount and hurry over to her. Her red hair, pale freckled face and wiry build told him she was a Briton.

"What has happened? Nobody will hurt you now."

"Savages with blue faces." Tears streamed down her face and she could barely articulate, "th-they killed my man and took our pigs. They b-burnt my house."

"Stay here, but keep out of sight till we return." Leo mounted and led a gallop down into the valley. The marauders were still looting and only a desultory arrow or two flew towards them as, with *spathae* swinging, they hacked down blue-painted tribesmen. Whether they were Picts or Scoti, Leo never discovered because he had no intention of taking one alive as he could not contain his rage at the despoiling of the village and fury at the sight of the bloodied bodies of the men, women and children. He beheaded a foe in the act of throwing a flaming torch onto the reed-thatched roof of a small dwelling so that the brand fell well short and blazed on the ground.

The encounter was over in a matter of minutes with not one of the plunderers left alive. Leo ordered his men to round up the stray animals and himself slipped a noose around a mule to lead back up the valley to where the poor woman was cowering with her babe.

"Do you have family in the area?" he asked.

She shook her head, mutely.

"Then, this is what we will do: mount the mule, and we'll accompany you to our destination, where you will be safe and comfortable because we have rounded up the village animals, which will all be yours as you are the only survivor."

Her mouth twitched, but it could not be called a smile. Feeling profoundly sorry for her, Leo turned to Maximus. "This will be your first official task, son. You will ensure that this woman and her child have a house and a pen sufficient for her animals and that nobody harms her in any way."

"Ay, father."

The rest of the journey north was uneventful. Maximus led the woman into the vicus and started his search for a small property. Leo instead, headed to the *principia*, to speak with Dux Quintus.

In the fortress headquarters, Leo learnt about the informer Lugh's role. His latest report had been concerning and, after the Count's experience on the road, more so.

"The Picts have been meeting regularly with other tribes, some from overseas and are planning a coordinated assault on Britannia." Quintus explained that this was the crux of Lugh's reports. "So, we'll also have to contend with the Saxons, heathens and fierce sea rovers, already known and dreaded along the coast of Gaul."

"Our friend, Count Doninas, will have to deal with them as they are more likely to attack along the east coast. I say, do you remember his predecessor as dux? I mean the general who retired, Gratianus Funarius."

"An Illyrian, was he not?"

"Ay, well, I don't know if the news has reached you up here in this remote outpost of the Empire, but his son Valentinian has been elected Western Emperor, while his younger brother, Valens, is the Eastern Emperor."

"What does this mean for us?"

"I'll send a report about the situation in Britannia. The fact that Valentinian's father was *dux* here may carry weight and we may receive the emperor's support."

"Would God it were so! There is a great conspiracy. The tribes of the far north have promised to join with the men between the walls. There are Areani working intensely for that purpose."

"What else do you know?"

"They have been bribing and suborning the auxiliaries. All the Brigantes among the garrison will mutiny when the time comes. The province is to be freed for ever from Roman rule."

"That is not a new idea, Quintus, it's as old as Boudicca and look what happened to her!"

"Nonetheless, it is true. I swear it! The tribes have taken the blood oath. And they have allied themselves with the Scoti."

"How many men in this garrison will stand by us?"

"Less than half."

Now Leo, too, was afraid. "When is the rising timed for?"

"The next but one new moon."

"That means I have two months to contact Rome and see what we can do to stem the heathen tide. I must return forthwith to Eboracum and reorganise our forces, but honestly, we are going to need outside help, otherwise, there promises to be a terrible bloodbath."

The bad weather came sooner at Hadrian's Wall. It was a harsh country of heather and rock; bleak and terrible in winter, yet austerely beautiful in summer; it was hard to determine whether the pitiless climate was worse for the men or their animals. Beyond the fortresses, the only sounds to be heard were the occasional forlorn cry of a curlew or the whistling of the unforgiving and everlasting wind. In the winter of 367, the Roman garrison on Hadrian's Wall rebelled and the Areani militia who manned the mile castles and signal towers along the frontier, recruited from local tribesmen from either side of the Wall, allowed the Picts from Caledonia to enter Britannia. Simultaneously, Attacotti, the Scoti from Hibernia and Saxons from Germania landed in what were coordinated and pre-arranged waves on the island's mid-western and south-eastern borders.

Dux Quintus had doubled his sentinels as the second new moon approached. Instinct had taken Valdor to stand over the southern gateway as he expected trouble south, not north of the Wall. He was right because as he peered into the moonless darkness, he heard screaming from the *vicus* and the sound of raised voices. There was no sign of fire, which was a mild relief. He hurried to the headquarters and spoke to his comrade, Centurion Lucius.

"I've heard screams and shouting from the *vicus*. Do you think it's the threatened attack? Should we take a patrol out?"

"Let's consult the dux. It's dark tonight and we shouldn't take the initiative in case it goes wrong."

They went together to Dux Quintus to seek his advice.

"Each of you take all of your men. A hundred and sixty can deal with any warband. If it's a full army, call for help!"

Both centurions were shocked to discover that a score of men were missing from the barracks. The only plausible explanation was that forty legionaries had deserted. Had they joined the enemy? If so, the situation was critical.

Valdor led a cavalry unit, but he recognised the unsuitability of horses for street fighting in the dark and did not want hoofbeats to alert anyone, so they moved on foot. They advanced in a tight formation to where they could hear sounds of commotion. At the head of his company, Valdor first saw the fighting. Dark shapes flitted between buildings and suddenly, his curved infantry shield was struck by an arrow, which remained impaled in the leather and wood. Keeping the shield high in front of him, he ran straight towards the archer, who ducked around the corner of a house. Valdor halted and waved some of his men to link shields so that they made an impenetrable barrier. Only then did he swing them around into the side street. There, they came across a full-scale fight between half-naked Picts and the townsfolk, many of whom had regular swords obtained on the black market some weeks before as rumours of impending danger circulated. Many a legionary had made a tidy sum in collaboration with the military storeman. Corruption of this sort was rife along the Wall, but this time, the situation had to be considered positive. Valdor used his shield to smash its edge under the chin of the archer, thus, symbolically returning the arrow to its owner. A downward thrust of his sword finished the unconscious raider. Now, Valdor was in his element. All the years of laborious weaponry training paid off. An inspirational example to his men and the townsfolk, he carved a trail of destruction among the ferocious tribesmen, who were, for all their fierce prowess, no match for him. Not far behind him, his younger brother, in the other unit, determined to match his sibling, also wreaked death upon the Picts. Caught between the defenders and the new arrivals, the highlanders succumbed to a dreadful slaughter. The *spathae* had taken a terrible toll on the enemy, so Vercovicium was saved. Valdor was not deluded into thinking that this skirmish was the only one along the Wall. To his mind, the question was just how many Picts, or indeed Scoti, had entered Britannia. Daylight would help him understand because with the dawn, he would lead out a patrol on horseback to find out the exact circumstances.

On a visit to the Othona shore fort, Count Doninas stared from the ramparts over the Blackwater Estuary, which the stronghold was designed to guard. When he turned to gaze out over the vast North Sea, his heart chilled at the sight of multiple sails, all heading towards the coast of Britannia. Quickly he had a cornicen sound the alarm and his *numerus fortensium*, the aptly named 'numerous brave ones', who garrisoned the fortress, rushed to arms. The Count had a difficult decision to make. His garrison, although one of the strongest along the coast, was still depleted by imperial demands and, to a lesser extent, by desertion. These men did not bear a grudge because they had recently received their pay. Doninas had to decide whether to face an assault on his strong walls, created by his predecessor, the noble Valdor, or to face the enemy as they attempted to disembark. He tended to favour the latter because, in the event of a defeat, his men could retreat within the walls until reinforcements arrived.

Count Doninas had little experience of fighting Saxons, but from descriptions provided by others, he recognised the marauders as such from their round shields, long hair and beards, and the battle axes that the Picts and Scoti did not use. He gathered his centurions and explained his plan. "The enemy will soon be here and I am sure that they will attempt to take the fortress. So, we'll give them a hot reception; they will almost certainly run their ships onto the sandy beach and if we place ourselves between the marsh and the beach, we can hit them with javelins and arrows as they try to disembark. That should weaken them sufficiently for us to advance towards the ships in tight formation and engage them from behind our *scuta*. The Saxons use battle axes, so we must be prepared to ward off mighty blows and profit from the raised arms to stab with our *gladii*."

As expected, the Saxon vessels ploughed into the sand and at Doninas' gesture, a hail of javelins took the first invaders by surprise, their corpses falling onto the soft sand or into the shallow water amidships. After the initial success, many arrows and javelins buried themselves in the gaudily-painted round shields. This was useful, too, because, especially in the case of javelins, they proved a hindrance and made the shield unwieldy. Doninas ordered the last hail of javelins and let his men choose when to throw their remaining darts with more precision at selected targets.

Undoubtedly, this tactic took its toll, but the Saxons still came. More ships ran ashore; Doninas counted a line of fifty-seven vessels. He did not want to spread his men too thinly, so at least half the boats were able to disgorge their crews unhindered. These warriors made the mistake of trying to surround the Roman soldiers with the aim of attacking from behind. They did not allow for the treacherous marshy ground and soon had to return to the beach, where they gathered into a semblance of a formation, shields raised and beaten rhythmically with axe hafts as they advanced chanting the name of their god, Woden. Doninas' centurions shouted at their men and tightened the Roman formation, which, extremely disciplined, waited calmly, shields joined until the more disorganised Saxons, those survivors of the earlier attack, united with their comrades in the steady advance up the beach.

The fury of the Saxons blossomed in a headlong rush over the last few yards so that they crashed into the interlocked Roman shields. The sound of crashing axe blows striking the sturdy Roman *scuta* misled the insurgents into a false sense of superiority, since many suffered fatal wounds from a gladius thrust, whereas the Roman shields remained defiantly interlocked. The Saxons were redoubtable fighters, however, and their chieftain wily. He ordered a detachment to wade into the shallow water behind the grounded ships and these, unseen by the Romans, emerged farther down the beach, to attack silently from behind. This manoeuvre turned the tide of battle, as the Romans, hitherto standing firm, were suddenly confronted by a furious onslaught from behind. Their disciplined line broke and despite the frantic orders from their centurions, the battle became one of disparate skirmishes. The Romans were now at a disadvantage as the taller Saxons with their long-handled axes were able to attack individuals in greater numbers.

Soon, their inroads brought them close to the eagle standard where Count Doninas was shouting orders to his depleted and demoralised force. The tall, blond Saxon chieftain, his hair swinging between his shoulders in a plait under a leather and steel helm, charged towards the standard, his axe creating a deadly swathe until he stood before the Count, who defiantly pushed aside a pair of bodyguards to face his foe one-on-one. Deftly, he skipped aside as the axe scythed downwards, but could not take immediate advantage of his adversary off balance. Again, the Saxon rushed at him and Doninas raised his *scutum*, taking a massive blow, that made him stagger, unscathed, backwards. The veteran Roman soldier sensed that he would have to use cunning to overcome such a formidable enemy, so rapidly sheathing his *gladius* and seizing a javelin planted in the turf by a legionary, ready for hurling, flung it with all his might at the advancing Saxon chieftain. The Saxon was so intent upon his next axe blow that the unexpected missile struck him off-guard between his ribs and sent him sprawling to the ground. As fast as a pouncing lion, Doninas, gladius drawn, was upon him and slashing his throat in seconds.

A howl of despair alerted the Count, who had to roll away from a descending axe-head. He could not know it, but his despairing assailant was the chieftain's son, fired by vengeance and his new responsibility as leader of the tribe. Somehow, Doninas had to regain his feet and above all, his *scutum*. It was his undoing because as he bent to retrieve the shield, the young chieftain sprang forward and struck the fateful blow that killed the Count of the Saxon Shore.

Several brave centurions around the standard also died along with many legionaries, while others, seeing the developments, managed to run away and seek their fortunes, like others before them by turning to banditry in the countryside.

The victorious Saxons seized the eagle standard and carried it as a triumphant totem into the defenceless fortress which they now meant to use as their base. They were no longer an army but a warband under a young and enterprising new chieftain.

At Dubris, the Roman fortress which the Classis Britannica used as a base, the news of the death of the Count of the Saxon Shore and the fall of Othona arrived within a few days. Admiral Maximus shelved plans to regain that fortress at the sight of a hundred Jutish vessels heading for the land of the Canti tribe. His war galleys were more than a match for the Jutes' light fast vessels if he could somehow entrap them since catching them in the North Sea was problematic. He therefore devised a plan in conjunction with his captains. He would hide the size of the Roman fleet, letting the enemy only see five ships under his command. The others would hide behind headlands and in estuaries and await the *cursus publicus*, the chain of fire signals at beacons along the coast. The interacting watchtowers and beacons would alert the commanders to swoop out into the open sea and engage the enemy.

As soon as the Romans lit the first beacon, the others followed and the ships' lookouts shouted a warning. This ploy was spectacularly successful so that the Jutes, too close to the shore to flee, were caught by an entire fleet of Roman vessels. The battle was short and decisive: ramming, blazing pitch launched by catapult, and speedy boarding, left the enemy sinking and drowning or burnt and drowning, or slaughtered in battle on confined decks. This wave of raiders, sadly only one among many, was thwarted. Elsewhere, warbands of Saxons, Frisians or Jutes reached the shores of Britannia and headed inland to plunder and ravish. Farther north, the *miles areani*, the local Roman agents who provided intelligence on barbarian movements, betrayed their paymasters for bribes, which made the attacks completely unexpected. Deserting soldiers and escaped slaves roamed the countryside and turned to robbery to support themselves. Although the chaos was widespread and initially concerted, the rebels had aims simply of personal enrichment and worked as small bands rather than larger armies.

The remaining loyal army units stayed garrisoned inside south-eastern cities and in Eboracum. In the latter city, Count Leo received daily reports, each more alarming than its predecessor. Deeply saddened, he learnt of the death of his old friend *Comes* Doninas at the defence of Othona. Worse than that, *Dux* Quintus had died, defending the fortress of Glannoventa against Scoti raiders from Hibernia. Despite the high-ranking official's death, a Roman victory ensued and Leo received a messenger, sent by Valdor, who informed him of the outcome and that his two sons and nephew were alive and well. With every passing week, it became clear to Leo that a barbarian conspiracy was unfolding and while he was happy to lead forays into the countryside to vanquish roaming warbands, he recognised that there was no longer an effective military force in the province of Britannia. It was, therefore, his duty as the most senior Roman officer, to contact his emperor in a plea for forces to alleviate the situation. What Leo did not know was that Valentinian was under immense pressure from the Alemanni, who had crossed the Rhine and invaded Gaul. Initially, they had defeated and killed two of the emperor's generals until after several victories along the Meuse River, General Jovinus fought and won a pitched battle with the Alemanni near Chalôn. After his victory, he pushed the Alemanni out of Gaul and was awarded the consulate the following year for his efforts. In early 367, Valentinian was distracted from launching a punitive expedition against the Alemanni due to Leo's plea. The young, and hitherto effective, emperor despite other distractions in the Eastern Empire, decided that he did not want to lose Britannia and therefore took decisive action.

14

BRITANNIA, AD 368

NEVER DURING THE ROMAN OCCUPATION OF BRITANNIA HAD the province experienced such loss of lands and anarchy. Almost a year had gone by since the hard-pressed Emperor Valentinian I had received Count Leo's urgent request for help. The emperor held Leo in high regard and reacted when he could by choosing a general, Theodosius, and giving him command of his *comitatensis* or Imperial Field Army so that early in the year, he marched on Bononia, Rome's harbour on the Channel. The impatient general, eager to embark, cast a glance over the churning waves and the unbroken low grey clouds and fixed the captain allocated to him with a gimlet eye, "It seems to me, although I'm no sailor, that the weather is breaking favourably. I need to reach Britannia as soon as possible."

"General, the Channel is temperamental and can turn on the unwary in the blink of an eye. I would not risk my army if I may make so bold."

The intrepid general was successful also because he had a stubborn streak. But he always put his men first, so, turning his piercing gaze on the captain, he said, "I always take advice from men more experienced than myself. This is what we shall do—we'll sail across but I'll leave my army to await clearer weather." The reluctant captain dared not contradict so important an officer and, being an expert mariner, knew that there was a chance they would arrive on Britannia's shore greeted by shimmering sunlight.

Not quite so, for they sailed into the harbour at *Rutupiae* still under a dull sky, where Theodosius started gathering intelligence on the situation in Britannia; he found out that the troops in the province had either refused to fight against an enemy superior in numbers, or had been on leave when the invasions began. Also, he found out that the enemy had broken up their forces into small raiding parties which were plundering at will.

Eager to be active, the general waited impatiently for three days, awakening to a splendid sunlit morning, he strode the ramparts of the fortress and gazed out to sea. At last, the welcome sight of his transport ships approaching the coast raised his spirits. Meanwhile, he had used his time to devise a strategy. Since his military career hitherto had never brought him to these isles, he had picked the legate's brain for invaluable information. Differently from his campaign in Gaul, he would profit from an established road network that led to the strategic port of *Londinium*. If he could recapture it from the barbarians, he would use it as a base to regain territory and restore law and order. He knew that he could easily deal with the various bands of marauders since he had won Valentinian's trust by succeeding in much more testing circumstances, but was fully aware of how significant this campaign was for the prestige and security of the Empire. He swore he would not fail! He allowed his men a day to recover from their voyage, despite his reluctance to delay. The march from Rutupiae to Londinium was blessed with fine weather and a good paved road, so by early afternoon, his army entered the fortress. Count Theodosius made straight for the governor's palace, where he discovered that Londinium had been subjected to a concerted and repeated attack by Picts, Scoti and Saxons, to the extent that the governor had been compelled to add twenty-two semi-circular towers to the city walls as platforms for *ballistae*. The governor also pointed out the hasty repair work that he had overseen to the wall.

"The barbarian scouts saw you coming, Count, and scared by the strength of your army, have abandoned the *vicus*, looting and destroying property before going their separate ways. I think it safe to say that *Augusta* is now safe at last." He preferred to use the recently adopted name for the city.

"I shall make Augusta my base as part of the process of restoring the province to Roman rule. By the way, how far from here is *Eboracum?*"

"It depends whether you go by land or sea. Certainly, you can reach that city sooner by sea."

"I need to consult with the Comes Britanniarum."

"Count Leo? He is fully occupied in the north, but I hear that he has won many skirmishes against the Picts and the Scoti."

"Ay, he enjoys the emperor's trust since he comes, like Valentinian himself, from a line of warriors. We must devise a joint strategy rather than working alone."

Theodosius gathered his officers and split his army into sizeable detachments.

"In Britannia, all roads lead to Londinium. Each of you will lead your men out in separate directions within reach of the city in search of raiding parties. You will either kill or capture them and then relieve them of their booty, supplies, and prisoners. This will be our top priority, but let it be known that I am offering an amnesty to soldiers who have deserted. They will be reintegrated into the Augusta garrison with no punishment." He turned to his son, who shared the same name, "Theodosius, you and our cousin"—he gestured towards Magnus Maximus —"will come with me to Eboracum to confer with Count Leo. We sail immediately."

Theodosius the Elder possessed enough charisma—that hard-to-define quality that makes a good general into a great one—to fill the room. Leo recognised a kindred spirit and warmed to the amiable features of the Carthaginian, which somehow took the chill out of the winter air and replaced it with optimism.

Yet, the situation along Britannia's northern frontier was desperate. Talking about how the Picts were pouring through Hadrian's Wall as if it weren't there and how the Scoti, even as they spoke, were besieging the western fortresses, would not solve the problem, however brave the words.

"My army is in Londinium Augusta," Theodosius declared, "a few more days and the areas around the city will be cleared of roaming bands. Theodosius, you and Magnus will sail there tomorrow. In three days, I want you to disembark the army at Arbeia."

Count Leo was impressed; Theodosius had studied the northern situation. How else would he know that Arbeia was the key supply station on the Tyne and commanded the east coast traffic?

Three days later, a strong Roman force alighted there and, marching along the Stanegate, running behind Hadrian's vallum, they made rapid progress westwards, collecting men from the garrisons of the forts linked by this road.

Meanwhile, Count Leo marched out of Eboracum with a strong force, north-westwards along the old northern Watling Street, mopping up two Scoti warbands on his way. He was worried for his two sons and nephew under siege for a week in Alauna Fort. An entire army of Scoti had surrounded the fortress, making it impossible for the garrison to emerge to protect the scattered farmsteads in the area. Would their supplies and drinking water be sufficient until relief came in the shape of two Roman armies?

Theodosius arrived before Leo and was impressed by the willingness of the Alauna garrison, on sighting his army, to gallop out of the fortress to attack the Scoti from behind, driving them into his tight formation. The ferocious enemy relied less on tactics and more on vigorous use of their long two-handed sword, the *claideamh*, supplemented by close stabbing with the *scian*, a long dagger. Theodosius' veterans, fortified by their successes on the Rhine against the equally formidable Germanic tribes, held firm and formed an impenetrable wall of shields so that the Gaels were trapped between them and the constant harrying by Valdor's cavalry. The clash of steel reverberated along the unwavering line of Theodosius' troops as the *claideamh* parried the *spathae*.

The situation was unsustainable for the Gaelic Scoti, for it only needed the slightest distraction as they resisted the whirlwind onslaught of incoming and outgoing riders, for one of Theodosius' legionaries to stab with his gladius. These sharp, piercing blows always proved fatal. So, long before Count Leo's army appeared over the hill on their southern flank, the Scoti were in a dire situation. Nor could they break to flee since the vengeful Alauna cavalrymen, liberated from a week's confinement, wanted nothing else since what was easier than cutting down a fleeing warrior from horseback?

For Valdor and his men, the greatest danger was the Scoti *scian*. After stabbing the first horse in the belly, the Hibernian raiders tried to make a tactic of it, but Valdor showed his men the response by encouraging his horse to rear up and use its bronze-shod hoofs to smash down the audacious foe.

The arrival of Count Leo's army effectively ended the battle, as Theodosius, quick to grasp the situation, swung his men in a wide arc, encircling the Scoti, making the cavalry retire to a role of pursuit only. Trapped between two superior forces, the barbarian raiders were doomed. The slaughter proceeded and the very few who managed to escape the closing vice of Roman *scuta*, were massacred by Centurion Valdor and his horsemen.

After the battle, the sky was obscured briefly by the swirling black smoke of burning Scoti ships, the biting wind off the Irish Sea sweeping it into nothingness over the corpse-strewn battlefield. As Gaius, who oversaw the burning in the aftermath of victory, said, "We cannot risk other tribes sailing here from Hibernia and reusing these vessels."

The following day, for practical reasons, but also as a premonitory monument, Theodosius ordered the heaping of Scoti bodies, covered by a giant stone cairn. It could be seen from a distance, so to add a pinch of vindictiveness, he ordered Scoti tribal colours to decorate the stones. The woollen garments and banners, trapped by the rocks, flapped uselessly in the wind, serving as an admonition against further incursions. Theodosius had wanted to place Scoti heads on stakes around the cairn, but as his relative, Magnus said, "Cousin, leave barbarous acts to the barbarians, isn't the height of the cairn warning enough?"

The defeat of this main Scoti force did not mark the end of Theodosius' operations. Britannia, with its many estuaries, was porous to invaders coming from all directions. Immediate action was called for when a messenger delivered an urgent appeal from the east coast fortress of Branodunum, whose garrison had lost a battle against Saxon invaders and fallen back behind their ramparts. Meanwhile, the Saxons were busy constructing ladders to scale the wall. As military envoy, Theodosius had overall command for the defence of Britannia. So, when Count Leo preferred to sail around Caledonia, risking the violent northern passage, Theodosius countermanded him, settling for a forced march to relieve Branodunum.

Three times, detachments had to cope with raiding bands. Not to lose precious time, the cavalry dealt with the marauders, who proved to be Picts. Leo was not surprised to find them in the south of Cumbria but was concerned that they might eventually join forces with the peaceful Celtic tribes to the southwest, hitherto menaced by raiders from Hibernia. The Romans had strengthened the bastions at strategic coastal forts such as Caerdydd for this reason. Leo sighed; how much easier life had been for his father—true, he had had to face up to usurpers and revolts, but Britannia's frontiers then had been sound and the navy had dealt with incoming raiders. Now the frontiers were assailed from every direction. *Thank goodness the emperor understands our situation!* Count Leo was happy to fulfil a subordinate role to a general evidently so competent as Theodosius. He commanded total obedience and enjoyed the unswerving loyalty of his legion.

When, at last, they arrived at Branodunum, the Saxon presence meant that the *vici* had been abandoned as the people took refuge in the fortress. As an important trading port, there was no shortage of supplies, so this stronghold could resist a prolonged siege. Theodosius' countenance clouded and his hand gripped the hilt of his sword until the knuckles were white. The cause of his fury was the desperate battle at the ramparts as the Saxons scaled the ladders in a frantic attempt to seize control of the walls. As he stared upwards, he saw two men heaving and swinging an anvil before dropping it on the swarming Saxons. It knocked several warriors to the ground, the fall leaving them senseless. Elsewhere, defenders were fighting off the insurgents with spears or in one case a pitchfork. So, the townsfolk were lending a hand. In one case, even a cow was pushed over the wall, falling in a terrified tangle of legs and horns to flatten the mounting barbarians.

Theodosius had seen enough and had his cornicen blow the charge. Only then aware of the Roman force, the Saxons not committed to the ladders grouped into a defensive formation. At the same time, the south gate swung open and the garrison troops marched out, bristling spears and hurling javelins. The battle was the hardest-fought encounter Theodosius had faced in Britannia, but his veterans had encountered Saxons in the forest near the Rhine and then had prevailed, which gave them the morale to win this battle. The losses were severe on both sides but as twilight began to darken the already gloomy day, the Romans marched triumphantly, victorious, into their fortress. Theodosius had stamped out another threat to Britannia.

15

BRITANNIA AD 368-370

FAMINE STALKED THE COUNTRYSIDE ON SKELETAL LEGS IN the Britannia countryside during the harsh winter of 368-369. The robber bands of the previous summer had left the suffering population in precarious circumstances and the task of returning to the prosperity of earlier Roman rule loomed like an unsurpassable mountain to those responsible for facing the challenge. Theodosius and Leo were not men to shirk their duty, so hampered by the bad weather, spent their time in Londinium planning the next phase of the campaign. Vital intelligence gathered from the large number of troops drifting back to their units helped Theodosius.

"Count Leo, look here!" He unrolled a chart on a table, carefully moving aside encumbrances like candlesticks, a pen-holder box and, impatiently, sundry empty bottles, which he swept unceremoniously to the floor with his forearm. He resumed, "This line here is the Watling Street, running from *Viroconium*, here, in the west." He jabbed his thick forefinger on the map, moving it along the line. "It passes through *Uxacona*," the finger hovered, "here and *Pennocrucium*, there, where the street is intersected by the Icknield Street, running north-south at this point. Therefore, *Letocetum* is already an invaluable fortress for us. Moving eastwards, do you follow, my friend? We have *Manduessedum* before we reach the vital intersection at Venonis, where the Fosse Way crosses Watling Street."

"We have an impressive network of roads," mused Count Leo.

"Ay, and I mean to turn them to our advantage, Leo. The best way to pacify Britannia is by eliminating roving warbands completely. To do that, we have to move quickly with sufficient men and, at the same time, provide refuge to farm labourers and their beasts. Look again, Viroconium to Venonis," his finger moved rapidly, stabbing at the intermediate places he had mentioned, creating a drum beat on the tabletop. "At these places, I will create *burgi*, walled, garrisoned, and easily defensible bases. Any daring raiders in the area will find themselves caught like flies in a web strung along the main roads and our troops, like ravenous spiders, will entrap and devour them."

Leo, who was quick on the uptake, saw the quality of the plan and thumped his fist down on the chart. "By God! I can do the same, north of Eboracum."

Theodosius smiled smugly, "I was going to make that suggestion, my friend. You have sufficient roads, as we have seen on our recent Cumbrian campaign, although, I dare say your energy would be better repaid by concentrating on the north-east, where there are more important trading ports and a larger population."

The pernicious winter bade its farewell towards the end of March with a series of violent thunderstorms. They seemed to clear the air and herald a mild beginning to spring. Theodosius took advantage of the returned, previously disaffected, troops by setting them to work on his construction projects, sweetening their deployment by finding funds for increased pay, which always ensured cooperation and loyalty, not to mention an increased work rate from his men. The general enjoyed their respect, too, as his name was associated with victorious campaigns.

Count Leo departed with his legion to Eboracum and in agreement with Theodosius, began work on constructing a similar chain of *burgi*. His plan was to string them north between Isurium Brigantum and Concangis. He was convinced that this 'spine' would impede the movement of raiders inland and towards the north. If Theodosius' plan proved successful, he might be able to avoid building another fortified chain towards the north-west.

The second aspect of Theodosius' plan was to restore the chief towns, ensuring that their civic administration was corruption-free and that hand-in-hand, the legal system was running efficiently.

He began this work in Camolodunum, once the capital of the

southern region of Britannia and still a most important town. He made good progress by installing trustworthy officials and, undoubtedly, by the end of the summer, the town had returned to thriving prosperity. Theodosius was ready to transfer his attention to Deva, but a more pressing matter came to his attention.

A Pannonian named Valentinus whose brother-in-law Maximinus was close to Emperor Valentinian, began plotting a new revolt. Having committed serious crimes, multiple rapes and theft in Rome, he was able to have his death sentence commuted to exile in Britannia, where he resided at the time of the Great Conspiracy. He took no part in that plot, largely because he was 'too Roman' and his ambitions went far beyond those of barbarian chieftains, who only wanted plunder and slaves.

After the arrival of Theodosius, Valentinus overworked his spies and could see that the general's policies were effective. If his plotting to seize Britannia for himself to use as a bargaining tool with Rome, were to have any success, he would have to steadily undo Theodosius' work and, that done, have the general arrested on trumped-up charges. He attracted his intended victim's attention by organising fellow exiles and attempting to bribe local troops to his cause. The latter proved to be his undoing.

Centurion Valdor was stationed in Deva when his cousin spoke to him about the unscrupulous exile who was attempting to overthrow the authorities.

"Some of my men are unsettled," said Gaius, "they are being offered twenty denarii each to convince their comrades to seize and hold the fortress in the name of this Valentinus. He claims to be related to the emperor and unjustly exiled to Britannia. He wishes to march on Londinium, arrest General Theodosius and declare himself ruler of Britannia."

"Does he, by Jupiter!" Valdor regularly fell back on the old gods to express his surprise, for he would not take God's name in vain. "We'll have to do something about this fellow, Gaius. Where is he now?"

"They say he's in Glevum, no doubt offering incentives to troops there."

"I have a plan, cousin. Gather thirty men and we'll ride there, saying that we'll lead this usurper's revolt for him. He won't know how to resist when I tell him that my century is behind me. With that excuse, we'll bring him to Deva, where we'll imprison him before bringing him to justice."

"Can we be so convincing?"

"Leave the talking to me, Gaius. But first, let's visit the canteen and then the infirmary."

"The infirmary?"

"Ay, we'll need to drug three flagons of red wine, which we'll keep well separated from the untainted wine we'll share with Valentinus."

"And the drugged wine?"

"For his followers, of course. He might have more men than your thirty."

"So why not take more men, Valdor?"

Valdor laughed, "Dear cousin, I can see you have no mind for deviousness! If I take all my men, we'll scare him away. If he has an escort of fifty, he will not be frightened of our thirty. We'll drug the fifty and seize him."

"Oh, I see now! It's a workable scheme. I'll prepare my men for a diplomatic mission to Glevum. We can ride there with an overnight stop."

"Exactly an overnight encampment!" Valdor crowed.

Given the unsettled nature of the times, Valdor chose the leeward side of a hilltop site to camp and organised a rota of sentries. In this way, they passed an undisturbed night and set off at dawn for the second leg of their journey to Glevum, stopping only to water their horses.

At Glevum, discreet inquiries brought them to the attention of Valentinus, who warily sent several of his best scouts to interrogate the centurion and his fellow officer.

"We're from Deva." Valdor told a burly, scarred veteran, possibly judging by his features and accent, an Illyrian, "I'm twenty-five years old and although I've fought with distinction against the Picts and the Scoti —put plainly—there's been no progression in my career."

"Twenty-five is young to be a centurion," the veteran growled.

"By Jupiter! I've been one for ten years without any thanks or recognition."

"You had a very early promotion," his lip curled.

"I proved my worth on Hadrian's Wall, but that was when we had an emperor who recognised talent when he saw it! To be honest with you, I've had enough. They say that this Valentinus is on the lookout for people like me."

"I should think he'll be interested, but tell me, how many men can you bring to his cause?"

"We came with only thirty as an escort because these are troubled times. Back at Deva I have 200 who will follow me without question and I believe that with even a small incentive, I can double that number. Of course, I'd have to return there to make sure. If our *leader*, Valentinus were to come, to make his presence felt, I think we might persuade even more."

"Really?" The veteran sounded doubtful. "So how come we only managed to convince two score when we were there a few days ago?"

"Because you spoke to the wrong people. I only found out about you and your plans thanks to an old friend of mine, a comrade from the Wall. He said that this was the leader we'd been looking for since Constantius left these shores."

"Ay, Constantius was a good man, I'll give you that," the veteran said grudgingly. "I fought under him in Pannonia." He gave Valdor his first warm smile. "Wait here; I'll be back soon, and I reckon to bring good news for you." They clasped hands and Valdor managed to meet the Illyrian's eyes with a frank unwavering stare. The veteran grunted, satisfied and, collecting his comrades, who were speaking to Gaius, strolled away, speaking in a low voice. The small group looked backwards over their shoulders from Valdor to Gaius. Valdor watched them until they left the building, then he sprang up and went to Gaius, "Did you convince them that we were ready to follow Valentinus?"

"Ay, the nest of traitors was keen to know why we wanted to desert and how many men we could bring."

"What did you say?" Valdor asked anxiously.

"If all went well, at least two hundred. Did I say that right?"

Valdor smiled, "Ay, our stories match. They'll grasp at such a chance, I'm sure."

Shortly, the veteran returned, "Told you so, we'll leave for Deva at dawn tomorrow."

"But don't we get to meet our new leader?" Valdor protested.

The Illyrian smiled, "He's very busy today. He will ride with you tomorrow then you can talk. By the way, we have 50 riders who will come with us."

They don't trust us and want to outnumber our thirty. Valdor kept his thoughts to himself and said, "We have plenty of wine for your fellows but we might be short of provisions."

"I'll see my men have sufficient bread and cheese. Your wine will be welcome."

More welcome than you'll ever know!

The eighty-strong band of cavalry rode out of Glevum with Valdor and Valentinus at the front. The Roman had a clean-shaven, oval face and his short dark hair was combed forward so that the waves ended at his forehead in one carefully trimmed downward curve. Streaks of grey interlaced the black hair, betraying that he was no longer in the prime of his youth. Valdor guessed he was in his early forties.

At first, apart from a cursory nod, the patrician did not speak, but after riding a mile or so in silence, he said, "So, you are Centurion Valdor. I suppose you will be a descendant of Valdor the Batavian who won fame under Carausius?"

"He was my great-grandfather," Valdor said without elaborating, wondering how this man had heard of his ancestor.

"So, you're from a noble lineage. And you are seeking a new Carausius to further your career."

Valdor laughed bitterly, "I hope I have found him because no-one seems to recognise my worth."

"Serve me well and you'll be a general in no time, young Valdor."

The centurion acted the part of the hungrily ambitious young upstart in their conversation and, out-of-character, boasted about his military achievements, embellishing a few details to his advantage. In this way, the miles passed and, since the enemy had no relish to attack a strong band of Roman cavalry, they remained hidden and watchful, leaving them undisturbed. From the height of the sun Valdor judged it to be mid-afternoon when he pointed at a hill—where they had camped recently— "I think we should pitch camp on yonder hill. We slept there two nights ago. It boasts a relatively sheltered hollow on its lee side."

"Very well."

"We could all do with a rest and a few beakers of wine."

"Ah, indeed! You have brought wine!"

"Only the finest from Italy, lord."

"Then, I'll be happy to partake."

Valdor considered his next words carefully, "We have enough wine to keep the men happy. I suppose you have no objections?" He held his breath because his plan depended on acceptance.

"None whatsoever. I believe in keeping my followers as cheerful as possible. They usually spend their extra pay on strong drink anyway, so why not simply give the drink directly rather than in the form of coins?" His laugh grated, rather like the caw of a crow, Valdor thought.

When the tents were pitched, the leather and canvas rustling or cracking in the breeze, Valdor said, "It's lucky the hillside has formed this hollow. I doubt that the exposed part," he pointed vaguely, "would be bearable. A couple of beakers of red wine will soon warm us up. Will one of your centurions supervise the passing around of these three flagons?"

He had been careful to melt a red wax seal over the neck of his flagon. Such a seal was common practice to stop air from deteriorating the wine, but it served for Valdor to distinguish the untainted liquid. He broke the seal and poured a cup for the patrician, who did not wait for the centurion to pour his own.

"Ha! An excellent vintage," he purred, smacking his lips, "I don't doubt it's from my own region of *Latium*."

"Quite possible, lord, we have it shipped from Ostia."

Valdor watched as the drugged wine was passed from hand to hand. The troops did not bother with anything as sophisticated as beakers, preferring to drink directly from the flagons. He hoped the infirmarian had dosed each one to perfection. The fellow had questioned him closely and Valdor had affirmed that he did not want to kill, but to anaesthetize his victims. He had assured the infirmarian that it was all legitimately in the emperor's service, which appeared to satisfy the elderly pharmacist. The centurion hoped that the guzzling soldiers would not keel over and arouse suspicion, he had asked for a slow-acting soporific. Drowsiness came slowly but inevitably, allowing time for the men to retire to their tents. Soon, the camp was asleep, early because the first stars could not yet be seen.

Valentinus had drunk too greedily to notice anything amiss and with his speech slurring noticeably, announced, "I think I'll retire, too. A good night's sleep will aid our travels on the morrow."

Valdor watched as the selected guardsman at Valentinus' tent sank to his haunches, his eyes heavy, before gently toppling unconscious on his flank. He fetched Gaius who had a coil of stout rope in his hand.

"Quickly, while there's no danger, we'll truss Valentinus up and gag him ready for the morning."

"We'd better place our own sentry on his tent. We don't want any early bird finding him bound like an oven-ready pheasant."

Valdor chuckled and his mirth became greater at the sight of the would-be usurper on his back snoring blissfully.

With a minimum of fuss, Gaius bound his legs and arms tightly to his body before ramming a silk cloth in his mouth and binding that in place with another one. To do this, he had to lift Valentinus' head gently, but his snoring didn't cease, although it was certainly quieter than when his empty mouth had sagged open.

Valdor slept very little and at six in the morning, the first light was breaking as expected in early March. He and Gaius quietly woke their men and ordered them to take their horses silently to the foot of the hill without disturbing the other horses and above all, the other men. Valdor himself led Valentinus' horse to its rider's tent. There, he hoisted the limp patrician over the beast's back before mounting his horse and leading the other by its reins downhill.

Gaius had explained the situation to his men, so nobody was surprised to see Valentinus in that condition. "I have a change of plan, Gaius," Valdor said, "let's go directly to Theodosius in Londinium. There's no point in returning to Deva. When his men come to their senses later, that is where they'll think we've gone and they might be prepared to attempt a rescue."

"Good thinking, I agree, so it's back the way we came."

"More or less, but before Glevum, we can by-pass the town and regain the Watling Street to Londinium."

It took them three days to reach the city and the only fighting that occurred was wrestling with the bound and indignant captive. They ungagged him in order to give him food and drink, but his abuse was so obnoxious that Gaius slapped him hard across his cheeks. He lapsed into resentful silence rather than receive further blows.

In the fortress of Londinium, Valdor consigned his prisoner immediately to a gaoler, who locked him in a cell in solitary confinement. Valdor and Gaius renewed acquaintance with Theodosius after the victory in Cumbria and explained why they were not in Deva.

"I had learnt of this criminal's activities," said the general, "but I had lost his trail in the north. It appears that he intended to supplant me in Britannia to further his ambitions with Rome."

"Will you execute him, general?" Gaius asked.

"Nay, I would not wish to produce more unrest in the province but I will hand him over to Dux Dulcitius for investigation and eventual execution." Dulcitius had sailed across with Theodosius and was appointed to the role of Dux Britanniarum on the unfortunate decease of Dux Quintus.

Summoned to Londinium Augusta from the northern province of *Maxima Caesariensis* and ordered to investigate Valentinus for treason, the dux began by questioning Valdor and Gaius. He did not take long to condemn the usurper, instead ordering a smith to fabricate an iron hose that was locked around Valentinus' body. From the fortress he was taken, blaspheming, to a small boat on the Tamesis, where they rowed out into midstream and lowered him, still cursing, in his metal sheath, to the bed of the river. A few bubbles, the remains of his curses, broke the surface of the river. This choice of execution was dishonourable and suitable for a traitor. A beheading might have inspired a cult following, something to be avoided at all costs.

Even without the threat of Valentinus, Theodosius still had much to do to restore Britannia, but he consoled himself, with men like Valdor and Gaius to rely on, that task was not impossible.

16

VERCOVICIUM, HADRIAN'S WALL, AD 370

Valdor stood on the ramparts over the south gates as so many times before and took a deep breath. Something was missing; but instantly, he knew what it was. The aroma of burning turf no longer filled the air. He felt nostalgia for that smell but even back when all the roofs of the crowded *vicus* emitted the grey smoke, he found the odour hard to define. He could draw on his memory and swear it smelt of pine, yet more bitter, maybe of ocean, of the fragrance of moss—undefinable but unforgettable. As he stared, he saw grey smoke wreathing from a handful of tiny homes. No wonder he could not smell or hear anything. Where once there was a bustling, thriving community no longer came the beat of hammers from the smithies, which stood abandoned, silent, forges unlit. He had seen the army supplies, increasingly shipped in from imperial factories on the continent delivered by carts into the fortress.

His new hero, Theodosius, had pacified the north of Britannia, but at a cost.

Occupation had declined, not just at Vercovicium, but also in the other *vici*. Theodosius' vigorous clearing out of the Areani had undoubtedly contributed, but also the continuous loss of numbers of troops, drawn away to fight elsewhere, and the ravages of inflation, meant that there was little reason left for local inhabitants of the *vici* to remain.

The hoot of an owl, a signal of permanence, reminded him of

bygone times. His mother's tales of how, all alone, she had run a market stall in this same *vicus*, where now there was no market. In the now-forsaken streets, she had met his father and they had fallen in love. The military life had been generous to his father, whereas his son and nephew had been sent back to the Wall. In this bleakest of outposts, they were here to ensure that tribalism did not return to Britannia. He was a centurion and feared no enemy, but in the vastness of the starry night, overlooking the abandonment of a once thriving centre, he felt small and insignificant. Thank the Lord that there were men like Theodosius with the energy to undertake the considerable reorganisation needed in Britannia, including the creation of a new province, *Valentia*, which Theodosius named in honour of Emperor Valentinian, to better address the state of the far north.

Valdor smiled at the thought; even a successful and valiant general felt the need to flatter the emperor. But Theodosius was a man of substance, who mounted punitive expeditions against the barbarians and imposed terms upon them. The Areani were removed from duty and the frontiers refortified with co-operation from border tribes such as the *Votadini*.

Meanwhile, the emperor granted a governor, Civilis, *vicarius* status under Dux Dulcitius, to head a new civilian administration. The combined thoroughness of Theodosius and Civilis restored peace to Britannia. As part of their reorganisation, Theodosius dispatched Valdor and Gaius once more to Vercovicium on Hadrian's Wall. The cousins enjoyed hero status among their men that their initiative against Valentinus had procured. Gaius received his promotion to centurion from Dulcitius almost as a matter of course, yet, he got drunk to celebrate at the first opportunity. Valdor was glad that his cousin, his elder by three years, had reached the same rank because it had always sat uneasily that he was his senior officer.

The advancing year brought the relief of milder weather but with it, increased watchfulness. The sensation, however, was that Theodosius' measures had been so effective that the Picts would remain in the highland glens and leave Britannia to enjoy its newly-gained peace.

Although a great supporter of Theodosius, Valdor was uneasy about one of his measures and could not stop thinking and worrying. After the Great Conspiracy, Theodosius had decided not to maintain some of the 'outpost forts' north of the Wall. In compensation, the general did a fair amount of rebuilding and recovery work elsewhere. He narrowed the gateway at *Banna* and made structural changes at *Maia* and *Glannaventa*. He also built a chain of fortlets that served as signal stations some 1400 paces apart, at Wreay Hall and Barrock Fell, and one to protect a farmstead at Cummersdale.

One only had to travel around the new province of Valentia to see that Theodosius' methods were repaying his efforts. Despite the renewed confidence and faith, Valdor could not quell his nagging doubt. The Areani had been expelled from the Wall, but they would not simply vanish. What would become of those men who wished to reclaim Britannia for the Britons? Was it right to abandon the outpost forts? Valdor increasingly believed not. He was torn: on the one hand, he was a solid admirer of Theodosius; on the other, he knew what he would do if he were one of the sheepfold men.

Valdor kept his worries to himself for a long time, but as summer approached, he could contain them no more. His natural confidant was Gaius, his cousin.

"I'm only a centurion and no strategist, but I'm worried about leaving a fortress like *Habitancum* unmanned. When Antonine built his wall farther north, he had a reason. We've seen what the Picts are capable of. Our general, Theodosius, has also shown what determination, organisation and courage can do. Oh, I don't know, maybe I'm as anxious as an old maid!"

Gaius laughed, but it was a sound tinged with uncertainty. "Do you know, it's something I've been thinking about, too. But as you say, who are we to question our superiors, especially when they are so esteemed?"

"The easiest thing would be to send a scout to check the fortress. Maybe it's the most sensible option. God knows, I've thought of leading my men there, but what if I lead them unwittingly to a slaughter? Even if I survived that, my career would end in disgrace."

Gaius gazed with concern over the northern wilderness from his vantage point on the ramparts. "Sending a scout out there is like condemning a man to death. I'll not send a man where I fear to tread. I'll go alone, Valdor!"

"Nay, I'll not let you go alone! If we die, we die together, cousin."

"Heed me well, Valdor, the absence of *two* centurions will be noted. One may go unnoticed, especially if covered by the other. Also, one scout may go unnoticed by the enemy; two, doubles the risk of being seen."

There was little Valdor could do in the face of such reasoning, but when his cousin slipped away on his horse, he sank into depression. Gaius was the rock he clung to on this troubled 'shoreline' of Hadrian's Wall. His cousin, only three years his senior, was more a companion than a relative. He would miss him sorely if anything happened to him and worse, would never forgive himself for acquiescing to let him venture out alone in hostile territory. True, he had his younger brother, Maximus and, although he loved him dearly, they had never established the same confidential relationship that he enjoyed with Gaius.

Conversely, as he rode northwards, alert and furtive, Gaius was unusually cheerful. Peace was everyone's most cherished desire, but it did not suit his temperament. Like his forebears of whom he was so proud, he was a man of action. With the Valentinus escapade fresh in his mind and the plaudits that had come his way, this adventure suited his restless temperament. Truth be told, he would have preferred to have Valdor with him, but the logic he had used in his argumentation had been sincere.

Valdor, meanwhile, had received a message from Eboracum. Count Leo wanted Maximus to join him there urgently, without providing another explanation. Sadly, Valdor waved a fond farewell to his younger brother and felt incredibly alone.

Habitancum was an Antonine auxiliary fort, built just south of the river Rede, where the Roman road, just to the west, crossed its valley, which cut through the plateau. Gaius warily abandoned the road as soon as he sighted the stronghold in the distance and urged his horse into a woodland of hardy dwarf conifers. Soon, he had found a small stream flowing through a narrow gorge, which formed an enclosed valley and would serve as an ideal overnight campsite, hidden from enemy eyes. Having watered his horse and found his refuge, he sought a vantage point overlooking the fortress and found it in the shape of a low ridge where another stream flowed around a crag, which was the ideal observation platform. He tethered his horse and climbed up the rocky outcrop, taking off his helm for fear the sun might glint off it and betray his presence. He laid it behind a shrub and, dropping onto his stomach, squirmed forward until he had a clear view over the river valley and its intersecting road to the fortress.

A red kite soared and screeched; he watched it glide over the valley and envied both its wings and its sight as it searched for prey. If he had a hawk's eyes, he could be sure whether that was a figure on the ramparts. Only when the shape moved, exactly as a sentinel would, was he sure that the stronghold was occupied. The question was how many men held the fortress? He was too obviously a Roman officer and could not pass himself off as anything else, so all he could do was lurk and observe from a distance.

He patiently lay, never taking his eyes off the approaches to the fort, although in this remote sweeping landscape of extensive views, his mind roved from the past to the future, seeking to place himself and his ambitions in some kind of perspective. His eyes felt heavy and his forehead touched the ground. If he slept, it was only for a few minutes. Jerking awake, he thought he heard voices and peering intently in search of the source, he found it, consisting of three ragged figures, one of whom raised a cow's horn to his lips and blew a lowing note that enabled them to enter the fortress. Gaius had seen enough for now—he knew that people came and went from this remote outpost—built to guard the road and Rede valley, just as he and his cousin feared. What did it mean? Who were these ragged individuals? What was their purpose in this fortress? *Obviously*, he thought as he stood, *it's a better refuge than a sheepfold and can hold more of them, but how many?*

That was what he had to discover somehow—he would not leave until he knew. For the moment, he'd return to the gorge he had identified as a base and set up camp. He had brought a leather tent and some provisions. There was water for man and beast and beside the stream was enough grass for his horse to graze. *Can I risk a small fire?* There was precious little warmth in the gorge, its air chilled by the rushing stream. His experience told him that a small fire of dry twigs would create a light grey smoke, swiftly dispersed by the breeze created by the rushing water. It would be unseen from the fortress and provide him with sufficient warmth because he had nothing to cook. Doubtless there were fish in the stream and he had heard tales of tickling trout, but he hadn't a clue about how to do it. The bread and hard cheese he had obtained from the canteen and the bottle of red wine would be sufficient to keep body and soul together.

His horse grazed happily by the stream, so Gaius pitched his small tent and gathered twigs to set a fire. It caught easily and crackled merrily as he warmed his hands before unstopping the leather bottle and downing a gulp of red wine. Immediately, he felt all his cares roll away—this strong feeling of remoteness and tranquillity was priceless. He looked forward to the dark night sky and the constellations and planets he would see before snuggling in the sheepskin he had brought.

In July, over where he lay, Ursa Minor was directly overhead, with Polaris finishing its tail, while off to the left was its 'big brother', the Great Bear, under the Plough; he drew satisfaction from recognition of the familiar stars so distinct in the sky. *That's bright! Is it a star or a planet just above the Little Bear and to the right? I'll ask Valdor when I get back.* His cousin had studied the stars among other things. He was quieter and more studious than Gaius. With this thought he retired for the night, snug inside his tent, hearing only the gurgling of the brook and the breeze rustling in the trees. His mind, however, would not be still as he tried to work out how to discover the number of men inside the fort.

He awoke with an idea. It was not a good one, but the best he could manage. To carry it out, he packed his tent and tethered his horse at the base of the crag on the far side from the fortress. Next, he gathered as much wood as possible, including some damp branches. As dawn broke, he lit the fire and waited until it caught well. Then, he hurried to his observation post and waited. He only took his eye off the fort to ensure that the hoped-for smoke was billowing from the gorge below. A satisfactory column of dark smoke rose from among the trees. His gaze turned back to the stronghold, where he saw activity on the ramparts: men shouting and pointing.

He watched and waited, watched and waited until his patience paid off, suddenly, men ran out of the gate to the road. That was what he had planned! They streamed towards the river, where the road crossed a ford. He counted a score of men, aware that there would be others within the walls of Habitancum Fort. Leaping to his feet, he hurried down the crag to his horse and urged his mount carefully away along a trail away from the valley. Once back on the plateau, he was able to give the mare her head and gallop away. There clearly was no cavalry in the fortress, so his return to Vercovicium would go unseen, for he had ridden in a wide arc to regain the road well out of sight of the Areani.

Valdor rose early and immediately stationed himself on the northern ramparts to peer out along the road. He was terribly worried. Had he let his cousin ride out to his death? He reassured himself; Gaius was too experienced to ride straight into a trap. *He will have spied on the fortress and, after all, he's only been out there one night.* Nonetheless, the centurion did not move away but stood, gaze fixed on the horizon. The early July day was a joy to behold, as the purple heather flowers graced the rolling land. For a moment, he was distracted by a hunting hen harrier, its brown and white wings widespread as it glided low over the moor in search of prey. When he stared back along the road, he blinked. Was that a rider? He looked down at his feet, blinked again, and stared hard. *Ay! A lone rider—pray God it's Gaius!* His spirits raised when he saw that it was indeed his cousin.

Gaius related the events in the smallest detail to a rapt Valdor, who said nothing until he had finished.

"It's as I feared. If they sent twenty out to check on the camp fire, there are sure to be many more of them inside. This is too important to keep to ourselves, Gaius. I say we go to Dux Dulcitius and that you tell him precisely what you told me."

The dux listened attentively, his expression becoming graver as Gaius went on. When he had finished, Dulcitius smiled at the elder cousin. "I was right to promote you. You two are exceptional officers and heedless of personal risk, ensure that our enemies are foiled. Good work! I am quite prepared to let you see it to a resolution—I mean, I won't take it upon myself. Muster enough men to deal with the Areani and ensure that you bring one of them back for questioning."

Gaius and Valdor summoned their most trusted decurions and ordered them to mount up their thirty men. Sixty-four Roman cavalrymen should be enough to overwhelm a garrison of ragged half-starved Britons. To make sure of entry into Habitancum Fort, Valdor ordered a *ballista* loaded onto a cart and another cartload of large stone balls.

The Areani refuted an attempt by Gaius to negotiate their surrender, so the centurions were forced to unload the ballista and hurl missiles at the wooden gates until they crashed inwards. Valdor led the charge and his cavalry made short work of those bold enough to face them in the courtyard. Other Britons took to the ramparts, where some unleashed arrows to little avail after slaying one cavalryman by surprise because the other darts were blocked by raised clipeī. Gaius led the charge up the steps to the rampart, remembering Dulcitius' order to take one alive, although neither he nor Valdor had seen March the carter, they had heard tales about the tall Briton. He saw that the remaining Britons had gathered around a taller man and called upon them to lay down their arms in exchange for their lives. The taller man issued a command and the last of the defenders surrendered.

Down in the courtyard, a desultory Valdor, who had tired of watching the massacre, was instead, reading an inscription. The Latin was carved neatly on an altar stone dedicated to the Nymphs:

> *SOMNIO PRAE*
> *MONITVS*
> *MILES HANC*
> *PONERE IVS*
> *SIT*
> *ARAM QVAE*
> *FABIO NVP*
> *TA EST NYM*
> *PHIS VENE*
> *RANDIS*

He translated rapidly, good scholar that he was: *Forewarned by a dream the soldier bade her who is married to Fabius to set up this altar to the Nymphs who are to be worshipped.*

Which made him wonder about the circumstances that had made the legionary, clearly a pagan, go to the trouble of creating this altar at the time of Antonine, so many years ago. It was one of several altars, Valdor's eyes swept over one dedicated to Hercules, another to *Jupiter Optimus Maximus* and yet another to *the Emperor Caesar Galerius Valerius Maximianus Pius Felix*. Curious, he was about to read it, when he heard Gaius call an order, "Bind the tall one and release the others!" March the carter struggled to resist, but his struggling stopped at the sight of the only Briton prepared to save his leader, mercilessly cut down by a Roman gladius.

On shouted orders, the surviving dozen Britons ran out of the devastated gateway and out into the heathery moorland. The captive was hoisted onto the spare horse caused by the one fatality and led to the road by three designated cavalrymen. Gaius spoke to his cousin, "We must demolish this fortress, Centurion. See to it, whilst I take the prisoner to the dux with those three men."

A Roman fortress of the size of Habitancum, measuring 443 feet from north-west to south-east, by about 384 feet transversely, cannot be demolished in one day by sixty men, although they made a good start around the devastated gateway. The barracks were still intact and showed signs of recent habitation, so Valdor and his men had shelter for the night. They also made use of the abandoned stables, leading their horses there, which had already cropped enough grass around the fort.

Work resumed at first light, steadily the stone wall, block by block tumbled to the turf, but there was much toil ahead of the sixty. What a relief, then, when an entire legion led by Gaius arrived, mid-morning to help complete the razing. The buildings in the courtyard were timber-built, so demolition was far easier and after a making use of them overnight, the legion destroyed them in the early morning. What had once been a proud bastion against the Picts now lay in ruin. Neither Valdor nor Gaius could know that history has its ups and downs because what they thought was the original Antonine fort had been destroyed in 197 and rebuilt under Severus with the different orientation that the cousins had now reduced to rubble. Whatever use the Areani would have made of the base was well and truly thwarted, so Valdor, at least, could sleep easier. Perhaps he would not if he had known the fate awaiting his hero, Theodosius.

17

VERCOVICIUM AND BANNA FORTS, HADRIAN'S WALL, AD 370

AFTER SOME DAYS OF INTERROGATION OF THE CAPTIVE Briton, Dux Dulcitius called Gaius and Valdor to his quarters.

He looked at Gaius, "What do you know about the captive you brought, Centurion?"

"Very little, lord, I imagine from his height that he is the infamous March the carter who took part in the conspiracy against Roman rule."

"Ay, he admitted his identity. The man is a coward, yet he found the courage to make certain accusations. I was tempted to have him scourged, but I won't whip a man until I'm sure he's lying."

"May I ask what are these accusations, lord?" Valdor asked.

"He has the nerve to accuse the *praefectus* of Banna Fort of being nothing less than a warlord and his men, a local militia, operating a racket to take money for protection, which of course, finishes in their own pockets. He says that in order not to stir up revolt among the suffering population, taxation gathering has stopped. That is a serious charge, centurions. If true, Rome will intervene to crush him and his men. It is my duty as dux to act on behalf of the Empire."

"The carter will be well-informed about what goes on along the Wall, lord. What has he to gain by such calumny? Revealing information to you about the Picts would be more gainful."

"My very thought, Centurion," Dulcitius smiled grimly, "which is why I called you here. I'm sending you to investigate, but you'll need a pretext to avoid arousing suspicion. I thought that we might turn this March to our advantage. You will report to the praefectus and tell him that you have to question Britons in search of a certain Guaire, whom an informer declares has valuable information about another Pictish conspiracy. That will give you the freedom to wander around the *vicus* talking to the local populace. Unsuspected by Praefectus Crispinus Sylla, you will gather whether March is telling the truth or not. Afterwards, you'll return and report to me, any questions?"

"Ay, lord, does this Guaire truly exist?" Gaius asked.

His cousin snorted and the dux smiled at Valdor.

"Nay, as you realise, Centurion Valdor, it is but a ploy, I invented the name. Logically, if by chance you discover anything about Pictish plans from the Britons, we'll regard it as something gained."

The cousins brought a fist to their chests in time-honoured fashion and bowed out of the room.

"It's an odd business," Valdor said, "just when we thought Count Theodosius had re-established the rule of law and order in Britannia, we are sent to one of the most important fortresses on the Wall to root out corruption."

"You always name Theodosius as if he were your hero, cousin."

"Come, Gaius, you must admit that the Count has restored Britannia to its former standing."

"Unless March the carter is right."

"Ay, that's what we must find out. To horse, my friend!"

The fourteen miles from Vercovicium to Banna along the Stanegate was a pleasant ride in the warm July weather. They stopped at a fort known as *Magnis*, which predated Hadrian's Wall because it was on the intersection of the Stanegate and the Maiden Way, therefore, at an important strategic location. The large *vicus*, lying on three sides of the fort, though not as populated as before the conspiracy, still provided the centurions a choice of taverns to break their journey and refresh themselves and their horses. Valdor ordered twice-brewed ale and on paying, asked the landlord, "Have you heard anything strange about Banna Fort just down the road?"

The innkeeper looked from one centurion to the other and leant forward confidentially. He was a strapping, pot-bellied Briton with dark hair. In a low voice he said, "Strange? Depends what you mean. All I know is that I've lost a lot of regulars from *our* fort. Someone told me that they go to Banna because they don't pay for drink there. How can that be?" His face took on a sullen expression, "No-one in his right mind can afford to give soldiers free drinks every day. One or two to my particular friends or someone who does me a favour, well, that's a different matter."

They thanked him and resumed their journey, discussing what they had heard and its possible meaning. Only five miles lay ahead to Banna now, so they would be there easily on time to have lunch in a tavern. The *Wounded Boar* tavern stood on the Stanegate, so they found it without deviating farther into the *vicus*. The presence of Roman soldiers in the tavern was evident and a couple of legionaries leaving the establishment saluted the centurions politely enough. They entered and took seats at a table. They had to wait a while until Gaius became irritable, "What is it with service in this place?"

Almost as if he had heard him, although given the noise of voices, it was impossible, a stout, surly-faced man with a morose expression, wearing a dirty apron, once white, now stained, asked, "Well, Centurions, what can I get you?"

"We're hungry, what food do you have?"

His manner became dourer, "We have chickpea soup," he said curtly.

"Two, with bread and two beakers of ale," Valdor reached into his purse and took out a silver piece, but a strong hand grasped his wrist, "What are you doing, Centurion?" A decurion from Banna Fort said, "Give him that and he'll want us all to pay!"

Valdor snatched his arm away, but kept the silver coin closed in his hand while the innkeeper glared at the newcomer. "I'll get your order," he growled and shuffled away.

"I'm used to paying for what I consume," Valdor said archly.

"Not here in *The Wounded Boar*" the decurion insisted. "You see, he doesn't pay taxes to Rome. In exchange, Roman troops get free meals and drinks. We don't profit too much, it's best to spread our custom around the other inns if we want more. That way, the Britons keep their resentment to themselves."

"Don't they complain to the praefectus?"

"Not if they've got any sense! But you, Centurion, don't ask so many questions and keep your hard-earned coins for yourself." He winked, nodded and sauntered away.

"What about that, Gaius?" Valdor whispered.

"I'll only do something if the innkeeper serves us piss!"

Valdor frowned, "It looks as though March the carter was telling the truth. We'll have to go deeper into this."

In reality, the ale was good and strong and the chickpea soup, hot and creamy. With so many other soldiers from the nearby fort in the room, Valdor made no attempt to pay for his meal, but he had a strong sense of a wrong needing righting.

The cousins rode farther down the road and crossed into the fortress. The first thing that struck them was the new construction work at the centre of the courtyard.

Valdor addressed a soldier, "What are they building there?"

"You must be new to the fort, Centurion...yon's the new quarters for the praefectus. I haven't been inside, but they say that it's luxurious with baths, mosaics and a large dining hall. Trust Crispinus Sylla to look after himself!"

"Do we go in there if we wish to speak with him?" Gaius asked.

"Nay," the soldier shook his head, "you'll have to go to the *principia*, over there. He's collecting money from the men."

"Don't you mean he's giving pay to the men?" Gaius asked innocently.

The soldier sneered, "It's clear that you are new here." Suddenly, he looked shifty, "I've lingered too long." He saluted and hurried off.

"What do you think he meant by that?" Gaius asked.

"I don't know, but we'll have to tread carefully."

Gaius set off towards the *principia*, but Valdor caught his arm, "Where are you going?"

"To see Crispinus Sylla, of course."

"Not a good idea!"

"Why not?"

"If he's wrongdoing, our presence won't be appreciated. We should try to see him on another occasion. Let's go and see what we can find out."

They rode out of the fortress unchallenged, just as when they had arrived. This laxity on the gate was unheard of in Vercovicium.

"Where is the discipline in this place?" Gaius said through gritted teeth.

They rode into the *vicus* and took a couple of turnings down narrow streets until they came to a square. On the far side was another tavern with a sign depicting crossed spears.

"Let's see if it's true that they don't pay in there." Valdor said.

They tethered their horses and ordered ale. Nobody interfered when Valdor slid a silver coin across the table, but he sensed all eyes on them. The innkeeper paled and slid the coin back. He spoke as if choking on the words, "I'll not take that, Centurion, the drink is on the house."

"Well, that's kind of you!" Gaius said.

"Kind of me! Kind of me!" the skinny man said bitterly, shaking his head.

The centurions sensed an increase of tension around them.

"Come on! Drink up, let's get out of here!" Valdor said.

He stepped out of the dim tavern, blinking in the bright sunlight. As soon as his eyes adjusted, he saw a soldier fiddling to untie the reins of his horse, tethered to a hitching post.

"Hey! What do you think you're doing? That's my horse!"

The soldier straightened, "I'm taking it in lieu of taxes."

"What taxes?" Valdor asked, drawing his gladius. Out of the corner of his eye he saw two other soldiers coming their way. "I'm a Roman centurion and I don't pay taxes."

"You do here, in Banna!" sneered the legionary also drawing his gladius.

"Look out!" Gaius called and spinning around, Valdor was in time to parry a thrust from a gladius. Gaius was now fighting the man by the horses. The cousins each had the same thought: *we must end this before others come to aid them!*

Perhaps it was desperation as much as their greater battle skills that helped them, but speedily, they overcame their adversaries, leaving three bloodied corpses in front of the tavern. They leapt on their horses and galloped away to the sound of raised angry voices. A javelin fell short and buried into the beaten earth road as Valdor glanced back.

They regained the Stanegate and slowed their horses to a moderate trotting pace.

"Well, I'll be damned, we had to slay three of our own men!" Gaius said.

"Nobody steals my horse, cousin. They got what they deserved as common thieves."

"Ay, but they weren't common thieves, they were Roman soldiers."

Valdor snorted, "I've had my fill of this place, we've seen enough, and yet, we've barely scratched the surface. Let's report to the dux."

Dux Dulcitius stared incredulously at his travel-weary centurions, "And you had to slay three of them, you say?"

"If we hadn't acted quickly, we'd have lost our horses and our lives," Gaius said.

"As we rode away, more of them gathered with arms drawn. At least one javelin hit the ground behind me," his cousin added.

"It appears that the carter was telling the truth. Go and rest. Tomorrow we'll use every available man to arrest Crispinus Sylla, take Banna Fort and restore civic order in the *vicus*. Oh, one other thing, Valdor, while you were away, a messenger from Count Leo arrived. He has appointed your brother, Maximus, as the Count of the Saxon Shore."

Valdor lay on his bed and thought about what he and his cousin had experienced and the significance of it. He had fought against tribes in the past where Roman law did not hold sway. What he had seen at Banna seemed little different from tribal society. Instead of a chieftain, the soldiers had their praefectus, who was behaving exactly like a local warlord and his local troops behaved precisely like tribal warriors. But how could the people of the vicus tolerate it? Of course, they were frightened and could not resist, but they also had the incentive of not paying taxes even if the troops exploited them by demanding payment in kind. He wondered whether this extended to enslavement or abusing the womenfolk. He wouldn't wager against it.

How strange, he thought, *in a nation that had bred Pelagius, who preached self-salvation, that these people did not rise up in their own defence. But surely, it is only a matter of time. Thank goodness for the dux and for Count Theodosius!*

Valdor struggled with his love for Maximus and jealousy: *surely, I'm great-grandfather's namesake and that honour should have been mine. I wonder how father chose and what he has in mind for me?* Setting such thoughts aside, he would not have fallen into his uneasy sleep if he had learnt that Count Theodosius had returned to a hero's welcome in

Rome, where he succeeded Jovinus as the *magister equitum praesentalis* at the court of Emperor Valentinian. He would be too occupied successfully fighting the Alemanni the following year to return to Britannia. But, had he still been in the country, he most certainly would have been as outraged as Dux Dulcitius and equally as decisive.

18

VERCOVICIUM AND BANNA FORTS, HADRIAN'S WALL, AD 370-371

THE ENTIRE GARRISON MARCHED OUT OF VERCOVICIUM along the Stanegate in battle formation with Dux Dulcitius and his two most trusted centurions in the vanguard. This army swung unhindered into the Banna fortress, such was the laxity at the gates. Overawed and dismayed, the resident soldiers stood, weapons untouched, posing no opposition.

In a stern voice, Dulcitius pointed at the new building, "Centurions, take some men and arrest Praefectus Crispinus Sylla." Valdor and Gaius gathered a handful of men each and marched into the edifice. The dux followed, walking his horse inside slowly without bothering to dismount.

The praefectus leapt from a throne-like chair, drawing a sword and screaming to his bodyguard, "Stop these intruders!"

The cream of the Banna veterans rushed forward with swords drawn but, unlike the newcomers, without shields. Valdor raised his voice, "Halt! Do not be fools! You cannot survive if you fight—there is an entire army outside in the courtyard."

"Don't heed him!" Crispinus screeched, "Do your duty!"

Men of the calibre of these Roman veterans needed no exhortation. With a roar, they flung themselves at Valdor and Gaius to the fore. Although they had fought Gaels, Picts, and Alemanni in their day with success, these brave fellows had never encountered opponents reared from infancy to become invincible in battle. Regardless of the fate of the first two guards, Crispinus' shrieks desperately and pitilessly urged the others to their doom as Valdor, in particular, under the admiring gaze of the dux, accounted for twice as many as the other combatants, including Gaius. The battle was over as the last of the bodyguards fell. Dulcitius had lost not a single man, his force undoubtedly advantaged by having a *scutum* to parry their valiant adversaries' blows.

The praefectus looked around for a way out but knew that his fate was sealed, so he reared his chin defiantly, turned his gladius to his chest and cried gloatingly, "You will never take me alive, Dux Dulcitius!"

"Don't play the fool, Crispinus! I'll see you get a fair trial."

They all saw the praefectus sneer as he held the short sword tight and pitched forward so that his weight against the floor drove the blade deep into his heart. In moments, he lay in a pool of blood, one more corpse to add to the number in the beautifully mosaiced room.

"So, perish all corrupt traitors!" Dux Dulcitius declared succinctly, wheeling his horse and riding into the courtyard.

"Men of Banna," he bellowed, "heed me well! Today, justice is done..." he paused for a moment as Gaius and Valdor remounted and edged their horses either side of his. In a low voice, he said to Gaius, "Go back into the building and find the praefectus' treasure chest." When he had gone, he gazed around at the rapt, attentive faces of the congregated Banna men and resumed his speech, "...as I said, justice is done. Your corrupt commander has paid with his life for his misdeeds. A new regime begins at Banna henceforth. You will obey Praefectus Valdor, a man who is worth a score of Syllas on his own! From this moment forth, you will treat the Britons in the *vicus* with respect. All services will be paid for, and you will not be short of money"—here he gambled on his instinct—" for you will be paid later today!"

A loud roar acclaimed these words from the men of Banna as those from Vercovicium stared impassively. Meanwhile, Valdor recovered from the shock of the announcement as Gaius returned to say, "I've found a metal-bound strongbox, lord, but no keys to open the locks."

"Not a problem!" Dulcitius replied confidently. "Men of Banna, is there a smith among you? Step forward and draw near." A tall muscular man stepped forward and advanced under the muzzle of the steed.

"I am a smith, lord."

"And a popular one you will be with your comrades, for you will break into Sylla's strongbox."

"An easy job, Dux, I built that chest myself."

"It will be full of his ill-gotten gains and we'll distribute them to the men. Meanwhile, centurion, ride into the *vicus* and send back the absentees to the fortress forthwith."

Gaius was gone in a flash. The dux turned to Valdor, "Watch this carefully! You'll need iron discipline here."

Again, the dux raised his voice, "I now need two carpenters, step forward!" Two men broke ranks and hurried towards him. He leant down and said, "Here, where my horse is standing, you will hurriedly plant a post, but give it a crossbar to bind outstretched arms at the wrist, for it'll be a scourging post."

"Ay, lord." One of the two turned to face the other and stretched both arms out level with the ground so that the experienced eye could take the measure.

"You may wonder what that was about," the dux bellowed. "Here will stand a whipping post. Any man who disobeys the order to respect the Britons or in any way violates camp discipline, on the orders of Praefectus Valdor and, at my behest, will be condemned to one thousand lashes." A collective gasp came from the Banna garrison, for no man could survive such a flogging. Even Valdor paled and silently prayed that he would never need to impose such a sentence.

Soon, the two carpenters, armed with a heavy mallet, drove a sharpened post into the ground and nailed and bound a crossbar into place. An awed silence, unbroken even by the disciplined men of Vercovicium, greeted the construction as if each man was thinking *'a thousand lashes!'*

The dux turned to a decurion, "Search inside the building for the praefectus' helm."

Minutes later, the fellow returned with a familiar sight to the Banna Garrison in his hands. He carried a beautiful burnished bronze helm with a large eagle sat on top flanked by two pouncing lions. Dulcitius took it in both hands and studied it, saying ruefully, "It's lovelier than mine! Take off your helm, Valdor, my work is done here."

Valdor unlaced the cheek guards of his centurion's helmet and with both hands lifted it off his head. Dulcitius edged his horse close to Valdor's and, symbolically, placed the helm with its bronze crest on his head.

A surprise greeted this gesture because a loud cheer from the men of Banna rent the air. This unexpected approbation was taken up heartily by the men of Vercovicium, who considered Valdor a hero. Meanwhile, Gaius' rounding up was proving effective as men straggled back into the camp to seek tidings from their comrades.

After a while, Gaius returned and the dux said, "Only one thing remains for me to do," he raised his voice, "Centurion Gaius, I appoint you *vicarius* to Praefectus Valdor. If for any reason he cannot fulfil his role, you'll take his place."

Dux Dulcitius issued a ringing command and the Vercovicium garrison gave an example of perfectly coordinated discipline as they marched out onto the Stanegate.

Valdor's first orders were to a centurion to organise the closure and manning of the gates. "I want a twenty-four-hour rota for the gates, Centurion."

His next thought was for his quarters. He had no intention of occupying the luxurious residence Sylla had created, so ordered another centurion to find him a room in the old *praetorium*.

"But will you not take up residence in Praefectus Crispinus Sylla's quarters, lord?"

"Nay, I'm a soldier, not a popinjay! Oh, and you can tell the men that from now on, when not on duty, they can make use of the baths."

The centurion stifled a grin, but thumped his chest and said, "This way to the *praetorium*."

Word spread around the camp like wildfire about this choice and that Praefectus Valdor was a real soldier, who would lead them to glory.

Gaius, meanwhile, had not forgotten that the smith was breaking into the treasure chest and that the men would be paid. The burly fellow was levering an iron band with a crowbar where a sturdy padlock hung. He was sweating profusely and Gaius could see that he had already broken four of the five bands. He acknowledged Gaius' presence by stopping, straightening and rubbing the small of his back, "Just one more band and I'm in, Centurion."

"Good man! I see that your handiwork made Praefectus Crispinus Sylla sleep easily."

"Ay, only the keys or brute force will get into this beauty!" the smith laughed. "God knows where he hid his keys!"

"We'll probably never find out. See if you can break that band. I'll see you're the first paid."

With one last effort and with a grunt, the smith separated the band from the padlock.

"Well done!"

Gaius opened the well-oiled lid, but neither man expected to find so many silver coins—years'-worth of extortion money—the corrupt gains robbed from the Britons and successively from their Roman oppressors.

Gaius picked out ten silver denarii, as if they were ten grains of sand on a beach and handed them to the smith. "Remember to pay for your drink, friend, for else I'll not be able to save you!"

"Thank you, Centurion," the smith tugged a forelock.

Gaius exited the building to find a decurion. "Send me two men to do some lifting and spread the word that the men are to form an orderly queue to receive their pay." Since there was no question of lifting the strongbox full of silver, Gaius ordered the two men to place a table and chair next to the box.

"What about the bodies, lord?"

"Nay, leave them. As the men file past, they'll see what happens to those who defy Rome."

He quickly counted and stacked columns of ten denarii before calling in the first man. The Banna garrison was too wise to abandon discipline on pay day, so the long snaking file of men moved forward smoothly without incident. After a while, a centurion stood before Gaius, who, without ado, pushed two stacks towards him as the officers received higher pay. Gradually, the pay made inroads into the strongbox contents but there was never a doubt in Gaius' mind that all the men would be paid.

When, at last, he had finished doling out the coins, the chest remained about a third full. *There's money for necessities,* he thought, *now what about those corpses?* Stepping into the courtyard to friendly grins, he ordered a group of soldiers to remove the bodies from the building. "Load them on a cart, we'll take them out of the north gate and burn them outside the fortress on the moors."

That afternoon, Valdor, wearing his helm of high office, ordered a decurion to accompany him to *The Wounded Boar* tavern. With the soldiers confined momentarily to the fortress, the inn was eerily quiet.

Valdor addressed the innkeeper, who studied his face and helmet with interest.

"You recognise me as that centurion of yesterday who wanted to pay you—and now I am the commandant of the fortress. Hark, things have changed. Henceforward, my men will pay a fair price for your ale and food. Should any one of them cause you to complain, you will come to me and report to me. He will then be severely punished. Any questions, landlord?"

"Nay, your honour."

"Then give us a beaker of your best ale."

There was no sign of the sullen features of the day before, but rather a winning, friendly smile as the beakers were set before the officers. They drank with gusto and although the decurion wanted to replenish his beaker, Valdor would not allow it. "We have to visit every hostelry in the *vicus!*"

He took two silver coins from his money bag and slid them towards the landlord.

"It's too much, lord."

"Keep it. It includes yesterday's drinks."

"But they were on the house," the voice was so low it was scarcely audible.

"Things have changed, but there will be taxation next year as once before. So, enjoy your profit while you can. Set money aside to pay your taxes when the year changes number. You will be taxed at the old rate. There will be no increases while I am praefectus."

"Bless you, lord! When will the soldiers return? I want no trouble."

"And you will have none. But remember, as I will not raise taxes, you will not increase your prices!"

"So be it!"

They left the jubilant Briton and headed to *The Crossed Spears,* where the same scene was re-enacted in front of the skinny landlord. The reaction was the same. The praefectus and decurion visited three more taverns in the large *vicus,* one of the few towns in the north not to have been affected by population loss, ironically due to the anarchy caused by no taxation, imposed by Valdor's predecessor.

While speaking to the innkeepers, Valdor questioned them about other tradesmen so that he and the decurion spread the word about the return of Roman law to the *vicus*. Confident that word would circulate rapidly among the bakers, oyster sellers, chandlers, and other services that the soldiers might avail themselves of, the two officers returned to base.

On entering the courtyard, Valdor noticed smoke billowing beyond the north wall. He hurried to the steps to investigate, but Gaius caught his arm—"No need, Valdor, it's the funeral pyre of those guards and their commandant we slew yesterday."

"Ah, I see you have taken Dulcitius' words to heart; it's good to know I have a reliable *vicarius*." He went on to explain what he had done in the *vicus* and his eye involuntarily drifted to the whipping post. *I hope I won't have to use that!*

His eye wandered over to the north wall again.

"I know what you're thinking, Valdor. It seems too good to be true, right?"

"Ay. I can't help wondering what the Picts are scheming."

19

BANNA FORT, HADRIAN'S WALL AD 371-373

VALDOR ENJOYED HIS ROLE AS COMMANDANT OF BANNA Fort, and with the exercise of power not diminishing his popularity with his men and his immediate superior, Dux Dulcitius, he had swallowed the disappointment of his younger brother becoming the Count of the Saxon Shore. In Eboracum, his father was well-informed and would surely have known that his eldest son was now *praefectus* at Banna. The old fellow had always admired young Maximus' prowess and quick mind, so perhaps passing over himself was understandable. Logic also dictated that Hadrian's Wall and the western forts were just as important frontiers as the Saxon Shore—if not more so. In any case, he had the good fortune to have Gaius, his best friend, here as his *vicarius*, so life was not altogether unbearable.

News from other parts of the Empire seeped through to the Wall, and the dux made it his business to share it with Valdor. So, he learnt that Emperor Valentinian I was engaged in operations against the Alemanni, Quadi and Sarmatians this year and, more troubling, his subordinates had to deal with a usurper, Firmus, in Africa. Valdor was not surprised to learn that there was talk of dispatching his hero, Theodosius, there, after his successes against the Alemanni. How he would love to enjoy similar adulation and triumphs to his idol!

As he pondered these thoughts, Valdor could not imagine that there would soon be no need for him to travel to Africa to enhance his reputation. That opportunity was lurking at his doorstep, aided by events elsewhere.

Meanwhile, however, his soldiers, many veterans among them, appreciated the rigid discipline at Banna. They knew where they stood, and Valdor proved to be a humane and fair leader. One episode, in particular, became the turning point in the general acceptance of him as commandant. He had been in his post only a month when the first challenge to his authority surfaced.

The innkeeper of *The Wounded Boar* came to the gate and begged to see the *praefectus*. A guard accompanied him to the *principia* and ushered him into the commandant's presence. Valdor feared the worst, for what other reason would an innkeeper be present? So, it proved: "*Praefectus*, you told me to report any man who refused to pay for his consumption. Not only did he decline to pay, but he struck me in the face." The innkeeper showed his profile, with a hangdog expression, and pointed to a swelling under his right eye.

"Did you get a name? When did this happen?"

"Yesterday. Nay, lord, the other soldiers comforted me, but said they would not betray a friend."

"Do you know how many men I command here? What am I to do without a name?"

The innkeeper shrugged and muttered, "You said you'd punish anyone who refused to pay."

"And so, I will, but first, I have to catch the rogue."

Valdor summoned a decurion and handed him two denarii. "Accompany this worthy fellow to his inn and have a few drinks on me, Decurion. Spend all day there if need be. The landlord will indicate a soldier to you. Arrest him and bring him to me."

Since it was the soldier's three days off-duty, everything went to plan. The decurion brought the legionary to the *praefectus* and said, "Blasius Centho, lord. Guilty of refusing to pay for drink and striking the tavernkeeper. I have several witnesses prepared to speak up."

"What do you have to say in your defence, Blasius?"

The legionary looked sullen, "For two years I haven't paid that fat swine. Why should I give him my hard-earned coin?"

"Because that is how the world works and, more importantly, because your *praefectus* ordered you to pay."

"Ay, but the old *praefectus* didn't."

"Enough! Decurion, have him stripped to the waist and tied to the whipping post. We'll flog some sense into this miscreant! Then gather the men in the courtyard to watch the punishment carried out."

In the courtyard, the men murmured among themselves, but the general mood was of acceptance. The criminal, Blasius Centho, wept and screamed for mercy, but Valdor was resolute. In a loud voice, he declared, "At the behest of our dux and, according to law, I, Valdor Leonius Caurus, *Praefectus* of Banna Fortress, condemn the convict, Blasius Centho, guilty of flouting military authority and unjustly striking a Briton, to one thousand lashes."

There were no gasps this time. The men had expected the sentence. One or two groaned at the implication: no man could survive a thousand lashes. The burly legionary tasked with flogging the wretch stepped forward. He wore a leather head covering, which had holes for the eyes and nose, the traditional guarantee of anonymity—of the assembly, only Valdor knew his identity. In his right hand dangled a knotted scourge made up of six strands. The knots were designed to injure the victim's flesh.

Valdor raised and dropped his hand, and the muscular arm raised the scourge, lashing it across the bare back, leaving a trail of raised weals with pricks of blood. The thrashing continued as the captive's groans became screams. The weals became open wounds as the tortured flesh resembled meat on a butcher's slab. Twenty-nine- thirty! "Halt!" Valdor cried. "Unbind him and take him to the infirmary. It is punishment enough. Blasius Centho will live to fight Rome's enemies. I take no satisfaction in slaying a veteran legionary, no matter how wantonly he flaunted my rules. Let it be known that I will not commute the next sentence for the same offence."

Several men stepped forward, likely friends of the injured man, to unbind him. They placed shoulders under his arms and heaved him, fainting, across the courtyard on trembling legs to the infirmary. The infirmarian, who had heard the *praefectus'* speech, had already prepared disinfectant, a salve and bandages. The disinfectant chosen was aged vinegar and almost as bad as further lashes, but effective for cleansing the wounds.

In a matter of days, Blasius Centho was able to wear a linen shirt over his bandages and take the air in the courtyard, where Valdor found him and solicitously asked, "How are you mending, Blasius?"

"Lord, I can't complain and I wish to thank you for your mercy. I'll never again disobey orders."

"I should think not, my friend. It is easier to face woad-painted Picts than await a flogging."

The veteran eyed his commander appreciatively, "Lord, I have a request, though I doubt—" he hesitated, aware of how it might go against him.

"Well, when it comes to battle, lord, I beg you to place me in defence of the legion's standard."

"You didn't scream until the sixth lash. That tells me you are courageous, Blasius. So, your request to defend the eagle is accorded. You may be brave, but take my advice, change tavern!"

Valdor laughed and walked away to the admiring stare of the punished man. He knew he might not have survived sixty lashes, never mind a thousand. The whole garrison knew it, too. The *praefectus* had stuck to his rules but had shown compassion at the right moment. The men knew that if it came to war, their commander would not sacrifice them to foolhardiness. What more could a good soldier ask for?

Alarming rumours filtered through to Banna about the state of some other forts, especially along the western coast and in Cumbria in general. The state of his fort before taking over had been replicated elsewhere. Some forts had been abandoned, whereas others were now in the hands of auxiliaries more intent on personal gain than on upholding Roman law, which had been the case in Banna under the previous *praefectus*. Of course, the Picts were well-informed and chose to circumvent Hadrian's Wall to the west, a task made easier by the undisciplined garrison of *Coggabata*, where, at night, they used ropes and grappling irons to scale the walls while the lax legionaries slept. In a trice, they opened the gates and their army slipped into Cumbria unopposed. The Picts had chosen well because, had the garrison not been asleep, as they knew, only a detachment was quartered in so small a fort and in the event of battle, it would surely have been overwhelmed.

Dux Dulcitius also had an efficient network of scouts, so although he was farther away from the incursion than Valdor, he knew about the Pictish army before him. Immediately, he dispatched a rider who galloped at breakneck speed along the Stanegate with orders for Valdor to track down and destroy the enemy.

Valdor marched westwards along the Stanegate, collecting additional troops from the five garrisons before Coggabata. He met no opposition to his recruitment from other garrison commanders because his reputation as a valiant general preceded him and his dazzling helmet endorsed his prowess. His predecessor, Crispinus Sylla, had worn it without merit, purely for vanity, whereas Valdor had vowed to be as fierce as the pouncing lions it portrayed.

As they pursued the Picts southwards, Valdor prayed silently, as he did before every battle. It was at that moment when inspiration came to him. Suddenly, he halted his men and sent a messenger to Dux Dulcitius. He had thought of Pictish deviousness and realised with a start that the force he was pursuing was nothing more than a decoy. The real problem would be when the bulk of the enemy poured over the Sandwath ford. Having completed the about-turn, the Roman army first encountered a Pictish scout, who preferred to die rather than reveal the whereabouts and strength of the foe. When they arrived at the southern end of the ford, gazing northwards, Valdor saw the dark mass of men moving towards them. He called Gaius and said, "Look, the ford is wide enough for only two men at a time to cross, otherwise, more would impede the use of weapons. You and I will hold this end of the ford."

"By God, Valdor, we can't fight that host on our own!"

"We'll fight until we tire or fall. We have an army at our backs."

They led by example as the first half-naked tattooed Picts roared across the ford to meet their deaths on the blades of the high-ranking Roman officers. Valdor also used his *scutum* as a weapon, not only a shield. The Picts had more wieldable bucklers but they were no match for the skilled cousins. Victory and defeat are played out in the mind and after seeing every man attempting to defeat the two berserkers—for the Picts thought them to be madmen—they became more unsure and, therefore, easier prey. Dead bodies now obstructed the onrushing Picts and Roman javelins took a deadly toll.

Valdor was exhausted, but he would not admit it, so it was a relief when Gaius said, "I'm done for, cousin, let someone replace us."

To raucous cheers from their men, the two officers allowed two centurions to replace them. As a last defiant act, Valdor seized a javelin and hurled it with deadly accuracy, fatally piercing one of the foes wading across the ford. Now, he needed to think. The battle would only be won by astuteness—of that, he was certain.

Even as he received the warm congratulations of his officers, Valdor's mind was racing. He remembered another *wath,* or ford, two miles to the west. Quickly, he spoke to Gaius, "Organise a cohort to hold this ford, while I attempt to get the bulk of the men away unobserved to the Stonewath. We'll cross and attack their flank before they know what's hit them!"

Valdor had already noticed and considered the state of the tides, which could make or break his scheme. Using the natural depression of the firth to remain unseen by the Picts, he led a strong force the two miles to the west. There, he confirmed that the very low spring tide was in his favour, and, as usual, he led from the front, wading across the Solway firth through the swirling outgoing tide and the brownish flows of the rivers Eden and Esk. The ancient *wath* ended in cloying mud, but his men were soon through that and marching rapidly towards the Pictish flank. They approached silently like a famished wildcat stalking its prey.

With a ferocious roar, Valdor led a wedge of troops into the unsuspecting foe with devastating effect. At the same time, Gaius led a frontal attack across the sandy *wath*. Panic spread through the Pictish ranks and the battle favoured Roman blades. The enemy rear melted away into the northern uplands. This loss of men was too grave to support and the battle reached its foregone conclusion with Valdor's victory. If he had been a hero before the battle, he became a myth after it. Along Hadrian's Wall, an exaggerated and idealised account of Valdor at the Sandwath was retold countless times although it was far from the truth that he had won the battle single-handedly as a testy Gaius was quick to point out.

Elsewhere the dux also defeated the Pict decoy force, but the veracity of the Pictish defeat was less important than the years of peace gained by the victories, however achieved. Thus, early in 383, while enjoying the fruits of his triumph in Banna Fort—peace and prestige—Valdor learnt that the man he most wished to emulate, Theodosius the Elder, had been appointed commander of an expedition to suppress the rebellion of Firmus in Mauretania. The *praefectus* did not doubt that his hero would succeed, so received the tidings as good news. A few months later came a less welcome communication from Eboracum. Count Leo had died at the ripe old age of 71. His death hit Valdor hard and, together with Gaius, he sought and obtained permission from the dux to travel south for the funeral, where he would receive another dire blow.

One certain thing about a man's fate is that it is never linear, but rather evolves with the most unforeseen twists and turns. So, Valdor was dismayed by Leo's will, which left the role of *Comes Britanniarum* and the Eboracum property to Gaius. Stung by his father's coherent preference for his nephew, and reducing the dear cousins' separation to his forcedly unpleasant departure, Valdor returned alone with gritted teeth to the Wall to brood. As far as he was concerned, much as he loved his cousin, he would have made a better *Comes*. He could not know that this enforced separation would facilitate something much more pleasant —the most important event in his life—which was in the offing.

20

REGULBIUM FORT AND MUCKING, ESSEX, AD 374-376

MAXIMUS, THE COUNT OF THE SAXON SHORE, stared incredulously at the wealthy Romano-Briton, several years his elder. "You say that there are more than a hundred of them and that they crossed the marshes and took over the hill?"

"Ay, lord, and they've built a palisade and are constructing houses."

"Do you know who these people are?"

"Barbarians."

"More specifically?"

"I reckon they are Saxons."

Maximus took a deep breath and considered, "Over a hundred Saxons, just two miles from your villa. This requires immediate action, Senovara; you are under my jurisdiction and, as such, guaranteed my protection. Centurion! Gather your men, we march in one hour."

Maximus left the *Regulbium* fortress, standing redoubtably on its promontory. He rode at the head of two hundred marching men and next to the Briton, who knew the byways and, more importantly, the route through the treacherous marshland once they reached the Tamesis estuary.

Less than four years had passed in his role as Count of the Saxon Shore, in which time, he had encountered bands of sea rovers, many of whom were Saxons. Invariably, he had emerged victorious from these clashes but had acquired a healthy respect for the fighting abilities of the men from across the Rhine. His high regard for this adversary, who, for reasons he could only guess, had been driven to reach Britannia's shores in waves, had led him to exhort the shore fort commanders to tighten discipline and conduct rigid weaponry practice. During the years of his assignment as Count of the Saxon Shore, he had witnessed a marked improvement in the fighting capabilities of the various garrisons. Compared to his first bloody engagement, won but at a high cost, the men had grown to acknowledge his courage and leadership skills; therefore, they received his demands with the right attitude and in good spirits and developed into excellent soldiers.

More than a hundred Saxons against two hundred such men, he reckoned, should provide him with another victory. A wooden palisade might cost him some men to overcome it, but he was not unduly worried.

Irritating gnats, whining in swarms, were the only enemy they encountered as they followed Senovara through the Tamesis marshlands. At last, the Romano-Briton pointed at a hill. "They have settled on yonder hill, lord. Here onwards the going is firm. My villa lies two miles in that direction," he pointed westwards, towards the low sun. Maximus created two flanking columns to his central one, each headed by a centurion and, after one final reassurance to Senovara, left the farmer behind.

Marching steadily uphill, they heard excited shouts, but unexpectedly, the gates swung back and a lone figure emerged. He was a tall individual with long blond hair falling forward over his shoulders, flanking a full beard. He advanced with arms open, demonstrating empty hands and, neither sword nor axe on his person. Accordingly, Maximus dismounted and walked towards him.

"Hail! My name is Mucca and these," he waved a hand airily behind him, "are my followers. I am chieftain of the Mucking. We come in peace, Centurion."

"I am a Count, but no matter. This land is within my jurisdiction and belongs to the Empire."

"The land is heavy, but fertile. All we ask is to be allowed to farm and trade peacefully."

"As Count of these shores, I must receive guarantees and impose conditions."

"Let's hear them, then," the piercing ocean blue eyes did not lack sincerity, "for if they are acceptable to my people, we can avoid bloodshed."

"Firstly, since this is imperial land, you will be subject to taxation, although not for another year and a day."

"How much taxation?" the chieftain asked suspiciously.

"A tithe of your produce should suffice."

"Acceptable, but don't expect miracles in our first year. We have to learn to handle the climate and work the soil."

"Secondly, and most importantly: you will respect the *pax romana*, which means leaving your neighbours in peace."

"I, Mucca, personally guarantee that we'll be good neighbours, and maybe we can profitably trade with neighbouring farmers."

"Do you have children, Mucca?"

The Saxon's face clouded, for he knew what was coming. "Isn't my word good enough? You don't need hostages, Roman."

"It will be my condition to avoid bloodshed. Now, answer my question!"

"Three sons and a daughter."

"Which is the youngest?"

"The girl, Hicela, she has but five winters."

"One less mouth to feed, Mucca." Maximus said persuasively. "If you keep the peace for five more winters, I will restore her to you. Meanwhile, I'll keep her as my child, so she'll grow strong and healthy."

"Her mother will not be pleased, but as I command everyone here, I accept, Roman. Will you come with me?"

"Not alone, Mucca. I do not know yet whether I can trust you."

The Saxon scowled. "I also need to trust you, Roman. From time to time, I will come to visit my daughter with my wife."

"So be it! You will find her at *Regulbium* fortress."

The Saxon disappeared into the compound and returned shortly, hand-in-hand with a wide-eyed waiflike child. "Here, Hicela, do you want a ride on the big white horse?"

The girl nodded enthusiastically and her father lifted her up in front of Maximus, who silently vowed to feed up this little sack of skin and bones and to have her bathed, for her hair stank of smoke. She won his affection immediately by running a tiny hand gently back and forth along the horse's mane.

"Oh, Mucca, one last thing. From this hilltop, you have a good view over the estuary. I'd appreciate it if you'd send a messenger informing me of the arrival of any new Saxon fleets. As an accepted resident here, it is my job to protect you, too. You don't want another tribe plundering your land, do you?"

"Next time you chance by here, come in peace, Roman, we'll seal our pact with ale, as is our tradition, and you'll meet my people."

"I'll consider that, Mucca. But first, win my trust!"

With that parting shot, Maximus urged his horse away and began to reassure the little girl. To gain her confidence, he promised her a pony of her own when she was older and he questioned her closely about her family, learning all their names. The child seemed strangely happy to be coming with him. He wondered if it was merely due to the joy of riding on a horse. Unless he had seriously misjudged Mucca, he doubted the man would mistreat the child. What did he know about the mother, though? The girl had not mentioned her once. Still, there was time to find out everything and to settle the bairn into her new surroundings. A decent meal, a warming fire, a thorough scrubbing and a soft bed would go a long way in that respect.

The weeks slipped by and Hicela became the darling of the fortress. Her sunken cheeks filled out and took on a roseate tint, offsetting her long blonde hair and sparkling blue eyes. She flitted around the courtyard like a tiny fairy and became popular for her ready smile and piping songs. She showed a sharp brain, too, asking countless questions of any soldier patient enough to sit and answer. Nor did they consider her a barbarian as Maximus' serving women washed and perfumed her with scents made from wild flowers or bought at the market in the *vicus*, incense from distant exotic places.

One early summer's day as the swallows came and went with metronomic regularity to and from the nests in the granary eaves, Senovara arrived asking to see the Count.

"Is everything alright, Senovara," Maximus asked anxiously.

"Ay, lord, I thank you, things couldn't be better. Mucca is a good and honest man. He came recently to buy seed to sow in the fields the Saxons have prepared. They farm in long strips, each with his own. Anyway, the point is, he paid me immediately in good silver coin."

Maximus kept his thoughts to himself: *likely plunder robbed from the coasts of Gaul*. But the provenance did not concern him—it mattered only that there should be no marauding on *his* territory. Senovara continued talking and Maximus returned to following his words "...and not only that, he sent men to repair the roof on my barn. I couldn't ask for better neighbours. That's why I came here today, with my offer, lord, if it pleases you."

"What offer?"

The Romano-British farmer looked embarrassed, "Getting to know Mucca and his wife, Nelda—"

"Wait! Are you saying that you have been into their settlement?"

"Ay, and quite a sizeable village it is! Mucca has a quite respectable timber hall, I'd reckon it to be about 50 feet long and 25 feet wide with entrances in the middle of both longer sides. He's adorned the walls with hangings and colourful shields. There must be another dozen large timber buildings, but most of the houses are pit-houses, dug into the earth, whose roofs come right down to the ground." The wealthy farmer laughed, "I can't imagine grubbing around in the earth to create a home, although I guess our forefathers must have done so before you Romans came to show us mosaic floors with underfloor heating."

"Very interesting, but not what you came to speak to me about."

"Nay, I was saying, after getting to know Mucca and his wife, Nelda, I learnt what good people they are and how they miss their daughter, Hicela—"

"I'll not send her back! When she arrived here, she was underfed and stank. Now, she's happy and healthy—"

"I don't want you to send her back. It's just that if you let me take her into my home as a hostage, my wife and I will treat her as well as you, Count, but she'll only be two miles from her parents, who can visit her almost every day and, surely, it will further strengthen our friendship."

Maximus stroked his chin and, raising his head, said, "Very well, but there's one condition."

"Ay?"

"You will find her a pony and teach her to ride it."

"I have a gentle donkey, will that do?"

Maximus smiled, "I'm all in favour of good relations with these new neighbours, but be wary! Your villa is not a fortress. What is to stop Mucca from seizing his daughter and plundering your farm?"

"*You*, Count. The thought that you would wreak vengeance upon his people. With all due respect, I see them with different eyes from yours."

"I have had to deal with atrocities, friend, but I would not frighten you with bloody tales. Remember the donkey!"

The count decided there and then, that he would visit the Saxons before long. Releasing the child to Senovara and his wife was already a sign of goodwill. The problem was not Mucca. For every Saxon like him, there must be a score intent on plunder and slaughter; yet, thought Maximus, who tried to peer into a distant future: *if Romans have married Britons and Britons, Romans—why might not Saxons wed Britons or Romans? The world is changing before my eyes!*

Had Maximus been anything of a seer or a prophet, he could have foretold such changes affecting his own family in the not-too-distant future.

The winter came, bringing another year, and Maximus, strategically placed to receive tidings from other far-flung parts of the Empire, news which reached his brother much later at Hadrian's Wall, learnt that in November, Emperor Valentinian concluded peace with the Alemanni in Germany, then marched into Illyricum to repel an invasion of the Quadi and the Sarmatians on the Danube frontier. The frontier problems would have direct consequences for both brothers, for although Britannia was far away, it formed part of the same Empire and the consequences reached its shores and even into the heart of the family. While negotiating with the Quadi, Valentinian, aged 54, became so enraged that he died in a fit of apoplexy at *Brigetio*.

Another death soon followed and it was one that deeply touched Valdor. When Emperor Valentinian suddenly died, that great servant of the Empire, and Valdor's hero, Theodosius, was still in Africa. Orders arrived for him to be arrested; he was taken to Carthage, and put to death in early 376. The reason was likely a factional power struggle after the sudden death of Valentinian, in Italy where the great general was seen as a threat, with some justification, for later, his son and namesake would become Emperor Theodosius I.

The chaos at the heart of the Empire and the barbarian incursions along its frontiers could hardly lead immediately to Maximus' uncertain vision of an integrated future. Meanwhile, he and his similars would try to hold the provinces of Britannia as best they could, but the once irresistible Empire was crumbling.

21

EASTERN EMPIRE, ALONG THE DANUBE INTO THRACE, AD 376-379

GOSVINTHA, A SIXTEEN-YEAR-OLD, BROWN-HAIRED, HAZEL-eyed beauty, sat on a fallen tree, gazing over the river Danube. Her eyes veiled by the silent tears that brimmed down her cheeks, she shrugged her father's hand off her shoulder.

"Don't be afraid, daughter," said Geberic, chieftain of the Vesi Goths—one of several Gothic tribes, the name later corrupted into Visigoths— "there's no time to lose."

"It's madness, the river is swollen by all the rain that has fallen and look what we have to cross it on, rafts and dugout canoes. I'm staying here in Thrace!"

"You'll come with me! At least, you'll have a chance to get across into Moesia. If you stay here, the Huns will seize and pass you around. Then you'll wish you'd drowned!"

"What if we do get across? Won't the Romans destroy us?" Her words were hard to understand, interspersed with shuddering sobs.

The chieftain again tried to reassure her, raising and taking her in his arms. "My sweet child, I have struck an agreement with Emperor Valens: we can settle on Roman soil, on condition that we provide soldiers to their legions. We'll be safe and able to grow our own food."

Before she could answer, his strong arms swept her off her feet and he carried her to a hollowed-out tree trunk where her mother sat at the fore, while four men wielding paddles were kneeling and waiting for their leader. Depositing her behind the fourth man, Geberic hauled himself aboard while simultaneously pushing the rudimentary craft into the strong current. After a considerable, strength-sapping struggle, all the canoes and rafts reached the far shore and not without the fear of capsizing in every breast. One raft overturned only yards from the bank, so the bedraggled men and women managed to survive, unlike the few foolhardy men who had decided to swim across the gushing stream. Gosvintha watched in horror as heads disappeared underwater and hands waved frantically before slipping below the surface, the battle against the force of the stream being lost. Still, the vast majority of her tribe were safely across, including children and babes in arms.

The Visigoths marched away from the river, hunting for food in the dense woodland, fortunately with success. Fires lit, they cooked the game they had killed and survival was guaranteed for another day.

His people looked to Geberic for leadership, so he said thoughtfully, "We must search for fertile land, but not far from this source of food. The seed we have brought will take time to sow and grow—time that we can ill-afford."

Unknown to him, the Greuthungi, another Gothic tribe, led by Alatheus and Saphrax, and also displaced by the predations of the Huns and Alans, requested asylum within the Roman Empire, which Valens refused. With the Roman frontier forces stretched to breaking point, they slipped across the Danube and united with Geberic.

The chieftain weighed up the benefits of having more warriors against the necessity to feed more people. After consulting his trusted advisers and listening to Gosvintha's pleas in favour of the Greuthungi, he allowed them to stay, but soon, the situation became critical and, desperately short of food, discontent rose amongst the Goths. Some of them went off on raids, plundering local farmsteads. The Roman reaction was inevitable.

Gosvintha fled and hid behind a tree near the settlement. From the fringe of woodland, she peered fearfully, afraid for her parents' safety. But the Romans failed to disarm the Visigoths remaining in the village, yet managed to mistreat them by seizing several children as slaves. Gosvintha, relieved that she had run and hidden, realised that she could easily have been made captive despite her father's battle hardiness. For her, the last four years had been a compound of dissatisfaction and terror. She looked back on her childhood as if on a golden age, when their town was stable, food was plentiful and her parents were the richest and most powerful people among the Vesi.

This first Roman assault on her folks, near the Danube, brought matters to a head. The Goths were supposed to stay within a containment area decided by the authorities. But the seizing of some children could only be described by Lupicinus, the Count of Thrace as 'bungling' and he was not surprised when the Goths, led by Geberic, broke out of their demarcated area and struck towards the low-lying fertile region near Marcianople. In truth, this was defiance, but not open revolt. Even so, Lupicinus sought to bring the Visigoths back under control.

A messenger arrived and Gosvintha heard him say, "Lord Geberic, you, Alatheus and Saphrax and your most trusted retainers are invited to a banquet in your honour, where in addition to food and drink, you can discuss provisions for your people."

At last, we'll have supplies of food, Gosvintha thought as she shrank back into the shadows far from the sight of the messenger and her father, who would have struck her for eavesdropping, but she heard him say, "Tell your master that we accept his invitation gladly."

Gosvintha and her mother remained in the village because her father did not trust the Comes of Thrace—wisely, as it turned out because he had prepared a trap. Lupicinus treacherously attempted to assassinate the Gothic delegation but underestimated their cunning, courage and resourcefulness. Half-prepared for such a plot, Geberic seized a weapon and escaped. As he told his people in an audience the following day: "To Hell with the *pax romana*, they have betrayed it themselves. As far as I am concerned, they have given us licence to loot and burn the farms and villas in the area of Marcianople and that is what we shall do. Who is with me?"

The Goths were desperate and unanimously behind Geberic. For days they marauded until Lupicinus reacted. He hastily gathered a force of local troops, totalling 5,000 men, but Geberic was well informed by his scouts and chose an advantageous position nine miles outside the town, where the result was devastating, the Goths annihilated the Roman force and, importantly, at Geberic's command, equipped themselves with the deceaseds' armour and weapons. News of this Gothic victory resounded throughout the Empire.

In his hall, the chieftain assembled his warriors. Before his wife and daughter, he declared, "Tomorrow, we march south towards Adrianople. I'm tired of living from hand to mouth, so either we strike a lasting agreement with Valens or we defeat him." His men greeted these ringing words with raucous cheers.

On learning of his plan, and fearing they would join Geberic, Valens ordered the Roman troops of Gothic origin stationed in Adrianople to move east. The soldiers requested a two-day delay to prepare and asked for food and money for the journey. The chief magistrate of Adrianople refused and the Goths broke out in open rebellion. They inflicted heavy casualties among the citizens before arming themselves with Roman equipment and joining forces with Geberic.

Although he now had a sizeable army, winter was fast approaching, making resolute action necessary. Since he admired his daughter's intelligence, Geberic privately sought her advice after his council meetings, which she was allowed to attend but in silence.

"If you can storm the city walls, father, then do it, but you've seen them for yourself, the chances of breaking them are almost nil. I suggest you abandon the attacks and divide your force into small bands, better able to forage and feed themselves. The weather is sure to get worse."

As always, the chieftain argued with his daughter, as a matter of self-respect, but as usual, ended up taking her advice, so throughout the remainder of the autumn, he sent bands of predatory Goths in different directions in the province. During these raids, the Roman troops remained cautiously in the towns. Some elite units remained in the field and skirmished with the Goths, but could not cope with Geberic's cunning tactics. His greatest success came near the town of Dibaltum, where he successfully disguised his numbers and sprang a trap, luring the Scutarii heavy cavalry into a mad charge and total defeat.

"Father, we need a major victory to force the Empire to make terms with us," Gosvintha could not bear to see a future of raids and skirmishes for her people. Her dearest wish was to settle in a stable community as at the time of her childhood. Her dream would come true, but most unexpectedly and not without a series of dramatic events precipitated by the emperor, Valens, who decided to solve the problem of the Goths himself. He assembled additional troops from Syria and from the reserves of the Western Empire in Gaul. He also appointed a general, Sebastianus, newly arrived from Italy to reorganise the army in Thrace.

Sebastianus picked 2,000 of his legionaries and marched towards

Adrianople. Along the way, they came upon and ambushed small detachments of Goths. Geberic as the leader of the Goths, assembled his forces at Nicopolis and Beroe to deal with the Roman threat.

On 8 August, encouraged by his counsellors and urged on by his daughter, Geberic sent an emissary to propose peace and an alliance in exchange for Roman territory. Certain that he would be victorious due to his supposed numerical superiority, Valens rejected these proposals. Valens' estimates of manpower, however, neglected to take into consideration part of the Gothic cavalry, about 5,000 men, absent with extended distances to forage.

Gosvintha sat with bated breath in a wagon—forming part of the wagon circle set up on the top of a hill north of the city—trying to comfort three little children, just as the older women were doing, as they waited for the battle to begin. She had faith in her father and the other menfolk, who, except for their cavalry, defended their wagon circle, inside of which were their families and possessions. Luckily, she could not read her father's anxieties, as his objective was to delay the Romans, in order to give enough time for the Gothic cavalry to return. Nor could she possibly know that the Roman troops arrived tired and dehydrated after marching for eight miles over difficult terrain and now they drew up and faced the Gothic camp that had been set up on the top of the hill.

"Burn the fields!" Geberic roared. His daughter smelled the smoke and trembled. She peeped out through the gap in the canvas curtains covering the entrance to the wagon. What little she could see reassured her that the carts were not on fire. How could she imagine that the burning fields below were her father's ploy to delay and harass the Romans with smoke? He also began negotiations for an exchange of hostages with the simple intent of gaining precious time until the Goth cavalry could arrive. These talks exasperated the Roman soldiers who seemed to hold the stronger position. But the ploy was effective.

From within her sanctuary, Gosvintha could not know what was happening. Some Roman units began the battle without orders to do so, believing they would have an easy victory, and over-eager to exact revenge on the Goths after two years of unchecked devastation throughout the area. The imperial scholae of shield-archers under the command of the Iberian prince, Bacurius, attacked, but lacking support they were easily repelled.

Gosvintha tried to cover the ears of a three-year-old girl since by now, they could plainly hear the screams of wounded men. She might have covered her eyes instead, had she known that the Roman left wing had reached the circle of wagons. Fortunately for her and all of the wagon occupants, they were too late because the drumming hoofs she heard approaching were the Goth cavalry, returning from a foraging expedition, and arrived to support the infantry. The cavalry surrounded the Roman troops, who were already in disarray after the failure of the first assault and who retreated to the base of the hill where they were unable to manoeuvre, encumbered by their heavy armour and long shields. With their withdrawal, the horrendous sounds of battle diminished and Gosvintha was able to remove her hands and instead kiss the top of the child's head, telling her, "It's alright, our men are winning the battle. We will all be safe." She could not be sure of this, but had to give hope to the innocent children in her charge.

How right she was! The casualties, exhaustion, and psychological pressure led to a rout of the Roman army. The cavalry continued their attack, and the killing continued until nightfall.

In the rout, the emperor's guards abandoned him. Some tried to retrieve him, but the majority of the Roman cavalry fled. Valens had escaped the field with a bodyguard and some eunuchs and hid in a peasant's cottage. The Goths attempted to pillage the cottage unaware that Valens was inside. Valens' men shot arrows from the second floor to defend the cottage and Geberic's response was to shout: "Set the cottage on fire!" The bodyguard leapt out the window and one shouted to Geberic, "Inside the building is Emperor Valens! If you capture him, he will be worth much money." Smoke poured thick and black out of the roof devoured by flames. "Nobody can survive that!" Geberic replied with a wolfish grin. It was too late; Valens perished in the flames and the battle was won.

Once again, Gosvintha's wisdom proved correct. The large-scale victory and the death of Valens along with the depletion of the Roman army led to important changes. Not least, the western emperor, Gratian, appointed Flavius Theodosius—the son of Valens' hero—as Valens' successor with orders to take charge of the current military emergency.

Theodosius came to terms with the Visigoths, settling them in the Balkans as military allies known as *foederati*. Also, Theodosius, having inherited his father's acumen, made it a condition of the agreement that

Geberic and his immediate family transfer to the most far-flung of the empire's frontiers—the northern frontier of Britannia, namely, Hadrian's Wall. He was allowed to take 300 men with him as auxiliary troops and they would be stationed at Banna Fort. Tired of fighting and living hand-to-mouth, Geberic seized the opportunity, encouraged by Gosvintha, although none of his people knew anything about Britannia.

22

BANNA FORT, AD 379-380

Praefectus Valdor was shocked to receive 300 Visigoth cavalrymen added to his garrison. A first look at the barbarians did not reveal their worth on the battlefield, while their appearance, so bedraggled, unkempt and different from his own, made him wonder whether they would disturb the harmony and discipline he had created in Banna Fort.

Their leader, a man named Geberic, wore an extravagant helm with two eagle's wings, fashioned in bronze, extending upwards. Below, he wore a three-quarters length green tunic, edged with red borders, its sleeves ending at the elbows, over a pair of brown trousers bound with the thongs of his leather boots. His eyes were brown and shrewd and surveyed Valdor without a hint of challenge, but rather of careful assessment. Despite the obvious importance of this newcomer, Valdor had eyes less for him than for the women who descended from the waggon the Visigoths were zealously flanking.

Valdor knew nothing of his great-grandsire namesake's impetuous and passionate love story with Sfava, but his heart leapt in the best family tradition when he clapped eyes upon Gosvintha. Now, almost twenty and in the full bloom of womanhood, she could not fail to notice the Roman officer's admiring glances. Her mother also noted them and put a protective arm around her daughter's shoulders.

Valdor shifted his attention to Geberic's horse. It was a dappled grey

Nisean from Persia, standing at 14 hands and nobler in aspect than the bulk of his men's ponies, although they were sturdy beasts from the eastern steppes and no doubt formidable in battle. Valdor's first words of welcome to Geberic were: "Welcome to Banna, friend. You, your men and horses will be a great asset in the war against the Picts, which is ever in the offing." He ran a gentle hand over the horse's silky muzzle. "A beautiful horse, Chieftain. May I call a man to take it for refreshment?"

Geberic understood Valdor's speech well enough and nodded, so the praefectus turned, called to a soldier and gave orders. The legionary cautiously slid a hand under the bridle and led the dappled grey towards a water trough, indicating to the Visigoths to follow him. The horses bridged the diffidence between the very different soldiers, those of the legion and the Visigoths. The watering, provision of fodder, stabling and mingling of good-willed men broke down those barriers.

As for Valdor, he made settling the Visigoth womenfolk a priority and put Geberic's wife and daughter in superior quarters at the top of his list. These attentions were not lost on the travel-weary Visigoths. Speaking strictly as praefectus, Valdor explained to the warrior chieftain that his word was law in the fortress and on the battlefield, but that in no way would that diminish the chieftain's important role in managing the Visigoth contingent.

"I am informed about you, Praefectus Valdor, and have heard only good things about your courage and leadership. My men, family, and I seek stability. We are prepared to fight for Rome in exchange for fair treatment. We expect regular meals, pay and respect for our role."

"All these are criteria that I meet with all of my men in exchange for rigorous discipline and respect, Chieftain Geberic."

"Then, we have an understanding. I'll ensure that my men are cognisant of what is expected."

"One of my centurions will take names and hand out duty rosters. Each man will have free time to venture into the *vicus*. I would encourage yours to integrate by befriending the veterans in the fortress, who can show them around. Oh, and if your womenfolk have particular necessities, it's better that you bring them to my attention. My men know that they must respect their presence. I will not tolerate anyone lacking in their behaviour towards the opposite sex."

Everything clarified to his satisfaction, Valdor led Geberic to his quarters, set his best red wine in front of him and began to probe his battle experiences. He listened attentively to the description of the Battle of Adrianople and almost choked on his drink when Geberic explained how Valens had miscalculated the Goths' numbers.

"We are never so superficial with the Picts," Valdor said flatly. "One has to be well informed because they are a formidable adversary, quite capable of the unexpected."

They spoke at length about past encounters and tactics until each, appraising the other, acquired a healthy respect for his counterpart. At a lower level, the garrison and the Visigoth newcomers were doing the same thing; it paid immediate dividends as not one of the Roman soldiers spoke ill of their commandant. On the contrary, they impressed the Visigoths with tales of his prowess at the Solway fords. They enjoyed a hearty laugh at the undoing of the Picts.

Despite all the talk of Picts, when the call to action came, it was from Gaius, whose plea was for help against the Saxons, who had landed unexpectedly farther north than usual and been sighted by a watchtower, the most northerly of a number of signalling stations. This one being sited on a great promontory known as Huntcliff Nab.

The Saxons, estimated at 200 men, headed south and, therefore, towards Gaius' stronghold, the wealthy city of Eboracum. Behind them, they left a trail of destruction and death. The messenger reported 14 victims tossed down a well in one village. Valdor summoned Geberic and explained that he, too, would take 300 cavalrymen from Banna in pursuit of the Saxons. Their number added to the Visigoths, should be sufficient to annihilate the raiders. He also explained that Gaius would march out of Eboracum to face them, so in a certain sense, the situation might be compared to Adrianople.

Gosvintha came to embrace her father but could not take her eyes off Valdor in his armour and splendid helm. Aware of her insistent glances, he, too, found it difficult not to stare at the Gothic beauty, so left the fortress with mixed feelings: a sense of yearning to be near the chieftain's daughter mingled with the usual excitement of heading for battle.

The well-known road south to Eboracum made for swift progress and, despite knowing that the Saxons were on foot, and, therefore, eminently catchable, passing time meant more ravishing and destruction. Aware of this, Valdor urged his men harder than usual, but noted with pleasure that this seemed to exhilarate the Visigoths.

His advance scouts located the Saxon force just south of Isurium Brigantum, whose reduced garrison had bravely faced them and lost a skirmish. The scout estimated overhauling the Saxons within the hour. The problem was that the raiders also used scouts and were aware of the impending cavalry force and its superior numbers. The only tactic they could adopt was to make use of the terrain, so on the advice of another scout, they struck out westwards to a peculiar area of moorland where in ancient times the rocks had been shaped into curious formations by glaciation and erosion. The Saxon chieftain, Wulfgeat, split his force into groups of twenty and had them place their backs to the millstone grit sandstone as he was aware that facing Roman cavalry on open ground was tantamount to suicide.

Wulfgeat, instead, climbed up a crag right to the top, taking a handful of his best men with him, whence he howled his derision and shook his battle axe as the Roman force encircled the bluffs, for no horse could scale these outcrops. Insults poured down as, perplexed, Valdor consulted with Geberic. Valdor was in favour of waiting for Gaius' infantry to arrive, but the Visigoth wanted action. They struck a compromise. Stung by the Saxon taunts, Valdor called over two centurions and ordered: "Choose a score of your fittest men and scale yon crag. If we slay their chieftain, the rest will surrender. You'll have a score of our Visigoth comrades, too. It would be wise to climb on different sides of the crag so that the chieftain and his bodyguard are obliged to spread out."

Owing to the rocky terrain, so risky for the horses' legs, the Saxons had the positional advantage, so Valdor, in overall command, was not prepared to attack more than one crag at a time. The Saxons had gleefully taken possession of ten such rock formations. How Valdor bitterly regretted not having brought specialised archers with him. Fighting on horseback on this ground, so difficult under the hoof, was a serious handicap.

As for the Saxon leader, incessantly shouting insults, the difficulty of scaling the crag and attacking upwards was evident. But from his distance, Valdor could not ascertain the degree of difficulty of scaling the rock. There were plenty of cracks in them enabling a steady ascent. He watched one centurion lead the way, his *clipeus* slung over a shoulder. Carefully, he transferred the shield to his left hand and despite the hindrance continued the climb. A Saxon with a long axe bent over the edge of the crag and struck a mighty blow at the *clipeus*. It did not dislodge the centurion, who used a foothold as purchase to strike forward and upwards with his sharp-pointed gladius. He stabbed the Saxon's ankle, severing the tendon, causing him to scream, lose balance and precipitate off the rock.

First blood to us, thought Valdor, but in all honesty, he could not imagine a favourable outcome. *How can my men reach the top and stand upright?* The situation was made more difficult because, at best, only four men could arrive at the edge of the rock face at any one time. All the while, in front of the other surreally-shaped stone masses, interspersed among boulders that made a cavalry charge impossible, the Saxons jeered and shouted oaths, encouraging their chieftain and his defenders of the lone outcrop under attack. Before Valdor's horrified eyes, a Saxon axe severed a climber's wrist, sending him and his hand plunging down separately. At that moment, Valdor knew that the outcome would not be in his favour. *Why waste good men?*

He ordered the retreat and explained to Geberic. "We might dislodge them at night. They have no food and drink and no material to make torches."

"Ay, but we'd still have to climb up at night and face their wrath," the Visigoth replied. "The best thing is to starve them into surrender." He rode around the outcrop and ordered his men to withdraw. Just as with the Roman attempt, his men had slain one and lost one.

They didn't need to wait until nightfall because Gaius, too, had efficient scouts and the report that reached him made clear the need for archery. Eboracum was one of the few Roman bases that contained a *fabrica* that fashioned bone bow laths to make composite bows. The expert cavalry of the *Legio XXI Primigenia* was equipped with Syrian-type bows, with their powerful pull of 70 lbs that shot an arrow capable of penetrating mail from close range.

The Saxons gazed with dismay at the approaching Roman cavalry; already outnumbered three-to-one before the arrival of Gaius' force, they looked up the rock face to where Wulfgeat stood defiant, shaking his axe and hurling insults. The intrepid Saxon hearts sank, knowing that there was no alternative but to die gloriously, falling into the arms of the Valkyrie, who would carry them to Woden's golden feasting hall.

The cousins embraced and Valdor rapidly explained the situation to Gaius, pointing up the crag towards the jeering chieftain. "Do you have an archer who can hit that buffoon at the first attempt, before the Saxons have time to react?"

"I'm sure I do." Gaius called to a centurion and gave a succinct order. Before the majority of the Saxons realised what was happening, an arrow winged up and buried itself in Wulfgeat's chest. He staggered, but grasping hands saved him from plunging down the outcrop. Suddenly, the previously vocal Saxons fell silent as the gravity of their plight struck home as forcefully as the fateful arrow.

A barked command from Gaius, and his mounted archers picked their way past the defiant Saxons. Some cringed, seeking protection behind a boulder, others raised their shields, but the expert archers took a deadly toll. Another order came from Geberic. The Visigoths dismounted and, Geberic to the fore, ran towards the surviving Saxons. The slaughter was furious and relentless.

Valdor cut a forlorn figure as he had taken no part in the victory. His thirst for glory would have to be slaked on another occasion. Had he known how soon that would be, it would have raised his spirits.

The first inkling of further combat awaiting them came when a messenger galloped across the moors bearing news of the arrival in the Ouse of other Saxon vessels. These raiders were already intent on attacking the walls of Eboracum. Gaius betrayed little concern, saying, "My uncle strengthened and raised the walls, so, the barbarians won't make any impression before we arrive."

His assessment was not exact because the walled *vicus* was weak on the north side since its defence was entrusted to the waters of the Ouse. All well and good, unless the attackers arrived by boat, as in this case. The remainder of the garrison in the fortress reacted by marching out, only to find a Saxon bridgehead on the crossing, where a desperate battle broke out. The majority of the Saxon force was able to pour into the unprotected *vicus*, slaughtering, looting and destroying at will. The fighting, hampered by the narrow confines of the bridge, failed to breach the stubborn defence of the Saxon warriors while their comrades continued to wreak devastation beyond the amphitheatre. Meanwhile, the combined cavalry of Valdor and Gaius arrived.

Valdor leapt off his horse and, shouting orders, pushed past the Roman soldiers until he reached the front line on the bridge. His pent-up frustration after being ineffectual in *the Battle of the Weird Rocks* as he named it in his mind, was now unleashed on the Saxon bulwark.

Gaius had pushed through in his cousin's wake and, before his admiring gaze, watched Valdor make the inroads other hardened veterans had failed to achieve. Soon there was space for the cousins to fight shoulder-to-shoulder and, together, they cut down the Saxons until they had gained the opposite bank. At this point, their men poured out and joined in the open battle. Geberic did not, preferring to lead the Visigoths in search of the marauders inside the *vicus*.

The latter, informed of the arrival of a Roman auxiliary force, gathered into a compact formation in the open space in front of the amphitheatre. There, the Visigoths charged them, fighting from horseback. The two sides were equal in number but as cavalry, the Visigoths had some advantage. However, the Saxons further tightened their formation and dealt some hefty blows, which caused Geberic to lead his cavalry in a circle and attempt an attack from the rear.

Meanwhile, with their battle won, Valdor and Gaius had remounted and, on hearing screams from the *vicus*, galloped towards the battle. The result was devastating for the Saxons, who suddenly found themselves attacked from the front and rear. Despite their impossible situation, these were tribes who had previously fought the Romans on the Rhine and would not fold easily. Indeed, as Geberic wheeled his horse, an axeman delivered a slash into the beast's flank, causing it to rear wildly and unseat its rider. Geberic lay momentarily stunned on the ground, unnoticed by his men, intensely engaged in the battle. Valdor, who had also wheeled his horse momentarily, saw Geberic fall, but was instantly occupied by a Saxon warrior and could do nothing to help the chieftain.

The Visigoth regained his senses, but his vision was blurred. He groped for his shield, and finding it, was just able to parry an axe blow from a Saxon standing over him. He rolled to one side to avoid another mighty strike from the same adversary. The praefectus had dealt with his opponent and, seeing Geberic unable to rise, urged his horse towards the chieftain and his foe. The latter, intent on killing his hapless adversary, did not see Valdor arrive, so received a mortal blow from the praefectus' *spatha*. Geberic sprang to his feet and emitted a shrill whistle. His horse trotted towards him and in seconds the Visigoth was on its back and leaning to inspect the wound. It was a deep gash and would need disinfecting and stitching, but the horse would survive. Followed by Geberic, Valdor drove into the Saxon ranks, which were near breaking point, hacking and hewing with his long sword. The superior numbers told and the Saxons' dream of plundering Eboracum was over.

Back inside the fortress, Valdor went to check on the condition of Geberic's horse because he had admired the noble beast from the moment he had set eyes upon it and was displeased by the wounding. The Visigoth chieftain fussed around the horse doctor, who applied salve to the wound after cleaning it. The legionary spoke to Geberic, "Speak softly in his ear, for now is the difficult part: I must stitch the gash." Geberic gently stroked the muzzle and whispered in the animal's ear. The legionary worked swiftly and deftly with the short, curved needle and, while Valdor expected a roar from the frightened beast, only a nicker came, which underlined its nobility. Geberic continued his soothing words and received a whinny and a nuzzle.

"It's as if the horse knows it's being cured," Valdor remarked, "what a remarkable beast!"

"There, all done! Some days and you can remove the stitches," the horse doctor said exultantly.

Geberic kissed the horse's forehead and patted and stroked its jaw. Then he gazed at Valdor. "It's you I should kiss!" he grinned.

"Nay, if I thought you'd do that, I'd have let the Saxon slay you!"

They both laughed, but Geberic embraced his commandant, wisely refraining from a kiss.

"Come, my friend, we have two victories to celebrate! If I remember right, my father's cellar is well stocked. I doubt that Gaius has guzzled it all!"

"Watch your tongue and remember who is the senior officer!" came from the stable door. Gaius stood there grinning. "I was looking for you two to celebrate! Shame I've *guzzled* all the red wine."

"Don't listen to him, Geberic. He's not a serious drinker like us!"

Gaius snorted. "It looks like I'm heading towards my third victory in one day. Let's hope no more Saxons arrive to spoil my next celebratory wine-drinking victory!"

23
BARRA FORT; AD 381

Gosvintha's servant, who had just finished combing and plaiting her hair, unexpectedly returned, her expression flushed and excited.

"Mistress, the men are back!"

Gosvintha leapt off her seat and ran out into the courtyard towards the south gate. Previously unknown emotions filled her breast; she was delighted as usual that Geberic had returned safe from battle, but her eye went straight to Valdor and she breathed a sigh of relief that he, too, was unscathed. She overcame her unseemly desire to run to the praefectus, instead, reaching her father's grey dappled horse and laying her head on his thigh. "I'm so glad that you are back, safe and sound, father."

"Only thanks to my friend, Praefectus Valdor; he saved my life and poor Sigesar," he patted the horse's head, "received a deep wound, didn't you, my beloved steed?"

"You must tell me all about it, father, but meanwhile, I must thank the praefectus for what he did."

Valdor had not missed a word of this exchange because he only had eyes for Gosvintha. She had noticed his adoring glances, but more importantly Geberic had seen them too.

Gosvintha stepped over to Valdor's horse and looked up to him and smiled. To her surprise, he immediately dismounted, which made it easier for her. She gazed adoringly at him and said, "You saved my father; bless you!" Leaning forward, she gave him a chaste kiss on his cheek.

"It's just what happens in battle," he said, "nothing special, unlike that kiss!"

Before she could react, he turned away and started issuing orders. She went back to her father but when she turned around, Valdor had gone.

Had she offended him with a kiss? Nay, impossible, not the way he had been looking at her. She sighed deeply and hurried off to be there with her mother after her father had seen to stabling his horse and checking on the stitched wound. The horse doctor had given him a salve to smear over the cut at journey's end. She had no idea that he would go thence to Valdor's quarters to drink as arranged on their way to the fort.

Clasping a generous beaker of red wine in his large hand, Geberic stared at his host, "As far as I'm concerned, you can have her, you know. I can't think of a more suitable man for my daughter. I've only heard good things about you, Valdor, and now I've seen with my own eyes that they are true—besides, you saved my life."

Valdor's eyes widened; this declaration was most unexpected. "Don't you think we should take Gosvintha's feelings into account?"

Geberic's voice sounded like the growl of an angry bear, "Pah! She'll do as I tell her! In any case, to me the woman is as easy to read as Nature's signs of impending good weather. She's smitten by you, Praefectus. If you want her, she's yours."

Valdor stood, placed a hand on the chieftain's shoulder, looked him in the eye, and said, "It's my intention to see how *she* feels. You finish that bottle while I speak with her."

He didn't pause to take off his cuirass, but slipped across the corridor to knock at the door of the Visigoths' quarters. The servant who had adjusted her mistress' hair opened the door.

"Is Lady Gosvintha at home?"

The maid blushed and nodded mutely.

"Then tell her that Praefectus Valdor requires her presence immediately."

"I am here," said Gosvintha who drew closer at the sound of his voice.

"Then come out and follow me!" he made his command voice as stern as possible. The serving maid stepped hastily aside, looking concerned, whereas Gosvintha smiled and followed the commandant who was already turning away.

"Where are you taking me, Lord?"

"Call me Valdor," he growled, "we're going up the rampart to look at the heather. It's beautiful at this time of year." Gallantly, he offered an arm and she hooked hers under it eagerly, secretly enjoying the iron hardness of the muscles against her forearm. Neither said a word as they mounted the steps. Valdor led her close to the northern gateway tower and pointed out over the moor at the carpet of purple heather, "There, isn't that a sight?"

"Beautiful," she admitted, "but why did you want me to see it?"

"An excuse," he confessed, "I want your opinion on a serious matter."

"Serious?"

"Well, *I* am serious. Will you wed me, Gosvintha?"

Her eyes were fiery and she said fiercely, "You don't know me, and what about my father?"

"I already have his consent."

"You *asked* him!"

"Something like that."

Her eyes flashed again, and she said rebelliously, "Because you saved his life."

"That was my duty and I doubt that it is the only reason he agreed."

Her chin jutted and it raised, "Well, I can't wed you."

Valdor looked dismayed, "Why not?"

"So many reasons," a tear trickled down her cheek.

"Give me the most important one," he gently wiped the tear with his thumb.

"You haven't once said you love me."

His strong arms steered her towards the palisade, "Look out there! For the Celtic Druids, heather celebrates life and love. There is a Celtic legend, Gosvintha, about the daughter of a poet who loved a warrior that was killed in battle. The story goes that when a messenger brought the news of her lover's death, he presented her with a bouquet of heather to symbolize her betrothed's love. So, why, sweet maid, do you think I brought you to look at the heather? Of course, I love you—I'm besotted with you!"

She sighed, "The heather is more beautiful now. But I cannot wed you, Valdor."

"Why not? I know you love me."

"It's true! But what about your faith? You are a Christian and I am a heretic."

"A *heretic?*"

"It's true, my people converted to Arian Christianity, while you are a Trinitarian."

"Good God! Do you understand such things, Gosvintha? I confess that I do not, nor do I care."

"I can become an Arian, whatever that means, if that's what you want."

The fiery eyes misted, and tears threatened. "It's what my people want, Valdor. I also do my duty."

"You'll have to explain it to me, Gosvintha. I have little patience with Church matters."

"I can't explain properly, Valdor. We need to speak to a priest to know how serious the situation is."

Valdor frowned, but his expression suddenly cleared, "Hold! I've heard that Bishop Eborius of Eboracum is in the north—at Vinovia fortress, to be exact. They say he's here to stamp out Mithras worship. Rather him than me! There are many soldiers who still worship the old gods. But if anyone can sort out our problem, Gosvintha, it is he. It's not far to Vinovia. I'll tell your father why we're going. You can ride a horse, can't you?" Her eyes flashed again, "Better than you, Valdor!"

He wasn't convinced about that, but her Visigoth pony from the eastern steppes made light work of Britannia's northern moors and made him think again.

On arrival at Vinovia, they found Bishop Eborius most receptive. Thanks to Gaius in Eboracum, he had learnt about Valdor and his role in the relief of the city from the pagan Saxons. So, he listened most attentively to the praefectus and his problem. Looking from one despairing face to the other, the bishop had to smother a smile. First, he would explain the theology because he was a devotee of the study of the nature of God and religious belief.

"Arius was a priest who taught in Alexandria, and who denied that Jesus was of the same substance as God. That is why many believe that his teachings are heretical. Put simply, Valdor, Arianism teaches that

Jesus was not God. You and I, Praefectus, but not your betrothed, follow the Nicene Creed, which we use to defeat Arianism by stating: "We believe in one Lord Jesus Christ, the Son of God...begotten, not made, consubstantial with the Father. Do you understand, Valdor?"

"Ay, Excellency, I've repeated that countless times in church. But is this difference of belief serious? Can Gosvintha and I wed? We love each other."

The bishop laughed. "I can see that, my son, and it gives me joy to tell you that you have no problem."

"How can that be, Excellency?" Gosvintha blurted, hope springing in her breast. Valdor looked perplexed.

The bishop took the Visigoth's hand and smiled, "It just so happens that earlier this year, the second ecumenical council met at Constantinople. Arianism was proscribed, and that famous statement of faith, the Nicene Creed, was approved throughout the Empire. It means, my child, that if you so desire, you can repeat the Creed after me and I can hear it and absolve you of any sin, which will free you to wed your beloved."

"As simple as that, Excellency?"

"Indeed, I do not think that you wish to oppose the church throughout the Empire by stubbornly clinging to a mistake made many years ago, young maiden."

"Nay, Excellency, I am overjoyed at this good news."

"Then come into the church and solemnly copy my words so that I can absolve you."

The brief, improvised ceremony completed, the bishop took Valdor apart and said, "I have to remain in the area a while longer. If the notion suits you, I can come to Banna in two weeks and conduct the wedding. First, of course, I must speak with your Visigoth contingent to explain why they cannot continue to spout the heresy. It should be straightforward as in other parts of the Empire; nobody is prepared to risk eternal life for a contentious dogma."

Valdor and Gosvintha strode to retrieve their horses and shared their first passionate kiss near the stables before riding home blissfully conversing about future plans.

Two weeks later, Bishop Eborius addressed the Visigoths at Barra and, as he predicted, had no difficulty explaining the Trinitarian concept to the troops. His task was made easier by the lack of a Visigoth priest, so there could be no theological argument. The bishop was intelligent and cleverly showed them the sign of the cross when he explained Trinitarianism. The simple gesture caught on so well that men could be seen crossing themselves for no reason.

Valdor arranged a celebratory feast in the large, otherwise unused hall in Crispinus Sylla's edifice. He spared no expense and excluded no one, so the day before the wedding, waggons bearing produce—the best delicacies the province could provide—came and went, providing work for a small army of cooks and servants.

Bishop Eborius conducted the wedding inside the fort's small chapel, aided by the chaplain and attended only by a small congregation while the Visigoths waited in the courtyard, rubbing shoulders with the veteran garrison of Barra. Valdor's cousin, Gaius, invited personally by the bishop, was present as the only member of Valdor's family and in his role as *Comes Britanniarum*. As a friend of the groom, Dux Dulcitius made the short journey from Vercovicium.

The occasion was convivial and, for the first time, Valdor blessed the corrupt Crispinus Sylla for having created the munificent surroundings with its frescoes and mosaics that would remain long in his memory along with the radiant appreciative face of his bride and the jubilant, raucous congregation of troops swilling vast quantities of strong drink at his expense. For one fleeting moment, Valdor recalled why he was stationed at Barra—he hoped fervently that the Picts had not got wind of the feast, for it would be like them to attack while his men were incapacitated by drink. He dismissed the thought, which was not so far-fetched because as he contemplated it, the Picts were meeting with the Scoti and deciding to take advantage of another weakened area, that of the fertile North Cambria since the important garrisons of Deva and Glevum had been depleted by the urgent imperial demand for troops to fight on other continental frontiers.

The resulting turmoil in Cambria would mean that Hadrian's Wall was left untroubled and that Valdor could enjoy time with his bride, but would have far deeper implications for the near future.

24

EBORACUM, CAMBRIA AND GALLIA AD 381-387

VALDOR WAS WORRIED. AS A MARRIED MAN, HE HAD FAMILY responsibilities to add to those of the commandant of a border fort. His Areani spies were in agreement that the Picts were fomenting unrest and planning a major invasion of Britannia. As a man of action, Valdor told himself, *I have to be in the forefront of any engagement to protect civilisation as we know it, but at the same time, I must ensure that Gosvintha is safe.*

With these thoughts in mind, he went to explain to her.

"My love, I wish to transfer you to Eboracum, where you will be far safer than at Barra. I have news that the Picts are going to launch a major attack on the Wall and beyond."

"But we will be together, Valdor, will we not?"

"I shall accompany you to Eboracum with your parents, but cannot be sure how I will be deployed until I have spoken with Gaius and maybe with my brother, Maximus."

"Tell me about Maximus, for I have not yet met him."

"He's younger than me, but..." Valdor went on to explain Maximus' career and tried hard to conceal his resentment at not having become the Count of the Saxon Shore—a role he still coveted and felt should have been his by right. Although she made no comment, Gosvintha intuited that her husband begrudged Maximus his position.

The warm welcome accorded him by his cousin suggested to her that there was no ill feeling between Valdor and Gaius. Her husband insisted on her presence and her father's when he discussed their circumstances with Gaius.

Valdor opened the debate with: "I have learnt from my border scouts that the Picts are plotting a substantial incursion into Britannia."

Gaius laughed, but the tone was far from cheerful, "For someone claiming to be well-informed, cousin, you are remarkably unfamiliar with what is happening. Here in Britannia, we are conditioned by faraway events. I'll wager that you do not know that in Macedonia, the Goths led by Fritigern have won the Battle of Thessalonica with the result that Theodosius I retreated to Thessalonica, leaving Gratian in control of the Western Roman Empire. That alone will have an impact on us all in Britannia. Gratian is unpopular with the troops and, if you add to that Rome's enemies, the Alemanni, Sarmatians and Huns being taken into Imperial service, it will prove fundamental in shaping all our futures. Mark my words, Valdor," he looked uneasily at Geberic, "Barbarian leaders are beginning to play an increasingly active role in the Roman Empire. The people nominally in charge of our destinies, do not care sufficiently about Britannia, even if it is the *bread basket* of the Empire."

"I'm not sure that I follow you, Gaius. What has this to do with the Picts?"

Gaius threw back his head and laughed heartily, "My word, Valdor, you *have* been too long on that beastly Wall! I think that one of the first things you should do is to call on your brother so that you can get a grasp on reality! Let me explain to you in simple terms..."

"Do not patronise me, Gaius!"

His cousin frowned and looked apologetic, "I meant no offence, but it's complicated. The Picts and the Scoti are quick to profit from the withdrawal of troops from Britannia to staunch the haemorrhage of frontier provinces falling into barbarian hands." He paused and looked at Geberic, "Do not take offence, either, friend. I know little about what your people suffered at the hands of Rome, and I use the language of the Empire to express what is happening."

Geberic's scowl changed into a sunny smile as he remembered Gaius' valour against the Saxons. How should the man express himself when, as he said, he had no knowledge of life beyond the shores of Britannia? Encouraged, Gaius continued, "I imagine the desire to settle on fertile lands meant that Britannia has become a prime target. The Scoti only have to sail across the Irish Sea to land on the lush pastures of Mona. At the same time, Saxons and Frisians sail across the North Sea and have begun to settle farther north than their original settlements. Maximus has a considerable task to hold them back."

Valdor began to understand the desperate state of Britannia. The fate of the Romano-British— people like himself—lay in the balance. The prospect of constant warfare to hold onto British territory hung over him like a heavy thundercloud. Even if the Picts were currently more of a threat to Cambria than Hadrian's Wall and Cumbria beyond it, he would still leave Gosvintha and her father in Eboracum in Gaius' safekeeping. His immediate plan was to ride to Camulodunum to meet with his brother before deciding where his future lay. He was sure only of one thing: it was not as praefectus of Banna. Britannia, he knew, needed the might of his arm elsewhere. But where?

After a few weeks in Eboracum, the arrival in Britannia of a famous Roman general decided the answer for him. Magnus Maximus was assigned to Britannia by Gratian to deal with the Pict and Scoti incursions caused in Cambria by the weakening of the garrisons, particularly those of Deva and Glevum.

Ill-informed as he was, about events and personages elsewhere in the Empire, Valdor had paid close attention to the circumstances involving his hero Theodosius the Elder. Maximus had been a junior officer in Britannia during the Great Conspiracy when he assisted Theodosius in defeating barbarians and criminals. He became a distinguished general in the following year and later served with distinction under Count Theodosius in Africa in 373. So, on hearing of his arrival, Valdor rode to offer his services, taking with him the 250 men he had brought to Eboracum from Barra.

Valdor rode into Maximus' camp based around a marching fort between Deva and Glevum and, presenting himself, reminding the general that they had fought together under Theodosius against the Scoti at the relief of Alauna.

"Ah, welcome! I remember you as a dashing cavalry officer who broke the Scoti resistance. I see you have brought a cavalry force with you."

"Ay, General, I have 250 men at your service—they are veterans of Barra on the Wall and all experienced at fighting the Picts."

"Settle them for the night because we leave at dawn to enter Cambria, where the Picts and the Scoti have united to seize the rich farmlands of Mona and North Cambria."

Valdor took advantage of the renewed acquaintance to find out more about the unhappy end of his hero, Count Theodosius.

"If Emperor Valentinian I had kept a reign on his temper, neither he nor the Count would have died. Valentinian was so enraged that he suffered a fatal stroke while yelling at the Quadi envoys. We were still in Africa when he died, leaving factions to struggle for power. You see, Theodosius would have been the perfect choice to replace Valentinian and they knew it in Italy. So, the cowards arrested him and smuggled him to Carthage. As you would expect, Valdor, Theodosius was calm, had himself baptised, and went serenely to his death, like the great man he was."

Valdor said nothing, but sighed heavily.

"By the way," Magnus Maximus added, "His son, the younger Theodosius, retired to his estates where he married Aelia Flaccilla. Those who had killed the elder Theodosius had also plotted against the safety of his son during his retirement, so he returned to the Danube frontier, where in 378 he was appointed *magister equitum*. Following his successes in the field he was elevated at Sirmium to the rank of *Augustus* by Emperor Gratian. So now, you see," Maximus raised a glass, "at last, we have a Theodosius I, ruling the Eastern Empire, and another Valentinian, the second of his name, although a young boy, ruling the Western Empire but under the tutelage of Gratian. I can't stand the man, myself! But, at least, he had the sense to send me here to sort out the mess he created."

"Ay, the garrisons have been overly depleted."

They chatted on until the sun went down and continued next to a campfire, reminiscing about old campaigns and discussing the forthcoming one and how best to face up to the enemy. For the first time, Valdor found himself confiding his disappointment at being overlooked in favour of his younger brother as Count of the Saxon Shore.

In the future, Valdor would have a similar conversation about this campaign, although his most vivid memory was not the crushing victory that drove the Picts and the Scoti into the sea, but the difficult crossing to Mona.

Taking advantage of local knowledge, Magnus Maximus ordered the crossing of the main body of the cavalry via the Lavan Sands, which at low tide almost span the Menai Straits from the mainland. The infantry was equipped with rafts, but the general wanted the cavalry to secure the ground on the opposite bank before his men ferried across. With correct timing, the sands can dry enough to provide a firm surface for movement. Despite that local knowledge, the sands shift, being changed by strong tides, so there was no guarantee of a safe crossing. Valdor would never forget the horrible experience of riding across the sands, only to be caught in a sudden fierce current that swept him and his men away and posed the danger of drowning. However, the horses were trained to swim and the riders to cling onto the harness and swim with their mounts. There were frantic moments when the strength of the swirling current threatened to take a deadly toll, but, instead, the entirety of the 18 troops of 32 mounted men each gained the opposite bank. With hindsight, the enemy blundered; they gave more importance to finding a strategic site for the forthcoming battle, whereas if they had rained javelins and arrows upon the emerging horsemen, struggling up the bank, a massacre might have ensued. Instead, Valdor sent scouts to locate the foe and positioned his men to protect the infantry as they disembarked from the rafts.

At last, the 10,000 men were ready to march towards the enemy and, transport, pack animal handlers, caterers, armourers, and medical aides, brought up the rear.

Valdor was impressed by the general's deployment of his cavalry, which surprised him. Maximus held them back until the Picts and Scoti had exhausted their throwing weapons. Instead, the *equites* were armed with shield and javelin and, as the general had observed, their mounts were hardy beasts, used to galloping over worse terrain, so he sent them in an encircling manoeuvre at the base of the hill and had them charge, sending a hail of javelins into the exposed rear of the foe. This assault swung the tide of battle in his favour, routing the enemy, which the cavalry picked off with their long *sparthae*.

After his success on Mona, Magnus Maximus strengthened the forts and fortlets on the isle and in mainland Cambria before bringing the garrisons of Deva and Glevum back up to strength, thereby ensuring a ceasing of Scoti raids.

The reprieve for Britannia was only temporary as Valdor witnessed first-hand. The Western Emperor Gratian had received a number of

Alani into his bodyguard, and was accused of showing favouritism towards these Iranian-speaking foreigners at the expense of Roman citizens. In 383 the discontented Roman army in Britannia proclaimed Magnus Maximus emperor in Gratian's place.

"Valdor, I have not asked for the purple. It is contrary to my oath of allegiance, although I have little time for Gratian, who is unworthy of the throne."

Valdor smothered a smile and kept silent, but thought, *that's as may be, but you, Maximus, don't fool me! I know that you have incited the troops to rebel against Gratian and that you are envious of Theodosius becoming emperor while you were not promoted: more or less like my brother and I.*

Valdor was correct in his analysis, but could not foresee how this declaration would portend the death knell of the Roman Empire in Britannia and change the rest of his life dramatically.

Maximus went to Gaul to pursue his imperial ambitions, taking a large portion of the British garrison with him. Thus, Valdor, his brother, and their cousin were involved in five days of skirmishing near Paris, where they defeated Gratian. The Western Emperor fled the battlefield but Andragathius, Maximus' *magister equitum*, pursued and killed him at *Lugdunum* on 25 August 383. On the death of Gratian, Valentinian II became the sole legitimate *Augustus* in the West.

Continuing his campaign into Italy, Maximus was stopped from overthrowing Valentinian II, who was only twelve, when Flavius Bauto, a Romanised Frank, came with a powerful force to forestall him. Negotiations followed in 384, including the intervention of Ambrose, Bishop of Milan, leading to an agreement with Valentinian II and Theodosius I in which Maximus was recognized as *Augustus* in the West.

After he became Emperor of the West, Maximus returned to Britain to campaign against the Picts and Scoti, probably in support of Rome's long-standing allies the *Damnonii*, *Votadini*, and *Novantae*, tribes all located north of Hadrian's Wall. While there, he made similar arrangements for a formal transfer of authority to local chiefs. After doing this, also in Cambria and Britannia, Maximus transferred to Gallia and, unwilling to send back his warlike companions to their wives, families, and possessions in Britannia, he conferred upon them numerous districts from the lake on the summit of Mons Iovis, to the city called Cant Guic, and to the western Tumulus, that is Cruc Occident, in

Armorica. He made a special exception for Valdor, appointing him to the role he coveted: the Count of the Saxon Shore, while keeping his brother and cousin in Armorica. This reorganisation by Magnus Maximus had serious consequences since it marked the end of Roman rule in Britannia and opened the way for the province to be overcome by barbarian invaders. It also led to the declaration of independence of Armorica from the Roman Empire in 407, as few of the Romano-Briton neo-landowners returned to Britannia and its colder climes.

As for Valdor, at last, he had his heart's desire, but it was a poisoned chalice since he had to cope with the relentless raids on the Saxon Shore, but he would have little alternative but to abandon his long-coveted role, with his only option to emerge like those local chieftains in Cambria and Caledonia, but in his case, in Britannia. He had never had the fortune to experience the glory days of Roman Britannia like his father, Leo, who had even befriended the great emperor, Constantine. And now, although he had Gosvintha, he was without other beloved members of his family. Would he ever see Gaius and Maximus again? Would he, a formidable general, be able to organise Romano-British resistance to safeguard civilisation as he knew it?

THE END

HISTORICAL NOTE

The Fall of the Roman Empire is a complicated subject involving the migration of many so-called barbarian tribes from different directions. Fortunately, there are near-contemporary accounts we can draw upon. Pinning down the exact end of the Roman Occupation of Britannia is a controversial subject, which after a long period of accepting AD 410 as a cut-off point has been modified in recent years by scholars. In my novel, I have adopted AD 383, basically accepting that the withdrawal of an estimated 60,000 Roman troops and auxiliaries by Magnus Maximus was for practical purposes the end. Yet, a small voice warns me, 'Look, there is numismatic evidence post-383 AD from Hadrian's Wall that suggests some continued occupation.' Yes, but were those men Roman legionaries or were they part of a northern war band?

Stilicho, regent to Theodosius's son Honorius, instigated a campaign against the Picts in 400 AD. It is unlikely he came in person, but after the campaign, he may have withdrawn further troops from Britain. Britannia struggled on.

The situation in Western Europe became more desperate. Yet again, in 407, the British elevated another emperor in Constantine III and he crossed the Channel with another army. While Constantine was fighting on the continent in 409, a further revolt forced out Constantine's officials in Britain.

"The barbarians drive us to the sea, the sea drives us back to the barbarians..." so ran the supplication.

There is an account that states that the British made a request to Emperor Honorius for military assistance in 410, which he rejected, saying they must defend themselves. This is disputed, as the document called the Rescript of Honorius could have referred to another location. There is no chance that he could have helped as he was besieged by Visigoths under Alaric at the time in Ravenna, then the western capital. On the balance of probability, it was Britain who abandoned Rome.

THE WOKEN TALISMAN

THE SAXON SHORE TRILOGY
BOOK 3

CHAPTER-BY-CHAPTER GLOSSARY

PREFACE

Lindum Colonia = present-day Lincoln, Lincolnshire.
Corinium = present-day Cirencester in Gloucestershire.
Verulamium = present-day St Albans in Hertfordshire.

CHAPTER ONE

Paludamentum = a cloak or cape fastened at one shoulder, worn by military commanders.
Cincticulus = belt or girdle worn by military commanders.
Aquincum = present-day Budapest, Hungary.
Comitatenses = Latin nominative plural of comitatensis, meaning 'field armies'.

CHAPTER TWO

Pollentia = modern Pollenzo in the Province of Cuneo, Italy.
Logres = the Brittonic territory roughly corresponding to the later borders of Hwicce and Mercia.
Urbs Aeterna = the Eternal City, the Roman name for Rome.
Sabrina = Roman name for the River Severn.
Turma (pl. turmae) = cavalry unit of 30 men.
Venta Silurium = present-day Montgomery, Montgomeryshire, Wales.
Isca Silurium = present-day Caerleon, Monmouthshire, Wales.
Duplicarius = Roman rank, second-in-command, under decurion, a soldier on double pay.
Glastum = woad plant, source of a blue dye.
Dobunni = a Brittonic tribe living in central Britain in an area that today broadly coincides with the English counties of Bristol, Gloucestershire, and the north of Somerset, maybe extending into Warwickshire.

CHAPTER THREE

Florentia = present-day Florence in Tuscany, Italy.
Suebi = Suebians were a large group of Germanic peoples originally from the Elbe River region in what is now Germany.
Bononia/Gesoriacum = present-day Boulogne, France.

CHAPTER FOUR

Arelate = Roman name of modern Arles, a city in Provence, South of France.
Lugdunum = Roman name of modern Lyons, city in the Auvergne-Rhône-Alpes Region, France.
Seteia = the estuary of the River Mersey, Lancashire.

Belisama = Roman name for the Ribble Estuary, Lancashire.
Solium (pl. solia) = throne(s).

CHAPTER FIVE

Hispania = Roman name for Spain.
Uxella Estuary = River Parrett estuary, Somerset.
River Alavna = unidentified river in Somerset as land configuration has changed over time.
Baetica = Roman province in Southern Spain.
Lusitania = Roman province now Portugal.
Gallaecia = Roman province in North-western Spain.

CHAPTER SIX

Lindinis = modern Ilchester, capital of the Durotriges tribe, Somerset.
Durnovaria = modern Dorchester in Dorset, second capital of the Durotriges tribe.

CHAPTER SEVEN

Abora Channel = present-day Bristol Channel.
Dun Breaton = modern Dumbarton, north bank of the River Clyde, Scotland.
Guotodin = a Brittonic kingdom of north-eastern Britannia, the area known as the Hen Ogledd or Old North, in the sub-Roman period.
Speculatores = Roman naval patrol ships.
Alavna = Roman name for the River Esk in Cumbria.
Clota Estuary = modern Firth of Clyde, Scotland.
Novantarum Promontorium = Mull of Galloway.

CHAPTER EIGHT

The Norns = deities responsible for shaping the course of human destinies.

CHAPTER NINE

Brat = iconic Gaelic cloak or mantle.

CHAPTER TEN

Cyulis = keels or warships.
Colonia Victricensis = present-day region of Essex.
Territory of the Regni = present-day region of Sussex.
Oppidum = a Latin word meaning 'defended (fortified) administrative centre or town, specifically, in Ch 10, Abingdon-on-Thames.

CHAPTER ELEVEN

The glen blocker fort = modern Drumquhassle Roman fort.
The Lake of Elms = modern Loch Lomond.

Arbeia = Roman port and fortress at modern-day South Shields at the eastern end of Hadrian's Wall.

CHAPTER THIRTEEN

Linnius region = area occupied by Lindenses tribe.
Lindenses = tribe occupying the area of modern-day Lincolnshire.
Abus Estuary = present-day Humber Estuary.
River Adur = the modern River Ouse.
Weolud = the modern River Welland.
River Abi = present-day River Witham.
Æstuarium Metuonis = the present-day Wash, a shallow natural rectangular bay and multiple estuary on the east coast.

CHAPTER SIXTEEN

Boderia Estuary = present-day Firth of Forth, Scotland.
Tuessis Estuary = Tay Estuary, Scotland.
Petchaish Estuary = present-day Moray Firth, Scotland.
Virvedrum Promontory = St. John's Point, Caithness, Scotland.

CHAPTER SEVENTEEN

Antivestaeum Promontory = present-day Land's End, Cornwall.

CHAPTER EIGHTEEN

Segontium = Caernarfon, Gwynedd, N. Wales.

CHAPTER NINETEEN

Cair-Caratauc = ancient Anglo-Saxon tribal centre of the Gewisse at present-day Old Sarum in Wiltshire.

CHAPTER TWENTY-TWO

Bravonium = present-day Leintwardine, Herefordshire.
Aquae Sulis = present-day Bath, Somerset.
Abona = present-day Bristol, city bordering Gloucestershire and Somerset.
River Abona = present-day River Avon, Somerset.

PREFACE
BRITANNIA, LATE FOURTH CENTURY AD

Valdor took stock: as a man of action, he had to quell his impulsiveness in favour of quiet reflection. Around him, the world he had known in his infancy was crumbling. The all-conquering Roman Empire had declined irreparably—he had to face that unpalatable truth—and his beloved Britannia had changed beyond recognition and redemption.

The most difficult of his various conundrums was personal: as a prominent, well-respected personage, he had to understand his role in the dissolution engulfing him. He was, after all, the Count of the Saxon Shore, a role allotted to him by the dubious figure of Magnus Maximus, executed as a usurper. Was his destiny to be, as some would have him, a hero, a saviour, or contrariwise, a warlord, blending self-interest with protection of the vulnerable?

He did, however, have certainties, and those entailed his family. He had left it late to fall in love. With four and forty winters to his name, his Gosvintha, a Visigoth beauty and chieftain's daughter, twenty years his junior, was carrying his child and unquestionably, in these troubled times, he would ensure them a safe haven. Yet, even here there was uncertainty—would the babe be a son, as he fervently hoped, or a daughter to illuminate his old age? If a boy, he would call him Primus, not just because he would be the firstborn, but in honour of his uncle, the gallant centurion fallen in battle in Pannonia. If a girl, her name would be Sfava, after his great-grandmother, the renowned shield maiden.

The days slipped by and still, he had not arrived at the decision about where to shelter his family. The year 387 was drawing to a close and Gosvintha, advanced in her pregnancy, was in no condition to travel long distances. For now, she would stay in the luxurious surroundings of the *domus palatina*, the wonderful mansion that Emperor Constans had given to his father, Leo, when he, Valdor, was an aspiring soldier. Yet, he knew that Eboracum, which owed its wealth to the river Ouse, was also assailable thanks to that waterway, which meant that he would move mother and child before the year was out.

Before he could relocate his family, Valdor needed to choose a base for operations and this requirement started him thinking about the role of the shore forts. How was it possible that a few boatloads of Saxons necessitated such imposing defences? The more he thought about it, the more unlikely it seemed. A ballista or a hail of javelins from the ramparts would easily deal with them. He wondered why the walls of many of these forts were incomplete on the seaward side. Surely, if they had been built to keep pirates at bay, it was exactly there that the walls were needed. If only he could ask his great-grandfather, who was responsible for building some of them!

Then, the answer occurred to him—the purpose of the shore forts was not to fend off Saxon incursions, but to welcome imperial troops with open arms. Britannia had created more emperors than any other province—emperors and usurpers—including the great Constantine I. Even recently, Magnus Maximus had been declared emperor in Britannia. This also accounted for why Rome had withdrawn tens of thousands of troops from the garrisons.

Having arrived at these conclusions, Valdor no longer felt the responsibility of fulfilling the role of Count of the Saxon Shore; at least, not as he had previously interpreted it. He could not be considered a stalwart bulwark against waves of Angles, Saxons, Frisians and Jutes. Ay, however much of Britannia could be protected and the land preserved for its Romano-British occupants if he had anything to do with it.

He could rationalise the few troops at his disposal and concentrate them strategically as garrisons while abandoning other forts entirely. Also, he would investigate and decide where he could create around himself and his family a small, mobile army to protect swathes of Britannia from settlement: that would be his plan!

He would need to select a well-defended city, possibly not vulnerable from the water, so he would not choose Eboracum like his father. Those towns remaining were Londinium, Camulodunum, Glevum, Lindum Colonia and Corinium. He agonised over his choice for some time, but dismissed Londinium, Lindum Colonia and Camulodunum because of their positions and proximity to known North Sea piracy routes. Also, Glevum and Corinium were only 20 miles apart and the latter, particularly, had a well-organised administrative centre.

Therefore, he would base his family and his armed force in Glevum, which had the correct facilities to accommodate a cavalry-based force and strong, almost impenetrable walls.

(EBORACUM AND GLEVUM, AD 387-398)

In mid-October 387, Gosvintha gave her husband a healthy baby boy, promptly named Primus. When she recovered from the ordeal of childbirth, she spoke solemnly to her husband when he suggested moving to Glevum.

"I was lucky, Valdor, for I had palatial surroundings to deliver my child. The *domus* is clean and I had assistance and good food and drink. All women should be so fortunate. Do you know how many die in childbirth in squalid surroundings? How many infants die before even reaching their first year? All of them should have a capable midwife as I did, and when we leave, I want to take Cori with me. We want another child, do we not?"

Instead of dismissing his wife's observations as *women's business*, Valdor reflected deeply on her words and said, "If we want to give all expectant mothers the conditions you spoke of, Gosvintha, we have to create a prenatal infirmary with clean beds and enough to eat. The best place to do that is Corinium because there, we can find the scribes to write an announcement to be cried in the towns and villages so that the women come to us. If we can win the hearts and minds of the people by caring for them, we can grow strong as a nation, whatever comes our way." He paused and gave her an embarrassed smile, yet she beamed at him.

Momentarily, her brow creased and she said, "If you want to foster a sense of nation, you need to talk about heroes of the past. That's what my grandparents did when I was little, but also, the adults would always boast about our first king, Berig—"

"Ah, you mean like Boudicca, the queen of the Iceni, who burnt Londinium and Verulamium to the ground and destroyed an entire Roman legion?"

"That's what I mean. If they discover pride in their past, they will have a sense of identity and be able to resist the assaults of those we are about to flee from."

"You are so sensible, Gosvintha; I'm so grateful for your suggestions."

"When we arrive in Corinium, I want to help organise the place to receive the women and wish to reassure the poor creatures."

"Whatever you desire, my love. We'll begin a new life where little Primus can grow to be a man."

They discussed their plans for the foreseeable future and Valdor explained his principal idea to her. "The raiders wish to advance to seize and settle on the most fertile land. A line has to be drawn, beyond which they are not allowed to cross. They are sure to advance along the Tamesis valley but we must keep them from overwhelming our main centres such as Corinium before they even catch a glimpse of them."

Like it or not, Valdor, although in Glevum nearer to the opposite coast, was still officially the Count of the Saxon Shore. However, external events would hasten a decision to change his circumstances.

Following the death of Theodosius I, Honorius would become emperor of the Western Roman Empire. A general, Stilicho, distinguished himself at the Battle of the Frigidus, in which he defeated and killed the usurper Eugenius. The forces of Theodosius were bolstered by numerous auxiliaries, including 20,000 Visigoth *foederati* under Alaric. Gosvintha's father, Geberic, and several of his best men died in this battle after having been summoned from Britannia to bolster numbers.

Theodosius, exhausted by the campaign, saw Stilicho as a man worthy of responsibility for the future safety of the empire. As Honorius was underage, Stilicho remained the caretaker for Honorius until he came of age. He became the commander-in-chief of the Roman armies in the west. To strengthen his hold over the emperor, he gave Honorius his daughter Maria's hand in marriage in 398. He used his military leadership as well as Honorius' youth and inexperience to consolidate his authority over the empire, though he acquired many rivals and enemies in the process.

Although Stilicho did not go to Britannia, he followed events there closely and sent strict orders to Valdor, reviving Carausius' broad anti-Germanic pirate command, maintaining and expanding it up to the end of the fourth century. This situation kept Valdor active while away from his family as Primus grew older and stronger, although after one visit, Gosvintha bore him a daughter, named Sfava in 389. Again, outside events would change the Count's circumstances. Meanwhile, he had a senior *logistical* command concerned with the provisioning of the Rhineland from Britain.

For the moment, however, the climate played a greater role than any dominant individual.

This was because of the semi-abandonment of the Lower Rhine due to flooding caused by a rise in sea level, involving notable marine transgressions. This phenomenon had already provoked regional piracy in the later third century when Valdor's namesake and great-grandfather had been Comes. Once again, the security of Britain's four provinces was entrusted to him as a very senior officer, whose responsibilities were largely coastal in a period when piracy was becoming a major problem. In addition, there were the difficulties involved in maintaining a permanent cross-Channel defence system, the irregular maintenance of the British Shore forts and the absence of any advanced, second-wave British-type fort in Gaul. All in all, Valdor was struggling against impossible odds and becoming increasingly disenchanted with the empire and with Stilicho in particular. He also commanded a highly mobile cavalry force, which was involved in dealing with frequent incursions in other frontier areas.

The Count fully understood the circumstances he was ordered to work under and saw that it was only a matter of time before raiders overwhelmed Britannia—Rome now held the lower Rhine as a shipping route but no longer as a frontier. Germania II was effectively abandoned, along with its ducate, and an inner defence line was created in Belgica II.

Apart from his work provisioning the Rhineland and combatting Saxon raiders, who were now using larger ships with sails, Valdor had to fend off Pictish and Scoti incursions to the north and west of Britannia. His reputation as a successful general went before him, while in Corinium, Gosvintha was making herself equally popular with the

Britons. Many an expectant mother travelled miles on foot during her eighth month of pregnancy as word of mouth spoke of healthy and salubrious conditions for a birth. Gosvintha ensured that the midwife, Cori, became a rich woman and provided her with young trainees to assist her work.

At the same time, Primus grew and, following his father's rigid instructions, built up his strength and, trained by a veteran legionary, learnt to wield a variety of weapons. The boy was now eleven years old while Valdor had experienced his fifty-first winter. He was not as athletic as before and burdened by great responsibilities, but after dandling Sfava on his knee, he gazed discreetly upon his training son with fatherly pride and hope for the future.

I

GLEVUM, AD 400

VALDOR GAZED IN AMAZEMENT FROM THE SOUTH-FACING wall of the Glevum fortress as an entire Roman legion marched with admirable order towards the city. He squinted against the bright sunlight, peering in an attempt to decipher the design on their shields. What legion was this? He was not expecting reinforcements.

The cornicen dismounted and stood next to an obviously high-ranking officer, judging by his splendid helmet and body armour, as well as the scarlet *paludamentum*, fastened over one shoulder and *cincticulus* tied around the waist in a bow. The horn blower sounded three blasts and Valdor waved to the gatekeepers to admit the newcomers.

In the principia, the *legatus legionis* introduced himself, "*Salve*, I am Legate Marcus, commandant of the *Legio II Adiutrix*. We were stationed in *Aquincum* protecting the western frontier of Pannonia. I know not why Emperor Arcadius ordered us to be shipped here in Britannia. He ordered us to be divided into two *comitatenses* and told me to report to the Count of the Saxon Shore. I confess, we had difficulty finding you, but the legate of Dubris fortress directed us here."

Valdor took an immediate liking to the legate but did not feel any obligation to explain his presence in Glevum to a complete stranger. Instead, he said, "The new century has begun unpromisingly. Waves of barbarians continue to assail our eastern and southern shores, Legate, therefore your countertrend arrival is fortuitous and welcome."

He expected the legate to smile at these words but received a puzzled frown and a stern expression.

"Fine words, Count, but hardly a consolation; in Aquincum we expected the arrival of the Huns. A large force was spotted and we were prepared to defend the Danube crossing, but my orders were countermanded. The barbarians will have found the city empty and defenceless. I expect that by now, they will have crossed the river and be menacing the eastern empire. I should not say this, I know, for my role is to obey orders. Still," he paused and looked embarrassed, biting his lower lip before continuing, "some commands are impossible to fathom. Sometimes it feels as though we are led by incompetents or imbeciles."

"Have no fear, friend, your words are sacrosanct and I'll not repeat them. But your presence here is welcome for that very reason. Our forces have been systematically bled white, withdrawn to defend the heartland. What can one say?"

They continued their congenial discussion over a silver flagon of wine until Valdor came to the conclusion that before him sat a conscientious and courageous officer—exactly the kind of man he had been seeking.

"Legate, I have fifty-seven winters behind me and can feel my strength waning—"

"That is not what I have heard, Count Valdor," the legate smiled and sounded sincere, "There abound reports of your valour and leadership."

"I thank you, friend, but the truth is another. I will do my duty until my strength fails me, but a younger man is needed to fulfil my obligations. And I have found him seated in front of me," he smiled, avuncularly, at the legate.

"What do you mean, Count?"

"For some time, I have been seeking a man worthy of succeeding me in the role of *Comes Litoris Saxonici* without success. My son is too young and inexperienced for such a position, but now, I have found you, Marcus, I have no hesitation through my authority to invest you as the Count of the Saxon Shore."

Legate Marcus remained speechless and poured them both another beaker. At last, he smiled and said, "I'm honoured, Count—"

"Ay, *Count*, for I mean to take the position of *Comes Britanniarum*, since the previous occupant of that role has not been replaced. His death in battle was a great loss to us all. The role suits me better, given my age and experience. I shall stem the advance of Picts, Scoti and anyone who tries to march on *this*, my city! Ah, *Count* Marcus, the title is not all I shall take. I mean to relieve you of one *comitatensis*, to add to my cavalry force. You will have no objection?"

"None, they are good men and will not disappoint you. But as for me, where do you suggest I make my base?"

"Either at Dubris or Regulbium, maybe the latter is a better strategic choice, but you would be wise to decide *in situ*."

As the months slipped by, Valdor received three separate reports of victories won by Marcus: against the Saxons twice, and the Jutes on one occasion. He felt more than justified in his choice of Count. As for himself, he was called into action in Cumbria against a Pictish incursion. The battle was more of a skirmish because the outnumbered Picts surrendered and were taken to be sold into slavery. At Glevum, one of the Picts broke free and flung himself into the Severn to vanish underwater and not reappear rather than be sold as a slave. Valdor divided the takings at the slave market between his men, then went home to join his family.

He found Primus lined up with other boys in front of the eastern wall at the start of a race along the road, to the far side of the fortress. The boy was now thirteen and tall and strong for his age: he did not look out of place with the sixteen-year-olds he was among. At the drop of a hand, the boys hurtled along the Via Quintana to the opposite wall. From where he stood, Valdor could not see the leader of the three out ahead, but one was certainly Primus. During the race, he had stifled a desire to cheer on his son, but now he smiled broadly as the trainer took the boy by his wrist and raised his arm—a sure sign that he had won.

Valdor sauntered along the paved road towards the group, pretending he knew nothing. Primus broke away from the group and ran towards him. "Father, I won the race from the east to the west wall— I came first!"

"Winners usually do," Valdor said laconically: the boy had to learn modesty.

"Now I'm going to win the javelin throwing contest!"

Valdor sighed and shrugged. "I suppose confidence is a good thing, Primus, but overconfidence should be left to losers."

The youth's face clouded. Gone was the joy of moments before, replaced by a serious expression. His father was a hero, and Primus had a burning desire to emulate him.

"I don't mean to brag, Father, but I have faith in my skills. Will you stay and watch?"

Valdor shook his head. "I have much to do." He hadn't, but the boy would perform better if he thought he wasn't the object of his parent's severe judgement. Valdor strode away, found the sanctuary of a side street, where he stood behind a corner unseen by his son, but with an excellent view of proceedings. The trainer chose a youth renowned for his strong arm and in a ringing voice ordered him to set a difficult marker for the others to surpass if they were able. Six-seven-eight javelins fell short before Primus hurled his at a perfect angle. For a moment, the weapon seemed to float and vibrate in the air before plunging to strike the ground at least three yards beyond the marker.

Ay, the boy has a strong arm, better than mine at his age. Not that I'll tell him that!

The trainer was organising sword practice with wooden swords but Valdor wanted to embrace his wife and daughter and felt sure that Primus would be bursting to report another victory sooner rather than later.

The reunion with mother and daughter went to plan, which was a joy as Sfava was now eleven and full of the embarrassing fact that she was now officially a woman! She was certainly a beauty, just like her mother. Whenever he was with them, he managed to tinge happiness with worry about the future. He knew that he had made a sensible decision passing the responsibility for the Saxon Shore forts to Marcus. Occasionally, when at home, he felt an urge to resign his commission and retire to the life of a family man, but he knew that was not his destiny, at least, not yet. The only certainty he had about the future was that it would involve Primus, who had so admirably shown his qualities as an athlete earlier, but Primus needed to grow older.

It came as a surprise, therefore, when his son stormed into the room shortly afterwards with a face like thunder.

"What on Earth's the matter?" Gosvintha asked.

"Nothing!" Primus said curtly, on the verge of rudeness.

"Primus, don't use that tone with your mother," Valdor snapped.

"Sorry, it's just that—"

"Ay?"

"...this damned arm's aching, but the trainer says it's not broken. Father, the truth is, my pride hurts more than my arm."

"Let me see," Gosvintha fussed, taking the offended limb and turning it gently.

"Ouch!"

His mother shook her head. "That's an ugly bruise forming there."

Primus' eyes filled with tears of unswallowed pride, and he swiped an angry hand across them. "It's the first time I've lost a sword fight, Father. I'm glad you didn't stay to see it."

"That's true, but I'll come to see you get revenge in a few days from now, when the bruise has gone."

Primus moaned, "I'll never beat Caius, he's too expert for me!"

Valdor squatted in front of his son, who was sitting on the low hearth wall and looked him straight in the eye. "What I need is a bit of that earlier cockiness! You said you'd win at the javelin and you did!"

His son's eyes sparkled. "You stayed to watch!" Then, his face fell.

"So, I did, but I didn't stay for the sword fights."

"So, you didn't see me lose?"

"Nay, but as I said, I'll come to see you get the better of this Caius."

"How can that be?"

Valdor laughed. "Because, I'll teach you some tricks my mother taught me when I was your age. There's one, in particular, that has always served me well in battle."

Primus leapt to his feet. "Did you hear, Mother? Where is she?"

"Here, with a balm for that arm. It'll take the pain away and bring out the bruise so that it'll pass in no time! This is a cure for bruises and sprains that an old woman taught my mother when we lived near the Baltic Sea. It's called the *sunshine salve* and is made from herbs like calendula and comfrey-infused oil." She dribbled some drops of oil onto the injured arm and massaged it gently before smearing a golden-orangey salve over the area. "There, isn't that better?" she grinned into his face. He leant over and kissed her.

"I'm becoming quite the infirmarian, you know," she said to Valdor. "Well, more the midwife, to be honest. I delivered two babes last week— my first time alone! There's nothing more joyous than handing a newborn child to its mother and to see her face as she stares into her child's eyes, believe me. You men wouldn't be so busy killing each other if you saw the miracle of a perfect creature fresh straight from the womb," she said accusingly.

"Mother," a small voice said, "next time can I come with you to see a birth?" Sfava gazed pleadingly at her mother.

"You should know, it might be distressing, daughter. Mothers in labour scream in pain—all of them—and they sweat and howl."

"If it's so painful, it's a wonder anyone has children!" Sfava said, marvelling.

"It's usually easier after the first one. But don't worry, Sfava, your mother is a trained midwife and you'll be much older before you wed unless you have a hidden beloved!"

"Not yet, Mother, but this Caius sounds interesting," she looked at Primus and grinned wickedly.

"Never! I'll slay him first! Only the best for my sister!" Primus said jealously. "Father's going to improve my sword skills, is it not so, Father?"

Valdor looked guiltily at Gosvintha, who immediately stared across the room at nothing in particular.

Valdor chuckled, "Ay, as soon as that bruise is healed, I'll show you how to best anyone with a sword – *er* – except me!"

Three days later, Valdor sent a servant to fetch two practice swords.

"These are like *spathae*, the gladius is a different proposition altogether."

"Ay, Publius says it's a waste of time training with the gladius because it's a stabbing weapon used through gaps between shields."

"He's right up to a point, but you can train speed of hand. I'll have a word with him about that. Now, step over here, today, you'll train indoors."

Valdor spoke about agility of foot and arm and the importance of feigning and counter-feigning. Primus soaked up the information like a sponge absorbs water. But he truly came alive when his father demonstrated a move that disarmed his son, sending the sword arcing through the air. Valdor laughed, placed his mock blade at his son's throat and said, "Of course, you needn't go for the throat, you could, for instance, thwack an undefended arm!"

"Pray, Father, show me how you did that!"

"Just like my mother showed me. Your grandmother Lavinia was a great shield maiden, you know."

Patiently, he explained the manoeuvre slowly, feint and twist of the wrist: "It's here you need to *stiffen* your wrist, be strong, like *this!*" Again, Primus' sword fell with a clatter to the floor. "Do you know how many times I've slain a foe in battle, using that trick?"

"I'll never be that good!"

"Oh, ay, you *will!* Your grandmother could do it and her wrists were not as strong as yours. Come on, try it!"

Sure enough, Valdor's sword went arcing away and Primus cried out with joy. "I've done it!"

"Ay, because I didn't use the technique for blocking it. I'll teach you that after you've thwacked Caius!"

Primus' open, honest features lit up in a wide beam. "I'll give him what he gave me—I hope his pride will be as wounded as mine was."

"If it is, it means that Caius will be a good soldier, too."

Two days passed before the next sword practice and Valdor, alerted by his son, again stood in the shadow of a building and watched with satisfaction when Caius' sword flew away. He had to feel sorry for the older youth when his unforgiving son struck the unprotected arm, causing his opponent to howl and show his arm to the concerned trainer. Valdor smiled to himself when he heard Publius say, "I'll wager your father taught you that trick, my lad."

He was proud of him when he heard the honest reply, "Ay, he *did*, Master Publius, I wish I had half the skills of my father. One day, I wish to be like him."

Valdor was even more pleased when he heard the trainer's reply: "There's no reason why not, Primus, as long as you remain humble and work hard."

The Count strode over to them. "I heard your advice, Publius and hope that Primus takes it to heart. How's young Caius?"

"The arm isn't broken, so I hope he's learnt the lesson that practice is not a battle!"

"Regarding that, friend Publius, I'd appreciate it if you'd teach the boys all you know about using a gladius. We've won more victories thanks to that weapon than all the others put together."

"It's true, when I think about my experiences of combat, lord. But how can I train that?"

"Simple. Withdraw enough *scuta* and *gladii*; line them up with linked shields, attack them with a long sword and declare the winner who can stab you with the wooden gladius."

"We'll try that this afternoon and make legionaries of them yet!"

Valdor strode away, determined to ensure that, one day, his son would reach his level of weaponry skills.

2

GLEVUM AND VENTA SILURUM, AD 401-403

WHERE PREVIOUSLY BROWN BRACKEN BOWED BEFORE THE biting wind, fresh green ferns sparkled with dew in the early sunshine: a sure sign that spring had come to prompt the cuckoo call. With the arrival of spring, military thoughts turned to new campaigns. At Eastertide at the Battle of Pollentia, the Roman army under Stilicho engaged with the Visigoths under Alaric I. Despite his April victory, Stilicho recalled troops from Britannia and the Rhine frontier to defend Italy. The capture of Alaric's wife and children did little to placate the warlike Goths.

In Glevum, Valdor was dismayed to receive the command to release his newly acquired *comitatensis* with other regular troops of his garrison, but he was not as disgruntled as the remaining veterans, who sent a delegation to him, declaring that they had agreed to nominate him for the imperial purple. They reckoned without his reaction, for loyalty was paramount among Valdor's many virtues. He had taken an oath of fidelity and meant to keep it. Besides, as he sat and reflected on these events, he decided that when he responded, it would be on *his* terms, not according to a gut reaction among disillusioned men.

However, he understood the need to soothe the aggrieved feelings among them. With this in mind, he gathered some of the more outspoken and sat them at his table.

"Brothers in arms," he began, "we all know that the heartland of the empire has to be defended, but our rulers cannot abandon Britannia with impunity. I have considered your plea at length and must admit that there is value in what you say."

"So, you *will* assume the imperial vestments, Count?" said their ringleader, a veteran decurion of Hadrian's Wall who Valdor knew well and admired for his courage in action.

"Nay, Flavius, I have no appetite to play the usurper. Besides, I have eyes only for Britannia or, even more narrowly, for what the Britons call the *Kingdom of Logres*, which includes the very city we are located in today. My idea is to travel around the various garrisons to build up an army to defend Logres. We'll rely on British support from Cambria, Dumnonia and the north-west, where the Britons are already planning to create an independent kingdom. It is important that we prevent the barbarians from crossing the frontiers of Logres.

If I build up a strong force and we defeat the raiders on all fronts, one day, I'll be ready to take the kingship of Logres and not the title of Western Emperor. We can still remain loyal to Rome until that day comes."

He looked around from one weather-beaten face to another, relaxing as he saw that the men received his words with sage nods and cheerful countenances. He thanked the Lord for the popularity he enjoyed among the rank and file; he had earned it through his deeds.

"On the understanding, Count Valdor," said Flavius, "that should Rome fall to the barbarians, you'll at once accept the crown of Logres as *King* Valdor."

"It is agreed," Valdor smiled, "and in the period of waiting for such a catastrophe, I'll prepare my son to succeed me, for I am not immortal and my strength cannot last forever. It must endure for a while to protect and build up an army worthy of the name. Consider yourselves subjects of the Roman Empire, but also men of Logres."

Cheers and table-thumping greeted these words and men rose to shake Valdor by the hand. Once more, he had won a battle—happily a bloodless one.

Valdor's first task was to ride with his men down the Tamesis valley to Londinium, where he weakened the garrison by more than half. The legate could not disobey the orders of the *Comes Britanniarum*, the highest-ranking officer in Britannia.

"Legate," Valdor told the dignified, long-nosed and silver-haired commandant of the fortress, "I entrust the defence of the fortress to you and your remaining men. I fear needs must! We have all lost men to Rome's insatiable appetite for troops. Do not be lured into battle against superior numbers. Concentrate on holding this stronghold until better times arrive."

"Ay, if they ever do," the legate shook his head pessimistically and his tone was bitter.

Valdor left Londinium feeling slightly guilty, but with his force doubled. He meant to redouble it, too, and to this purpose, marched his men to Regulbium for a meeting with the Count of the Saxon Shore. Count Marcus bemoaned the increasing raids on the southern and eastern shores of the land and, more resentfully, the haemorrhage of troops into Italy.

At this point, without precise explanation, Valdor pulled rank and explained that he would now travel up the east coast, halving each garrison and adding men to his field army.

"I know precisely what effect this will have on you, Count Marcus. We can only hope that good sense returns to the corridors of the *Urbs Aeterna* and that they will send another legion to Britannia, as they did your Legio II Adiutrix."

Marcus grunted and said rebelliously, "I fear it's not a question of good sense, Count Valdor, but the need for a radical change of leadership."

"But Stilicho is a successful general."

"Ay, and so are you and I, but the Western Emperor is no more than a boy and the barbarians know his weakness."

"He will grow. Meanwhile, we must defend this province until Honorius comes to manhood."

Marcus scowled and looked unconvinced, if not outright seditious, but knowing the nature of the man who stood before him, wisely kept his counsel.

Valdor progressed up the east coast, stopping at seven shore fortresses, relieving each one of half its already depleted garrison, making himself unpopular with the stressed commandant of each stronghold. Valdor underlined the importance of coordinated action under the command of Count Marcus, for although he had sensed the unease of the Count of the Saxon Shore, he did not harbour the slightest doubt as to his military abilities.

With the equivalent force of two legions, 10,000 infantry and 600 cavalrymen, Valdor gazed with pride as his columns marched to Glevum. A pride that was reciprocated by men aware of their commanding officer's splendid reputation and self-belief in their unflinching discipline.

They were not immediately called into action, but after several weeks, one of the many scouts sent out in all directions reported to his commandant. After the ritual salute of fist to chest, he said, "Count, the Scoti have landed in the Sabrina estuary and intend to attack Venta Silurum."

"Mmm, it's a rich town. Refresh my memory, is it walled?"

"Ay, lord. Some seventy years ago, stone walls replaced the old ramparts."

"So, we can arrive in time to save the town."

The scout smiled and nodded, "Since the town lies on the road between us and the fortress of Isca Silurum, the cavalry will arrive promptly."

Valdor recognised the external tower of the south wall as he galloped at the head of his ten *turmae*. Their hooves thundered along the paved road, the iron shoes occasionally slipping on the smooth surface or, alternatively, sending sparks flying. In both cases, the riders needed all their skills to maintain their speed and formation.

At the sight of the approaching cavalry, the Scoti left the road to take up position on the softer ground of the open flatlands. Valdor spotted the danger to the horses' legs and slowed his riders almost to a halt, sent a *duplicarius* to his decurion and ordered three *turmae* to ride in a wide arc to attack the Scoti from behind. The cunning choice of terrain by the Scoti reduced the agility of the horses, but the superior height and better discipline of Valdor's force triumphed.

The Count led the frontal assault so vigorously that the enemy were totally concentrated on defending themselves. They inflicted some injuries to the horses with their spears, but the unseen arrival of the three *turmae*, unheard on the soft turf, devastated their force. The *spathae* took a deadly toll from behind and Valdor was quick to press home the advantage, targeting the Scoti chieftain, a tall red-haired warrior with a blue-painted face. More than a feeble attempt to transform his ferocious features with *glastum* dye was required to intimidate Valdor, who struck the mortal blow that broke the Scoti resistance when their leader collapsed, dying, to the ground.

The Scoti standing their ground were captured while those fleeing were cut down. The victorious Roman force trotted towards the south gate of Venta Silurium, only to find the entrance blocked by stone and mortar. From the ramparts, a voice called to them to enter through the smaller west gate. Valdor rode into the prosperous town towards the central *insula*, where the forum and basilica stood. The regular plan of the roads, he noticed, was broken by a new amphitheatre. All in all, he was impressed by the town, its wealth not reflected, however, in the common homes, more like hovels.

A delegation of townsfolk came to greet him, their leader beaming at him, grateful for once for not having to fight the fierce Scoti.

"These raids are becoming more frequent, Centurion."

"Count," Valdor said through clenched teeth, "and you are?"

The swarthy-featured individual with black, curly hair stared hard at Valdor, "Roman, my name is Bran ap Hefeydd, chieftain of the Silures. We know how to look after ourselves but your help is appreciated."

"I am Count Valdor, Comes Britanniarum, and while I am loyal to Rome, I am more interested in looking after the Kingdom of Logres. There are many Britons there, whom I wish to protect from raiders," he indicated with a tilt of his head, "such as these miserable captives. I am actively seeking alliances to combat incursions. I am willing to repeat today's action if called upon, Chieftain Bran ap Hefeydd, and would appreciate a mutual agreement. I will have you know that whereas your people have a long-standing grudge with Rome, while I am Comes Britanniarum, you may consider me a friend."

The chieftain looked from Valdor to his captives: two-score Scoti. When his gaze returned to the Count, it was suspicious and calculating. "Come to my hall, Count, there's much to discuss." Although he spoke his language, the words were harsh and guttural to Valdor's ears, but he had no hesitation in following the Silurian.

In time-honoured fashion, the chieftain offered his guest his best mead before opening negotiations. "We saw your strength today, Count, and would prefer you as an ally, not a foe. I have only one request, which I am sure will not test your patience."

"Which is?"

"I require you to hand over your captives. We can use them as a bargaining counter with the Scoti, whereas you will only sell them into slavery. If it's silver you want for them, speak!"

"Nay, I do not seek to profit from this friendship, Chieftain, except to widen alliances through your favourable word. I'll willingly hand you the captives in exchange for your goodwill."

They spoke at length about common interests and clasped wrists to seal the alliance. Before leaving the town, Valdor gave orders to hand over the Scoti destined as hostages. That done, his army returned to Glevum. But it was not the end of the matter.

A week later, another of his scouts reported, "Count, the Silures deceived you. Outside the walls of their *civitas* capital, sprout stakes like the quills of a porcupine, each bearing the head of a Scoti captive. Bran ap Hefeydd ordered them all beheaded."

"So much for wanting hostages! I wonder if I can trust the Silures on other matters? Only time will tell."

Valdor sat and reflected on the savage nature of the Silurian chieftain, but he was too wise to imagine that the Silures were worse in that respect than the Romans themselves. Had not the via Appia into Rome been lined with crucified men? Venta Silurum had been something of a paradox now he thought about it. The houses in the settlement were generally small and modestly appointed for such a thriving community. From his stolen glimpses through open doors, he concluded that few of them possessed tessellated or mosaic floors. He imagined hardly any having hypocaust heating or adjoining bathhouses. The Silures had not attained the refined Roman qualities and wealth of their close neighbours in *his* area—the Dobunni—who had built many villas in the hills surrounding their *civitas* capital at Corinium. Now he thought about it, Valdor had seen no such outlying villas surrounding the Silurian capital.

He poured himself a beaker of mead, sipping it slowly, realising that tasty as it was, it was lower quality than that offered by Bran ap Hefeydd. Was it possible that even a liquor could be paradoxical? Valdor sighed and put his head in his hands, resting on his elbows. The responsibility of his role as Comes Britanniarum abruptly weighing on him.

Suddenly, an image of the small altar he had seen in the corner of the chieftain's hall miraculously replaced that of heads on poles. In a way that he could not explain, this memory cleared his thinking. The crisply hewn block was dedicated to Mars-Ocelus—an example of religion in Britannia being a mixture of Roman gods and goddesses linked with their Celtic equivalents. Surely, if he needed it, this was a sign that the policy he had launched was correct. He regretted the deaths of the captives, but perhaps Bran ap Hefeydd was right. The Silures had lived and farmed for hundreds of years in the south of Cambria. *What a world!* Like the rest of Britannia, Cambria was threatened by merciless attacks from overseas.

The image in his head of the altar whispered to him, *people can absorb the best of other cultures and live in harmony. It is my job to protect this sacred right.* He had clasped hands with the Silurian chieftain in an alliance; that the Silurian had changed his mind about the captives and cruelly slaughtered them, need not undermine Valdor's wider vision— after all, the Scoti were a common enemy and he, Valdor, had slain his share on the battlefield. If anything positive could be saved from the Roman invasion of Britannia, then it was his duty to preserve it.

Some weeks later, news from elsewhere arrived. The Visigoths, under King Alaric I, advancing through the Brenner Pass, invaded Italy again. With 30,000 men, Stilicho defeated them at the Battle of Verona. Alaric was forced into signing a truce and withdrew eastwards. As a result, Stilicho and Honorius were honoured with a triumphal march.

On hearing the news, Valdor rubbed his hands and grinned. This might mean that Rome would not persist in recalling more troops from Britannia. He could not know that the Battle of Verona would be the last victory celebrated in Rome.

3

GLEVUM, CORINIUM AND REGULBIUM, AD 403-407

VALDOR ENJOYED A PERIOD OF PEACE AFTER HIS DEFEAT OF the Scoti, whereas Marcus, the Count of the Saxon Shore, had to win several battles against Saxon, Frisian and Jutish invaders in the same period. To the north, Hadrian's Wall was effectively abandoned, but the Picts were relatively quiet, so Valdor used this tranquil spell with his family. Occasionally, he settled disputes, especially those concerning taxation, where he'd earned a reputation as a hard but fair administrator. Taxation was essential for him to ensure the regular payment of his troops. He had an army on standby and, therefore, gave particular attention to events in Britannia and elsewhere in the Western Empire.

At home, he spent more time in Corinium than in Glevum, partly because Gosvintha had become a devoted midwife and was based there. As she pointed out to him, "Every mother I help safely through childbirth represents a family happy under your rule, Valdor. You cannot imagine how many hearts I've won for your cause."

He did not need persuasion to appreciate her work, also because the tragic news that reached Britannia from the Eastern Empire moved him deeply.

Eastern Empress, the daughter of a Romanised Frankish administrator, Aelia Eudoxia, a rare beauty, married Emperor Arcadius when they were both eighteen. Rumour had it that the eunuch Eutropius presented Arcadius with a portrait of Eudoxia and expounded on her charms until Arcadius fell in love. Valdor had subsequently heard that this was just an embroidered tale because Arcadius had become used to the intelligent orphaned girl at court for six years and needed no encouragement from the eunuch.

It was common knowledge that Eudoxia loved her husband and in the decade between her marriage and her death, she gave birth to five surviving children; sadly, she bore two stillborn babes and suffered miscarriages, too. Tragically, her last pregnancy ended in another miscarriage and she was left bleeding and died of an infection shortly thereafter.

As Gosvintha was quick to point out, "If that can happen in the palatial surroundings of Byzantine chambers, to an *empress*, no less—poor creature—imagine what might happen in the squalid streets of Corinium. Don't you see, Valdor, you who are a general, that my life mission is as important to me as your tactics when you lead your men. I guide my women through the agonies of childbirth and into the joys of motherhood."

Valdor could not be accused of disinterest in her work. Instead, fully understanding her nature, he had encouraged her. He noticed with pleasure that in the civilian setting of Corinium, he was always met by smiling faces. He was convinced and relaxed about his wife's activity and, although he had set aside personal ambitions for the moment, felt sure that should the day come when he had to seek popular support, he would find it, also thanks to Gosvintha's kindness.

Momentarily, his main preoccupation was Primus, now with seventeen winters behind him, whose frame had filled out and who already stood some inches taller than his father. The Count had taught his son every sword trick he knew and considered him ready from that point of view. Primus only lacked the strengthening that came from hard training, so Valdor waited for the bad weather. As soon as the rain transformed the trackways around the town into muddy trails, he sent him out with three comrades of his age to run on the ridgeway to Glevum.

The following day, he ordered them to run back, aware how much character was needed to complete the course in sapping conditions. When Primus came in second and had the nerve to blame his performance on the bad underfoot situation, Valdor punished him by having him pick up a heavy rock, as Lavinia had done with him, and made him run out again, following him on horseback to ensure he obeyed without deception. He smiled grimly at the glowers his gasping son gave him and only allowed him to pause when he reached the milestone that indicated three miles from Corinium. After a few minutes' respite, he had him turn around, heft up the rock and slog his way back to the town.

When he arrived, mud-spattered and exhausted, Valdor dismounted to put an arm around his son's shoulder, "Sometimes, in battle, you have to keep fighting when your muscles are on fire and your brain screams at you to rest. Obey that call and you are a dead man! Now, Primus, go to the baths and relax. Tomorrow, you and your friends will race with stones around the amphitheatre. There'll be no mud to drag at your feet there."

Valdor continued the harsh physical regime with variations, with and without armour, throughout the winter of 404. In the spring of 405, he entrusted the four youths to a centurion in Glevum, convinced that they were ready for combat.

"The next time you are called into action, Centurion, I want these four soldiers in the front line because they are ready."

The centurion smiled and nodded with an admiring glance at his commander because he knew that he was entrusting his son.

In June, Primus rode into Corinium and, with a broad grin, greeted his father.

"Father, I have fought my first battle and slew seven Picts. We met them in the Cumbrian hills near Alauna Fort—"

"Ah, that place brings back fond memories," Valdor smiled enigmatically. "Come on, we must drink together to celebrate your victory and you can tell me about the battle."

"We received a call for help at Glevum since the Picts were devastating farmsteads in the area of Alauna—"

He gave his father a detailed account, blow by blow, of his battle and then listened to Valdor's reminiscences of his engagement when he helped Theodosius' force years before. In comparison, Primus' encounter had only been a skirmish, but nothing could dampen his pride at his success—now, he was a soldier in his own right, he would make his father proud of him.

Elsewhere in the empire, events precipitated. Radagaisus, a Gothic king and dedicated pagan, decided to attack Italy, declaring that he would sacrifice the Roman senators to his gods before burning Rome to the ground. With a force of over 20,000 men, he crossed the Alps, swelling his numbers with Arian Christians on the way. Radagaisus' army devastated northern Italy for at least six months, well into 406, while the Empire mobilised its forces. Eventually, the Goths besieged Florentia, but Stilicho arrived with 15,000 men and relieved the city as it approached the point of surrender.

The Roman counterattack was extremely successful, and Radagaisus was forced to retreat into the hills of Fiesole, about five miles away. There, Radagaisus abandoned his followers and tried to escape but was captured by the Romans and executed on 23 August while 12,000 of his higher-status fighters were drafted into the Roman army. Most of the remaining followers were dispersed, and so many of the others were sold into slavery that the slave market briefly collapsed.

During the summer, while Radagaisus was rampaging in northern Italy, yet another urgent request for troops to help save Rome reached the Count of the Saxon Shore. For Marcus, this was the last straw and, far from complying, he instigated his troops to rebel. A mutiny followed with the legionaries declaring him Western Emperor.

Marcus' first act was to send a messenger to Glevum, ordering Valdor to march his army to Regulbium with the intention of sailing to Gallia to defeat Stilicho and remove Honorius from his throne.

When the messenger arrived in Glevum, he first met with a young decurion and demanded to meet Valdor.

"My father is not in the town," Primus told the messenger, "but deliver your message to me and I will see that the Count receives it." Primus listened gravely to the message and merely muttered, "Gaul, eh?" He shook his head and summoned a group of legionaries. "Take this messenger to the canteen, feed him and make sure he has the best wine." He turned and waved, "And you, fellow, see to his horse."

Primus watched the men, chatting amicably, lead the messenger away before going to his centurion. "Centurion Pontus, I have grave news..." he explained and ended, "...my father will have no truck with mutiny and usurpation. With your permission, I'll ride to Corinium to warn him. We should see that the messenger does not return to his fortress as we do not wish to alert the usurper to our refusal to obey him."

"Decurion, we can lock him in a cell until we deem it safe to release him. As you know, the messenger bears no blame."

Primus rode to Corinium, not sparing his horse. He went straight to his mother's *domus* and blurted the news of Marcus' rebellion to his father. Valdor's reaction was exactly as he expected: "Treason! I blame myself, for I appointed Marcus to be the Count."

"Nay, father, the men mutinied against Rome and Stilicho's constant demands to withdraw troops."

"But if he remained true to his oath, Marcus would have forsworn the imperial purple as I did when our men agitated against the empire."

"What are we to do, father?"

"Nothing. I'll have no truck with the usurper. My forces outnumber his."

"Will you not then march on Regulbium and arrest him?"

"Primus, I will not countenance a civil war. The Lord knows we have enough to contend with in Britannia without losing more men in a futile clash of brothers. Nay, we'll observe the situation and let Marcus go to Gallia alone if that is his plan."

"Let me go to Regulbium, father, I can keep an eye on what Marcus is planning."

"Only on condition that you do nothing rash and keep your name secret. Marcus could use you as a hostage to force my hand. Your presence there might be useful to determine how to react and if he decides to march against Glevum, you will be able to let me know promptly."

"It's agreed, then. I'll leave at dawn."

Primus wore the armour of a simple legionary and mingled with the other men, inventing a tale of desertion from Hadrian's Wall and reintegration in the south. Nobody challenged his tale: one which was common enough in Britannia. He was sure to ask about pay, although he had no real intention of drawing any. By not registering, he achieved his aim of remaining anonymous.

Yuletide approached, but there was no conviviality in the fortress. The men were angry. More of their comrades were forced to embark for Italy, desperate for troops in the face of the barbarian menace. There was also a smouldering resentment against Marcus for his high-handed approach to discipline, but the final affront came when the Count, hitherto a successful general, took a cohort from Regulbium onto the peninsula near Rutupiae fort and, commanding a joint force, ignored his centurions' warning that they were marching into a trap, led his men to a terrible slaughter. Holding himself back, Marcus escaped with a handful of survivors, who told the sorry tale.

Infuriated by his cowardice and arrogance, the garrison rebelled. They had another candidate ready for the imperial purple, but first, they had to get rid of Marcus. A mob of soldiers gathered, Primus among them, hurling insults outside the *principia*.

Suddenly, someone flung the door back and Marcus appeared with five burly bodyguards brandishing swords. Several of the men around Primus melted away, but the young decurion and some veterans stood their ground. The newly emerged force rushed the remaining assembled men, determined to make an example of them.

A mighty clash of steel and one of Primus' comrades fell, further infuriating the crowd of legionaries who had regrouped and gathered to watch and join in the fray if necessary. Primus severely wounded one of the guards, thus drawing the Count's attention to himself. With a roar, Marcus rushed at him, not imagining that a simple legionary was a sophisticated swordsman. Soon, he realised his error and was struggling to maintain his position in the face of a skilled onslaught. Primus watched the general's eyes carefully and chose his moment well. With the practised feint and wrist flick, to everyone's astonishment, Marcus' sword flew away. The Count only had time to utter, "Who the..." before Primus' strong arm thrust his sword fatally into the usurper's heart. A deafening roar rent the air and Marcus' failed bodyguard gestured surrender and laid their swords on the ground.

At that moment, mobbed by enthusiastic comrades, Primus did not notice what else was happening. So, given that the men's chosen candidate advised caution and refused to be proclaimed emperor immediately, it was only later that he learnt who the proposed nominee was.

Primus decided that it was time to return to Glevum to report Marcus' death to his father. He would let the Count decide whether he should return to Regulbium.

Valdor's tone was a mixture of admiration and censure, "I told you not to do anything rash in Regulbium and you only fight and slay a Roman general, who's a Count to boot! I'll be sure to let Emperor Honorius know! As for Regulbium, I'll send a spy who's more discreet than my son."

Time passed and it was October before Valdor summoned Primus. "I thought you'd like to know; the shore troops have replaced your usurper with another."

"Father?"

"He's called Gratian, a Romano-Briton, and an urban aristocrat. I suspect that the promotion of a non-military official by the army suggests that there are issues that the army felt will be better handled by a civilian official, such as pay, or perhaps disagreements between myself, the *Comes Litoris Saxonici*, and the *Dux Britanniarum*. Well, good luck to them if they think that this usurper can do a better job than us!"

On the last day of December 406, an army of Vandals, Alans and Suebi crossed the frozen Rhine and Valdor shared his thoughts on this again with his son.

"They say that Stilicho is behind this...that he's instigated the barbarian invasion of Gallia."

"But why, father?"

"I believe it's true that he's concerned about the British usurpers but unable to act against them because of the activities of Radagaisus and Alaric I. The invasion is therefore meant to distract the British army."

"Diabolical! Is this Stilicho prepared to risk so much?"

"Evidently, but remember, he's an able general and administrator, without him as his *magister militum*, Honorius would have been ousted years ago. We'll have to see what Gratian can do about the Western Empire that he's claimed for himself."

Valdor did not have long to wait to find out.

As news of the barbarian invasion reached Britannia, and their rapid approach to Bononia—the main port from which supplies and troops would arrive in Britain—the army became restless. The troops in Regulbium wanted to cross into Gallia to stop the barbarians, but Gratian ordered them to stay. Unhappy, the troops killed him after four months of rule and elected Flavius Claudius Constantinus, a common soldier, not an officer, who took the title of Constantine III as their leader in early February.

"It only goes to show, Primus, how wise was my decision to reject the imperial throne. The life expectancy of usurpers in Britannia has become ever shorter! This Constantine will have to be an able statesman to survive. Meanwhile, we'll look on: I have a feeling that if circumstances become much worse, I shall reluctantly be forced to maintain a promise to my men here in Glevum."

4

BONONIA AND GLEVUM, AD 407-408

CONSTANTINE MOVED QUICKLY, APPOINTING TWO OFFICERS already in Gallia as generals: Justinianus and Nebiogastes, instructing them to seize Arelate and the passes which controlled traffic to and from Italy. He crossed the Channel at Bononia, taking with him, apart from Valdor's men, all of the 6,000 mobile troops left in Britain, and their commander, General Gerontius. This denuded Roman Britain of front-line military protection. Constantine travelled to Lugdunum where he set up his headquarters and commenced minting coins in his own name.

Some men become great; others have greatness thrust upon them: Valdor was a strange mixture of both. In truth, he had withstood the lure of power for years, and in all honesty, he did little to resist assuming the proffered role of king. This time, the difference lay in the timing. Valdor looked around and considered the effect of Constantine's final depredation of troops from Britannia and what he saw was anarchy. The soldiers had not been paid for years, their comrades had been drained to the continent to fight barbarians while Britannia's coasts were subject to raids by chieftains like the Irish king, Niall of the Nine Hostages, or Pictish seaborne assaults along the east coast.

The reaction of the garrisons not under his direct control was understandable. Hearing of the Germanic invasion of Gallia across the Rhine, the Roman military in Britannia was desperate for some sense of security in a world that seemed to be rapidly falling apart. But their solution of appointing usurpers only to murder them for not fulfilling expectations only contributed to a growing certainty that Roman rule in Britannia was definitively over.

Gazing across the Channel to Constantine's campaign, Valdor was not reassured. The central Roman authorities did not respond to the Germanic invasion. At best, the usurper gained a tenuous control over Gallia but had to compromise by sharing power with bands of marauding barbarians. Conflicting news reached Glevum, each report more incredible than its predecessor. In practice, by securing the Rhine frontier, Constantine had to sacrifice northern Gaul. At the same time, Honorius and Stilicho with the Visigoths were in conflict with the Eastern Empire, trying to extort land for the Visigoths.

The alleged Roman leaders were too busy trying to maintain their positions and fighting among themselves while surrounded by migrating forces determined to seize fertile land. In this desperate situation, Centurion Pontus came to Valdor as the troops' spokesman. They had been paid regularly but were anxious about the political situation and yearned for security and stability. The centurion bowed and said, "Count Valdor, it is true that Rome has not yet fallen, but it is only a matter of time; meanwhile, Gallia is slipping from the empire's grasp and the only capable general has failed to halt Constantine. Stilicho is too occupied fending off Alaric and protecting Honorius to make a decisive move. Lord, now the time is right! Only you can save this land from devastation. The men beg you to take the throne of Logres."

Valdor sat and stared across the room, contemplating the situation. Everything Pontus had said was correct. Britannia was defenceless and would have to learn to protect itself. Instead, he had an army sufficient to hold the borders of Logres against any incursions and the land was fertile and productive even if the area around the Sabrina Estuary was prone to flooding. His territory, for he was beginning to consider it as *his*, stretched as far as Cornwall in the southwest and with a little consolidation, he could press down the Tamēsis valley and across to the east coast. In the north, he could hold a natural frontier with Cumbria at the river Seteia and to the north-east at the river Belisama.

The centurion coughed discreetly to snap the count out of his reverie.

"Uh? Oh, aye, Centurion, gather an assembly and I'll address the men. I've decided to accept the kingship."

"You have? That's magnificent news, King Valdor!"

The beaming centurion bowed out of the room as Valdor reached another decision: he would appoint a select group of 'knights' who would be privy to decision making and they would have no hierarchy but gather as peers. As such, he would seat them in such a way that nobody would feel emarginated from his king. To do this, the high table would have to be round in shape. Pontus would be one of his knights, as would his son, Primus.

Pontus sent a legionary to inform him that the men were gathered and waiting. Valdor stepped outside the *principia*, to see that a makeshift dais had been placed in front of the building, in the shape of a cart. Pontus, standing on it already, offered the count a hand to haul him up beside him. The centurion took the initiative, "Comrades, today is a momentous occasion. Heed well the words of Count Valdor. Silence!" he bellowed as some murmured that Valdor had not accepted the kingship, given Pontus' use of the title 'count'.

"Brothers in arms," Valdor began confidently, "having listened to your appeal and after deep consideration, I have decided to accept the kingship..." he wanted to continue but a thunderous roar of approval halted him. At once, the legionaries cried, "God save the King!" repeated over and over until, Pontus, with a thunderous expression, raised a hand for silence, "Heed the words of King Valdor."

"I am your king and claim your loyalty. Our task is to protect Logres from intruders, to defend the men, women and children of Britannia and their livestock. We shall bring justice and peace to the people and defend it with our sinews and our last drop of blood." Valdor quoted the creed, "we believe in one God, the Father Almighty..." and was delighted when the majority of the men recited it with him. A Christian kingdom, based on justice and peace was his heart's desire. He was acute enough to know that he and his men would have to fight to preserve these values. Nor could he expect to hold Logres alone, he would need reliable allies, such as his friend, Bran ap Hefeydd on the other side of the great estuary. Judging by the uproarious reception of his decision, he would have no trouble relying on his men. He had the prescription for success: regular pay and victories. This combination was infallible, but to ensure its effectiveness, he would need to call upon the ablest of his selected knights—he was a valid general, not a god. Unlike some previous insane emperors, he had no pretension to being superhuman—

Nero and Caligula came to mind, both undoubtedly insane and corrupted by total power.

Valdor's first task was to summon men skilled at woodworking and he told them what he wanted. They confabulated until one said, "Sire, we have oak that has seasoned for three years. It has lost its moisture and is ideal for the purpose."

The following day, they came to Valdor's Hall with lengths of oak already smoothed. All day they sawed and hammered and planed until night fell. In the morning, at first light, they continued until the massive circular, flat top was finished. "Sire, we need enough men to raise the table top onto its stand, but first, lord, decide where the table will be positioned in the hall since it will be no easy task to move it."

"Here," said the king, moving to the precise centre of the room. Grunting and sweating, the six carpenters heaved the oak base to where the king had indicated and checked for his approval, which he granted.

"We'll need thirty strong men, sire, for the top alone weighs more than a ton," the head carpenter said. Valdor did not doubt his words because they had told him 121 pieces of oak had gone into making the eighteen-foot diameter tabletop. The six carpenters steered the legionaries deftly to centre the top exactly in perfect equilibrium on its stand. Once satisfied, the head carpenter took a chair and surprised everyone by climbing onto it and then jumping onto the tabletop. To Valdor's amazement, the top did not budge under the muscular man's weight. "Look, Sire, you have a perfectly stable creation here," he bragged.

"You will all be well compensated, now I require twenty-one *solia*, each fit for a king. Can you have them ready in three days?"

Three days later, Valdor summoned a priest and had the table blessed and anointed before his chosen knights, then told them, "There is no precedence. You may sit where you like but my only rule is that once chosen, that seat will always be yours and not be occupied by another. This is my *solium*." He smiled happily when Primus rushed to sit next to him. The others hesitated, but Pontus took the seat on his left hand.

When they were all seated, Valdor smiled with satisfaction because as he had planned, he could see them all and they all could see him.

"Place your hands flat on the table so that your outer fingers touch those of the men next to you," he demonstrated with Primus and

Pontus, "Good, now we are bound in Brotherhood and you will swear never to harm or betray your comrades here today. Moreover, you will swear loyalty to your king and to defend the innocent and weak and live a chaste life governed by God's commandments."

"I do so swear," bellowed Pontus.

Valdor looked at the man next to Pontus, a centurion named Walwen, "I swear to abide by these rules."

One by one, around the table, the knights swore the oath until Primus completed the avowal.

"Excellent, my Knights of the Round Table. As you witnessed, this table is as holy as an altar and it is here that all our gravest decisions will be taken. We begin today because it is essential that the rich farmlands and villas of the Upper Tamēsis Valley are protected. I have given this much thought, and that is why I am sending Sir Pontus with a cohort of cavalry to a place where the river Leach flows into the Tamēsis. Above that point stands a most ancient fort dug into the hill. Within its perimeter stand the ruins of twenty-four ancient round houses. Using the stone, the legionaries will build an outer defensive wall. Since beyond this point, the Tamēsis is no longer navigable, it is of great strategic interest to us for the protection of the Coln and Leach valley villas." Valdor paused and gazed around the intent faces, pleased that his chosen comrades hung on his every word. Satisfied, he continued, "Sir Pontus, you and your men will combat any raiding ship, but if there is more than one vessel, you will send for reinforcements here. Whatever happens, we'll prevent barbarians from attacking Corinium from the east and equally, no barbarians will attack Glevum from the Sabrina Estuary. I think that is all for today unless—"

"Aye, Sire, what will become of the rest of Britannia beyond the confines of Logres?" Primus asked.

"The situation in Gallia is grave," Valdor bowed his head and shook it slowly, "we have no reason to believe that Britannia will be different, Sir Primus, except for Logres, where anarchy will not prevail thanks to our resolution. Beyond our borders, we must be watchful and also rely on old and new alliances. That is why I intend to visit our neighbour, Bran ap Hefeydd very soon, to ensure our friendship and keep the western bank of Sabrina safe. It is too close to Glevum for comfort."

A week later, Valdor rode at the head of three *turmae* of cavalry to Venta Silurium, where, on approaching the walls, he could not fail but notice the grisly pecked skulls of the Scoti captives on their stakes. As they drew near, carrion crows flapped away, cawing their disapproval at the disturbance.

Valdor was anything but squeamish, but he was glad to enter the gate to renew acquaintance with the uncompromising Cambrian leader. His welcome was warm, so he decided not to make an issue of the treatment of the Scoti hostages. He was also pleased to accept Bran's exquisite mead and rapidly explained what was happening in Gallia.

"It means, friend, that our defences will soon be put to the test, especially by Germanic raiders, although I expect the Scoti and the Picts to attack too. About that, I wished to assure you that our bank of the great estuary will be held securely—"

"And ours, friend, Arthur."

Valdor stared hard at Bran ap Hefeydd, "Why do you call me Arthur, Bran?"

The Cymry chieftain smiled and said, "Here in Cymru, it is a princely name and one borne by my forebears. It is similar to Valdor and it suits me to call you by that name."

Valdor looked momentarily nonplussed, then remarked, "Ay, it suits me, too. I shall adopt the name. Let it be known that I am King Arthur."

Later, alone, Valdor could not decide whether he had adopted the name to please his ally or, because, as he suspected, it had a certain resonance to it and he liked it.

When he returned to Glevum, the alliance reinforced, he summoned his knights to the table and told them, "Henceforth, I renounce the name Valdor and will be known as Arthur. Spread the word among the men, King Arthur has spoken."

5

GLEVUM AND THE WESTERN ROMAN EMPIRE AD 409

KING ARTHUR USED HIS PERIODIC ASSEMBLIES AT THE Round Table to inform his knights of events elsewhere in the empire. Thus, he told them how Constantine III had extended his new empire to include Hispania. His triumph was short-lived and, as Arthur explained, "Constantine's control of his empire has fallen apart. Part of his force is in Hispania and unavailable for action in Gallia. Some of those in Gallia have been swayed against him by loyalist Roman generals."

"My friends, you may ask how does that affect us in Britannia? The Germans living west of the Rhine River have risen and those living east of the river crossed the ice into Gallia. We are fortunate here in Logres compared to the rest of Britannia, for we have secure boundaries and a well-fed and paid army under our command. Last year, Britannia suffered particularly severe Saxon raids and without sufficient troops, the other areas view the situation in Gallia with renewed alarm." The king paused and looked grave; reassured by the serious faces, he resumed. "It is our duty, fellow knights, to assure that the Saxons do not set foot in Logres. To achieve this, we must understand two things: first, there is no hope of relief under Constantine—indeed, there is talk that his magistrates will soon be expelled from Britannia.

Constantine has allowed the Saxons to raid and it is no surprise that Britons are arming themselves and preparing to revolt against—" Arthur broke off and stared, along with his knights, at a bloodied staggering figure who had entered his Hall without his permission.

"What is the meaning of this?" Arthur said, slowly rising and staring at the intruder who, on the point of fainting, swayed and grasped Sir Boduoc's shoulder. The knight stood and called, "Water! Someone, fetch the poor man water!"

Arthur nodded and said, "Seat him, good Sir Boduoc, in these exceptional circumstances an outsider may sit at the Round Table, only briefly, for the time required to utter his tale."

Liquid gulped from a beaker brought to his lips by Sir Maccus revived the man, a Briton by appearance, his pale countenance more pallid due to the loss of blood. Suddenly, the hall fell silent as he muttered his first words, "A monster, Sire! I've come to Glevum to seek aid for my village," he struggled for breath, but after a moment continued, "It is a fearsome, hideous creature, terrorising our village."

"A monster!" Primus exclaimed. "I would fight a monster!"

"Nay, Sire, I claim the right to slay the monster," cried Sir Geraint.

Primus was about to object but pressed his lips tight, breathing hard when his father laid a restraining hand on his arm.

"Sir Geraint, you will ride forth in the name of the Round Table, investigate and destroy this monster. Take a *turma* with you as support. But hold! Fellow, where is your village?"

The swooning man raised his head and said weakly, "Where the Alavna flows into the Uxella estuary."

"Go then, noble Sir Geraint, and may God be with you," Arthur said, inviting the assembled knights to pray.

The low evening sunlight sparkled on the water of the estuary, flashing and twinkling like the stars in the night sky. Geraint had not reached the village but halted his horse and, staring in disbelief, saw two eyes flashing in a monstrous snarling head rising out of a reed bed. The knight drew his sword and, turning to his decurion, said, "I'll go alone to fight the monster. Wait here and if it devours me, charge it with all of your men."

"Ay, lord, may God be with you," the decurion said, crossing himself and squinting fearfully against the strong, low sunlight made more dazzling by the reflections off the rippling water.

Geraint adjusted his helmet and urged his steed slowly forward. The animal was not restive, showing no fear of the monster as they drew nearer. A cloud passing in front of the sun had momentarily darkened the landscape, but once passed, driven by the stiff breeze that ruffled the plume of Geraint's helm, the sun illuminated the land, its rosy hues picking out details of the monster.

Geraint laughed with relief; the monster was nothing but a snarling head with bronze eyes carved into a tree trunk. It was clearly a pagan totem, for all he knew, one of the heathens' gods. They had placed it in the reed bed, he supposed, for two reasons: to drive it easily into the soft ground, and to disguise its tree trunk nature, the awesome head rising out of the reeds to inculcate terror into the simple-minded. From a distance, even he, a warrior with a lion heart, had been duped. At close quarters, his only desire was to find the pagans who had erected the totem... to slaughter them.

Still, he stared in wonder at the skilfully wrought whorls of the burnished bronze eyes, sparkling in the sunlight, crafted by a capable wright. His gaze slipped down to the snarling mouth where the chiselled pointed teeth left no doubt about the bloodlust of the heathen god. *How can anyone worship so savage a deity?* Geraint asked himself, forgetting for a moment the human sacrifices his forebears had perpetrated under the stern directions of the druids at the summer solstice.

Before urging his horse forward, Geraint signalled to his horsemen, who in response came to him at a gallop. "Look," Geraint said to his decurion, "the monster is only a glorified pole planted among the reeds. When we have slain its creators, we'll return to extract and burn it. For now, we must find the village and who or whatever is terrorising it."

The situation became clearer downstream, where they found a Saxon ship moored in the shallows.

"Lord, should we seize the vessel?" the decurion asked.

"Nay, we won't waste time and energy on it. It will be defended by few men. Once we have dealt with its crew on land, we'll return to fight them and sink their craft."

They continued downstream and, finding a woman struggling to lug her possessions wrapped and secured in a blanket while driving along two little children, Geraint called, "What is happening, woman?"

"Savages looted and burnt our village and, after fighting, my husband fled to seek aid from King Arthur."

"Your husband is alive and well. He completed his quest, so, we are here to fight the heathen. How many are there, do you know?"

The poor woman shook her head and her tear-filled eyes looked desperate, "At least a score," she murmured.

Geraint heard her and, turning to his men, said, "We can deal with a score of pagans. Woman, are your menfolk still fighting?"

"Ay, but they have lost good men."

"Quickly! We may be in time to save at least some of them!"

Without a backward glance, Geraint galloped his horse forward in the direction of the black smoke swirling over the settlement.

The sight of the small houses ablaze, pouring smoke, inflamed his wrath. "Over yonder!" he led the charge, "In the name of the Lord and King Arthur!" he yelled, sword aloft. The Saxons, engaged in fighting the villagers, armed only with agricultural implements, turned to face the greater menace, forgetting the fury of men who had seen their livelihood destroyed. From behind, pitchforks and timber axes drove into their unprotected backs as the Roman cavalry charged into their ranks, wreaking a similar devastation to that they had brought to this sleepy rural village. Geraint, possessed by rage and affronted by the pagan totem, slew five Saxons in rapid succession before pausing to inspect his surroundings.

He saw his men making short work of the raiders and raised his sword in salute to the cheering villagers who had retreated to the shelter of a forge, leaving the hot work of battle to the better-equipped Roman cavalrymen. The fight was almost over when Geraint spotted the enemy chieftain surrounded by his stalwarts. The knight charged, swatting aside a vicious axe blow and decapitating the warrior responsible, before slaying another as he arrived to face the tall, muscular leader.

Angered by the attempt to wound his horse with a long-handled axe, Geraint not only parried the blow but rendered the weapon unserviceable by hewing through the pole. The Saxon stared in disbelief at such a prodigious deflection and tossed the useless weapon to the ground, snatching another battleaxe from a comrade only in time to ward off Geraint's fierce downward strike. He may have thought he'd survived, but the battle was irretrievably lost and it was the decurion, from his left, who struck the death blow, denying Geraint the satisfaction of slaying the man who had crossed the North Sea to create widows and plunder.

Geraint calmed his panting horse and trotted him over to the cowering Britons.

"Friends, let it be known far and wide that anyone who dares invade King Arthur's kingdom will meet the same end!"

"God save King Arthur!" cried a man who Geraint took to be the village smith, judging by his robust build and soot-blackened face and arms. The villagers chorused the chant and from the small church emerged several women and children, *Thank God they are saved,* Geraint thought. *Now, to destroy their idol and ship.*

A sharp order to his men and the Romans rode away, the cheers of the Britons drowned by their hoofbeats. Soon, they arrived at the ship, dismounted and waded to the vessel, boarding despite fierce resistance from three desperate Saxons. The Romans were too many, so that those unhindered by the downward blows of the defenders managed to pull themselves on board. At that point, seeing their dire situation, two of the Saxons threw themselves into the river and struck out for the far bank. The other, remaining, stood defiantly to face Geraint, but was no match for the Roman knight, a former centurion. The victor, in his moment of triumph recognising the bravery of his adversary, ordered the body to be carried ashore. "Uproot the idol from the reed bed and lay it on the turf. Gather wood from yonder trees to build a pyre for this abomination and the corpse of this honourable opponent. Ah, before that, use their axe to smash a hole in the hull to sink this vessel."

The sun was setting when the reed bed was illuminated by red and orange flickering flames. Geraint waited to ensure that the pine totem caught. He watched, satisfied when a tongue of flame emerged from the serrated mouth of the idol and the bronze eyes distorted and melted in the searing heat. His mission completed as the dusk enfolded the Earth, Geraint wheeled his horse, about to lead the return to Glevum when he noticed movement at the edge of the woods: the woman and her children they had encountered before the battle. He rode over to them and, ignoring her thanks, lifted an infant girl onto his horse, whispering in her ear, "You have nothing more to fear, child. I'll take you to your father," and ordered his men to mount the woman and her other child. A horseman gathered the woman's blanket and they all headed swiftly back to Arthur's court where the woman immediately bathed her husband's wounds.

"Let this be a lesson to us," Arthur said. "My subjects shall not be victims of these raids in Logres. Tomorrow, we'll build a watchtower at the Uxella confluence and scout out other strategic points in all directions from Glevum. An early warning will save lives and secure our kingdom against such incursions. Geraint, I am well pleased with you. A monster! Harumph, stuff of folklore!" The king smiled under his curly chestnut beard, secretly pleased that no hideous monster stalked his land. He had needlessly fretted for Geraint's safety.

Elsewhere in Britannia, as he would later learn, courtyards rotted and lofty gates fell while villa roofs were stripped. Other halls stood empty, their red curved roofs shedding tiles, decay bringing them to the ground, piles of rubble testimony to the once proud edifices. Civilisation clung on in Logres but meanwhile, other kingdoms would rise and fall; none of them matching the splendour of the Roman Empire.

Principal among the threatened cities was Rome, as Arthur learnt later in 409. The heart of the empire was besieged by Visigoths and the population came close to starvation while Honorius, safe in inaccessible Ravenna, refused to negotiate. Elsewhere chaos reigned: General Gerontius, former supporter of Constantine, revolted and set up another usurper. Famine struck in Hispania, Gallia, and the Italian peninsula. Alaric came to terms with the Senate and installed a rival emperor: Priscus Attalus.

Meanwhile, at Arthur's peaceful and stable court, preparations were underway to celebrate Yuletide. In contrast, the Vandals, led by King Gunderic, crossed the Pyrenees into Hispania. They received land from the Romans, as foederati in Baetica. The Alans occupied lands in Lusitania and the Suebi controlled parts of Gallaecia. So, the Britons were right to quail; the barbarians were getting closer and Rome and Britannia ever weaker.

6

GLEVUM AND LINDINIS AD 410-411

King Arthur stood in front of his throne with a grim expression. He held aloft a document with an elaborate seal. "Brothers, what we have known for some time is now official," he shook the parchment above his head, "This is a letter from Emperor Honorius in Ravenna. Friends, Britannia no longer exists, that is the simple truth. I beg you not to mention the name again. From now on, we must consider kingdoms like Logres that are a reality. Britons appealed to the emperor to send troops to fend off invading barbarians, but in his reply, the emperor tells us in no uncertain terms that the British *civitates* must look to their own defence as his regime is still fighting usurpers in Gaul and trying to deal with the Visigoths who are in the far south of Italy."

Primus leapt to his feet and addressed his father, the king, "Sire, this is good news for you and for your knights gathered here. It means that this court cannot be considered illegitimate. We have the emperor's blessing to be independent and to cope with our territory as *we* see fit."

"Indeed, Sir Primus. As I said before, this is nothing new. It was clear three years ago when Constantine removed troops from these shores that we were alone to defend ourselves. We began to do so last year and will continue for as long as it takes to maintain control of the land that belongs to the Britons."

Sir Vindacius stood and asked to speak and, on royal assent, added, "It is clearer than ever that we must expand the frontiers of Logres to build strategic outposts that will thwart the inroads of the pagans. Sooner or later, the occasional raiding craft will give way to roving warbands, and we must be ready to defeat them from a position of strength."

"Well said, Sir Vindacius," Arthur boomed, "and to do so, we should draw upon the wisdom of the ancients. Our forefathers built fortresses that remain on the hills of our fair land. We must identify and reinforce them. I assign the task of heading out on this quest to the south-west to Sir Vindacius and two others of our number. Who will accompany him?"

"I, lord!" cried Sir Geraint, "For my home was in Devon before I came to Glevum and I know some fitting places."

"So be it!"

"And I, Sire," said Sir Belalucius, "Since I have family in Dumnonia and know Cornwall well."

"You three, choose the places and we shall arrange for them to become impregnable strongholds. May God guide you!"

Shortly afterwards, Sir Segovax caught Primus by the arm, "Primus, my friend, I should have spoken, for I know a place most suitable in the land of the Durotriges. Will you come with me? The military road runs straight from Corinium to Lindinis, their capital."

"I will come willingly, but only if I have my father's permission, remember our oath."

"Ay, it goes without saying."

Primus hastened to his father and explained Segovax's idea.

"Mmm. The territory of the Durotriges? That would give us a stronghold on their eastern frontier. It is a valuable territory, for salt production is important there, not to mention lead from the Mendip mines."

"Those mines still yield silver, father. Also, Lindinis is linked to Corinium by the Fosse Way, which proceeds across country as far as Lindum Colonia."

"You have my blessing, Primus, and if the site is as good as our noble Sir Segovax says, I want you to ride back and fetch me. I rely on your opinion."

The two knights rode out from Glevum and took the Fosse Way out of Corinium as planned. After a gentle ride of less than two hours, they approached the *civitas* of the Durotriges. Primus cast a military eye over the stone-walled fort guarding the crossing of the Fosse Way and the River Yeo. The first impact came from the thriving industrial area of the suburbs, where iron, glass, and bone working and pottery production were among the activities. These workshops gave way to agricultural plots within the town, followed by private homes of owners rich enough to install fine mosaic floors, made by craftsmen from Corinium. Such wealth explained why the *civitas* was surrounded by stone walls and a defensive bank and ditch with stone gateways, erected less than a century before—it had become the only walled town in the territory of the Durotriges other than Durnovaria.

"We should seek a tavern to spend the night," Sir Segovax suggested.

"Nay, we were both centurions, we can rightfully claim a bed in the barracks. I'd like to see the state of the garrison. But hark! Can we not arrive at your hillfort before nightfall?"

"It's possible, Primus, but bear in mind the terrain; true, the hill is only eight miles to the east, but the ground will be damp—the name *Lindinis* says it all, it means *soggy ground*—so, the going will be slow across such land. It's waterlogged at certain times of year. Where do you suppose we'd sleep on that windy hillfort?"

"You are right, let's seek hospitality at the fort by the river."

The garrison was commanded by a legate who, by his own admission, was formerly a centurion, but had adopted the superior rank at his men's insistence. "We no longer receive orders from Rome."

He was mightily interested to learn about King Arthur's court at Glevum. "So, you are *equites* and serve the King of Logres? I've heard my men say that Arthur is the only hope for Britannia."

"The name is now meaningless, Legate, but Arthur is my father and sworn to protect the Britons. We also prefer the name *knights* to *equites*."

"My garrison is depleted; we'd have difficulty defending ourselves against the Scoti or the Saxons."

"Hence our quest, Legate. I'll confide in you. We have come to survey the ancient fortress some miles to the east. We need to see if it could be made into a stronghold for King Arthur."

"Ah, you mean Cador's Hill. It's about eight miles from here. Do you know, I've often thought that it would make an excellent Roman fortress. The ancients knew how to choose their defensive sites. I hope you'll agree, Sir Primus, it will be a comfort to have your troops nearby."

"We'll visit it early tomorrow, I'll let you know because we'll take the Fosse Way on our return, rather than strike out across country."

"Ay, that makes sense."

The following morning, refreshed after a deep sleep, the two knights set off for their destination. Sir Segovax's words proved correct, the going was soft and slow, made worse in places by them having to dismount as their horses' hoofs sank into the ground beyond the fetlocks.

With the sun overhead and the going easier, Primus halted and pointed, "In the name of the Blessed Virgin, yon hill must be at least five hundred feet above this level ground!"

"Ay, rest assured that it is so, our horses will have a stiff climb ahead."

The sturdy creatures plodded uphill until Primus halted again. "We'll leave the horses here, Segovax. I'll not risk the poor beast's legs slithering down such a slope." Indeed, the ditch ahead posed a challenge to the men. "The ancients must have spent years digging out this fosse! And to think, they most likely did it with animal bones: a shoulder blade for a shovel and an antler for a pick!" he said, in wonder.

"It runs for a mile around the whole summit," his companion replied.

They panted up the terraced earthwork banks and crossed further ditches. Primus counted four ramparts and his military sense told him that with a timber palisade, the hillfort would be close to impregnable.

The comrades gazed in awe at the view that stretched for miles in every direction.

"Impossible to attack by surprise," Primus murmured, more to himself.

"Do you think King Arthur will like my choice of hill?"

Primus laughed sarcastically, "*Your* choice, good Sir Segovax? Unless you lived many centuries ago and have come back to haunt me..."

His companion laughed good-naturedly, "You know what I mean!"

"There's only one way to find out. The king commanded me to fetch him if my reaction was favourable. He said he'd rely on my opinion. Well, my response is more than favourable. To the horses!"

Before returning to Glevum, they stopped for refreshment and to report to the legate at the Lindinis fort.

"Legate, when we return with the king, we'll stop here again and present you to him. I'm sure that the king will appreciate the hillfort. What did you say its name is?"

"The locals call it Cador's Hill, but I've heard it's called after the Celtic god Camul, just like Camolodunum where I was once based."

"If all goes well, we'll see you on the morrow or the day after."

Impressed by his two knights' account of the hillfort, King Arthur agreed to ride to Lindinis, where he was given a throaty reception by the garrison, cheering and chanting his name.

In the legate's larder hung a swan that had been there for three days. Legate Galenus, a tall, broad-shouldered officer with brindled brown hair—some curls were entirely grey—summoned a cook and ordered the bird to be plucked and roasted. "I believe swan's meat is fit for a king, Sire, if only I could offer you a decent wine, for I fear the only decent beverage is the local twice-brewed ale."

"That will be most acceptable, will it not, Primus? There was a time, Legate, that I preferred ale to wine. While we await the meal, tell me about your career and something about yon hillfort."

The legate was happy to oblige and when he spoke about his experiences on Hadrian's Wall and, in particular, about a term spent at the Banna Fort as part of the *Cohors I Aelia Dacorum*, he spoke in condemnatory terms about the praefectus commandant of the fort, Crispinus, who killed himself to avoid arrest, but then, he explained, a certain Valdor took his place and the difference was like the moon and the sun. "Praefectus Valdor was the best commander I've ever served under; he restored discipline and treated us well—"

The legate broke off and stared hard at Arthur, who had spluttered over his ale, recognition fighting with denial.

"Ay, it was my father, the king," Primus grinned. "He is no longer Praefectus Valdor, but King Arthur!"

"Sire, you may count on me and my men to serve you faithfully. I was a simple decurion back then, but I'll never forget how you spared my comrade from the death sentence he did his best to earn."

"How curious we should meet again under these circumstances, Legate. I take it to be a sign from God that I am on the correct path."

They talked about the hillfort and Arthur grew ever more convinced that Segovax's choice was inspired, and this before seeing it and assessing the site for himself.

The following day, the steep climb impressed the king, but his companions played the part of experienced surveyors and minimised what still remained an arduous approach.

When Arthur scanned the landscape below the stronghold, he raised his arms and praised the heavens. "This place is perfect!" he told a delighted Segovax "and here in the centre, we'll build..." the king took twenty-two measured strides, turned sharply and took another eleven. "...a Great Hall, measuring sixty-six feet by thirty-three. Timber ramparts and a stone gateway will protect my castle. Primus, what did you say this place is called?"

"Galenus said the locals call it Cador's Hill, but he'd heard it called after the Celtic god Camul, just like Camolodunum where he was once based."

"Nay!" cried Arthur, "I'll not name my castle after a pagan god; I shall pray for illumination."

He knelt and the fresh breeze ruffled the hair crowning his bowed head. He stayed in this position for some time as Primus and Segovax exchanged glances.

"What's wrong with Cador's Hill?" Primus whispered and his comrade shrugged.

"I have it," Arthur shouted jubilantly, "The Holy Spirit inspires me! We'll call this place *Camelot,* a concession to the Celts but, above all, in these times of darkness, we need a place of light that captures the spirit of Lot, whose righteousness led him to leave Sodom."

"Father, the name has a pleasant chime; we'll erect a Hall fit for a king, here at Camelot!"

7

AD 411-412

King Arthur quickly realised that Constantine III had left Britannia manned by boys and retired veterans. He needed urgent action, so he sent riders to all the towns of Logres to find men willing to enrol in his army. The king was astonished at the positive response. Within days he ordered Primus and Sir Vindalus to train hundreds of men to ride and fight in formation. The ruler looked on with a satisfied smile as the Britons showed signs of shaping up into a formidable force. It had to be remembered that the Britons were hampered by a lack of a tradition of warfare, lost over four centuries of mostly stable Roman rule. Weapons amongst the civilian population had been routinely banned by the Roman state. Arthur wondered whether what he was seeing was some kind of vestigial memory.

The training coincided with the new work on the hilltop forts. His knights had surveyed the territories of the Dobunni, Durotriges and Dumnonii tribes and found many such strongholds, so they chose only three with enormous potential and each within easy reach of Camelot. Arthur felt sure he could transfer his court to Camelot before 411 slipped into 412. His confidence was based on the completion of the timber hall in the centre of the fortress. Only some days before, he had sent skilled woodcarvers to embellish the uprights with carvings of religious motifs, although he had requested a head with his likeness over the main entrance. The wooden head would be adorned with a crown painted gold, something he never wore but was considering.

Sir Belalucius enthused about a fortress called *Rugan beorh* in the native tongue, explaining to the king that it meant 'rough hill'. This particular hill stood among the others of the Quantocks and, although it was smaller than most, had a triangular shape over four acres, but boasted a tunnel that gave safe access to a nearby spring, meaning that, if necessary, the stronghold could resist a lengthy siege.

To the north of the territory, overlooking the *Môr Hafren*, known as *the Abora Channel* to the Romans, and standing 358 feet above that water boundary, was a stronghold built by the Britons. This construction, therefore, was one of the most recent of its kind and rapidly occupied by the Romans after the invasion of Britannia. Bordered on the north and west sides by steep cliffs dropping to the sea, its south side was protected by a single rampart and ditch and the level eastern approach by two ramparts and five ditches. From the interior of the stronghold, the views extended along the Channel, meaning that raiders from Hibernia—the Scoti—could be easily seen. Also, the eye could sweep over the Black Mountains, the Mendip Hills, Dunkery Beacon, Sand Point and even into Cambria. A curious feature that Sir Belalucius waxed lyrical about to his king were the triangular platforms on the slopes around the fort. "Sire, I am informed that they served the Britons as bases for their slingers. The apexes are flush with the slope and the front faces some five and a half feet above the hillside. We could use them for our javelin throwers in case of attack."

"How high are the ramparts, good Sir Belalucius?"

"From the bottom of the ditch, Sire, I estimate thirty-five feet. A weakness might have been that the three-foot-deep walls are dry-laid, but they have been protected by four-foot-thick rubble barriers. Anyone trying to remove the rubble would be under attack from above."

"Most satisfactory. We shall move a garrison there. I congratulate you both on your choices." He beamed from Sir Geraint to his comrade.

Their third and final choice, farther along the same Abora channel on the land of the Dobunni, was astonishingly dominant, standing 1,115 feet above the sea on an easterly spur of a hill in the Quantocks. It lay over a six-acre site and dominated the valley of the Uxella. As Arthur pointed out, "With these four fortresses actively manned, any warbands in the area will be lured into entrapment and swiftly defeated."

As good as his word, within the month, the newly trained Britons were dispatched to the three strongholds. They were expected to build their quarters and make any necessary repairs to the existing structure.

The king was ready to transfer his court to Camelot, but his queen refused to leave her midwifery in Corinium. "But Arthur, I am the most experienced midwife and the women respect and love me. It's a delicate matter and a question of trust. How can I leave Corinium?"

"There is no garrison in the city and these isles are constantly threatened. A queen should be beside her husband in a safe place." As he spoke, he saw the sorrow and desperation in her face. Despite her commitment to the Britons and often interrupted nights, Gosvintha had kept her youthful appearance and willowy silhouette. He loved her deeply and, although he would struggle with the separation, he wanted to give her everything she desired.

"Very well, this is what we will do. I'll send my noblest and most trusted knight, Sir Regalis, to watch over you. He'll ensure you come to Camelot if there is any danger of barbarians attacking the city."

The queen merely smiled, *noblest and most trusted* she thought and silently added, *ay, and the most handsome*, but immediately felt ashamed of herself. Instead, she said, "Oh, husband, thank you for understanding the importance of my work. Women come, sometimes in the most difficult circumstances from miles around. The babes have every chance of survival when they come to me. If only you could see their big eyes as soon as they are born and their perfect little hands and feet! You should see the love in the faces of the mothers—Arthur, being queen is nothing compared to the joy of helping to bring new life into the world!" She rushed to embrace and kiss him.

"It is decided then. We leave for Camelot on the morrow. I shall expect to see you at the Easter festivities—that is a command, Gosvintha, and no number of pregnant Britons will keep you from attending. I'll inform Sir Regalis."

King Arthur left Glevum stronger than he had found it; otherwise, he had no regrets, for his overall scheme for protecting Logres was taking shape. His eyes were turned to the north for the next stage of his plan. Before he truly settled in Camelot, he would travel to Eboracum where he would ensure Logres made alliances to increase the safety of his kingdom.

After a wearisome journey to the banks of the Ouse, Arthur was dismayed to see how the once-thriving city had declined. Vulnerable thanks to the river artery that had made it prosper, the city now lay abandoned by its people. The king entered the principia to meet the dux, who greeted him warmly. The high-ranking official, whose lineaments revealed him to be as Celtic as his name, Coel Hen, suggested. His forthright speech pleased Arthur, who recognised a fellow warrior and kindred spirit. The flashing blue eyes fixed on his visitor as he said with a hint of bitterness, "My title is *Dux Britanniarum*, King Arthur, but it is meaningless and I prefer to be known as the Prefect of Valentia Province. That reflects the work I do to keep the province in a strong protective grip. The truth is, Rome has no further bearing on affairs in Britannia. Honorius has washed his hands of us and the news will not have reached you yet in Glevum, but a usurper Jovinus has taken control of Gaul and is menacing Honorius; meanwhile, another self-proclaimed emperor has revolted in Africa and has cut off grain supplies to Rome. Honorius has condemned this man, Heraclianus, to death. I say we are fortunate to be on the edge of the empire, but we must keep a watchful eye on our enemies. You can rely on my support if needed, King Arthur."

"I thank you, my friend, but what can you say about the Picts?"

"North of the Wall, lies the Kingdom of Guotodin, firmly in the hands of the Votadini. They control the region around the start of the Firth of Forth to the eastern end of the Antonine Wall under Ceneu ap Coel."

"Ap Coel? Your son, then?"

Coel smiled, "Ay, which is why any friend of mine is a friend of his. You need have no fear for that territory, which acts as a barrier against Pictish invasions. If anything, Arthur, you should travel to Strathclyde, where Ceretic Guletic holds the western half of the Antonine Wall down to Cumbria. His stronghold is at Dun Breaton. He is reputed to have a fiery temper, but I dare say you'll strike an agreement with him if you ignore his rude ways."

"I know Cumbria well from my younger days," Arthur said, "A good night's rest and we'll set out tomorrow."

"And a good meal, my friend," Coel Hen linked arms with Arthur and steered him to his quarters. Left alone, Arthur dropped gratefully onto a soft bed and soon sank into restorative sleep. When he awoke to the discreet cough of a servant, he shook his befuddled head, wondering where he was. The servant informed him that the prefect expected him at his table soon, for it was now evening.

As he washed his face in cold water, Arthur smiled, his scheme to create alliances in the north was two-thirds complete. The following day would prove decisive after another long journey. A good meal now would build up his strength, but before going to the table, he needed to be more presentable.

"Is there a barber, who can shave me?" he asked the servant.

"Ay, lord, I'll send him at once."

The barber slave used an ancient razor. It was a half-moon instrument called a *novacula* made of tempered iron that he sharpened on a grindstone. To rub off stubble, he used a pumice stone.

When the slave finished shaving, Arthur's face was a deep red from the scraping, but that would soon pass with another splash of cold water. The next torture, which made the slave smile secretly, was the use of a pair of tweezers to pluck out, one by one, the hairs around his eyebrows and neck. Arthur winced, but the slave was an expert and Arthur paid a lot of attention to his appearance and care of his body. The journey had taxed him, but now after a deep sleep and his shave, he felt ready to reappear before his host.

Coel Hen was pleased to announce that three days before, he had slain the deer now set before them in a hunt out on the moors to the north of the city. Arthur was partial to venison and also to the excellent imported red wine.

"Soon, it will be a problem to import produce from Gallia, for whenever I see the blue-painted *speculatores* of the *Classis Britannica*, I realise that they are manned by experienced crews of enlisted Anglo-Saxon ship-folk, on the watch for sea-borne intrusions of Saxons from their continental homelands. Can we really expect them to slaughter their own kind and deliver the merchandise we so desperately need?" Coel sighed and shook his head, unable to disguise his regret for better past days.

"We can but hope and pray for stability overseas, who knows what new kingdoms will spring up to replace the Roman sway?" Arthur could not foretell the future, but he was determined to consolidate in the present as he explained to Coel. "If we can hold onto the last vestiges of Roman civilisation and make our kingdoms more secure, we shall have accomplished a fine enterprise, my friend. Mmm, your venison is delicious!"

The following morning, Arthur, with his escort, set out along the roads well known to him from his youthful exploits, which took him well into Cumbria and to the dramatically sited Mediobogdum fort overlooking the Alauna Valley. The commandant explained that the fort was manned principally by Britons and Roman veterans, many of whom had served on Hadrian's Wall and were now more or less retired from active service, as indeed he, a veteran centurion, had found safety and peace in this superb setting.

"Indeed, your location can compete for beauty with my fortress at Camelot, Centurion," Arthur said appreciatively. "But will you be able to hold it against a hostile enemy?"

"We repelled the Picts three summers ago, but with help from a detachment from Glannoventa. Since then, we have been untroubled, although I and my men defeated a band of Britons who had turned to banditry some months ago. We try to keep the area safe for travellers on their way to and from the coast."

"On the morrow we are headed for Glannoventa and thence to Strathclyde," Arthur said, wondering whether the journey might be more arduous than he'd imagined.

He need not have worried, and when the commandant of Glannoventa Fort suggested avoiding the wearying overland march to Dun Breaton by taking a ship around the *Novantarum Promontorium* and into the Clota Estuary, where the court of Ceretic Guletic overlooked the north bank of the river Clota.

During the voyage, Arthur and his men kept their eyes peeled for pirate ships and more than one, in his heart, was convinced they would not reach their destination without a fight, but in reality, although they saw some distant vessels, the journey proved uneventful. There was, though, a moment when Arthur felt they would be attacked by a sea monster. A large shape rose from the depths, leapt out of the sea and plunged back down displaying a huge fan-shaped tail fin. Their captain laughed at the quaking men, "Yon's harmless enough, it's nought but a whale!" Many sighs of relief greeted these words and the gigantic mammal was quickly forgotten.

At the dock, Arthur received information about how to reach Ceretic's stronghold. It was a stiff climb up a rocky promontory and was known as *the fort of the Britons*. Again, the view over the river was spectacular and, Arthur complimented his host for the choice of location.

"It is essential to keep the seaways under observation, King Arthur, for we have the Scoti and the Picts to look out for and I defy any of them to besiege this fortress and live to tell the tale!"

"I can see that King Ceretic, and know you that I have come to befriend the right man."

"I extend the hand of friendship willingly, having heard of your remarkable exploits. They say that you have never lost a battle."

"It's true, but there was a close-run affair once—" he entertained his new friend with an account of a battle fought many years before.

"Ay, the Hibernian Scoti are formidable fighters, sure enough, which is why we must prevent them from settling in Cumbria or worse, here in Strathclyde."

"Or in Dumnonia or in Cambria," Arthur laughed. "If we can unite to destroy them so severely, it will be a task well done, but the truth is that you also have the Picts to contend with and I have the Frisians, Angles, Jutes and Saxons. The latest news that the Visigoths have settled in Gallia is hardly encouraging. Friend, Ceretic, give me your hand and we'll stand firm alone, but together when needed."

The two men clasped hands and grinned in friendship. Arthur's visit to the north had borne rich fruit.

8

VENTA SILURIUM AND CAMELOT AD 413

KING BRAN AP HEFEYDD, AT A TIME OF MUCH HEARTACHE and self-doubt, consumed several beakers of his strong ale—too much—and he fell into a deep and troubling sleep, in which he dreamt that a wizened old man stood before his throne.

Unsure of whether he was awake or still in a dream, the king shook his head, rubbed his eyes, stared hard at his visitor and his expression lit up in a broad grin.

"You can change disguise as many times as you like, Myrddin Wyllt, but I shall always recognise you!"

"Only if I want you to, Sire," the descendant of a long line of Druids cackled and shape-shifted into a young boy. "Now, explain why you wanted to see me so very much, my lord."

"It's true I did, but as I recall, I did not send for you, Myrddin."

"Not necessary, for I see into the future and saw that you yearned for my presence."

"Correct, but you didn't take the trouble to find out why," the king grumbled.

Merlin's boyish face grew wrathful and he changed into a man of some thirty winters, angrily pointing at the king, his deep voice resonating menacingly, "Do not provoke me, Lord of Venta Silurium, or you'll know what it is to live as a toad!"

King Bran wilted under the wrathful gaze and had no doubt that the wizard would fulfil his threat if further provoked, so he blurted a humble apology and explained.

"The Kingdom of Logres is ruled by King Arthur, and if my own kingdom is to be saved, I need you to visit him and strengthen his arm against the Saxon invaders. Was it not you, Myrddin, who foresaw that the white dragon would conquer the red?"

"Ay, it was, and while my powers are prodigious, I cannot change the tide of the future, however," he chuckled at his wittiness, "I can divert the waters somewhat. Where can I find this Arthur?"

"Use your famous—" the words died on his lips, as Myrddin's finger pointed at him again, "*er*, they say he has made his court at Camelot in the territory of the Dobunni."

"Then, there shall I go—" before the sentence finished, in a puff of smoke, Myrddin vanished.

Bran inspected himself to ensure there was nothing toadlike about his appearance and sighed with relief.

Myrddin reappeared in his handsome thirty-year-old form beside a lake deep in a forest and startled, looked around. "This cannot be Camelot," he spoke aloud.

"Indeed, it is not," spoke a sweet, lilting voice.

He spun around and his eyes settled on a beautiful half-naked faery. "Who are you, who has interfered with my magic?" he said, tempering his anger in the face of such beauty.

"I confess my interference, Myrddin Wyllt, or rather, the meddling of the Norns. I am known as the Lady of the Lake. So, I know your purpose here and also that you will fall in love with me, but there is a price you must pay!" She wove her hands in front of her, wiggling her long fingers.

"What the—" Myrddin found himself bound by a magic web to a tree trunk. In vain, he uttered spells to free himself.

"No use fighting the Norns, Myrddin Wyllt, their magic is more powerful than yours and they predicted that in exchange for my love, you would teach me all you know of magic."

"If this is true—and I recognise that I am smitten—I am helpless."

An impish smile crossed her elfin features. She approached him and gently kissed his lips. "Wait!" she cried in a falsetto voice, although he had no other choice, and she vanished below the surface of the lake. Reappearing moments later, she bore a magnificent shining sword.

Again, she waved her hands and the invisible web disappeared, releasing the wizard. "Here, you may not take this, but hold it in both hands and concentrate, for you must transform Arthur's sword to be identical, although he will not know it. This sword is named Excalibur and has invincible properties." She laid it in Myrddin's outstretched palms. His brow furrowed and he murmured a spell in a language older than the lake.

"Good," she snatched the sword back and hurled it into the placid water where, with a loud splash, it sank into the depths. "We'll meet again, soon, Myrddin, for you cannot resist the allure of the Lady of the Lake," she smiled wickedly, and he knew she was right. "Now go! Go to Camelot!"

When he looked around, once again, he was not in Camelot, but in another part of the same forest. Moments later, he heard hoofbeats, "Wretched woman!" he grumbled, "What now?" A deer broke cover and raced past him, followed by a knight on a charger, who hurled a javelin with deadly accuracy. The deer squealed and fell, mortally wounded. Arthur reined in and stared at the unknown man, so deep in the forest. "Who are you?" the king demanded brusquely.

"One whose destiny is interwoven with yours," came the curt reply. "Now," the hypnotic eyes of the wizard held Arthur's, "give me your sword. I'll put the poor beast out of its agony." Arthur obeyed since he could not resist the sway of the stranger. He drew his sword and tamely handed it to Myrddin, who hurried over to the agonised deer and slit its throat. He stood for a moment over the prey as if in prayer, but, in reality, he was transforming the sword into Excalibur. Satisfied, he strode back to Arthur, who took the sword and noticed first, the exquisite hilt and new, fine balance. "W-what—" he stuttered, but never finished because Myrddin had erased all memory of him handing his sword over and replaced it with joyous acceptance of the 'new' weapon. Without further ado, Arthur sheathed his sword and asked, "So, stranger, who are you and what did you mean about our interlaced destiny?"

"I'm a seer who King Bran ap Hefeydd sent to help you wage war against Saxon invaders."

"How can you help me, seer?"

"Since I can read the future, I'll counsel you. The proof is, I knew where to find you and within moments your knights will arrive here."

"Ha!" scoffed Arthur, "that takes no seer! I, too, hear their approaching hoofbeats."

"Ay, but it doesn't explain how I knew where to find you,"—which was something, in truth, he found hard to explain himself. *Was it the Lady of the Lake or the Norns?*

"Sire, are you alright?" exclaimed Sir Eppilus, gazing suspiciously at Myrddin.

"Ay, this is my new friend and counsellor, although I do not know your name, yet, fellow."

"I am Myrddin Wyllt, and come from Venta Silurium, the court of King Bran."

"Help my counsellor onto your horse, while I collect my deer."

"I need no horse, for I shall be in Camelot before you," said Myrddin mysteriously and before the king's disbelieving eyes, vanished.

"Where did he go?" Arthur exclaimed and looked at the other three knights.

"I don't know," each muttered and shrugged.

When Arthur returned to Camelot and entered his Hall, empty but for the figure of Myrddin occupying the one seat at the Round Table without a name, left vacant until someone worthy should claim it.

"Do you then claim the empty seat?" Arthur asked.

He received no reply because the seer's head was tilted back and his eyes glazed as one in a trance. Suddenly, an ethereal voice piped from the stranger's throat:

> *"I behold what common men cannot—*
> *What is to become in after times,*
> *Beheld only by those whose soul*
> *Harbour the light and dissolve the mist*
> *Shrouding mortal sight. And yet,*
> *I can see dimly, as the Pleiades*
> *Appear to come and go and hide*
> *Behind the veil of the rising sun."*

Arthur gaped at this strange utterance, "Do you then pretend to be a prophet, Myrddin?"

Again, the seer refused to answer or could not because a howl issued from his throat like a starved wolf greeting the moon. "Hooowww!

Arthur is the one true king who will unite the lands and bring magic back to Albion."

Myrddin's eyes cleared and he sat upright, peered at the king and asked, "What did I say, for I have no memory of it?"

Arthur explained and added, "but first I asked you if you had the gift of prophecy. You did not reply."

"What do you think, great-grandson of Valdor?"

Arthur started, few people knew that and he wondered how a seer from Cambria could possibly know his lineage, so carefully concealed in the present, unless, of course, he was what he claimed to be. Arthur would wish it so since in his trance the prophet had named him as *the one true king*— precisely what Arthur yearned to be—the one to *unite the lands*. But as he reflected on this, Myrddin's eyes rolled back so that only the whites could be seen, and with a guttural *"aaargh!"* spoke in a sing-song voice, *"Conflict will continue until arises the Boar of Somerset who will bring peace and harmony to this land. He will be the noblest king and tales of his exploits will be as meat and drink to storytellers who relate them in ages to come."*

Arthur waited patiently until the trance passed and Myrddin's eyes settled on his perplexed face.

"What is it, Arthur?"

"Who is the Boar of Somerset?"

A thin smile played at the corner of the seer's mouth, "Of course, you cannot know that, for Somerset is the future name, given by the Saxons to this territory where Camelot stands—"

"The Saxons, then, will conquer the land of the Dobunni?" Arthur asked fearfully.

"Ay, but not in your lifetime, nor for many centuries."

"But is it true, what you said, that *the Boar of Somerset who will bring peace and harmony to this land* and if so, who is the Boar of Somerset?"

Myrddin laughed heartily and pointed to the king, "Do you doubt my prophecy? *You*, Arthur, are he, and that is why I am here."

Arthur sat thoughtfully for some time and finally said, "What must I do differently to achieve such fame, and why *boar?*"

"Do what you have set out to do. If you are about to misstep, I shall advise you. Boar? That creature is a symbol of courage and ferocity and may mean war in some ways."

For a while, they sat in uncomfortable silence: the king awed by the words of the seer and Myrddin discouraged by Arthur's diffidence. Suddenly, the wizard rubbed his eyes and in a strange voice said, "These are difficult times, Arthur," from which the king realised that he had not slipped again into a trance, "the Moon's chariot shall run amok in the Zodiac; the Pleiades will burst into tears. None of these will return to the duty expected of it."

Arthur leapt to his feet, "Enough! I can make no sense of your words. It's a fact that we live in troubled times, but why should that trouble the heavens? I shall go to my chapel and pray for enlightenment. God will guide my actions. Why should I heed the words of a Cambrian seer?"

Myrddin sighed heavily and muttered, "And yet you will!" Arthur heard this as he walked away, but did not turn. Instead, in the chapel on his knees, he asked for guidance, murmuring, I liked some of his prophecies, but if I believe one, I must believe all. Guide me, Lord, for as king I must lead my people in righteousness and defeat the pagans who threaten our land." He closed his eyes and waited in stillness but he could not settle his overactive mind: *peace and harmony to the land through conquest? Ay, it's possible but only victory will ensure them for my people.* He looked up at a crucifix hanging above the altar. "Your greatest defeat was your greatest victory, was it not, Lord Jesus? You, however, defeated death and rose again. If I die, I'll not arise." He waited a long time in silence and nothing came to him. In desperation, he said, "Lord, I beg you, send me a sign that will tell me what I must do. Amen." He recited the Pater Noster and rose, bowed and left the chapel, where he encountered his son, Primus.

"Father, some while ago, I was in the chapel and met with a strange sensation while praying. I need a strong drink after what I have seen."

"Come then, and tell me everything."

Father and son strode to the refectory where Arthur called for a flagon of his best ale and two glass cups, which he kept for special banquets. He poured the double-brewed ale and looked at Primus, "I, too, have something disturbing to relate, my son. But right enough, you must speak first."

Primus took a deep breath and began, "After I heard that you'd gone hunting, I went into the chapel and prayed for your safety. In a vision, I, too, rode into the forest alone to chance my arm. I strayed off my usual trail, lured by a tumult of squeals and howls. When I came to a clearing, father, there was a lone boar fighting a pack of wolves. I counted seven grey wolves, snapping and snarling and biting that boar, but although sorely wounded and outnumbered, it fought so courageously and gored one wolf after another until they fled and the poor beast stood alone. I could have slaughtered it with my spear and it stared at me as if it knew, but, father, how could I slay so noble a fighter? We stared at each other and I spoke gently to it, encouraging it to go away and lick its wounds. Father? Are you following me? What can the vision mean?"

"Hey, what? Oh, ay, God has spoken through you, Primus. He has answered my prayer. Do you know, I am a boar and the wolves are the Saxons. I, too, will triumph even at great personal cost."

"You, a boar, father? What are you saying?"

"Seers speak in strange riddles, my boy, and what I had to tell you is that we have a prophet come to live and counsel us at court. His name is Myrddin from Cambria and he has revealed much of interest to me today. You have just given me confirmation of his greatest prophecy. Primus, we will save Logres and bring peace and harmony to this land."

"I would meet with him, maybe he can tell me my future, too, father."

"You will meet him on the morrow, when the knights gather at the Round Table, for he will take the vacant seat."

"The one between Sir Senicus and Sir Dias?"

"Ay, that one, but there will still be an empty seat."

"How so?"

Arthur felt a strange premonition, but replied, "Sir Regalis is away in Corinium championing your mother."

"Father, what ails you?"

"Ah, nothing, but I have just thought of a matter I must raise with the seer. I value his gifts."

9

CAMELOT AND CAMBRIA AD 413

The knights sat at the Round Table, patiently awaiting the arrival of the king. Myrddin chatted with Primus and ignored the curious stares. He had changed aspect again, preferring to vaunt a long white beard on the grounds that it lent him a certain *gravitas* for this first encounter with the knights. When Arthur arrived, he glanced twice at the wizard-cum-prophet, surprised by this change of appearance. Then, he proceeded to introduce the newcomer.

"Fellow knights, we have a newcomer in our midst, it is Myrddin Wyllt, whose counsel I'll lean on. Welcome him among us, for he is also a seer. Indeed, Myrddin, I wish to ask you what will happen in the Empire in the immediate years to come?"

"I fail to see how what happens abroad will affect Logres, but since you put me to the test..."

He sat silently for some minutes so that the doubters at the table began to smile and exchange glances. Suddenly, in a strange, portentous voice, he proclaimed, "Later this year, the usurper will invade with a large army. Honorius will tremble, but his generals will triumph in Umbria. The emperor's envoys follow Heraclianus to Carthage and leave him lying in a pool of blood." Now the white-bearded seer had their rapt attention, especially when he screamed, "Aaargh! More blood! Honorius will receive the heads of Jovinius and his brother in Ravenna, the Visigoths will capture and behead them." He slumped back in his chair and a faraway gaze changed his expression into a trance-like state.

"That should be the fate of all usurpers," said Arthur, reflecting on how he had refused to become one and his role as King of Logres was respondent to Honorius' letter ordering Britons to defend themselves. His reflections did not last long because Myrddin spoke again, "Next year, the half-sister of Honorius will wed with the King of the Visigoths, Ataulf, and great festivities will follow for him and his bride, Gallia Placidia. Constantius will campaign in Gaul against the Visigoths, who will blockade the ports. The year after, Constantius will drive the Visigoths out of Gaul. And more blood!" Myrddin's beard trembled and he laid his hands on the table while his eyes roved, but stared unseeingly, around the room.

The knights sat silently in awe as they contemplated the future. What blood had the prophet foreseen? They did not have long to wait to discover the answer.

"Aaargh! Alas, poor Ataulf! As he takes his bath, he is slain; the water turns crimson. Sigeric succeeds him, but what a short reign! Only seven days before he, too, is murdered. But fear not, friends; Wallia, Ataulf's brother, makes peace with Honorius in exchange for six hundred thousand measures of grain. The bold knight has to choose between his duty to the king and the love of his heart."

Perplexed at this riddle, the knights exchanged glances. Everything had been clear up to this point. Was the prophet referring to Queen Gallia Placidia, so swiftly and cruelly widowed? Every knight at the table thought so, except King Arthur, who sat pale and speechless until he summarised.

"Thank you, Myrddin. As we can see, events overseas in the next few years have little bearing upon our land, although we may face shortages on some imported goods while the Visigoths blockade the ports of Gallia. Still, that warlike people will not invade these islands. We have to deal with the boat people, as and when they come. Our very own seer will advise us. As you see, noble knights, our newest member of the Round Table is a great asset to Camelot."

Myrddin bowed his head slightly in the direction of the king but frowned at the anxious face staring back hard at him.

The knights dispersed and Arthur took Myrddin aside.

Gently laying a hand on the seer's sleeve, he asked, "The knight who has to choose, is Regalis, is he not? What am I to do, Myrddin?"

"Sire, I cannot advise you to slay your boldest knight, but be prepared for betrayal."

Arthur sank into gloom for days. He could not receive counsel on the matter closest to his heart, but he had gained confirmation. Sir Regalis was in love with Gosvintha, but was her heart given to him? He decided to wait for Easter and her arrival at Camelot to find out. Meanwhile, he would decide what to do with them both if his worst fears should prove well-founded. There was still time to get a more complete answer from Myrddin. In any case, he would keep the matter between himself and the seer; his knights must suspect nothing, especially Gosvintha's son, Primus.

Before Lent had passed, a messenger arrived at Camelot from Bran ap Hefeydd.

"King Arthur, the Scoti have landed on our bank of the Abora Channel. According to the terms of our alliance, King Bran appeals for your aid."

"And he shall have it, my friend. You may deliver this affirmation to your king."

Having honourably decided to send a force, Arthur, nonetheless, consulted with Myrddin. He explained and the seer replied, "You are bound by an oath of friendship to aid King Bran."

"Ay, his messenger is now returning with my acceptance of his plea. But I ask you, Myrddin, for counsel about *who* to send."

The counsellor smiled, "It is obvious to me that you, who are recently so preoccupied must send Sir Regalis and the Britons of the Glevum garrison. There are good reasons for doing so. They are the closest force to where the Scoti are marauding; also, Sir Regalis can thus prove his devotion to your service."

"A splendid idea, Myrddin! I'll send a messenger to Corinium at once."

"Also, Sire, you should ride to that city to bring your queen back here to Camelot, but, hark, ride out a day after your envoy."

For the rest of the day, after he had sent the rider, Arthur sat brooding about in what state of mind he would approach Gosvintha.

The following day he rode into Corinium and embraced his queen.

He immediately noticed the rigidity of her body and misinterpreted it. Standing back, he fixed her with an accusatory stare.

"Oh, Valdor!" she cried, which startled him because she was the only one still to use his former name. "How *could* you send Sir Regalis possibly to his death to fight the Scoti?"

"Simply because he was the nearest of my knights to the invasion and the Glevum garrison the nearest force. I trust Regalis as I trust no other," he growled.

"I already miss him," the queen confessed, "he is so chivalrous with me."

"Does he love you, Gosvintha?"

She looked terrified and said in a shaky voice, "He has never said that, and, anyway, it would be high treason." Her voice grew stronger, "I am your queen and the mother of *our* son."

"So, you do not love him?"

She gasped and looked sternly at her husband, "Sir Regalis is a handsome, brave and noble knight. It's hard not to love him, but not in the sense that you mean. He's too chivalrous, and I am too loyal."

Arthur stepped forward and took her by the waist, pulling her towards him. Gone was the former rigidity. "It's alright, my sweet. We both love Regalis in that sense; why else would I have entrusted you to his care? Also, Sir Regalis will defeat the Scoti. There is no bolder knight in the land, excepting myself. Now, I wish for you to accompany me to Camelot—no excuses, there are other midwives in Corinium! You will be present when Regalis comes with news of his victory. He does not fight alone, but has King Bran's fierce Cambrians by his side."

"And he wears my favour, a silk scarf, to inspire him."

"Will you give me a favour, too, the next time I ride into battle?"

"Of course, but I pray that none is in the offing, husband."

"Not that I know of, but we have a seer at court and he will advise me when the time comes."

"A seer?" she sounded anxious, renewing the smallest doubt in Arthur's mind until she said boldly, "I'd like to meet and talk with him."

"And that you shall, my dear." *It would be a shame to sentence you to death. I've always loved you.* He was immediately ashamed of this thought and suddenly kissed her lips, pleased that she responded willingly.

They rode together to Camelot and Arthur immediately presented

Myrddin to her. The wizard led her aside and handed her a small glass vial containing a blue liquid. She took it as he whispered in her ear.

Afterwards, Arthur wanted to know what the seer had said. She blushed and shook her head, "Just that I must lie with you tonight, Valdor, for we must make another son."

"I need a woman to warm my bed, Gosvintha, for I have taken no other in your absence."

"Oh, Valdor!" she flung her arms about his neck and kissed him passionately.

Meanwhile, in Cambria, Sir Regalis met with King Bran.

"I am Regalis, Sire, the most trusted of King Arthur's knights, indeed, I wear Queen Gosvintha's favour. I bring the Britons of Glevum garrison, sworn to defend our lands against all-comers."

"Welcome, Sir Regalis, your fame precedes you. They say that you are invincible in battle."

"Rightly so, and I would fight by your side, this day."

Bran clicked his tongue, "Nay, friend, we must outsmart the Scoti. You will take your men behind yonder knoll, while I lead mine directly into the valley."

"It is a clever plan and should win the day. So be it!"

From his position in the trees on the valley side of the knoll, Regalis watched as the Cambrians, guided by Bran, marched straight towards the Scoti line. Both sides hurled insults while the Cambrians used slingshots to open the attack with only small success. They provoked the Scoti into charging, their bright-coloured short-sleeved tunics knee-length over speckled trousers, and cloaks streaming behind them, either red or black and the richest hemmed with drake feathers, made for an impressive array. The Scoti king's *brat* was entirely covered in heron feathers, marking him out as the target for King Bran. Undismayed, the Cambrians charged forward, too, screaming war cries, many of their faces liberally daubed with blue woad.

Sir Regalis took the merciless cut and thrust of the two clashing forces as the signal to order his cavalry to move. With him in the lead, they circled the knoll to charge into the Scoti flank. For such a cunning foe, it was surprising that their scouts had failed to warn their chieftain of this ploy. The effect was devastating as the peerless Sir Regalis hacked a swathe in the Scoti ranks, followed by his Britons, relishing their first taste of battle other than on the training ground. Yet, their tireless training repaid a thousandfold as the enemy infantry crumbled before the mounted legion.

King Bran, mightily encouraged, drove towards the heron-feathered chieftain and engaged in single combat on foot. Regalis saw this and urged his horse near to the fight, destroying anyone daring enough to impede his progress. Eventually, he stopped his horse only feet away from the exposed back of the Scoti warrior, but had no desire to intervene as it would have been a slight to the noble Cambrian, who, anyway, blow by blow and parry for parry, was holding his ground. For a fleeting moment, Regalis' eyes met Bran's and he smiled encouragement as much as to say, "I'm here if you need me!" This momentary exchange seemed to drive Bran to greater endeavour and sure enough, the Scoti leader lost ground, fatally backing into a fallen comrade, tripping over the body and lying defenceless as Bran drove his sword into his chest to wild whoops and cheers of the surrounding Cambrians and Britons. The battle was won and the men spoke of nothing but Regalis' and Bran's prowess.

The feasting under the stars that night was as wild as the celebrations on the battlefield. The following morning, Regalis crossed the Channel and, leaving a centurion to lead the jubilant cavalry back to Glevum, headed for Corinium, believing his queen to be there. When he learnt that Arthur had accompanied her to Camelot, he drove his steed at a gallop.

At Camelot, leaving the weary beast in the stable boy's capable hands, Regalis strode into the Hall. Unwisely, he made directly for the queen, instead of his king, a choice noted by both Arthur and Myrddin. As a man coming out of a trance, Regalis smiled at the queen and deviated to bow before his king.

"Sire, we have won a great battle."

Arthur nodded and Myrddin said, "You were right not to strike the Scoti chieftain's undefended back—it would have been the act of a coward."

"How can you know that!" Regalis gazed incredulously at the white-bearded man.

"Well, I am a *seer!*" was the curt reply. "Sir Regalis, I need to speak with you in yon quiet corner."

Meekly, the knight followed the apparently ancient man, surprised by the firmness and speed of his gait.

"Since I am a seer, sir knight, I foretell that if you remain in Logres, it will be the ruin of Camelot. You must beg your king to release you into the service of King Ceretic of Strathclyde."

"But I am the queen's champion, how can I leave her side?"

"If you do not, it will be the death of her. Is that what you want, Sir Regalis?"

"Give me a couple of days to reflect, Seer."

Still deep in thought, the knight strode over to the queen. Always decisive, he did not need two days to consider his future.

"What ails you, Sir Regalis?" she asked gently.

"My lady, I must return your favour and beg to be released as your champion."

"B-but why?"

"Ay, why?" Arthur intervened, who had overheard.

"Because I have spoken with the seer, who tells me my quest must be fulfilled in distant Strathclyde."

"So be it!" Arthur said too quickly.

"B-but Val—"

"Silence, my lady!" Arthur boomed, turning again to Regalis, "Hand the favour to me, sir knight, for as from today, I alone shall champion my queen. Your strong arm will be sorely missed, but the seer is rarely wrong. You are freed of your vow—make the Picts pay for their incursions!"

Arthur smiled, for he had reason to be happy.

10

CAMELOT AD 415-417

ONE BY ONE, WITH ASTONISHING ACCURACY, MYRDDIN'S prophecies for the Empire came true. Not only that, but whatever the blue potion he had concocted contained, Queen Gosvintha, after lying with Arthur, became pregnant again. Nine months later, she gave birth to a son. The queen insisted that he should be named Valdor, and, in exchange, she promised to call her husband constantly Arthur.

"It's remarkable, my darling," said Arthur, "At my advanced age, I did not expect to become a father."

"Truly, although I'm younger than you, I am still beyond what normally is considered child-bearing age. *It must have been Myrddin's potion.*" But she kept her thought to herself. Arthur, instead, who had passed his seventieth year, had another idea. He went to see Myrddin, who had transformed his room into some sort of laboratory.

"You are full of uncertainties, my king, is it not so?"

"Ay, Myrddin, I have become a father and I am too old!"

"But it is not fatherhood that truly bothers you," the blue eyes seemed to peer into the king's soul. "You are more concerned about your prowess as a warrior, are you not?"

The king gaped at the Cambrian; he sometimes wondered whether Myrddin's was a God-given or a diabolical gift; either way, he could read his mind. There was no going back because the indecipherable creature, descendant of the druids, standing before him had touched on the matter dearest to his heart.

"Ay, it is so, Myrddin. My men view me as a charismatic and fearless leader. I lead by example, often fighting alongside them in the thick of battle, which earns me their respect and admiration. My soldiers are willing to follow me into the most challenging situations because they believe in my vision and trust my judgement, but how can a man of ten and three score winters hope to defeat a younger foe in the prime of life?"

"Sire, he cannot! But you have come to Myrddin Wyllt, where the impossible does not exist. The question we must ask ourselves is this: should Myrddin make Arthur appear younger than Primus, his son? Or should his art make it so that he appears older, but retains a younger man's strength?"

"Is that possible, Myrddin?"

"Have I not just explained?" the wizard snapped. "Arthur, as the one true king, you must still fulfil your destiny, and you cannot do that as a dodderer! Let me see," The Cambrian turned the yellowed parchment of an ancient book and his finger rested on a script unknown to the king. "Ah, here I have it! Ay, I have this, this and this in stock," his finger jabbed continually at the page. Before the bewildered ruler, he began to mix fluids, grind powders and pluck leaves from herbs before chopping them finely. Eventually, he mixed and swirled them all together before demanding to hold Arthur's wrist. "Your pulse is strong, Sire, there is no risk. Drink this potion, quaff it down to the very last drop."

Myrddin gazed satisfied at the king, never leaving his hold on the wrist, nodding sagely and watching as the wrinkles disappeared from the king's face. "Go to Gosvintha and observe her reaction. I tell you only that you have the strength of two-score years ago!"

"Bless you, Myrddin, if that be true."

"Do not doubt my word or I'll transform you into the strongest toad in Christendom!"

Arthur quailed; he feared no man except Myrddin. "I did not mean to offend, O wise one! I'm just so astonished. I feel as though I could run to Gosvintha! I haven't run for years!"

"Then, do so! The sooner you leave me in peace, the better!" Myrddin returned to leafing through the parchments, smiling smugly as Arthur ran across the room and skidded out of the door.

Arthur hurried to Gosvintha, who stared at her husband. "Val—er—Arthur, you look as if all the cares of the world have rolled off your shoulders. You seem years younger!"

"That is how I feel! Myrddin made me a potion so that I can fight again. I'm going to ask Primus to put me through my paces."

"Take care not to harm our son," Gosvintha said, thinking, *I wonder if Myrddin can make me shed a few years, too?* She should have known better, for hers was only vanity, the safety of a whole realm depended on Arthur's strength.

It took Arthur some time to overcome Primus in their mock battle but not due to any infirmity or lack of agility, more to Primus' skill and tenacity. After conceding that he could not win, the younger man, panting from exertion, said, "I hope that I can fight like that when—" he bit his tongue, not wishing to upset his father.

"...you're my age!" Arthur finished for him with a grin.

Primus strode over and placed a gentle kiss on his father's brow, "If we have to fight anytime soon, I wish to fight by your side, father."

"I'll ask Myrddin what the future holds, but first, I need a drink!"

After having slaked his thirst, Arthur hurried to Myrddin for counsel.

"Welcome, mighty warrior, soon, your strong arm will be needed!"

"What is happening, Myrddin, will the Saxons march against us?"

Myrddin sat heavily on a stool and before his eyes rolled back to show only the whites, he said, "Nay, Jutes!" His voice changed dramatically and in the familiar sing-song tone of his prophecies, the seer chanted:

> *"Three sea steeds, the cyulis, wave crossers, come by chance;*
> *The tyrant pleads for help against the Picts,*
> *Whose blood stains the turf.*
> *Gurthigerno makes a gift to the horse and stallion: the fire isle.*
> *It is the place of holm oaks where the foam bathes the beach*
> *And while it has none of its own, soil taken from the isle*
> *To any place whatsoever kills writhing snakes there.*
> *The faithless oath-breakers, sons of Wictglis,*

> *Call their fellows, and the stallion ousts the tyrant from*
> > *his throne*
> *To wear his crown yet the horse is slain by the Britons—*
> *Those worthless cowards of the rich lands."*

When he had finished with a hiss and the rolling of his eyes, Arthur blasphemed, "By the Lord's Sacred Blood, Myrddin! Why must you always speak in riddles? Who are the stallion and the horse? And where is the isle of fire?"

"Is that what I said?" Myrddin asked innocently.

"Ay, and some things I understood. A tyrant king with a long name, I can't recall it now, enlisted the help of three shiploads of Jutes to defeat the Picts. They were victorious and the king gifted them an island, but they broke their oath and called more Jutes—"

"Not just Jutes, but also, Angles and Saxons," Myrddin explained helpfully. "You have the gist, Arthur, but the defeated king will come to seek your aid. You will learn everything from him."

"What is his name?"

"His father named him Gurthigerno, but he took the title, King Vortigern. These events have not yet taken place, Arthur, but they will! Prepare for his visit within two twelvemonths and be ready for an attack along the Tamēsis."

King Arthur strolled to the stables, where he recalled a Saxon slave worked, a man renowned for his knowledge of horses. On an impulse, the king called the tall blond man to him, and pointed to a fine black stallion. "You, who speak my language, fellow, know that we call it a stallion. What is that word in your language?"

"Hengist, sire."

"Mmm. Hengist. I'll remember the name. Is it the same in the Jutish tongue?"

"I believe it is, lord, for I once lived but a few miles from a Jutish town and many words were the same as ours."

Arthur told him to resume his work and watched attentively as the Saxon inspected the hoofs and brushed down a chestnut mare.

A year and some months after this brief encounter, a small group of riders came to Camelot. Their leader presented himself as Vortigern, *king without a kingdom.*

"King Arthur, if only I had possessed a fortress such as this, I would not be standing before you today." His brown eyes flashed proudly and he tried to moderate his natural arrogance since he had come in the guise of a supplicant.

"What is it you want of me, King Vortigern?"

"Sire, I cannot pretend to regain my kingdom, for it is lost, but if there were a small corner of this fair land where I could re-establish my dignity and found a dynasty, I'd be grateful, for I have three sons in my party."

"I can make no promises today, King Vortigern, for I must consult with my allies before taking such a decision, but come, sit with me and recount the mishap that has befallen you."

They sat at a dining table, where Vortigern presented his sons, Vortimer, Pascent, and Faustus.

"My sorry tale begins with the representatives of all the *civitates*, who, in a Council, begged me to grant land in Britain to the Jutes, first on Thanet in exchange for service as *foederati* troops, which we sorely needed. Then to the rest of Cantium in exchange for marriage to Hengist's daughter, but King Arthur, I may have lacked judgement or am, at best, unlucky—"

"Father, you were unlucky. How could you know that you were dealing with faithless men?" interjected Vortimer, his eldest son.

Arthur smiled; he would expect Primus to defend him similarly if circumstances ever called for an intervention.

"And those oath-breaking mercenaries, invited to a banquet, treacherously slew all the leaders of the Britons but spared me and my sons to take Colonia Victricensis and the territory of the Regni as ransom. But then Vortimer—"

"Ay, I ignored their threats and gathered an army. We fought four battles and although, sadly, my brother, Catigern, was slain, I slew the Jutish leader Horsa, myself," Vortimer explained. "Yet, our victories were in vain because they had summoned ever more ships containing their people and we were forced to retreat."

King Arthur began to form a deep respect for Vortimer and silently vowed that he would try his best to help his father. So, it proved, for after contacting his Cambrian allies, they offered the small kingdom of Powys to Vortigern, but Arthur made acceptance dependent on Vortimer remaining at his court and taking a seat at the Round Table.

After Vortigern agreed and left for Powys with his other two sons,

Myrddin came to Arthur and said, "It is well done, my king. Vortigern and his descendants will rule well in Powys for generations to come while Sir Vortimer's deeds will be the toast of Camelot." Arthur took advantage of Myrddin's presence to ask, "How long before the Saxons march on Corinium and which direction will they take?"

"Sire, they will come up the great river valley to the place where the white horse gallops across the hills. Better to move at once to reinforce the *oppidum*."

"Riddles, always riddles!" Arthur groaned as Myrddin strode away. But then, he put together the elements he had heard. "Of course, the *oppidum* in the White Horse Vale. I know it well, it lies by the Tamēsis!"

He gathered his knights and a strong contingent of cavalry and took them to join the Ermin Way, whence they rode to the *oppidum* in the vale. It already had a garrison and a thriving marketplace.

"It is here we shall await the Saxons," Arthur explained to his knights. "I will lead a cohort and you, Sir Vortimer, as the latest knight to join the Table, and yet, the most experienced against the Saxons, will lead the other." This raised a few eyebrows among the knights, but as Vortimer was a popular addition to their ranks with a personable character, nobody murmured an objection.

When his scouts reported the advance of a large Saxon force, Arthur, who was not one to await an enemy, consulted with Sir Vortimer, a man of similar temperament. They soon agreed to lead their men down the vale, along the river.

Arthur placed a hand on the hilt of Excalibur and reflected on how it had never been drawn in anger, but occasionally, unsheathed in the chapel at Camelot and held upright before the altar, in prayer. In these circumstances, Arthur felt a strange force emanating from the sword and sweeping through him unless it was, as he suspected, just his imagination.

However, as they approached the enemy, it was clear that their scouts had done their work because the foe was drawn up in a defensive formation with shields interlocked and sprouting long spears.

Arthur unsheathed his sword and felt a tingling sensation course down his arm. He exchanged glances with Vortimer, who nodded and together they galloped at the head of their men straight at the enemy line. Arthur reached it before anyone else and a hostile spear jabbed at him; to his amazement and that of the enemy concerned, his sword sliced through the thick pole as a knife cuts through butter, removing the wicked spearhead that fell uselessly to the ground. Another spear thrust at him and again, without its wielder hesitating, the sword severed the stout wooden pole. That was how the king realised that he was brandishing no ordinary sword, for in such circumstances, a blade would not remain undamaged. Mightily encouraged, Arthur urged his steed forcefully into the massed enemy rank and with devastating violence, carved helmets, shields and armour almost casually. Primus and his cavalry followed through the breach, while on the right flank, without the aid of Excalibur; nonetheless, Sir Vortimer, by dint of his strength and experience, also made inroads and created a second breach. The two gaps effectively ended the battle because the Saxons for all their might could not hold against the well-disciplined Romano-British cavalry, who knew how to take advantage of the enemy's disarray.

The few Saxons who managed to escape the battlefield did so by diving into the river and reaching the far bank. They would be useful witnesses destined to counsel wisdom against attacking Logres. This victory would resound for years and guarantee the safety of Arthur's kingdom while, at the same time, denying the myth that the Britons were a cowardly and easy prey. Instead, the praise for Arthur and Vortimer's prowess in battle was the talk of Camelot and beyond for many long months. The rejoicing went beyond Logres, where the bordering kingdoms felt safer in the knowledge that the formidable Saxons could be defeated.

II

CAMELOT AD 417

King Arthur had a daily routine of visiting the chapel early each morning, where in solitude, he gave thanks for a victory or sought enlightenment for the future. Basking in his defeat of the Saxons, he remained humble enough to ask the Lord for guidance to secure his kingdom. Head bowed, he was unaware of another presence as he prayed for clarification. His sharp mind told him that the marauders were likely to increase and benefit from the Roman road system, which was once favourable to the builders for swift military manoeuvres but now worked against them and in favour of the raiders, as recent events had proved.

The king remained immobile, concentrated, his request for guidance apparently unanswered until a gentle hand on his shoulder made him look up into the reassuring features of Myrddin.

"Forgive me, Sire, for interrupting your prayers, but I know that you seek answers and I am here to furnish them."

"Myrddin, how can you know my inner thoughts?"

"I also meditate, Sire, in my own way, and I, too, have a spiritual guide. Pray, let us be seated and I will tell you what you need to know."

Arthur readily agreed, wondering secretly whether Myrddin's spiritual enlightenment had anything vaguely Christian about it. He knew of the man's druidic lineage and often feared that he might compromise his soul by consorting with such a creature. Still, the benefits were such that he always succumbed to temptation. Had not the seer provided him, at his age, with the strength to defeat mighty younger foes in battle? He also suspected that the wizard, if that was what he was, had interfered with his sword. How else could it have so easily sliced through wooden poles? Yet, Myrddin had touched it only once to slay a wounded deer; was that long enough to achieve such a miracle?

Myrddin laid a hand on the king's arm and reassured him—again, displaying that disturbing habit of reading his innermost feelings—" Sire, this is a sacred place, do not fear that my prophecies will defile what is holy, for they come from the same Godhead."

"I am relieved to hear your words, Myrddin, therefore, prophesy and I shall heed them."

"Not long ago, lord, I congratulated you on your great victory but do not be deceived, it's only a temporary respite. My king, you are fated to fight twelve more battles before the *great battle*." The seer heaved a heavy sigh and the gentle hand on the king's sleeve suddenly turned into an iron grip. "Your final victory will be so overwhelming that it will obtain peace for a whole generation after your death."

"Am I to die in battle, Myrddin?"

The lined visage grew sorrowful and, in a sharp tone, he replied, "No man should know his doom beforehand. The time is not right."

"Will I have the strength to fight twelve battles, old friend?"

Myrddin smiled and said, "It's not simply the fighting, Arthur, to honour your alliances, you will also travel into Cambria and Caledonia. You will, indeed, need endurance."

"Will you give me more of that miraculous draught?"

Myrddin's upper lip curled slightly, "After your fifth battle, you will take an oak apple from a tree to chew and swallow."

"Ugh! Is it not a poison?"

"Nay, quite the opposite—an antidote if anything. Does not the squirrel feast on them? They are bitter, which is why we call the oak apple a gall, but you'll find needs must."

Arthur clicked his tongue and puffed out his cheeks, "It's always riddles with you, Myrddin! How can an oak apple give me strength?"

"I can reveal little else, Sire, but remember, only after your *fifth* battle. You cannot go around the land seeking and devouring oak apples or you will truly poison yourself! This particular one will reveal itself to you. Now I must go."

Suddenly, Arthur found himself alone in the chapel and, on turning to stare at the door, found no sign of his counsellor. Another mystery!

Well, he's never been wrong or let me down. He knew to come and settle my doubts. Still, to salve his conscience, Arthur returned to kneel before the altar to ask the Lord whether he should follow the words of a descendant of the druids. Arthur left the chapel with the certainty in his heart that he must prepare for war since twelve battles constituted a war, not a skirmish.

With this in mind, he ordered his centurions to redouble military training and urged greater efforts from his smiths: more javelins and arrowheads would be needed. Domestic life at Camelot was sweet. Some weeks after the birth of Valdor, heavily pregnant women began to appear at Camelot and Gosvintha arranged for transport from the foot of the hill into the courtyard. She had a small building constructed and furnished with beds. Soon, the king could hear the squalling of newborn babes in his fortress and the sound filled his heart with joy. In truth, if he needed an incentive, it was this: he would be fighting to secure their futures.

One morning, he strolled into his Hall and found Primus cradling his little brother in his arms. He chucked the babe under his chin before looking up and smiling at his father.

"Where's your mother? Is there no nurse for Valdor?"

"Mother is delivering a babe and I offered to nurse my brother. He's been fed and if you sniff down here, you'll see he's digested his milk!"

"Primus, you are a good son and brother, but don't you think you should be out training for battle or, at least, courting some maid? You are getting no younger and should think about making a babe of your own!"

Primus looked askance at the king. "Father, I'm unlikely to find her at Camelot! I would set out on a quest to find my bride, but not until I know that you don't need me in battle."

"Very well, Primus, after my twelfth battle, you shall seek your true love."

"*Twelfth!*" cried Primus, so loud that he woke Valdor, who immediately started crying. Despite his soothing voice and gentle rocking, he could not get the babe back to sleep. Arthur called a maid and consigned the infant to her.

"Come, father, a rematch on the practice ground would be good."

The king slogged his way to another closely-fought win and his respect for Primus grew accordingly.

For this reason, when a messenger arrived from distant Caledonia, he consigned the fortress to his son with a sufficient garrison to defeat potential Saxon raids.

"Primus, I must travel beyond Hadrian's Wall to honour my alliance, since the Kingdom of Gododdin and King Ceneu is hard-pressed by an alliance of Picts and Saxons. I know not how long I shall be away." The messenger spoke of a Roman fortress *the glen blocker*, close to the *Lake of the Elms*, where Arthur should arrive to draw the Picts south and into a trap. Time was important, so the king decided to sail from the south coast, through the channel and up the east coast as far as the port of Arbeia, which he knew well from his younger days on Hadrian's Wall.

At Arbeia, the commandant advised him to continue by ship to Caled's fort, on an inlet much farther north, which would leave his force with an inland march of seventy miles to the lake. The Picts had built the fort, but the Romans had taken it recently. Trying to reach his destination overland from Arbeia was far too arduous.

The glen blocker fort, skilfully built in the first century AD was one of a double row of defensive forts to protect the invading Romans from the Highland tribes and the nearest to the beautiful great lake. Arthur's experienced military eye immediately observed the strategic brilliance of the choice of location. He also concluded that, owing to the heavily wooded terrain, venturing forth along the lakeside might lead to a massacre of his men since the trees would provide the ideal cover for the Pictish strike-and-run tactics. Somewhat against his natural bold inclinations, Arthur decided to accept the messenger's advice to await an attack on the fortress.

The king wondered what his ally, King Ceneu, had in mind. Arthur had brought his army so far in only three days, so doubted that in any way the king's plans would have been altered. But what were they? Arthur sent the messenger with one of his trusted scouts to find out. They returned together the following day. His scout bowed and said, "Sire, the enemy is aware of your presence here and after sending a decoy force to engage King Ceneu in the north, with the aim of delaying him from joining you, they are marching in strength toward this fort. They aim to defeat you to proceed down the glen and strike into Strathclyde."

"The ground immediately ahead of the fort is suitable for a battle," Arthur said, "and if we keep the walls close to our rear, the enemy will not be able to attack us from behind. We shall fight on foot this time, so we did well to bring the scuta with us from Arbeia. Sir Segovax, you will form a shield wall on our left flank; Sir Vindacius, you will do the same for the right flank. I shall hold the centre." Privately, he wished he had Sir Regalis to call upon. If the foe managed to defeat him this day, they would most likely encounter Regalis and King Ceretic in Strathclyde.

"Form up immediately," Arthur ordered, "we must not be caught unprepared." He knew that it could be enervating to wait too long in a disciplined formation with nothing happening, so he supervised the interlocking shields and, satisfied, stood in front of his men to address them, mainly to raise morale, but also, to defeat boredom. He drew his magnificent sword and held it above his head, "My trusted brothers, we are indeed far from home, but the defence of Logres begins here! By displaying good faith—keeping our word—to our sworn friends, we know we can call upon them, should the day ever arise, when we have to defend the borders of Logres—"

He had to break off because war cries and the banging of weapons against shields interrupted his speech as the enemy appeared at the end of the valley. Arthur resumed, unconcerned, "Here are the men who have chosen to end their days bloodied at our feet! Brothers, fight for each other, remember that the man next to you depends on your strength and courage." Arthur took his place in the front line next to the eagle standard bearer. "To take our standard, the enemy will have to pass over my body," he cried in a ringing voice.

Arthur smiled at the ill-disciplined approach of the foe. There was no wedge formation, or any other for that matter, as they swarmed forward, the swiftest and strongest runners first, but suddenly, according to some pre-arranged plan, they stopped some hundred yards away. Slowly, the less energetic runners joined them and, at last, they were gathered into something resembling a formation. Arthur eyed them suspiciously. What was their plan? Was it to lure them away from the wall? That was not going to be an option. "Hold your position," he cried. At his command, the enemy began to jeer and taunt the Romano-British. Some of the Picts dropped their breeches, waved their genitals at their enemy before turning and displaying their buttocks.

"How terrifying!" Arthur sneered, "if they are so manly, they will attack!" After a while, he realised that the plan was to play on their nerves, to make them break ranks and charge. But he was having none of that. They had no idea of how disciplined was his force. The king explained what was happening to the men near him and word spread out to the flanks. Not a chink appeared in the Roman shield wall. His men trusted Arthur's leadership.

The king decided to make something happen, so he stepped forward three paces and ordered the shields to close behind him. He then called Sir Segovax and Sir Vindacius to join him. With one either side, he said, "My most trusted knights of the Round Table, we shall challenge the enemy alone. We'll take ten paces forward and signal to the foe to come and fight three men." Vindacius grinned, "They'll charge at us and try to surround us, but we'll cut them down!" Segovax, known as a knight of few words, said laconically, "Ay, let 'em come!"

The three men were about to enter into legend and folklore. They took ten paces and Arthur bellowed, "Come on cowards, can you not fight three men?"

There was a moment's bewilderment and exchange of uneasy glances before a giant Saxon, wielding a long-hafted axe, roared and raced towards them followed by an ill-disciplined rabble. The Saxon never reached them because a well-flighted javelin from the Roman ranks impaled his chest, just as happened by surprise to several others before they raised shields. Another roar from an enemy throat and a foe hurled himself at Arthur, who casually cleaved off his axe arm with Excalibur. Segovax and Vindacius each slew the foremost enemy with the ease of seasoned centurions. Vastly outnumbered, they fought like demons, not yielding an inch and preventing the enemy from surrounding them. This possibility was an ever-present threat, and inevitable without a counter-measure, so Arthur ordered his companions to retreat quickly without turning their backs until they stood in front of their own defensive shields. "Javelins!" Arthur yelled as the frustrated enemy ran towards them. Their rage against the three bold knights blinded them to the danger and thus, many fell because their headlong rush came heedless of the missiles. Many had their shields uselessly lowered by their side as they ran. Arthur, instead, with his scutum well raised, stepped forward again and slew any foe that he chanced upon. More than ever, he realised the peerlessness of the blade he wielded that appeared to cleave effortlessly through any protective armour. He lost count of axe hafts and steel blades that he destroyed as, at last, his officers ordered his men to advance. They eagerly engaged the enemy, inspired by the prowess of their three fearless commanders, especially that of their king. The Picts and Saxons were equally cowed by the matchless courage they had seen. Superstitiously, they wondered if they were fighting immortals. As their bravery drained, they lost ground, but the situation changed dramatically, as from among the trees, at the valley side, emerged a figure familiar to Arthur: Sir Regalis and at his back, the army of Strathclyde! Farther down the valley, well beyond the enemy also came Ceneu's force, weary from their victory over the Pictish decoy, but with their morale sky high.

In a terrible trap, the desperate enemy knew not where to turn and Arthur blessed the Romans who had sited this fortress so well, for it was as much geography as tactics that would win the day. When the carnage was over, Arthur embraced Regalis and the other kings. "We have won a major battle, brothers."

"The Picts infest the Highlands and will never leave us in peace," King Ceretic grumbled.

"Ay, and the Angles and Jutes come in waves to threaten our coast," King Ceneu growled. "This is a temporary respite," he added, "We needed you, King Arthur. Without your aid," he pointed at the heaped bodies on the battlefield, "these barbarians would be pressing into Strathclyde."

"Only to be smitten by Sir Regalis and Ceretic's men," Arthur smiled fondly at his former knight and his new monarch.

"But who's to say that the devils are not in league with the Scoti?" Ceretic said. "We are assailed from many directions. We cannot rest on our laurels, my friends."

Nobody understood when Arthur muttered, "Eleven to go!"

12

CAMELOT AND ENVIRONS AD 417

The eight-year-old stood before Primus, trembling and bedraggled, her eyes like those of a frightened fawn, and her clothes stained with blood.

Gently, gently, the knight asked her, "What's your name, child?"

"Elvira, lord," she spoke so quietly that he struggled to hear her, so he stood and squatted beside her, noting how the movement made her cringe with fear.

"Do not be afraid; I am here to help you. Now tell me what happened."

"They slew my father!" She burst into uncontrollable sobbing and Primus took her in his arms and carried her to the throne he had vacated, where he sat and held her tightly and stroked her hair until she regained her composure. "They left him for dead. I watched it all from behind a water barrel. When they went, I ran to him a-a-and," she stuttered, "he was still alive. His last words were, 'Go to King Arthur!'"

"Now, you are here."

"Ay, but where is the king?"

"He's away in Caledonia, a long way from here, but I am Primus, his son, and I can help you." He squeezed her gently, reassuringly.

"They took my mother and my sister, Willow." She snuffled and wiped her nose with her sleeve, "and they took the cow and the goats."

"Who are *they*, Elvira?"

"The Saxons! Father used to say that they were good neighbours, hardworking and honest, b-but he was wrong, wasn't he?"

"Settlers, then. How old is Willow?"

"She's eighteen, lord. Ten winters older than me."

"Good Lord!" Primus lifted her off his knee, setting her gently on the floor and sprang to his feet. "There's no time to lose! Sir Geraint!" he bellowed. "Fetch our horses and grab your sword, we have a family to avenge and a maid to rescue!"

With Elvira sat in front of him, Primus galloped to the child's farmstead...and beyond, following her indications. The fields were well-tended, and tethered in front of the house to stakes were three goats and a cow. "Those are our animals!" Elvira wailed.

Primus and Geraint dismounted and the former lifted her down, bent to the girl and told her, "Run, find a safe place to hide!"

No sooner had she disappeared than a tall strapping blond man emerged from the building. He had to lower his head to pass through the door. He swung an axe in his right hand—not a serviceable axe for chopping wood, but a battle axe. On seeing the two knights drawing their swords, he called over his shoulder, "Arnulf, Willa! There's trouble here."

"Where are Willow and her mother?"

"What business is it of yours?"

"It's my business because I am the law in Logres—" he stopped because a red-haired man of equally imposing stature pushed past the blond.

"And *I* am the law here!" he said, brandishing a sword menacingly. Primus appraised it, surely a Frankish sword of fine manufacture. "If you know what's good for you, you'll take those horses and ride away from here. I can call on a score of men!"

"What's a score to us?" Primus scoffed and the man's eyes narrowed. "It's your last warning, get ye gone!"

"*You* do not command *me*, oaf!" Primus said, loftily. "We're going nowhere without Willow and her mother and their animals and the man who slew her husband must be brought to justice."

"If that is what you want, you'll have to fight for it!" The red-haired man took up a defensive stance and turned his head sideways, "Willa, fetch the men!"

"No, you don't!" Geraint snarled and quick as a flash sliced into

Willa's thigh as he made to run off. The man collapsed on the ground, trying to staunch his wound while his red-haired chieftain roared and threw himself, sword raised at Primus, who fended off a mighty blow, admiring the strength behind it and the quality of the sword. As they engaged in a vigorous contest, Geraint faced the axeman and narrowly avoided a deadly swipe.

The importance of having downed the runner became clear. Another twenty of such fierce fighters would have put their mettle sorely to the test. Primus hoped that his idea to come with only Geraint had not been foolhardy. There was no time to elaborate his thoughts as the Saxon feinted a move Primus knew well from years of practice. It was easy enough for him to thwart it, but served to demonstrate how able was his adversary. In which case, thought Primus, I'll show you a trick or two of mine. The Saxon couldn't cope and his sword clattered to the ground. He sank to his knees and feigning defeat, cunningly drew a long knife from his boot before lunging the blade towards Primus' groin. The knight was ready for a disloyal gesture and imperiously sliced off the Saxon's weapon-bearing hand with a downward, sideways stroke.

The chieftain's scream choked in his mouth as Primus' blade pressed against his windpipe.

"Who slew Willow's father? You?"

The man bit his lip until it bled, staring unbelievingly at his severed wrist, but chokingly managed:

"Ay, what of it?"

"Go to meet your pagan gods!" Primus thrust the sword into his throat and twisted, watching the life die in the man's eyes. The blond Saxon, hard-pressed by Geraint saw the deed and, flinging down his axe, cried, "Enough! You have slain Arnulf. Spare me and I'll come and fight for you, Romans. That's what you want isn't it?"

"Where are the women?" Primus snapped.

The Saxon nodded at the door. Before entering, Primus said, "Geraint, don't trust him. One false move, slay him!"

Primus barged into the house and saw two women bound to chairs. The younger one, a beautiful young woman, her tunic torn off her shoulders to reveal her breasts. Primus strode towards her tear-stained face and gently pulled up her tunic to cover her. "Elvira is safe and so are you; your sister is a brave little creature. She ran all the way to Camelot to fetch us," he said, all the time carefully sawing through the rope binding her until she was free. Her dazzling smile stole his heart as he turned to release her mother. As he finished his task, he heard his name shouted from outside.

Rushing to the door, he waved to the two women to stay behind. Bursting into the open, he saw the reason for Geraint's call. His comrade was holding the blond Saxon by the arms behind his back and his sword across his throat. Geraint yelled, "Don't take another step and lay down your arms, or he's dead!"

Primus' gaze followed Geraint's and he counted eight men wielding arms coming into the farmyard. *We can deal with four each!* Primus took the initiative. "I am Primus, son of King Arthur! We are here in the name of justice. Your chieftain lies dead at my hands and you will all join him if you disobey." There followed a moment's bewilderment among them, but then, the foremost fellow laid down his axe and showed empty hands. The others followed, just as Primus heard a sound behind him and saw Willa, the wounded Saxon, had somehow dragged himself to his feet and with a seax was about to strike the knight in the back. With a guttural roar, he spun around and drove his sword into his would-be assailant's chest.

At the same time, he saw the shocked expression on the most beautiful face he'd ever seen, peering through the half-open door.

Primus walked over to the blond captive, "Who is your leader, now that Arnulf is dead?"

"I suppose I am, I'm the eldest son."

"Where are your womenfolk?"

"Working in the barn—father sent them there while—"

"While he had his way with those two poor women," Primus finished. "This is what we will do...what's your name?"

"Caena, lord."

"Caena, I will not take you into service in our army, but in exchange, you will send two men to work on your neighbour's farm to compensate for the loss of the farmer. I'll tell the women to contact me at once if anything goes amiss, understood?"

"Ay, lord, I understand."

"Good, choose two men and they can drive the stolen animals back to the farm."

While Caena carried out these orders, Primus called in a loud voice, "Elvira! Where are you? Come to me now!"

The girl broke cover and flung herself around Primus' legs, gasping out her thanks. Soon she was joined by mother and sister. Primus lifted Elvira onto his horse and helped Willow up behind her, noting the soft slenderness of her body as he did so. "I'll lead the horse. You, Geraint, help the woman onto yours and lead the beast alongside us."

They tramped willingly to the neighbouring farm and Primus said, "Nothing can restore your poor father, Willow, but justice has been done. I'll send a priest and a handful of men to give your father a Christian burial."

A long silence followed after the gasped thanks of the young woman until they reached the farm. Primus ordered Geraint to remain with the women and horses. He hurried to the farmyard and saw the body of the farmer. Dashing into the house, he took a blanket and, hurrying outside, covered the body. Only then did he call Geraint to fetch the womenfolk. All three gazed sadly at the covered body and Primus thanked the Lord that he'd had the sense to cover it.

He bent over and kissed Elvira on the top of her head, "You are a brave little creature," he said.

"But not as brave as you, Sir Primus!"

Everyone laughed at this, then, before the two knights took their leave, Primus turned to the widow, "May I come occasionally to check on your wellbeing, woman?"

"On mine, or on Willow's?" the woman said with a twinkle in her eye.

Primus gave an embarrassed little cough, "Ahem, are you a mind reader, goodwife?"

"Nay, lord, but I've seen the way you look at my daughter," she whispered with a smile. "You are the king's son and you don't need my permission to come here when you want." She grasped his hand and carried it to her lips, "We are so grateful. You saved Willow's virtue and our animals."

"I'm sorry for your loss," he glanced at the body. "I told Willow, I'll send a priest and some men to dig a grave." With that, he mounted his horse and rode away with Geraint. When they arrived in Camelot, Geraint teased him.

"Who would have thought we had such a gem so close to Camelot?"

"I don't know what you mean, Geraint."

"Strange, for you could not take your eyes off that bright gem!"

Primus laughed, "Willow is indeed as beautiful as any gem, but today she lost her father. I cannot in all conscience play upon her gratitude."

"Nay, but did you not confide to me that King Arthur told you to find a wife?"

"So must you, Geraint, but look elsewhere; I'll not fight my best friend over a woman!"

Primus sent six men and a priest, to whom he entrusted a large bunch of roses. "Give them to Lady Willow, Father, she'll know what to do with them."

The priest smiled; he knew the family well and remembered how beautiful the young maiden was. *Has the king's son been smitten by her beauty?* he asked himself.

Three days later, a weary messenger arrived from Caledonia with news of a great victory, but also with the disturbing news that another invasion had to be contested, so the king had to delay his return until he defeated the foe.

Primus called his friend to share the news.

"Sometimes, I regret that my father didn't take us to Caledonia, Geraint, but we cannot complain at lack of action. That Arnulf was a worthy fighter."

"Ay, and Caena was no less! He tested my mettle."

"It's just a shame we weren't there to save Lady Willow's father."

"*Lady* Willow?"

"Well, she *will* be when I wed her," Primus said defensively.

First, he had to win her heart and that was his intention when he rode out of Camelot the following morning. It was immediately clear when he entered the farmhouse that he had won one heart, at least. Elvira sidled to embrace him and shyly whispered, "It's not fair, just because I'm young."

"What's unfair, Elvira?" Primus said, gently freeing himself from her embrace.

The girl blushed bright red, "I love you more than she does," she murmured so low that Primus was unsure he'd heard correctly.

"Elvira, leave Sir Primus to drink our cider," her mother scolded. "Willow, where are you, girl?"

"Here, mother."

The beauty appeared from the kitchen carrying a flagon of cider and three beakers on a tray.

"Father was proud of his cider," Willow said with a catch in her voice. "He would have loved to drink with you, Sir Primus," she said with a dazzling smile.

"Well, let's drink to his soul, I'm sure he's looking down on us."

"Ay, with his approval," said the widow meaningfully.

The cider was excellent, dry, as Primus preferred and he accepted another beaker willingly. It gave him the courage to speak his mind—if only he had his battle courage with women!

"Willow, are you betrothed?"

She blushed a fiery red, but it was her mother who answered, "Nay, she has led a sheltered life, have you not, Willow?"

"Ay, it's true," Willow murmured, gazing at Primus from under a lowered brow and her eyelids almost closed. She brushed her long blonde hair over her shoulder.

"W-would you consider betrothal with me, my lady fair?"

A stunned silence descended on the room.

"We are so grateful for what you have done for us," Willow managed.

"But...?" Primus said, dismay on his face.

"But I am only a farm girl and *you* are a prince."

Primus laughed, "Ay, but I am a prince only because my father is king; otherwise, I am a simple soldier. Willow, I fell in love with you as soon as I saw you, but it is only fair to tell you that you have a rival."

Now it was Willow's turn to look dismayed, "Who is she, lord?"

"Why, that courageous little creature you should be proud to call your sister!"

Primus grinned at Elvira, "Let *her* decide if we should be betrothed!"

Willow spun around in her chair and fixed her sister with a threatening scowl, "Elvira, choose your words carefully."

"I'm too young, else I'd fight you for him. But I love you, Willow, and it's your happiness that counts. *You* must decide."

"Then, I will. Mother, do I have your blessing?"

"Ay, my child, with all my heart."

Willow gazed lovingly at Primus, "We are betrothed, my lord, kiss me!"

Only too happy to oblige, Primus leant across and his chaste kiss soon became passionate.

Detaching himself, he asked, "Will you come to Camelot to meet my mother?"

"I have no horse."

"You'll ride in front on mine, then I'll gift you a horse, so that you can visit your family whenever you want." He turned to the widow, "How are the Saxons?"

The woman blushed—apparently, a family trait among the women — "They are good workers, I can't complain. I like one of them very much," she said hesitatingly.

Willow and Primus exchanged their first complicit look and both laughed.

13

LINNIUS REGION, AD 418

King Arthur wished he could question Myrddin because the seer had given him no timescale for his twelve battles and, apart from saying that he would need to travel, no sense of place. Here in Caledonia, he experienced a watchful tacit truce. The enemy had suffered sufficient losses not to seek another engagement without outside reinforcements. Arthur grew restless and longed to return to his kingdom, so he was relieved when the decision was made easy for him by further events. His ally, the Governor of Valentia, was alarmed by the mobilisation of Angle settlers south of the Abus estuary in the Linnius region.

Coel Hen was rightly troubled at the prospect of an invasion across his southern border. A messenger came, calling upon Arthur to hurry south to Eboracum to unite his army with Coel's. The overland journey from the port of Arbeia was expedited by Arthur's knowledge of the roads from Hadrian's Wall to Eboracum. In all, it took three days to arrive. The relieved former Dux Britanniarum welcomed him and his men warmly.

"My scouts have warned me of a considerable enemy build-up gathering to the south of Lindum. Their numbers swell on a daily basis as countless boats arrive on the east coast of that region."

"Can the shore forts not confront them?"

"Arthur, you know as well as I that they are undermanned and underpaid. They are more likely to join the enemy than fight them."

Arthur looked up into the ascetic face, the brown eyes troubled and the high brow creased with worry. "My friend, I have heard plenty about your leadership. Now that we have united our forces, we should lose no time in heading into the land of the Lindenses."

"I do not have the ships to carry two legions to an east coast port," objected the governor.

"We'll march down to Lindum."

The lined face grew graver and combined with the grey hair, made Coel look careworn and older than his years. "Therein is the problem, the tides are dangerous. Crossing the Abus on foot is too risky in this season."

"Marching around the estuary will lengthen our journey both in miles and hours," Arthur pointed out.

"Time to build sufficient rafts and the risk of drowning has to be taken into consideration."

"You are right, my friend, there's little to be gained. We'll march around the Abus and immediately head inland to join the road to Lindum. There's still a garrison in the *colonia* unless I'm mistaken."

"Ay, it's true. If we can get there before the Angle host, those men will make a welcome addition to our army."

"It will be in their best interests to defeat the Angles or their city will be a prime target for those people. Their commander doesn't need to be a genius to figure that out," Arthur added waspishly. He ran a critical hand over the stubble on his chin. "You don't have a decent barber, by any chance?" Enviously, he studied the clean-shaven visage of the governor.

"I'll call him at once; then, King Arthur, we should march for the bridge over the Adur before striking overland to the Ermine Street and down to Lindum."

After two overnight camps, the Romano-British army marched through an archway in the defensive walls spanning the Ermine Street into Lindum. The thriving city seemed to be clinging onto its Roman heritage, and Arthur gazed at the nineteen columns gracing the forum entrance while calculating that the population must be at least 6,000. They marched wearily up a steep hill to the fortress that dominated the *civitas*. This was what he was fighting for, the preservation of law and a culture that had been consolidated over centuries. Almost without thinking of the implications of his religion, he prayed that the garrison commander would be helpful. There was that, too, the influx of marauding strangers devoted to bloodthirsty gods, pagans, who had little knowledge of Christianity, and scorned the concept of *love thy neighbour*.

Scouts brought consistent reports that the Angles were amassing their host near the confluence of the Glen with the Weolud, so the allied commanders headed with all speed to that area.

The Angles' choice of battleground was not random. They were used to fighting on marshy ground in their homeland and feared the Roman cavalry. Soggy ground was not suited to mounted warfare. However, their attempt at cunning misfired because Arthur would have paid a fortune for them to choose the position that was nothing less than a trap between the two rivers.

All that could be said in favour of the terrain was that it limited the mobility of men as well as beasts and when the battle was in full sway, the losses were great on both sides. The Anglian chieftains attempted to attack Arthur, but his battle skills were too much for his opponents, who made no inroads towards the eagle standard. Yet, the Angles were hardy fighters and the Romano-British force lost many men on either flank. One of King Arthur's boldest knights, Sir Comux, a member of the Round Table, gave his life dearly. In the end, as the sun dipped, symbolically turning the river waters red, it was the terrain that proved the victor. Losses on both sides were more or less equal, but the strength of the Romano-British centre was sufficient to drive the Angles back into the river, where many fell to javelins in their attempt to swim away to the opposite bank. Some made it across, others drowned and yet others bloodied the water as the javelins took their toll.

When the battle ended, a grim-faced Arthur turned to Coel and said, "Today, we triumphed again, but at what cost! A seer told me that I must fight twelve battles. This is the second, but if the next ten are so costly, I'll have no army left."

The Governor of Valentia Province hung his head, "There seems to be no end to the arrival of these boat people. If it's not Angles, it's Frisians or Jutes, not to mention the Saxons, and even the Picts sail this far south. Where will it end?"

Arthur laid a hand on his ally's arm. "It'll end in our victory, according to my seer, but the next battles must be swift and costly only for the foe, else, we shall not sustain the haemorrhage."

For the moment, Lindum was safe. The two commanders decided to stay there for some days, which proved to be a wise decision because the surviving Angles were joined by an influx of Saxons, who immediately took up the challenge and marched inland to plunder the villages in the valley of the small river Dubglas. This insurgence was a calculated provocation, based on the terrain once more. The ground was firm, but the valley surrounded by woodland, enabling a quick escape route if necessary to the Saxon vessels moored in the broad River Abi.

The Angles and Saxons faced King Arthur in the early morning, the low sun behind them, shining into the faces of the advancing Romano-British. Arthur's scouts had reported on the nature of the terrain, so the king decided to deploy his cavalry. The early fighting was, therefore, favourable to the Romano-British, who were unprepared for the Saxons deserting the battlefield. In a prearranged tactic, therefore, with surprising discipline, they vanished into the nearby woods.

The presence of Arthur's cavalry saved the day, preventing the Angles from springing a trap and attacking the pursuing Romano-British infantry from behind. Arthur had his cornicen sound the retreat, bringing the infantry back out of the woods and into the engagement with the hard-pressed Angles. Arthur admired the cunning strategy of the enemy but realised that without his cavalry, the outcome would have been disastrous. Instead of the massacre of the Anglian warriors, led by his redoubtable battle skills, the ground would have been littered with the bodies of his men. Although the Saxon invaders had escaped to fight another day, which they undoubtedly would, Arthur dispassionately watched the wheeling carrion raptors feast on the fallen Angles. He had won the foretold third battle only a matter of a few miles and days distant from the second.

In his heart, he hoped that more of the seer's battles would follow rapidly—a desire soon verified because the incoming invaders had set their sights upon the fertile plains of the Linnius region.

The fourth battle saw the same Saxon force, augmented by the fresh reinforcement of a fleet of Jutish ships from the south, march on Lindum. Arthur's scouts were efficient so that he and Coel and the Lindum garrison prepared to meet the invaders outside the walls of the *colonia*.

The Romano-British force had prepared this battle on their own terms, knowing that the enemy would take the road from the river Nene to its junction at Ancaster with the Ermine Street that led straight to Lindum. At Ancaster, there were two Roman forts. One in the valley near the cemetery and one on the hill overlooking the town. Arthur split his army, taking all the cavalry into the upper fort and leaving the infantry to hold the lower one that guarded the road junction.

As expected, the enemy, unaware of this ploy, advanced on the road fort and waited outside, attempting to lure the Britons into an open battle. They believed they had succeeded when the gate opened and the serried Romano-British force emerged prepared for battle. Seeing their numerical superiority, the Saxons and Jutes did not hesitate, but bent on avenging the massacre of the Angles, flung themselves into battle. Arthur ordered his men to ride across the meadow, avoiding the stone road, and thus, muffle his hoofbeats. Intent on the enemy on foot, the foe concentrated on their frontal attack on the interlinked Romano-British *scuta*. Once again, Arthur's cavalry with their long *spathae*, wreaked a deadly toll, winning the battle with few losses.

Reflecting afterwards, Arthur had not expected four battles in so short a span of time. There would have been a fifth if the defeated survivors had their way. They sent messages to their homeland, promising fertile land to those who joined them, but wisely, despite their daring, those men refused to face the wild and wasteful North Sea until the calmer months of the following spring. The V-shaped profile of their ships' hulls meant that they were prone to capsizing and more men might be drowned than ever set foot on a new shore.

They arrived in large numbers, taking the easy approach into the *Æstuarium Metuonis*, where they moored in the mouth of the Weolud. They were disappointed at a first glance, since the area had only a very small population, but in the past, the Romans had imported slaves from foreign parts and other areas of Britannia to construct a high bank against the sea, drain the countryside, build roads and bridges for the transport of troops and the use of the people. They erected a large stone bridge with four arches and this the invaders crossed to move inland; a manoeuvre seen by Arthur's scouts.

The raiders could see the potential of the agricultural land and were determined not to be beaten as their predecessors. Arthur had used the winter months wisely, feeding his people and ensuring the survival of many poor families. Sending officers out in all directions far and wide, the able-bodied Britons were made to realise the importance of defending their land. Arthur set smiths to work to manufacture armour and arms so that by the time the enemy ships anchored, Arthur had doubled his force and used veterans to train his recruits in combat techniques.

These operations did not go unnoticed, whereas some Saxon auxiliaries joined the Romano-British ranks, the majority of the settlers rebuffed the opportunity to fight their own kith and kin. Aware that their scouts had failed to inform them of Arthur's movements before the last defeat, the invaders learnt the lesson and ensured that they kept a closer eye on his manoeuvres this time.

The result was that Arthur knew the exact location of the Saxon host and their movement, which was rapid along a sixty-foot-wide military road running inland from the Weolud in a westerly direction. The Saxon scouts brought back detailed information about the Romano-British cavalry and the main force. King Arthur had prudently garrisoned two wayside fortresses with his latest recruits in the charge of seasoned centurions. Obeying orders to keep a low profile in their respective forts, the one or two lookouts on the ramparts did not arouse enemy scouts' suspicion and so, the presence of these additional troops went unreported.

Arthur relied on this tactic and halted his army on the road equidistant between the two forts. His army was arranged in a classic formation, with the infantry ranked on the road and the cavalry positioned on either flank. Before midday, Arthur's scouts galloped back, reporting the enemy's approach and approximate numbers. The Saxons marched past the first fort on its hill without a sideways glance, a fatal error because they soon came face to face with the main force, which captured their attention. The Saxons halted just beyond the throwing distance of the enemy lines and copying them, erected a shield wall.

There followed several long minutes of impasse until one Saxon warrior, demonstrating his bravery and, perhaps, trying to inspire his comrades, broke ranks, and with a cry ran towards the Romano-British line. By hurling his javelin towards the Roman eagle standard, he exposed his body to several counter-throws. He died a hero and achieved his purpose of inspiring his companions, who howled in rage and charged forward, shields raised. This was a sign for the flanking cavalry to sweep around and attack, but the Saxons were not an undisciplined rabble and, surprisingly, formed into two tight squares, their long spears held along the forearm defensively. The riders could not risk their steeds and rode around the Saxons, some jeering and launching javelins to little avail. The knights leading them ordered the retreat to their previous position amid the whoops of the unharmed Saxons. The horsemen regrouped along the flanks and the Saxon squares advanced warily.

A hail of Roman javelins failed to have any great effect so that the Saxons arrived shield to shield for hand-to-hand combat. Swords, axes, and clubs battered against the stout Roman *scuta*. This was what Arthur had planned because his Britons had trained for hours to hold their shields against enemy pressure and to stab with the gladius whenever an opportunity arose. Many of the Saxons had faced this kind of combat in the Rhineland and a stalemate ensued until, by surprise, a centurion led his garrison furtively into the Saxon rear. Inevitably, the Saxon shield wall disintegrated, leaving the shield bearers vulnerable to attack from front and rear.

The cavalry galloped into the fray again, but this time, they met a disastrous disarray and the slaughter was terrible to behold. Arthur won his fifth consecutive battle, effectively ensuring the safety of the eastern and southern part of the Valentia Province as a jubilant Coel Hen was quick to point out.

Arthur's most pressing task regarded Myrddin's words, which were impressed on his memory—*after the fifth battle, find an oak gall.* There were no oak trees in this area, so he changed plan and accompanied Coel to Eboracum: Camelot was in no danger and could wait.

14

EBORACUM AND BASSA REGION OF LOGRES, AD 418

KING ARTHUR DREW ON LOCAL KNOWLEDGE BEFORE SETTING out into a nearby forest, half an hour from Eboracum. They assured him that he would find oak trees in the woodland, and he did. The problem was the difficulty of finding an accessible oak gall. At last, he found two on adjoining branches, plucked them, and studied their unappetising appearance.

"If I were you," a deep disembodied voice said, "I'd munch the one with a hole in it because it means the insect inside has bored its way out."

"Ugh!" Arthur rapidly tossed the intact gall to the ground and looked around fearfully, "W-what, can oak trees talk, then?"

"Nay! Ha-ha-ha!" Myrddin stepped out from behind another large oak trunk. "Come, come, chew the gall!"

"You startled me, Myrddin."

"Can it take so little to frighten the great King Arthur?"

"I fear only the unknown."

"*Only!* There is so much unknown in the universe that you should be permanently afeared!"

"Ugh! It's bitter—vile—"

"Do not spit it out! Swallow it! Here, take this," Myrddin handed him a vial of phosphorescent green liquid, "Drink it to the very last drop!"

Arthur did this willingly because it had a pleasant flavour that annulled the horrid gall. The mere thought of that taste made Arthur say, "Yak!"

Myrddin grinned, "Such ado about nothing, squirrels eat them all the time!"

"It may have escaped your attention, Myrddin, but I am no squirrel! Anyway, what will this mixture do for me?"

"Follow this trail in search of adventure, and you will find out soon enough."

Without a word of assent or dissent, Arthur set off along the leaf-canopied trail.

Soon, he heard a scream and the clash of steel—combat in progress!

He urged his steed forward and broke into a clearing where a man lay on the ground, seven dead men around him and the eighth standing with a foot on either side of the familiar prostrate figure. The assailant's hands were raised overhead, holding an inverted sword, ready to plunge it down into his victim's chest. King Arthur recognised the supine figure of Sir Mandacus—one of his Knights of the Round Table.

Frantically, Arthur unlatched his spear from its harness and, defying the weight of the pole, hurled it with such vigour that it penetrated the mail shirt at the base of the ribs, transfixed the warrior's body and emerged through the other side of the mail shirt, carrying the fellow off his feet and away from Arthur's liege knight. The king blinked in amazement at his prodigious feat; by rights, the heavy spear should have fallen harmlessly short. It must have been due to Myrddin, his oak gall and potion! So, that was what he meant by *Follow this trail, and you will find out soon enough.* His concoction had given King Arthur unsuspected and abnormal strength.

He hurried over to his wounded knight, dismounted and bent over him, "Sir Mandacus, up on my horse, you must have treatment."

"Sire, I'm too sorely wounded to mount a steed."

"Nonsense! I'll lift you up."

"But that's imposs—"

In a trice, Arthur hoisted the knight, armour and all, onto the patient beast. The king sprang up behind him and prevented the knight, in his weakened state, from slipping off the animal's back. The king's charger plodded back towards Eboracum.

For a while, Sir Mandacus did not attempt to speak, but after a while, he said bitterly, "My father was right! If I wish to have better fortune, I should change my name."

The king wondered if he had heard aright. "How so?"

Weakly, the knight said, "I have ne'er liked my name—Man-da-cus! What kind of name is that? My grandsire was bold and ever fortunate."

"What was his name?"

"Gawain."

"Sir Gawain! It has a pleasant ring to it. From now on, I shall call you Gawain. However, I would not say that you are *not* bold. Did you not slay seven of your assailants?"

"Ay, it's true, lord, but if it had not been for your timely arrival, my luck would have abruptly ended."

"One man against eight! You are a worthy knight, Gawain. Try to rest; soon I'll have someone tend your wounds."

As the king's horse made steady progress into Eboracum, Myrddin wandered in a completely different direction until he reached a vantage point over a valley on the farthest side of the forest. The sight that met his eyes distressed him. Below, he saw a mixed host of Saxons and Scoti, but that did not concern him. His anxiety was reserved for six sinister figures—hooded pipers dressed in white robes. Myrddin groaned, *the six Pipers of Bassa!* He spoke aloud to himself, for only a few common, timid woodland birds could hear his voice. "The Pipers would not join the Saxons for money, what then could induce them? They should naturally ally with the Britons, not fight them! But, of course! They hate the Romans because they were the ones who drove their druidic forefathers from the Isle of Mona." Myrddin had no time to lose. He had to hasten to Arthur to warn him. Without thinking, he rushed along the woodland trail, back into the forest, where his shoe caught in an exposed root, tripping him and sending him sprawling, to strike his head against a rock. The wizard lay unconscious on the ground, unaware of nightfall and the cold darkness enfolding him. When, in the morning, at last he came to his senses, he shook his head, remembered that he needed to make haste, but not why. He imprecated against his blighted fate, and wandered over to a brook, where he dabbed his bloodied brow. Despite the shock of the icy water, he could not remember the cause of his precipitous flight, rather like Sir Gawain, who after treatment, tried to recall why he had become embroiled in a fight.

As his strength returned, Gawain suddenly remembered how he had been on a scouting mission, had seen and evaluated the Saxon and Scoti numbers before fleeing to the safety of the forest. It had not proved so safe since eight warriors had pursued him and surrounded him in a clearing. Sitting up suddenly, which made his head hurt, he swung his legs to the floor and staggered to the door. He did not get far because a doctor steered him back to bed.

"But I must speak with the king. I have urgent news."

"Lie still, I'll fetch him."

As good as his word, the doctor returned with the monarch a few paces behind.

"Sire, I have recalled the purpose of my journey. Several of us went out in different directions on a routine scouting mission. Beyond the confines of the forest in the area of Bassa—in your kingdom! —I saw thousands of Saxons and Scoti gathering. When I retreated into the forest, they spotted me and eight men pursued me until they caught up with me in the clearing where you found me."

"I'll muster my army and head for Bassa. Gawain, concentrate on regaining your strength." Abruptly, Arthur turned away to make his preparations.

The blow to Myrddin's head had been so severe that he suffered from memory loss. He could not recall why he was in a forest or where that woodland was situated. He wandered around for days, feeding on berries and nuts.

Meanwhile, Arthur assembled a large army and marched into the same forest on their way to Bassa, which region lay to the extreme west of Logres, almost on the border with Cambria. In the western side of the forest, Myrddin was perched on a rocky outcrop, still slightly dazed and somewhat detached from reality, watching a trickle of what might have been a waterfall in the winter, dripping down the crag and sparkling in the sunlight. After long minutes of this hypnotic pastime, he heard horses neighing and the tramping of feet. As he gazed along the trail, he saw the Roman eagle standard at the head of a column of men.

He was so far from his usual self that Arthur's banner meant nothing to him; he felt sluggish, nauseous and dizzy when he tried to stand. Myrddin promptly sat down again and waited for the marching men to disappear from sight. Gradually, as his cerebral commotion subsided, the Cambrian remembered what was so urgent. He recalled that he had a message for the king. He stood slowly and, on reaching the trail, set out after the Romano-British force.

The wizard reached the edge of the forest and went to his earlier vantage point with the view over the valley. He was too late! The two armies faced each other and, in the second file of Scoti soldiers, stood six hooded, white-clad figures: the pipers of Bassa! Myrddin could do nothing except look on anxiously as the opposing forces advanced.

Endowed with the force of ten men, Arthur smashed into the front line of the Saxons and Scoti with devastating effect. Then, the pipers began to play their fluting tune. Arthur must have been protected by the magic he had consumed earlier, but the enchanted tune lulled his soldiers into a trance, except for the knights near to the king, who heard only his bellowed commands. Unable or unwilling to fight, Arthur's men sat on the turf and the enemy proceeded to slaughter them mercilessly. After all, their ferocious gods were insatiable for human blood. In vain, Arthur waved his arms and shouted orders.

From high on his rock, in his befuddled state, Myrddin could not remember the spells to counteract the piping music. He blamed himself for the massacre below and the thought tipped his fragile mind into insanity.

With the strength of ten men, thanks to Myrddin, Arthur advanced with his noblest knights, cutting swathes in the enemy ranks and directing his efforts towards those whom he recognised as sorcerers. The king himself silenced the pipers and the spell was broken. His surviving warriors began to fight back, enraged by the deaths of their companions and infuriated by the use of druidic magic. The tide began to turn, but it was too late to help Myrddin, who had long since run into the woods, casting off his clothes, and ranting like a madman. The anguished seer beat his brow against a tree trunk before lapsing again into unconsciousness.

The Saxons retreated in orderly fashion and Arthur wisely refrained from pursuit. To no avail, his knights tried to cheer the gloom-wracked king. They claimed a sixth successive victory, but Arthur's army had lost too many men for him to accept such superficiality. It was a victory that smacked of defeat. *If only Myrddin had been by my side to combat the sorcery!* In his dismay, he did not think that, had it not been for Myrddin, he would not have had the strength to perform the prodigious deeds his men so admired. Rather, his thoughts were on the other five battles that the seer had foretold.

He needed to levy more men—or, if only Myrddin would give his boldest knights squirrel food...! The latter was not an option as Arthur soon found in Eboracum, nobody had seen the wizard for many days. The king sent men into the forest to find him but the wild, naked, and unkempt madman was too wily to be found. Arthur begged Honorius for just one legion, but the emperor's situation was worse than his own, so his request received an instant rebuttal.

When he reached Camelot, Gosvintha provided him with a solution, as was often the case.

"Why not appeal to your ally, the King of Dumnonia? He has little love for the Scoti."

Arthur looked at her appraisingly, "The men of Cornwall are too attached to their land," he said, admiration underlying his scornful tone. "What if we have to march north again?" he asked prophetically.

"From what I'm hearing, men are so impressed by your feats, husband, that they would follow you even into the bowels of the Earth!"

"Pah! That's nonsense!"

"Nay, father," said Primus. "Remember what Myrddin said—you will fight twelve battles and then peace will be gained against the barbarians."

"There's a moot point! Where the devil is Myrddin?"

15

FROM A FOREST IN LOGRES TO A RIVER IN CALEDONIA, AD 419

HIS ATTENTION CAUGHT BY A FEEBLE SQUEALING SOUND, Myrddin halted and bent to peer under a bush. "Ah, the poor mite!" he said aloud, reaching down and gently picking up a tiny albino boar. "You can't be more than a day or two old and abandoned by your mother on account of your pigment." Myrddin's finger gently stroked the creature's chest and its disproportionately large eyes melted his heart. "Don't worry, little fellow, you're safe with Myrddin!" He carried the newborn boar back to his cavern and dribbled honey from his fingertip into the boar's famished mouth. He needed milk for the poor creature, so he wrapped it in dried leaves to keep it warm and went off to beg or steal milk.

An old woman in a forest hovel took pity on him when he explained that his pet dog was dying of hunger. She didn't believe the unkempt wild man, thinking that he needed the milk for himself, which was partly true, so she gave him a bottle of milk, fresh from her goat. Delighted, Myrddin carried it back to the limestone cave that was his home, where he lit a fire, placed the boar near it and trickled milk into its mouth. Despite his insanity, Myrddin could remember a few elementary spells: fire lighting was one of them, and it served him well in the wilderness.

At last, after a year of wandering in the wild, he had a home and a family—himself and Baedd—for that was what he named his little white friend with its pinkish eyes. The next time he visited the old woman, she had compassion for such a filthy wretch, dressed only in a loincloth and all skin and bones. She could make little sense of his crazed rambling speech, but realised that he was a Briton like herself, so she gave him some gruel, the first hot meal that he'd eaten in months, wrapped him in a blanket and refilled his bottle with milk. Moved by her kindness, Myrddin swore that he would regain his magic arts and repay her a thousandfold for her kind heart.

With each passing day, Baedd grew stronger, which pleased Myrddin, for soon the winter season would be passed and he would move on. The seer was delighted that his divining was slowly returning and although he no longer had visions, he could claim to have *insights*. That was how he knew that he had to move north when the spring began to show signs of greenery. Luckily, Baedd was developing and Myrddin found him rooting around under a nearby oak, grubbing for acorns stored underground by a jay in the autumn.

Baedd had taken to sleeping with Myrddin and rarely left him for such independent adventures. The wizard was grateful for the boar's initiative. He could not continue to trouble the old woman and Baedd would need much more food on a regular basis. It was essential that he foraged for his sustenance.

One morning, the boar wandered away to grub for food while Myrddin set a trap for a pheasant or a rabbit. Startled by the boar's protesting squeal and its insistent walking to and fro, the wizard realised that the animal was trying to communicate and wanted him to follow. The enchanter obliged his little friend until they came to a gorge. The boar peered over the edge and Myrddin heard whimpering. Cautiously gazing down the ravine, he saw a small black dog, clearly in pain.

Myrddin patted Baedd's head, told him to wait and carefully climbed down, grasping roots and clefts in the rock until he came to the injured animal. One glance was enough to tell him that the unnatural position of its right foreleg meant it was broken. Myrddin cursed the bad luck that had turned him into an animal rescuer, not that he could now live without Baedd. Gently, he took the dog and draped it over his shoulder, thus keeping one arm free to climb up the rocky cliff. Careful not to distress the injured canine, the man inched his way upwards. Knees trembling, he managed to reach level ground and, adjusting the dog in his arms, carried him back to the cavern, where he laid him on his bed of ferns. Probing delicately with his fingers, he ascertained the fracture and, to his surprise, found himself chanting a spell, not from memory, but automatically. To his immense satisfaction, he felt the broken bone knit under his touch and, within moments, the black dog was bounding gratefully around his feet as if nothing had happened.

Well, Myrddin, your gifts are returning! the wizard told himself gleefully. "Well done, Baedd," the enchanter hugged his boar, "This poor fellow couldn't scramble back up in his condition. Another night down there would have done for him." The boar looked at Myrddin and squeaked, *oink!* The wizard believed the intelligent swine could understand his every word. He turned to stroke the dog, "Ci du, are you hungry, *bach?*" That solved the problem of a name for his new friend. *Ci du* meant nothing other than *black dog* in Myrddin's ancient tongue, but its sound pleased him, so the matter was settled.

He now had companions to feed, which made the success of his trap vitally important. Both animals watched intently as he removed and strangled a pheasant, then plucked it before cleaning it ready for cooking. Within the hour, the cavern filled with the delicious aroma of roasting game.

He shared out the meat fairly, but Baedd gobbled his down, while Ci du nibbled delicately at his pieces before having to defend them with bared teeth and growls from the greedy boar. Myrddin's hiss of disapproval had more effect because the boar knew he depended on the man. He slunk away to grub for acorns so that man and dog finished their meal in peace.

Resting afterwards, Myrddin squatted down and rocked on his heels, his eyes rolled in his head and he went into a trance. When he returned to his normal state, he knew that he had to move north because that was where he was needed. He set off with his black dog and white boar in his wake, the woollen blanket folded neatly over his shoulder. He did not cast a backward glance at the limestone cavern that had been his cosy home for the better part of two years.

Elsewhere, deep in the forest, an elderly woman emerged bright and early from her abject dwelling and blinked hard at the sight that greeted her. Two kids were tied, one on either side of her nanny goat. How was it possible? Who could have hitched them there? On closer inspection, she discovered that one was a billy and the other a female. Her lined face lit up into a gummy smile as she contemplated a rosier future, still, she was unable to explain the mystery. Fleetingly, she thought about the pathetic shambling man she had pitied and wondered whether in some angelic way she had been repaid for her kindness to him. She shrugged and hurried over to lead the goats to pasture.

Myrddin's journey was long and slow and had to be frequently interrupted for material needs. The pathways were unknown to him but his reading of nature was such that he navigated northwards successfully. Signs such as on which side of tree trunks moss grew indicated north.

The wild man and his strangely assorted animals travelled throughout the spring and summer until, unwittingly, they crossed the border into Caledonia. Myrddin's hunting and fire-lighting skills ensured that they never went hungry. Even so, the wizard's appearance made him repugnant to everyone but the most kind-hearted soul. Providence ensured that it was such a person who encountered the outlandish trio.

Myrddin first noticed Ci du's hackles raised and a low rumbling growl deep in the dog's throat, together with a reluctance to proceed along the trail.

"Who's there?" the enchanter called, alarmed.

"No-one of any importance," came the reply in Myrddin's same language. "You have nought to fear. Come, ease your weary bones in my humble abode."

The little black dog ran, wagging its tail, towards a cleft in a rock face, somewhat similar to the cavern they had left in the forest weeks before. Closely behind the pup ran Baedd and both, earlier diffidence gone, vanished into the cavern, where Myrddin found them embraced by a figure rivalling him for unkemptness.

"Who are you?" Myrddin asked.

"No-one of any importance," repeated the hermit. "I was forewarned of your arrival in a dream."

"Are you then, also a seer?"

"Nay, but I speak with the Lord," said the saint, "and He told me that a soul in torment would come to visit me."

"In torment? Ay, it's true." Tears flooded uncontrollably down Myrddin's face. "It's my fault! All those dead, including my three brothers! Had I been more careful I could have warned my king to avoid the slaughter."

"I see no fault in you, friend, only penitence and a dark shadow around your soul."

"You say you are not a seer, yet you see clearly!"

"It is the Lord who has cast the scales from my eyes."

"You say you are no-one of any importance, but our meeting is not by chance. I am Myrddin, descendant of the druids and a lifelong sun-worshipper."

"Then you have erred for an entire lifetime, Myrddin, but the Lord is ready to embrace you if you will do the same for Him."

Myrddin felt a tug at his heart, matched by an equal reluctance to surrender his magical arts. As if reading his mind, the hermit smiled sadly and shook his head. "You must realise, Druid, that your gifts are freely given by the Creator and you are called to use them for good.

"What is your name?"

"Whatever you wish it to be. I have different names, but the saint who rescued me and my mother from the furious sea called me Mungo. It means *my beloved* and he gave me communion and opened my heart to God's love. You are possessed by an evil spirit who torments you wilfully, undermining your faith in yourself to prevent you from achieving what the Lord has planned for you."

Myrddin lapsed into silence and contemplated the wall behind the shoulder of the seated hermit. He recognised the truth in the words of the recluse and posited himself a series of questions: if Mungo's words were untrue, why was he directed into Caledonia? Was it possible that his insights and gifts were God-given? Had he not used his powers frequently for good—such as repaying the old woman's kindness?

After a long respectful silence, Mungo said, "Well, Myrddin, will you come to the stream and be baptised in the name of Christ?"

"My king, the saviour of my nation, is a Christian. I have heard you speak from the heart, Mungo. I will come with you. I shall wash away this dirt along with my sins." Myrddin emerged from the fast-flowing stream as clean as a rainbow trout and as spiritually unsullied as his dripping body.

Mungo led the naked, shivering figure back to his cave and, rummaging in the depths, pulled out a black monastic habit. "Here, wear this. Saint Serf raised me in a monastery. I have chosen to live in isolation and no longer need it. By wearing it, you'll openly renounce the temptation to return and live in self-pity. Repeat after me, I bear no blame for the deaths in Arthur's last battle."

"Ay, I see it now! The devil hooked my foot in the tree root. I bear no blame for the deaths in Arthur's last battle: I bear no blame."

"Good, now, Myrddin, on your way, and remember to pray for guidance, for God has a greater plan for you than you imagine when you emerge from a trance. In a state of stupor, you open yourself to the devil's insinuations. In prayer, you commune with the Lord. Dwell only on these words. Go in love and peace, my brother."

Myrddin set off, again towards the north, but he had only gone a mile before he stopped to sit on a rock overlooking a river, where he gazed on the beauty of Creation and, whereas normally he would have fallen into a trance, he remembered the saint's words and bowed his head to pray for guidance.

16

CAMELOT AND CALEDONIA, AD 420

King Octa of Kent, son of Hengest, listened attentively to his elders. More than ever, he needed good advice because Kent was fertile territory and the Picts and Scoti had increased their raids on his coasts. The British Isles were increasingly parcelled into kingdoms, many of them Saxon ones, especially on the east coast. None of them, as his greybeards pointed out, were as strong as the Romano-British Kingdom of Logres, led by King Arthur, who regularly defeated the enemies who dared to challenge him in combat.

Octa smiled at his uncle, Oisc, and insisted, "You are right, I'll go to persuade Arthur to deal with the Picts and Scoti together with our warriors, but *you* will come with me to convince him."

Back in Camelot, Arthur sorely missed Myrddin, who had vanished three years before. He yearned for his wise counsel, but also for the insights the seer's prophecies provided. Yet, it was fair to say that the Cambrian had provided him with the most important revelation: he had to fight twelve battles to achieve his aim. Seven were now history, so another five awaited him.

Arthur sat deep in thought, trying to place those future events into some kind of context. Apart from his own kingdom, the south-west was in the hands of Britons, as was Cambria. None of them led an existence untroubled by marauders, but Logres, at least, clung on to the villas and civilisation that the Romans had constructed. Elsewhere, there were

Anglian, Saxon, and Jutish kingdoms that were clearly demarcated towards the eastern and south-eastern parts of Albion. The Britannia of his youth no longer existed; nor, for that matter, did the Roman Empire. The Western Empire was still nominally led by the ineffectual Honorius, but such were the power struggles in Italy that last year, a five-year-old had married an infant girl, aged two. Arthur snorted: how had the mighty fallen! Momentarily, real control lay in the hands of the boy emperor's widowed mother, but she would be just another brief comet in the night sky before her light was extinguished by the forces of darkness. Emperor Honorius struggled to keep the Huns at bay, but if not them, he had to contend with the Vandals in Hispania and Gallia, the Franks had crossed the Rhine, and the Goths and Visigoths would have to deal with them.

Arthur had given considerable thought to where his next battle should be fought. He had allies to the north and to the south; Myrddin would have advised him, but as it was, he would have to decide for himself. Or so he thought, until he received a visit from the Jutish king of Kent and his retainers.

The King of Logres could only nod wisely when King Octa complained about Pictish incursions along the coast of Kent. The formidable Caledonians were not dissuaded by the long sea journey either to the east or the west. Arthur could understand the balanced reasoning of the Saxon counsellors. It was true that defeating several shiploads of Picts in Kent or in Logres' own great estuary would hardly resolve the problem in the long run.

"You understand that by taking the fight to the Picts, in their inhospitable terrain, the situation changes enormously," Arthur pointed out. "More than one battle will be needed to quell those savages!"

"Aye, sire, but taking the fight to them is the only way to stop them from raiding our homes."

"I, too, am convinced of that," Arthur said. "However, the overland journey is too exhausting; we will need ships to take us to their borders. I have friends in the north who will fight beside us. We should dock in the Boderia Estuary and march inland from there."

The monarchs agreed to sail north from Kent as soon as the spring presented them with favourable weather. Just before his departure, Arthur received a communication from Ravenna, which revealed that a law had been passed making it illegal to instruct barbarians in shipbuilding. The king smiled ruefully. What would Honorius think of the Romano-British army travelling in Saxon ships to Caledonia; moreover, in the company of the barbarians?

They saw three Saxon vessels near the coast of Essex, but since King Octa had no desire to attack his similars, they allowed them to enter an inlet unimpeded—more settlers, Arthur thought.

After mooring in the Boderia Estuary and setting up an overnight camp, Arthur spoke with King Octa. "Of course, we could send a messenger to the Picts to demand hostages in exchange for a peaceful outcome."

"It's not in their nature," Octa shook his head, "but you can always try."

The Saxon was correct; the mortified messenger had been stripped and bound to his horse, his ears ringing with taunts and insults before the Picts slapped his horse's rump and sent it galloping into the enemy camp.

Arthur sent out scouts in the hope of tracking the Picts to their stronghold, but without success.

The following morning, therefore, the joint force made a decoy run along the wooded valley of the River Tuessis. It was enough to encounter an outlying Pictish force.

The Saxons expected an easy victory against them, going into this first battle. Indeed, the Picts retreated nearly as soon as they'd started fighting, and then Octa declared: "Our troops proved their superiority."

But Arthur would not allow his ally to be fooled by an illusion and ordered an immediate retreat to the ships. While he served on Hadrian's Wall, he had heard of Romans setting up their camp, thinking they had frightened off the enemy, only for the Picts to return, pouring out of the woods and seemingly out of thin air. They caught the Romans completely unaware and massacred them. "We must be ready for their tricks on their own ground, King Octa," Arthur said. He had his men pretend to be otherwise engaged, making a camp, but retained the majority aboard ship, ready for immediate action.

Arthur explained, "That is why I left the cavalry behind; I remember a centurion reporting to me when I was his commandant, time and time again, the Picts would lure our men into a false sense of security before striking when their guard was down. For instance, they would often charge our cavalry on horseback and immediately retreat, luring them away from their infantry. Then, a second squad of Picts would leap out of the woods and slaughter any Romans that had been foolish enough to give chase. That is what we are up against, my friend. You cannot expect the Picts to fight you on your terms. We must be prepared for traps, fireballs, and decoys. I remember once," Arthur recalled, "they had planted sharpened stakes under the snow and I saved a whole troop of men by noticing a depression at the last minute."

"By Odin! They fight like cowards!" Octa grimaced.

"Nay! Not so," Arthur said. "They are bold fighters, who never surrender, but they fight with immense cunning. Also, be prepared to see them painted blue, for they shave and paint their bodies with woad, except for the head. It makes them look more ferocious and instils fear into their enemies."

"Not into us! We're not afraid of blue men," Octa said. "They bleed red like the rest of us. But thank you for warning me. I'll prepare my men for such an encounter."

"That's not all I need to tell you, King Octa," Arthur sounded concerned. "You see, if you go ahead boldly and try to fight the Picts as an honourable Saxon, you will meet with a terrible defeat. You have to fight them taking into account their way of going about war."

"I'm not sure that I understand, friend Arthur."

"A campaign this far north can be a nightmare. This is barren heathland with sporadic small farms in sheltered areas and widely dispersed herds of semi-wild animals. It cannot support 20,000 troops *off the land*. If we planned to stay long enough, food to support the troops would have to be brought up from the Lowlands by cart or mule across barren terrain with no roads, often under driving rain. Caledonian war bands would harass these essential supply trains and eat our grain or cattle. Do you see what I mean, King Octa?"

The Saxon's face had seriously changed expression. For a moment, he looked distinctly crestfallen, but equally quickly, his countenance became pugnacious. Arthur could sense frustration and tension building up in his ally.

"What are you saying, King of Logres? Have we come all this way to lose our men to small groups using sting-and-fly tactics?"

Arthur snorted, "Nay, that is what they want. We must outwit them and make them long for peace."

Octa frowned and appeared bewildered, "I can't imagine an easy solution."

"It's no coincidence we haven't seen them yet. They are watching and waiting. We must lead them to believe that we are building an encampment by the riverside, but we'll trick them."

"Explain, Arthur!" King Octa was growing impatient.

"Look, I have kept most of the men aboard ship, with instructions to remain silent. The small number you see out here are going through the motions of digging a ditch."

"How will that help our cause?"

Arthur displayed his confidence by replying at once, "The Picts prefer naval warfare to fighting on land. It's no coincidence that they sail down as far as your kingdom, Octa. I'm convinced that they will come with their vessels, either late in the day or, indeed, at night to catch us by surprise."

"By Thor! But we'll be ready for them!"

"If I'm wrong, we'll have to think again," Arthur said, but added buoyantly, "I know I'm not wrong."

Arthur was right, but not in the way he believed. The Picts had a surprise in store for him.

At night, at least a hundred skin boats, each piloted by a single occupant and driven by the current, drifted down the river, with only four of them illuminated by a torch, placed at regular intervals; these served as guides for the others. If the Pictish plan was to take the allied ships by surprise, they failed miserably because Arthur's lookouts spotted them at once and archers picked off the illuminated torchbearers easily enough. Javelins accounted for many more. The others fled across to the far bank, away from the purported Roman camp and made good their escape. The expedition had failed miserably, but neither could it be considered a Romano-Saxon victory. On the other hand, if Arthur had not been so aware of the enemy's cunning, the entire fleet might have been burnt in the night.

The following morning, his men collected some of the skin boats to study them. They resembled nothing so much as a collection of greater and lesser baskets; small boats made of wickerwork and covered with hide.

They were light craft with textile coverings, as the Picts vaunted weaving skills and had the means to make a waterproofing tree sap-based tar. The majority were constructed of flannel and tar and were about half the weight of the hide-covered version. Arthur had never seen such a vessel before and had to admire the ingenuity of his foe. One such boat could be carried by a lightly-armed man overland to a nearby river, where he could move silently and rapidly with the current. The king began to regret coming so far north to challenge this wily foe on his own turf and in his rivers. The more he thought about it, the more convinced he became that the previous generations of Romans had not conquered the Highlands, despite the efforts of successive emperors, for a good reason. It was a reason that urged him to return south, despite his agreement with the Saxons.

Arthur and Octa stood, daggers almost drawn, glaring at each other. The cause of their dispute was disagreement over how to proceed with the campaign. Octa was a bluff character who relished nothing more than a good fight, whereas Arthur urged caution and pointed out that if they could locate the Pictish fleet, they could inflict such destruction that the coasts of their respective kingdoms would be free of them for years.

"I'll lead my men up the valley in pursuit of these cowards!" King Octa snarled.

Arthur could see an advantage in this as it would keep the Saxon leader occupied and the enemy distracted while he patrolled the inlets directly to the north.

Given his way, Octa became friendly again and readily agreed to let Arthur take the ships up the coast. They would meet again at the same place in three days. "In any case, you won't find anyone," Octa muttered.

I could say the same to you, my friend, Arthur thought, but settled for an enigmatic smile.

From the stern of his ship, Arthur watched Octa and half of his men march blithely into the woodlands. The Romanised Briton could not shake off a feeling of foreboding, but he consoled himself, the Saxon's character was not one to easily suffer advice.

Their fleet sailed north throughout the day, ignoring the small Tuessis Estuary in favour of making for the Pict heartland around the Petchaish Estuary. Arthur had never been this far north but had heard awed tales of green fireballs lighting the night skies, although he thought these were tales for old women. The landscape was certainly breathtaking and the estuary vast. They directed their ships into the narrower channel at the south of the extensive bay, but Arthur was sorely disappointed not to find enemy ships, except for a couple of harmless fishing craft of no interest. In the distance, inland, they could see the hills of Caithness and the easily identified peaks of Morven and Scaraben.

Arthur decided not to venture farther north to the Virvedrum promontory because, although he believed he might find the Pictish fleet so distant, he would never make his assignation with Octa in time and he was not loath to abandon his ally to the mercy of the Picts.

Therefore, they sailed south and for scrupulousness, sailed two miles into the Tuessis Estuary, where they found their prey. They were upon the Pictish vessels before the enemy could react and Arthur's swift commands soon had the enemy ships blazing, the stiff breeze making the allies' task simple as the flames leapt from one ship to another. Arthur smiled wryly as Picts leapt overboard to drown, for he had heard that the Picts ritually drowned their high-ranking enemy captives. He counted the number of vessels burnt to the waterline and had passed forty when he declared himself satisfied and ordered the withdrawal. He had accomplished what he had set out to do. If Octa had succeeded in avoiding the wily Picts, their expedition would have been a great success.

The fleet arrived at the meeting place earlier than agreed and both kings were delighted to see each other hale and hearty. Octa spoke of the enemy's cunning, but bragged about outwitting them and showed Arthur the ghastly blue-painted head of the enemy chieftain that he claimed to have slain himself after laying his own trap. With a nonchalant gesture, he threw the head into the river and chortled, "Let the fish god feast on him!"

For his part, Arthur explained how they had sailed miles out of their way before returning to deal with the Pictish fleet. He did not need to brag because the Saxon's uncle elaborated on their triumph, at least doubling the true number of ships they had destroyed.

17

THE RIVER BASSAS. KINGDOM OF LOGRES AND ISCA SILURIUM, AD 420

REPORTS REACHED ARTHUR AT THEIR OVERNIGHT STOP IN Arbeia that Scoti marauders were pillaging in the area around Glevum. He drew on the goodwill banked with Octa to persuade him to sail past Kent and help fight the Scoti in Logres. The long voyage took them around the Antivestaeum promontory—the extremity of Cornwall—bringing them into the Sabrina estuary. Primus and a cavalry unit met his father to inform him that the Scoti had bypassed Glevum and its stout walls in favour of pillaging inland. Primus' scouts were ready to lead the army into combat, heading in a north-easterly direction.

During the long voyage, in response to a dream, King Arthur found himself a painter and had him decorate his shield with the image of the Mother of God. Primus admired it and asked about it.

"It was rather strange as far as dreams go, Primus. You know how it is when you are half-awake and images come to you? Well, mine was of Myrddin. I'm convinced it was he speaking to me in my sleep. Except that he was so bedraggled that I scarcely recognised him at first. His hair was long and tangled and he wore only a loincloth—quite the wild man! I wonder what has become of him? Has he returned to Camelot?"

"Nay, Father. It must be three years since I last saw him. But what has this to do with your shield?"

"Everything. Myrddin informed me in the dream that I should bear this image into my next battle. I'd have given it no credence because when was Myrddin ever a Christian? The dream was too vivid to ignore and besides, these are desperate times."

At last, they came to the river Bassas, where a vast array of rovers, skirts swirling about their knees, beat upon their shields and hurled insults at the Romano-Saxon force. As in all his recent battles, Arthur, with the strength of an oak, led his men from the fore, inspiring them with his courage and resolve. The king must have been a terrible sight to the enemy as he charged forward, bearing the image of the Holy Virgin, Mother of God, upon his shield, and through the power of the Lord Jesus Christ, and Holy Mary, put the Scoti to flight, and pursued them the whole day with great slaughter. Thus was Myrddin's eighth prophesied victory completed and another alliance strengthened, although the two kings went their separate ways.

On their return to Camelot, Arthur and Primus were met by the beaming Gosvintha. "Husband, son, come with me, for I wish to show you a glad sight."

Father and son exchanged glances but meekly followed the queen to Camelot's ladies' room. With an expansive gesture, the queen swept her arm at the many sleeping infants. "Is it not a sight to behold!" she said proudly. "It is their future you are fighting for, my king."

Arthur was not so interested in babies but wished to please his wife and bent over several cots to inspect the contents. When Primus did likewise but turned away from a pretty little babe, Gosvintha caught his arm, "Why such a cursory glance, my boy? Do you not recognise your own daughter?"

"What? Has Willow delivered her child?" He almost knocked his mother off her feet as he turned back to the cot and fended off his father with a strong wrist, scooping up the babe into his arms.

"Hey! It's my grandchild!" Arthur complained before turning to his wife, "When was she born?"

"During the night, but Primus left in such haste this morning for your men's business that I could not forestall him."

"Is Willow well?" Primus asked.

"She's resting. Let her regain her strength. Why don't you start to think of a name for the child?"

"I already have a name for her, but I'll not say a word until I've spoken with Willow."

"That is only right and proper," Arthur laughed.

"Hand the babe to his grandfather, Primus. See how well all the babes sleep in this room. It is a safe, reassuring place. Not one of them is wailing. We fetch in the mothers when necessary, of course, but for now most of them are relaxing."

So, too was Willow, who smiled weakly after her travails. Her wide eyes gazed adoringly at her husband. "Have you seen our daughter, Primus?"

"Ay, she's as beautiful as her mother."

Willow sighed happily and sank deeper into her goose-down pillow, "Have you decided on a name?"

"I have, but I wanted to test your reaction. I'd like to call her Elvira, like your sister, because she is so brave and tenacious."

"Elvira would love that. It's a clever way of ensuring an aunt's love."

Primus crossed to the bed and sat, caressed his wife's hair, and kissed her gently on her forehead, breathing in the scent of rosewater in her hair. "Thank you for your gift to me, my love," he said. In this moment of bliss, war seemed to belong to another world and time.

Yet, it was not so—there was barely a week for him to become familiar with another scent, that of his newborn daughter when the call for help came to Arthur from across the estuary, since the Scoti had invaded Mona across the Irish Sea. Primus could not expect the same intensity of warfare as his father because Arthur had revealed Myrddin's prophecy of twelve battles to nobody else. He alone was aware that seven of these battles had already been fought. Only after the twelfth battle could Primus expect to enjoy peace with his family. King Vortigern in Powys called for help, so Arthur mustered his men once again, Primus included, and took them across at the *Trajectus*, where the Roman legions used to be ferried across the Sabrina. The journey, a distance of little over a mile at a point where the tides run swiftly, was a dangerous one, and its reputation, the roughness of the water, and the smallness of the boats deterred most travellers. As fortune would have it, the weather was favourable, so nobody was lost in transit.

The King of Dumnonia had repelled a Saxon leader, Hwita, with his six ships from the north-west coast of his kingdom. The would-be invader had sailed to Hibernia, where he had bargained with a Scoti leader, so together they sailed for Mona and swept all before them, taking the isle and then marching south-eastwards on the mainland. Arthur's scouts informed him that this allied enemy force was heading for the old Roman fortress of Isca Silurium, where the descendants of the Second Augustan Legion still lived. How many of them could be called upon to fight was a moot point.

Arthur lined his men up in front of the stone walls of the fortress and awaited the Saxon-Scoti attack. The thought of the whole of Cambria falling into their hands inspired the king to deliver a stirring speech about preventing the enemy from settling on their doorstep. His men were sufficiently roused when a scout came galloping up to his king.

"Sire, the enemy are in a meadow some two leagues to the north. They have formed up to face King Vortigern, who has pursued them from Segontium. The Saxons and Scoti outnumber King Vortigern but if we make haste, we shall triumph."

Their forced march brought them to the top of a low rise, from where it was clear that the battle had broken into dispersed bands confronting each other. The field was already littered with corpses and the usual shrieks and clashing of steel echoed around the valley. Arthur spotted Vortigern's standard, depicting a red and white dragon in combat, which he recognised from his visit to Camelot. He urged his men forward, as usual, himself to the fore, and swung the battle in favour of the hard-pressed Vortigern.

The Romans advanced, and as expected found themselves suddenly confronted by a hastily-formed wall of shields. Used to such an adversary, they readied their javelins. The Roman *pilum* punched through the enemy shield by virtue of its pyramidal point, the hole was wider than the narrow shaft, allowing it to pass through almost to a weighted ball. The iron shaft could easily bend, making the *pilum* very difficult to pull out, and impossible to throw back. It also made the shield near impossible to use with a *pilum* hanging out of it. The javelin had done its job, and the enemy was disrupted and deprived of a good number of its shields, Arthur led the advance of his shield wall with a thrusting sword blade protruding out from between every large shield. This is when the gladius would do its work, although the king preferred to use his magnificent sword—Excalibur.

Primus had tied one of his daughter's ribbons around his sword wrist and, inspired by the thought of Elvira's future, set about the foe as irresistibly as his father. Soon Arthur had hewn his way to Vortigern's standard, where the two kings exchanged triumphant grins. The battle was irretrievably lost for Hwita and his allies.

Respite had been gained from the constant threat brought across the waves from different far-off lands. But if the invaders, so disparate among themselves, could ally, so too could Arthur, who had little in common with the Jutish Vortigern and his Cambrian subjects. Even his people of Logres, although principally Britons, were also Romanised descendants of mixed origins. Arthur's own forebears were originally from across the North Sea. His forebear and namesake, Valdor, was a Batavian born and bred, but the Roman Empire had created a huge melting pot of races. Surveying the bodies dotting the battlefield, it was clear to the king that very few of them had originated among the green and pleasant valleys of Cambria.

This land meant much more to the missing Myrddin than to him. As far as Arthur was concerned, Cambria served as a buffer that guaranteed protection to his western border. As such, it was vitally important and well worth risking life and limb for. However, the king would have loved to share this victory with his Cambrian counsellor if only he knew how to contact him.

That particular problem was solved when he returned to Camelot, where one of his knights, Sir Aesu, a ginger-haired warrior with green eyes, came to him saying apologetically, "I would not trouble you with this, Sire, but the little wretch is so insistent—"

"Who, Sir Aesu?"

"An urchin from the forest, lord. He says he has a message from your Cambrian counsellor—by which I suppose he means Myrddin—and that it's urgent. His father is a charcoal burner and this imp is black-faced and ragged, in no state to stand before his king without a good scrubbing." The knight, dressed in fine silk and smelling of expensive scent, wrinkled his nose in distaste.

"Be that as it may, I'll hear him at once as I've been worried about Myrddin. He's been away from Camelot for far too long. Fetch the child, sir knight."

Aesu hurried away and returned with a skinny ragamuffin, the only white part of his face immediately under his nose where he had wiped mucus on his blackened and somewhat shiny sleeve.

"Do you have a message for me, child?"

"Ay, Sire." The boy's bright eyes were lively and suggested intelligence. An impression at once betrayed by his words—the few listeners thought him unhinged—except for Arthur, for whom they meant something.

"I spoke to an oak tree, Sire. It told me that it was the king's counsellor and belonged to a long line of druids. The tree made me learn these words, the child began to recite: *In the clearing where the hart died, use the same blade under the double gall; insert it in the flag bird's store to unbind the old man.* That's it, lord. Shall I say it again?"

"Ay," said Arthur, memorising the words before handing a silver coin to the boy. "You have done well. Give this coin to your father. He will spend it on your family, now, off you go and if you pass the oak tree, tell it I'm on my way!"

Sir Aesu and Sir Boduoc exchanged glances, raised an eyebrow and shrugged.

18

CAMELOT AND ISCA SILURIUM, AD 420

As he rode down the steep trail out of Camelot, King Arthur repeated Myrddin's message to himself in an attempt to decipher it. *In the clearing where the hart died, use the same blade under the double gall; insert it in the flag bird's store to unbind the old man.* It was not so mysterious as it at first struck him; a little logical thought was all that was needed. Myrddin had slain the wounded hart in a clearing with Arthur's sword, so he had to use Excalibur, evidently at an oak tree in the clearing. Once again, he would have to find oak galls, which shouldn't be too difficult. But what was the flag bird? That was the hardest part of the riddle. Was it a bird typically found on a flag—say, like the eagle? But did the eagle have a store? A nest, maybe, high up in the mountains. Nay, if not a bird on a flag, then, a flag on a bird! "Ay!" Arthur cried aloud, that would be it, the *flag* must refer to the plumage. So, a brightly coloured bird that had a store, what would that be? He rode on and thought for a few minutes until, suddenly, he exclaimed again, *I have it!* The woodpecker drummed into trees to store nuts for the winter. Ay, that made sense, especially because the woodpecker had a bright red cap of feathers. The old man would be Myrddin himself, but the king's purpose was to *unbind* him. What was he doing bound up? And what did it have to do with the oak tree?

Arthur groaned, nothing was ever straightforward with the Cambrian; weird was more likely. Yet, his desire to regain his magical counsellor was so strong that it never occurred to him to turn back to Camelot.

The last few years had been so intense that hunting had been out of the question for Arthur; yet, as he approached the woodland, as if he had never been away, he immediately recognised the entry among the trees that he had previously used. Although the king was distracted by the glimpse of a distant stag and tempted to head off in pursuit of it, his sense of duty prevailed. He recognised the minor trail where the hart had bolted long ago on that happy occasion and geed his horse along it until he came to the clearing. In the distance, between the trees, he caught sight of sunlight flashing on water. Vaguely, he remembered there being a lake in the vicinity, but his concentration was on the trees. Gazing around the clearing, his eyes rested on horse chestnuts, sycamore and ash trees, but none of them had the imposing trunk of the mighty oak that stood majestically to his right.

Arthur urged his horse up to the oak tree and was immediately struck by a narrow cleft, wide enough for a man to insert two fingers, that ran from the roots to the lowest branch. Higher up, a twig bore two oak galls, so the king knew that he had the correct tree. Now, he had to find the woodpecker's hole. His eye roamed upwards, above the lowest branch to where there was another branch that bore no leaves and looked more dead than alive and there, sure enough, was a neat, round hole under the galls, but it was out of his reach.

If he was to fulfil his instructions, Arthur would have to climb up the tree. To do so, he inched his horse under the lowest branch and, adjusting himself on the steed's back, sprang to clasp the bough with both hands. Frantically seeking purchase for his foot, the toe of his boot found the crack in the trunk—it was enough—thanks to his potion, the king's unnatural strength at his age enabled him to haul on another sound branch and stand on the solid lower one. Regaining his breath, the monarch searched for the woodpecker's hole and found it. Taking a firm grip on the tree trunk with one hand, Arthur drew his sword with the other and inserted the blade into the perfectly round hole in the dead branch.

With a mighty splitting sound, the crack in the oak trunk opened wide like the gates of Camelot and the figure of Myrddin stepped out of the inner hollowness. Arthur called down to him, but the wizard did not react; he stood still like a man without hearing. Suddenly, the Cambrian looked up and, spotting the king in the tree, called to him to come down quickly, "There's no time to lose," the enchanter shouted and did not reply when Arthur asked why haste was necessary.

Speed might have been required, but his foothold in the tree trunk had gone because the crack had opened to release his counsellor. He decided, therefore, to withdraw and sheath Excalibur, then, to sit astride the branch he was standing on. Somehow, he had to transfer his entire weight to his arms and dangle from the lower branch. He struggled to do this but succeeded, whistling his horse as he sagged from the branch. As the intelligent creature stationed itself under the king's swaying legs, the monarch released his hold and dropped the short distance onto its back.

He called to Myrddin, who came over and offered an arm. Arthur hauled him up behind him. "Go! Waste no time!" came the urgent plea.

Arthur knew better than to argue, so kicked his heels and they sped out of the clearing back along the trail. The king half-turned his head and began to question his counsellor, who, much to his irritation, failed to reply to a single question. He had never known Myrddin to be so discourteous—it was as if he was speaking to a deaf man.

Within sight of the fortress, Myrddin tapped his shoulder, "Rein in and dismount," he said, "I'll explain everything."

The two men sat on a grassy bank as the horse cropped at the unexpected treat.

Myrddin pulled tightly packed moss out of his ears.

"What are you doing with moss plugging your ears and why were you lurking in a hollow oak?"

Myrddin clicked his tongue in annoyance. "Patience was never your greatest virtue, Arthur. Give me time to explain!"

"Well, you gave me no time to get out of that oak. I could have broken my back if I'd fallen."

"But you didn't. I would not have summoned you if it had meant you hurting yourself."

"Ah, I forget that you can read the future!"

Myrddin sighed heavily and his green eyes bored into Arthur's, "The Lady of the Lake trapped me in the oak with magic she had extorted from me."

"The Lady of the Lake?"

"Ay, one of the faery folks—a water nymph and a rare beauty. I am an old fool. I lost my heart to her. I should have known she only wanted me for my magic. Arthur, there is a price to pay for everything. I wanted you to have a magic sword and that led me down the slippery slope."

"Why the moss in your ears, Myrddin?"

"Sire, I could not remove it until out of earshot of the lake, for her siren song would have lured me back to her. Take my advice and never go near that lake, for now she knows that you have a copy of Excalibur and she will entice you to her to relieve you of it. Only that sword could unlock her spell on the oak. Her rage will be boundless now you have thwarted her, but she is doomed to live out her life in or near that lake, so you are safe far from the enchantress."

"Don't tell me that you have lived locked in that tree for three years, Myrddin."

"Nay, Sire, I have roamed far and wide. I was near your battle in Caledonia. That is when I met Saint Mungo and became a Christian."

Arthur's eyes widened and he blinked hard, "*You*, a Christian? How can a druid embrace the faith? Surely, you'll lose your magic powers?"

"Not so," Myrddin's lip twisted, "my gifts are God-given. I must use them only for good, after prayer and contemplation, else, as you say, I'll lose them."

"Is that how Christ performed His miracles, after prayer and contemplation?"

"Ay, something like that. You have fought eight of your twelve battles, Arthur. Remember, whatever happens, if you want my prophecy to come true, go nowhere near the Lady of the Lake. I shall not, even if she will not be the death of me. It is not given to us to know our own fate, but *she* told me that I'll suffer a triple death; it gave her pleasure since she's a wanton fay creature."

"When? Did she say *when*, Myrddin?"

The enchanter laughed sadly and shook his grey head, "It is not for me to know. But not soon, for I have seen things far ahead, acts that your grandson, Valdor, will perform. Meanwhile, great king, you will triumph in your twelfth and final battle."

Arthur groaned, "That means I have another three battles first—" he stopped short, "Ah, but I've always known that," he said. "When and where will the next one be, Myrddin? Tell me, so that I might better make ready."

"Where you went for your last battle."

"Venta Silurium?"

"Not exactly, but near there, Isca Silurium."

Arthur pursed his lips. "Ay, that is nearby, and it's as well to know it, for I can march around the estuary and not risk the dangerous ferry."

"Take the ferry, Sire. I foresee no tragedy."

Arthur would have set off there and then but realised that his counsellor had told him where but not when. So, he asked, "When should I leave Camelot?"

"If you wish to avoid a long march and cross the *Trajectus*, leave at dawn. The weather will be favourable, so nobody will be lost in transit. Time is important, time you cannot afford by circling the estuary because the Anglo-Saxons are intent on making Isca a stronghold. The Britons living there are no match for them. You must stop the barbarian westward expansion, Arthur. Their chieftains are cunning and they having avoided your kingdom of Logres is no coincidence. Evidently, neither is my release from that oaken prison. You liberated me in time to march on Isca."

The crossing went exactly as Myrddin predicted and Arthur's army entered Isca Silurium unopposed to the rejoicing of the townsfolk. Arthur inspected the defences because he had to decide whether to fight outside the fortress or to defend it against the invaders. He had been there once before, long ago, and needed to refresh his memory. He saw that the original earth and timber ramparts of the fortress were strengthened by the addition of a stone revetment at the front. Defences of this composite rampart consisted of a stone wall 5½ feet thick, backed by a clay bank and fronted by a single ditch.

Next, he strolled over to an inscription in a wall plaque recording that the barracks were rebuilt by the Second Augustan Legion in stone during 259. Suddenly, a wave of sadness swept over him, *Ah, those were the days—if only the Empire had been correctly governed, civilisation would still be flourishing in Britannia!*

He wandered away from the barracks, where his men were relaxing, over to the particularly impressive amphitheatre, whose arena was oval in shape with eight entrances and capable of holding six thousand spectators. *What a shame! This hasn't been used since the legion left some seventy years ago.* At this thought, another idea came to him, but it remained to be seen whether he could bring it to fruition.

To set his plan in motion, he drew on his knowledge of the characters of Vortigern and Octa. The two barbarian chieftains had much in common; both were valiant and proud, to the point of arrogance. They were quick-tempered and unlikely to back down if their mettle was put to the test. With this in mind, Arthur summoned Primus and ordered him to convene only the Knights of the Round Table. *It's a pity Regalis is no longer with me; that's owing to my foolish jealous nature! But I do have Gawain and Geraint among the others!*

Arthur led them into the amphitheatre and sat the twenty-one knights in the front row, while he addressed them from the arena. "Brother knights, I have a proposal for your consideration. What say you if we were to challenge the Anglo-Saxons to select their best twenty-two warriors to fight us in this arena? Whoever wins the day, wins the battle! In this way, many lives on both sides can be saved. Of course, we'll entrust our victory to God."

A shocked silence met his words, but one or two of the knights were smiling broadly.

Primus broke the silence, "Assuming they accept, Sire, can we trust the barbarians to keep their word?"

"They are proud people, Primus, remember how well Octa fought beside us in Caledonia?"

"Ay, but he's a Jute," Primus muttered so low that his father could not hear.

"I say we issue the challenge!" Gawain cried.

Soon, the amphitheatre echoed to the sound of cheering voices as the knights spoiled for the fight. Arthur raised a hand for silence and obtained it. "Then it is decided, I'll carry the message to the Saxons myself."

"*Anglo*-Saxons!" Primus muttered, and said aloud, "If there are Angles, Sire, it will be well to acknowledge them lest they take offence."

"Ay, that is what I meant and will be careful to respect their chieftains."

Arthur would not hear of anyone accompanying him to meet the Anglo-Saxons. He rode out, a lone figure, to the north-west. In his left hand, he carried a spear, but attached to it was the white banner that signified his peaceful intentions.

"I am Arthur, King of Logres and have a proposal for your chieftains," he declared boldly and watched as three men exchanged words in low voices.

"King Arthur, either you are very brave or foolhardy coming here alone," said one of them, a bare-armed muscular figure with a wolf-pelt draped over his shoulders, the glassy eyes of the dead creature seemed to fix him balefully, "I am Aldfrid, chieftain of these vagabonds and as I speak for them, I say that it must be an interesting proposal to take such a risk. We'll hear it!"

"Then this is it," Arthur said in a strong voice, "you can, of course, fight us, which you came here to do, but your scouts have told you that we have as many men as you, hidden inside yon fortress, armed and ready for war—"

"Or?" Aldfrid snapped impatiently.

"*Or*, you can fight my twenty-two best men inside the arena in the fortress. *I* and my son will be among our twenty-two. If your warriors win, Chieftain, you can take the crown of Logres and Camelot for your own. There is also a third option."

"Which is?"

"That you and your men are afraid of a fair fight, and you turn around and hurry away. We will let you go to Hibernia."

"Ha!" snarled Aldfrid, and his face contorted unpleasantly. "You are lucky you bear the white flag of parley, else I would smite you down, King of Logres, for no-one calls me a coward and lives."

"So, what is your decision?"

"One moment, Roman!"

The Saxon turned and spoke rapidly to the other two chieftains, who spent the entire time staring unflinchingly at Arthur before replying to Aldfrid. When they had finished, their gaze returned to Arthur's face.

Aldfrid spoke, "My comrades, Irmin and Ruma, accept your challenge, King. I will take your crown willingly," his laugh grated on Arthur's ears. "There's just one thing—"

"Ay?"

The Saxon's blue eyes seemed to draw closer together, but that was because they had narrowed, "You want my best twenty-two warriors, who will include we three, to enter that amphitheatre alone. How do we know that it is not a cunning trap to destroy our best men in one fell swoop?"

"I came here alone and you did not murder me. We can travel back together. You have my word, but to make you feel safer, I will accompany your men under the white flag into the amphitheatre and they can take seats to watch the spectacle. The theatre can hold six thousand spectators. My men can watch, too. Let's entertain our men, Chieftains Aldfrid, Irmin and Ruma." He looked at them in turn as he spoke, making sure they recognised that he honoured them by remembering their names. For their part, they judged him well, as a noble foe.

"It is agreed. Lead on, King Arthur."

Primus, anxious upon seeing his father with the enemy force behind him, rode out to meet him.

Arthur turned to the three chieftains. "This is my son, Primus, undoubtedly anxious for my safety, but do not be deceived, he is courageous, one of my score-and-two warriors. I will accompany him back to open the gates and warn my men that yours come in peace." He thrust the pole bearing the white flag into Aldfrid's hand. "I expect you in the arena after all your men are seated."

Aldfrid nodded respectfully and turned to bellow instructions, handing the white banner to a Saxon warrior. Arthur and Primus galloped to the citadel and through the gates, which closed behind them. Aldfrid was mouthing oaths just as the gates swung back open. "All is well, then!"

The three chieftains held back nineteen warriors and sent the others with instructions not to touch their weapons but to take seats peacefully in the amphitheatre. There they found their would-be enemies already peaceably seated, filling the southern and eastern sectors. They trooped into the north and western tiers and took their places. The silence was unexpected. Arthur had foreseen both sides trading insults. They would, in due course, as soon as the fighting began. His knights all wielded swords and shields, whereas the Anglo-Saxon warriors chose battle axes as their weapon, except for the three chieftains, who had decided on swords.

The twenty-two each side began to circle warily. Arthur called to them in their own language, "The boldest of you must come to fight me, for I am the greatest warrior here."

"Nay! *I* am," Aldfrid thumped his shield with the hilt of his sword and many of his warriors leapt to their feet in the seating tiers to jeer and hurl insults, swiftly traded by Arthur's army, who knew what to expect of their king. As the two strong warriors exchanged blows, Primus singled out Irmin, whom he recognised as standing next to Aldfrid earlier and sent Gawain to fight him, while he rushed at Ruma himself. Following the lead of these two, the other knights chose a battle-axe-swinging foe and, to a deafening roar around the arena, engaged a foe. The spectacle was ensured; however, the rules of engagement had not been established. Arthur and Aldfrid had not specified single combat. For the King of Logres, it was implicit but not everyone was likeminded. This detail became clear when it was one of the Round Table, Sir Prasto, to fall to a devastating axe blow and to the resounding cheers from the north and west of the monumental arena, matched by groans from the other sides.

With the death of Sir Prasto, his victor immediately turned to help Sir Geraint's opponent, who until that point had been hard-pressed. Arthur saw this from the corner of his eye and told himself, *all is fair in love and war! This is war and not only my crown, but my love is at stake.* This thought spurred him on to redouble his efforts and his oak-like strength belied his grey hair. With his added vigour, he soon bypassed his enemy's shield and drove Excalibur into Aldfrid's heart, reversing the cheers and groans around the stadium. He hurried to help Primus, for his son was his first thought. "Nay! Shrieked his heir, aid Geraint!" Arthur rushed to even the fight and, to the incredulity of the knight's new opponent, Excalibur sliced through the axe haft as if it were a mere willow wand, not seasoned birch. His courage was not at fault, as he parried another mighty blow from the deadly blade, and drew his seax to continue the fight. The seax was no match for a spatha, so the severely-pressed warrior had to concentrate on fending off shuddering blows, which contradicted the apparent age of his adversary. He would have been aghast had he seen the effect of those blows on the outside of his shield. The layer of leather gummed to the linden wood was now shredded and hanging in ribbons.

Meanwhile, more groans came from the Anglo-Saxon spectators as another chieftain, Ruma, fell at Primus' feet, where he met his end. At this point in the combat, the Anglo-Saxons were outnumbered because, now evenly matched, Geraint slew his single adversary. Primus and Geraint both had the same idea—if they could help Gawain defeat Irmin, maybe the battle would be over. Primus pulled rank on his comrade and, as his prince, ordered him to help the king. Arthur was on the threshold of victory, but did not slacken his efforts, so even as

Geraint approached, he delivered the fatal blow and dispatched his adversary. "What now, Sire?" Geraint called.

"Choose anyone to aid," Arthur replied and, setting the example, rushed to help Sir Boduoc. Together, they soon overcame his Anglian opponent and each turned to go to the aid of another. Since this state of affairs kept on repeating, the battle was soon won to the uproarious catcalls of Arthur's army, met by sullen silence from across the bloodied arena.

A man bearing the white flag stepped onto the battleground and walked over to Arthur, "I am Fridbarn, Aldfrid's son, chieftain in his place. He would not let me fight, but made me swear, in the event, to honour his pact. Therefore, King Arthur, I shall take my army to Hibernia and make an oath not to attack Logres. I have no quarrel with you, as you sent our best warriors to a noble death. They are now supping with our gods, as is fitting for such men." Fridbarn held out his hand and Arthur clasped it.

"Will the Angles accept you as their leader?"

The Saxon's lip curled, "It's agreed on oath, King Arthur. We are men of our word. We'll never know if our lesser warriors might yet have been better than yours. What I do know is that yours and father's pact has saved many lives, at least, until we meet the Scoti!"

Fridbarn led his subdued army away from Isca Silurium.

"The tenth battle is won," Arthur said in a low voice to Primus.

"What's that, father?"

"Oh, nothing, just something Myrddin once said," Arthur smiled and embraced his son. That day, he had taken a risk with Primus that the Saxon chieftain had not wished to run. He swore he would never do that again!

19

CAMELOT AND CHEDWORTH ROMAN VILLA, 421 AD

SIR GAWAIN APPROACHED HIS KING WITH A DEFERENTIAL expression, "Sire, I have a favour to ask on behalf of my father. You will remember that he was a centurion colleague under you on Hadrian's Wall. Well, since his retirement, he has given himself to commerce at the port of Glevum with such success that he has become a wealthy man."

"I'm glad to hear that your father prospers, Gawain, but what is the favour he seeks?"

Gawain smiled at the king's ready indulgence.

"He always says that he could not enjoy the fruits of his success were it not for the peace and security your reign brings to the land, so he wishes you to grant him the boon of a visit to his villa."

"Is that all, Gawain? Remind me of your father's name."

"Sire, you knew him as Centurion Volisius—"

"Ay, a good friend and a courageous soldier. But hark! Isn't he of royal blood?"

"He likes to boast as much. My grandsire was a Briton, Sire, and a chieftain. I'm not sure that counts as royalty. Ah, and remember that if you grant his wish, you should not call me Gawain, but *Mandacus*, the name my parents saddled me with!"

"If *Gawain* escapes me, I'll tell him that I gave you the name for the Round Table, which isn't far from the truth."

"So, you will come, Sire! Thank you!"

"Both you and your father deserve as much if not more. How far is the villa?"

"Not far, it's but three leagues to the east of Glevum and even closer to Corinium—"

"So, about 20 leagues from Camelot. We can ride there in a day. Send a message to Volisius to warn him of our arrival in four days. We'll take three knights with us. Five of us should not eat him out of his home!"

Four days later, Gawain led the small but jovial band, composed of Arthur's favourite knights, although he left Primus with his family, east from the coastal air of Camelot to join the Roman road, the Fosse Way, running from Isca Dumnoniorum to Lindum Colonia. "We can stay on this road for the rest of the ride," Gawain explained, "as father's villa is just off the road and eight miles north of Corinium Dobunnorum."

Arthur had chosen a lovely spring day for the excursion so that as they approached the *villa rustica*, he fully appreciated the sapient choice of location in a sheltered, shady position in the valley overlooking the River Coln among the Cotswold Hills. The king knew from his accounts how important this Cotswold area was for agriculture. Indeed, there were some fifty villas dotted around these hills, each a fecund source of produce; it was, the king learnt later from his host, one of nine, in just a five-mile radius.

Former centurion Volisius hurried out of the ornamental gates to welcome his king.

When Arthur dismounted, as did the others, he hurried over to him and knelt, taking and kissing his hand. Arthur hauled him to his feet and embraced him, "Nay, old comrade, I'll not have you kneeling before me. I remember how bravely you charged forth against the Picts, leading by example and your son, Ga-w—*er*—Mandacus is a truly worthy offspring."

The father hurried to hug his son and then, having welcomed his companions, said, "Please follow me so that I can show you why my predecessors chose this location for my villa." He led them to a *nymphaeum*, dedicated to a natural spring in the north-west corner of the complex which was the villa's main source of water, and around which was later built an apsidal shrine to the water-nymphs. "See, Sire, I am a Christian, but my forerunners were right to worship the water! It is a God-given source of life. Here, we have had various building phases, but this was the first. The spring became the location for this shrine with the curved rear wall 2 metres high and it is the original Roman masonry. All of the water needs of the villa are provided for by this spring. See, the octagonal pool is located at the centre, and is fed by the spring." He led them over to gaze into the limpid depths of the pool, where Sir Geraint cupped his hands and sucked greedily at the pure liquid.

"Ah, it's cool and sweet!" he said appreciatively.

"Not only that," said Volisius proudly, "but successive previous owners rebuilt the baths in the north wing and changed them to a *laconicum*, with dry heat, which means we have both damp-heat and dry-heat bathing suites. After your ride from Camelot, you might wish to relax in them. There's plenty of time before our banquet. Of course, the blessed water provides us with a *hypocaust* under the dining room, which is the one recent addition I have made. I brought in skilled mosaic craftsmen to depict the four seasons in the floor."

"Hypocaust, that's underfloor heating," Gawain explained in a whisper to his best friend Geraint, "would that I had it in my chamber in Camelot."

"You're soft enough as it is!" Geraint teased him, wary of the dangerous look in Gawain's eye.

"Come! Let me show you quickly around my home and then you can sample our best wine and relax with a gentle bathe," Volisius said. Thus, they admired the twenty-five rooms and heard how the proprietor intended to expand further in the next few years to a total of thirty. Even the king was awestruck at the splendour of the mosaics, which almost every room boasted.

"You must give me the name of your mosaic craftsman, Volisius, for I would like to create a particular Christian design at Camelot in my queen's chamber."

"Sire, I am a Christian too, and have converted a temple, some 800 paces outside the villa into a small church if you wish to visit it after you have rested."

"Willingly, good Volisius. Your home convinces me that while I am king, and hopefully while my heir follows me, we shall not permit barbarians to come pillaging and despoiling such beauty and luxury. It is as well to know precisely what one is fighting to preserve."

"Bless you, Sire, now let us drink to your long life!"

Meanwhile, back in Camelot, Myrddin subjected Arthur's youngest grandson, Valdor, to his hypnotic powers, leading him, entranced, outside the walls to a hollow where they basked in the mild spring sunshine and listened to a distant cuckoo calling across the valley.

"Valdor, what I am about to tell you, you will share with nobody, and it'll remain in your mind for the rest of your days. You will soon leave Camelot for Cair-Caratauc to go in search of a Saxon bride. She will be one of the westernmost Saxons, the daughter of a chieftain. Her family will accept you because you are Arthur's grandson. Together you will have a son and you will call the babe Cynoda. One day he and his descendants will rule this kingdom; it will no longer be called Logres, but will be known as the Kingdom of the Gewisse. Your son will be a great king. It is the only way that your family will remain as kings of this land, for one day in the distant future," Myrddin's eyes rolled back in his head, revealing only the whites, "Britannia will be united, at last, under a different name and a Saxon king. Aargh!" He slumped onto his side and lay still in the grass. Valdor snapped out of his trance and turned his attention to the state of the elderly enchanter, "Are you alright, Myrddin?" He shook his shoulder and the counsellor sat up, his eyes as bright and piercing as ever.

"Hey? Alright, ay. What about you, my prince?"

"I know not. It is as if I have heard something important, but for the life of me—"

"You need not fret, Prince Valdor, for it will come to you without any effort on your part, trust me!"

"Oh, I do trust you, my grandfather's dearest counsellor."

"Thank you, lord."

Back in Camelot, two items of strange news greeted Arthur: the first, Primus communicated to him, "Father, my brother has vanished."

"Valdor has vanished? How so?"

Primus looked pleased with himself, "I think we need not fear because I sought Myrddin's counsel and he told me not to worry, for Valdor has gone off in search of a Saxon bride."

"A Saxon? That's a good idea!"

Primus looked shocked. "How can you say that? We are a Christian family."

"Which is why we'll win her round to our way of thinking. Mine is that the offspring of hybrid stock bring vigour into the family. Look at you! I did it with your mother."

"Ay, but she was a Christian."

"I had to save her from heresy, my boy!"

Primus knew better than to argue with his father, so he delivered his second item of news. "We have a minstrel come to Camelot from overseas."

"Now, that's music to my ears!" Arthur jested. "Bring him to me, Primus. He'll play for the Knights of the Round Table and me."

The minstrel bowed before the king and gazed overawed around the circular table at the renowned and muscular knights. He spoke with a pleasant accent, "Sire, I am a bard and come from the Rhineland, where I have seen the ruin of many a fine building inside city walls once insurmountable, but now overrun and destroyed by the enemies of the once-mighty Empire. What I have seen inspired me to write a song about the importance of defending what I call *the giants' work,* for the barbarians cannot appreciate beauty and would use the tessellated floors as a surface to thresh grain." The harpist bowed and Arthur inclined his head graciously because after his eye-opening visit to Volisius' villa, he was receptive to the theme of the song.

The harpist strummed his strings, swiftly converting the sound into a melody and breaking into a chant with a rich, deep voice:

> *Though once splendid, fate laid waste to the wall,*
> *City buildings tumbled; giants' works did fall.*
> *Towers crumbled, roofs lay ruined and bare,*
> *Gates broken, frost and moss now everywhere.*
> *Ceilings gaping wide, plaster cracked and old,*
> *Through storms and kingdoms, this wall did hold.*
> *Builders raised arches, halls with chimneys bright,*
> *Bathhouses and beer houses, alive with delight.*
> *Fate's hand brought change, spread slaughter and disease,*
> *Warriors' halls empty, echoing with unease.*
> *City crumbled, builders gone, armies at rest,*

Halls now empty, roofs now distressed.
Decay brought it down, smashed to rubble's heap,
Where once stood stone buildings, now in silence sleep.
Hot streams once flowed, fountains within the wall,
Now all that remains, a memory's call.

He played a few concluding notes and sighed deeply, bowing his head.

Arthur clapped his hands and the knights took up the applause.

"Tell me, sir minstrel, have you seen such sights with your own eyes or are your words the licence of a poet?" Arthur asked.

"Sire, I call my song *The Ruin*, because sadly, this is what the future holds unless Roman generals can stem the tide of barbaric peoples who worship bloodthirsty gods. I fear that they have been unworthy and unable to do so, except in some happy islands of peace, such as yours, Sire."

"Tell me, fellow, what is your name and whence your origins?"

"Lord, my name is Marius and I am nobility of Gallic descent, but after Emperor Honorius found himself an able commander, Constantius, who defeated Maximus and Gerontius, and then Constantine, last year, I fled to Britannia, seeking a place of peace for my old age. I believe I have found it in Logres if you will let me stay."

"I will, Marius, although we know little of your news here in my kingdom."

"Well, Sire, you will have surely heard of the sack of Rome by Alaric and his Goths, some years ago, the product of Honorius's indecisive character. This so-called emperor hides in Ravenna and even when he finds a decent general, he undoes his work. In my native Gaul, for example, he recalled Constantius's troops to Italy, and Jovinus revolted in northern Gaul, with the support of the Alans, Burgundians, and the nobility of Gallic descent, but I no longer wish to be a part of it—as you heard from my song."

"It is fortunate, Marius, that our ambitions coincide. I wish to encourage the arts and crafts in my kingdom, to restore and retain the splendour that was Rome. There is a place for poetry and song in Logres."

20

CAIR-CARATAUC AND ENVIRONS, AND CAMELOT, 421 AD

MYRDDIN PLACED HIS HANDS OVER HIS TEMPLES AND groaned. When more than one person wanted him at one time, his head spun and felt as if it was splitting. It happened that Valdor and Arthur both needed him at the same time but in a different and distant place. Valdor's need appeared to Myrddin more urgent, so in the seclusion of his chamber, he opened his window with a view over the surrounding countryside, and performed magic that he ensured nobody ever saw: he shifted shape into a falcon and flew high and free, speeding towards the Saxon stronghold of Cair-Caratauc.

Valdor sat alone on a rock, contemplating his misfortune. He had set off impulsively from Camelot without consulting anyone and without considering how he could successfully conclude the wooing of his Saxon princess. He had made a good impression on Cwen's parents, most importantly, on her father; Cenhelm was keen to unite with King Arthur's family, but custom had it that a prospective husband had to offer his wife a valuable gift, the *morgengifu*—morning-gift—which consisted of paying money or giving land for the lady's hand in marriage.

Valdor groaned and buried his face in his hands. Why hadn't Myrddin, so much wiser than he, advised him that he would need such a gift? He did not notice a falcon perching on a branch above him and only raised his bowed head when a voice said:

"Because you slipped away without a word of farewell. What chance did you give me, Prince?"

Valdor leapt to his feet, "Myrddin! What brings you here?"

"Your moaning and misery, of course! Do you not know, Valdor, that sorrowful thoughts wing their way faster than light? It only takes an attuned ear to receive the message."

"I've made a mess of things, Myrddin. I've found the most wonderful, the most beautiful, kind and loving maiden that ever lived and she loves me, too. Her father likes me, but—"

"But you have no morning-gift for this paragon of feminine charm and that is why you summoned Myrddin."

"Summoned?"

"Ay, did you not? If you prefer, I can walk away."

Valdor took a step forward, held out a hand, which quickly dropped limply and futilely to his side. "There's nothing to be done. Where am I to obtain a *morgengifu* worthy of Cwen?"

Myrddin's whiskers seemed to bristle. "Do you have no faith in Myrddin, then?"

"Can you help me, Myrddin? I'll be forever in your debt."

Myrddin's lip curled, "Do not doubt it! Here," he reached inside his cloak and took out a silver coin. "Use this."

Valdor stared at the silver piece with contempt. "How is this supposed to help me with the *morgengifu*?" His tone was scornful, bordering on insolence.

"Do not test my patience, Prince. Take the coin to that little house near the woods and give it to the ceorl who lives there in exchange for a spade."

"A spade?"

"There is nothing wrong with your hearing, lord."

"Oh, very well," Valdor said, his mood verging on the exasperated.

Myrddin watched him go and chuckled to himself. Thwarted love could play strange tricks, since the usually polite, charming young man had become an insolent boor. But he, Myrddin, would restore his good nature very soon.

Valdor came back bearing a spade worth much less than the silver coin, but, nevertheless, worth a fortune.

"Follow me, Prince Valdor!"

Myrddin led the prince along a woodland trail until they came to a rocky outcrop, screened by a hazel grove. The enchanter pushed his way between two trees and Valdor followed. "There!" pointed Myrddin, his tone triumphant, "Dig there, Prince Valdor."

Curious and eager to oblige, the young man's strong arms heaved light, loamy soil into a heap beside him. After a while, he unearthed soiled sacking. Carefully scraping away the soil, he revealed more of the sack and tried to insert his spade under it. The battle to release the container from the soil, at last, won, Valdor raised it clinking intriguingly from the ground.

"Aaargh!" Overcome by some emotion, Myrddin slumped to the leaf mould.

Valdor laid the sack down and bent urgently over the seer.

"What is it, Myrddin? Are you ill?"

"Aaargh! Blood and death! I see the bloodied faces of the robbers' victims and those slain among themselves, all for greed!" His eyes rolled, but he sat up, "Only one man knows where this treasure is hidden, and, to his rage, he will find it gone!"

"Treasure? Let's see."

"It's a hoard, stolen and concealed here, not so long ago."

Valdor gently shook the sack and was met by the glint of gold. Coins, bracelets, armlets, necklaces, and sword pommels resplendent in gold and garnet greeted his astonished eyes, among the other assorted objects. "There's a fortune here, Myrddin!"

"Ay!" chuckled the seer.

"But what use is it to me?" the prince said gloomily.

"What do you mean?"

"I can't give this to Cwen in a muddy old sack."

Myrddin's stare bored into the prince. "Valdor, since boyhood, I have known you as a bright intelligent youth. Love must have clouded your intellect. Look! Just one of those gold coins is enough to have a craftsman sell you a beautiful strongbox. Now, out of my sight, while I conceal myself somewhere with the treasure until you return."

Valdor stumbled over an apology, bent to pick out a gold coin and hurried back to the settlement, where he found a furniture maker and explained that he needed a portable chest fit for a lady's jewels. The elderly craftsman's eyes widened unmistakably with greed when he saw the gold coin and he was not about to allow scruples to prevent him pocketing it.

"The only thing like that I possess is this velvet-lined chest. I've just finished it. It was commissioned by a Christian priest to hold a chalice and other objects he uses in his ceremonies. I can make another one for him. Naturally, I wouldn't keep Thor waiting, but his puny god is another matter."

"Watch your tongue, old fellow! I'm a Christian, but my need is greater than the priest's. Make sure you make him one just as good. Here's your coin. I know I've overpaid, but it matters little to me."

"Whatever you say, lord," the craftsman's eye gleamed as he handed over the chest.

Valdor decided to take no chances, so he entered the wood with his sword drawn and the chest under his left arm. He need not have worried because had there been any danger of the marauder returning, Myrddin would have foreseen it; just as he foresaw when Valdor would arrive by the outcrop.

"Over here," said the wizard, drawing aside a shrub to reveal the sack. Valdor knelt on the turf and transferred the treasure, item by item, into the blue-velvet-lined chest.

"I'm keeping this!" he wriggled a solid gold armlet up over his elbow. It was in the form of a serpent biting its tail.

"Very becoming, Sire."

"Myrddin, I'm so grateful. If there's anything among these articles that you like, please take it."

"Why would I do that when I can turn base metal into gold back in Camelot? Nay, you hurry to your beloved's father and show him your morning gift. I foresee no problems for your hand-fasting. Then you must bring Lady Cwen to Camelot to meet your father, who needs me now, it would appear."

Valdor gazed open-mouthed at Myrddin, who never ceased to amaze him. Yet he would have been more astonished had he lingered in the clearing. As it was, as he trudged back to Cair-Caratauc, he heard a falcon screech overhead and looked up to see the stately bird speed across the sky with mighty and steady strokes of its wings. *What I would give to fly like you! But nay, I'd not part with the treasure in this chest!* He smiled to himself and hurried to Cenhelm's Hall.

Setting the chest down on the chieftain's table, he flicked the catch and tipped back the lid.

"With your blessing, I'll wed Cwen, father."

"King Arthur honours us!" Cenhelm said, appraising the munificent gift.

"My father knows nothing of this," Valdor said honestly, "this is all mine!"

Valdor had cunningly withheld several gold coins from the well-stocked chest. Now, he handed them to Cwen's father. "These are for you as a token of our friendship, Lord Cenhelm. I take it you have no objection to Cwen coming with me to Camelot to meet my parents?"

"None, if I can come, too. I wish to meet your famous father. What better way to form an alliance than through family bonds?"

"Perfect!" The men clasped hands and Cenhelm called for drinking horns.

A minor event intrigued Valdor when they set off for Camelot. One of the warriors, a certain Agga, who had agreed to travel with his chieftain disappeared and did not make the journey.

Cenhelm shrugged and laughed off the matter, saying, "It's probably women trouble, he's well known for his amorous adventures."

The falcon flew straight through the open window in Camelot and perched on a high-backed seat. It looked around the room, then satisfied, transformed into Myrddin.

By the moon and stars! I need a rest before I seek out Arthur.

Feeling better, the seer hastened to Arthur's Hall.

"Sire, I felt that you needed my counsel."

"Ay, I've sought you high and low in Camelot, but could not find you."

Myrddin smiled, "I was away on urgent business with Prince Valdor."

"Where is my grandson?"

"In Cair-Caratauc."

"Among the Saxons?"

Myrddin chortled, "Such is the heat of young blood! The prince has found himself a wife—a rare beauty named Cwen. You should be pleased, Arthur, because this union will bring you a firm ally and a lineage that will rule for generations."

"That's the Myrddin I like: the one who foretells the future and the one I need right now."

"What troubles you, Sire? What is it you need to know beforehand?"

"Soon I must fight the eleventh battle you predicted, O Wise One. I wish to know where and when it will be fought so that I can make my plans."

"May I be seated, Sire?"

Arthur waved a hand airily at a seat and the seer dropped into it. Immediately, his eyes rolled back in their sockets, his hands gripped the chair arms and his lips trembled, but no speech came until he suddenly cried, "Traeth Tryfrwyd!"

The name impressed itself on Arthur's mind. It sounded like something uttered in an ancient tongue. He said nothing but waited; instead, Myrddin disappointed him by saying no more. Gradually, the colour came back to his pallid cheeks and his eyes fixed Arthur, as his grip loosened on the chair.

"Is that it?" Arthur asked.

"Is that what? When I go into a trance and foretell events, I do not understand what I am saying, I just spout the words. What is it I said?"

"Something in a strange, ancient tongue, my friend. All you said was *Traeth Tryfrwyd*."

"Ah, that is the old tongue of my forefathers, but I'm puzzled as to its meaning."

"You're puzzled! Come on, Myrddin, I need better than that!"

"It's open to interpretation. I think it could be the river Tribruit, but in the Old Cambrian tongue. But I am not familiar with such a place."

"But you suppose it to be somewhere in Cambria?" Arthur persisted.

"Not necessarily, you see, Sire, my old tongue has different meanings for the same word. Traeth could be a riverbank or it could be a seashore. In the latter case, the whole phrase may mean the speckled strand."

"So, it may refer to a bay rather than a river?" Arthur's patience was wearing thin and it was clear from his tone.

"Indeed, and it may not be in Cambria, but anywhere where the old tongue was spoken."

"Even in the far north and the far south? Good Lord, Myrddin! That's not much use to me." Arthur's shoulders slumped, "we'll just have to wait for the invaders to come and let them take the initiative," he said in a defeated voice.

"Not necessarily, I'm still thinking about those two words. *Tryfrwyd* has another meaning. It can be interpreted as *through pierced*. What then if that refers to a stretch of river or a firth? It would refer to a *trajectus* or river crossing."

"Such as the one where we crossed the Sabrina before?"

"Exactly, but not that one, because as you say, it is the Sabrina not the Tribruit."

"What then, am I to do?"

Myrddin's gimlet eyes stared hard from under his bushy brows and his jaw set in determined fashion.

"Send riders out in all directions in search of a river crossing where there is speckled sand. One of them will find it and you will march there to prepare for battle."

"Which I will win?"

"Of course. You must win all twelve for my prophecy to come true. You want to win a lasting peace, Arthur, do you not?"

"More than anything else in the world."

The seer gazed affectionately at his king. His divining skills had told him years before that this was the one true king who could save the Britons from total disaster. He had won nine consecutive battles so he urged, "Then, make haste, my liege, and send your horsemen!"

The first riders to come to Camelot did not bring the expected news, but were Saxons accompanying Prince Valdor. The king's grandson walked into the Great Hall with a lady on his arm. The corn-coloured blonde held herself erect, her neck like a swan and her mesmerising iris-blue eyes fixed on the king.

No wonder she has stolen Valdor's heart, why, she has robbed mine!

Hitherto, in his dealings with Saxons, Arthur had always found them admirable, perhaps because they were fearless warriors like himself; he might also have considered that the original Valdor among his forebears was also a native of the Rhine region and there might, therefore, have been some affinity in his blood, obscured by time and Romanisation. Whatever the case, Arthur and Cenhelm struck a firm friendship and promised to aid each other in the case of necessity. Arthur, however, felt loath to call on Saxons to fight other Saxons. He would keep his appeal back until he was sure that he needed help against the Picts or Scoti.

He had no idea which foe to expect for his eleventh battle. Maybe his ideas would be clear once he knew where the battle would be fought. While he waited for news he would enjoy the gracious company of the latest addition to his family.

21

THE TRYFRWYD CROSSING, BODERIA ESTUARY, 421 AD

A LONE RIDER ARRIVED AT CAMELOT, RUSHED INTO Arthur's Hall, and gasped out his message, "Sire, I have made all haste, coming to Durnovaria by ship from the northeast, thence galloping to Camelot. There is little time, lord. A vast Saxon fleet is heading for the Boderia Estuary."

"We must sail at once, and do as my good servant has done. We shall not waste time sailing around Cornwall, but march on Durnovaria, thence to sail up to the Boderia Estuary. We know the journey will be tiring, but my men can rest aboard the vessels."

Once in the estuary, Arthur peered at the Saxon vessels pulled up on the strand and saw little movement aboard. "The Saxons have landed and moved inland." He chose scouts and sent them to the north and south of the firth to locate the foe.

Meanwhile, welcome reinforcements arrived from his Brythonic allies of Guotodin, who assured him that the Saxons were north of the inlet. Arthur disembarked his men on the northern strand and marched uphill where he encountered his returning scouts.

"Sire, the enemy is beyond the rise and in great numbers."

Undaunted, Arthur spoke with his ally, Cenen ap Coel, "The land cannot conceal us; we must therefore square our shoulders and face the enemy breast-to-breast."

The Votadini chieftain grinned at his friend, "Arthur, we have the sinews to defeat even the hardiest of adversaries. Onward! May God give us greater strength!"

The Romano-Britons and Saxons clashed on the battlefield, their swords and axe heads gleaming in the sunlight as they prepared for the brutal confrontation ahead. The air was thick with tension, and the sound of war cries filled the air, echoing across the open field.

The Romano-Britons, led by the valiant Arthur, stood in tight formation, their shields raised high to form an impenetrable wall against the oncoming Saxon horde. The Saxons, fierce and determined, charged forward with resounding battle cries, their weapons held high as they sought to break through the enemy lines.

As the two armies collided, the clash of metal on metal rang out like thunder, filling the air with the sound of war. The Romano-Britons fought with a fierce determination, their swords slashing through the air as they pushed back against the Saxons with all their might.

The Saxon warriors, ferocious and skilful in battle, fought back with equal vigour, their axes swinging with deadly precision as they sought to break through their opponents' ranks. The battlefield was a chaotic swirl of blood and steel, with neither side willing to give an inch in the fierce struggle for supremacy.

Amidst the chaos of battle, Arthur stood tall, Excalibur flashing in the sunlight as he led his men with bravery and relentless carnage. His fortitude inspired his warriors to fight with renewed fervour, pushing back against the Saxon assault with unbending determination.

But the Saxons were not easily defeated, their warriors fighting with a savage intensity that seemed to know no bounds. The battlefield was unforgiving, the ground littered with the fallen bodies of brave men on both sides.

As the battle raged on, the tide of the conflict ebbed and flowed, with neither side able to gain a decisive advantage. The Romano-Britons fought with all their strength; their determination unwavering even in the face of overwhelming odds. As the sun began to set on the blood-soaked battlefield, it became clear that the Romano-Britons had gained the upper hand. The Saxons, their numbers depleted and their morale flagging, began to fall back in disarray, their commander fighting valiantly to hold the line as his men retreated.

In the end, Arthur emerged victorious, his warriors celebrating their hard-won triumph as they claimed the killing ground. The Saxons, although defeated, had fought with honour and courage, their sacrifice a testament to their bravery in the face of adversity. And so, the battle between the Romano-Britons and Saxons came to a close, leaving behind a field of carrion and destruction as the echoes of war faded into the stillness of the evening, broken only by the shrieks of kites and the caw of crows in a dense whirl of scavengers.

Arthur's men were too exhausted to pursue the remnant of the Saxon force, so the king knew they could come back but cared little. He had won his tenth victory, and if the defeated adversary should dare to return for his eleventh triumph, so much the worse for them. Nevertheless, it proved tempting to ride his steed to the crest of the nearby hill to gain a vantage point over the sea. There was satisfaction to be had in watching the demoralised foe sail away, their dream of conquest in tatters. But Arthur was a realist; whence these had come, others would come, likely enough joining them to swell their ranks. So hard had been this battle that the king's rational mind told him that he would have to draw on the goodwill of his allies as he could not sustain such great losses if he had to fight more battles. His fervent hope was that the next clash would be nearer home since the long journey had sapped valuable energy better employed on the battlefield.

Back home, King Arthur stood on the parapets of Camelot and gazed out over a lovely spring day unfolding like a painting come to life. The gentle warmth of the sun kissed the rolling hills and meadows, coaxing vibrant hues of green to burst forth, creating a backdrop of gaudy colours. The air was crisp and invigorating, carrying the sweet scent of blooming flowers and freshly cut grass.

His ears were greeted by the cheerful chirping of finches flitting about in the clear blue sky. Their melodies, blending harmoniously with the soft rustling of leaves in the gentle breeze, created a soothing accompaniment to the day's tranquillity.

Meadows of golden wildflowers nodded their heads, their bright petals dancing in the sunlight. Magnificent cherry blossoms adorned the king's orchard, adding delicate shades of pink and white to the canvas. The gentle gurgling of streams and rivers provided a calming rhythm to the scene, inviting the king to pause and drink in the beauty of nature's symphony, balm to his soul, scarred by years of bloodshed and torment.

In the surrounding villages and towns under his protection, life bustled with a sense of renewal and energy. Colourful market stalls lined the streets of Camelot, offering an array of fresh produce and craft goods. The aroma of freshly baked bread and perfume of blooming flowers wafted through the air, mingling with the laughter and chatter of locals and visitors alike.

As his eye passed over the winding lanes and footpaths, it encountered the recently built stone bridges crossing over babbling brooks, passing cottages with thatched roofs, interspersed by the occasional churches heavy with incense whose sickly scent mingled with the other aromas even up on the ramparts to be swept away on the breeze.

In the distance, the majestic silhouette of Glastonbury Tor rose against the horizon, shrouded in a soft haze of springtime mist. Its ancient ruins and mystical allure added a touch of magic to the already enchanted landscape, beckoning him to explore and discover the secrets hidden within its historic past.

He returned to the same position later, as the day drew to a close, as if drawn by one of Myrddin's spells, he found himself immersed in the peaceful serenity of a Somerset spring evening. The setting sun bathed the landscape in a warm golden light, casting long shadows across the fields and hedgerows. The sky was depicted in hues of pink and orange as the birdsong faded into the gentle hush of twilight, signalling the end of a perfect, peaceful day in this idyllic corner of his kingdom.

Arthur sighed wistfully. If he had to fight more battles, then let it be for his people and this, his charmed land. He needed to speak with Myrddin. Moments like this made him feel the weight of the years on his shoulders, deceived by the enchanter's magic providing him with youthful vim. How much longer could he go on with so many cares? So much death and destruction? Yet, he knew his duty was to lead his army twice more into battle; whatever the cost, it would be compensated by the generation of peace the seer had prophesied. Then would be the time to hand over to Primus and surrender to his fate. The sooner it was all over, the better.

Before descending from the parapet, Arthur spied a lone rider approaching Camelot. It turned out to be Agga, the warrior who had surprisingly not travelled with Cenhelm. He appeared sullen and taciturn and refused to answer when questioned about his tardy arrival. All this tended to confirm Cenhelm's theory that the fellow was embroiled in trouble with one or more women.

Only Valdor was slightly concerned about this Agga because he had caught him glaring his way on more than one occasion, and he wondered about it since he had not spoken to the man, so there seemed to be no reason for his antipathy.

The following morning, Valdor decided to go for a stroll through the market. He used to do this occasionally not because he wished to purchase anything, but because he enjoyed the bustle—the sights and sounds—the tradesmen's cries, the colourful wares and artisanal skills.

At first, he did not notice Agga dogging his steps, but being out and about precisely because he wanted to see things, he recognised him as the sullen Saxon and, on being seen, he gave Valdor a curt nod, who moved on. After several more stalls, Valdor turned to observe the Saxon still close behind. The prince moved towards him and said, "Are you following me, fellow?"

The surly manner he had witnessed in his grandfather's hall continued: "I am. I want a word with you in private. Far from all these people."

"What about?"

"That'll keep till we're alone."

Something about the curtness of manner and expression of the warrior alerted Valdor.

"We can walk over to my grandfather's cherry orchard. Nobody will disturb us there."

In three minutes, they had arrived under the blossom-laden trees; the heady scent of the blooms filled the air. But Valdor was oblivious to such beauty, all his senses were focused on the Saxon's slightest movement. Thus, he was ready when the brute pulled out a seax from his belt. Valdor's sword was already in his hand.

"What is your quarrel with me, fellow?" Valdor slowly circled him in the ritual dance of the expert swordsman. "I don't even know you."

"Give me my armlet and tell me where the rest of my treasure is."

"*Your* treasure? It was stolen and hidden away to cover your crimes. If you want the armlet, you'll have to take it by force. As for the rest, it has gone forever."

"Rrrarr!" the warrior roared and lunged with his seax, which Valdor swatted aside without difficulty.

"If I were you," Valdor said, "I'd accept my offer to walk away and forget about this, mindful of the good relations between our peoples. Besides, I've grown fond of *my* armlet."

Another roar and another lunge proved a fatal mistake for Agga because Valdor would not make the error of underestimating his opponent, nor of being too tender. Expert swordsman that he was, the mismatch was evident—brute force against sumptuous skill and a seax against a Frankish sword. Although he had rid himself of a vindictive foe, Valdor gazed at the bloodied corpse in dismay. What consequences would this deed have? He had only one choice: to go straight to the king and explain what had happened.

As luck would have it, Arthur was speaking with Cenhelm, so the two men listened to Valdor's agitated account of the events.

"I swear, Sire, I gave him the opportunity to walk away and forget our differences, but he disloyally lunged at me and I was forced to defend myself."

Cenhelm laughed bitterly, "Ay, that's Agga's way, sure enough! Hark, Prince Valdor, between ourselves, every family has its black sheep, and Agga was only trouble. I've come close to executing him myself, but held back to avoid internal strife. This is the perfect excuse for me to explain how he brought this upon himself by attacking the grandson of my closest ally. It will soon be forgotten, and you'll keep your gold, young lord."

Valdor thought it wiser not to mention the rest of the treasure since, for now, nobody would ever know where his morning gift had come from, except Myrddin, who was listening and smiling to himself in a shady corner of the hall. The alliance between the western Saxons and Logres was as sound as ever and would soon be called upon, Myrddin knew.

22

CAMELOT, AND NEAR BRAVONIUM, MONS BADONICUS 421 AD

Myrddin drew King Arthur aside and said, "Sire, I think you should speak with your guest while he is here, for your next battle looms. You will not need to ask him to fight his fellow Saxons."

"Who is it then, the Picts or the Scoti?"

"Both together and your wish not to have a long march will be granted because they are bringing war to your back garden."

"What, here to Camelot?"

"Nay, but they'll penetrate inland from the Sabrina Estuary. To the north on your western borders stands the fortress of Bravonium—"

"I know it well; it lies on the Watling Street."

"Not exactly, Sire, close, but somewhat to the east of the street."

"Don't quibble, Myrddin. I must raise as many men as possible to thwart the foe. The garrison is small in Bravonium. Apart from Cenhelm and his men, I can call upon my Cambrian allies. They, too, could be at risk if we do not stop the Scoti—"

"And the Picts."

"Myrddin! Do not test my patience!"

Despite their bickering, after the event, Arthur wanted to talk to Myrddin. He was unsure whether the outcome could be considered his eleventh victory. It was important to know this, because the twelfth battle was the all-important one.

The Picts and Scoti had taken up position near Bravonium and, although ready to fight, reconsidered because Arthur commanded an enormous force of Britons, Cambrians and Saxons. Also, his reputation as a relentless winning general preceded him. This resulted in the enemy chieftains suing for peace and handing over hostages as surety for their oaths. Arthur was relieved to see them sail away without bloodshed, but worried that no blood meant no victory.

"Nay, Sire, you may count that as your eleventh victory because your able diplomacy led to you leading a formidable force of allies, enough to scare away the foe. Besides, I have seen the future and know full well that your twelfth battle is on the horizon and is not far off."

"Where?"

"Close to Aquae Sulis. You will choose the hill for the battle."

"I'll have my scouts survey the area, although I'm quite familiar with it."

As for the Saxons, intermittent seaborne migratory waves from the Continent had brought more troops, accompanied by their families, who sought settlement in largely rural locations. Thereafter, the incomers' way was opened by loosely interdependent military groups, born, hardened and dedicated to battle, who, as oceanic seafarers, easily exploited the east-west river systems of the country. These united for the occasion in order to assemble an army for an assault on what they mistakenly considered the weakened Logres. Amongst the early warleaders of the Anglo-Saxon invaders were Germanic veterans trained in the tactics of the late Roman army. These Saxons, not Cenhelm's, on hearing of Arthur's engagement with the Picts and Scoti, but being ignorant of the truce, thought to take advantage of the King of Logres' weakness, little realising that the king had emerged stronger. Thus, they, too, sailed into the Sabrina Estuary or marched inland, joining together near Aquae Sulis.

Strengthened by Myrddin's reassurances, Arthur knew no fear and marched his army to the summit of Mons Badonicus, a hill not far from Aquae Sulis.

As the sun began to rise over the rolling hill of that place, the warriors of King Arthur's army prepared for battle. They knew that the fate of Britain hung in the balance, as the Saxon invaders had been gaining ground elsewhere and threatening to overrun the land.

King Arthur himself stood tall and resolute, his sword Excalibur gleaming in the early morning light. His knights gathered around him, ready to defend their homeland against the enemy. On the other side of the field, the Saxon warlord Cerdic surveyed his forces with a cruel smile. He was confident in his superior numbers and strength, and he was determined to crush Arthur's army once and for all.

The battle began with a deafening roar as the two armies clashed in a brutal melee. Swords clashed, shields splintered, and blood ran freely across the field. The air was filled with the screams of the wounded and dying, but both sides fought on with all their might.

Arthur led his knights into the heart of the Saxon army, cutting a path through their ranks with Excalibur. His courage and skill inspired his men to fight even harder, and soon the tide of battle began to turn in their favour. Cerdic fought ferociously, his axe swinging with deadly precision as he sought to cut down Arthur and claim victory for his own. But Arthur was a skilled warrior, and he parried Cerdic's blows with grace and strength.

As the sun reached its zenith in the sky, the battle reached its climax. The Saxon lines began to falter and break, and Arthur's knights surged forward with renewed vigour. With a final, mighty blow, Arthur slew Cerdic and the remaining Saxons fled in terror.

The Battle of Mons Badonicus was won, but the cost had been high. Many brave knights had fallen, and the land was scarred with the blood of the fallen. Yet Arthur and his warriors knew that they had saved Britain from ruin, and that their victory would be remembered for generations to come.

Word of the great victory spread throughout the land and it did not need Myrddin to assure everyone that the various barbarian tribes were in no condition to challenge the King of Logres. Arthur's Rhenish bard, Marius, composed a song, with which he regaled the valiant knights at the celebratory feast. An expectant hush fell over the hall as the bard strummed the first notes before tilting back his head and singing:

> *In these days of Arthur's reign,*
> *We Britons fought with might and main,*
> *At Mons Badon hill we stood our ground,*
> *With swords that clashed with thunderous sound.*
> *The Saxon hordes came fierce and bold,*
> *Their numbers vast, their hearts so cold,*
> *But Arthur's knights would not retreat,*

We faced our enemy in the heat.
On that day at Mons Badon's peak,
We Britons fought so brave to wreak
Our victory over the valley deep,
As Saxons fled from our fierce keep.
So sing we now of Arthur's might,
And how he won that glorious fight,
At Mons Badon, the Britons' pride,
We stood strong and did abide.

Tumultuous applause greeted his song and the merry company pressed drinks upon him. The bard had captured the mood and significance of the victory, but his was only jubilant guesswork. Arthur and Myrddin had counted the twelve victories and anticipated a generation of peace. Arthur's good mood spread through his family and he began to plan for his succession because he felt old and weary.

He took Primus aside to discuss how best to face the future.

"Myrddin assures me that we have won fifty years of peace by our victory at Mons Badonicus, but, my son, prepare yourself to lead our people and consider your own succession, for neither are you a mere youth. When we go, we must leave the kingdom in safe hands and in a stronger state than we found it. Remember how Britannia faltered when Honorius wrote to tell us to defend ourselves. Rome is no more, except a remnant barricaded within the impenetrable walls of Constantinople. We must be realistic. The future is with the slow-spreading stain of the Anglo-Saxons. Britons will wed with Saxons and your son has a Saxon spouse; when they have children, they will be readily accepted by both sides. Myrddin foresees a long and healthy lineage, but those kings must rule over well-preserved towns and villas. The fortifications should be strong," Arthur paused and his eyes scanned his son's face to ensure that Primus was following him. Satisfied, he concluded, "I see you are in agreement, so, my son, with your greater energy, begin to survey the kingdom and reinforce and build where necessary."

"Father, I saw no lack of energy at Badon Hill. Do you know what folks are saying? That you slew 940 Saxons on your own!"

Arthur threw back his head and guffawed. "People will exaggerate, but I wish to be remembered as a king who played his part in preserving the Roman heritage, but, oh, Primus, I am weary to my bones and need to rest."

"And so, you shall, father."

As good as his word, Primus spent the next months repairing the walls of major towns, taking over and strengthening the ancient hillforts of long-forgotten people, and encouraging trade between the south-west and the reduced Roman Empire. Shiploads of large amphorae containing wine and olive oil arrived while others containing glossy red tableware. At Camelot, Primus substantially rebuilt the rampart and gateway with a timber framework and dry stone facing.

Primus' most ambitious project was the construction of an earthen rampart with a ditch along the high ground of the south bank of the river Abona upstream to Aquae Sulis. He took the king to see it and, pointing upwards, said, "The westernmost end of this dyke lies at the ancient hillfort of Maes Knoll, see it rises yonder. This western dyke runs from Combe to the hillfort." As Arthur was aware, Combe lay close to the Roman road from Aquae Sulis to Londinium, which had prompted the building of a splendid villa in Combe Down some years before. He nodded his head in approval and said, "Son, I could not have conceived a better project myself."

The enterprise required considerable capital and manpower and demanded the king's full backing as well as all of Primus' grasp of military design and his authority over experts in land-surveying and experienced supervision of labour. Only his high-ranking position gave him the necessary procuratorial authority. When questioned by his father about the expenditure, it prompted him to take the king to see it and to reply, "Sire, the dyke is designed to protect Somerset from Saxon invasion." He was right, as the protected area was the wealthiest in Logres. Thanks to Arthur's victory and Primus' consolidation, the kingdom embarked on a golden age for the Britons as the Saxons were in no condition to undertake a complicated invasion of Arthur's kingdom. Complicated, since the profile of the turf wall along the defended ridge above the Abona was pre-determined by already existing features: the three or four pre-Roman hillforts—which were turned to the wall's advantage—the valley of the river Chew and the three pre-existing Roman roads. Nevertheless, the regularity of its fortifications at approximately five-mile intervals was militarily impressive, and Primus had to take the credit for this.

Despite the secure golden age flourishing, there were some troubling clouds gathering outside the walls of Camelot. Now that his military success was guaranteed, Arthur's exceptional strength began to fail. At last, he showed signs of his age as did Gosvintha, who finally succumbed to various ailments and died peacefully in her sleep. The beloved queen was mourned far and wide in Logres and people came in masses to Camelot often trailing healthy children the queen and her team of midwives had brought safely into the world. Arthur planned to be entombed with her, but little did he know of his destiny. Without her, he had no desire to ask Myrddin for more potion.

Meanwhile, Myrddin, responding to Arthur's grief, prophesied his own death. "Sire, my death is in the offing. I am older than my appearance and am not easily slain, but mine will be *a triple death*."

"A triple death, Myrddin? What does that even mean?"

"I shall not explain because it grieves me; but you will live to see it, my king."

Arthur grasped the seer by the arm, "Nay, I would not live to see that day!"

"But you will, Sire, even if your remaining days thereafter to mourn my passing will be brief, owing to your disobedience."

"Disobedience? I don't understand your meaning, O Wise One."

"Nay, because you are heedless of my warnings, but I'll not repeat myself for such a wayward soul."

Arthur dwelt on these words, his mood already dark and, although his family tried to raise his spirits, he was inconsolable, unrecognisable from the hero of Mons Badonicus. Yet, while as the ancients said, *old age stinks like a carcass*, it also brings a certain equanimity with life seen from a fresh perspective. Arthur found this to be true. After his active military service, he now relaxed by his hearth with his grandchildren at his feet, tranquil that governance was in the safe hands of his heir.

For his part, Primus, who had noticed his father's physical decline, smiled indulgently as the white-haired king dandled his youngest grandson on his knee and told him tales of past glory.

23

THE ENCHANTED LAKE NEAR CAMELOT, 421 AD

MYRDDIN DISAPPEARED FOR WEEKS ON END, LOCKED AWAY IN his quarters because he was preparing to triumph in a battle of contrasting magical arts. He did not mean to lose, so he worked on countering every possible spell thrown at him. When he decided, at last, that he was ready, he set off down the hill from Camelot and into the forest to the forbidden enchanted lake.

Rather like Arthur, he had grown disillusioned and weary of life, but unlike the king, he was in love. It happens that some vain, misguided old men can believe a younger woman will freely give herself to him without wanting material benefits in exchange. Myrddin was not deluded in that respect; he'd already once fallen into the trap of the Lady of the Lake, that fay, malign creature, so beautiful to behold. This time, he wanted to outwit her and win her if possible. He was even prepared to live with her in her realm below the surface of the lake.

The enchanter stood with his feet firmly planted on the shore of the lake, muttering a spell in his ancient tongue. A circular ripple, such as those created by fish feeding just under the surface, slowly spread outwards. Instead of a fish, the turquoise hair of a pale-skinned woman broke the surface and a slender arm pointed at Myrddin, "You!" she screamed, "how dare you disturb my slumber?" She opened her mouth to enchant him with her song, but nothing emerged. Her turquoise eyes betrayed her panic, and Myrddin cackled in glee; his plan was working.

"It's your turn," he said, "to know the inside of the hollow oak tree." He waved his hands in a peculiar fashion and the sylphlike form of the water nymph flew out of the lake and vanished among the trees. Myrddin slowly and confidently strolled to his former prison and stood before the crack in the oak. "How does it feel being entrapped inside the tree?" he asked gleefully, all the time muttering an unbreakable sealing spell.

She wailed, "You can't leave me here, you know that if I am too long out of the lake, I will die."

"I know that, so it's best you don't deceive me. I'll leave you here the rest of the day and all the night. That should be long enough for you to decide that you will content this old man. I want to lie with you, Lady. I'll come prepared to counter any trick you think you might perpetrate to foil me. You will give your heart to Myrddin Wyllt."

"Please don't leave me here!" she sobbed, "I'll do anything."

Myrddin chuckled maliciously; "I can't trust one of the faery folk, not until your spirit is broken. First, you must wait in anxiety, hoping that I will come to release you, for no-one else can. Will I truly return? Or am I a savage druid who wants revenge for your previous artful behaviour? Think carefully about Myrddin Wyllt, Lady of the Lake."

He laughed at her sobs and walked away blithely from the majestic oak.

Back in Camelot, Myrddin dedicated himself to reading ancient books of faery lore. He needed to be certain that on the morrow he could deal with all of her wiles. However, he had forgotten one essential detail and this would prove costly the following day.

The dawn broke with the promise of a bright and sunny day. Myrddin rose with a spring in his step and a tune in his heart. That day, if all went to plan, the Lady of the Lake, that slender, beguiling creature, would voluntarily give herself to him. He knew this because he had found the spell that would force her to keep her promises or consign her to dust.

His heart on fire and with the gait of a youngster, Myrddin strode into the forest. When he reached the clearing with the oak on the right, he hurried to the tree.

"See, I have come to release you, my dear; now, all you have to do is repeat an ancient rhyme after me and great happiness will be yours. I will transform myself into an irresistible young swain to make matters easier for you."

"You have forgotten something very important, Myrddin Wyllt. You neglected to mute me before you left yesterday eve. It was a fatal mistake."

"I think not, Lady," Myrddin sweated and cursed himself, it was indeed a foolish mistake, "Even if you can call upon an army of your kind, they cannot release you. Only I can do that! If I choose not to, survey the interior of the oak, for that will be your tomb."

"I hate you! What do you suppose to gain from a woman who does not love you?"

"Let me be the judge of that! For the moment I will conjure another trap proof against all your wiles, Lady of the Lake—"

"I beg you! —" she screamed.

"Ha-ha!" He began to weave his arms in a peculiar manner and murmured an ancient druidic spell. With it, he created an invisible bed, with a sealing spell ready to be activated in an instant.

"Have you decided to oblige me or will you die in yon tomb?" Myrddin was merciless because he knew how many lost souls were ascribable to the Lady of the Lake.

"Help! Help!" she squealed. Myrddin looked around fearfully, but there was no sign of any aid from fairyland.

"I will repeat my question only once, fay creature—have you decided to oblige me or will you die in yon tomb?"

"Release me and I'll do your will." Her tone was snivelling and miserable.

Myrddin chanted a spell and the oak sprung open, revealing the nymph sat on her haunches. She was staring around, so Myrddin knew he had to act quickly. He grabbed her slender wrist and hauled her onto the strategically-placed enchanted bed. She fell on her back on the bed, and in a trice, Myrddin chanted the sealing spell. From the inside, they could see the forest glade, but from the outside, anyone who stumbled across the bed could not see it.

The water nymph gazed at Myrddin with wide eyes. What she saw was not an old decrepit wizard, but a perfectly proportioned young man with the physique of a Greek god, as he had promised. Moreover, he was completely naked and most becoming to her eyes. They fell together, she, to her surprise, willingly. She had been forced to make a life-threatening promise, but there was no question of breaking it. She was delighted to keep her word. Little did it matter to her that it was the deception of magic because wrapped in her arms was her ideal of manliness.

After they had made wild, passionate love, she gazed into his eyes with her lovely turquoise eyes. "My sweet," she said, "release the bed from the spell. I begin to feel ill; I need to immerse myself in the lake. I will only take a few minutes to feel better, then I'll return and we can make love just as before."

Myrddin was not easily deceived, but since their lovemaking had been, he was sure, as satisfying for her as for him, and her plea was quite plausible, he agreed, but first, he muttered a spell to protect his ears from her siren song because he had no wish to drown in the placid waters of the lake. Instead, he watched her sensuous lithe form wade slowly into the lake and slide below the surface. He smiled to himself; in a few minutes, she would return to transport him in bliss again.

But he was wrong. His eyes caught movement in the glade and he knew that his triple death awaited him. She had foiled him. There were no birds, rabbits, owls, or hedgehogs in the glade, just a circle of malevolent elves skipping in a circle. One of them played an enchanting tune on a flute, but it had no effect on Myrddin, who had protected himself from the Lady's enthralling song with a spell. It also countered the flute.

Enraged, the elves, who bore gnarled clubs in their hands, swarmed over the now-visible bed and battered the young man so violently that his appearance spell faded and they found themselves pummelling the ancient wizard they had expected to encounter. Myrddin could do nothing against such overwhelming odds and malevolence. With his remaining energy, he tumbled out of the bed and staggered to his feet. Being far taller than the elves, he was, at least, able to stumble away blindly, as misfortune would have it, towards the lake, where he tripped over a fallen branch and fell face down into the water. The elves swarmed over him, thrashing his head with the clubs so that he could not raise it and was condemned to breathe in lake water and drown. The clubbing had killed him, but so too, the water. To avoid any doubt, the Lady of the Lake brought Excalibur—the original blade—and drove it between his shoulder blades to the gleeful chanting of the malicious elves. Thus, as prophesied by Saint Mungo, Myrddin, the last of a long line of druids, would die a triple death: clubbed, drowned and pierced.

"Begone, my little friends!" cried the Lady of the Lake. "But first, drag the body into the clearing and one of you leave the message at Camelot, for my work does not end here!" Her laughter was tinkling but spiteful, to match eyes as hard as the gems of the same colour. Delicately, she slid the blade of Excalibur out of Myrddin's body and, with a graceful underarm swing, flung the sword into the lake. It flew in a perfect arc, its bejewelled hilt sparkling momentarily in the sunlight before dropping into the water. Equally elegantly, with a tinkling laugh, to the cheers of the elves, the water nymph dived below the surface of the lake, her home for centuries, creating barely a ripple.

In a symbolic gesture, one after the other, the elves threw their clubs into the lake and then, with great fatigue, they hauled what to them was the gigantic body of the enchanter into the clearing. There, they saw three things had happened: first, the bed had vanished; second, the *door* in the oak had closed; and third, the wizard's clothes had appeared in a pile with his boots. Remembering their instructions, the elves swarmed over Myrddin's corpse and dressed it as the Lady had requested. They sat and rested while one, the most educated, wrote in gall ink on vellum: *You will find the body of Myrddin the druid in the forest clearing by the lake.* So far, he had obeyed his instructions to the letter. He glanced at the crack in the oak trunk, whence all his instructions had come from the imprisoned Lady of the Lake the evening before. The fay elves were obliged to obey a superior being of their own kind, especially when in mortal danger. He glared at Myrddin's body—the druid had got what he deserved.

Now, the elf would make the only mistake committed by his kind that day. His instructions were to take the message to the ruler of Camelot. Endowed with the art of invisibility, the elf sped to Camelot, entered unseen, but not bestowed with enlightenment, he did not know that King Arthur was the ruler of Camelot. Instead, he delivered the message to the *de facto* ruler, Prince Primus, by placing it on his knee, removing its invisibility, secretly and delightedly watching the ruler snatch up and read the note before racing out of the chamber, calling for his knights.

The elf, cloaked by invisibility, sat behind Primus on his steed to gallop with a dozen knights into the forest. To the elf's glee, the clearing only contained the body of Myrddin. His companion elves had long gone to their remote forest refuge. Thinking his duty fulfilled, the elf flew off to join them.

Days later, he had to face the wrath of the Lady of the Lake, who had wanted to lure King Arthur to her for vengeance. Bitterly disappointed, she swore that time would come. The question was whether to let it happen naturally or to force fate. She would spend time deliberating the matter.

The sorrowful knights carried Myrddin's body to Camelot, where an inconsolable Arthur wept over his tomb for days on end. Myrddin was entombed in the same crypt as Gosvintha, the underground chapel that the king had supposed would be his final resting place.

24

LAKE AND FOREST IN ENVIRONS OF CAMELOT, AD 412

AFTER WEEKS OF PROLONGED MOURNING FOR HIS WIFE AND old counsellor, King Arthur began to spend less time in the subterranean crypt and more with the living. He had grown increasingly fond of his son's wife, Willow, and now that she was expecting another child, he could not look at her without thinking how Gosvintha would have delighted in the moment.

As he emerged from the candlelit crypt into the light of day, Arthur resumed his favourite activities. First among these was reading the works of Greek and Roman authors, whose books he had gone to lengths to acquire. Seated near his hearth, Arthur caught up on the poet Virgil and the tale of his visit to the underworld; a work that reminded him of Myrddin and his occult activities.

For a man of action, quiet contemplation was all very well, but he needed the great outdoors and the thrill of the chase. He'd had quite enough of the thrill of warfare, but hunting a boar or a deer was well within his capabilities even at his age. The added benefit of capturing a succulent meal attracted him, too. He collected a spear and his horse, setting off without a care in the world for the forest, but also heedless of Myrddin's warning, which had been delivered too long ago for Arthur to bear in mind.

Thus, he rode into the forest on his regular trail and penetrated farther than usual in search of game. At last, he glimpsed what he took to be boar spoor marking the trail and urged his horse on cautiously. Soon, he saw his prey—a large tusked hog. Its tiny eyes met his, the creature squealed and darted into a bush. Arthur rode over, probed into the foliage with his spear, elicited a pained squeak and kicked his horse in pursuit of the beast. Fleeing for its life, the boar was fleeter of foot than Arthur expected. When it plunged down a steep slope, the king reined in, unprepared to risk his horse's limbs for a meal. He looked around and realised that he had come much deeper into the forest than intended. He had no landmark to guide him and still had not sated his desire for game, so he pressed on until the movement of a red deer caught his eye. He licked a finger and held it up to gauge the wind direction. Satisfied that he was downwind of the deer, he moved slowly forward until almost within throwing range of the animal.

Suddenly, startled, it leapt into the air and sped away down the trail, taking a right fork with Arthur in hot pursuit. It led him a merry chase, but at last, the king hurled his spear with great precision, piercing it behind the scapula and bringing it crashing, screaming to earth. Arthur drew Excalibur and, springing down, quickly put the beast out of its agony. He lifted the hart over the neck of his steed and, remounting, realised that he did not have a clue where he was.

Instinct told him to follow this right fork because it seemed to be looping slowly back on itself. At a certain point, through the trees, he glimpsed the sheen of water—it had to be the lake he knew, but seen from the opposite shore. Undeterred, he pressed on, heedless of Myrddin's warning to stay away from it. Indeed, it did not occur to him that he should. He had completely forgotten.

As he left the shelter of the trees, he halted his horse to stare out at the beauty of the lacustrine scene. The water was so calm that it reflected like a mirror and he saw the opposite bank—the one he knew—in the clearest of inverted images. The king breathed in the fresh air of the trees, shrubbery and the water with relish. It was good to be alive! He sighed happily and, not for the first time, thanked God for the beauty of his kingdom. The monarch did not notice the eerie silence of the glades, which should have been full of birdsong, nor did he sense the unease of his shuffling steed. A vague sense of anxiety gripped him, a sudden awareness that he should not be there, but it was too late, the seductive siren song of a modern-day Circe reached his ears. Earlier in the day, he had read about the enchantress, daughter of the sun god and an oceanic nymph beguiling Odysseus on his return from the Trojan War.

A sudden recollection of Myrddin's warning turned his blood to ice, but against his will, he found himself dismounting and sleepwalking towards the edge of the lake. The song filled his senses, gone was the beauty of the day, the reflections, the scent of woodland, all replaced by the enthralling beauty of the siren song.

King Arthur gazed in wonder and entrancement at the naked beauty, her waist upwards out of the water, revealing her turquoise locks and eyes and her delightful curves. His blood pounded in his skull and, unaware that he was wading into the water, the nymph called to him, "King Arthur, at last we meet! You must content me and throw Excalibur into the lake. It was stolen by the sorcerer, Myrddin, against my will. The sword is mine!"

"Lady, I beg you," Arthur pleaded, "I had destined the sword to my heir, who will need it to keep the barbarians at bay."

"Arthur, past and future king, there is much you do not know, but I will tell you everything, for you must come and live with me beneath the surface of this lake. Do not let your eyes deceive you. There are many more realities than mere mortals can conceive." She began to sing again and her flashing eyes seemed to shoot out rays of turquoise light. Her voice, so lilting and melodic, ensnared him and there was no Hermes to give him moly to save him from her snare.

Unwillingly, he unsheathed Excalibur and, with a mighty overarm throw, hurled it towards the nymph. It splashed into the lake a yard in front of her, close enough to make her flinch and glare at him. She stopped her music and snapped, "I have countless ways of punishing you for your foolish actions, Arthur, but Fate has decreed differently, so now you will come to me and we'll regret together that you are no longer the young centurion of yore."

She waved long, sinuous fingers in the air and drew him towards her. How she was miraculously above water, he could not tell, but his head sank below the surface as he marched on. The strangest thing was that he did not drown but could somehow breathe like a fish or amphibian. Suddenly, he reached her and a slender arm snatched at him, taking his wrist and pulling him towards her. He only had time to appreciate her perfect body when he lost consciousness and she towed him unawares to the deepest part of the lake.

When the king regained consciousness, he was lying flat on his back and staring up along tall arches. He expected this large hall to be lit by torchlight or candles; whereas, he saw that natural light was rippling in through a glass dome supported on the arches. When a silvery shape darted across his view—one of several fish—he realised that he was seeing them from below and staring up from the bed of the lake towards its surface.

A discreet cough captured his attention and there beside him on the bed was the beautiful naked siren. He gasped and his eyes widened.

"Do you like what you see, King Arthur?"

"I—I," he coughed in embarrassment.

"Don't worry, I have appropriated Myrddin's powers to myself; so, I can transform you into the young Centurion Valdor."

"Valdor? How come you know my name!"

"Not only that, but I know what you looked like before you met your wife. I know things you cannot suspect, Valdor. You are a widower and you can dedicate yourself to pleasing me. You have much time before you return to battle."

"I must return to battle?"

"Aye, you are the future king who must save the land from the Norsemen."

"And will I be King Arthur again?"

"What is in a name? Valdor—Arthur—Alfred?"

"Alfred?"

"Aye, what of it? Take off your clothes, Valdor."

He looked down at his flaccid stomach and, to his astonishment, found the iron muscles of his youth. His heart beat with joy. Was this truly happening? Was he in thrall to the Lady of the Lake or did he have free will? He would find out in due course. In any case, she was incredibly beautiful and, as she said, he was a widower. He had never betrayed Gosvintha and since she had departed this world, this was not betrayal. He had another pressing question before giving himself to the enchantress.

"Lady, when I fight these—what did you call them—Norsemen, will I wield Excalibur?"

"I demanded you return the sword because the future is already written. Your son Primus, who is at present mourning your inexplicable disappearance, is not entitled to do so. They who seem enemies may only be defeated by courage and natural means until your nation needs *you* many centuries hence. Now, *I* need you, Valdor; enough idle chatter."

"Do you know, it's a relief to return to my old name and a blessing that you have brought me here."

"Something had to be saved of this ancient land. You have been its greatest defender. In the years to come, I will teach you some of the oldest mysteries, but for now, love me, Valdor."

She was in love with him and as the years slipped by, kept him informed about his descendants and the problems successive kings faced. Only slowly did it occur to the past and future king that he was no longer mortal. She would break it to him when the time came to fulfil his destiny that not only would he return to mortality as the future king, but that he might not enjoy the strength and health he had as Valdor and Arthur, but would be more intelligent and learned than both together.

THE END

ABOUT THE AUTHOR

Award-winning author, John Broughton, was born in Cleethorpes, Lincolnshire, UK, in 1948, just one of the post-war baby boomers. After attending grammar school and studying to the sound of Bob Dylan, he went to Nottingham University and studied Medieval and Modern History (Archaeology subsidiary). The subsidiary course led to one of his greatest academic achievements: tipping the soil content of a wheelbarrow from the summit of a spoil heap on an old lady hobbling past the dig. Fortunately, they subsequently became firm friends.

He did many different jobs while living in Radcliffe-on-Trent, Leamington, Glossop, the Scilly Isles, Puglia, and Calabria. They include teaching English and History, managing a Day-Care Centre, being a Director of a Trade Institute, and teaching university students English. He even tried being a fisherman and a flower-picker when he was on St. Agnes Island, Scilly. He has lived in Calabria since 1992, where he settled into a long-term job, for once, at the University of Calabria teaching English. No doubt, his "lovely Calabrian wife Maria" stopped him from being restless.

His two kids are grown up now, but he wrote books for them when they were little. Hamish Hamilton and then Thomas Nelson published six of these in England in the 1980s. They are now out of print. He's a granddad and happily the parents wisely named his grandson Dylan. He decided to take up writing again late in his career. When you are teaching and working as a translator, you don't have time for writing. As soon as he stopped the translations, he resumed writing in 2014. The fruit of that decision was his first historical novel, *The Purple Thread*. The novel is set in his favourite Anglo-Saxon period. Subsequently, he has published eighteen novels set between 450 and 1066 AD, including three trilogies, with Next Chapter Publishers. They also published *Angenga*, a time-travel novel linking the ninth century to the twenty-first. This novel inspired John Broughton to write a series of novels about psychic investigator Jake Conley, whose retrocognition takes him back to Anglo-Saxon times.

In order to put his writing versatility to the test, he embarked on a series of detective mystery novels set in London with the Metropolitan Police, who have to deal with a criminally insane serial killer in *The Quasimodo Killings*; *The London Tram Murders* and *The Thames Crossbow Murders*. The latter was voted among the best twenty-five independent books of 2022. Heartened by this venture, he completed a fourth and fifth mystery *The Thames-Tigris Connection* and *London's Psycho Cyclist*. To widen his experience of genres, he decided to write an apocalyptic novel entitled *The Remnant*, a science-fiction novel. However, he returned to his first love with a historical saga, *Expulsion*, about the expulsion of the Vikings from Dublin and the subsequent diaspora. *The Reversed Hermit* is his first novella. Newly committed to historical fiction, he embarked on *Rhodri's Furies*, which is Book 1 of an early medieval Welsh trilogy, *The Bretland Trilogy*, of which *Avenging Rhodri* is Book 2, *Hywel the Good* is Book 3. *The Wyvern's End* is Book 3 of the Wyrd Trilogy. Straying slightly outside his favoured Anglo-Saxon period and inspired by Gibbon's *Decline and Fall*, he has begun a new Saxon Shore Trilogy of which *The Great Conspiracy* is Book 2 and *The Woken Talisman*, Book 3.

To learn more about John Broughton and discover more Next Chapter authors, visit our website at www.nextchapter.pub.

The Saxon Shore Trilogy
ISBN: 978-4-82419-646-0
Hardcover Edition

Published by
Next Chapter
2-5-6 SANNO
SANNO BRIDGE
143-0023 Ota-Ku, Tokyo
+818035793528

8th August 2024